AGATHA CHRISTIE

AGATHA CHRISTIE

MURDER ON THE ORIENT EXPRESS
CARDS ON THE TABLE • FIVE LITTLE PIGS
HERCULE POIROT'S CHRISTMAS

DIAMOND ◆ BOOKS

Murder on the Orient Express first published in
Great Britain in 1934 by William Collins Sons & Co Ltd
Copyright 1934

Cards on the Table first published in
Great Britain in 1936 by William Collins Sons & Co Ltd
Copyright 1936

Five Little Pigs first published in
Great Britain in 1942 by William Collins Sons & Co Ltd
Copyright 1942

Hercule Poirot's Christmas first published in
Great Britain in 1939 by William Collins Sons & Co Ltd
Copyright 1939

© Introduction William Collins Sons & Co Ltd 1980
This edition produced in 1991 by Diamond Books,
an imprint of HarperCollins*Publishers* Ltd
ISBN 0 583 31348 5

Printed and bound in Great Britain by
HarperCollinsManufacturing Glasgow

CONTENTS

INTRODUCTION

Mr Shaitana, a man of sinister tastes and Mephistophelian appearance, invites to dinner four murderers who have got away with their crimes and four people whose business is the detection of crime. In the course of the evening . . .

But perhaps by now you are beginning to say: 'This is ridiculous – totally unrealistic.' If so, perhaps you should give up this collection of Christie stories at once. You are the sort of person who sits through a performance of *The Importance of Being Earnest* worrying about the well-being of the baby in the handbag. The story of *Cards on the Table* is an elegant stylisation that touches real life only obliquely from time to time, for Agatha Christie is not a realistic writer and did not intend to be, and her novels are glittering exercises in a convention as artificial as the comedies of Wilde or Congreve. Any idea that her novels should reflect the real world of the twentieth century for purposes of social or moral criticism she would have ridiculed: she had no pretensions to being a teacher or a prophet. Her purpose is solely to intrigue, tantalise and entertain, and in these roles her success is legendary. In this omnibus volume are collected four of the very finest, most tantalising, most entertaining volumes she wrote. I would be inclined to call them the cream of Poirot.

Hercule Poirot is undoubtedly the best-known fictional detective of our century, one whose peculiarities and catch-phrases have entered popular consciousness. Many find him irritating, and it is probably true that he *is* a collection of catch-phrases and mental oddities rather than a deeply-felt character. He is a machine for detecting. But the reason his supremacy is deserved is precisely that he is, of all fictional sleuths, the one who is a great detective because his detection is great. It is he whose processes of reasoning are most brilliantly and persuasively put before us, and it is Christie's triumph as a popular writer that this process never becomes heavy: his bravura displays of impeccable logic delight the mind; he jumps delicately from proposition to proposition; but never plods.

These Poirot mysteries are all from that period in Christie's career when she was, luckily, at the height both of her powers and her productivity. *Murder on the Orient Express* is, deservedly, the best-known of Christie's excursions abroad; but it stands out from the others by reason not only of its outrageous solution, but of the sequel to that solution. W. W. Robson has written of Christie that 'her stories, like Jane Austen's *Emma*, offer a puzzle to be solved, and affirm reason and morality in the solution. The detective story cannot do without poetic justice.' Sometimes, one feels, she was inclined to affirm law rather than broader morality in her final chapters, but here Poirot forgets for once his *bourgeois* disapproval of murder, and lets the justice be indeed poetic rather than literal.

Hercule Poirot's Christmas is a splendid display of her most characteristic gift, the production in the last chapter of the staggering solution that the reader has not for a moment considered. In *Cards on the Table* she deliberately denies herself this, her best card: here there are only four possible suspects, and each is equally suspicious. To keep the reader's interest, therefore, she has to rely on devices other than the reader's expectation of a climactic surprise. If *Hercule Poirot's Christmas* is an exercise on classic themes (the country house party murder, the locked room murder), *Cards* is an attempt to do without the classic ingredient of surprise, and it brilliantly succeeds.

In *Five Little Pigs* she takes as her model the Wilkie Collins formula of letting the various people involved in the case tell their own story. Dickens found the construction of *The Moonstone* 'wearisome beyond endurance' and though most critics put this down to jealousy of his young friend's success, many modern readers surely agree with him: one tires of the device long before the story nears its somewhat protracted end. Christie humanises the device, making it both more likely and less schematised. The individuals who narrate their parts in the Crale case are economically individualised, and the discrepancies in their accounts are superbly utilised when the time for a solution comes round. In all, this is one of the peaks of Christie's achievement, and not as widely appreciated as it deserves.

One last word about Christie's art. In spite of the near-universality of her appeal, or more likely because of it, people sometimes take a slightly dismissive attitude to her books: 'What are you reading?' 'Oh, just a Christie.' Thus in Jane Austen's time did people say, 'Just a novel,' rousing her memorable ire in *Northanger Abbey*. There is no 'just' about Christie's stories at their best, and nothing easy about their conception and construction. They may not be beautifully written or subtly characterised, but they are put together with the art of the miniature-painter or the clock-maker. They are marvels of planning and forethought, little gems of misleading suggestion and double-edged conversation. Anyone who imagines such miracles of double deception are remotely easy should try for themselves. Christie is the supreme craftswoman of the detective story, and these books have become part of our twentieth-century folk heritage.

ROBERT BARNARD

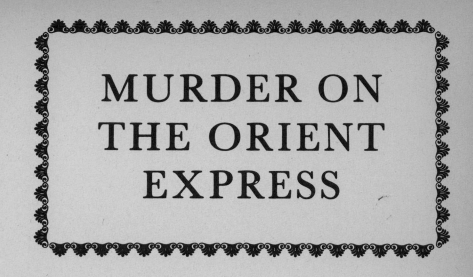

MURDER ON THE ORIENT EXPRESS

PART I

THE FACTS

— I —

AN IMPORTANT PASSENGER
ON THE TAURUS EXPRESS

IT was five o'clock on a winter's morning in Syria. Alongside the platform at Aleppo stood the train grandly designated in railway guides as the Taurus Express. It consisted of a kitchen and dining-car, a sleeping-car and two local coaches.

By the step leading up into the sleeping-car stood a young French lieutenant, resplendent in uniform, conversing with a small man, muffled up to the ears, of whom nothing was visible but a pink-tipped nose and the two points of an upward-curled moustache.

It was freezingly cold, and this job of seeing off a distinguished stranger was not one to be envied, but Lieutenant Dubosc performed his part manfully. Graceful phrases fell from his lips in polished French. Not that he knew what it was all about. There had been rumours, of course, as there always were in such cases. The General's – *his* General's – temper had grown worse and worse. And then there had come this Belgian stranger – all the way from England, it seemed. There had been a week – a week of curious tensity. And then certain things had happened. A very distinguished officer had committed suicide, another had resigned – anxious faces had suddenly lost their anxiety, certain military precautions were relaxed. And the General – Lieutenant Dubosc's own particular General – had suddenly looked ten years younger.

Dubosc had overheard part of a conversation between him and the stranger. 'You have saved us, *mon cher*,' said the General emotionally, his great white moustache trembling as he spoke. 'You have saved the honour of the French Army – you have

11

averted much bloodshed! How can I thank you for acceding to my request? To have come so far—'

To which the stranger (by name M. Hercule Poirot) had made a fitting reply including the phrase, 'But indeed do I not remember that once you saved my life?' And then the General had made another fitting reply to that disclaiming any merit for that past service, and with more mention of France, of Belgium, of glory, of honour and of such kindred things they had embraced each other heartily and the conversation had ended.

As to what it had all been about, Lieutenant Dubosc was still in the dark, but to him had been delegated the duty of seeing off M. Poirot by the Taurus Express, and he was carrying it out with all the zeal and ardour befitting a young officer with a promising career ahead of him.

'Today is Sunday,' said Lieutenant Dubosc. 'Tomorrow, Monday evening, you will be in Stamboul.'

It was not the first time he had made this observation. Conversations on the platform, before the departure of a train, are apt to be somewhat repetitive in character.

'That is so,' agreed M. Poirot.

'And you intend to remain there a few days, I think?'

'*Mais oui.* Stamboul, it is a city I have never visited. It would be a pity to pass through – *comme ça.*' He snapped his fingers descriptively. 'Nothing presses – I shall remain there as a tourist for a few days.'

'La Sainte Sophie, it is very fine,' said Lieutenant Dubosc, who had never seen it.

A cold wind came whistling down the platform. Both men shivered. Lieutenant Dubosc managed to cast a surreptitious glance at his watch. Five minutes to five – only five minutes more!

Fancying that the other man had noticed his surreptitious glance, he hastened once more into speech.

'There are few people travelling this time of year,' he said, glancing up at the windows of the sleeping-car above them.

'That is so,' agreed M. Poirot.

'Let us hope you will not be snowed up in the Taurus!'

'That happens?'

'It has occurred, yes. Not this year, as yet.'

'Let us hope, then,' said M. Poirot. 'The weather reports from Europe, they are bad.'

'Very bad. In the Balkans there is much snow.'

'In Germany too, I have heard.'

'*Eh bien*,' said Lieutenant Dubosc hastily as another pause seemed to be about to occur. 'Tomorrow evening at seven-forty you will be in Constantinople.'

'Yes,' said M. Poirot, and went on desperately, 'La Sainte Sophie, I have heard it is very fine.'

'Magnificent, I believe.'

Above their heads the blind of one of the sleeping-car compartments was pushed aside and a young woman looked out.

Mary Debenham had had little sleep since she left Baghdad on the preceding Thursday. Neither in the train to Kirkuk, nor in the Rest House at Mosul, nor last night on the train had she slept properly. Now, weary of lying wakeful in the hot stuffiness of her overheated compartment, she got up and peered out.

This must be Aleppo. Nothing to see, of course. Just a long, poor-lighted platform with loud furious altercations in Arabic going on somewhere. Two men below her window were talking French. One was a French officer, the other was a little man with enormous moustaches. She smiled faintly. She had never seen anyone quite so heavily muffled up. It must be very cold outside. That was why they heated the train so terribly. She tried to force the window down lower, but it would not go.

The *wagon lit* conductor had come up to the two men. The train was about to depart, he said. Monsieur had better mount. The little man removed his hat. What an egg-shaped head he had. In spite of her preoccupations Mary Debenham smiled. A ridiculous-looking little man. The sort of little man one could never take seriously.

Lieutenant Dubosc was saying his parting speech. He had thought it out beforehand and had kept it till the last minute. It was a very beautiful, polished speech.

Not to be outdone, M. Poirot replied in kind.

'*En voiture, monsieur*,' said the *wagon lit* conductor.

With an air of infinite reluctance M. Poirot climbed aboard the train. The conductor climbed after him. M. Poirot waved his hand. Lieutenant Dubosc came to the salute. The train, with a terrific jerk, moved slowly forward.

'*Enfin!*' murmured M. Hercule Poirot.

'Brrrrr,' said Lieutenant Dubosc, realizing to the full how cold he was . . .

'*Voilà, monsieur*.' The conductor displayed to Poirot with a dramatic gesture the beauty of his sleeping-compartment and the neat arrangement of his luggage. 'The little *valise* of monsieur, I haved placed it *here*.'

His outstretched hand was suggestive. Hercule Poirot placed in it a folded note.

'*Merci, monsieur*.' The conductor became brisk and businesslike. 'I have the tickets of monsieur. I will also take the passport, please. Monsieur breaks his journey in Stamboul, I understand?'

M. Poirot assented.

'There are not many people travelling, I imagine?' he said.

'No, monsieur. I have only two other passengers – both English. A colonel from India, and a young English lady from Baghdad. Monsieur requires anything?'

Monsieur demanded a small bottle of Perrier.

Five o'clock in the morning is an awkward time to board a train. There was still two hours before dawn. Conscious of an inadequate night's sleep, and of a delicate mission successfully accomplished, M. Poirot curled up in a corner and fell asleep.

When he awoke it was half-past nine, and he sallied forth to the restaurant-car in search of hot coffee.

There was only one occupant at the moment, obviously the young English lady referred to by the conductor. She was tall, slim and dark – perhaps twenty-eight years of age. There was a kind of cool efficiency in the way she was eating her breakfast and in the way she called to the attendant to bring her more coffee, which bespoke a knowledge of the world and of travelling. She wore a dark-coloured travelling-dress of some thin material eminently suitable for the heated atmosphere of the train.

M. Hercule Poirot, having nothing better to do, amused himself by studying her without appearing to do so.

She was, he judged, the kind of young woman who could take care of herself with perfect ease wherever she went. She had poise and efficiency. He rather liked the severe regularity of her features and the delicate pallor of her skin. He liked the burnished black head with its neat waves of hair, and her eyes, cool, impersonal and grey. But she was, he decided, just a little too efficient to be what he called '*jolie femme*'.

Presently another person entered the restaurant-car. This was a tall man of between forty and fifty, lean of figure, brown of skin, with hair slightly grizzled round the temples.

'The colonel from India,' said Poirot to himself.

The newcomer gave a little bow to the girl.

'Morning, Miss Debenham.'

'Good morning, Colonel Arbuthnot.'

The colonel was standing with a hand on the chair opposite her.

'Any objection?' he asked.

'Of course not. Sit down.'

'Well, you know, breakfast isn't always a chatty meal.'

'I should hope not. But I don't bite.'

The colonel sat down.

'Boy,' he called in peremptory fashion.

He gave an order for eggs and coffee.

His eyes rested for a moment on Hercule Poirot, but they passed on indifferently. Poirot, reading the English mind correctly, knew that he had said to himself, 'Only some damned foreigner.'

True to their nationality, the two English people were not chatty. They exchanged a few brief remarks, and presently the girl rose and went back to her compartment.

At lunch time the other two again shared a table and again they both completely ignored the third passenger. Their conversation was more animated than at breakfast. Colonel Arbuthnot talked of the Punjab, and occasionally asked the girl a few questions about Baghdad, where it became clear that she had been in a post as governess. In the course of conversation they discovered some mutual friends, which had the immediate effect of making them more friendly and less stiff. They discussed old Tommy Somebody and Jerry Someone Else. The colonel inquired whether she was going straight through to England or whether she was stopping in Stamboul.

'No, I'm going straight on.'

'Isn't that rather a pity?'

'I came out this way two years ago and spent three days in Stamboul then.'

'Oh, I see. Well, I may say I'm very glad you are going right through, because I am.'

He made a kind of clumsy little bow, flushing a little as he did so.

'He is susceptible, our colonel,' thought Hercule Poirot to himself with some amusement. 'The train, it is as dangerous as a sea voyage!'

Miss Debenham said evenly that that would be very nice. Her manner was slightly repressive.

The colonel, Hercule Poirot noticed, accompanied her back to her compartment. Later they passed through the magnificent scenery of the Taurus. As they looked down towards the Cilician Gates, standing in the corridor side by side, a sigh came suddenly from the girl. Poirot was standing near them and heard her murmur: 'It's so beautiful! I wish – I wish—'

'Yes?'

'I wish I could enjoy it!'

Arbuthnot did not answer. The square line of his jaw seemed a little sterner and grimmer.

'I wish to Heaven you were out of all this,' he said.

'Hush, please. Hush.'

'Oh! it's all right.' He shot a slightly annoyed glance in Poirot's direction. Then he went on: 'But I don't like the idea of your being a governess – at the beck and call of tyrannical mothers and their tiresome brats.'

She laughed with just a hint of uncontrol in the sound.

'Oh! you mustn't think that. The downtrodden governess is quite an exploded myth. I can assure you that it's the parents who are afraid of being bullied by *me*.'

They said no more. Arbuthnot was, perhaps, ashamed of his outburst.

'Rather an odd little comedy that I watch here,' said Poirot to himself thoughtfully.

He was to remember that thought of his later.

They arrived at Konya that night about half-past eleven. The two English travellers got out to stretch their legs, pacing up and down the snowy platform.

M. Poirot was content to watch the teeming activity of the station through a window pane. After about ten minutes, however, he decided that a breath of air would not perhaps be a bad thing, after all. He made careful preparations, wrapping himself in several coats and mufflers and encasing his neat boots in goloshes. Thus attired he descended gingerly to the platform and began to pace its length. He walked out beyond the engine.

It was the voices which gave him the clue to the two indistinct figures standing in the shadow of a traffic van. Arbuthnot was speaking.

'Mary—'

The girl interrupted him.

'Not now. Not now. When it's all over. When it's behind us – *then*—'

Discreetly M. Poirot turned away. He wondered.

He would hardly have recognised the cool, efficient voice of Miss Debenham . . .

'Curious,' he said to himself.

The next day he wondered whether, perhaps, they had quarrelled. They spoke little to each other. The girl, he thought, looked anxious. There were dark circles under her eyes.

It was about half-past two in the afternoon when the train came to a halt. Heads were poked out of windows. A little knot of men were clustered by the side of the line looking and pointing at something under the dining-car.

Poirot leaned out and spoke to the *wagon lit* conductor who was hurrying past. The man answered and Poirot drew back his head and, turning, almost collided with Mary Debenham who was standing just behind him.

'What is the matter?' she asked rather breathlessly in French. 'Why are we stopping?'

'It is nothing, mademoiselle. It is something that has caught fire under the dining-car. Nothing serious. It is put out. They are now repairing the damage. There is no danger, I assure you.'

She made a little abrupt gesture, as though she were waving the idea of danger aside as something completely unimportant.

'Yes, yes, I understand that. But the *time*!'

'The time?'

'Yes, this will delay us.'

'It is possible – yes,' agreed Poirot.

'But we can't afford delay! The train is due in at 6.55 and one has to cross the Bosphorus and catch the Simplon Orient Express the other side at nine o'clock. If there is an hour or two of delay we shall miss the connection.'

'It is possible, yes,' he admitted.

He looked at her curiously. The hand that held the window bar was not quite steady, her lips too were trembling.

'Does it matter to you very much, mademoiselle?' he asked.

'Yes. Yes, it does. I – I must catch that train.'

She turned away from him and went down the corridor to join Colonel Arbuthnot.

Her anxiety, however, was needless. Ten minutes later the train started again. It arrived at Haydapassar only five minutes late, having made up time on the journey.

The Bosphorus was rough and M. Poirot did not enjoy the crossing. He was separated from his travelling companions on the boat, and did not see them again.

On arrival at the Galata Bridge he drove straight to the Tokatlian Hotel.

THE TOKATLIAN HOTEL

At the Tokatlian, Hercule Poirot asked for a room with bath. Then he stepped over to the concierge's desk and inquired for letters.

There were three waiting for him and a telegram. His eyebrows rose a little at the sight of the telegram. It was unexpected.

He opened it in his usual neat, unhurried fashion. The printed words stood out clearly.

'*Development you predicted in Kassner Case has come unexpectedly please return immediately.*'

'*Voilà ce qui est embêtant,*' murmured Poirot vexedly. He glanced up at the clock.

'I shall have to go on tonight,' he said to the concierge. 'At what time does the Simplon Orient leave?'

'At nine o'clock, monsieur.'

'Can you get me a sleeper?'

'Assuredly, monsieur. There is no difficulty this time of year. The trains are almost empty. First class or second?'

'First.'

'*Très bien, monsieur.* How far are you going?'

'To London.'

'*Bien, monsieur.* I will get you a ticket to London and reserve your sleeping-car accommodation in the Stamboul–Calais coach.'

Poirot glanced at the clock again. It was ten minutes to eight.

'I have time to dine?'

'But assuredly, monsieur.'

The little Belgian nodded. He went over and cancelled his room order and crossed the hall to the restaurant.

As he was giving his order to the waiter a hand was placed on his shoulder.

'Ah! *mon vieux*, but this is an unexpected pleasure,' said a voice behind him.

The speaker was a short, stout, elderly man, his hair cut *en brosse*. He was smiling delightedly.

Poirot sprang up.

'M. Bouc!'

'M. Poirot!'

M. Bouc was a Belgian, a director of the Compagnie Internationale des Wagons Lits, and his acquaintance with the former star of the Belgian Police Force dated back many years.

'You find yourself far from home, *mon cher*,' said M. Bouc.

'A little affair in Syria.'

'Ah! And you return home – when?'

'Tonight.'

'Splendid! I, too. That is to say, I go as far as Lausanne, where I have affairs. You travel on the Simplon Orient, I presume?'

'Yes. I have just asked them to get me a sleeper. It was my intention to remain here some days, but I have received a telegram recalling me to England on important business.'

'Ah!' sighed M. Bouc. '*Les affaires – les affaires!* But you – you are at the top of the tree nowadays, *mon vieux*!'

'Some little success I have had, perhaps.' Hercule Poirot tried to look modest but failed signally.

Bouc laughed.

'We will meet later,' he said.

Hercule Poirot addressed himself to the task of keeping his moustaches out of the soup.

That difficult task accomplished, he glanced round him whilst waiting for the next course. There were only half a dozen people in the restaurant, and of those half-dozen there were only two that interested Hercule Poirot.

These two sat at a table not far away. The younger was a likeable-looking young man of thirty, clearly an American. It was, however, not he but his companion who had attracted the little detective's attention.

He was a man of between sixty and seventy. From a little distance he had the bland aspect of a philanthropist. His slightly bald head, his domed forehead, the smiling mouth that displayed a very white set of false teeth, all seemed to speak of a benevolent personality. Only the eyes belied this assumption. They were small, deep set and crafty. Not only that. As the man, making some remark to his young companion, glanced across the room, his gaze stopped on Poirot for a moment, and just for that second there was a strange malevolence and unnatural tensity in the glance.

Then he rose.

'Pay the bill, Hector,' he said.

His voice was slightly husky in tone. It had a queer, soft, dangerous quality.

When Poirot rejoined his friend in the lounge, the other two men were just leaving the hotel. Their luggage was being brought down. The younger was supervising the process. Presently he opened the glass door and said: 'Quite ready now, Mr Ratchett.'

The elder man grunted an assent and passed out.

'*Eh bien*,' said Poirot. 'What do you think of those two?'

'They are Americans,' said M. Bouc.

'Assuredly they are Americans. I meant what did you think of their personalities?'

'The young man seemed quite agreeable.'

'And the other?'

'To tell you the truth, my friend, I did not care for him. He produced on me an unpleasant impression. And you?'

Hercule Poirot was a moment before replying.

'When he passed me in the restaurant,' he said at last, 'I had a curious impression. It was as though a wild animal – an animal savage, but savage! you understand – had passed me by.'

'And yet he looked altogether of the most respectable.'

'*Précisément!* The body – the cage – is everything of the most respectable – but through the bars, the wild animal looks out.'

'You are fanciful, *mon vieux*,' said M. Bouc.

'It may be so. But I could not rid myself of the impression that evil had passed me by very close.'

'That respectable American gentleman?'

'That respectable American gentleman.'

'Well,' said M. Bouc cheerfully. 'It may be so. There is much evil in the world.'

At that moment the door opened and the concierge came towards them. He looked concerned and apologetic.

'It is extraordinary, monsieur,' he said to Poirot. 'There is not one first class berth to be had on the train.'

'*Comment?*' cried M. Bouc. 'At this time of year? Ah, without doubt there is some party of journalists – of politicans—?'

'I don't know, sir,' said the concierge, turning to him respectfully. 'But that's how it is.'

'Well, well.' M. Bouc turned to Poirot. 'Have no fear, my friend. We will arrange something. There is always one compartment – the No. 16 – which is not engaged. The conductor sees to that!' He smiled, then glanced up at the clock. 'Come,' he said, 'it is time we started.'

At the station M. Bouc was greeted with respectful *empressement* by the brown-uniformed *wagon lit* conductor.

'Good evening, monsieur. Your compartment is the No. 1.'

He called to the porters and they wheeled their load halfway along the carriage on which the tin plates proclaimed its destination:

ISTANBUL TRIESTE CALAIS

'You are full up tonight, I hear?'

'It is incredible, monsieur. All the world elects to travel tonight!'

'All the same, you must find room for this gentleman here. He is a friend of mine. He can have the No. 16.'

'It is taken, monsieur.'

'What? The No. 16?'

A glance of understanding passed between them, and the conductor smiled. He was a tall, sallow man of middle age.

'But yes, monsieur. As I told you, we are full – full – everywhere.'

'But what passes itself?' demanded M. Bouc angrily. 'There is a conference somewhere? It is a party?'

'No, monsieur. It is only chance. It just happens that many people have elected to travel tonight.'

M. Bouc made a clicking sound of annoyance.

'At Belgrade,' he said, 'there will be the slip coach from Athens. There will also be the Bucharest–Paris coach – but we do not reach Belgrade until tomorrow evening. The problem is for tonight. There is no second class berth free?'

'There *is* a second class berth, monsieur—'

'Well, then—'

'But it is a lady's berth. There is already a German woman in the compartment – a lady's-maid.'

'*Là, là,* that is awkward,' said M. Bouc.

'Do not distress yourself, my friend,' said Poirot. 'I must travel in an ordinary carriage.'

'Not at all. Not at all.' He turned once more to the conductor. 'Everyone has arrived?'

'It is true,' said the man, 'that there is one passenger who has not yet arrived.'

He spoke slowly with hesitation.

'But speak then?'

'No. 7 berth – a second class. The gentleman has not yet come, and it is four minutes to nine.'

'Who is it?'

'An Englishman.' The conductor consulted his list. 'A Mr Harris.'

'A name of good omen,' said Poirot. 'I read my Dickens. Mr Harris, he will not arrive.'

'Put monsieur's luggage in No. 7,' said M. Bouc. 'If this Mr Harris arrives we will tell him that he is too late – that berths cannot be retained so long – we will arrange the matter one way or another. What do I care for a Mr Harris?'

'As monsieur pleases,' said the conductor.

He spoke to Poirot's porter, directing him where to go.

Then he stood aside the steps to let Poirot enter the train.

'*Tout à fait au bout, monsieur*,' he called. 'The end compartment but one.

Poirot passed along the corridor, a somewhat slow progress, as most of the people travelling were standing outside their carriages.

His polite '*Pardons*' were uttered with the regularity of clockwork. At last he reached the compartment indicated. Inside it, reaching up to a suitcase, was the tall young American of the Tokatlian.

He frowned as Poirot entered.

'Excuse me,' he said. 'I think you've made a mistake.' Then, laboriously in French, '*Je crois que vous avez un erreur.*'

Poirot replied in English.

'You are Mr Harris?'

'No, my name is MacQueen. I—'

But at that moment the voice of the *wagon lit* conductor spoke from over Poirot's shoulder. An apologetic, rather breathless voice.

'There is no other berth on the train, monsieur. The gentleman has to come in here.'

He was hauling up the corridor window as he spoke and began to lift in Poirot's luggage.

Poirot noticed the apology in his tone with some amusement. Doubtless the man had been promised a good tip if he could keep the compartment for the sole use of the other traveller. However, even the most munificent of tips lose their effect when a director of the company is on board and issues his orders.

The conductor emerged from the compartment, having swung the suitcases up on to the racks.

'*Voilà, monsieur*,' he said. 'All is arranged. Yours is the upper berth, the number 7. We start in one minute.'

He hurried off down the corridor. Poirot re-entered the compartment.

'A phenomenon I have seldom seen,' he said cheerfully. 'A *wagon lit* conductor himself puts up the luggage! It is unheard of!'

His fellow traveller smiled, He had evidently got over his annoyance – had probably decided that it was no good to take the matter other than philosophically.

'The train's remarkably full,' he said.

A whistle blew, there was a long, melancholy cry from the engine. Both men stepped out into the corridor.

Outside a voice shouted.

'*En voiture.*'

'We're off,' said MacQueen.

But they were not quite off. The whistle blew again.

'I say, sir,' said the young man suddenly, 'if you'd rather have the lower berth – easier, and all that – well, that's all right by me.'

A likeable young fellow.

'No, no,' protested Poirot. 'I would not deprive you—'

'That's all right—'

'You are too amiable—'

Polite protests on both sides.

'It is for one night only,' explained Poirot. 'At Belgrade—'

'Oh, I see. You're getting out at Belgrade—'

'Not exactly. You see—'

There was a sudden jerk. Both men swung round to the window, looking out at the long, lighted platform as it slid slowly past them.

The Orient Express had started on its three-days' journey across Europe.

— 3 —

POIROT REFUSES A CASE

M. HERCULE POIROT was a little late in entering the luncheon-car on the following day. He had risen early, breakfasted almost alone, and had spent the morning going over the notes of the case that was recalling him to London. He had seen little of his travelling companion.

M. Bouc, who was already seated, gesticulated a greeting and summoned his friend to the empty place opposite him. Poirot sat down and soon found himself in the favoured position of the table which was served first and with the choicest morsels. The food, too, was unusually good.

It was not till they were eating a delicate cream cheese that M. Bouc allowed his attention to wander to matters other than nourishment. He was at the stage of a meal when one becomes philosophic.

'Ah!' he sighed. 'If I had but the pen of a Balzac! I would depict this scene.'

He waved a hand.

'It is an idea, that,' said Poirot.

'Ah, you agree? It has not been done, I think? And yet – it lends itself to romance, my friend. All around us are people, of all classes, of all nationalities, of all ages. For three days these people, these strangers to one another, are brought together. They sleep and eat under one roof, they cannot get away from each other. At the end of three days they part, they go their several ways, never, perhaps, to see each other again.'

'And yet,' said Poirot, 'suppose an accident—'

'Ah no, my friend—'

'From your point of view it would be regrettable, I agree. But nevertheless let us just for one moment suppose it. Then, perhaps, all these here are linked together – by death.'

'Some more wine,' said M. Bouc, hastily pouring it out. 'You are morbid, *mon cher*. It is, perhaps, the digestion.'

'It is true,' agreed Poirot, 'that the food in Syria was not, perhaps, quite suited to my stomach.'

He sipped his wine. Then, leaning back, he ran his eye thoughtfully round the dining-car. There were thirteen people seated there and, as M. Bouc had said, of all classes and nationalities. He began to study them.

At the table opposite them were three men. They were, he guessed, single travellers graded and placed there by the unerring judgment of the restaurant attendants. A big, swarthy Italian was picking his teeth with gusto. Opposite him a spare, neat Englishman had the expressionless disapproving face of the well-trained servant. Next to the Englishman was a big American in a loud suit – possibly a commercial traveller.

'You've got to put it over *big*,' he was saying in a loud nasal voice.

The Italian removed his toothpick to gesticulate with it freely.

'Sure,' he said. 'That whatta I say alla de time.'

The Englishman looked out of the window and coughed.

Poirot's eye passed on.

At a small table, sitting very upright, was one of the ugliest old ladies he had ever seen. It was an ugliness of distinction – it fascinated rather than repelled. She sat very upright. Round her neck was a collar of very large pearls which, improbable though it seemed, were real. Her hands were covered with rings. Her sable coat was pushed back on her shoulders. A very small expensive black toque was hideously unbecoming to the yellow, toad-like face beneath it.

She was speaking now to the restaurant attendant in a clear, courteous but completely autocratic tone.

'You will be sufficiently amiable to place in my compartment a bottle of mineral water and a large glass of orange juice. You will arrange that I shall have chicken cooked without sauces for dinner this evening – also some boiled fish.'

The attendant replied respectfully that it should be done.

She gave a slight gracious nod of the head and rose. Her glance caught Poirot's and swept over him with the nonchalance of the uninterested aristocrat.

'That is Princess Dragomiroff,' said M. Bouc in a low tone. 'She is a Russian. Her husband realized all his money before the Revolution and invested it abroad. She is extremely rich. A cosmopolitan.'

Poirot nodded. He had heard of Princess Dragomiroff.

'She is a personality,' said M. Bouc. 'Ugly as sin, but she makes herself felt. You agree?'

Poirot agreed.

At another of the large tables Mary Debenham was sitting with two other women. One of them was a tall middle-aged woman in a plaid blouse and tweed skirt. She had a mass of faded yellow hair unbecomingly arranged in a large bun, wore glasses, and had a long, mild, amiable face rather like a sheep. She was listening to the third woman, a stout, pleasant-faced, elderly woman who was talking in a slow clear monotone which showed no signs of pausing for breath or coming to a stop.

'. . . and so my daughter said, "Why," she said "you just can't apply Amurrican methods in this country. It's just natural to the folks here to be indolent," she said. "They just haven't got any hustle in them." But all the same you'd be surprised to know what our college there is doing. They've gotten a fine staff of teachers. I guess there's nothing like education. We've got to apply our Western ideals and teach the East to recognize them. My daughter says—'

The train plunged into a tunnel. The calm monotonous voice was drowned.

At the next table, a small one, sat Colonel Arbuthnot – alone. His gaze was fixed upon the back of Mary Debenham's head. They were not sitting together. Yet it could easily have been managed. Why?

Perhaps, Poirot thought, Mary Debenham had demurred. A

governess learns to be careful. Appearances are important. A girl with her living to get has to be discreet.

His glance shifted to the other side of the carriage. At the far end, against the wall, was a middle-aged woman dressed in black with a broad expressionless face. German or Scandinavian, he thought. Probably a German lady's-maid.

After her came a couple leaning forward and talking animatedly together. The man wore English clothes of loose tweed – but he was not English. Though only the back of his head was visible to Poirot, the shape of it and the set of the shoulders betrayed him. A big man, well made. He turned his head suddenly and Poirot saw his profile. A very handsome man of thirty-odd with a big fair moustache.

The woman opposite him was a mere girl – twenty at a guess. A tight-fitting little black coat and skirt, white satin blouse, small chic black toque perched at the fashionable outrageous angle. She had a beautiful foreign-looking face, dead white skin, large brown eyes, jet-black hair. She was smoking a cigarette in a long holder. Her manicured hands had deep red nails. She wore one large emerald set in platinum. There was coquetry in her glance and voice.

'*Elle est jolie – et chic*,' murmured Poirot. 'Husband and wife – eh?'

M. Bouc nodded.

'Hungarian Embassy, I believe,' he said. 'A handsome couple.'

There were only two more lunchers – Poirot's fellow traveller MacQueen and his employer Mr Ratchett. The latter sat facing Poirot, and for the second time Poirot studied that unprepossessing face, noting the false benevolence of the brow and the small, cruel eyes.

Doubtless M. Bouc saw a change in his friend's expression.

'It is at your wild animal you look?' he asked.

Poirot nodded.

As his coffee was brought to him, M. Bouc rose to his feet. Having started before Poirot, he had finished some time ago.

'I return to my compartment,' he said. 'Come along presently and converse with me.'

'With pleasure.'

Poirot sipped his coffee and ordered a liqueur. The attendant was passing from table to table with his box of money, accepting payment for bills. The elderly American lady's voice rose shrill and plaintive.

'My daughter said, "Take a book of food tickets and you'll have

26

no trouble – no trouble at all.'' Now, that isn't so. Seems they have to have a ten per cent tip, and then there's that bottle of mineral water – and a queer sort of water too. They hadn't got any Evian or Vichy, which seems queer to me.'

'It is – they must – how you say – serve the water of the country,' explained the sheep-faced lady.

'Well, it seems queer to me.' She looked distastefully at the heap of small change on the table in front of her. 'Look at all this peculiar stuff he's given me. Dinars or something. Just a lot of rubbish, it looks. My daughter said—'

Mary Debenham pushed back her chair and left with a slight bow to the other two. Colonel Arbuthnot got up and followed her. Gathering up her despised money, the American lady followed suit, followed by the lady like a sheep. The Hungarians had already departed. The restaurant-car was empty save for Poirot and Ratchett and MacQueen.

Ratchett spoke to his companion, who got up and left the car. Then he rose himself, but instead of following MacQueen he dropped unexpectedly into the seat opposite Poirot.

'Can you oblige me with a light?' he said. His voice was soft – faintly nasal. 'My name is Ratchett.'

Poirot bowed slightly. He slipped his hand into his pocket and produced a matchbox which he handed to the other man, who took it but did not strike a light.

'I think,' he went on, 'that I have the pleasure of speaking to M. Hercule Poirot. Is that so?'

Poirot bowed again.

'You have been correctly informed, monsieur.'

The detective was conscious of those strange shrewd eyes summing him up before the other spoke again.

'In my country,' he said, 'we come to the point, quickly. M. Poirot, I want you to take on a job for me.'

Hercule Poirot's eyebrows went up a trifle.

'My clientèle, monsieur, is limited nowadays. I undertake very few cases.'

'Why, naturally, I understand that. But this, M. Poirot, means big money.' He repeated again in his soft, persuasive voice, 'Big money.'

Hercule Poirot was silent a minute or two, then he said:

'What is it you wish me to do for you, Mr – er – Ratchett?'

'M. Poirot, I am a rich man – a very rich man. Men in that position have enemies. I have an enemy.'

'Only one enemy?'

'Just what do you mean by that question?' asked Ratchett sharply.

'Monsieur, in my experience when a man is in a position to have, as you say, enemies, then it does not usually resolve itself into one enemy only.'

Ratchett seemed relieved by Poirot's answer. He said quickly:

'Why, yes, I appreciate that point. Enemy or enemies – it doesn't matter. What does matter is my safety.'

'Safety?'

'My life has been threatened, M. Poirot. Now, I'm a man who can take pretty good care of himself.' From the pocket of his coat his hand brought a small automatic into sight for a moment. He continued grimly. 'I don't think I'm the kind of man to be caught napping. But as I look at it I might as well make assurance doubly sure. I fancy you're the man for my money, M. Poirot. And remember – *big* money.'

Poirot looked at him thoughtfully for some minutes. His face was completely expressionless. The other could have had no clue as to what thoughts were passing in that mind.

'I regret, monsieur,' he said at length. 'I cannot oblige you.'

The other looked at him shrewdly.

'Name your figure, then,' he said.

Poirot shook his head.

'You do not understand, monsieur. I have been very fortunate in my profession. I have made enough money to satisfy both my needs and my caprices. I take now only such cases as – interest me.'

'You've got a pretty good nerve,' said Ratchett. 'Will twenty thousand dollars tempt you?'

'It will not.'

'If you're holding out for more, you won't get it. I know what a thing's worth to me.'

'I also – Mr Ratchett.'

'What's wrong with my proposition?'

Poirot rose.

'If you will forgive me for being personal – I do not like your face, Mr Ratchett,' he said.

And with that he left the restaurant-car.

— 4 —

A CRY IN THE NIGHT

THE Simplon Orient Express arrived at Belgrade at a quarter to nine that evening. It was not due to depart again until 9.15, so Poirot descended to the platform. He did not, however, remain there long. The cold was bitter and, though the platform itself was protected, heavy snow was falling outside. He returned to his compartment. The conductor, who was on the platform stamping his feet and waving his arms to keep warm, spoke to him.

'Your *valises* have been moved, monsieur, to the compartment No. 1, the compartment of M. Bouc.'

'But where is M. Bouc, then?'

'He has moved into the coach from Athens which has just been put on.'

Poirot went in search of his friend. M. Bouc waved his protestations aside.

'It is nothing. It is nothing. It is more convenient like this. You are going through to England, so it is better that you should stay in the through coach to Calais. Me, I am very well here. It is most peaceful. This coach is empty save for myself and one little Greek doctor. Ah! my friend, what a night! They say there has not been so much snow for years. Let us hope we shall not be held up. I am not too happy about it, I can tell you.'

At 9.15 punctually the train pulled out of the station, and shortly afterwards Poirot got up, and said good night to his friend and made his way along the corridor back into his own coach, which was in front next to the dining-car.

On this, the second day of the journey, barriers were breaking down. Colonel Arbuthnot was standing at the door of his compartment talking to MacQueen.

MacQueen broke off something he was saying when he saw Poirot. He looked very surprised.

'Why,' he cried, 'I thought you'd left us. You said you were getting off at Belgrade.'

'You misunderstood me,' said Poirot, smiling. 'I remember now, the train started from Stamboul just as we were talking about it.'

'But, man, your baggage – it's gone.'

'It has been moved into another compartment – that is all.'

'Oh, I see.'

He resumed his conversation with Arbuthnot and Poirot passed on down the corridor.

Two doors from his own compartment, the elderly American lady, Mrs Hubbard, was standing talking to the sheep-like lady, who was a Swede. Mrs Hubbard was pressing a magazine on the other.

'No, do take it, my dear,' she said. 'I've got plenty other things to read. My, isn't the cold something frightful?' She nodded amicably to Poirot.

'You are most kind,' said the Swedish lady.

'Not at all. I hope you'll sleep well and that your head will be better in the morning.'

'It is the cold only. I make now myself a cup of tea.'

'Have you got some aspirin? Are you sure, now? I've got plenty. Well, good night, my dear.'

She turned to Poirot conversationally as the other woman departed.

'Poor creature, she's a Swede. As far as I can make out, she's a kind of missionary – a teaching one. A nice creature, but doesn't talk much English. She was *most* interested in what I told her about my daughter.'

Poirot, by now, knew all about Mrs Hubbard's daughter. Everyone on the train who could understand English did! How she and her husband were on the staff of a big American college in Smyrna and how this was Mrs Hubbard's first journey to the East, and what she thought of the Turks and their slipshod ways and the condition of their roads.

The door next to them opened and the thin, pale manservant stepped out. Inside Poirot caught a glimpse of Mr Ratchett sitting up in bed. He saw Poirot and his face changed, darkening with anger. Then the door was shut.

Mrs Hubbard drew Poirot a little aside.

'You know, I'm dead scared of that man. Oh, not the valet – the other – his master. Master, indeed! There's something *wrong* about that man. My daughter always says I'm very intuitive. "When Momma gets a hunch, she's dead right," that's what my daughter says. And I've got a hunch about that man. He's next door to me, and I don't like it. I put my grips against the communicating door last night. I thought I heard him trying the handle. Do you know, I shouldn't be a bit surprised if that man turns out to be a murderer – one of these train robbers you read about. I dare say I'm foolish, but there it is. I'm downright scared of the man! My daughter said I'd have an easy journey, but somehow I don't feel happy about it. It may be foolish, but I feel anything might happen. Anything at all. And how that nice young fellow can bear to be his secretary I can't think.'

Colonel Arbuthnot and MacQueen were coming towards them down the corridor.

'Come into my carriage,' MacQueen was saying. 'It isn't made up for the night yet. Now what I want to get right about your policy in India is this—'

The men passed and went on down the corridor to MacQueen's carriage.

Mrs Hubbard said good night to Poirot.

'I guess I'll go right to bed and read,' she said. 'Good night.'

'Good night, madame.'

Poirot passed into his own compartment, which was the next one beyond Ratchett's. He undressed and got into bed, read for about half an hour and then turned out the light.

He awoke some hours later, and awoke with a start. He knew what it was that had wakened him – a loud groan, almost a cry, somewhere close at hand. At the same moment the ting of a bell sounded sharply.

Poirot sat up and switched on the light. He noticed that the train was at a standstill – presumably at a station.

That cry had startled him. He remembered that it was Ratchett who had the next compartment. He got out of bed and opened the door as the *wagon lit* conductor came hurrying along the corridor and knocked on Ratchett's door. Poirot kept his door open a crack and watched. The conductor tapped a second time. A bell rang and a light showed over another door farther down. The conductor glanced over his shoulder.

At the same moment a voice from within the next-door compartment called out: *'Ce n'est rien. Je me suis trompé.'*

'Bien, monsieur.' The conductor scurried off again, to knock at the door where the light was showing.

Poirot returned to bed, his mind relieved, and switched off the light. He glanced at his watch. It was just twenty-three minutes to one.

— 5 —

THE CRIME

HE found it difficult to go to sleep again at once. For one thing, he missed the motion of the train. If it *was* a station outside it was curiously quiet. By contrast, the noises on the train seemed unusually loud. He could hear Ratchett moving about next door – a click as he pulled down the washbasin, the sound of the tap running, a splashing noise, then another click as the basin shut to again. Footsteps passed in the corridor outside, the shuffling footsteps of someone in bedroom slippers.

Hercule Poirot lay awake staring at the ceiling. Why was the station outside so silent? His throat felt dry. He had forgotten to ask for his usual bottle of mineral water. He looked at his watch again. Just after a quarter-past one. He would ring for the conductor and ask him for some mineral water. His finger went out to the bell, but he paused as in the stillness he heard a ting. The man couldn't answer every bell at once.

Ting . . . ting . . . ting . . .

It sounded again and again. Where was the man? Somebody was getting impatient.

Ting . . .

Whoever it was was keeping their finger solidly on the push.

Suddenly with a rush, his footsteps echoing up the aisle, the man came. He knocked at a door not far from Poirot's own.

Then came voices – the conductor's, deferential, apologetic, and a woman's – insistent and voluble.

Mrs Hubbard!

Poirot smiled to himself.

The altercation – if it was one – went on for some time. Its proportions were ninety per cent of Mrs Hubbard's to a soothing ten per cent of the conductor's. Finally the matter seemed to be adjusted. Poirot heard distinctly: '*Bonne nuit, madame,*' and a closing door.

He pressed his own finger on the bell.

The conductor arrived promptly. He looked hot and worried.

'*De l'eau minérale, s'il vous plaît.*'

'*Bien, monsieur.*' Perhaps a twinkle in Poirot's eye led him to unburden himself.

'*La dame américaine–*'

'Yes?'

He wiped his forehead.

'Imagine to yourself the time I have had with her! She insists – but *insists* – that there is a man in her compartment! Figure to yourself, monsieur. In a space of this size.' He swept a hand round. 'Where would he conceal himself? I argue with her. I point out that it is impossible. She insists. She woke up and there was a man there. And how, I ask, did he get out and leave the door bolted behind him? But she will not listen to reason. As though there were not enough to worry us already. This snow—'

'Snow?'

'But yes, monsieur. Monsieur has not noticed? The train has stopped. We have run into a snowdrift. Heaven knows how long we shall be here. I remember once being snowed up for seven days.'

'Where are we?'

'Between Vincovci and Brod.'

'*Là là*,' said Poirot vexedly.

The man withdrew and returned with the water.

'*Bonsoir, monsieur.*'

Poirot drank a glass of water and composed himself to sleep.

He was just dropping off when something again woke him. This time it was as though something heavy had fallen with a thud against the door.

He sprang up, opened it and looked out. Nothing. But to his right some way down the corridor a woman wrapped in a scarlet kimono was retreating from him. At the other end, sitting on his little seat, the conductor was entering up figures on large sheets of paper. Everything was deathly quiet.

'Decidedly I suffer from the nerves,' said Poirot and retired to bed again. This time he slept till morning.

When he awoke the train was still at a standstill. He raised a blind and looked out. Heavy banks of snow surrounded the train.

He glanced at his watch and saw that it was past nine o'clock.

At a quarter to ten, neat, spruce, and dandified as ever, he made his way to the restaurant-car, where a chorus of woe was going on.

Any barriers there might have been between the passengers had now quite broken down. All were united by a common misfortune. Mrs Hubbard was loudest in her lamentations.

'My daughter said it would be the easiest way in the world. Just sit in the train until I got to Parrus. And now we may be here for days and days,' she wailed. 'And my boat sails day after to-morrow. How am I going to catch it now? Why, I can't even wire to cancel my passage. I feel too mad to talk about it.'

The Italian said that he had urgent business himself in Milan. The large American said that that was 'too bad, ma'am,' and soothingly expressed a hope that the train might make up time.

'My sister – her children wait me,' said the Swedish lady and wept. 'I get no word to them. What they think? They will say bad things have happen to me.'

'How long shall we be here?' demanded Mary Debenham. 'Doesn't anybody *know*?'

Her voice sounded impatient, but Poirot noted that there were no signs of that almost feverish anxiety which she had displayed during the check to the Taurus Express.

Mrs Hubbard was off again.

'There isn't anybody knows a thing on this train. And nobody's trying to do anything. Just a pack of useless foreigners. Why, if this were at home, there'd be someone at least *trying* to do something.'

Arbuthnot turned to Poirot and spoke in careful British French.

'*Vous êtes un directeur de la ligne, je crois, monsieur. Vous pouvez nous dire—*'

Smiling, Poirot corrected him.

'No, no,' he said in English. 'It is not I. You confound me with my friend M. Bouc.'

'Oh! I'm sorry.'

'Not at all. It is most natural. I am now in the compartment that he had formerly.'

M. Bouc was not present in the restaurant-car. Poirot looked about to notice who else was absent.

Princess Dragomiroff was missing and the Hungarian couple. Also Ratchett, his valet, and the German lady's-maid.

The Swedish lady wiped her eyes.

'I am foolish,' she said. 'I am baby to cry. All for the best, whatever happen.'

This Christian spirit, however, was far from being shared.

'That's all very well,' said MacQueen restlessly. 'We may be here for days.'

'What is this country anyway?' demanded Mrs Hubbard tearfully.

On being told it was Yugoslavia she said: 'Oh! one of these Balkan things. What can you expect?'

'You are the only patient one, mademoiselle,' said Poirot to Miss Debenham.

She shrugged her shoulders slightly.

'What can one do?'

'You are a philosopher, mademoiselle.'

'That implies a detached attitude. I think my attitude is more selfish. I have learned to save myself useless emotion.'

She was not even looking at him. Her gaze went past him, out of the window to where the snow lay in heavy masses.

'You are a strong character, mademoiselle,' said Poirot gently. 'You are, I think, the strongest character amongst us.'

'Oh, no. No, indeed. I know one far far stronger than I am.'

'And that is—?'

She seemed suddenly to come to herself, to realize that she was talking to a stranger and a foreigner with whom, until this morning, she had only exchanged half a dozen sentences.

She laughed a polite but estranging laugh.

'Well – that old lady, for instance. You have probably noticed her. A very ugly old lady, but rather fascinating. She has only to lift a little finger and ask for something in a polite voice – and the whole train runs.'

'It runs also for my friend M. Bouc,' said Poirot. 'But that is because he is a director of the line, not because he has a masterful character.'

Mary Debenham smiled.

The morning wore away. Several people, Poirot amongst them, remained in the dining-car. The communal life was felt, at the moment, to pass the time better. He heard a good deal more about Mrs Hubbard's daughter and he heard the lifelong habits of Mr Hubbard, deceased, from his rising in the morning and commencing breakfast with a cereal to his final rest at night in the bed-socks that Mrs Hubbard herself had been in the habit of knitting for him.

It was when he was listening to a confused account of the missionary aims of the Swedish lady that one of the *wagon lit* conductors came into the car and stood at his elbow.

'*Pardon, monsieur.*'

'Yes?'

'The compliments of M. Bouc, and he would be glad if you would be so kind as to come to him for a few minutes.'

Poirot rose, uttered excuses to the Swedish lady and followed the man out of the dining-car.

It was not his own conductor, but a big fair man.

He followed his guide down the corridor of his own carriage and along the corridor to the next one. The man tapped at a door, then stood aside to let Poirot enter.

The compartment was not M. Bouc's own. It was a second class one – chosen presumably because of its slightly larger size. It certainly gave the impression of being crowded.

M. Bouc himself was sitting on the small seat in the opposite corner. In the corner next the window facing him was a small, dark man looking out at the snow. Standing up and quite preventing Poirot from advancing any farther was a big man in blue uniform (the *chef de train*) and his own *wagon lit* conductor.

'Ah, my good friend,' cried M. Bouc. 'Come in. We have need of you.'

The little man in the window shifted along the seat, Poirot squeezed past the other two men and sat down facing his friend.

The expression on M. Bouc's face gave him, as he would have expressed it, furiously to think. It was clear that something out of the common had happened.

'What has occurred?' he asked.

'You may well ask that. First this snow – this stoppage. And now—'

He paused – and a sort of strangled gasp came from the *wagon lit* conductor.

'And now what?'

'*And now a passenger lies dead in his berth – stabbed.*'

M. Bouc spoke with a kind of calm desperation.

'A passenger? Which passenger?'

'An American. A man called – called—' He consulted some notes in front of him. 'Ratchett – that is right – Ratchett?'

'Yes, monsieur,' the *wagon lit* man gulped.

Poirot looked at him. He was as white as chalk.

'You had better let that man sit down,' he said. 'He may faint otherwise.'

The *chef de train* moved slightly and the *wagon lit* man sank down in the corner and buried his face in his hands.

'Brr!' said Poirot. 'This is serious!'

'Certainly it is serious. To begin with, a murder – that by itself is a calamity of the first water. But not only that, the circumstances are unusual. Here we are, brought to a standstill. We may be here for hours – and not only hours – days! Another circumstance. Passing through most countries we have the police of that country on the train. But in Yugoslavia – no. You comprehend?'

'It is a position of great difficulty,' said Poirot.

'There is worse to come. Dr Constantine – I forgot, I have not introduced you – Dr Constantine, M. Poirot.'

The little dark man bowed and Poirot returned it.

'Dr Constantine is of the opinion that death occurred at about 1 a.m.'

'It is difficult to say exactly in these matters,' said the doctor, 'but I think I can say definitely that death occurred between midnight and two in the morning.'

'When was this Mr Ratchett last seen alive?' asked Poirot.

'He is known to have been alive at about twenty minutes to one, when he spoke to the conductor,' said M. Bouc.

'That is quite correct,' said Poirot. 'I myself heard what passed. That is the last thing known?'

'Yes.'

Poirot turned toward the doctor, who continued: 'The window of Mr Ratchett's compartment was found wide open, leading one to suppose that the murderer escaped that way. But in my opinion that open window is a blind. Anyone departing that way would have left distinct traces in the snow. There were none.'

'The crime was discovered – when?' asked Poirot.

'Michel!'

The *wagon lit* conductor sat up. His face still looked pale and frightened.

'Tell this gentleman exactly what occurred,' ordered M. Bouc.

The man spoke somewhat jerkily.

'The valet of this Mr Ratchett, he tapped several times at the door this morning. There was no answer. Then, half an hour ago, the restaurant-car attendant came. He wanted to know if monsieur was taking *déjeuner*. It was eleven o'clock, you comprehend.

'I open the door for him with my key. But there is a chain, too, and that is fastened. There is no answer and it is very still in there, and cold – but cold. With the window open and snow drifting in. I thought the gentleman had had a fit, perhaps. I got the *chef de train*. We broke the chain and went in. He was – *ah! c'était terrible!*'

He buried his face in his hands again.

'The door was locked and chained on the inside,' said Poirot thoughtfully. 'It was not suicide – eh?'

The Greek doctor gave a sardonic laugh.

'Does a man who commits suicide stab himself in ten – twelve – fifteen places?' he asked.

Poirot's eyes opened.

'That is great ferocity,' he said.

'It is a woman,' said the *chef de train*, speaking for the first time. 'Depend upon it, it was a woman. Only a woman would stab like that.'

Dr Constantine screwed up his face thoughtfully.

'She must have been a very strong woman,' he said. 'It is not my desire to speak technically – that is only confusing – but I can assure you that one or two of the blows were delivered with such force as to drive them through hard belts of bone and muscle.'

'It was not, clearly, a scientific crime,' said Poirot.

'It was most unscientific,' said Dr Constantine. 'The blows seem to have been delivered haphazard and at random. Some have glanced off, doing hardly any damage. It is as though somebody had shut their eyes and then in a frenzy struck blindly again and again.'

'*C'est une femme,*' said the *chef de train* again. 'Women are like that. When they are enraged they have great strength.' He nodded so sagely that everyone suspected a personal experience of his own.

'I have, perhaps, something to contribute to your store of knowledge,' said Poirot. 'Mr Ratchett spoke to me yesterday. He told me, as far as I was able to understand him, that he was in danger of his life.'

'"Bumped off" – that is the American expression, is it not? said M. Bouc. 'Then it is not a woman. It is a "gangster" or a "gunman".'

The *chef de train* looked pained at his theory having come to naught.

'If so,' said Poirot, 'it seems to have been done very amateurishly.'

His tone expressed professional disapproval.

'There is a large American on the train,' said M. Bouc, pursuing his idea – 'a common-looking man with terrible clothes. He chews the gum, which I believe is not done in good circles. You know whom I mean?'

The *wagon lit* conductor to whom he had appealed nodded.

'*Oui*, monsieur, the No. 16. But it cannot have been he. I should have seen him enter or leave the compartment.'

'You might not. You might not. But we will go into that presently. The question is, what to do?' He looked at Poirot.

Poirot looked back at him.

'Come, my friend,' said M. Bouc. 'You comprehend what I am about to ask of you. I know your powers. Take command of this investigation! No, no, do not refuse. See, to us it is serious – I speak for the Compagnie Internationale des Wagons Lits. By the time the Yugoslavian police arrive, how simple if we can present them with the solution! Otherwise delays, annoyances, a million and one inconveniences. Perhaps, who knows, serious annoyance to innocent persons. Instead – *you* solve the mystery! We say, "A murder has occurred – *this* is the criminal!"'

'And suppose I do not solve it?'

'Ah! *Mon cher.*' M. Bouc's voice became positively caressing. 'I know your reputation. I know something of your methods. This is the ideal case for you. To look up the antecedents of all these people, to discover their *bona fides* – that all takes time and endless inconvenience. But have I not heard you say often that to solve a case a man has only to lie back in his chair and think? Do that. Interview the passengers on the train, view the body, examine what clues there are and then – well, I have faith in you! I am assured that it is no idle boast of yours. Lie back and think – use (as I have heard you say so often) the little grey cells of the mind – and you will *know*!'

He leaned forward, looking affectionately at his friend.

'Your faith touches me, my friend,' said Poirot emotionally. 'As you say, this cannot be a difficult case. I myself, last night – but we will not speak of that now. In truth, this problem intrigues me. I was reflecting, not half an hour ago, that many hours of boredom lay ahead whilst we are stuck here. And now – a problem lies ready to my hand.'

'You accept then?' said M. Bouc eagerly.

'*C'est entendu.* You place the matter in my hands.'

'Good – we are all at your service.'

'To begin with, I should like a plan of the Istanbul–Calais coach, with a note of the people who occupied the several compartments, and I should also like to see their passports and their tickets.'

'Michel will get you those.'

The *wagon lit* conductor left the compartment.

'What other passengers are there on the train?' asked Poirot.

'In this coach Dr Constantine and I are the only travellers. In the coach from Bucharest is an old gentleman with a lame leg. He is well known to the conductor. Beyond that are the ordinary carriages, but these do not concern us, since they were locked after dinner had been served last night. Forward of the Istanbul–Calais coach there is only the dining-car.'

'Then it seems,' said Poirot slowly, 'as though we must look for our murderer in the Istanbul–Calais coach.' He turned to the doctor. 'That is what you were hinting, I think?'

The Greek nodded.

'At half an hour after midnight we ran into the snowdrift. No one can have left the train since then.'

M. Bouc said solemnly.

'*The murderer is with us – on the train now . . .*'

— 6 —

A WOMAN?

'First of all,' said Poirot, 'I should like a word or two with young Mr MacQueen. He may be able to give us valuable information.'

'Certainly,' said M. Bouc.

He turned to the *chef de train*.

'Get Mr MacQueen to come here.'

The *chef de train* left the carriage.

The conductor returned with a bundle of passports and tickets. M. Bouc took them from him.

'Thank you, Michel. It would be best now, I think, if you were to go back to your post. We will take your evidence formally later.'

'Very good, monsieur.'

Michel in his turn left the carriage.

'After we have seen young MacQueen,' said Poirot, 'perhaps *M. le docteur* will come with me to the dead man's carriage.'

'Certainly.'

'After we have finished there—'

But at this moment the *chef de train* returned with Hector MacQueen.

M. Bouc rose.

'We are a little cramped here,' he said pleasantly. 'Take my seat, Mr MacQueen. M. Poirot will sit opposite you – so.'

He turned to the *chef de train*.

'Clear all the people out of the restaurant-car,' he said, 'and let it be left free for M. Poirot. You will conduct your interviews there, *mon cher*?'

'It would be the most convenient, yes,' agreed Poirot.

MacQueen had stood looking from one to the other, not quite following the rapid flow of French.

'*Qu'est ce qu'il y a?*' he began laboriously. '*Pourquoi–?*'

With a vigorous gesture Poirot motioned him to the seat in the corner. He took it and began once more.

'*Pourquoi–?*' Then, checking himself and relapsing into his own tongue, 'What's up on the train? Has anything happened?'

He looked from one man to another.

Poirot nodded.

'Exactly. Something has happened. Prepare yourself for a shock. *Your employer, Mr Ratchett, is dead!*'

MacQueen's mouth pursed itself in a whistle. Except that his eyes grew a shade brighter, he showed no signs of shock or distress.

'So they got him after all,' he said.

'What exactly do you mean by that phrase, Mr MacQueen?'

MacQueen hesitated.

'You are assuming,' said Poirot, 'that Mr Ratchett was murdered?'

'Wasn't he?' This time MacQueen did show surprise. 'Why, yes,' he said slowly. 'That's just what I did think. Do you mean he just died in his sleep? Why, the old man was as tough as – as tough—'

He stopped, at a loss for a simile.

'No, no,' said Poirot. 'Your assumption was quite right. Mr Ratchett was murdered. Stabbed. But I should like to know why you were so sure it *was* murder, and not just – death.'

MacQueen hesitated.

'I must get this clear,' he said. 'Who exactly are you? And where do you come in?'

'I represent the Compagnie Internationale des Wagons Lits.' He paused, then added, 'I am a detective. My name is Hercule Poirot.'

If he expected an effect he did not get one. MacQueen said merely, 'Oh, yes?' and waited for him to go on.

'You know the name, perhaps.'

'Why, it does seem kind of familiar – only I always thought it was a woman's dressmaker.'

Hercule Poirot looked at him with distaste.

'It is incredible!' he said.

'What's incredible?'

'Nothing. Let us advance with the matter in hand. I want you to tell me, Mr MacQueen, all that you know about the dead man. You were not related to him?'

'No. I am – was – his secretary.'

'For how long have you held that post?'

'Just over a year.'

'Please give me all the information you can.'

'Well, I met Mr Ratchett just over a year ago when I was in Persia—'

Poirot interrupted.

'What were you doing there?'

'I had come over from New York to look into an oil concession. I don't suppose you want to hear all about that. My friends and I had been let down rather badly over it. Mr Ratchett was in the

41

same hotel. He had just had a row with his secretary. He offered me the job and I took it. I was at a loose end, and glad to find a well-paid job ready made, as it were.'

'And since then?'

'We've travelled about. Mr Ratchett wanted to see the world. He was hampered by knowing no languages. I acted more as a courier than as a secretary. It was a pleasant life.'

'Now tell me as much as you can about your employer.'

The young man shrugged his shoulders. A perplexed expression passed over his face.

'That's not so easy.'

'What was his full name?'

'Samuel Edward Ratchett.'

'He was an American citizen?'

'Yes.'

'What part of America did he come from?'

'I don't know.'

'Well, tell me what you do know.'

'The actual truth is, M. Poirot, that I know nothing at all! Mr Ratchett never spoke of himself, or of his life in America.'

'Why do you think that was?'

'I don't know. I imagined that he might have been ashamed of his beginnings. Some men are.'

'Does that strike you as a satisfactory solution?'

'Frankly, it doesn't.'

'Has he any relations?'

'He never mentioned any.'

Poirot pressed the point.

'You must have formed *some* theory, Mr MacQueen.'

'Well, yes, I did. For one thing, I don't believe Ratchett was his real name. I think he left America definitely in order to escape someone or something. I think he was successful – until a few weeks ago.'

'And then?'

'He began to get letters – threatening letters.'

'Did you see them?'

'Yes. It was my business to attend to his correspondence. The first letter came a fortnight ago.'

'Were these letters destroyed?'

'No, I think I've got a couple still in my files – one I know Ratchett tore up in a rage. Shall I get them for you?'

'If you would be so good.'

MacQueen left the compartment. He returned a few minutes

later and laid down two sheets of rather dirty notepaper before Poirot.

The first letter ran as follows:

'Thought you'd doublecross us and get away with it, did you? Not on your life. We're out to GET you, Ratchett, and we WILL get you!'

There was no signature.

With no comment beyond raised eyebrows, Poirot picked up the second letter.

'We're going to take you for a ride, Ratchett. Some time soon. We're going to GET you, see?'

Poirot laid the letter down.

'The style is monotonous!' he said. 'More so than the handwriting.'

MacQueen stared at him.

'You would not observe,' said Poirot pleasantly. 'It requires the eye of one used to such things. This letter was not written by one person, Mr MacQueen. Two or more persons wrote it – each writing a letter of a word at a time. Also, the letters are printed. That makes the task of identifying the handwriting much more difficult.'

He paused, then said: 'Did you know that Mr Ratchett had applied for help to me?'

'To *you?*'

MacQueen's astonished tone told Poirot quite certainly that the young man had not known of it. He nodded.

'Yes. He was alarmed. Tell me, how did he act when he received the first letter?'

MacQueen hesitated.

'It's difficult to say. He – he – passed it off with a laugh in that quiet way of his. But somehow' – he gave a slight shiver – 'I felt that there was a good deal going on underneath the quietness.'

Poirot nodded. Then he asked an unexpected question.

'Mr MacQueen, will you tell me, quite honestly, exactly how you regarded your employer? Did you like him?'

Hector MacQueen took a moment or two before replying.

'No,' he said at last. 'I did not.'

'Why?'

'I can't exactly say. He was always quite pleasant in his manner.' He paused, then said, 'I'll tell you the truth, M. Poirot. I disliked and distrusted him. He was, I am sure, a cruel and a dangerous man. I must admit, though, that I have no reasons to advance for my opinion.'

'Thank you, Mr MacQueen. One further question – when did you last see Mr Ratchett alive?'

'Last evening about' – he thought for a minute – 'ten o'clock, I should say. I went into his compartment to take down some memoranda from him.'

'On what subject?'

'Some tiles and antique pottery that he bought in Persia. What was delivered was not what he had purchased. There has been a long, vexatious correspondence on the subject.'

'And that was the last time Mr Ratchett was seen alive?'

'Yes, I suppose so.'

'Do you know when Mr Ratchett received the last threatening letter?'

'On the morning of the day we left Constantinople.'

'There is one more question I must ask you, Mr MacQueen. Were you on good terms with your employer?'

The young man's eyes twinkled suddenly.

'This is where I'm supposed to go all goosefleshy down the back. In the words of a bestseller, "You've nothing on me." Ratchett and I were on perfectly good terms.'

'Perhaps, Mr MacQueen, you will give me your full name and your address in America.'

MacQueen gave his name – Hector Willard MacQueen – and an address in New York.

Poirot leaned back against the cushions.

'That is all for the present, Mr MacQueen,' he said. 'I should be obliged if you would keep the matter of Mr Ratchett's death to yourself for a little time.'

'His valet, Masterman, will have to know.'

'He probably knows already,' said Poirot dryly. 'If so, try to get him to hold his tongue.'

'That oughtn't to be difficult. He's a Britisher, and does what he calls "Keeps himself to himself". He's a low opinion of Americans and no opinion at all of any other nationality.'

'Thank you, Mr MacQueen.'

The American left the carriage.

'Well?' demanded M. Bouc. 'You believe what he says, this young man?'

'He seems honest and straightforward. He did not pretend to any affection for his employer as he probably would have done had he been involved in any way. It is true Mr Ratchett did not tell him that he had tried to enlist my services and failed, but I do not think that is really a suspicious circumstance. I fancy Mr Ratchett was a gentleman who kept his own counsel on every possible occasion.'

'So you pronounce one person at least innocent of the crime,' said M. Bouc jovially.

Poirot cast on him a look of reproach.

'Me, I suspect everybody till the last minute,' he said. 'All the same, I must admit that I cannot see this sober, long-headed MacQueen losing his head and stabbing his victim twelve or fourteen times. It is not in accord with his psychology – not at all.'

'No,' said M. Bouc thoughtfully. 'That is the act of a man driven almost crazy with a frenzied hate – it suggests more the Latin temperament. Or else it suggests, as our friend the *chef de train* insisted, a woman.'

— 7 —

THE BODY

FOLLOWED by Dr Constantine, Poirot made his way to the next coach and the compartment occupied by the murdered man. The conductor came and unlocked the door for them with his key.

The two men passed inside. Poirot turned inquiringly to his companion.

'How much has been disarranged in this compartment?'

'Nothing has been touched. I was careful not to move the body in making my examination.'

Poirot nodded. He looked round him.

The first thing that struck the senses was the intense cold. The window was pushed down as far as it would go and the blind was drawn up.

'Brrr,' observed Poirot.

The other smiled appreciatively.

'I did not like to close it,' he said.

Poirot examined the window carefully.

'You are right,' he announced. 'Nobody left the carriage this way. Possibly the open window was intended to suggest the fact, but, if so, the snow has defeated the murderer's object.'

He examined the frame of the window carefully. Taking a small case from his pocket he blew a little powder over it.

'No fingerprints at all,' he said. 'That means it has been wiped. Well, if there had been fingerprints it would have told us very little. They would have been those of Mr Ratchett or his valet or the conductor. Criminals do not make mistakes of that kind nowadays.

'And that being so,' he added cheerfully, 'we might as well shut the window. Positively it is the cold storage in here!'

He suited the action to the word and then turned his attention for the first time to the motionless figure lying in the bunk.

Ratchett lay on his back. His pyjama jacket, stained with rusty patches, had been unbuttoned and thrown back.

'I had to see the nature of the wounds, you see,' explained the doctor.

Poirot nodded. He bent over the body. Finally he straightened himself with a slight grimace.

'It is not pretty,' he said. 'Someone must have stood there and stabbed him again and again. How many wounds are there exactly?'

'I make it twelve. One or two are so slight as to be practically scratches. On the other hand, at least three would be capable of causing death.'

Something in the doctor's tone caught Poirot's attention. He looked at him sharply. The little Greek was standing staring down at the body with a puzzled frown.

'Something strikes you as odd, does it not?' he asked gently. 'Speak, my friend. There is something here that puzzles you?'

'You are right,' acknowledged the other.

'What is it?'

'You see these two wounds – here and here. He pointed. 'They are deep, each cut must have severed blood-vessels – and yet – the edges do not gape. They have not bled as one would have expected.'

'Which suggests?'

'That the man was already dead – some little time dead – when they were delivered. But this is surely absurd.'

'It would seem so,' said Poirot thoughtfully. 'Unless our murderer figured to himself that he had not accomplished his job properly and came back to make quite sure; but that is manifestly absurd! Anything else?'

46

'Well, just one thing.'

'And that?'

'You see this wound here – under the right arm – near the right shoulder. Take this pencil of mine. Could you deliver such a blow?'

Poirot raised his hand.

'*Précisément*,' he said. 'I see. With the *right* hand it is exceedingly difficult – almost impossible. One would have to strike back-handed, as it were. But if the blow were struck with the *left* hand—'

'Exactly, M. Poirot. That blow was almost certainly struck with the *left* hand.'

'So that our murderer is left-handed? No, it is more difficult than that, is it not?'

'As you say, M. Poirot. Some of these other blows are just as obviously right-handed.'

'Two people. We are back at two people again,' murmured the detective. He asked abruptly: 'Was the electric light on?'

'It is difficult to say. You see, it is turned off by the conductor every morning about ten o'clock.'

'The switches will tell us,' said Poirot.

He examined the switch of the top light and also the roll-back bed-head light. The former was turned off. The latter was closed.

'*Eh bien*,' he said thoughtfully. 'We have here a hypothesis of the First and Second Murderer, as the great Shakespeare would put it. The First Murderer stabbed his victim and left the compartment, turning off the light. The Second Murderer came in in the dark, did not see that his or her work had been done and stabbed at least twice at a dead body. *Que pensez-vous de ça?*'

'Magnificent,' said the little doctor with enthusiasm.

The other's eyes twinkled.

'You think so? I am glad. It sounded to me a little like non-sense.'

'What other explanation can there be?'

'That is just what I am asking myself. Have we here a coinci-dence or what? Are there any other inconsistencies, such as would point to two people being concerned?'

'I think I can say yes. Some of these blows, as I have already said, point to a weakness – a lack of strength or a lack of determi-nation. They are feeble glancing blows. But this one here – and this one—' Again he pointed. 'Great strength was needed for those blows. They have penetrated the muscle.'

'They were, in your opinion, delivered by a man?'

'Most certainly.'

'They could not have been delivered by a woman?'

'A young, vigorous, athletic woman might have struck them, especially if she were in the grip of a strong emotion, but it is my opinion highly unlikely.'

Poirot was silent a moment or two.

The other said anxiously: 'You understand my point?'

'Perfectly,' said Poirot. 'The matter begins to clear itself up wonderfully! The murderer was a man of great strength, he was feeble, it was a woman, it was a right-handed person, it was a left-handed person – *Ah! c'est rigolo, tout ça!*'

He spoke with sudden anger.

'And the victim – what does he do in all this? Does he cry out? Does he struggle? Does he defend himself?'

He slipped his hand under the pillow and drew out the automatic pistol which Ratchett had shown him the day before.

'Fully loaded, you see,' he said.

They looked round them. Ratchett's day clothing was hanging from the hooks on the wall. On the small table formed by the lid of the washing-basin were various objects – false teeth in a glass of water; another glass, empty; a bottle of mineral water, a large flask and an ash-tray containing the butt of a cigar and some charred fragments of paper; also two burnt matches.

The doctor picked up the empty glass and sniffed it.

'Here is the explanation of the victim's inertia,' he said quietly.

'Drugged?'

'Yes.'

Poirot nodded. He picked up the two matches and scrutinized them carefully.

'You have a clue, then?' demanded the little doctor eagerly.

'Those two matches are of a different shape,' said Poirot. 'One is flatter than the other. You see?'

'It is the kind you get on the train,' said the doctor, 'in paper covers.'

Poirot was feeling in the pockets of Ratchett's clothing. Presently he pulled out a box of matches. He compared them carefully.

'The rounder one is a match struck by Mr Ratchett,' he said. 'Let us see if he had also the flatter kind.'

But a further search showed no other matches.

Poirot's eyes were darting about the compartment. They were bright and sharp like a bird's. One felt that nothing could escape their scrutiny.

With a little exclamation he bent and picked up something from the floor.

It was a small square of cambric, very dainty. In the corner was an embroidered initial – H.

'A woman's handkerchief,' said the doctor. 'Our friend the *chef de train* was right. There is a woman concerned in this.'

'And most conveniently she leaves her handkerchief behind!' said Poirot. 'Exactly as it happens in the books and on the films – and to make things even easier for us it is marked with an initial.'

'What a stroke of luck for us!' exclaimed the doctor.

'Is it not?' said Poirot.

Something in his tone surprised the doctor.

But before he could ask for elucidation, Poirot had made another dive on to the floor.

This time he held out on the palm of his hand – a pipe cleaner.

'It is perhaps the property of Mr Ratchett?' suggested the doctor.

'There was no pipe in any of his pockets, and no tobacco or tobacco pouch.'

'Then it is a clue.'

'Oh! decidedly. And again dropped most conveniently. A masculine clue this time, you note! One cannot complain of having no clues in this case. There are clues here in abundance. By the way, what have you done with the weapon?'

'There was no sign of any weapon. The murderer must have taken it away with him.'

'I wonder why,' mused Poirot.

'Ah!' The doctor had been delicately exploring the pyjama pockets of the dead man.

'I overlooked this,' he said. 'I unbuttoned the jacket and threw it straight back.'

From the breast pocket he brought out a gold watch. The case was dented savagely, and the hands pointed to a quarter-past one.

'You see?' cried Constantine eagerly. 'This gives us the hour of the crime. It agrees with my calculations. Between midnight and two in the morning is what I said, and probably about one o'clock, though it is difficult to be exact in these matters. *Eh bien,* here is confirmation. A quarter-past one. That was the hour of the crime.'

'It is possible, yes. It is certainly possible.'

The doctor looked at him curiously.

'You will pardon me, M. Poirot, but I do not quite understand you.'

'I do not understand myself,' said Poirot. 'I understand nothing at all, and, as you perceive, it worries me.'

He sighed and bent over the little table, examining the charred fragment of paper. He murmured to himself.

'What I need at this moment is an old-fashioned woman's hat-box.'

Dr Constantine was at a loss to know what to make of this singular remark. In any case, Poirot gave him no time for questions. Opening the door into the corridor, he called for the conductor.

The man arrived at a run.

'How many women are there in this coach?'

The conductor counted on his fingers.

'One, two, three – six, monsieur. The old American lady, a Swedish lady, the young English lady, the Countess Andrenyi and Madame la Princesse Dragomiroff and her maid.'

Poirot considered.

'They all have hat-boxes, yes?'

'Yes, monsieur.'

'Then bring me – let me see – yes, the Swedish lady's and that of the lady's-maid. Those two are the only hope. You will tell them it is a Customs regulation – something – anything that occurs to you.'

'That will be all right, monsieur. Neither lady is in her compartment at the moment.'

'Then be quick.'

The conductor departed. He returned with the two hat-boxes. Poirot opened that of the lady's-maid and tossed it aside. Then he opened the Swedish lady's and uttered an exclamation of satisfaction. Removing the hats carefully, he disclosed round humps of wire-netting.

'Ah, here is what we need. About fifteen years ago hat-boxes were made like this. You skewered through the hat with a hatpin on to this hump of wire-netting.'

As he spoke he was skilfully removing two of the attachments. Then he repacked the hat-box and told the conductor to return them both where they belonged.

When the door was shut once more he turned to his companion.

'See you, my dear doctor, me, I am not one to rely upon the expert procedure. It is the psychology I seek, not the fingerprint or the cigarette ash. But in this case I would welcome a little scientific assistance. This compartment is full of clues, but can I be sure that those clues are really what they seem to be?'

'I do not quite understand you, M. Poirot.'

'Well, to give you an example – we find a woman's handkerchief. Did a woman drop it? Or did a man, committing the crime, say to himself: "I will make this look like a woman's crime. I will stab my enemy an unnecessary number of times, making some of the blows feeble and ineffective, and I will drop this handkerchief where no one can miss it"? That is one possibility. Then there is another. Did a woman kill him and did she deliberately drop a pipe cleaner to make it look like a man's work? Or are we seriously to suppose that two people – a man and a woman – were separately concerned, and that each was so careless as to drop a clue to their identity? It is a little too much of a coincidence, that!'

'But where does the hat-box come in?' asked the doctor, still puzzled.

'Ah! I'm coming to that. As I say, these clues, the watch stopped at a quarter-past one, the handkerchief, the pipe cleaner, they may be genuine, or they may be fake. As to that I cannot yet tell. But there is *one* clue here which I believe – though again I may be wrong – has *not* been faked. I mean this flat match, *M. le docteur.* *I believe that that match was used by the murderer, not by Mr Ratchett.* It was used to burn an incriminating paper of some kind. Possibly a note. If so, there was something in that note, some mistake, some error, that left a possible clue to the assailant. I am going to endeavour to resurrect what that something was.'

He went out of the compartment and returned a few moments later with a small spirit stove and a pair of curling-tongs.

'I use them for the moustaches,' he said, referring to the latter.

The doctor watched him with great interest. He flattened out the two humps of wire, and with great care wriggled the charred scrap of paper on to one of them. He clapped the other on top of it and then, holding both pieces together with the tongs, held the whole thing over the flame of the spirit lamp.

'It is a very makeshift affair, this,' he said over his shoulder. 'Let us hope that it will answer its purpose.'

The doctor watched the proceedings attentively. The metal began to glow. Suddenly he saw faint indications of letters. Words formed themselves slowly – words of fire.

It was a very tiny scrap. Only three words and a part of another showed.

'-member little Daisy Armstrong.'

'Ah!' Poirot gave a sharp exclamation.

'It tells you something?' asked the doctor.

Poirot's eyes were shining. He laid down the tongs carefully.

'Yes,' he said. '*I know the dead man's real name. I know why he had to leave America.*'

'What was his name?'

'Cassetti.'

'Cassetti.' Constantine knitted his brows. 'It brings back to me something. Some years ago. I cannot remember . . . It was a case in America, was it not?'

'Yes,' said Poirot. 'A case in America.'

Further than that Poirot was not disposed to be communicative. He looked round him as he went on: 'We will go into all that presently. Let us first make sure that we have seen all there is to be seen here.'

Quickly and deftly he went once more through the pockets of the dead man's clothes but found nothing there of interest. He tried the communicating door which led through to the next compartment, but it was bolted on the other side.

'There is one thing that I do not understand,' said Dr Constantine. 'If the murderer did not escape through the window, and if this communicating door was bolted on the other side, and if the door into the corridor was not only locked on the inside but chained, how, then, did the murderer leave the compartment?'

'That is what the audience says when a person bound hand and foot is shut into a cabinet – and disappears.'

'You mean—'

'I mean,' explained Poirot, 'that if the murderer intended us to believe that he had escaped by way of the window he would naturally make it appear that the other two exits were impossible. Like the "disappearing person" in the cabinet – it is a trick. It is our business to find out how the trick is done.'

He locked the communicating door on their side.

'In case,' he said, 'the excellent Mrs Hubbard should take it into her head to acquire first-hand details of the crime to write to her daughter.'

He looked round once more.

'There is nothing more to do here, I think. Let us rejoin M. Bouc.'

THE ARMSTRONG KIDNAPPING CASE

THEY found M. Bouc finishing an omelet.

'I though it best to have lunch served immediately in the restaurant-car,' he said. 'Afterwards it will be cleared and M. Poirot can conduct his examination of the passengers there. In the meantime I have ordered them to bring us three some food here.'

'An excellent idea,' said Poirot.

Neither of the other two men was hungry, and the meal was soon eaten, but not till they were sipping their coffee did M. Bouc mention the subject that was occupying all their minds.

'*Eh bien?*' he asked.

'*Eh bien*, I have discovered the identity of the victim. I know why it was imperative he should leave America.'

'Who was he?'

'Do you remember reading of the Armstrong baby? This is the man who murdered little Daisy Armstrong – Cassetti.'

'I recall it now. A shocking affair – though I cannot remember the details.'

'Colonel Armstrong was an Englishman – a V.C. He was half American, as his mother was a daughter of W. K. Van der Halt, the Wall Street millionaire. He married the daughter of Linda Arden, the most famous tragic American actress of her day. They lived in America and had one child – a girl – whom they idolised. When she was three years old she was kidnapped, and an impossibly high sum demanded as the price of her return. I will not weary you with all the intricacies that followed. I will come to the moment, when, after having paid over the enormous sum of two hundred thousand dollars, the child's dead body was discovered, it having been dead at least a fortnight. Public indignation rose to fever point. And there was worse to follow. Mrs Armstrong was expecting another child. Following the shock of the discovery, she gave birth to a dead child born prematurely, and herself died. Her broken-hearted husband shot himself.'

'*Mon Dieu*, what a tragedy. I remember now,' said M. Bouc. 'There was also another death, if I remember rightly?'

'Yes – an unfortunate French or Swiss nursemaid. The police were convinced that she had some knowledge of the crime. They refused to believe her hysterical denials. Finally, in a fit of despair, the poor girl threw herself from a window and was killed. It was proved afterwards that she was absolutely innocent of any complicity in the crime.'

'It is not good to think of,' said M. Bouc.

'About six months later, this man Cassetti was arrested as the head of the gang who kidnapped the child. They had used the same methods in the past. If the police seemed likely to get on their trail, they had killed their prisoner, hidden the body, and continued to extract as much money as possible before the crime was discovered.

'Now, I will make clear to you this, my friend. Cassetti was the man! But by means of the enormous wealth he had piled up and by the secret hold he had over various persons, he was acquitted on some technical inaccuracy. Notwithstanding that, he would have been lynched by the populace had he not been clever enough to give them the slip. It is now clear to me what happened. He changed his name and left America. Since then he has been a gentleman of leisure, travelling abroad and living on his *rentes*.'

'*Ah! quel animal!*' M. Bouc's tone was redolent of heart-felt disgust. 'I cannot regret that he is dead – not at all!'

'I agree with you.'

'*Tout de même*, it is not necessary that he should be killed on the Orient Express. There are other places.'

Poirot smiled a little. He realized that M. Bouc was biased in the matter.

'The question we have now to ask ourselves is this,' he said. 'Is this murder the work of some rival gang whom Cassetti had double-crossed in the past, or is it an act of private vengeance?'

He explained his discovery of the few words on the charred fragment of paper.

'If I am right in my assumption, then the letter was burnt by the murderer. Why? Because it mentioned the word "Armstrong", which is the clue to the mystery.'

'Are there any members of the Armstrong family living?'

'That, unfortunately, I do not know. I think I remember reading of a younger sister of Mrs Armstrong's.'

Poirot went on to relate the joint conclusions of himself and Dr Constantine. M. Bouc brightened at the mention of the broken watch.

'That seems to give us the time of the crime very exactly.'

'Yes,' said Poirot. 'It is very convenient.'

There was an indescribable something in his tone that made both the other two look at him curiously.

'You say that you yourself heard Ratchett speak to the conductor at twenty minutes to one?'

Poirot related just what had occurred.

'Well,' said M. Bouc, 'that proves at least that Cassetti – or Ratchett, as I shall continue to call him – was certainly alive at twenty minutes to one.'

'Twenty-three minutes to one, to be precise.'

'Then at twelve thirty-seven, to put it formally, Mr Ratchett was alive. That is *one* fact, at least.'

Poirot did not reply. He sat looking thoughtfully in front of him.

There was a tap on the door, and the restaurant attendant entered.

'The restaurant-car is free now, monsieur,' he said.

'We will go there,' said M. Bouc, rising.

'I may accompany you?' asked Constantine.

'Certainly, my dear doctor. Unless M. Poirot has any objection?'

'Not at all. Not at all,' said Poirot.

After a little politeness in the matter of procedure, '*Après vous, monsieur*.' '*Mais non, après vous,*' they left the compartment.

PART II

THE EVIDENCE

— I —

THE EVIDENCE OF THE
WAGON LIT CONDUCTOR

In the restaurant-car all was in readiness.

Poirot and M. Bouc sat together on one side of a table. The doctor sat across the aisle.

On the table in front of Poirot was a plan of the Istanbul–Calais coach with the names of the passengers marked in in red ink.

The passports and tickets were in a pile at one side. There was writing-paper, ink, pen and pencils.

'Excellent,' said Poirot. 'We can open our court of inquiry without more ado. First, I think, we should take the evidence of the *wagon lit* conductor. You probably know something about the man. What character has he? Is he a man in whose word you would place reliance?'

'I should say so most assuredly. Pierre Michel has been employed by the company for over fifteen years. He is a Frenchman – lives near Calais. Thoroughly respectable and honest. Not, perhaps, remarkable for brains.'

Poirot nodded comprehendingly.

'Good,' he said. 'Let us see him.'

Pierre Michel had recovered some of his assurance, but he was still extremely nervous.

'I hope monsieur will not think that there has been any negligence on my part,' he said anxiously, his eyes going from Poirot to M. Bouc. 'It is a terrible thing that has happened. I hope monsieur does not think that it reflects on me in any way?'

Having soothed the man's fears, Poirot began his questions. He first elicited Michel's name and address, his length of service, and the length of time he had been on this particular route. These

56

particulars he already knew, but the routine questions served to put the man at his ease.

'And now,' went on Poirot, 'let us come to the events of last night. Mr Ratchett retired to bed – when?'

'Almost immediately after dinner, monsieur. Actually before we left Belgrade. So he did on the previous night. He had directed me to make up the bed while he was at dinner, and I did so.'

'Did anybody go into his compartment afterwards?'

'His valet, monsieur, and the young American gentleman his secretary.'

'Anyone else?'

'No, monsieur, not that I know of.'

'Good. And that is the last you saw or heard of him?'

'No, monsieur. You forget, he rang his bell about twenty to one – soon after we had stopped.'

'What happened exactly?'

'I knocked at the door, but he called out and said he had made a mistake.'

'In English or in French?'

'In French.'

'What were his words exactly?'

'Ce n'est rien. Je me suis trompé.'

'Quite right,' said Poirot. 'That is what I heard. And then you went away?'

'Yes, monsieur.'

'Did you go back to your seat?'

'No, monsieur, I went first to answer another bell that had just rung.'

'Now, Michel, I am going to ask you an important question. Where were you at a quarter-past one?'

'I, monsieur? I was at my little seat at the end – facing up the corridor.'

'You are sure?'

'Mais oui – at least—'

'Yes?'

'I went into the next coach, the Athens coach, to speak to my colleague there. We spoke about the snow. That was at some time soon after one o'clock. I cannot say exactly.'

'And you returned – when?'

'One of my bells rang, monsieur – I remember – I told you. It was the American lady. She had rung several times.'

'I recollect,' said Poirot. 'And after that?'

'After that, monsieur? I answered your bell and brought you

57

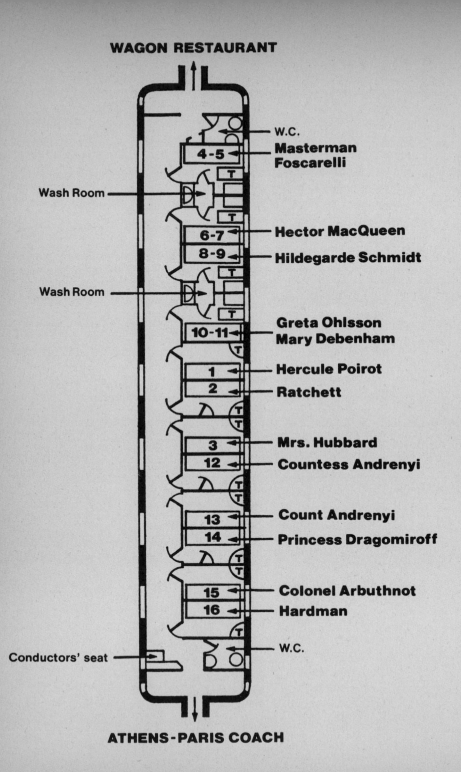

WAGON RESTAURANT

W.C.

4-5 — **Masterman Foscarelli**

Wash Room

Hector MacQueen

6-7 — **Hector MacQueen**

8-9 — **Hildegarde Schmidt**

Wash Room

10-11 — **Greta Ohlsson Mary Debenham**

1 — **Hercule Poirot**

2 — **Ratchett**

3 — **Mrs. Hubbard**

12 — **Countess Andrenyi**

13 — **Count Andrenyi**

14 — **Princess Dragomiroff**

15 — **Colonel Arbuthnot**

16 — **Hardman**

W.C.

Conductors' seat

ATHENS-PARIS COACH

some mineral water. Then, about half an hour later, I made up the bed in one of the other compartments – that of the young American gentleman, Mr Ratchett's secretary.'

'Was Mr MacQueen alone in his compartment when you went to make up his bed?'

'The English colonel from No. 15 was with him. They had been sitting talking.'

'What did the colonel do when he left Mr MacQueen?'

'He went back to his own compartment.'

'No. 15 – that is quite close to your seat, is it not?'

'Yes, monsieur, it is the second compartment from that end of the corridor.'

'His bed was already made up?'

'Yes, monsieur. I had made it up while he was at dinner.'

'What time was all this?'

'I could not say exactly, monsieur. Not later than two o'clock, certainly.'

'And after that?'

'After that, monsieur, I sat in my seat till morning.'

'You did not go again into the Athens coach?'

'No, monsieur.'

'Perhaps you slept?'

'I do not think so, monsieur. The train being at a standstill prevented me from dozing off as I usually do.'

'Did you see any of the passengers moving up or down the corridor?'

The man reflected.

'One of the ladies went to the toilet at the far end, I think.'

'Which lady?'

'I do not know, monsieur. It was far down the corridor, and she had her back to me. She had on a kimono of scarlet with dragons on it.'

Poirot nodded.

'And after that?'

'Nothing, monsieur, until the morning.'

'You are sure?'

'Ah, pardon, you yourself, monsieur, opened your door and looked out for a second.'

'Good, my friend,' said Poirot. 'I wondered whether you would remember that. By the way, I was awakened by what sounded like something heavy falling against my door. Have you any idea what that could have been?'

The man stared at him.

'There was nothing, monsieur. Nothing, I am positive of it.'

'Then I must have had the *cauchemar*,' said Poirot philosophically.

'Unless,' said M. Bouc, 'it was something in the compartment next door that you heard.'

Poirot took no notice of the suggestion. Perhaps he did not wish to before the *wagon lit* conductor.

Let us pass to another point,' he said. 'Supposing that last night an assassin joined the train. Is it quite certain that he could not have left it after committing the crime?'

Pierre Michel shook his head.

'Nor that he can be concealed on it somewhere?'

'It has been well searched,' said M. Bouc. 'Abandon that idea, my friend.'

'Besides,' said Michel, 'no one could get on to the sleeping-car without my seeing them.'

'When was the last stop?'

'Vincovci.'

'What time was that?'

'We should have left there at 11.58. But owing to the weather we were twenty minutes late.'

'Someone might have come along from the ordinary part of the train?'

'No, monsieur. After the service of dinner the door between the ordinary carriages and the sleeping-cars is locked.'

'Did you yourself descend from the train at Vincovci?'

'Yes, monsieur. I got down on to the platform as usual and stood by the step up into the train. The other conductors did the same.'

'What about the forward door? The one near the restaurant-car?'

'It is always fastened on the inside.'

'It is not so fastened now.'

The man looked surprised, then his face cleared.

'Doubtless one of the passengers has opened it to look out on the snow.'

'Probably,' said Poirot.

He tapped thoughtfully on the table for a minute or two.

'Monsieur does not blame me?' said the man timidly.

Poirot smiled on him kindly.

'You have had the evil chance, my friend,' he said. 'Ah! One other point while I remember it. You said that another bell rang just as you were knocking at Mr Ratchett's door. In fact, I heard it myself. Whose was it?'

'It was the bell of Madame la Princesse Dragomiroff. She desired me to summon her maid.'

'And you did so?'

'Yes, monsieur.'

Poirot studied the plan in front of him thoughtfully. Then he inclined his head.

'That is all,' he said. 'For the moment.'

'Thank you, monsieur.'

The man rose. He looked at M. Bouc.

'Do not distress yourself,' said the latter kindly. 'I cannot see that there has been any negligence on your part.'

Gratified, Pierre Michel left the compartment.

— 2 —

THE EVIDENCE OF THE SECRETARY

For a minute or two Poirot remained lost in thought.

'I think,' he said at last, 'that it would be well to have a further word with Mr MacQueen, in view of what we now know.'

The young American appeared promptly.

'Well,' he said, 'how are things going?'

'Not too badly. Since our last conversation I have learnt something – the identity of Mr Ratchett.'

Hector MacQueen leaned forward interestedly.

'Yes?' he said.

'Ratchett, as you suspected, was merely an alias. Ratchett was Cassetti, the man who ran the celebrated kidnapping stunts – including the famous affair of little Daisy Armstrong.'

An expression of utter astonishment appeared on MacQueen's face; then it darkened.

'The damned skunk!' he exclaimed.

'You had no idea of this, Mr MacQueen?'

'No, sir,' said the young American decidedly. 'If I had I'd have cut off my right hand before it had a chance to do secretarial work for him!'

'You feel strongly about the matter, Mr MacQueen?'

'I have a particular reason for doing so. My father was the district attorney who handled the case, M. Poirot. I saw Mrs Armstrong more than once – she was a lovely woman. So gentle and heartbroken.' His face darkened. 'If ever a man deserved what he got, Ratchett or Cassetti is the man. I'm rejoiced at his end. Such a man wasn't fit to live!'

'You almost feel as though you would have been willing to do the good deed yourself?'

'I do. I—' He paused, then flushed rather guiltily. 'Seems I'm kind of incriminating myself.'

'I should be more inclined to suspect you, Mr MacQueen, if you displayed an inordinate sorrow at your employer's decease.'

'I don't think I could do that, even to save myself from the chair,' said MacQueen grimly.

Then he added: 'If I'm not being unduly curious, just how did you figure this out? Cassetti's identity, I mean.'

'By a fragment of a letter found in his compartment.'

'But surely – I mean – that was rather careless of the old man?'

'That depends,' said Poirot, 'on the point of view.'

The young man seemed to find this remark rather baffling. He stared at Poirot as though trying to make him out.

'The task before me,' said Poirot, 'is to make sure of the movements of everyone on the train. No offence need be taken, you understand? It is only a matter of routine.'

'Sure. Get right on with it and let me clear my character if I can.'

'I need hardly ask you the number of your compartment,' said Poirot, smiling, 'since I shared it with you for a night. It is the second class compartment Nos. 6 and 7, and after my departure you had it to yourself.'

'That's right.'

'Now, Mr MacQueen, I want you to describe your movements last night from the time of leaving the dining-car.'

'That's quite easy. I went back to my compartment, read a bit, got out on the platform at Belgrade, decided it was too cold, and got in again. I talked for a while to a young English lady who is in the compartment next to mine. Then I fell into conversation with that Englishman, Colonel Arbuthnot – as a matter of fact I think you passed us as we were talking. Then I went in to Mr Ratchett and, as I told you, took down some memoranda of letters he wanted written. I said good night to him and left him. Colonel Arbuthnot was still standing in the corridor. His compartment was already made up for the night, so I suggested that he should come along to mine. I ordered a couple of drinks and we got right down to it. Discussed world politics and the Government of India and our own troubles with the financial situation and the Wall Street crisis. I don't as a rule cotton on to Britishers – they're a stiff-necked lot – but I liked this one.'

'Do you know what time it was when he left you?'

'Pretty late. Getting on for two o'clock, I should say.'

'You noticed that the train had stopped?'

'Oh, yes. We wondered a bit. Looked out and saw the snow lying very thick, but we didn't think it was serious.'

'What happened when Colonel Arbuthnot finally said good night?'

'He went along to his compartment and I called to the conductor to make up my bed.'

'Where were you whilst he was making it?'

'Standing just outside the door in the corridor smoking a cigarette.'

'And then?'

'And then I went to bed and slept till morning.'

'During the evening did you leave the train at all?'

'Arbuthnot and I thought we'd get out at – what was the name of the place? – Vincovci to stretch our legs a bit. But it was bitterly cold – a blizzard on. We soon hopped back again.'

'By which door did you leave the train?'

'By the one nearest to our compartment.'

'The one next to the dining-car?'

'Yes.'

'Do you remember if it was bolted?'

MacQueen considered.

'Why, yes, I seem to remember it was. At least there was a kind of bar that fitted across the handle. Is that what you mean?'

'Yes. On getting back into the train did you replace that bar?'

'Why, no – I don't think I did. I got in last. No, I don't seem to remember doing so.'

He added suddenly: 'Is that an important point?'

'It may be. Now, I presume, monsieur, that while you and Colonel Arbuthnot were sitting talking the door of your compartment into the corridor was open?'

Hector MacQueen nodded.

'I want you, if you can, to tell me if anyone passed along that corridor *after* the train left Vincovci until the time you parted company for the night.'

MacQueen drew his brows together.

'I think the conductor passed along once,' he said, 'coming from the direction of the dining-car. And a woman passed the other way, going towards it.'

'Which woman?'

'I couldn't say. I didn't really notice. You see, I was just arguing a point with Arbuthnot. I just seem to remember a glimpse of some scarlet silk affair passing the door. I didn't look, and anyway I wouldn't have seen the person's face. As you know, my carriage faces the dining-car end of the train, so a woman going along the corridor in that direction would have her back to me as soon as she'd passed.'

Poirot nodded.

'She was going to the toilet, I presume?'

'I suppose so.'

'And you saw her return?'

'Well, no, now that you mention it, I didn't notice her returning, but I suppose she must have done so.'

'One more question. Do you smoke a pipe, Mr MacQueen?'

'No, sir, I do not.'

Poirot paused a moment.

'I think that is all at present. I should now like to see the valet of Mr Ratchett. By the way, did both you and he always travel second class?'

'He did. But I usually went first – if possible in the adjoining compartment to Mr Ratchett. Then he had most of his baggage put in my compartment and yet could get at both it and me easily whenever he chose. But on this occasion all the first-class berths were booked except the one which he took.'

'I comprehend. Thank you, Mr MacQueen.'

— 3 —

THE EVIDENCE OF THE VALET

THE American was succeeded by the pale Englishman with the inexpressive face whom Poirot had already noticed on the day before. He stood waiting very correctly. Poirot motioned to him to sit down.

'You are, I understand, the valet of Mr Ratchett?'

'Yes, sir.'

'Your name?'

'Edward Henry Masterman.'

'Your age?'

'Thirty-nine.'

'And your home address?'

'21 Friar Street, Clerkenwell.'

'You have heard that your master has been murdered?'

'Yes, sir. A very shocking occurrence.'

'Will you now tell me, please, at what hour you last saw Mr Ratchett?'

The valet considered.

'It must have been about nine o'clock, sir, last night. That or a little after.'

'Tell me in your own words exactly what happened.'

'I went in to Mr Ratchett as usual, sir, and attended to his wants.'

'What were your duties exactly?'

'To fold or hang up his clothes, sir. Put his dental plate in water and see that he had everything he wanted for the night.'

'Was his manner much the same as usual?'

The valet considered a moment.

'Well, sir, I think he was upset.'

'In what way – upset?'

'Over a letter he'd been reading. He asked me if it was I who had put it in his compartment. Of course I told him I hadn't done any such thing, but he swore at me and found fault with everything I did.'

'Was that unusual?'

'Oh, no, sir, he lost his temper easily – as I say, it just depended what had happened to upset him.'

'Did your master ever take a sleeping draught?'

Dr Constantine leaned forward a little.

'Always when travelling by train, sir. He said he couldn't sleep otherwise.'

'Do you know what drug he was in the habit of taking?'

'I couldn't say, I'm sure, sir. There was no name on the bottle. Just "*The Sleeping Draught to be taken at bedtime*".'

'Did he take it last night?'

'Yes, sir. I poured it into a glass and put it on top of the toilet table ready for him.'

'You didn't actually see him drink it?'

'No, sir.'

'What happened next?'

'I asked if there was anything further, and asked what time Mr Ratchett would like to be called in the morning. He said he didn't want to be disturbed till he rang.'

'Was that usual?'

'Quite usual, sir. He used to ring the bell for the conductor and then send him for me when he was ready to get up.'

'Was he usually an early or a late riser?'

'It depended, sir, on his mood. Sometimes he'd get up for breakfast, sometimes he wouldn't get up till just on lunch time.'

'So that you weren't alarmed when the morning wore on and no summons came?'

'No, sir.'

'Did you know that your master had enemies?'

'Yes, sir.'

The man spoke quite unemotionally.

'How did you know?'

'I had heard him discussing some letters, sir, with Mr MacQueen.'

'Had you an affection for your employer, Masterman?'

Masterman's face became, if possible, even more inexpressive than it was normally.

'I should hardly like to say that, sir. He was a generous employer.'

'But you didn't like him?'

'Shall we put it that I don't care very much for Americans, sir?'

'Have you ever been in America?'

'No, sir.'

'Do you remember reading in the paper of the Armstrong kidnapping case?'

A little colour came into the man's cheeks.

'Yes, indeed, sir. A little baby girl, wasn't it? A very shocking affair.'

'Did you know that your employer, Mr Ratchett, was the principal instigator in that affair?'

'No, indeed, sir.' The valet's tone held positive warmth and feeling for the first time. 'I can hardly believe it, sir.'

'Nevertheless, it is true. Now, to pass to your own movements last night. A matter of routine, you understand. What did you do after leaving your master?'

'I told Mr MacQueen, sir, that the master wanted him. Then I went to my own compartment and read.'

'Your compartment was—'

'The end second class one, sir. Next to the dining-car.'

Poirot was looking at his plan.

'I see – and you had which berth?'

'The lower one, sir.'

'That is No. 4?'

'Yes, sir.'

'Is there anyone in with you?'

'Yes, sir. A big Italian fellow.'

'Does he speak English?'

'Well, a kind of English, sir.' The valet's tone was deprecating. 'He's been in America – Chicago – I understand.'

'Do you and he talk together much?'

'No, sir. I prefer to read.'

Poirot smiled. He could visualise the scene – the large voluble Italian, and the snub direct administered by the gentleman's gentleman.

'And what, may I ask, are you reading?' he inquired.

'At present, sir, I am reading *Love's Captive,* by Mrs Arabella Richardson.'

'A good story?'

'I find it highly enjoyable, sir.'

'Well, let us continue. You returned to your compartment and read *Love's Captive* till – when?'

'At about ten-thirty, sir, this Italian wanted to go to bed. So the conductor came and made the beds up.'

'And then you went to bed and to sleep?'

'I went to bed, sir, but I didn't sleep.'

'Why didn't you sleep?'

'I had the toothache, sir.'

'Oh, *là là* – that is painful.'

'Most painful, sir.'

'Did you do anything for it?'

'I applied a little oil of cloves, sir, which relieved the pain a little, but I was still not able to get to sleep. I turned the light on above my head and continued to read – to take my mind off it, as it were.'

'And did you not go to sleep at all?'

'Yes, sir, I dropped off about four in the morning.'

'And your companion?'

'The Italian fellow? Oh, he just snored.'

'He did not leave the compartment at all during the night?'

'No, sir.'

'Did you?'

'No, sir.'

'Did you hear anything during the night?'

'I don't think so, sir. Nothing unusual, I mean. The train being at a standstill made it all very quiet.'

Poirot was silent a moment or two, then he said: 'Well, I think there is very little more to be said. You cannot throw any light upon the tragedy?'

'I'm afraid not. I'm sorry, sir.'

'As far as you know, was there any quarrel or bad blood between your master and Mr MacQueen?'

'Oh, no, sir. Mr MacQueen is a very pleasant gentleman.'

'Where were you in service before you came to Mr Ratchett?'

'With Sir Henry Tomlinson, sir, in Grosvenor Square.'

'Why did you leave him?'

'He was going to East Africa, sir, and did not require my services any longer. But I am sure he will speak for me, sir. I was with him some years.'

'And you have been with Mr Ratchett – how long?'

'Just over nine months, sir.'

'Thank you, Masterman. By the way, are you a pipe smoker?'

'No, sir. I only smoke cigarettes – gaspers, sir.'

'Thank you. That will do.'

Poirot gave him a nod of dismissal.

The valet hesitated a moment.

'You'll excuse me, sir, but the elderly American lady is in what I might describe as a state, sir. She's saying she knows all about the murderer. She's in a very excitable condition, sir.'

'In that case,' said Poirot, smiling, 'we had better see her next.'

'Shall I tell her, sir? She's been demanding to see someone in authority for a long time. The conductor's been trying to pacify her.'

'Send her to us, my friend,' said Poirot. 'We will listen to her story now.'

— 4 —

THE EVIDENCE OF THE AMERICAN LADY

M<small>RS</small> H<small>UBBARD</small> arrived in the dining-car in such a state of breathless excitement that she was hardly able to articulate her words.

'Now just tell me this. Who's in authority here? I've got some vurry important information, *vurry* important, indeed, and I just want to tell it to someone in authority as soon as may be. If you gentlemen—'

Her wavering glance fluctuated between the three men. Poirot leaned forward.

'Tell it to me, madame,' he said. 'But, first, pray be seated.'

Mrs Hubbard plumped heavily down on to the seat opposite to him.

'What I've got to tell you is just this. There was a murder on the train last night, and the murderer was *right there in my compartment*!'

She paused to give dramatic emphasis to her words.

'You are sure of this, madame?'

'Of course I'm sure! The idea! I know what I'm talking about. I'll tell you just everything there is to tell. I'd gotten into bed and gone to sleep, and suddenly I woke up – all in the dark, it was – and I knew there was a man in my compartment. I was just so scared I couldn't scream, if you know what I mean. I just lay there and thought, "Mercy, I'm going to be killed." I just can't describe to you how I felt. These nasty trains, I thought, and all the outrages I'd read of. And I thought, "Well, anyway, he won't get my jewellery," because, you see, I'd put that in a stocking and hidden it under my pillow – which isn't so mighty comfortable, by the way, kinder bumpy, if you know what I mean. But that's neither here nor there. Where was I?'

'You realized, madame, that there was a man in your compartment.'

'Yes, well, I just lay there with my eyes closed, and I thought whatever should I do, and I thought, "Well, I'm just thankful that my daughter doesn't know the plight I'm in." And then, somehow, I got my wits about me and I felt about with my hand and I pressed the bell for the conductor. I pressed it and I pressed it, but nothing happened, and I can tell you I thought my heart was going to stop beating. "Mercy," I said to myself, "maybe they've murdered every single soul on the train." It was at a standstill, anyhow, and a nasty quiet feel in the air. But I just went on pressing that bell, and oh! the relief when I heard footsteps coming running down the corridor and a knock on the door. "Come in," I screamed, and I switched on the lights at the same time. And, would you believe it, there wasn't a soul there.'

This seemed to Mrs Hubbard to be a dramatic climax rather than an anti-climax.

'And what happened next, madame?'

'Why, I told the man what had happened, and he didn't seem to believe me. Seemed to imagine I'd dreamt the whole thing. I made him look under the seat, though he said there wasn't room for a man to squeeze himself in there. It was plain enough the man had got away, but there *had* been a man there and it just made me mad the way the conductor tried to soothe me down! I'm not one to imagine things – I don't think I know your name?'

'Poirot, madame, and this is M. Bouc, a director of the company, and Dr Constantine.'

Mrs Hubbard murmured: 'Pleased to meet you, I'm sure,' to all three of them in an abstracted manner, and then plunged once more into her recital.

'Now I'm just not going to pretend I was as bright as I might have been. I got it into my head that it was the man from next door – the poor fellow who's been killed. I told the conductor to look at the door between the compartments, and sure enough it wasn't bolted. Well, I soon saw to that. I told him to bolt it then and there, and after he'd gone out I got up and put a suitcase against it to make sure.'

'What time was this, Mrs Hubbard?'

'Well, I'm sure I can't tell you. I never looked to see. I was so upset.'

'And what is your theory now?'

'Why, I should say it was just as plain as plain could be. The man in my compartment was the murderer. Who else could he be?'

'And you think he went back into the adjoining compartment?'

'How do I know where he went? I had my eyes tight shut.'

'He must have slipped out through the door into the corridor.'

'Well, I couldn't say. You see, I had my eyes tight shut.'

Mrs Hubbard sighed convulsively.

'Mercy, I was scared! If my daughter only knew—'

'You do not think, madame, that what you heard was the noise of someone moving about next door – in the murdered man's compartment?'

'No, I do not, M. – what is it? – Poirot. The man was *right there in the same compartment with me*. And, what's more, I've got proof of it.'

Triumphantly she hauled a large handbag into view and proceeded to burrow in its interior.

She took out in turn two large clean handkerchiefs, a pair of horn-rimmed glasses, a bottle of aspirin, a packet of Glauber's salts, a celluloid tube of bright green peppermints, a bunch of keys, a pair of scissors, a book of American Express cheques, a snapshot of an extraordinary plain-looking child, some letters, five strings of pseudo-Oriental beads and a small metal object – a button.

'You see this button? Well, it's not one of *my* buttons. It's not off anything I've got. I found it this morning when I got up.'

As she placed it on the table, M. Bouc leaned forward and gave an exclamation.

'But this is a button from the tunic of a *wagon lit* attendant!'

'There may be a natural explanation for that,' said Poirot.

He turned gently to the lady.

'This button, madame, may have dropped from the conductor's uniform, either when he searched your cabin, or when he was making the bed up last night.'

'I just don't know what's the matter with all you people. Seems as though you don't do anything but make objections. Now listen here. I was reading a magazine last night before I went to sleep. Before I turned the light out I placed that magazine on a little case that was standing on the floor near the window. Have you got that?'

They assured her that they had.

'Very well, then. The conductor looked under the seat from near the door and then he came in and bolted the door between me and the next compartment, but he never went up near the window. Well, this morning that button was lying right on top of the magazine. What do you call that, I should like to know?'

'That, madame, I call evidence,' said Poirot.

The answer seemed to appease the lady.

'It makes me madder than a hornet to be disbelieved,' she explained.

'You have given us most interesting and valuable evidence,' said Poirot soothingly. 'Now, may I ask you a few questions?'

'Why, willingly.'

'How was it, since you were nervous of this man Ratchett, that you hadn't already bolted the door between the compartments?'

'I had,' returned Mrs Hubbard promptly.

'Oh, you had?'

'Well, as a matter of fact, I asked that Swedish creature – a pleasant soul – if it was bolted, and she said it was.'

'How was it you couldn't see for yourself?'

'Because I was in bed and my sponge-bag was hanging on the door handle.'

'What time was it when you asked her to do this for you?'

'Now let me think. It must have been round about half-past ten or a quarter to eleven. She'd come along to see if I'd got an aspirin. I told her where to find it, and she got it out of my grip.'

'You yourself were in bed?'

'Yes.'

Suddenly she laughed.

'Poor soul – she was in quite a taking. You see, she'd opened the door of the next compartment by mistake.'

'Mr Ratchett's?'

'Yes. You know how difficult it is as you come along the train and all the doors are shut. She opened his by mistake. She was very distressed about it. He'd laughed, it seemed, and I fancy he may have said something not quite nice. Poor thing, she was all in a flutter. "Oh! I make mistake," she said. "I ashamed make mistake. Not nice man," she said. "He say, 'You too old.'"'

Dr Constantine sniggered and Mrs Hubbard immediately froze him with a glance.

'He wasn't a nice kind of man,' she said, 'to say a thing like that to a lady. It's not right to laugh at such things.'

Dr Constantine hastily apologized.

'Did you hear any noise from Mr Ratchett's compartment after that?' asked Poirot.

'Well – not exactly.'

'What do you mean by that, madame?'

'Well—' she paused. 'He snored.'

'Ah! He snored, did he?'

'Terribly. The night before it quite kept me awake.'

'You didn't hear him snore after you had had the scare about a man being in your compartment?'

'Why, M. Poirot, how could I? He was dead.'

'Ah, yes, truly,' said Poirot. He appeared confused. 'Do you remember the affair of the Armstrong kidnapping, Mrs Hubbard?' he asked.

'Yes, indeed I do. And how the wretch that did it escaped scot free! My, I'd have liked to get my hands on him.'

'He has not escaped. He is dead. He died last night.'

'You don't mean—?' Mrs Hubbard half rose from her chair in excitement.

'But yes, I do. Ratchett was the man.'

'*Well!* Well, to think of that! I must write and tell my daughter. Now, didn't I tell you last night that that man had an evil face? I was right, you see. My daughter always says: "When Momma's got a hunch, you can bet your bottom dollar it's O.K."'

'Were you acquainted with any of the Armstrong family, Mrs Hubbard?'

'No. They moved in a very exclusive circle. But I've always heard that Mrs Armstrong was a perfectly lovely woman and that her husband worshipped her.'

'Well, Mrs Hubbard, you have helped us very much – very much indeed. Perhaps you will give me your full name?'

'Why, certainly. Caroline Martha Hubbard.'

'Will you write your address down here?'

Mrs Hubbard did so, without ceasing to speak.

'I just can't get over it. Cassetti – on this train. I had a hunch about that man, didn't I, M. Poirot?'

'Yes, indeed, madame. By the way, have you a scarlet silk dressing-gown?'

'Mercy, what an odd question! Why, no. I've got two dressing-gowns with me – a pink flannel one that's kind of cosy for on board ship, and one my daughter gave me as a present – a kind of local affair in purple silk. But what in creation do you want to know about my dressing-gowns for?'

'Well, you see, madame, someone in a scarlet kimono entered either your or Mr Ratchett's compartment last night. It is, as you said just now, very difficult when all the doors are shut to know which compartment is which.'

'Well, no one in a scarlet dressing-gown came into my compartment.'

'Then she must have gone into Mr Ratchett's.'

Mrs Hubbard pursed her lips together and said grimly:

'That wouldn't surprise me any.'

Poirot leaned forward.

'So you heard a woman's voice next door?'

'I don't know how you guessed that, M. Poirot. I don't really. But – well – as a matter of fact, I *did*.'

'But when I asked you just now if you heard anything next door, you only said you heard Mr Ratchett snoring.'

'Well, that was true enough. He *did* snore part of the time. As for the other—' Mrs Hubbard got rather pink. 'It isn't a very nice thing to speak about.'

'What time was it when you heard a woman's voice?'

'I can't tell you. I just woke up for a minute and heard a woman talking, and it was plain enough where she was. So I just thought, "Well that's the kind of man he is. Well, I'm not surprised," and then I went to sleep again, and I'm sure I should never have mentioned anything of the kind to three strange gentlemen if you hadn't dragged it out of me.'

'Was it before the scare about the man in your compartment, or after?'

'Why, that's like what you said just now! He wouldn't have had a woman talking to him if he were dead, would he?'

'*Pardon*. You must think me very stupid, madame.'

'I guess even you get kinda muddled now and then. I just can't get over it being that monster Cassetti. What my daughter will say—'

Poirot managed adroitly to help the good lady to restore the contents of her handbag and he then shepherded her towards the door.

At the last moment he said: 'You have dropped your handkerchief, madame.'

Mrs Hubbard looked at the little scrap of cambric he held out to her.

'That's not mine, M. Poirot. I've got mine right here.'

'*Pardon*. I thought as it had the initial H on it—'

'Well, now, that's curious, but it's certainly not mine. Mine are marked C.M.H., and they're sensible things – not expensive Paris fallals. What good is a handkerchief like that to anybody's nose?'

Neither of the three men seemed to have an answer to this question, and Mrs Hubbard sailed out triumphantly.

— 5 —

THE EVIDENCE OF THE SWEDISH LADY

M. BOUC was handling the button Mrs Hubbard had left behind her.

'This button. I cannot understand it. Does it mean that, after all, Pierre Michel is involved in some way?' he said. He paused, then continued, as Poirot did not reply, 'What have you to say, my friend?

'That button, it suggests possibilities,' said Poirot thoughtfully. 'Let us interview next the Swedish lady before we discuss the evidence we have heard.'

He sorted through the pile of passports in front of him.

'Ah! here we are. Greta Ohlsson, age forty-nine.'

M. Bouc gave directions to the restaurant attendant, and presently the lady with the yellowish-grey bun of hair and the long mild sheep-like face was ushered in. She peered short-sightedly at Poirot through her glasses, but was quite calm.

It transpired that she understood and spoke French, so that the conversation took place in that language. Poirot first asked her the questions to which he already knew the answers – her name, age and address. He then asked her her occupation.

She was, she told him, matron in a missionary school near Stamboul. She was a trained nurse.

'You know, of course, of what took place last night, mademoiselle?'

'Naturally. It is very dreadful. And the American lady tells me that the murderer was actually in her compartment.'

'I hear, mademoiselle, that you were the last person to see the murdered man alive?'

'I do not know. It may be so. I opened the door of his compartment by mistake. I was much ashamed. It was a most awkward mistake.'

'You actually saw him?'

'Yes. He was reading a book. I apologized quickly and withdrew.'

'Did he say anything to you?'

A slight flush showed on the worthy lady's cheek.

'He laughed and said a few words. I – I did not quite catch them.'

'And what did you do after that, mademoiselle?' asked Poirot, passing from the subject tactfully.

'I went in to the American lady, Mrs Hubbard. I asked her for some aspirin and she gave it to me.'

'Did she ask you whether the communicating door between her compartment and that of Mr Ratchett was bolted?'

'Yes.'

'And was it?'

'Yes.'

'And after that?'

'After that I go back to my own compartment, I take the aspirin and lie down.'

'What time was all this?'

'When I got into bed it was five minutes to eleven, because I look at my watch before I wind it up.'

'Did you go to sleep quickly?'

'Not very quickly. My head got better, but I lay awake some time.'

'Had the train come to a stop before you went to sleep?'

'I do not think so. We stopped, I think, at a station, just as I was getting drowsy.'

'That would be Vincovci. Now your compartment, mademoiselle, is this one?' He indicated it on the plan.

'That is so, yes.'

'You had the upper or the lower berth?'

'The lower berth, No. 10.'

'And you had a companion?'

'Yes, a young English lady. Very nice, very amiable. She had travelled from Baghdad.'

'After the train left Vincovci, did she leave the compartment?'

'No, I am sure she did not.'

'Why are you sure if you were asleep?'

'I sleep very lightly. I am used to waking at a sound. I am sure if she had come down from the berth above I should have awakened.'

'Did you yourself leave the compartment?'

'Not until this morning.'

'Have you a scarlet silk kimono, mademoiselle?'

'No, indeed. I have a good comfortable dressing-gown of Jaeger material.'

'And the lady with you, Miss Debenham? What colour is her dressing-gown?'

'A pale mauve *abba* such as you buy in the East.'

Poirot nodded. Then he said in a friendly tone: 'Why are you taking this journey? A holiday?'

'Yes, I am going home for a holiday. But first I go to Lausanne to stay with a sister for a week or so.'

'Perhaps you will be so amiable as to write me down the name and address of your sister?'

'With pleasure.'

She took the paper and pencil he gave her and wrote down the name and address as requested.

'Have you ever been in America, mademoiselle?'

'No. Very nearly once. I was to go with an invalid lady, but it was cancelled at the last moment. I much regretted. They are very good, the Americans. They give much money to found schools and hospitals. They are very practical.'

'Do you remember hearing of the Armstrong kidnapping case?'

'No, what was that?'

Poirot explained.

Greta Ohlsson was indignant. Her yellow bun of hair quivered with her emotion.

'That there are in the world such evil men! It tries one's faith. The poor mother. My heart aches for her.'

The amiable Swede departed, her kindly face flushed, her eyes suffused with tears.

Poirot was writing busily on a sheet of paper.

'What is it you write there, my friend?' asked M. Bouc.

'*Mon cher*, it is my habit to be neat and orderly. I make here a little table of chronological events.'

He finished writing and passed the paper to M. Bouc.

9.15	Train leaves Belgrade.
about 9.40	Valet leaves Ratchett with sleeping draught beside him.
about 10.00	MacQueen leaves Ratchett.
about 10.40	Greta Ohlsson sees Ratchett (last seen alive). N.B. – He was awake reading a book.
0.10	Train leaves Vincovci (late).
0.30	Train runs into a snowdrift.
0.37	Ratchett's bell rings. Conductor answers it. Ratchett says, '*Ce n'est rien. Je me suis trompé.*'
about 1.17	Mrs Hubbard thinks man is in her carriage. Rings for conductor.

M. Bouc nodded approval.

'That is very clear,' he said.

'There is nothing there that strikes you as at all odd?'

'No, it seems all quite clear and above board. It seems quite plain that the crime was committed at 1.15. The evidence of the watch shows us that, and Mrs Hubbard's story fits in. For my mind, I will make a guess at the identity of the murderer. I say, my friend, that it is the big Italian. He comes from America – from Chicago – and remember an Italian's weapon is the knife, and he stabs not once but several times.'

'That is true.'

'Without a doubt, that is the solution of the mystery. Doubtless he and this Ratchett were in this kidnapping business together. Cassetti is an Italian name. In some way Ratchett did on him what they call the double-cross. The Italian tracks him down, sends him warning letters first, and finally revenges himself upon him in a brutal way. It is all quite simple.'

Poirot shook his head doubtfully.

'It is hardly as simple as that, I fear,' he murmured.

'Me, I am convinced it is the truth,' said M. Bouc, becoming more and more enamoured of his theory.

'And what about the valet with the toothache who swears that the Italian never left the compartment?'

'That is the difficulty.'

Poirot twinkled.

'Yes, it is annoying, that. Unlucky for your theory, and extremely lucky for our Italian friend, that Mr Ratchett's valet should have had the toothache.'

'It will be explained,' said M. Bouc with magnificent certainty.

Poirot shook his head again.

'No, it is hardly so simple as that,' he murmured again.

— 6 —

THE EVIDENCE OF THE RUSSIAN PRINCESS

'Let us hear what Pierre Michel has to say about this button,' he said.

The *wagon lit* conductor was recalled. He looked at them inquiringly.

M. Bouc cleared his throat.

'Michel,' he said. 'Here is a button from your tunic. It was found in the American lady's compartment. What have you to say for yourself about it?'

The conductor's hand went automatically to his tunic.

'I have lost no button, monsieur,' he said. 'There must be some mistake.'

'That is very odd.'

'I cannot account for it, monsieur.'

The man seemed astonished, but not in any way guilty or confused.

M. Bouc said meaningly: 'Owing to the circumstances in which it was found, it seems fairly certain that this button was dropped by the man who was in Mrs Hubbard's compartment last night when she rang the bell.'

'But, monsieur, there was no one there. The lady must have imagined it.'

'She did not imagine it, Michel. The assassin of Mr Ratchett passed that way – *and dropped that button.*'

As the significance of M. Bouc's words became plain to him, Pierre Michel flew into a violent state of agitation.

'It is not true, monsieur, it is not true!' he cried. 'You are accusing me of the crime. Me? I am innocent. I am absolutely innocent. Why should I want to kill a monsieur whom I have never seen before?'

'Where were you when Mrs Hubbard's bell rang?'

'I told you, monsieur, in the next coach, talking to my colleague.'

'We will send for him.'

'Do so, monsieur, I, implore you, do so.'

The conductor of the next coach was summoned. He immediately confimed Pierre Michel's statement. He added that the conductor from the Bucharest coach had also been there. The three of them had been discussing the situation caused by the snow. They had been talking some ten minutes when Michel fancied he heard a bell. As he opened the doors connecting the two coaches, they had all heard it plainly. A bell ringing repeatedly. Michel had run post-haste to answer it.

'So you see, monsieur, I am not guilty,' cried Michel anxiously.

'And this button from a *wagon lit* tunic – how do you explain it?'

'I cannot, monsieur. It is a mystery to me. All my buttons are intact.'

Both of the other conductors also declared that they had not lost a button. Also that they had not been inside Mrs Hubbard's compartment at any time.

'Calm yourself, Michel,' said M. Bouc, 'and cast your mind back to the moment when you ran to answer Mrs Hubbard's bell. Did you meet anyone at all in the corridor?'

'No, monsieur.'

'Did you see anyone going away from you down the corridor in the other direction?'

'Again, no, monsieur.'

'Odd,' said M. Bouc.

'Not so very,' said Poirot. 'It is a question of time. Mrs Hubbard wakes to find someone in her compartment. For a minute or two she lies paralysed, her eyes shut. Probably it was then that the man slipped out into the corridor. Then she starts ringing the bell. But the conductor does not come at once. It is only the third or fourth peal that he hears. I should say myself that there was ample time—'

'For what? For what, *mon cher*? Remember that there are thick drifts of snow all round the train.'

'There are two courses open to our mysterious assassin,' said Poirot slowly. 'He could retreat into either of the toilets or he could disappear into one of the compartments.'

'But they were all occupied.'

'Yes.'

'You mean that he could retreat into his *own* compartment?'

Poirot nodded.

'It fits, it fits,' murmured M. Bouc. 'During that ten minutes' absence of the conductor, the murderer comes from his own compartment, goes into Ratchett's, kills him, locks and chains the door on the inside, goes out through Mrs Hubbard's compartment and is back safely in his own compartment by the time the conductor arrives.'

Poirot murmured: 'It is not quite so simple as that, my friend. Our friend the doctor here will tell you so.'

With a gesture M. Bouc signified that the three conductors might depart.

'We have still to see eight passengers,' said Poirot. 'Five first-class passengers – Princess Dragomiroff, Count and Countess Andrenyi, Colonel Arbuthnot and Mr Hardman. Three second-class passengers – Miss Debenham, Antonio Foscarelli and the lady's-maid, Fräulein Schmidt.'

'Who will you see first – the Italian?'

'How you harp on your Italian! No, we will start at the top of the tree. Perhaps Madame la Princesse will be so good as to spare us a few moments of her time. Convey that message to her, Michel.'

'*Oui, monsieur*,' said the conductor, who was just leaving the car.

'Tell her we can wait on her in her compartment if she does not wish to put herself to the trouble of coming here,' called M. Bouc.

But Princess Dragomiroff declined to take this course. She appeared in the dining-car, inclined her head slightly and sat down opposite Poirot.

Her small, toad-like face looked even yellower than the day before. She was certainly ugly, and yet, like the toad, she had eyes like jewels, dark and imperious, revealing latent energy and an intellectual force that could be felt at once.

Her voice was deep, very distinct, with a slight grating quality in it.

She cut short a flowery phrase of apology from M. Bouc.

'You need not offer apologies, messieurs. I understand a murder has taken place. Naturally, you must interview all the passengers. I shall be glad to give all the assistance in my power.'

'You are most amiable, madame,' said Poirot.

'Not at all. It is a duty. What do you wish to know?'

'Your full Christian names and address, madame. Perhaps you would prefer to write them yourself?'

Poirot proffered a sheet of paper and pencil, but the Princess waved them aside.

'You can write it,' she said. 'There is nothing difficult – Natalia Dragomiroff, 17 Avenue Kleber, Paris.'

'You are travelling home from Constantinople, madame?'

'Yes, I have been staying at the Austrian Embassy. My maid is with me.'

'Would you be so good as to give me a brief account of your movements last night from dinner onwards?'

'Willingly. I directed the conductor to make up my bed whilst I was in the dining-car. I retired to bed immediately after dinner. I read until the hour of eleven, when I turned out my light. I was unable to sleep owing to certain rheumatic pains from which I suffer. At about a quarter to one I rang for my maid. She massaged me and then read aloud till I felt sleepy. I cannot say exactly when she left me. It may have been half an hour, it may have been later.'

'The train had stopped then?'

'The train had stopped.'

'You heard nothing – nothing unusual during the time, madame?'

'I heard nothing unusual.'

'What is your maid's name?'

'Hildegarde Schmidt.'

'She has been with you long?'

'Fifteen years.'

'You consider her trustworthy?'

'Absolutely. Her people come from an estate of my late husband's in Germany.'

'You have been in America, I presume, madame?'

The abrupt change of subject made the old lady raise her eyebrows.

'Many times.'

'Were you at any time acquainted with a family of the name of Armstrong – a family in which a tragedy occurred?'

With some emotion in her voice the old lady said: 'You speak of friends of mine, monsieur.'

'You knew Colonel Armstrong well, then?'

'I knew him slightly; but his wife, Sonia Armstrong, was my god-daughter. I was on terms of friendship with her mother, the actress, Linda Arden. Linda Arden was a great genius, one of the greatest tragic actresses in the world. As Lady Macbeth, as Magda, there was no one to touch her. I was not only an admirer of her art, I was a personal friend.'

'She is dead?'

'No, no, she is alive, but she lives in complete retirement. Her health is very delicate, she has to lie on a sofa most of the time.'

'There was, I think, a second daughter?'

'Yes, much younger than Mrs Armstrong.'

'And she is alive?'

'Certainly.'

'Where is she?'

The old woman bent an acute glance at him.

'I must ask you the reason of these questions. What have they to do with the matter in hand – the murder on this train?'

'They are connected in this way, madame, the man who was murdered was the man responsible for the kidnapping and murder of Mrs Armstrong's child.'

'Ah!'

The straight brows drew together. Princess Dragomiroff drew herself a little more erect.

'In my view, then, this murder is an entirely admirable happening! You will pardon my slightly biased point of view.'

'It is most natural, madame. And now to return to the question you did not answer. Where is the younger daughter of Linda Arden, the sister of Mrs Armstrong?'

'I honestly cannot tell you, monsieur. I have lost touch with the younger generation. I believe she married an Englishman some years ago and went to England, but at the moment I cannot recollect the name.'

She paused a minute and then said: 'Is there anything further you want to ask me, gentlemen?'

'Only one thing, madame, a somewhat personal question. The colour of your dressing-gown.'

She raised her eyebrows slightly.

'I must suppose you have a reason for such a question. My dressing-gown is of blue satin.'

'There is nothing more, madame. I am much obliged to you for answering my questions so promptly.'

She made a slight gesture with her heavily beringed hand.

Then, as she rose, and the others rose with her, she stopped.

'You will excuse me, monsieur,' she said, 'but may I ask your name? Your face is somehow familiar to me.'

'My name, madame, is Hercule Poirot – at your service.'

She was silent a minute, then: 'Hercule Poirot,' she said. 'Yes. I remember now. This is Destiny.'

She walked away, very erect, a little stiff in her movements.

'*Voilà une grande dame*,' said M. Bouc. 'What do you think of her, my friend?'

But Hercule Poirot merely shook his head.

'I am wondering,' he said, 'what she meant by Destiny.'

— 7 —

THE EVIDENCE OF COUNT AND COUNTESS ANDRENYI

COUNT and Countess Andrenyi were next summoned. The count, however, entered the dining-car alone.

There was no doubt that he was a fine-looking man seen face to face. He was at least six feet in height, with broad shoulders and slender hips. He was dressed in very well-cut English tweeds, and might have been taken for an Englishman had it not been for the length of his moustache and something in the line of the cheek-bone.

'Well, messieurs,' he said, 'what can I do for you?'

'You understand, monsieur,' said Poirot, 'that in view of what has occurred I am obliged to put certain questions to all the passengers.'

'Perfectly, perfectly,' said the count easily. 'I quite understand your position. Not, I fear, that my wife and I can do much to assist you. We were asleep and heard nothing at all.'

'Are you aware of the identity of the deceased, monsieur?'

'I understand it was the big American – a man with a decidedly unpleasant face. He sat at that table at meal times.'

He indicated with a nod of his head the table at which Ratchett and MacQueen had sat.

'Yes, yes, monsieur, you are perfectly correct. I meant did you know the name of the man?'

'No.' The count looked thoroughly puzzled by Poirot's queries.

'If you want to know his name,' he said, 'surely it is on his passport?'

'The name on his passport is Ratchett,' said Poirot. 'But that, monsieur, is not his real name. He is the man Cassetti, who was responsible for a celebrated kidnapping outrage in America.'

He watched the count closely as he spoke, but the latter seemed quite unaffected by the piece of news. He merely opened his eyes a little.

'Ah!' he said. 'That certainly should throw light upon the matter. An extraordinary country America.'

'You have been there, perhaps, *Monsieur le Comte*?'

'I was in Washington for a year.'

'You knew, perhaps, the Armstrong family?'

'Armstrong – Armstrong – it is difficult to recall – one met so many.'

He smiled, shrugged his shoulders.

'But to come back to the matter in hand, gentlemen,' he said. 'What more can I do to assist you?'

'You retired to rest – when, *Monsieur le Comte*?'

Hercule Poirot's eyes stole to his plan. Count and Countess Andrenyi occupied compartments No. 12 and 13 adjoining.

'We had one compartment made up for the night whilst we were in the dining-car. On returning we sat in the other for a while—'

'What number would that be?'

'No. 13. We played picquet together. About eleven o'clock my wife retired for the night. The conductor made up my compartment and I also went to bed. I slept soundly until morning.'

'Did you notice the stopping of the train?'

'I was not aware of it till this morning.'

'And your wife?'

The count smiled.

'My wife always takes a sleeping draught when travelling by train. She took her usual dose of trional.'

He paused.

'I am sorry I am not able to assist you in any way.'

Poirot passed him a sheet of paper and a pen.

'Thank you, *Monsieur le Comte*. It is a formality, but will you just let me have your name and address?'

The count wrote slowly and carefully.

'It is just as well I should write this for you,' he said pleasantly. 'The spelling of my country estate is a little difficult for those unacquainted with the language.'

He passed the paper across to Poirot and rose.

'It will be quite unnecessary for my wife to come here,' he said. 'She can tell you nothing more than I have.'

A little gleam came into Poirot's eye.

'Doubtless, doubtless,' he said. 'But all the same I think I should like to have just one little word with *Madame la Comtesse*.'

'I assure you it is quite unnecessary.'

His voice rang out authoritatively.

Poirot blinked gently at him.

'It will be a mere formality,' he said. 'But you understand, it is necessary for my report.'

'As you please.'

The count gave way grudgingly. He made a short, foreign bow and left the dining-car.

Poirot reached out a hand to a passport. It set out the count's name and titles. He passed on to the further information – *accompanied by wife*. Christian name Elena Maria; maiden name Goldenberg; age twenty. A spot of grease had been dropped some time by a careless official on it.

'A diplomatic passport,' said M. Bouc. 'We must be careful, my friend, to give no offence. These people can have nothing to do with the murder.'

'Be easy, *mon vieux*, I will be most tactful. A mere formality.'

His voice dropped as the Countess Andrenyi entered the dining-car. She looked timid and extremely charming.

'You wish to see me, messieurs?'

'A mere formality, *Madame la Comtesse*.' Poirot rose gallantly, bowed her into the seat opposite him. 'It is only to ask you if you saw or heard anything last night that may throw light upon this matter.'

'Nothing at all, monsieur. I was asleep.'

'You did not hear, for instance, a commotion going on in the compartment next to yours? The American lady who occupies it had quite an attack of hysterics and rang for the conductor.'

'I heard nothing, monsieur. You see, I had taken a sleeping draught.'

'Ah! I comprehend. Well, I need not detain you further.' Then, as she rose swiftly, 'Just one little minute – these particulars, your maiden name, age and so on, they are correct?'

'Quite correct, monsieur.'

'Perhaps you will sign this memorandum to that effect, then.'

She signed quickly, a graceful slanting handwriting.

Elena Andrenyi.

'Did you accompany your husband to America, madame?'

'No, monsieur.' She smiled, flushed a little. 'We were not married then; we have only been married a year.'

'Ah yes, thank you, madame. By the way, does your husband smoke?'

She stared at him as she stood poised for departure.

'Yes.'

'A pipe?'

'No. Cigarettes and cigars.'

'Ah! Thank you.'

She lingered; her eyes watched him curiously. Lovely eyes they were, dark and almond-shaped, with very long black lashes that swept the exquisite pallor of her cheeks. Her lips, very scarlet, in the foreign fashion, were parted just a little. She looked exotic and beautiful.

'Why did you ask me that?'

'Madame,' Poirot waved an airy hand, 'detectives have to ask all sorts of questions. For instance, perhaps you will tell me the colour of your dressing-gown?'

She stared at him. Then she laughed.

'It is corn-coloured chiffon. Is that really important?'

'Very important, madame.'

She asked curiously: 'Are you really a detective, then?'

'At your service, madame.'

'I thought there were no detectives on the train when it passed through Yugoslavia – not until one got to Italy.'

'I am not a Yugoslavian detective, madame. I am an international detective.'

'You belong to the League of Nations?'

'I belong to the world, madame,' said Poirot dramatically. He went on, 'I work mainly in London. You speak English?' he added in that language.

'I speak a leetle, yes.'

Her accent was charming.

Poirot bowed once more.

'We will not detain you further, madame. You see, it was not so very terrible.'

She smiled, inclined her head and departed.

'*Elle est jolie femme*,' said M. Bouc appreciatively.

He sighed.

'Well, that did not advance us much.'

'No,' said Poirot. 'Two people who saw nothing and heard nothing.'

'Shall we now see the Italian?'

Poirot did not reply for a moment. He was studying a grease spot on a Hungarian diplomatic passport.

— 8 —

THE EVIDENCE OF COLONEL ARBUTHNOT

POIROT roused himself with a slight start. His eyes twinkled a little as they met the eager ones of M. Bouc.

'Ah! my dear old friend,' he said. 'You see, I have become what they call the snob! The first class, I feel it should be attended to before the second class. Next, I think, we will interview the good-looking Colonel Arbuthnot.'

Finding the colonel's French to be of a severely limited description, Poirot conducted his interrogation in English.

Arbuthnot's name, age, home address and exact military standing were all ascertained. Poirot proceeded: 'It is that you come home from India on what is called the leave – what we call *en permission*?'

Colonel Arbuthnot, uninterested in what a pack of foreigners called anything, replied with true British brevity: 'Yes.'

'But you do not come home on the P. & O. boat?'

'No.'

'Why not?'

'I chose to come by the overland route for reasons of my own.'

'And that,' his manner seemed to say, 'is one for you, you interfering little jackanapes.'

'You came straight through from India?'

The colonel replied dryly: 'I stopped for one night to see Ur of the Chaldees and for three days in Baghdad with the A.O.C., who happens to be an old friend of mine.'

'You stopped three days in Baghdad. I understand that the young English lady, Miss Debenham, also comes from Baghdad. Perhaps you met her there?'

'No, I did not. I first met Miss Debenham when she and I shared the railway convoy car from Kirkuk to Nissibin.'

Poirot leaned forward. He became persuasive and a little more foreign than he need have been.

'Monsieur, I am about to appeal to you. You and Miss Debenham are the only two English people on the train. It is necessary that I should ask you each your opinion of the other.'

'Highly irregular,' said Colonel Arbuthnot coldly.

'Not so. You see, this crime, it was most probably committed by a woman. The man was stabbed no less than twelve times. Even the *chef de train* said at once, "It is a woman." Well, then, what is my first task? To give all the women travelling in the Stamboul–Calais coach what Americans call the "once over". But to judge of an Englishwoman is difficult. They are very reserved, the English. So I appeal to you, monsieur, in the interests of justice. What sort of a person is this Miss Debenham? What do you know about her?'

'Miss Debenham,' said the Colonel with some warmth, 'is a lady.'

'Ah!' said Poirot with every appearance of being much gratified. 'So you do not think that she is likely to be implicated in this crime?'

'The idea is absurd,' said Arbuthnot. 'The man was a perfect stranger – she had never seen him before.'

'Did she tell you so?'

'She did. She commented at once upon his somewhat unpleasant appearance. If a woman *is* concerned, as you seem to think (to my mind without any evidence but mere assumption), I can assure you that Miss Debenham could not possibly be indicated.'

'You feel warmly in the matter,' said Poirot with a smile. Colonel Arbuthnot gave him a cold stare.

'I really don't know what you mean,' he said.

The stare seem to abash Poirot. He dropped his eyes and began fiddling with the papers in front of him.

'All this is by the way,' he said. 'Let us be practical and come to facts. This crime, we have reason to believe, took place at a quarter-past one last night. It is part of the necessary routine to ask everyone on the train what he or she was doing at that time.'

'Quite so. At a quarter-past one, to the best of my belief, I was talking to the young American fellow – secretary to the dead man.'

'Ah! Were you in his compartment, or was he in yours?'

'I was in his.'

'That is the young man of the name of MacQueen?'

'Yes.'

'He was a friend or acquaintance of yours?'

'No, I never saw him before this journey. We fell into casual conversation yesterday and both became interested. I don't as a rule like Americans – haven't any use for 'em—'

Poirot smiled, remembering MacQueen's strictures on 'Britishers'.

'—But I liked this young fellow. He'd got hold of some tomfool idiotic ideas about the situation in India; that's the worst of Americans – they're so sentimental and idealistic. Well, he was interested in what I had to tell him. I've had nearly thirty years' experience of the country. And I was interested in what he had to tell me about the financial situation in America. Then we got down to world politics in general. I was quite surprised to look at my watch and find it was a quarter to two.'

'That is the time you broke up this conversation?'

'Yes.'

'What did you do then?'

'Walked along to my own compartment and turned in.'

'Your bed was made up ready?'

'Yes.'

'That is the compartment – let me see – No. 15 – the one next but one to the end away from the dining-car?'

'Yes.'

'Where was the conductor when you went to your compartment?'

'Sitting at the end at a little table. As a matter of fact, MacQueen called him just as I went to my own compartment.'

'Why did he call him?'

'To make up his bed, I suppose. The compartment hadn't been made up for the night.'

'Now, Colonel Arbuthnot, I want you to think carefully. During the time you were talking to Mr MacQueen did anyone pass along the corridor outside the door?'

'A good many people, I should think. I wasn't paying attention.'

'Ah! but I am referring to – let us say the last hour and a half of your conversation. You got out at Vincovci, didn't you?'

'Yes, but only for about a minute. There was a blizzard on. The cold was something frightful. Made one quite thankful to get back to the fug, though as a rule I think the way these trains are overheated is something scandalous.'

M. Bouc sighed.

'It is very difficult to please everybody,' he said. 'The English, they open everything – then others, they come along and shut everything. It is very difficult.'

Neither Poirot nor Colonel Arbuthnot paid any attention to him.

'Now, monsieur, cast your mind back,' said Poirot encouragingly. 'It was cold outside. You have returned to the train. You sit down again, you smoke – perhaps a cigarette, perhaps a pipe—'

He paused for the fraction of a second.

'A pipe for me. MacQueen smoked cigarettes.'

'The train starts again. You smoke your pipe. You discuss the state of Europe – of the world. It is late now. Most people have retired for the night. Does anyone pass the door – think?'

Arbuthnot frowned in the effort of remembrance.

'Difficult to say,' he said. 'You see, I wasn't paying any attention.'

'But you have the soldier's observation for detail. You notice without noticing, so to speak.'

The colonel thought again, but shook his head.

'I couldn't say. I don't remember anyone passing except the conductor. Wait a minute – and there was a woman, I think.'

'You saw her? Was she old – young?'

'Didn't see her. Wasn't looking that way. Just a rustle and a sort of smell of scent.'

'Scent? A *good* scent?'

'Well, rather fruity, if you know what I mean. I mean you'd smell it a hundred yards away. But mind you,' the colonel went on hastily, 'this may have been earlier in the evening. You see, as you said just now, it was just one of those things you notice without noticing, so to speak. Some time that evening I said to myself, "Woman – scent – got it on pretty thick." But *when* it was I can't be sure, except that – why, yes, it must have been after Vincovci.'

'Why?'

'Because I remember – sniffing, you know – just when I was talking about the utter washout Stalin's five-year plan was turning out. I know the idea – woman – brought the idea of the position of women in Russia into my mind. And I know we hadn't got on to Russia until pretty near the end of our talk.'

'You can't pin it down more definitely than that?'

'N-no. It must have been roughly within the last half-hour.'

'It was after the train had stopped?'

The other nodded.

'Yes, I'm almost sure it was.'

'Well, we will pass from that. Have you ever been in America, Colonel Arbuthnot?'

'Never. Don't want to go.'

'Did you ever know a Colonel Armstrong?'

'Armstrong – Armstrong – I've known two or three Armstrongs. There was Tommy Armstrong in the 60th – you don't mean him? And Selby Armstrong – he was killed on the Somme.'

'I mean the Colonel Armstrong who married an American wife and whose only child was kidnapped and killed.'

'Ah, yes, I remember reading about that – shocking affair. I don't think I actually ever came across the fellow, though, of course, I knew of him. Toby Armstrong. Nice fellow. Everybody liked him. He had a very distinguished career. Got the V.C.'

'The man who was killed last night was the man responsible for the murder of Colonel Armstrong's child.'

Arbuthnot's face grew rather grim.

'Then in my opinion the swine deserved what he got. Though I would have preferred to have seen him properly hanged – or electrocuted, I suppose, over there.'

'In fact, Colonel Arbuthnot, you prefer law and order to private vengeance?'

'Well, you can't go about having blood feuds and stabbing each other like Corsicans or the Mafia,' said the colonel. 'Say what you like, trial by jury is a sound system.'

Poirot looked at him thoughtfully for a minute or two.

'Yes,' he said. 'I am sure that would be your view. Well, Colonel Arbuthnot, I do not think there is anything more I have to ask you. There is nothing you yourself can recall last night that in any way struck you – or shall we say strikes you now looking back – as suspicious?'

Arbuthnot considered for a moment or two.

'No,' he said. 'Nothing at all. Unless—' He hesitated.

'But yes, continue, I pray of you.'

'Well, it's nothing really,' said the colonel slowly. 'But you said *anything*.'

'Yes, yes. Go on.'

'Oh, it's nothing. A mere detail. But as I got back to my compartment I noticed that the door of the one beyond mine – the end one, you know—'

'Yes, No. 16.'

'Well, the door of it was not quite closed. And the fellow inside peered out in a furtive sort of way. Then he pulled the door to quickly. Of course, I know there's nothing in that – but it just struck me as a bit odd. I mean, it's quite usual to open a door and stick your head out if you want to see anything. But it was the furtive way he did it that caught my attention.'

'Ye-es,' said Poirot doubtfully.

'I told you there was nothing to it,' said Arbuthnot apologetically. 'But you know what it is – early hours of the morning – everything very still – the thing had a sinister look – like a detective story. All nonsense, really.'

He rose.

'Well, if you don't want me any more—'

'Thank you, Colonel Arbuthnot, there is nothing else.'

The soldier hesitated for a minute. His first natural distaste for being questioned by 'foreigners' had evaporated.

'About Miss Debenham,' he said rather awkwardly. 'You can take it from me that she's all right. She's a *pukka sahib*.'

Flushing a little, he withdrew.

'What,' asked Dr Constantine with interest, 'does a *pukka sahib* mean?'

'It means,' said Poirot, 'that Miss Debenham's father and brothers were at the same kind of school as Colonel Arbuthnot.'

'Oh!' said Dr Constantine, disappointed. 'Then it has nothing to do with the crime at all.'

'Exactly,' said Poirot.

He fell into a reverie, beating a light tattoo on the table. Then he looked up.

'Colonel Arbuthnot smokes a pipe,' he said. 'In the compartment of Mr Ratchett I found a pipe-cleaner. Mr Ratchett smoked only cigars.'

'You think—'

'He is the only man so far who admits to smoking a pipe. And he knew of Colonel Armstrong – perhaps actually did know him though he won't admit it.'

'So you think it possible—'

Poirot shook his head violently.

'That is just it – it is *im*possible – quite impossible – that an honourable, slightly stupid, upright Englishman should stab an enemy twelve times with a knife! Do you not feel, my friends, how impossible it is?'

'That is the psychology,' said M. Bouc.

'And one must respect the psychology. This crime has a signature and it is certainly not the signature of Colonel Arbuthnot. But now to our next interview.'

This time M. Bouc did not mention the Italian. But he thought of him.

— 9 —

THE EVIDENCE OF MR HARDMAN

THE last of the first-class passengers to be interviewed – Mr Hardman – was the big flamboyant American who had shared a table with the Italian and the valet.

He wore a somewhat loud check suit, a pink shirt, a flashy tiepin, and was rolling something round his tongue as he entered the dining-car. He had a big, fleshy, coarse-featured face, with a good-humoured expression.

'Morning, gentlemen,' he said. 'What can I do for you?'

'You have heard of this murder, Mr – er – Hardman?'

'Sure.'

He shifted the chewing-gum deftly.

'We are of necessity interviewing all the passengers on the train.'

'That's all right by me. Guess that's the only way to tackle the job.'

Poirot consulted the passport lying in front of him.

'You are Cyrus Bethman Hardman, United States subject, forty-one years of age, travelling salesman for typewriting ribbons?'

'O.K., that's me.'

'You are travelling from Stamboul to Paris?'

'That's so.'

'Reason?'

'Business.'

'Do you always travel first class, Mr Hardman?'

'Yes, sir. The firm pays my travelling expenses.'

He winked.

'Now, Mr Hardman, we come to the events of last night.'

The American nodded.

'What can you tell us about the matter?'

'Exactly nothing at all.'

'Ah, that is a pity. Perhaps, Mr Hardman, you will tell us exactly what you did last night, from dinner onwards?'

For the first time the American did not seem ready with his reply. At last he said: 'Excuse me, gentlemen, but just who are you? Put me wise.'

'This is M. Bouc, a director of the Compagnie Internationale des Wagons Lits. This gentleman is the doctor who examined the body.'

'I am Hercule Poirot. I am engaged by the company to investigate this matter.'

'I've heard of you,' said Mr Hardman. He reflected a minute or two longer. 'Guess I'd better come clean.'

'It will certainly be advisable for you to tell us all you know,' said Poirot dryly.

'You'd have said a mouthful if there was anything I *did* know. But I don't. I know nothing at all – just as I said. But I *ought* to know something. That's what makes me sore. I *ought* to.'

'Please explain, Mr Hardman.'

Mr Hardman sighed, removed the chewing-gum, and dived into a pocket. At the same time his whole personality seemed to undergo a change. He became less of a stage character and more of a real person. The resonant nasal tones of his voice became modified.

'That passport's a bit of bluff,' he said. 'That's who I really am.'

Poirot scrutinised the card flipped across to him. M. Bouc peered over his shoulder.

Mr Cyrus B. Hardman,
McNeil's Detective Agency,
New York.

Poirot knew the name. It was one of the best known and most reputable private detective agencies in New York.

'Now, Mr Hardman,' he said. 'Let us hear the meaning of this.'

'Sure. Things came about this way. I'd come over to Europe trailing a couple of crooks – nothing to do with this business. The chase ended in Stamboul. I wired the chief and got his instructions to return, and I would have been making my tracks back to little old New York when I got this.'

He pushed across a letter.

The heading at the top was the Tokatlian Hotel.

Dear Sir – *You have been pointed out to me as an operative of the McNeil Detective Agency. Kindly report to my suite at four o'clock this afternoon.*

It was signed 'S. E. Ratchett'.

'*Eh bien?*'

'I reported at the time stated and Mr Ratchett put me wise to the situation. He showed me a couple of letters he'd got.'

'He was alarmed?'

'Pretended not to be, but he was rattled all right. He put up a proposition to me. I was to travel by the same train as he did to Parrus and see that nobody got him. Well, gentlemen, I *did* travel by the same train and, in spite of me, somebody *did* get him. I certainly feel sore about it. It doesn't look any too good for me.'

'Did he give you any indication of the line you were to take?'

'Sure. He had it all taped out. It was his idea that I should travel in the compartment alongside his – well, that was blown upon straight away. The only place I could get was berth No. 16, and I had a bit of a job getting that. I guess the conductor likes to keep that compartment up his sleeve. But that's neither here nor there. When I looked all round the situation, it seemed to me that No. 16 was a pretty good strategic position. There was only the dining-car in front of the Stamboul sleeping-car, the door on to the platform at the front end was barred at night. The only way a thug could come was through the rear end door to the platform or along the train from the rear – in either case he'd have to pass right by my compartment.'

'You had no idea, I suppose, of the identity of the possible assailant.'

'Well, I knew what he looked like. Mr Ratchett described him to me.'

'What?'

All three men leaned forward eagerly.

Hardman went on: 'A small man, dark, with a womanish kind of voice – that's what the old man said. Said, too, that he didn't think it would be the first night out. More likely the second or third.'

'He knew something,' said M. Bouc.

'He certainly knew more than he told his secretary,' said Poirot thoughtfully. 'Did he tell you anything about this enemy of his? Did he, for instance, say *why* his life was threatened?'

'No, he was kinda reticent about that part of it. Just said the fellow was out for his blood and meant to get it.'

'A small man – dark – with a womanish voice,' said Poirot thoughtfully.

Then, fixing a sharp glance on Hardman, he said: 'You knew who he really was, of course?'

'Which, mister?'

'Ratchett. You recognized him?'

'I don't get you.'

'Ratchett was Cassetti, the Armstrong murderer.'

Mr Hardman gave way to a prolonged whistle.

'That certainly is some surprise!' he said. 'Yes, *sir*! No, I didn't recognize him. I was away out West when that case came on. I suppose I saw photos of him in the papers, but I wouldn't recognize my own mother when a press photographer had done with her. Well, I don't doubt that a few people had it in for Cassetti all right.'

'Do you know of anyone connected with the Armstrong case who answers to that description – small, dark, womanish voice?'

Hardman reflected a minute or two.

'It's hard to say. Pretty nearly everyone to do with that case is dead.'

'There was the girl who threw herself out of the window, remember.'

'Sure. That's a good point, that. She was a foreigner of some kind. Maybe she had some wop relations. But you've got to remember that there were other cases besides the Armstrong case. Cassetti had been running this kidnapping stunt some time. You can't concentrate on that only.'

'Ah, but we have reason to believe that this crime is connected with the Armstrong case.'

Mr Hardman cocked an inquiring eye. Poirot did not respond. The American shook his head.

'I can't call to mind anybody answering that description in the Armstrong case,' he said slowly. 'But of course I wasn't in it and didn't know much about it.'

'Well, continue your narrative, Mr Hardman.'

'There's very little to tell. I got my sleep in the daytime and stayed awake on the watch at night. Nothing suspicious happened the first night. Last night was the same, as far as I was concerned. I had my door a little ajar and watched. No stranger passed.'

'You are sure of that, Mr Hardman?'

'I'm plumb certain. Nobody got on that train from outside and nobody came along the train from the rear carriages. I'll take my oath on that.'

'Could you see the conductor from your position?'

'Sure. He sits on that little seat almost flush with my door.'

'Did he leave that seat at all after the train stopped at Vincovci?'

'That was the last station? Why, yes, he answered a couple of bells – that would be just after the train came to a halt for good. Then, after that, he went past me into the rear coach – was there about a quarter of an hour. There was a bell ringing like mad and he came back running. I stepped out into the corridor to see what it was all about – felt a mite nervous, you understand – but it was only the American dame. She was raising hell about something or other. I grinned. Then he went on to another compartment and came back and got a bottle of mineral water for someone. After that he settled down in his seat till he went up to the far end to make somebody's bed up. I don't think he stirred after that until about five o'clock this morning.'

'Did he doze off at all?'

'That I can't say. He may have done.'

Poirot nodded. Automatically his hands straightened the papers on the table. He picked up the official card once more.

'Be so good as just to initial this,' he said.

The other complied.

'There is no one, I suppose, who can confirm your story of your identity, Mr Hardman?'

'On this train? Well, not exactly. Unless it might be young MacQueen. I know him well enough – seen him in his father's office in New York – but that's not to say he'll remember me from a crowd of other operatives. No, M. Poirot, you'll have to wait and cable New York when the snow lets up. But it's O.K. I'm not telling the tale. Well, so long, gentlemen. Pleased to have met you, M. Poirot.'

Poirot proffered his cigarette case.

'But perhaps you prefer a pipe?'

'Not me.'

He helped himself, then strode briskly off.

The three men looked at each other.

'You think he is genuine?' asked Dr Constantine.

'Yes, yes. I know the type. Besides, it is a story that would be very easily disproved.'

'He has given us a piece of very interesting evidence,' said M. Bouc.

'Yes, indeed.'

'A small man, dark, with a high-pitched voice,' said M. Bouc thoughtfully.

'A description which applies to no one on the train,' said Poirot.

— 10 —

THE EVIDENCE OF THE ITALIAN

'AND now,' said Poirot with a twinkle in his eye, 'we will delight the heart of M. Bouc and see the Italian.'

Antonio Foscarelli came into the dining-car with a swift, cat-like tread. His face beamed. It was a typical Italian face, sunny-looking and swarthy.

He spoke French well and fluently, with only a slight accent.

'Your name is Antonio Foscarelli?'

'Yes, monsieur.'

'You are, I see, a naturalized American subject?'

The American grinned.

'Yes, monsieur. It is better for my business.'

'You are an agent for Ford motor cars?'

'Yes, you see—'

A voluble exposition followed. At the end of it, anything that the three men did not know about Foscarelli's business methods, his journeys, his income, and his opinion of the United States and most European countries seemed a negligible factor. This was not a man who had to have information dragged from him. It gushed out.

His good-natured childish face beamed with satisfaction as, with a last eloquent gesture, he paused and wiped his forehead with a handkerchief.

'So you see,' he said, 'I do big business. I am up to date. I understand salesmanship!'

'You have been in the United States, then, for the last ten years on and off?'

'Yes, monsieur. Ah! well do I remember the day I first took the boat – to go to America, so far away! My mother, my little sister—'

Poirot cut short the flood of reminiscence.

'During your sojourn in the United States did you ever come across the deceased?'

'Never. But I know the type. Oh, yes.' He snapped his fingers expressively. 'It is very respectable, very well dressed, but underneath it is all wrong. Out of my experience I should say he was the big crook. I give you my opinion for what it is worth.'

'Your opinion is quite right,' said Poirot dryly. 'Ratchett was Cassetti, the kidnapper.'

'What did I tell you? I have learned to be very acute – to read the face. It is necessary. Only in America do they teach you the proper way to sell.'

'You remember the Armstrong case?'

'I do not quite remember. The name, yes? It was a little girl – a baby – was it not?'

'Yes, a very tragic affair.'

The Italian seemed the first person to demur to this view.

'Ah, well, these things they happen,' he said philosophically, 'in a great civilization such as America—'

Poirot cut him short.

'Did you ever come across any members of the Armstrong family?'

'No, I do not think so. It is difficult to say. I will give you some figures. Last year alone I sold—'

'Monsieur, pray confine yourself to the point.'

The Italian's hands flung themselves out in a gesture of apology.

'A thousand pardons.'

'Tell me, if you please, your exact movements last night from dinner onwards.'

'With pleasure. I stay here as long as I can. It is more amusing. I talk to the American gentleman at my table. He sells typewriter ribbons. Then I go back to my compartment. It is empty. The miserable John Bull who shares it with me is away attending to his master. At last he comes back – very long face as usual. He will not talk – says yes and no. A miserable race, the English – not sympathetic. He sits in the corner, very stiff, reading a book. Then the conductor comes and makes our beds.'

'Nos. 4 and 5,' murmured Poirot.

'Exactly – the end compartment. Mine is the upper berth. I get up there. I smoke and read. The little Englishman has, I think, the toothache. He gets out a little bottle of stuff that smells very strong. He lies in bed and groans. Presently I sleep. Whenever I wake I hear him groaning.'

'Do you know if he left the carriage at all during the night?'

'I do not think so. That, I should hear. The light from the corridor – one wakes up automatically thinking it is the Customs examination at some frontier.'

'Did he ever speak of his master? Ever express any animus against him?'

'I tell you he did not speak. He was not sympathetic. A fish.'

'You smoke, you say – a pipe, cigarettes, cigars?'

'Cigarettes only.'

Poirot proffered him one, which he accepted.

'Have you ever been in Chicago?' inquired M. Bouc.

'Oh, yes – a fine city – but I know best New York, Washington, Detroit. You have been to the States? No? You should go, it—'

Poirot pushed a sheet of paper across to him.

'If you will sign this, and put your permanent address, please.'

The Italian wrote with a flourish. Then he rose – his smile was as engaging as ever.

'That is all? You do not require me further? Good day to you, messieurs. I wish we could get out of the snow. I have an appointment in Milan—' He shook his head sadly. 'I shall lose the business.'

He departed.

Poirot looked at his friend.

'He has been a long time in America,' said M. Bouc, 'and he is an Italian, and Italians use the knife! And they are great liars! I do not like Italians.'

'*Ça se voit*,' said Poirot with a smile. 'Well, it may be that you are right, but I will point out to you, my friend, that there is absolutely no evidence against the man.'

'And what about the psychology? Do not Italians stab?'

'Assuredly,' said Poirot. 'Especially in the heat of a quarrel. But this – this is a different kind of crime. I have the little idea, my friend, that this is a crime very carefully planned and staged. It is a far-sighted, long-headed crime. It is not – how shall I express it? – a *Latin* crime. It is a crime that shows traces of a cool, resourceful, deliberate brain – I think an Anglo-Saxon brain.'

He picked up the last two passports.

'Let us now,' he said, 'see Miss Mary Debenham.'

— I I —

THE EVIDENCE OF MISS DEBENHAM

WHEN Mary Debenham entered the dining-car she confirmed Poirot's previous estimate of her.

Very neatly dressed in a little black suit with a French grey shirt, the smooth waves of her dark head were neat and unruffled. Her manner was as calm and unruffled as her hair.

She sat down opposite Poirot and M. Bouc and looked at them inquiringly.

'Your name is Mary Hermione Debenham, and you are twenty-six years of age?' began Poirot.

'Yes.'

'English?'

'Yes.'

'Will you be so kind, mademoiselle, as to write down your permanent address on this piece of paper?'

She complied. Her writing was clear and legible.

'And now, mademoiselle, what have you to tell us of the affair last night?'

'I am afraid I have nothing to tell you. I went to bed and slept.'

'Does it distress you very much, mademoiselle, that a crime has been committed on this train?'

The question was clearly unexpected. Her grey eyes widened a little.

'I don't quite understand you.'

'It was a perfectly simple question that I asked you, mademoiselle. I will repeat it. Are you very much distressed that a crime should have been committed on this train?'

'I have not really thought about it from that point of view. No, I cannot say that I am at all distressed.'

'A crime – it is all in the day's work to you, eh?'

'It is naturally an unpleasant thing to have happen,' said Mary Debenham quietly.

'You are very Anglo-Saxon, mademoiselle. *Vous n'éprouvez pas d'emotion.*'

She smiled a little.

'I am afraid I cannot have hysterics to prove my sensibility. After all, people die every day.'

'They die, yes. But murder is a little more rare.'

'Oh, certainly.'

'You were not acquainted with the dead man?'

'I saw him for the first time when lunching here yesterday.'

'And how did he strike you?'

'I hardly noticed him.'

'He did not impress you as an evil personality?'

She shrugged her shoulders slightly.

'Really, I cannot say I thought about it.'

Poirot looked at her keenly.

'You are, I think, a little bit contemptuous of the way I prosecute my inquiries,' he said with a twinkle. 'Not so, you think, would an English inquiry be conducted. There everything would be cut and dried – it would be all kept to the facts – a well-ordered business. But I, mademoiselle, have my little originalities. I look first at my witness, I sum up his or her character, and I frame my questions accordingly. Just a little minute ago I am asking questions of a gentleman who wants to tell me all his ideas on every subject. Well, him I keep strictly to the point. I want him to answer yes or no, this or that. And then you come. I see at once that you will be orderly and methodical. You will confine yourself to the matter in hand. Your answers will be brief and to the point. And because, mademoiselle, human nature is perverse, I ask of you quite different questions. I ask what you *feel*, what you *thought*. It does not please you, this method?'

'If you will forgive my saying so, it seems somewhat of a waste of time. Whether or not I liked Mr Ratchett's face does not seem likely to be helpful in finding out who killed him.'

'Do you know who the man Ratchett really was, mademoiselle?'

She nodded.

'Mrs Hubbard has been telling everyone.'

'And what do you think of the Armstrong affair?'

'It was quite abominable,' said the girl crisply.

Poirot looked at her thoughtfully.

'You are travelling from Baghdad, I believe, Miss Debenham?'

'Yes.'

'To London?'

'Yes.'

'What have you been doing in Baghdad?'

'I have been acting as governess to two children.'

'Are you returning to your post after your holiday?'

'I am not sure.'

'Why is that?'

'Baghdad is rather out of things. I think I should prefer a post in London if I can hear of a suitable one.'

'I see. I thought, perhaps, you might be going to be married.'

Miss Debenham did not reply. She raised her eyes and looked Poirot full in the face. The glance said plainly, 'You are impertinent.'

'What is your opinion of the lady who shares your compartment – Miss Ohlsson?'

'She seems a pleasant, simple creature.'

'What colour is her dressing-gown?'

Mary Debenham stared.

'A kind of brownish colour – natural wool.'

'Ah! I may mention without indiscretion, I hope, that I noticed the colour of your dressing-gown on the way from Aleppo to Stamboul. A pale mauve, I believe.'

'Yes, that is right.'

'Have you any other dressing-gown, mademoiselle? A scarlet dressing-gown, for example?'

'No, that is not mine.'

Poirot leant forward. He was like a cat pouncing on a mouse.

'Whose, then?'

The girl drew back a little, startled.

'I don't know. What do you mean?'

'You do not say, "No, I have no such thing." You say, "That is not mine" – meaning that such a thing *does* belong to someone else.'

She nodded.

'Somebody else on this train?'

'Yes.'

'Whose is it?'

'I told you just now. I don't know. I woke up this morning about five o'clock with the feeling that the train had been standing still for a long time. I opened the door and looked out into the

103

corridor, thinking we might be at a station. I saw someone in a scarlet kimono some way down the corridor.'

'And you don't know who it was? Was she fair or dark or grey-haired?'

'I can't say. She had on a shingle cap and I only saw the back of her head.'

'And in build?'

'Tallish and slim, I should judge, but it's difficult to say. The kimono was embroidered with dragons.'

'Yes, yes, that is right, dragons.'

He was silent a minute. He murmured to himself: 'I cannot understand. I cannot understand. None of this makes sense.'

Then, looking up, he said: 'I need not keep you further, mademoiselle.'

'Oh!' she seemed rather taken aback, but rose promptly.

In the doorway, however, she hesitated a minute and then came back.

'The Swedish lady — Miss Ohlsson, is it? — seems rather worried. She says you told her she was the last person to see this man alive. She thinks, I believe, that you suspect her on that account. Can't I tell her that she has made a mistake? Really, you know, she is the kind of creature who wouldn't hurt a fly.'

She smiled a little as she spoke.

'What time was it that she went to fetch the aspirin from Mrs Hubbard?'

'Just after half-past ten.'

'She was away — how long?'

'About five minutes.'

'Did she leave the compartment again during the night?'

'No.'

Poirot turned to the doctor.

'Could Ratchett have been killed as early as that?'

The doctor shook his head.

'Then I think you can reassure your friend, mademoiselle.'

'Thank you.' She smiled suddenly at him, a smile that invited sympathy. 'She's like a sheep, you know. She gets anxious and bleats.'

She turned and went out.

THE EVIDENCE OF THE GERMAN LADY'S-MAID

M. Bouc was looking at his friend curiously.

'I do not quite understand you, *mon vieux*. You were trying to do – what?'

'I was searching for a flaw, my friend.'

'A flaw?'

'Yes – in the armour of a young lady's self-possession. I wished to shake her *sang froid*. Did I succeed? I do not know. But I know this – she did not expect me to tackle the matter as I did.'

'You suspect her,' said M. Bouc slowly. 'But why? She seems a very charming young lady – the last person in the world to be mixed up in a crime of this kind.'

'I agree,' said Constantine. 'She is cold. She has not emotions. She would not stab a man; she would sue him in the law courts.'

Poirot sighed.

'You must, both of you, get rid of your obsession that this is an unpremeditated and sudden crime. As for the reason why I suspect Miss Debenham, there are two. One is because of something that I overheard, and that you do not as yet know.'

He retailed to them the curious interchange of phrases he had overheard on the journey from Aleppo.

'That is curious, certainly,' said M. Bouc when he had finished. 'It needs explaining. If it means what you suspect it means, then they are both of them in it together – she and the stiff Englishman.'

Poirot nodded.

'And that is just what is not borne out by the facts,' he said. 'See you, if they were both in this together, what should we expect to find – that each of them would provide an alibi for the other. Is not that so? But no – that does not happen. Miss Debenham's alibi is provided by a Swedish woman whom she has never seen before, and Colonel Arbuthnot's alibi is vouched for by MacQueen, the dead man's secretary. No, that solution of the puzzle is too easy.'

'You said there was another reason for your suspicions of her,' M. Bouc reminded him.

Poirot smiled.

'Ah! but that is only psychological. I ask myself, is it possible for Miss Debenham to have planned this crime? Behind this business, I am convinced, there is a cool, intelligent, resourceful brain. Miss Debenham answers to that description.'

M. Bouc shook his head.

'I think you are wrong, my friend. I do not see that young English girl as a criminal.'

'Ah, well,' said Poirot, picking up the last passport. 'To the final name on our list. Hildegarde Schmidt, lady's-maid.'

Summoned by the attendant, Hildegarde Schmidt came into the restaurant-car and stood waiting respectfully.

Poirot motioned her to sit down.

She did so, folding her hands and waiting placidly till he questioned her. She seemed a placid creature altogether – eminently respectable – perhaps not over-intelligent.

Poirot's methods with Hildegarde Schmidt were a complete contrast to his handling of Mary Debenham.

He was at his kindest and most genial, setting the woman at her ease. Then, having got her to write down her name and address, he slid gently into his questions.

The interview took place in German.

'We want to know as much as possible about what happened last night,' he said. 'We know that you cannot give us much information bearing on the crime itself, but you may have seen or heard something that, while conveying nothing to you, may be valuable to us. You understand?'

She did not seem to. Her broad, kindly face remained set in its expression of placid stupidity as she answered: 'I do not know anything, monsieur.'

'Well, for instance, you know that your mistress sent for you last night?'

'That, yes.'

'Do you remember the time?'

'I do not, monsieur. I was asleep, you see, when the attendant came and told me.'

'Yes, yes. Was it usual for you to be sent for in this way?'

'It was not unusual, monsieur. The gracious lady often required attention at night. She did not sleep well.'

'*Eh bien*, then, you received the summons and you got up. Did you put on a dressing-gown?'

'No, monsieur, I put on a few clothes. I would not like to go in to Her Excellency in my dressing-gown.'

'And yet it is a very nice dressing-gown – scarlet, is it not?'

She stared at him.

'It is a dark-blue flannel dressing-gown, monsieur.'

'Ah! Continue. A little pleasantry on my part, that is all. So you

went along to *Madame la Princesse*. And what did you do when
you got there?'

'I gave her massage, monsieur, and then I read aloud. I do not
read aloud very well, but Her Excellency says that is all the better.
So it sends her better to sleep. When she became sleepy, monsieur,
she told me to go, so I closed the book and I returned to my own
compartment.'

'Do you know what time that was?'

'No, monsieur.'

'Well, how long had you been with *Madame la Princesse*?'

'About half an hour, monsieur.'

'Good, continue.'

'First, I fetched Her Excellency an extra rug from my compartment. It was very cold in spite of the heating. I arranged the
rug over her and she wished me good night. I poured her out some
mineral water. Then I turned out the light and left her.'

'And then?'

'There is nothing more, monsieur. I returned to my carriage
and went to sleep.'

'And you met no one in the corridor?'

'No, monsieur.'

'You did not, for instance, see a lady in a scarlet kimono with
dragons on it?'

Her mild eyes bulged at him.

'No, indeed, monsieur. There was nobody about except the
attendant. Everyone was asleep.'

'But you did see the conductor?'

'Yes, monsieur.'

'What was he doing?'

'He came out of one of the compartments, monsieur.'

'What?' M. Bouc leaned forward. 'Which one?'

Hildegarde Schmidt looked frightened again and Poirot cast a
reproachful glance at his friend.

'Naturally,' he said. 'The conductor often has to answer bells at
night. Do you remember which compartment it was?'

'It was about the middle of the coach, monsieur. Two or three
doors from *Madame la Princesse*.'

'Ah! tell us, if you please, exactly where this was and what
happened.'

'He nearly ran into me, monsieur. It was when I was returning
from my compartment to that of the princess with the rug.'

'And he came out of a compartment and almost collided with
you? In which direction was he going?'

'Towards me, monsieur. He apologized and passed on down

the corridor towards the dining-car. A bell began ringing, but I do not think he answered it.'

She paused and then said: 'I do not understand. How is it—?

Poirot spoke reassuringly.

'It is just a question of times,' he said. 'All a matter of routine. This poor conductor, he seems to have had a busy night – first waking you and then answering bells.'

'It was not the same conductor who woke me, monsieur. It was another one.'

'Ah, another one! Had you seen him before?'

'No, monsieur.'

'Ah! Do you think you would recognize him if you saw him?'

'I think so, monsieur.'

Poirot murmured something in M. Bouc's ear. The latter got up and went to the door to give an order.

Poirot was continuing his questions in an easy friendly manner.

'Have you ever been to America, Frau Schmidt?'

'Never, monsieur. It must be a fine country.'

'You have heard, perhaps, of who this man who was killed really was – that he was responsible for the death of a little child.'

'Yes, I have heard, monsieur. It was abominable – wicked. The good God should not allow such things. We are not so wicked as that in Germany.'

Tears had come into the woman's eyes. Her strong motherly soul was moved.

'It was an abominable crime,' said Poirot gravely.

He drew a scrap of cambric from his pocket and handed it to her.

'Is this your handkerchief, Frau Schmidt?'

There was a moment's silence as the woman examined it. She looked up after a minute. The colour had mounted a little in her face.

'Ah! No, indeed. It is not mine, monsieur.'

'It has the initial H, you see. That is why I thought it was yours.'

'Ah! Monsieur, it is a lady's handkerchief, that. A very expensive handkerchief. Embroidered by hand. It comes from Paris, I should say.'

'It is not yours and you do not know whose it is?'

'I? Oh, no, monsieur.'

Of the three listening, only Poirot caught the nuance of hesitation in the reply.

M. Bouc whispered in his ear. Poirot nodded and said to the

woman: 'The three sleeping-car attendants are coming in. Will you be so kind as to tell me which is the one you met last night as you were going with the rug to the princess?'

The three men entered. Pierre Michel, the big blond conductor of the Athens–Paris coach, and the stout burly conductor of the Bucharest one.

Hildegarde Schmidt looked at them and immediately shook her head.

'No, monsieur,' she said. 'None of these is the man I saw last night.'

'But these are the only conductors on the train. You must be mistaken.'

'I am quite sure, monsieur. These are all tall, big men. The one I saw was small and dark. He had a little moustache. His voice when he said "*Pardon*" was weak like a woman's. Indeed, I remember him very well, monsieur.'

— 13 —

SUMMARY OF THE PASSENGERS' EVIDENCE

'A SMALL dark man with a womanish voice,' said M. Bouc.

The three conductors and Hildegarde Schmidt had been dismissed.

M. Bouc made a despairing gesture.

'But I understand nothing – but nothing of all this! The enemy that this Ratchett spoke of, he was, then, on the train after all? But where is he now? How can he have vanished into thin air? My head, it whirls. Say something, then, my friend, I implore you. Show me how the impossible can be possible!'

'It is a good phrase that,' said Poirot. 'The impossible cannot have happened, therefore the impossible must be possible in spite of appearances.'

'Explain to me, then, quickly, what actually happened on the train last night.'

'I am not a magician, *mon cher*. I am, like you, a very puzzled man. This affair advances in a very strange manner.'

'It does not advance at all. It stays where it was.'

Poirot shook his head.

'No, that is not true. We are more advanced. We know certain things. We have heard the evidence of the passengers.'

'And what has that told us? Nothing at all.'

'I would not say that, my friend.'

'I exaggerate, perhaps. The American, Hardman, and the German maid – yes, they have added something to our knowledge. That is to say, they have made the whole business more unintelligible than it was.'

'No, no, no,' said Poirot soothingly.

M. Bouc turned upon him.

'Speak, then, let us hear the wisdom of Hercule Poirot.'

'Did I not tell you that I was, like you, a very puzzled man? But at least we can face our problem. We can arrange such facts as we have with order and method.'

'Pray continue, monsieur,' said Dr Constantine.

Poirot cleared his throat and straightened a piece of blotting-paper.

'Let us review the case as it stands at this moment. First, there are certain indisputable facts. This man Ratchett, or Cassetti, was stabbed in twelve places and died last night. That is fact one.'

'I grant it to you – I grant it, *mon vieux*,' said M. Bouc with a gesture of irony.

Hercule Poirot was not at all put out. He continued calmly: 'I will pass over for the moment certain rather peculiar appearances which Dr Constantine and I have already discussed together. I will come to them presently. The next fact of importance, to my mind, is the *time* of the crime.'

'That, again, is one of the few things we do know,' said M. Bouc. 'The crime was committed at a quarter-past one this morning. Everything goes to show that that was so.'

'Not *everything*. You exaggerate. There is, certainly, a fair amount of evidence to support that view.'

'I am glad you admit that at least.'

Poirot went on calmly, unperturbed by the interruption.

'We have before us three possibilities. One: That the crime was committed, as you say, at a quarter-past one. This is supported by the evidence of the German woman, Hildegarde Schmidt. It agrees with the evidence of Dr Constantine. Possibility two: The crime was committed later and the evidence of the watch was deliberately faked. Possibility three: The crime was committed earlier and the evidence faked for the same reason as above.

'Now, if we accept possibility one as the most likely to have occurred and the one supported by most evidence, we must also accept certain facts arising from it. To begin with, if the crime was committed at a quarter-past one, the murderer cannot have left the train, and the question arises: Where is he? And *who* is he?

'To begin with, let us examine the evidence carefully. We first hear of the existence of this man – the small dark man with a womanish voice – from the man Hardman. He says that Ratchett told him of this person and employed him to watch out for the man. There is no *evidence* to support this – we have only Hardman's word for it. Let us next examine the question: Is Hardman the person he pretends to be – an operative of a New York Detective Agency?

'What to my mind is so interesting in this case is that we have none of the facilities afforded to the police. We cannot investigate the *bona fides* of any of these people. We have to rely solely on deduction. That, to me, makes the matter very much more interesting. There is no routine work. It is a matter of the intellect. I ask myself, "Can we accept Hardman's account of himself?" I make my decision and I answer, "Yes." I am of the opinion that we *can* accept Hardman's account of himself.'

'You rely on the intuition – what the Americans call the hunch?' said Dr Constantine.

'Not at all. I regard the probabilities. Hardman is travelling with a false passport – that will at once make him an object of suspicion. The first thing that the police will do when they do arrive upon the scene is to detain Hardman and cable as to whether his account of himself is true. In the case of many of the passengers, to establish their *bona fides* will be difficult; in most cases it will probably not be attempted, especially since there seems nothing in the way of suspicion attaching to them. But in Hardman's case it is simple. Either he is the person he represents himself to be or he is not. Therefore I say that all will prove to be in order.'

'You acquit him of suspicion?'

'Not at all. You misunderstand me. For all I know, any American detective might have his own private reasons for wishing to murder Ratchett. No, what I am saying is that I think we *can* accept Hardman's own account of *himself*. This story, then, that he tells of Ratchett's seeking him out and employing him, is not unlikely and is most probably, though not of course certainly, true. If we are going to accept it as true, we must see if there is any confirmation of it. We find it in rather an unlikely place – in the evidence of Hildegarde Schmidt. Her description of the man she saw in *wagon lit* uniform tallies exactly. Is there any further confirmation of these two stories? There is. There is the button found in her compartment by Mrs Hubbard. And there is also another corroborating statement which you may not have noticed.'

'What is that?'

'The fact that both Colonel Arbuthnot and Hector MacQueen mention that the conductor passed their carriage. They attached no importance to the fact, but, *messieurs, Pierre Michel has declared that he did not leave his seat except on certain specified occasions*, none of which would take him down to the far end of the coach past the compartment in which Arbuthnot and MacQueen were sitting.

'Therefore this story, the story of a small dark man with a womanish voice dressed in *wagon lit* uniform, rests on the testimony – direct or indirect – of four witnesses.'

'One small point,' said Dr Constantine. 'If Hildegarde Schmidt's story is true, how is it that the real conductor did not mention having seen her when he came to answer Mrs Hubbard's bell?'

'That is explained, I think. When he arrived to answer Mrs Hubbard, the maid was in with her mistress. When she finally returned to her own compartment, the conductor was in with Mrs Hubbard.'

M. Bouc had been waiting with difficulty until they had finished.

'Yes, yes, my friend,' he said impatiently to Poirot. 'But whilst I admire your caution, your method of advancing a step at a time, I submit that you have not yet touched the point at issue. We are all agreed that this person exists. The point is – *where did he go?*'

Poirot shook his head reprovingly.

'You are in error. You are inclined to put the cart before the horse. Before I ask myself, *"Where did this man vanish to?"* I ask myself, *"Did such a man really exist?"* Because, you see, if the man were an invention – a fabrication – how much easier to make him disappear! So I try to establish first that there really *is* such a flesh and blood person.'

'And having arrived at the fact that there is – *eh bien* – where is he now?'

'There are only two answers to that, *mon cher*. Either he is still hidden on the train in a place of such extraordinary ingenuity that we cannot even think of it, or else he is, as one might say, *two persons*. That is, he is both himself—the man feared by Mr Ratchett—and a passenger on the train so well disguised that Mr Ratchett did not recognize him.'

112

'It is an idea, that,' said M. Bouc, his face lighting up. Then it clouded over again. 'But there is one objection—'

Poirot took the words out of his mouth.

'The height of the man. It is that you would say? With the exception of Mr Ratchett's valet, all the passengers are big men – the Italian, Colonel Arbuthnot, Hector MacQueen, Count Andrenyi. Well, that leaves us the valet – not a very likely supposition. But there is another possibility. Remember the "womanish" voice. That gives us a choice of alternatives. The man may be disguised as a woman, or, alternatively, he may actually *be* a woman. A tall woman dressed in man's clothes would look small.'

'But surely Ratchett would have known—'

'Perhaps he *did* know. Perhaps, already, this woman had attempted his life wearing men's clothes the better to accomplish her purpose. Ratchett may have guessed that she would use the same trick again, so he tells Hardman to look for a man. But he mentions, however, a womanish voice.'

'It is a possibility,' said M. Bouc. 'But—'

'Listen, my friend, I think that I should now tell you of certain inconsistencies noticed by Dr Constantine.'

He retailed at length the conclusions that he and the doctor had arrived at together from the nature of the dead man's wounds. M. Bouc groaned and held his head again.

'I know,' said Poirot sympathetically. 'I know exactly how you feel. The head spins, does it not?'

'The whole thing is a fantasy,' cried M. Bouc.

'Exactly. It is absurd – improbable – it cannot be. So I myself have said. And yet, my friend, *there it is*! One cannot escape from the facts.'

'It is madness!'

'Is it not? It is so mad, my friend, that sometimes I am haunted by the sensation that really it must be very simple . . .

'But that is only one of my "little ideas" . . .'

'Two murderers,' groaned M. Bouc. 'And on the Orient Express.'

The thought almost made him weep.

'And now let us make the fantasy more fantastic.' said Poirot cheerfully. 'Last night on the train there are two mysterious strangers. There is the *wagon lit* attendant answering to the discription given us by Mr Hardman, and seen by Hildegarde Schmidt, Colonel Arbuthnot and Mr MacQueen. There is also a woman in a red kimono – a tall, slim woman – seen by Pierre

Michel, by Miss Debenham, by Mr MacQueen and by myself –
and smelt, I may say, by Colonel Arbuthnot! Who was she? No
one on the train admits to having a scarlet kimono. She, too, has
vanished. Was she one and the same with the spurious *wagon lit*
attendant? Or was she some quite distinct personality? Where are
they, these two? And, incidentally, where is the *wagon lit* uniform
and the scarlet kimono?'

'Ah! that is something definite.' M. Bouc sprang up eagerly.
'We must search all the passengers' luggage. Yes, that will be
something.'

Poirot rose also.

'I will make a prophecy,' he said.

'You know where they are?'

'I have a little idea.'

'Where, then?'

'You will find the scarlet kimono in the baggage of one of the
men and you will find the uniform of the *wagon lit* conductor in
the baggage of Hildegarde Schmidt.'

'Hildegarde Schmidt? You think—?'

'Not what you are thinking. I will put it like this. If Hildegarde
Schmidt is guilty, the uniform *might* be found in her baggage – but
if she is innocent it *certainly* will be.'

'But how—?' began M. Bouc and stopped.

'What is this noise that approaches?' he cried. 'It resembles a
locomotive in motion.'

The noise drew nearer. It consisted of shrill cries and protests in
a woman's voice. The door at the end of the dining-car flew open.
Mrs Hubbard burst in.

'It's too horrible,' she cried. 'It's just too horrible. In my
sponge-bag. My sponge-bag. A great knife – all over blood.'

And, suddenly toppling forward, she fainted heavily on M.
Bouc's shoulder.

— 14 —

THE EVIDENCE OF THE WEAPON

WITH more vigour than chivalry, M. Bouc deposited the fainting
lady with her head on the table. Dr Constantine yelled for one of
the restaurant attendants, who came at a run.

'Keep her head so,' said the doctor. 'If she revives give her a little cognac. You understand?'

Then he hurried off after the other two. His interest lay wholly in the crime – swooning middle-aged ladies did not interest him at all.

It is possible that Mrs Hubbard revived rather quicker with these methods than she might otherwise have done. A few minutes later she was sitting up, sipping cognac from a glass proffered by the attendant, and talking once more.

'I just can't say how terrible it was. I don't suppose anybody on this train can understand my feelings. I've always been vurry, vurry sensitive ever since a child. The mere sight of blood – ugh – why, even now I come over queer when I think about it.'

The attendant proffered the glass again.

'Encore un peu, madame.'

'D'you think I'd better? I'm a lifelong teetotaller. I just never touch spirits or wine at any time. All my family are abstainers. Still, perhaps as this is only medicinal—'

She sipped once more.

In the meantime Poirot and M. Bouc, closely followed by Dr Constantine, had hurried out of the restaurant-car and along the corridor of the Stamboul coach towards Mrs Hubbard's compartment.

Every traveller on the train seemed to be congregated outside the door. The conductor, a harassed look on his face, was keeping them back.

'Mais il n'y a rien à voir,' he said, and repeated the sentiment in several other languages.

'Let me pass, if you please,' said M. Bouc.

Squeezing his rotundity past the obstructing passengers, he entered the compartment, Poirot close behind him.

'I am glad you have come, monsieur,' said the conductor with a sigh of relief. 'Everyone has been trying to enter. The American lady – such screams as she gave – *ma foi*! I thought she too had been murdered! I came at a run and there she was screaming like a mad woman, and she cried out that she must fetch you and she departed, screeching at the top of her voice and telling everybody whose carriage she passed what had occurred.'

He added, with a gesture of the hand: *'It* is in there, monsieur. I have not touched it.'

Hanging on the handle of the door that gave access to the next compartment was a large-size checked rubber sponge-bag. Below it on the floor, just where it had fallen from Mrs Hubbard's hand, was a straight-bladed dagger – a cheap affair, sham Oriental, with an embossed hilt and a tapering blade. The blade was stained with patches of what looked like rust.

Poirot picked it up delicately.

'Yes,' he murmured. 'There is no mistake. Here is our missing weapon all right – eh, *docteur*?'

The doctor examined it.

'You need not be so careful,' said Poirot. 'There will be no fingerprints on it save those of Mrs Hubbard.'

Constantine's examination did not take long.

'It is the weapon all right,' he said. 'It would account for any of the wounds.'

'I implore you, my friend, do not say that.'

The doctor looked astonished.

'Already we are heavily overburdened by coincidence. Two people decide to stab Mr Ratchett last night. It is too much of a good thing that each of them should select an identical weapon.'

'As to that, the coincidence is not, perhaps, so great as it seems,' said the doctor. 'Thousands of these sham Eastern daggers are made and shipped to the bazaars of Constantinople.'

'You console me a little, but only a little,' said Poirot.

He looked thoughtfully at the door in front of him, then, lifting off the sponge-bag, he tried the handle. The door did not budge. About a foot above the handle was the door bolt. Poirot drew it back and tried again, but still the door remained fast.

'We locked it from the other side, you remember,' said the doctor.

'That is true,' said Poirot absently. He seemed to be thinking about something else. His brow was furrowed as though in perplexity.

'It agrees, does it not?' said M. Bouc. 'The man passes through this carriage. As he shuts the communicating door behind him he feels the sponge-bag. A thought comes to him and he quickly slips the bloodstained knife inside. Then, all unwitting that he has awakened Mrs Hubbard, he slips out through the other door into the corridor.'

'As you say,' murmured Poirot. 'That is how it must have happened.'

But the puzzled look did not leave his face.

'But what is it?' demanded M. Bouc. 'There is something, is there not, that does not satisfy you?'

Poirot darted a quick look at him.

'The same point does not strike you? No, evidently not. Well, it is a small matter.'

The conductor looked into the carriage.

'The American lady is coming back.'

Dr Constantine looked rather guilty. He had, he felt, treated Mrs Hubbard rather cavalierly. But she had no reproaches for him. Her energies were concentrated on another matter.

'I'm just going to say one thing right out,' she said breathlessly as she arrived in the doorway. 'I'm not going on any longer in this compartment! Why, I wouldn't sleep in it tonight if you paid me a million dollars.'

'But, madame—'

'I know what you are going to say, and I'm telling you right now that I won't do any such thing! Why, I'd rather sit up all night in the corridor.'

She began to cry.

'Oh! if my daughter could only know – if she could see me now, why—'

Poirot interrupted firmly.

'You misunderstand, madame. Your demand is most reasonable. Your baggage shall be changed at once to another compartment.'

Mrs Hubbard lowered her handkerchief.

'Is that so? Oh, I feel better right away. But surely it's all full up, unless one of the gentlemen—'

M. Bouc spoke.

'Your baggage, madame, shall be moved out of this coach altogether. You shall have a compartment in the next coach which was put on at Belgrade.'

'Why, that's splendid. I'm not an out of the way nervous woman, but to sleep in that compartment next door to a dead man—' She shivered. 'It would drive me plumb crazy.'

'Michel,' called M. Bouc. 'Move this baggage into a vacant compartment in the Athens–Paris coach.'

'Yes, monsieur – the same one as this – the No. 3?'

'No,' said Poirot before his friend could reply.' I think it would be better for madame to have a different number altogether. The No. 12, for instance.'

'*Bien*, monsieur.'

The conductor seized the luggage. Mrs Hubbard turned gratefully to Poirot.

'That's vurry kind and delicate of you. I appreciate it, I assure you.'

'Do not mention it, madame. We will come with you and see you comfortably installed.'

Mrs Hubbard was escorted by the three men to her new home. She looked round her happily.

'This is fine.'

'It suits you, madame? It is, you see, exactly like the compartment you have left.'

'That's so – only it faces the other way. But that doesn't matter, for these trains go first one way and then the other. I said to my daughter, "I want a carriage facing the engine," and she said, "Why, Momma, that'll be no good to you, for if you go to sleep one way, when you wake up the train's going the other." And it was quite true what she said. Why, last evening we went into Belgrade one way and out the other.'

'At any rate, madame, you are quite happy and contented now?'

'Well, no, I wouldn't say that. Here we are stuck in a snowdrift and nobody doing anything about it, and my boat sailing the day after tomorrow.'

'Madame,' said M. Bouc, 'we are all in the same case – every one of us.'

'Well, that's true,' admitted Mrs Hubbard. 'But nobody else has had a murderer walking right through their compartment in the middle of the night.'

'What still puzzles me, madame,' said Poirot, 'is how the man got into your compartment if the communicating door was bolted as you say. You are sure that it *was* bolted?'

'Why, the Swedish lady tried it before my eyes.'

'Let us just reconstruct that little scene. You were lying in your bunk – so – and you could not see for yourself, you say?'

'No, because of the sponge-bag. Oh, my, I shall have to get a new sponge-bag. It makes me feel sick in my stomach to look at this one.'

Poirot picked up the sponge-bag and hung it on the handle of the communicating door into the next carriage.

'*Précisément* – I see,' he said. 'The bolt is just underneath the handle – the sponge-bag masks it. You could not see from where you were lying whether the bolt were turned or not.'

'Why, that's just what I've been telling you!'

'And the Swedish lady, Miss Ohlsson, stood so, between you and the door. She tried it and told you it was bolted.'

'That's so.'

'All the same, madame, she may have made an error. You see what I mean.' Poirot seemed anxious to explain. 'The bolt is just a projection of metal – so. Turned to the right the door is locked, left straight, it is not. Possibly she merely tried the door, and as it was locked on the other side she may have assumed that it was locked on your side.'

'Well, I guess that would have been rather stupid of her.'

'Madame, the most kind, the most amiable are not always the cleverest.'

'That's so, of course.'

'By the way, madame, did you travel out to Smyrna this way?'

'No. I sailed right to Stamboul, and a friend of my daughter's – Mr Johnson (a perfectly lovely man; I'd like to have you know him) – met me and showed me all round Stamboul, which I found a very disappointing city – all tumbling down. And as for those mosques and putting on those great shuffling things over your shoes – where was I?'

'You were saying that Mr Johnson met you.'

'That's so, and he saw me on board a French Messagerie boat for Smyrna, and my daughter's husband was waiting right on the quay. What he'll say when he hears about all this! My daughter said this would be just the safest, easiest way imaginable. "You just sit in your carriage," she said, "and you get right to Parrus and there the American Express will meet you." And, oh dear, what am I to do about cancelling my steamship passage? I ought to let them know. I can't possibly make it now. This is just too terrible—'

Mrs Hubbard showed signs of tears once more.

Poirot, who had been fidgeting slightly, seized his opportunity.

'You have had a shock, madame. The restaurant attendant shall be instructed to bring you along some tea and some biscuits.'

'I don't know that I'm so set on tea,' said Mrs Hubbard tearfully. 'That's more an English habit.'

'Coffee, then, madame. You need some stimulant.'

'That cognac's made my head feel mighty funny. I think I would like some coffee.'

'Excellent. You must revive your forces.'

'My, what a funny expression.'

'But first, madame, a little matter of routine. You permit that I make a search of your baggage?'

'Whatever for?'

'We are about to commence a search of all the passengers'

luggage. I do not want to remind you of an unpleasant experience, but your sponge-bag – remember.'

'Mercy! Perhaps you'd better! I just couldn't bear to get any more surprises of that kind.'

The examination was quickly over. Mrs Hubbard was travelling with the minimum of luggage – a hat-box, a cheap suitcase, and a well-burdened travelling-bag. The contents of all three were simple and straightforward, and the examination would not have taken more than a couple of minutes had not Mrs Hubbard delayed matters by insisting on due attention being paid to photographs of 'My daughter' and two rather ugly children – 'My daughter's children. Aren't they cunning?'

— 15 —

THE EVIDENCE OF THE PASSENGERS' LUGGAGE

HAVING delivered himself of various polite insincerities, and having told Mrs Hubbard that he would order coffee to be brought to her, Poirot was able to take his leave accompanied by his two friends.

'Well, we have made a start and drawn a blank,' observed M. Bouc. 'Whom shall we tackle next?'

'It would be simplest, I think, just to proceed along the train carriage by carriage. That means that we start with No. 16 – the amiable Mr Hardman.'

Mr Hardman, who was smoking a cigar, welcomed them affably.

'Come right in, gentlemen – that is, if it's humanly possible. It's just a mite cramped in here for a party.'

M. Bouc explained the object of their visit, and the big detective nodded comprehendingly.

'That's O.K. To tell the truth, I've been wondering you didn't get down to it sooner. Here are my keys, gentlemen, and if you like to search my pockets too, why, you're welcome. Shall I reach the grips down for you?'

'The conductor will do that. Michel!'

The contents of Mr Hardman's two 'grips' were soon examined

and passed. They contained perhaps an undue proportion of spirituous liquor. Mr Hardman winked.

'It's not often they search your grips at the frontiers – not if you fix the conductor. I handed out a wad of Turkish notes right away, and there's been no trouble so far.'

'And at Paris?'

Mr Hardman winked again.

'By the time I get to Paris,' he said, 'what's left over of this little lot will go into a bottle labelled hairwash.'

'You are not a believer in Prohibition, Mr Hardman,' said M. Bouc with a smile.

'Well,' said Hardman. 'I can't say Prohibition has ever worried me any.'

'Ah!' said M. Bouc. 'The speakeasy.' He pronounced the word with care, savouring it. 'Your American terms are so quaint, so expressive,' he said.

'Me, I would much like to go to America,' said Poirot.

'You'd learn a few go-ahead methods over there,' said Hardman. 'Europe wants waking up. She's half asleep.'

'It is true that America is the country of progress,' agreed Poirot. 'There is much that I admire about Americans. Only – I am perhaps old-fashioned – but me, I find the American woman less charming than my own countrywomen. The French or Belgian girl, coquettish, charming – I think there is no one to touch her.'

Hardman turned away to peer out at the snow for a minute.

'Perhaps you're right, M. Poirot,' he said. 'But I guess every nation likes its own girls best.'

He blinked as though the snow hurt his eyes.

'Kind of dazzling, isn't it?' he remarked. 'Say, gentlemen, this business is getting on my nerves. Murder and the snow and all, and nothing *doing*. Just hanging about and killing time. I'd like to get busy after someone or something.'

'The true Western spirit of hustle,' said Poirot with a smile.

The conductor replaced the bags and they moved on to the next compartment. Colonel Arbuthnot was sitting in a corner smoking a pipe and reading a magazine.

Poirot explained their errand. The colonel made no demur. He had two heavy leather suitcases.

'The rest of my kit has gone by long sea,' he explained.

Like most Army men, the colonel was a neat packer. The examination of his baggage took only a few minutes. Poirot noted a packet of pipe-cleaners.

'You always use the same kind?' he asked.

'Usually. If I can get 'em.'

'Ah!' Poirot nodded.

These pipe-cleaners were identical with the one he had found on the floor of the dead man's compartment.

Dr Constantine remarked as much when they were out in the corridor again.

'*Tout de même*,' murmured Poirot, 'I can hardly believe it. It is not *dans son caractère*, and when you have said that you have said everything.'

The door of the next compartment was closed. It was that occupied by Princess Dragomiroff. They knocked on the door and the Princess's deep voice called, '*Entrez.*'

M. Bouc was spokesman. He was very deferential and polite as he explained their errand.

The Princess listened to him in silence, her small toad-like face quite impassive.

'If it is necessary, messieurs,' she said quietly when he had finished, 'that is all there is to it. My maid has the keys. She will attend to it with you.'

'Does your maid always carry your keys, madame?' asked Poirot.

'Certainly, monsieur.'

'And if during the night at one of the frontiers the Customs officials should require a piece of luggage to be opened?'

The old lady shrugged her shoulders.

'It is very unlikely. But in such a case this conductor would fetch her.'

'You trust her, then, implicitly, madame?'

'I have told you so already,' said the Princess quietly. 'I do not employ people whom I do not trust.'

'Yes,' said Poirot thoughtfully. 'Trust is indeed something in these days. It is, perhaps, better to have a homely woman whom one can trust than a more *chic* maid – for example, some smart Parisienne.'

He saw the dark intelligent eyes come slowly round and fasten themselves upon his face.

'What exactly are you implying, M. Poirot?'

'Nothing, madame. I? Nothing.'

'But yes. You think, do you not, that I should have a smart Frenchwoman to attend to my toilet?'

'It would be, perhaps, more usual, madame.'

She shook her head.

'Schmidt is devoted to me.' Her voice dwelt lingeringly on the words. 'Devotion – *c'est impayable.*'

The German woman had arrived with the keys. The Princess spoke to her in her own language, telling her to open the *valises* and help the gentlemen in their search. She herself remained in the corridor looking out at the snow and Poirot remained with her, leaving M. Bouc to the task of searching the luggage.

She regarded him with a grim smile.

'Well, monsieur, do you not wish to see what my *valises* contain?'

He shook his head.

'Madame, it is a formality, that is all.'

'Are you so sure?'

'In your case, yes.'

'And yet I knew and loved Sonia Armstrong. What do you think, then? That I would not soil my hands with killing such *canaille* as that man Cassetti? Well, perhaps you are right.'

She was silent a minute or two, then she said: 'With such a man as that, do you know what I should have liked to have done? I should have liked to call to my servants: "Flog this man to death and fling him out on the rubbish heap." That is the way things were done when I was young, monsieur.'

Still he did not speak, just listened attentively.

She looked at him with a sudden impetuosity.

'You do not say anything, M. Poirot. What is it that you are thinking, I wonder.?'

He looked at her with a very direct glance.

'I think, madame, that your strength is in your will – not in your arm.'

She glanced down at her thin, black-clad arms ending in those claw-like yellow hands with the rings on the fingers.

'It is true,' she said. 'I have no strength in these – none. I do not know if I am sorry or glad.'

Then she turned abruptly back towards her carriage, where the maid was busily packing up the cases.

The Princess cut short M. Bouc's apologies.

'There is no need for you to apologise, monsieur,' she said. 'A murder has been committed. Certain actions have to be performed. That is all there is to it.'

'*Vous êtes bien amiable, madame.*'

She inclined her head slightly as they departed.

The doors of the next two carriages were shut. M. Bouc paused and scratched his head.

'*Diable!*' he said. 'This may be awkward. These are diplomatic passports. Their baggage is exempt.'

'From Customs examination, yes. But a murder is different.'

'I know. All the same – we do not want to have complications—'

'Do not distress yourself, my friend. The count and countess will be reasonable. See how amiable Princess Dragomiroff was about it.'

'She is truly *grande dame*. These two are also of the same position, but the count impressed me as a man of somewhat truculent disposition. He was not pleased when you insisted on questioning his wife. And this will annoy him still further. Suppose – eh – we omit them. After all, they can have nothing to do with the matter. Why should I stir up needless trouble for myself?'

'I do not agree with you,' said Poirot. 'I feel sure that Count Andrenyi will be reasonable. At any rate, let us make the attempt.'

And, before M. Bouc could reply, he rapped sharply on the door of No. 13.

A voice from within cried, '*Entrez.*'

The count was sitting in the corner near the door reading a newspaper. The countess was curled up in the opposite corner near the window. There was a pillow behind her head, and she seemed to have been asleep.

'Pardon, *Monsieur le Comte*,' began Poirot. 'Pray forgive this intrusion. It is that we are making a search of all the baggage on the train. In most cases a mere formality. But it has to be done. M. Bouc suggests that, as you have a diplomatic passport, you might reasonably claim to be exempt from such a search.'

The count considered for a moment.

'Thank you,' he said. 'But I do not think that I care for an exception to be made in my case. I should prefer that our baggage should be examined like that of the other passengers.'

He turned to his wife.

'You do not object, I hope, Elena?'

'Not at all,' said the countess without hesitation.

A rapid and somewhat perfunctory search followed. Poirot seemed to be trying to mask an embarrassment in making various small pointless remarks, such as: 'Here is a label all wet on your suitcase, madame,' as he lifted down a blue morocco case with initials on it and a coronet.

The countess did not reply to this observation. She seemed, indeed, rather bored by the whole proceeding, remaining curled up in her corner, staring dreamily out through the window whilst the men searched her luggage in the compartment next door.

Poirot finished his search by opening the little cupboard above the wash-basin and taking a rapid glance at its contents – a sponge, face cream, powder and a small bottle labelled trional.

Then, with polite remarks on either side, the search party withdrew.

Mrs Hubbard's compartment, that of the dead man, and Poirot's own came next.

They now came to the second class carriages. The first one, Nos. 10, 11, was occupied by Mary Debenham, who was reading a book, and Greta Ohlsson, who was fast asleep but woke with a start at their entrance.

Poirot repeated his formula. The Swedish lady seemed agitated, Mary Debenham calmly indifferent.

Poirot addressed himself to the Swedish lady.

'If you permit, mademoiselle, we will examine your baggage first, and then perhaps you would be so good as to see how the American lady is getting on. We have moved her into one of the carriages in the next coach, but she is still very upset as the result of her discovery. I have ordered coffee to be sent to her, but I think she is of those to whom someone to talk to is a necessity of the first water.'

The good lady was instantly sympathetic. She would go immediately. It must have been indeed a terrible shock to the nerves, and already the poor lady was upset by the journey and leaving her daughter. Ah, yes, certainly she would go at once – her case was not locked – and she would take with her some sal ammoniac.

She bustled off. Her possessions were soon examined. They were meagre in the extreme. She had evidently not yet noticed the missing wires from the hat-box.

Miss Debenham had put her book down. She was watching Poirot. When he asked her, she handed over her keys. Then, as he lifted down a case and opened it, she said: 'Why did you send her away, M. Poirot?'

'I, mademoiselle? Why, to minister to the American lady.'

'An excellent pretext – but a pretext all the same.'

'I don't understand you, mademoiselle.'

'I think you understand me very well.'

She smiled.

'You wanted to get me alone. Wasn't that it?'

'You are putting words into my mouth, mademoiselle.'

'And ideas into your head? No, I don't think so. The ideas are already there. That is right, isn't it?'

'Mademoiselle, we have a proverb—'

'*Qui s'excuse s'accuse;* is that what you were going to say? You must give me the credit for a certain amount of observation and common sense. For some reason or other you have got it into your head that I know something about this sordid business – this murder of a man I never saw before.'

'You are imagining things, mademoiselle.'

'No, I am not imagining things at all. But it seems to me that a lot of time is wasted by not speaking the truth – by beating about the bush instead of coming straight out with things.'

'And you do not like the waste of time. No, you like to come straight to the point. You like the direct method. *Eh bien*, I will give it to you, the direct method. I will ask you the meaning of certain words that I overheard on the journey from Syria. I had got out of the train to do what the English call "stretch the legs" at the station of Konya. Your voice and the colonel's, mademoiselle, they came to me out of the night. You said to him, "*Not now. Not now. When it's all over. When it's behind us.*" What did you mean by those words, mademoiselle?'

She said very quietly: 'Do you think I meant – murder?'

'It is I who am asking you, mademoiselle.'

She sighed – was lost a minute in thought. Then, as though rousing herself, she said: 'Those words had a meaning, monsieur, but not one that I can tell you. I can only give you my solemn word of honour that I had never set eyes on this man Ratchett in my life until I saw him on this train.'

'And – you refuse to explain those words?'

'Yes – if you like to put it that way – I refuse. They had to do with – with a task I had undertaken.'

'A task that is now ended?'

'What do you mean?'

'It is ended, is it not?'

'Why should you think so?'

'Listen, mademoiselle, I will recall to you another incident. There was a delay to the train on the day we were to reach Stamboul. You were very agitated, mademoiselle. You, so calm, so self-controlled. You lost that calm.'

'I did not want to miss my connection.'

'So you said. But, mademoiselle, the Orient Express leaves Stamboul every day of the week. Even if you had missed the connection it would only have been a matter of twenty-four hours' delay.'

Miss Debenham for the first time showed signs of losing her temper.

'You do not seem to realize that one may have friends awaiting one's arrival in London, and that a day's delay upsets arrangements and causes a lot of annoyance.'

'Ah, it is like that? There are friends awaiting your arrival? You do not want to cause them inconvenience?'

'Naturally.'

'And yet – it is curious—'

'What is curious?'

'On this train – again we have a delay. And this time a more serious delay, since there is no possibility of sending a telegram to your friends or of getting them on the long – the long—'

'The long-distance? The telephone, you mean.'

'Ah, yes, the *portmanteau* call, as you say in England.'

Mary Debenham smiled a little in spite of herself.

'Trunk call,' she corrected. 'Yes, as you say, it is extremely annoying not to be able to get any word through, either by telephone or telegraph.'

'And yet, mademoiselle, *this* time your manner is quite different. You no longer betray the impatience. You are calm and philosophical.'

Mary Debenham flushed and bit her lip. She no longer felt inclined to smile.

'You do not answer, mademoiselle?'

'I am sorry. I did not know that there was anything to answer.'

'The explanation of your change of attitude, mademoiselle.'

'Don't you think that you are making rather a fuss about nothing, M. Poirot?'

Poirot spread out his hands in an apologetic gesture.

'It is perhaps a fault with us detectives. We expect the behaviour to be always consistent. We do not allow for changes of mood.'

Mary Debenham made no reply.

'You know Colonel Arbuthnot well, mademoiselle?'

He fancied that she was relieved by the change of subject.

'I met him for the first time on this journey.'

'Have you any reason to suspect that he may have known this man Ratchett?'

She shook her head decisively.

'I am quite sure he didn't.'

'Why are you sure?'

'By the way he spoke.'

'And yet, mademoiselle, we found a pipe-cleaner on the floor of the dead man's compartment. And Colonel Arbuthnot is the only man on the train who smokes a pipe.'

He watched her narrowly, but she displayed neither surprise nor emotion, merely said: 'Nonsense. It's absurd. Colonel Arbuthnot is the last man in the world to be mixed up in a crime – especially a theatrical kind of crime like this.'

It was so much what Poirot himself thought that he found himself on the point of agreeing with her. He said instead: 'I must remind you that you do not know him very well, mademoiselle.'

She shrugged her shoulders.

'I know the type well enough.'

He said very gently: 'You still refuse to tell me the meaning of those words – "When it's behind us"?'

She said coldly: 'I have nothing more to say.'

'It does not matter,' said Hercule Poirot. 'I shall find out.'

He bowed and left the compartment, closing the door after him.

'Was that wise, my friend?' asked M. Bouc. 'You have put her on her guard – and through her you have put the colonel on his guard also.'

'*Mon ami*, if you wish to catch a rabbit you put a ferret into the hole, and if the rabbit is there he runs. That is all I have done.'

They entered the compartment of Hildegarde Schmidt.

The woman was standing in readiness, her face respectful but unemotional.

Poirot took a quick glance through the contents of the small case on the seat. Then he motioned to the attendant to get down the bigger suitcase from the rack.

'The keys?' he said.

'It is not locked, monsieur.'

Poirot undid the hasps and lifted the lid.

'Aha!' he said, and turning to M. Bouc, 'You remember what I said? Look here a little moment!'

On the top of the suitcase was a hastily rolled up brown wagon lit *uniform.*

The stolidity of the German woman underwent a sudden change.

'Ach!' she cried. 'That is not mine. I did not put it there. I have never looked in that case since we left Stamboul. Indeed, indeed, it is true.'

She looked from one to another pleadingly.

Poirot took her gently by the arm and soothed her.

'No, no, all is well. We believe you. Do not be agitated. I am as sure you did not hide the uniform there as I am sure that you are a good cook. See. You are a good cook, are you not?

Bewildered, the woman smiled in spite of herself.

'Yes, indeed, all my ladies have said so. I—'

She stopped, her mouth open, looking frightened again.

'No, no,' said Poirot. 'I assure you all is well. See, I will tell you how this happened. This man, the man you saw in *wagon lit* uniform, comes out of the dead man's compartment. He collides with you. That is bad luck for him. He has hoped that no one will see him. What to do next? He must get rid of his uniform. It is now not a safeguard, but a danger.'

His glance went to M. Bouc and Dr Constantine, who were listening attentively.

'There is the snow, you see. The snow which confuses all his plans. Where can he hide these clothes? All the compartments are full. No, he passes one where the door is open and shows it to be unoccupied. It must be the one belonging to the woman with whom he has just collided. He slips in, removes the uniform and jams it hurriedly into a suitcase on the rack. It may be some time before it is discovered.'

'And then?' said M. Bouc.

'That we must discuss,' said Poirot with a warning glance.

He held up the tunic. A button, the third down, was missing. Poirot slipped his hand into the pocket and took out a conductor's pass key, used to unlock the doors of the compartments.

'Here is the explanation of how our man was able to pass through locked doors,' said M. Bouc. 'Your questions to Mrs Hubbard were unnecessary. Locked or not locked, the man could easily get through the communicating door. After all, if a *wagon lit* uniform, why not a *wagon lit* key?'

'Why not, indeed?' said Poirot.

'We might have known it, really. You remember Michel said that the door into the corridor of Mrs Hubbard's compartment was locked when he came in answer to her bell.'

'That is so, monsieur,' said the conductor. 'That is why I thought the lady must have been dreaming.'

'But now it is easy,' continued M. Bouc. 'Doubtless he meant to relock the communicating door also, but perhaps he heard some movement from the bed and it startled him.'

'We have now,' said Poirot, 'only to find the scarlet kimono.'

'True. And these last two compartments are occupied by men.'

'We will search all the same.'

'Oh! assuredly. Besides, I remember what you said.'

Hector MacQueen acquiesced willingly in the search.

'I'd just as soon you did,' he said with a rueful smile. 'I feel I'm just definitely the most suspicious character on the train. You've only got to find a will in which the old man left me all his money, and that'll just about fix things.'

M. Bouc bent a suspicious glance upon him.

'That's just my fun,' said MacQueen hastily. 'He'd never have left me a cent, really. I was just useful to him – languages and so on. You're apt to be done down, you know, if you don't speak anything but good American. I'm no linguist myself, but I know what I call shopping and hotel snappy bits in French and German and Italian.'

His voice was a little louder than usual. It was as though he was slightly uneasy at the search in spite of his willingness.

Poirot emerged.

'Nothing,' he said. 'Not even a compromising bequest!'

MacQueen sighed.

'Well, that's a load off my mind,' he said humorously.

They moved on to the last compartment. The examination of the luggage of the big Italian and of the valet yielded no result.

The three men stood at the end of the coach looking at each other.

'What next?' asked M. Bouc.

'We will go back to the dining-car,' said Poirot. 'We know now all that we can know. We have the evidence of the passengers, the evidence of their baggage, the evidence of our eyes. We can expect no further help. It must be our part now to use our brains.'

He felt in his pocket for his cigarette case. It was empty.

'I will join you in a moment,' he said. 'I shall need the cigarettes. This is a very difficult, a very curious affair. Who wore that scarlet kimono? Where is it now? I wish I knew. There is something in this case – some factor – that escapes me! It is difficult because it has been made difficult. But we will discuss it. Pardon me a moment.'

He went hurriedly along the corridor to his own compartment. He had, he knew, a further supply of cigarettes in one of his *valises*.

He got it down and snapped back the lock.

Then he sat back on his heels and stared.

Neatly folded on the top of the case was a thin scarlet silk kimono embroidered with dragons.

'So,' he murmured. 'It is like that. A defiance. Very well. I take it up.'

PART III

HERCULE POIROT SITS BACK AND THINKS

— I —

WHICH OF THEM?

M. Bouc and Dr Constantine were talking together when Poirot entered the dining-car. M. Bouc was looking depressed.

'*Le voilà*,' said the latter when he saw Poirot.

Then he added as his friend sat down: 'If you solve this case, *mon cher*, I shall indeed believe in miracles!'

'It worries you, this case?'

'Naturally it worries me. I cannot make head or tail of it.'

'I agree,' said the doctor.

He looked at Poirot with interest.

'To be frank,' he said, 'I cannot see what you are going to do next.'

'No?' said Poirot thoughtfully.

He took out his cigarette case and lit one of his tiny cigarettes. His eyes were dreamy.

'That, to me, is the interest of this case,' he said. 'We are cut off from all the normal routes of procedure. Are these people whose evidence we have taken speaking the truth or lying? We have no means of finding out – except such means as we can devise ourselves. It is an exercise, this, of the brain.'

'That is all very fine,' said M. Bouc. 'But what have you to go upon?'

'I told you just now. We have the evidence of the passengers and the evidence of our own eyes.'

'Pretty evidence – that of the passengers! It told us just nothing at all.'

Poirot shook his head.

'I do not agree, my friend. The evidence of the passengers gave us several points of interest.'

131

'Indeed,' said M. Bouc sceptically. 'I did not observe it.'

'That is because you did not listen.'

'Well, tell me – what did I miss?'

'I will just take one instance – the first evidence we heard – that of the young MacQueen. He uttered, to my mind, one very significant phrase.'

'About the letters?'

'No, not about the letters. As far as I can remember, his words were: *"We travelled about. Mr Ratchett wanted to see the world. He was hampered by knowing no languages. I acted more as a courier than a secretary."*'

He looked from the doctor's face to that of M. Bouc.

'What? You still do not see? That is inexcusable – for you had a second chance again just now when he said, *"You're apt to be done down if you speak nothing but good American."*'

'You mean—?' M. Bouc still looked puzzled.

'Ah, it is that you want it given to you in words of one syllable. Well, here it is! *Mr Ratchett spoke no French.* Yet, when the conductor came in answer to his bell last night, it was a voice speaking in *French* that told him that it was a mistake and that he was not wanted. It was, moreover, a perfectly idiomatic phrase that was used, not one that a man knowing only a few words of French would have selected! *"Ce n'est rien. Je me suis trompé."*'

'It is true,' cried Constantine excitedly. 'We should have seen that! I remember your laying stress on the words when you repeated them to us. Now I understand your reluctance to rely upon the evidence of the dented watch. Already, at twenty-three minutes to one, Ratchett was dead—'

'And it was his murderer speaking!' finished M. Bouc impressively.

Poirot raised a deprecating hand.

'Let us not go too fast. And do not let us assume more than we actually know. It is safe, I think, to say that at that time, twenty-three minutes to one, *some other person* was in Ratchett's compartment and that that person was either French, or could speak the French language fluently.'

'You are very cautious, *mon vieux.*'

'One should advance only one step at a time. We have no actual *evidence* that Ratchett was dead at that time.'

'There is the cry that awakened you.'

'Yes, that is true.'

'In one way,' said M. Bouc thoughtfully, 'this discovery does not affect things very much. You heard someone moving about next door. That someone was not Ratchett, but the other man.

132

Doubtless he is washing blood from his hands, clearing up after the crime, burning the incriminating letter. Then he waits till all is still, and when he thinks it is safe and the coast is clear he locks and chains Ratchett's door on the inside, unlocks the communicating door through into Mrs Hubbard's compartment and slips out that way. In fact it is exactly as we thought – *with the difference that Ratchett was killed about half an hour earlier*, and the watch put on to a quarter-past one to create an alibi.'

'Not such a famous alibi, said Poirot. 'The hands of the watch pointed to 1.15 – the exact time when the intruder actually left the scene of the crime.'

'True,' said M. Bouc, a little confused. 'What, then, does the watch convey to you?'

'If the hands were altered – I say *if* – then the time at which they were set *must* have a significance. The natural reaction would be to suspect anyone who had a reliable alibi for the time indicated – in this case 1.15.'

'Yes, yes,' said the doctor. 'That reasoning is good.'

'We must also pay a little attention to the time the intruder *entered* the compartment. When had he an opportunity of doing so? Unless we are to assume the complicity of the real conductor, there was only one time when he could have done so – during the time the train stopped at Vincovci. After the train left Vincovci the conductor was sitting facing the corridor and whereas any one of the passengers would pay little attention to a *wagon lit* attendant, the *one* person who would notice an impostor would be the real conductor. But during the halt at Vincovci the conductor is out on the platform. The coast is clear.'

'And, by our former reasoning, it *must* be one of the passengers,' said M. Bouc. 'We come back to where we were. Which of them?'

Poirot smiled.

'I have made a list,' he said, 'If you like to see it, it will, perhaps, refresh your memory.'

The doctor and M. Bouc pored over the list together. It was written out neatly in a methodical manner in the order in which the passengers had been interviewed.

HECTOR MACQUEEN – American subject. Berth No. 6. Second Class.

Motive	Possibly arising out of association with dead man?
Alibi	From midnight to 2 a.m (Midnight to 1.30 vouched for by Col. Arbuthnot and 1.15 to 2 vouched for by conductor.)

Evidence	
against him	None.
Suspicious	
circumstances	None.

CONDUCTOR – PIERRE MICHEL – French subject.

Motive	None.
Alibi	From midnight to 2 a.m. (Seen by H.P. in corridor at same time as voice spoke from Ratchett's compartment at 12.37. From 1 a.m. to 1.16 vouched for by other two conductors.)
Evidence against him	None.
Suspicious circumstances	The *wagon lit* uniform found is a point in his favour since it seems to have been intended to throw suspicion on him.

EDWARD MASTERMAN – English subject. Berth No. 4. Second Class.

Motive	Possibly arising out of connection with deceased, whose valet he was.
Alibi	From midnight to 2 a.m. (Vouched for by Antonio Foscarelli.)
Evidence against him or suspicious circumstances	None, except that he is the only man the right height or size to have worn the *wagon lit* uniform. On the other hand, it is unlikely that he speaks French well.

MRS HUBBARD – American subject. Berth No. 3. First Class.

Motive	None.
Alibi	From midnight to 2 a.m. – None.
Evidence against her or suspicious circumstances	Story of man in her compartment is substantiated by the evidence of Hardman and that of the woman Schmidt.

GRETA OHLSSON – Swedish subject. Berth No. 10. Second Class.

Motive	None.
Alibi	From midnight to 2 a.m. (Vouched for by Mary Debenham.)
	Note. – Was last to see Ratchett alive.

PRINCESS DRAGOMIROFF – Naturalized French subject. Berth No. 14. First Class.

Motive	Was intimately acquainted with Armstrong family, and godmother to Sonia Armstrong.
Alibi	From midnight to 2 a.m. (Vouched for by conductor and maid.)
Evidence against her or suspicious circumstances	None.

COUNT ANDRENYI – Hungarian subject. Diplomatic passport. Berth No. 13. First Class.

Motive	None.
Alibi	Midnight to 2 a.m. (Vouched for by conductor – this does not cover period from 1 to 1.15.)

COUNTESS ANDRENYI – As above. Berth No. 12.

Motive	None.
Alibi	Midnight to 2 a.m. Took trional and slept. (Vouched for by husband. Trional bottle in her cupboard.)

COLONEL ARBUTHNOT – British subject. Berth No. 15. First Class.

Motive	None.
Alibi	Midnight to 2 a.m. Talked with MacQueen till 1.30. Went to own compartment and did not leave it. (Substantiated by MacQueen and conductor.)
Evidence against him or suspicious circumstances	Pipe-cleaner.

CYRUS HARDMAN – American subject. Berth No. 16. Second Class.

Motive	None known.
Alibi	Midnight to 2 a.m. Did not leave compartment. (Substantiated by MacQueen and conductor.)

*Evidence
against him
or suspicious
circumstances*   None.

ANTONIO FOSCARELLI – American subject. (Italian birth.) Berth No. 5. Second Class.

Motive	None known.
Alibi	Midnight to 2 a.m. (Vouched for by Edward Masterman.)
Evidence against him or suspicious circumstances	None, except that weapon used might be said to suit his temperament. (*Vide* M. Bouc.)

MARY DEBENHAM – British subject. Berth No. 11. Second Class.

Motive	None.
Alibi	Midnight to 2 a.m. (Vouched for by Greta Ohlsson.)
Evidence against her or suspicious circumstances	Conversation overheard by H.P. and her refusal to explain same.

HILDEGARDE SCHMIDT – German subject. Berth No. 8. Second Class.

Motive	None.
Alibi	Midnight to 2 a.m. (Vouched for by conductor and her mistress.) Went to bed. Was aroused by conductor at 12.38 approx. and went to mistress.

NOTE: The evidence of the passengers is supported by the statement of the conductor that no one entered or left Mr Ratchett's compartment between the hours of midnight to 1 o'clock (when he himself went into the next coach) and from 1.15 to 2 o'clock.

'That document, you understand,' said Poirot, 'is a mere *précis* of the evidence we heard, arranged that way for convenience.'

With a grimace M. Bouc handed it back.

'It is not illuminating,' he said.

'Perhaps you may find this more to your taste,' said Poirot with a slight smile as he handed him a second sheet of paper.

— 2 —

TEN QUESTIONS

ON THE paper was written:

Things needing explanation.
1. The handkerchief marked with the initial H. Whose is it?
2. The pipe-cleaner. Was it dropped by Colonel Arbuthnot? Or by someone else?
3. Who wore the scarlet kimono?
4. Who was the man or woman masquerading in *wagon lit* uniform?
5. Why do the hands of the watch point to 1.15?
6. Was the murder committed at that time?
7. Was it earlier?
8. Was it later?
9. Can we be sure that Ratchett was stabbed by more than one person?
10. What other explanation of his wounds can there be?

'Well, let us see what we can do,' said M. Bouc, brightening a little at this challenge to his wits. 'The handkerchief to begin with. Let us by all means be orderly and methodical.'

'Assuredly,' said Poirot, nodding his head in a satisfied fashion.

M. Bouc continued somewhat didactically.

'The initial H is connected with three people – Mrs Hubbard, Miss Debenham, whose second name is Hermione, and the maid Hildegarde Schmidt.'

'Ah! And of those three?'

'It is difficult to say. But I *think* I should vote for Miss Debenham. For all one knows, she may be called by her second name and not her first. Also there is already some suspicion attaching to her. That conversation you overheard, *mon cher*, was certainly a little curious, and so is her refusal to explain it.'

'As for me, I plump for the American,' said Dr Constantine. 'It is a very expensive handkerchief that, and Americans, as all the world knows, do not care what they pay.'

'So you both eliminate the maid?' asked Poirot.

'Yes. As she herself said, it is the handkerchief of a member of the upper classes.'

'And the second question – the pipe-cleaner. Did Colonel Arbuthnot drop it, or somebody else?'

'That is more difficult. The English, they do not stab. You are right there. I incline to the view that someone else dropped the pipe-cleaner – and did so to incriminate the long-legged Englishman.'

'As you said, M. Poirot,' put in the doctor, '*two* clues is too much carelessness. I agree with M. Bouc. The handkerchief was a genuine oversight – hence no one will admit that it is theirs. The pipe-cleaner is a faked clue. In support of that theory, you notice that Colonel Arbuthnot shows no embarrassment and admits freely to smoking a pipe and using that type of cleaner.'

'You reason well,' said Poirot.

'Question No. 3 – who wore the scarlet kimono?' went on M. Bouc. 'As to that, I will confess I have not the slightest idea. Have you any views on the subject, Dr Constantine?'

'None.'

'Then we confess ourselves beaten there. The next question has, at any rate, possibilities. Who was the man or woman masquerading in *wagon lit* uniform? Well, one can say with certainty a number of people whom it could *not* be. Hardman, Colonel Arbuthnot, Foscarelli, Count Andrenyi and Hector MacQueen are all too tall. Mrs Hubbard, Hildegarde Schmidt and Greta Ohlsson are too broad. That leaves the valet, Miss Debenham, Princess Dragomiroff and Countess Andrenyi – and none of them sounds likely! Greta Ohlsson in one case and Antonio Foscarelli in the other both swear that Miss Debenham and the valet never left their compartments. Hildegarde Schmidt swears to the Princess being in hers, and Count Andrenyi has told us that his wife took a sleeping draught. Therefore it seems impossible that it can be anybody – which is absurd!'

'As our old friend Euclid says,' murmured Poirot.

'It must be one of those four,' said Dr Constantine. 'Unless it is someone from outside who has found a hiding-place – and that, we agreed, was impossible.'

M. Bouc had passed on to the next question on the list.

'No. 5 – why do the hands of the broken watch point to 1.15? I can see two explanations of that. Either it was done by the murderer to establish an alibi and afterwards he was prevented from leaving the compartment when he meant to do so by hearing people moving about, or else – wait – I have an idea coming—'

The other two waited respectfully while M. Bouc struggled in mental agony.

'I have it,' he said at last. 'It was *not* the *wagon lit* murderer who tampered with the watch! It was the person we have called the

Second Murderer – the left-handed person – in other words the woman in the scarlet kimono. She arrives later and moves back the hands of the watch in order to make an alibi for herself.'

'Bravo,' said Dr Constantine. 'It is well imagined, that.'

'In fact,' said Poirot, 'she stabbed him in the dark, not realizing that he was dead already, but somehow deduced that he had a watch in his pyjama pocket, took it out, put back the hands blindly and gave it the requisite dent.'

M. Bouc looked at him coldly.

'Have you anything better to suggest yourself?' he asked.

'At the moment – no,' admitted Poirot.

'All the same,' he went on, 'I do not think you have either of you appreciated the most interesting point about that watch.'

'Does question No. 6 deal with it?' asked the doctor. 'To that question – was the murder committed at that time – 1.15 – I answer, *"No."*'

'I agree,' said M. Bouc. ' "Was it earlier?" is the next question. I say yes. You, too, doctor?'

The doctor nodded.

'Yes, but the question "Was it later?" can also be answered in the affirmative. I agree with your theory, M. Bouc, and so, I think, does M. Poirot, although he does not wish to commit himself. The First Murderer came earlier than 1.15, the Second Murderer came *after* 1.15. And as regards the question of left-handedness, ought we not to take steps to ascertain which of the passengers is left-handed?'

'I have not completely neglected that point,' said Poirot. 'You may have noticed that I made each passenger write either a signature or an address. That is not conclusive, because some people do certain actions with the right hand and others with the left. Some write right-handed, but play golf left-handed. Still, it is something. Every person questioned took the pen in their right hand – with the exception of Princess Dragomiroff, who refused to write.'

'Princess Dragomiroff, impossible,' said M. Bouc.

'I doubt if she would have had the strength to inflict that particular left-handed blow,' said Dr Constantine dubiously. 'That particular wound had been inflicted with considerable force.'

'More force than a woman could use?'

'No, I would not say that. But I think more force than an elderly woman could display, and Princess Dragomiroff's physique is particularly frail.'

'It might be a question of influence of mind over body,' said Poirot. 'Princess Dragomiroff has great personality and immense willpower. But let us pass from that for the moment.'

'To questions Nos. 9 and 10. Can we be sure that Ratchett was stabbed by more than one person, and what other explanation of the wounds can there be? In my opinion, medically speaking, there *can be no other* explanation of those wounds. To suggest that one man struck first feebly and then with violence, first with the right hand and then with the left, and after an interval of perhaps half an hour inflicted fresh wounds on a dead body – well, it does not make sense.'

'No,' said Poirot. 'It does not make sense. And you think that two murderers do make sense?'

'As you yourself have said, what other explanation can there be?'

Poirot stared straight ahead of him.

'That is what I ask myself,' he said. 'That is what I never cease to ask myself.'

He leaned back in his seat.

'From now on, it is all here,' he tapped himself on the forehead. 'We have thrashed it all out. The facts are all in front of us – neatly arranged with order and method. The passengers have sat here, one by one, giving their evidence. We know all that can be known – *from outside* . . .'

He gave an affectionate smile at M. Bouc.

'It has been a little joke between us, has it not – this business of sitting back and *thinking* out the truth? Well, I am about to put my theory into practice – here before your eyes. You two must do the same. Let us all three close our eyes and *think* . . .

'One or more of those passengers killed Ratchett. *Which of them?*'

— 3 —

CERTAIN SUGGESTIVE POINTS

It was quite a quarter of an hour before anyone spoke.

M. Bouc and Dr Constantine had started by trying to obey Poirot's instructions. They had endeavoured to see through a maze of conflicting particulars to a clear and outstanding solution.

M. Bouc's thoughts had run something as follows: 'Assuredly I must think. But as far as that goes I have already thought . . . Poirot obviously thinks this English girl is mixed up in the matter. I cannot help feeling that that is most unlikely . . . The English are extremely cold. Probably it is because they have no figures . . . But that is not the point. It seems that the Italian could not have done it – a pity. I suppose the English valet is not lying when he said the other never left the compartment? But why should he? It is not easy to bribe the English, they are so unapproachable. The whole thing is most unfortunate. I wonder when we shall get out of this. There must be *some* rescue work in progress. They are so slow in these countries . . . it is hours before anyone thinks of doing anything. And the police of these countries, they will be most trying to deal with – puffed up with importance, touchy, on their dignity. They will make a grand affair of all this. It is not often that such a chance comes their way. It will be in all the newspapers . . .'

And from there on M. Bouc's thoughts went along a well-worn course which they had already traversed some hundred times.

Dr Constantine's thoughts ran thus: 'He is queer, this little man. A genius? Or a crank? Will he solve this mystery? Impossible. I can see no way out of it. It is all too confusing . . . Everyone is lying, perhaps . . . But even then that does not help one. If they are all lying it is just as confusing as if they were speaking the truth. Odd about those wounds. I cannot understand it . . . It would be easier to understand if he had been shot – after all, the term "gunman" must mean that they shoot with a gun. A curious country, America. I should like to go there. It is so progressive. When I get home I must get hold of Demetrius Zagone – he has been to America, he has all the modern ideas . . . I wonder what Zia is doing at this moment. If my wife ever finds out—'

His thoughts went on to entirely private matters.

Hercule Poirot sat very still.

One might have thought he was asleep.

And then, suddenly, after a quarter of an hour's complete immobility, his eyebrows began to move slowly up his forehead. A little sigh escaped him. He murmured beneath his breath: 'But, after all, why not? And if so – why, if so, that would explain everything.'

His eyes opened. They were green like a cat's. He said softly: '*Eh bien.* I have thought. And you?'

Lost in their reflections, both men started violently.

'I have thought also,' said M. Bouc just a shade guilty. 'But I have arrived at no conclusion. The elucidation of crime is your *métier*, not mine, my friend.'

'I, too, have reflected with great earnestness,' said the doctor unblushingly, recalling his thoughts from certain pornographic details. 'I have thought of many possible theories, but not one that really satisfies me.'

Poirot nodded amiably. His nod seemed to say: 'Quite right. That is the proper thing to say. You have given me the cue I expected.'

He sat very upright, threw out his chest, caressed his moustache and spoke in the manner of a practised speaker addressing a public meeting.

'My friends, I have reviewed the facts in my mind, and have also gone over to myself the evidence of the passengers – with this result. I see, nebulously as yet, a certain explanation that would cover the facts as we know them. It is a very curious explanation, and I cannot be sure as yet that it is the true one. To find out definitely, I shall have to make certain experiments.

'I would like first to mention certain points which appear to me suggestive. Let us start with a remark made to me by M. Bouc in this very place on the occasion of our first lunch together on the train. He commented on the fact that we were surrounded by people of all classes, of all ages, of all nationalities. That is a fact somewhat rare at this time of year. The Athens–Paris and the Bucharest–Paris coaches, for instance, are almost empty. Remember also one passenger who failed to turn up. It is, I think, significant. Then there are some minor points that strike me as suggestive – for instance, the position of Mrs Hubbard's sponge-bag, the name of Mrs Armstrong's mother, the detective methods of Mr Hardman, the suggestion of Mr MacQueen that Ratchett himself destroyed the charred note we found, Princess Dragomiroff's Christian name, and a grease spot on a Hungarian passport.'

The two men stared at him.

'Do they suggest anything to you, those points?' asked Poirot.

'Not a thing,' said M. Bouc frankly.

'And *M. le docteur?*'

'I do not understand in the least of what you are talking.'

M. Bouc, meanwhile, seizing upon the one tangible thing his friend had mentioned, was sorting through the passports. With a grunt he picked up that of Count and Countess Andrenyi and opened it.

'Is this what you mean? This dirty mark?'

'Yes. It is a fairly fresh grease spot. You notice where it occurs?'

'At the beginning of the description of the Count's wife – her Christian name, to be exact. But I confess that I still do not see the point.'

'I am going to approach it from another angle. Let us go back to the handkerchief found at the scene of the crime. As we have stated not long ago – three people are associated with the letter H. Mrs Hubbard, Miss Debenham and the maid, Hildegarde Schmidt. Now let us regard that handkerchief from another point of view. It is, my friends, an extremely expensive handkerchief – an *objet de luxe*, hand-made, embroidered in Paris. Which of the passengers, apart from the initial, was likely to own such a handkerchief? Not Mrs Hubbard, a worthy woman with no pretensions to reckless extravagance in dress. Not Miss Debenham; that class of Englishwoman has a dainty linen handkerchief, but not an expensive wisp of cambric costing perhaps two hundred francs. And certainly not the maid. But there *are* two woman on the train who would be likely to own such a handkerchief. Let us see if we can connect them in any way with the letter H. The two women I refer to are Princess Dragomiroff—'

'Whose Christian name is Natalia,' put in M. Bouc ironically.

'Exactly. And her Christian name, as I said just now, is decidedly suggestive. The other woman is Countess Andrenyi. And at once something strikes us—'

'*You!*'

'*Me*, then. Her Christian name on her passport is disfigured by a blob of grease. Just an accident, anyone would say. But consider that Christian name. Elena. Suppose that, instead of Elena, it were *Helena*. That capital H could be turned into a capital E and then run over the small e next to it quite easily – and then a spot of grease dropped to cover up the alteration.'

'Helena,' cried M. Bouc. 'It is an idea, that.'

'Certainly it is an idea! I look about for any confirmation, however slight, of my idea – and I find it. One of the luggage labels on the Countess's baggage is slightly damp. It is one that happens to run over the first initial on top of the case. That label has been soaked off and put on again in a different place.'

'You begin to convince me,' said M. Bouc. 'But the Countess Andrenyi – surely—'

'Ah, now, *mon vieux*, you must turn yourself round and approach an entirely different angle of the case. How was this murder intended to appear to everybody? Do not forget that the snow has upset all the murderer's original plan. Let us imagine, for a little minute, that there is no snow, that the train proceeded on its normal course. What, then, would have happened?

'The murder, let us say, would still have been discovered in all probability at the Italian frontier early this morning. Much of the same evidence would have been given to the Italian police. The threatening letters would have been produced by Mr MacQueen, Mr Hardman would have told his story, Mrs Hubbard would have been eager to tell how a man passed through her compartment, the button would have been found. I imagine that two things only would have been different. The man would have passed through Mrs Hubbard's compartment just before one o'clock – and the *wagon lit* uniform would have been found cast off in one of the toilets.'

'You mean?'

'I mean that the murder was *planned to look like an outside job*. The assassin would have been presumed to have left the train at Brod, where the train is timed to arrive at 00.58. Somebody would probably have passed a strange *wagon lit* conductor in the corridor. The uniform would be left in a conspicuous place so as to show clearly just how the trick had been played. No suspicion would have been attached to the passengers. That, my friends, was how the affair was intended to appear to the outside world.

'But the accident to the train changes everything. Doubtless we have here the reason why the man remained in the compartment with his victim so long. He was waiting for the train to go on. But at last he realized *that the train was not going on*. Different plans would have to be made. The murderer would now be *known* to be still on the train.'

'Yes, yes,' said M. Bouc impatiently. 'I see all that. But where does the handkerchief come in?'

'I am returning to it by a somewhat circuitous route. To begin with, you must realize that the threatening letters were in the nature of a blind. They might have been lifted bodily out of an indifferently written American crime novel. They are not *real*. They are, in fact, simply intended for the police. What we have to ask ourselves is, "Did they deceive Ratchett?" On the face of it, the answer seems to be, "No." His instructions to Hardman seem to point to a definite "private" enemy of the identity of whom he was well aware. That is if we accept Hardman's story as true. But Ratchett certainly received *one* letter of a very different character – the one containing a reference to the Armstrong baby, a fragment of which we found in his compartment. In case Ratchett had not realized it sooner, this was to make sure that he understood the reason of the threats against his life. That letter, as I have said all along, was *not* intended to be found. The murderer's first care was to destroy it. This, then, was the second hitch in his plans. The first was the snow, the second was our reconstruction of that fragment.

'That note being destroyed so carefully can only mean one thing. *There must be on the train someone so intimately connected with the Armstrong family that the finding of that note would immediately direct suspicion upon that person.*

'Now we come to the other two clues that we found. I pass over the pipe-cleaner. We have already said a good deal about that. Let us pass on to the handkerchief. Taken at its simplest, it is a clue which directly incriminates someone whose initial is H, and it was dropped there unwittingly by that person.'

'Exactly,' said Dr Constantine. 'She finds out that she has dropped the handkerchief and immediately takes steps to conceal her Christian name.'

'How fast you go. You arrive at a conclusion much sooner than I would permit myself to do.'

'Is there any other alternative?'

'Certainly there is. Suppose, for instance, that you have committed a crime and wish to cast suspicion for it on someone else. Well, there is on the train a certain person connected intimately with the Armstrong family – a woman. Suppose, then, that you leave there a handkerchief belonging to that woman . . . She will be questioned, her connection with the Armstrong family will be brought out – *et voilà*. Motive – *and* an incriminating article of evidence.'

'But in such a case,' objected the doctor, 'the person indicated, being innocent, would not take steps to conceal her identity.'

'Ah, really? That is what you think? That is truly the opinion of the police court. But I know human nature, my friend, and I tell you that, suddenly confronted with the possibility of being tried for murder, the most innocent person will lose their head and do the most absurd things. No, no, the grease spot and the changed label do not prove guilt – they only prove that the Countess Andrenyi is anxious for some reason to conceal her identity.'

'What do you think her connection with the Armstrong family can be? She has never been in America, she says.'

'Exactly, and she speaks broken English, and she has a very foreign appearance which she exaggerates. But it should not be difficult to guess who she is. I mentioned just now the name of Mrs

145

Armstrong's mother. It was Linda Arden, and she was a very celebrated actress – among other things a Shakespearean actress. Think of *As You Like It* – the Forest of Arden and Rosalind. It was there she got the inspiration for her acting name. Linda Arden, the name by which she was known all over the world, was not her real name. It may have been Goldenberg – she quite likely had central European blood in her veins – a strain of Jewish, perhaps. Many nationalities drift to America. I suggest to you, gentlemen, that that young sister of Mrs Armstrong's, little more than a child at the time of the tragedy, was Helena Goldenberg the younger daughter of Linda Arden, and that she married Count Andrenyi when he was an attaché in Washington.'

'But Princess Dragomiroff says that she married an Englishman.'

'Whose name she cannot remember! I ask you, my friends – is that really likely? Princess Dragomiroff loved Linda Arden as great ladies do love great artists. She was godmother to one of her daughters. Would she forget so quickly the married name of the other daughter? It is not likely. No, I think we can safely say that Princess Dragomiroff was lying. She knew Helena was on the train, she had seen her. She realized at once, as soon as she heard who Ratchett really was, that Helena would be suspected. And so, when we question her as to the sister she promptly lies – is vague, cannot remember, but "thinks Helena married an Englishman" – a suggestion as far away from the truth as possible.'

One of the restaurant attendants came through the door at the end and approached them. He addressed M. Bouc.

'The dinner, monsieur, shall I serve it? It is ready some little time.'

M. Bouc looked at Poirot. The latter nodded.

'By all means, let dinner be served.'

The attendant vanished through the doors at the other end. His bell could be heard ringing and his voice upraised: *'Premier Service. Le dîner est servi. Premier dîner* – First service.'

— 4 —

THE GREASE SPOT ON A
HUNGARIAN PASSPORT

POIROT shared a table with M. Bouc and the doctor.

The company assembled in the restaurant-car was a very subdued one. They spoke little. Even the loquacious Mrs Hubbard
was unnaturally quiet. She murmured as she sat: 'I don't feel as
though I've got the heart to eat anything,' and then partook of
everything offered her, encouraged by the Swedish lady, who
seemed to regard her as a special charge.

Before the meal was served Poirot had caught the chief
attendant by the sleeve and murmured something to him. Constantine had a pretty good guess what the instructions had been,
as he noticed that the Count and Countess Andrenyi were always
served last and that at the end of the meal there was a delay in
making out their bill. It therefore came about that the count and
countess were the last left in the restaurant-car.

When they rose at length and moved in the direction of the
door, Poirot sprang up and followed them.

'Pardon, madame, you have dropped your handkerchief.'

He was holding out to her the tiny monogrammed square.

She took it, glanced at it, then handed it back to him.

'You are mistaken, monsieur, that is not my handkerchief.'

'Not your handkerchief? Are you sure?'

'Perfectly sure, monsieur.'

'And yet, madame, it has your initial – the initial H.'

The count made a sudden movement. Poirot ignored him. His
eyes were fixed on the countess's face.

Looking steadily at him she replied: 'I do not understand,
monsieur. My initials are E. A.'

'I think not. Your name is Helena – not Elena. Helena Goldenberg, the younger daughter of Linda Arden – Helena Goldenberg,
the sister of Mrs Armstrong.'

There was a dead silence for a minute or two. Both the count
and countess had gone deadly white. Poirot said in a gentler tone:
'It is of no use denying. That is the truth, is it not?'

The count burst out furiously: 'I demand, monsieur, by what
right you—'

She interrupted him, putting up a small hand towards his
mouth.

'No, Rudolph. Let me speak. It is useless to deny what this gentleman says. We had better sit down and talk the matter out.'

Her voice had changed. It still had the southern richness of tone, but it had become suddenly more clear-cut and incisive. It was, for the first time, a definitely American voice.

The count was silenced. He obeyed the gesture of her hand; they both sat down opposite Poirot.

'Your statement, monsieur, is quite true,' said the countess. 'I am Helena Goldenberg, the younger sister of Mrs Armstrong.'

'You did not acquaint me with that fact this morning, *Madame la Comtesse*.'

'No.'

'In fact, all that your husband and you told me was a tissue of lies.'

'Monsieur,' cried the count angrily.

'Do not be angry, Rudolph. M. Poirot puts the fact rather brutally, but what he says is undeniable.'

'I am glad you admit the fact so freely, madame. Will you now tell me your reasons for so doing and also for altering your Christian name on your passport.'

'That was my doing entirely,' put in the count.

Helena said quietly: 'Surely, M. Poirot, you can guess my reason – our reason. This man who was killed is the man who murdered my baby niece, who killed my sister, who broke my brother-in-law's heart. Three of the people I loved best and who made up my home – my world!'

Her voice rang out passionately. She was a true daughter of that mother, the emotional force of whose acting had moved huge audiences to tears.

She went on more quietly.

'Of all the people on the train, I alone had probably the best motive for killing him.'

'And you did not kill him, madame?'

'I swear to you, M. Poirot, and my husband knows and will swear also – that, much as I may have been tempted to do so, I never lifted a hand against that man.'

'I too, gentlemen,' said the count. 'I give you my word of honour that last night Helena never left her compartment. She took a sleeping draught exactly as I said. She is utterly and entirely innocent.'

Poirot looked from one to the other of them.

'On my word of honour,' repeated the count.

Poirot shook his head slightly.

'And yet you took it upon yourself to alter the name in the passport?'

'M. Poirot,' the count spoke earnestly and passionately. 'Consider my position. Do you think I could stand the thought of my wife dragged through a sordid police case. She was innocent, I knew it, but what she said was true – because of her connection with the Armstrong family she would have been immediately suspected. She would have been questioned – arrested, perhaps. Since some evil chance had taken us on the same train as this man Ratchett, there was, I felt sure, but one thing for it. I admit, monsieur, that I lied to you – all, that is, save in one thing. My wife never left her compartment last night.'

He spoke with an earnestness that it was hard to gainsay.

'I do not say that I disbelieve you, monsieur,' said Poirot slowly. 'Your family is, I know, a proud and ancient one. It would be bitter indeed for you to have your wife dragged into an unpleasant police case. With that I can sympathize. But how, then, do you explain the presence of your wife's handkerchief actually in the dead man's compartment?'

'That handkerchief is not mine, monsieur,' said the countess.

'In spite of the initial H?'

'In spite of the initial. I have handkerchiefs not unlike that, but not one that is exactly of that pattern. I know, of course, that I cannot hope to make you believe me, but I assure you that it is so. That handkerchief is not mine.'

'It may have been placed there by someone in order to incriminate you?'

She smiled a little.

'You are enticing me to admit that, after all, it is mine? But indeed, M. Poirot, it isn't.'

She spoke with great earnestness.

'Then why, if the handkerchief was not yours, did you alter the name in the passport?'

The count answered this.

'Because we heard that a handkerchief had been found with the initial H on it. We talked the matter over together before we came to be interviewed. I pointed out to Helena that if it were seen that her Christian name began with an H she would immediately be subjected to much more rigorous questioning. And the thing was so simple – to alter Helena to Elena was easily done.'

'You have, *Monsieur le Comte*, the makings of a very fine criminal,' remarked Poirot dryly. 'A great natural ingenuity, and an apparently remorseless determination to mislead justice.'

149

'Oh, no, no.' The girl leaned forward. 'M. Poirot, he's explained to you how it was.' She broke from French into English. 'I was scared – absolutely dead scared, you understand. It had been so awful – that time – and to have it all raked up again. And to be suspected and perhaps thrown into prison. I was just scared stiff, M. Poirot. Can't you understand at all?'

Her voice was lovely – deep – rich – pleading, the voice of the daughter of Linda Arden the actress.

Poirot looked gravely at her.

'If I am to believe you, madame – and I do not say that I will *not* believe you – then you must help me.'

'Help you?'

'Yes. The reason for the murder lies in the past – in that tragedy which broke up your home and saddened your young life. Take me back into the past, mademoiselle, that I may find there the link that explains the whole thing.'

'What can there be to tell you? They are all dead.' She repeated mournfully. 'All dead – all dead – Robert, Sonia – darling, darling Daisy. She was so sweet – so happy – she had such lovely curls. We were all just crazy about her.'

'There was another victim, madame. An indirect victim, you might say.'

'Poor Susanne? Yes, I had forgotten about her. The police questioned her. They were convinced she had something to do with it. Perhaps she had – but, if so, only innocently. She had, I believe, chatted idly with someone, giving information as to the time of Daisy's outings. The poor thing got terribly wrought up – she thought she was being held responsible.' She shuddered. 'She threw herself out of the window. Oh, it was horrible.'

She buried her face in her hands.

'What nationality was she, madame?'

'She was French.'

'What was her last name?'

'It's absurd, but I can't remember – we all called her Susanne. A pretty laughing girl. She was devoted to Daisy.'

'She was the nursery-maid, was she not?'

'Yes.'

'Who was the nurse?'

'She was a trained hospital nurse. Stengelberg her name was. She, too, was devoted to Daisy – and to my sister.'

'Now, madame, I want you to think carefully before you answer this question. Have you, since you were on this train, seen anyone that you recognized?'

150

She stared at him.

'I? No, no one at all.'

'What about Princess Dragomiroff?'

'Oh, her? I know her, of course. I thought you meant anyone – anyone from – from that time.'

'So I did, madame. Now think carefully. Some years have passed, remember. The person might have altered their appearance.'

Helena pondered deeply. Then she said: 'No – I am sure – there is no one.'

'You yourself – you were a young girl at the time – did you have no one to superintend your studies or to look after you?'

'Oh, yes, I had a dragon – a sort of governess to me and secretary to Sonia combined. She was English or rather Scotch – a big, red-haired woman.'

'What was her name?'

'Miss Freebody.'

'Young or old?'

'She seemed frightfully old to me. I suppose she couldn't have been more than forty. Susanne, of course, used to look after my clothes and maid me.'

'And there were no other inmates of the house?'

'Only servants.'

'And you are certain – quite certain, madame – that you have recognized no one on the train?'

She replied earnestly: 'No one, monsieur. No one at all.'

— 5 —

THE CHRISTIAN NAME OF
PRINCESS DRAGOMIROFF

When the count and countess had departed, Poirot looked across at the other two.

'You see,' he said, 'we make progress.'

'Excellent work,' said M. Bouc cordially. 'For my part, I should never have dreamed of suspecting Count and Countess Andrenyi. I will admit I thought them quite *hors de combat*. I suppose there is no doubt that she committed the crime? It is rather sad. Still, they will not guillotine her. There are extenuating circumstances. A few years' imprisonment – that will be all.'

'In fact you are quite certain of her guilt.'

'My dear friend, surely there is no doubt of it? I thought your reassuring manner was only to smooth things over till we are dug out of the snow and the police take charge.'

'You do not believe the count's positive assertion – on his word of honour – that his wife is innocent?'

'*Mon cher* – naturally – what else *could* he say?' He adores his wife. He wants to save her! He tells his lie very well – quite in the *grand seigneur* manner, but what else than a lie could it be?'

'Well, you know, I had the preposterous idea that it might be the truth.'

'No, no. The handkerchief, remember. The handkerchief clinches the matter.'

'Oh, I am not so sure about the handkerchief. You remember, I always told you that there were two possibilities as to the ownership of the handkerchief.'

'All the same—'

M. Bouc broke off. The door at the end had opened, and Princess Dragomiroff entered the dining-car. She came straight to them and all three men rose to their feet.

She spoke to Poirot, ignoring the others.

'I believe, monsieur,' she said, 'that you have a handkerchief of mine.'

Poirot shot a glance of triumph at the other two.

'Is this it, madame?'

He produced the little square of fine cambric.

'That is it. It has my initial in the corner.'

'But, *Madame la Princesse*, that is the letter H,' said M. Bouc. 'Your Christian name – pardon me – is Natalia.'

She gave him a cold stare.

'That is correct, monsieur. My handkerchiefs are always initialled in the Russian characters. H is N in Russian.'

M. Bouc was somewhat taken aback. There was something about this indomitable old lady which made him feel flustered and uncomfortable.

'You did not tell us that this handkerchief was yours at the inquiry this morning.'

'You did not ask me,' said the princess dryly.

'Pray be seated, madame,' said Poirot.

She sighed.

'I may as well, I suppose.'

She sat down.

'You need not make a long business of this, messieurs. Your next question will be – how did my handkerchief come to be lying by a murdered man's body? My reply to that is that I have no idea.'

'You have really no idea.'

'None whatever.'

'You will excuse me, madame, but how much can we rely upon the truthfulness of your replies?'

Poirot said the words very softly. Princess Dragomiroff answered contemptuously.

'I suppose you mean because I did not tell you that Helena Andrenyi was Mrs Armstrong's sister?'

'In fact you deliberately lied to us in the matter.'

'Certainly. I would do the same again. Her mother was my friend. I believe, messieurs, in loyalty – to one's friends and one's family and one's caste.'

'You do not believe in doing your utmost to further the ends of justice?'

'In this case I consider that justice – strict justice – has been done.'

Poirot leaned forward.

'You see my difficulty, madame. In this matter of the handkerchief, even, am I to believe you? Or are you shielding your friend's daughter?'

'Oh! I see what you mean.' Her face broke into a grim smile. 'Well, messieurs, this statement of mine can be easily proved. I will give you the address of the people in Paris who make my handkerchiefs. You have only to show them the one in question and they will inform you that it was made to my order over a year ago. The handkerchief is mine, messieurs.'

She rose.

'Have you anything further you wish to ask me?'

'Your maid, madame, did she recognize this handkerchief when we showed it to her this morning?'

'She must have done so. She saw it and said nothing? Ah, well, that shows that she too can be loyal.'

With a slight inclination of her head she passed out of the dining-car.

'So that was it,' murmured Poirot softly. 'I noticed just a trifling hesitation when I asked the maid if she knew to whom the handkerchief belonged. She was uncertain whether or not to admit that it was her mistress's. But how does that fit in with that strange central idea of mine? Yes, it might well be.'

'Ah!' said M. Bouc with a characteristic gesture, 'she is a terrible old lady, that!'

'Could she have murdered Ratchett?' asked Poirot of the doctor.

He shook his head.

'Those blows – the ones delivered with great force penetrating the muscle – never, never could anyone with so frail a physique inflict them.'

'But the feebler ones?'

'The feebler ones, yes.'

'I am thinking,' said Poirot, 'of the incident this morning when I said to her that the strength was in her will rather than in her arm. It was in the nature of a trap, that remark. I wanted to see if she would look down at her right or her left arm. She did neither. She looked at them both. But she made a strange reply. She said, "No, I have no strength in these. I do not know whether to be sorry or glad." A curious remark that. It confirms me in my belief about the crime.'

'It did not settle the point about the left-handedness.'

'No. By the way, did you notice that Count Andrenyi keeps his handkerchief in his right-hand breast pocket?'

M. Bouc shook his head. His mind reverted to the astonishing revelations of the last half-hour. He murmured: 'Lies – and again lies – it amazes me, the amount of lies we had told to us this morning.'

'There are more still to discover,' said Poirot cheerfully.

'You think so?'

'I shall be very disappointed if it is not so.'

'Such duplicity is terrible,' said M. Bouc. 'But it seems to please you,' he added reproachfully.

'It has this advantage,' said Poirot. 'If you confront anyone who has lied with the truth, they usually admit it – often out of sheer surprise. It is only necessary to guess *right* to produce your effect.

'That is the only way to conduct this case. I select each passenger in turn, consider their evidence and say to myself, "*If* so and so is lying, on what point are they lying and what is the *reason* for the lie?" And I answer *if* they are lying – *if*, you mark – it could only be for such a reason and on such a point. We have done that once very successfully with Countess Andrenyi. We shall now proceed to try the same method on several other persons.'

'And supposing, my friend, that your guess happens to be wrong?'

'Then one person, at any rate, will be completely freed from suspicion.'

'Ah! A process of elimination.'

'Exactly.'

'And whom do we tackle next?'

'We are going to tackle that *pukka sahib*, Colonel Arbuthnot.'

— 6 —

A SECOND INTERVIEW WITH
COLONEL ARBUTHNOT

COLONEL Arbuthnot was clearly annoyed at being summoned to the dining-car for a second interview. His face wore a most forbidding expression as he sat down and said: 'Well?'

'All my apologies for troubling you a second time,' said Poirot. 'But there is still some information that I think you might be able to give us.'

'Indeed? I hardly think so.'

'To begin with, you see this pipe-cleaner?'

'Yes.'

'Is it one of yours?'

'Don't know. I don't put a private mark on them, you know.'

'Are you aware, Colonel Arbuthnot, that you are the only man amongst the passengers in the Stamboul–Calais carriage who smokes a pipe?'

'In that case it probably is one of mine.'

'Do you know where it was found?'

'Not the least idea.'

'It was found by the body of the murdered man.'

Colonel Arbuthnot raised his eyebrows.

'Can you tell us, Colonel Arbuthnot, how it is likely to have got there?'

'If you mean did I drop it there myself, no, I didn't.'

'Did you go into Mr Ratchett's compartment at any time?'

'I never even spoke to the man.'

'You never spoke to him and you did not murder him?'

The colonel's eyebrows went up again sardonically.

'If I had, I should hardly be likely to acquaint you with the fact. As a matter of fact I *didn't* murder the fellow.'

'Ah, well,' murmured Poirot. 'It is of no consequence.'

'I beg your pardon?'

'I said that it was of no consequence.'

'Oh!' Arbuthnot looked taken aback. He eyed Poirot uneasily.

'Because, you see,' continued the little man, 'the pipe-cleaner, it is of no importance. I can myself think of eleven other excellent explanations of its presence.'

Arbuthnot stared at him.

'What I really wished to see you about was quite another matter,' went on Poirot. 'Miss Debenham may have told you, perhaps, that I overheard some words spoken to you at the station of Konya?'

Arbuthnot did not reply.

'She said, "*Not now. When it's all over. When it's behind us.*" Do you know to what those words referred?'

'I am sorry, M. Poirot, but I must refuse to answer that question.'

'*Pourquoi?*'

The colonel said stiffly: 'I suggest that you should ask Miss Debenham herself for the meaning of those words.'

'I have done so.'

'And she refused to tell you?'

'Yes.'

'Then I should think it would have been perfectly plain – even to you – that my lips are sealed.'

'You will not give away a lady's secret?'

'You can put it that way, if you like.'

'Miss Debenham told me that they referred to a private matter of her own.'

'Then why not accept her word for it?'

'Because, Colonel Arbuthnot, Miss Debenham is what one might call a highly suspicious character.'

'Nonsense,' said the colonel with warmth.

'It is not nonsense.'

'You have nothing whatever against her.'

'Not the fact that Miss Debenham was companion governess in the Armstrong household at the time of the kidnapping of little Daisy Armstrong?'

There was a minute's dead silence.

Poirot nodded his head gently.

'You see,' he said, 'we know more than you think. If Miss Debenham is innocent, why did she conceal that fact? Why did she tell me that she had never been in America?'

The colonel cleared his throat.

'Aren't you possibly making a mistake?'

'I am making no mistake. Why did Miss Debenham lie to me?'

Colonel Arbuthnot shrugged his shoulders.

'You had better ask her. I still think that you are wrong.'

Poirot raised his voice and called. One of the restaurant attendants came from the far end of the car.

'Go and ask the English lady in No. 11 if she will be good enough to come here.'

'*Bien, monsieur.*'

The man departed. The four men sat in silence. Colonel Arbuthnot's face looked as though it were carved out of wood, it was rigid and impassive.

The man returned.

'The lady is just coming, monsieur.'

'Thank you.'

A minute or two later Mary Debenham entered the dining-car.

— 7 —

THE IDENTITY OF MARY DEBENHAM

SHE wore no hat. Her head was thrown back as though in defiance. The sweep of her hair back from her face, the curve of her nostril suggested the figurehead of a ship plunging gallantly into a rough sea. In that moment she was beautiful.

Her eyes went to Arbuthnot for a moment – just a moment. She said to Poirot: 'You wished to see me?'

'I wished to ask you, mademoiselle, why you lied to us this morning?'

'Lied to you? I don't know what you mean.'

'You concealed the fact that at the time of the Armstrong tragedy you were actually living in the house. You told me that you had never been in America.'

He saw her flinch for a moment and then recover herself.

'Yes,' she said. 'That is true.'

'No, mademoiselle, it was false.'

'You misunderstood me. I mean that it is true that I lied to you.'

'Ah, you admit it?'

Her lips curved into a smile.

'Certainly. Since you have found me out.'

'You are at least frank, mademoiselle.'

'There does not seem anything else for me to be.'

'Well, of course, that is true. And now, mademoiselle, may I ask you the reason for these evasions?'

'I should have thought the reason leapt to the eye, M. Poirot?'

'It does not leap to mine, mademoiselle.'

She said in a quiet, even voice with a trace of hardness in it: 'I have my living to get.'

'You mean—'

She raised her eyes and looked him full in the face.

'How much do you know, M. Poirot, of the fight to get and keep decent employment? Do you think that a girl who had been detained in connection with a murder case, whose name and perhaps photographs were reproduced in the English papers – do you think that any nice ordinary middle-class Englishwoman would want to engage that girl as governess to her daughters?'

'I do not see why not – if no blame attached to you.'

'Oh, blame – it is not blame – it is publicity! So far, M. Poirot, I have succeeded in life. I have had well-paid, pleasant posts. I was not going to risk the position I had attained when no good end could have been served.'

'I will venture to suggest, mademoiselle, that I would have been the best judge of that, not you.'

She shrugged her shoulders.

'For instance, you could have helped me in the matter of identification.'

'What do you mean?'

'Is it possible, mademoiselle, that you did not recognize in the Countess Andrenyi Mrs Armstrong's young sister whom you taught in New York?'

'Countess Andrenyi? No.' She shook her head. 'It may seem extraordinary to you, but I did not recognize her. She was not grown up, you see, when I knew her. That was over three years ago. It is true that the countess reminded me of someone – it puzzled me. But she looks so foreign – I never connected her with the little American schoolgirl. It is true that I only glanced at her casually when coming into the restaurant-car. I noticed her

158

clothes more than her face' – she smiled faintly – 'women do! And then – well, I had my own preoccupations.'

'You will not tell me your secret, mademoiselle?'

Poirot's voice was very gentle and persuasive.

She said in a low voice: 'I can't – I can't.'

And suddenly, without warning, she broke down, dropping her face down upon her outstretched arms and crying as though her heart would break.

The colonel sprang up and stood awkwardly beside her.

'I – look here—'

He stopped and, turning round, scowled fiercely at Poirot.

'I'll break every bone in your damned body, you dirty little whipper-snapper,' he said.

'Monsieur,' protested M. Bouc.

Arbuthnot had turned back to the girl.

'Mary – for God's sake—'

She sprang up.

'It's nothing. I'm all right. You don't need me any more, do you, M. Poirot? If you do, you must come and find me. Oh, what an idiot – what an idiot I'm making of myself.'

She hurried out of the car. Arbuthnot, before following her, turned once more on Poirot.

'Miss Debenham's got nothing to do with this business – nothing, do you hear? And if she's worried and interfered with, you'll have me to deal with.'

He strode out.

'I like to see an angry Englishman,' said Poirot. 'They are very amusing. The more emotional they feel the less command they have of language.'

But M. Bouc was not interested in the emotional reactions of Englishmen. He was overcome by admiration of his friend.

'*Mon cher, vous êtes épatant*,' he cried. 'Another miraculous guess. *C'est formidable*.'

'It is incredible how you think of these things,' said Dr Constantine admiringly.

'Oh, I claim no credit this time. It was not a guess. Countess Andrenyi practically told me.'

'*Comment?* Surely not?'

'You remember I asked her about her governess or companion? I had already decided in my mind that *if* Mary Debenham were mixed up in the matter, she must have figured in the household in some such capacity.'

'Yes, but the Countess Andrenyi described a totally different person.'

'Exactly. A tall, middle-aged woman with red hair – in fact, the exact opposite in every respect of Miss Debenham, so much so as to be quite remarkable. But then she had to invent a name quickly, and there it was that the unconscious association of ideas gave her away. She said Miss Freebody, you remember.'

'Yes?'

'*Eh bien,* you may not know it, but there is a shop in London that was called, until recently, Debenham & Freebody. With the name Debenham running in her head, the countess clutches at another name quickly, and the first that comes is Freebody. Naturally I understood immediately.'

'That is yet another lie. Why did she do it?'

'Possibly more loyalty. It makes things a little difficult.'

'*Ma foi,*' said M. Bouc with violence. 'But does everybody on this train tell lies?'

'That,' said Poirot, 'is what we are about to find out.'

— 8 —

FURTHER SURPRISING REVELATIONS

'NOTHING would surprise me now,' said M. Bouc. 'Nothing! Even if everybody in the train proved to have been in the Armstrong household I should not express surprise.'

'That is a very profound remark,' said Poirot. 'Would you like to see what your favourite suspect, the Italian, has to say for himself?'

'You are going to make another of these famous guesses of yours?'

'Precisely.'

'It is really a *most* extraordinary case,' said Constantine.

'No, it is most natural.'

M. Bouc flung up his arms in comic despair.

'If this is what you call natural, *mon ami*—'

Words failed him.

Poirot had by this time requested the dining-car attendant to fetch Antonio Foscarelli.

The big Italian had a wary look in his eye as he came in. He shot nervous glances from side to side like a trapped animal.

'What do you want?' he said. 'I have nothing to tell you – nothing, do you hear! *Per Dio*—' He struck his hand on the table.

'Yes, you have something more to tell us,' said Poirot firmly. 'The truth!'

'The truth?' He shot an uneasy glance at Poirot. All the assurance and geniality had gone out of his manner.

'*Mais oui*. It may be that I know it already. But it will be a point in your favour if it comes from you spontaneously.'

'You talk like the American police. "Come clean," that is what they say – "come clean."'

'Ah! so you have had experience of the New York police?'

'No, no, never. They could not prove a thing against me – but it was not for want of trying.'

Poirot said quietly: 'That was in the Armstrong case, was it not? You were the chauffeur?'

His eyes met those of the Italian. The bluster went out of the big man. He was like a pricked balloon.

'Since you know – why ask me?'

'Why did you lie this morning?'

'Business reasons. Besides, I do not trust the Yugoslav police. They hate the Italians. They would not have given me justice.'

'Perhaps it is exactly justice that they *would* have given you!'

'No, no, I had nothing to do with this business last night. I never left my carriage. The long-faced Englishman, he can tell you so. It was not I who killed this pig – this Ratchett. You cannot prove anything against me.'

Poirot was writing something on a sheet of paper. He looked up and said quietly: 'Very good. You can go.'

Foscarelli lingered uneasily.

'You realize that it was not I – that I could have had nothing to do with it?'

'I said that you could go.'

'It is a conspiracy. You are going to frame me? All for a pig of a man who should have gone to the chair! It was an infamy that he did not. If it had been me – if I had been arrested—'

'But it was not you. You had nothing to do with the kidnapping of the child.'

'What is that you are saying? Why, that little one – she was the delight of the house. Tonio, she called me. And she would sit in the car and pretend to hold the wheel. All the household worshipped her! Even the police came to understand that. Ah, the beautiful little one.'

His voice had softened. The tears came into his eyes. Then he wheeled round abruptly on his heel and strode out of the dining-car.

'Pietro,' called Poirot.

The dining-car attendant came at a run.

'The No. 10 – the Swedish lady.'

'*Bien, monsieur.*'

'Another?' cried M. Bouc. 'Ah, no – it is not possible. I tell you it is not possible.'

'*Mon cher*, we have to know. Even if in the end everybody on the train proves to have a motive for killing Ratchett, we have to know. Once we know, we can settle once for all where the guilt lies.'

'My head is spinning,' groaned M. Bouc.

Greta Ohlsson was ushered in sympathetically by the attendant. She was weeping bitterly.

She collapsed on the seat facing Poirot and wept steadily into a large handkerchief.

'Now do not distress yourself, mademoiselle. Do not distress yourself.' Poirot patted her on the shoulder. 'Just a few little words of truth, that is all. You were the nurse who was in charge of little Daisy Armstrong?'

'It is true – it is true,' wept the wretched woman. 'Ah, she was an angel – a little sweet, trustful angel. She knew nothing but kindness and love – and she was taken away by that wicked man – cruelly treated – and her poor mother – and the other little one who never lived at all. You cannot understand – you cannot know – if you had been there as I was – if you had seen the whole terrible tragedy – I ought to have told you the truth about myself this morning. But I was afraid – afraid. I did so rejoice that that evil man was dead – that he could not any more kill or torture little children. Ah! I cannot speak – I have no words . . .'

She wept with more vehemence than ever.

Poirot continued to pat her gently on the shoulder.

'There – there – I comprehend – I comprehend everything – everything, I tell you. I will ask you no more questions. It is enough that you have admitted what I know to be the truth. I understand, I tell you.'

By now inarticulate with sobs, Greta Ohlsson rose and groped her way blindly towards the door. As she reached it she collided with a man coming in.

It was the valet – Masterman.

He came straight up to Poirot and spoke in his usual, quiet, unemotional voice.

'I hope I'm not intruding, sir. I thought it best to come along at once, sir, and tell you the truth. I was Colonel Armstrong's batman in the war, sir, and afterwards I was his valet in New York. I'm afraid I concealed that fact this morning. It was very wrong of me, sir, and I thought I'd better come and make a clean breast of it. But I hope, sir, that you're not suspecting Tonio in any way. Old Tonio, sir, wouldn't hurt a fly. And I can swear positively that he never left the carriage all last night. So, you see, sir, he couldn't have done it. Tonio may be a foreigner, sir, but he's a very gentle creature – not like those nasty murdering Italians one reads about.'

He stopped.

Poirot looked steadily at him.

'Is that all you have to say?'

'That is all, sir.'

He paused, then, as Poirot did not speak, he made an apologetic little bow, and after a momentary hesitation left the dining-car in the same quiet, unobtrusive fashion as he had come.

'This,' said Dr Constantine, 'is more wildly improbable than any *roman policier* I have ever read.'

'I agree,' said M. Bouc. 'Of the twelve passengers in that coach, nine have been proved to have had a connection with the Armstrong case. What next, I ask you? Or, should I say, who next?'

'I can almost give you the answer to your question,' said Poirot. 'Here comes our American sleuth, Mr Hardman.'

'Is he, too, coming to confess?'

Before Poirot could reply, the American had reached their table. He cocked an alert eye at them and, sitting down, he drawled out: 'Just exactly what's up on this train? It seems bughouse to me.'

Poirot twinkled at him: 'Are you quite sure, Mr Hardman, that you yourself were not the gardener at the Armstrong home?'

'They didn't have a garden,' replied Mr Hardman literally.

'Or the butler?'

'Haven't got the fancy manner for a place like that. No, I never had any connection with the Armstrong house – but I'm beginning to believe I'm about the only one on this train who hadn't! Can you beat it – that's what I say? Can you beat it?'

'It is certainly a little surprising,' said Poirot mildly.

'*C'est rigolo!*' burst from M. Bouc.

'Have you any ideas of your own about the crime, Mr Hardman?' inquired Poirot.

'No, sir. It's got me beat. I don't know how to figure it out. They can't all be in it; but which one is the guilty party is beyond me. How did you get wise to all this, that's what I want to know?'

'I just guessed.'

'Then, believe me, you're a pretty slick guesser. Yes, I'll tell the world you're a slick guesser.'

Mr Hardman leaned back and looked at Poirot admiringly.

'You'll excuse me,' he said, 'but no one would believe it to look at you. I take off my hat to you. I do, indeed.'

'You are too kind, Mr Hardman.'

'Not at all. I've got to hand it to you.'

'All the same,' said Poirot, 'the problem is not yet quite solved. Can we say with authority that we know who killed Mr Ratchett?'

'Count me out,' said Mr Hardman. 'I'm not saying anything at all. I'm just full of natural admiration. What about the other two you've not had a guess at yet? The old American dame and the lady's-maid? I suppose we can take it that they're the only innocent parties on the train?'

'Unless,' said Poirot, smiling, 'we can fit them into our little collection as – shall we say? – housekeeper and cook in the Armstrong household.'

'Well, nothing in the world would surprise me now,' said Mr Hardman with quiet resignation. 'Bughouse – that's what this business is – bughouse!'

'Ah, *mon cher*, that would be indeed stretching coincidence a little too far,' said M. Bouc. 'They cannot all be in it.'

Poirot looked at him.

'You do not understand,' he said. 'You do not understand at all. Tell me,' he said, 'do you know who killed Ratchett?'

'Do you?' countered M. Bouc.

Poirot nodded.

'Oh, yes,' he said. 'I have known for some time. It is so clear that I wonder you have not seen it also.' He looked at Hardman and asked, 'And you?'

The detective shook his head. He stared at Poirot curiously.

'I don't know,' he said. 'I don't know at all. Which of them was it?'

Poirot was silent a minute. Then he said: 'If you will be so good, Mr Hardman, assemble everyone here. There are two possible solutions of this case. I want to lay them both before you all.'

9

POIROT PROPOUNDS TWO SOLUTIONS

THE passengers came crowding into the restaurant-car and took their seats round the tables. They all bore more or less the same expression, one of expectancy mingled with apprehension. The Swedish lady was still weeping and Mrs Hubbard was comforting her.

'Now you must just take a hold on yourself, my dear. Everything's going to be perfectly all right. You mustn't lose your grip on yourself. If one of us is a nasty murderer we know quite well it isn't you. Why, anyone would be crazy even to think of such a thing. You sit here and I'll stay right by you; and don't you worry any.'

Her voice died away as Poirot stood up.

The *wagon lit* conductor was hovering in the doorway.

'You permit that I stay, monsieur?'

'Certainly, Michel.'

Poirot cleared his throat.

'Messieurs et mesdames, I will speak in English, since I think all of you know a little of that language. We are here to investigate the death of Samuel Edward Ratchett – alias Cassetti. There are two possible solutions of the crime. I shall put them both before you, and I shall ask M. Bouc and Dr Constantine here to judge which solution is the right one.

'Now you all know the facts of the case. Mr Ratchett was found stabbed this morning. He was last known to be alive at 12.37 last night, when he spoke to the *wagon lit* conductor through the door. A watch in his pyjama pocket was found to be badly dented and it had stopped at a quarter past one. Dr Constantine, who examined the body when found, puts the time of death as having occurred between midnight and two in the morning. At half an hour after midnight, as you all know, the train ran into a snowdrift. After that time *it was impossible for anyone to leave the train.*

'The evidence of Mr Hardman, who is a member of a New York Detective Agency' (several heads turned to look at Mr Hardman) 'shows that no one could have passed his compartment (No. 16 at the extreme end) without being seen by him. We are therefore forced to the conclusion that the murderer is to be found among the occupants of one particular coach – the Stamboul–Calais coach.

'That, I will say, *was* our theory.'

'*Comment?*' ejaculated M. Bouc, startled.

'But I will put before you an alternative theory. It is very simple. Mr Ratchett had a certain enemy whom he feared. He gave Mr Hardman a description of this enemy and told him that the attempt, if made at all, would most probably be made on the second night out from Stamboul.

'Now I put it to you, ladies and gentlemen, that Mr Ratchett knew a good deal more than he told. The enemy, as Mr Ratchett expected, joined the train at *Belgrade, or possibly at Vincovci*, by the door left open by Colonel Arbuthnot and Mr MacQueen who had just descended to the platform. He was provided with a suit of *wagon lit* uniform, which he wore over his ordinary clothes, and a pass key which enabled him to gain access to Mr Ratchett's compartment in spite of the door being locked. Mr Ratchett was under the influence of a sleeping draught. This man stabbed him with great ferocity and left the compartment through the communicating door leading to Mrs Hubbard's compartment—'

'That's so,' said Mrs Hubbard, nodding her head.

'He thrust the dagger he had used into Mrs Hubbard's sponge-bag in passing. Without knowing it, he lost a button of his uniform. Then he slipped out of the compartment and along the corridor. He hastily thrust the uniform into a suitcase in an empty compartment, and a few minutes later, dressed in ordinary clothes, he left the train just before it started off. Again using the same means of egress – the door near the dining-car.'

Everybody gasped.

'What about that watch?' demanded Mr Hardman.

'There you have the explanation of the whole thing. *Mr Ratchett had omitted to put his watch back an hour as he should have done* at Tzaribrod. His watch still registered Eastern European time, which is one hour *ahead* of Central European time. It was a quarter-past *twelve* when Mr Ratchett was stabbed – not a quarter-past one.'

'But it is absurd, that explanation,' cried M. Bouc. 'What of the voice that spoke from the compartment at twenty-three minutes to one. It was either the voice of Ratchett – or else of his murderer.'

'Not necessarily. It might have been – well – a third person. One who had gone in to speak to Ratchett and found him dead. He rang the bell to summon the conductor, then, as you express it, the wind rose in him – he was afraid of being accused of the crime and he spoke pretending to be Ratchett.'

'*C'est possible*,' admitted M. Bouc grudgingly.

Poirot looked at Mrs Hubbard.

'Yes, madame, you were going to say—?'

'Well, I don't quite know what I was going to say. Do you think I forgot to put my watch back too?'

'No, madame. I think you heard the man pass through – but unconsciously; later you had a nightmare of a man being in your compartment and woke up with a start and rang for the conductor.'

'Well, I suppose that's possible,' admitted Mrs Hubbard.

Princess Dragomiroff was looking at Poirot with a very direct glance.

'How do you explain the evidence of my maid, monsieur?'

'Very simple, madame. Your maid recognized the handkerchief I showed her as yours. She somewhat clumsily tried to shield you. She did encounter the man – but earlier – while the train was at Vincovci station. She pretended to have seen him at a later hour with a confused idea of giving you a watertight alibi.'

The Princess bowed her head.

'You have thought of everything, monsieur. I – I admire you.'

There was a silence.

Then everyone jumped as Dr Constantine suddenly hit the table a blow with his fist.

'But no,' he said. 'No, no, and again no! That is an explanation that will not hold water. It is deficient in a dozen minor points. The crime was not committed so – M. Poirot must know that perfectly well.'

Poirot turned a curious glance on him.

'I see,' he said, 'that I shall have to give you my second solution. But do not abandon this one too abruptly. You may agree with it later.'

He turned back again to face the others.

'There is another possible solution of the crime. This is how I arrived at it.

'When I had heard all the evidence, I leaned back and shut my eyes and began to *think*. Certain points presented themselves to me as worthy of attention. I enumerated these points to my colleagues. Some I have already elucidated – such as a grease-spot on a passport, etc. I will run over the points that remain. The first and most important is a remark made to me by M. Bouc in the restaurant-car at lunch on the first day after leaving Stamboul – to the effect that the company assembled was interesting because it was so varied – representing as it did all classes and nationalities.

'I agreed with him, but when this particular point came into my mind, I tried to imagine whether such an assembly were ever likely to be collected under any other conditions. And the answer I made to myself was – only in America. In America there might be a household composed of just such varied nationalities – an Italian chauffeur, an English governess, a Swedish nurse, a French lady's-maid and so on. That led me to my scheme of "guessing" – that is, casting each person for a certain part in the Armstrong drama much as a producer casts a play. Well, that gave me an extremely interesting and satisfactory result.

'I had also examined in my own mind each separate person's evidence with some curious results. Take first the evidence of Mr MacQueen. My first interview with him was entirely satisfactory. But in my second he made rather a curious remark. I had described to him the finding of a note mentioning the Armstrong case. He said, "But surely—" and then paused and went on, "I mean – that was rather careless of the old man."

'Now I could feel that that was not what he had started out to say. *Supposing what he had meant to say was, "But surely that was burnt!"* In which case, *MacQueen knew of the note and of its destruction* – in other words, he was either the murderer or an accomplice of the murderer. Very good.

'Then the valet. He said his master was in the habit of taking a sleeping draught when travelling by train. That might be true, but *would Ratchett have taken one last night*? The automatic under his pillow gave the lie to that statement. Ratchett intended to be on the alert last night. Whatever narcotic was administered to him must have been done so without his knowledge. By whom? Obviously by MacQueen or the valet.

'Now we come to the evidence of Mr Hardman. I believed all that he told me about his own identity, but when it came to the actual methods he had employed to guard Mr Ratchett, his story was neither more nor less than absurd. The only way effectively to have protected Ratchett was to have passed the night actually in his compartment or in some spot where he could watch the door. The only thing that his evidence *did* show plainly was that no one *in any other part of the train could possibly have murdered Ratchett.* It drew a clear circle round the Stamboul–Calais carriage. That seemed to me a rather curious and inexplicable fact, and I put it aside to think over.

'You probably have all heard by now of the few words I overheard between Miss Debenham and Colonel Arbuthnot. The interesting thing to my mind was the fact that Colonel Arbuthnot called her *Mary* and was clearly on terms of intimacy with her. But the colonel was only supposed to have met her a few days previously – and I know Englishmen of the colonel's type. Even if he had fallen in love with the young lady at first sight, he would have advanced slowly and with decorum – not rushing things. Therefore I concluded that Colonel Arbuthnot and Miss Debenham were in reality well acquainted, and were for some reason pretending to be strangers. Another small point was Miss Debenham's easy familiarity with the term "long distance" for a telephone call. Yet Miss Debenham had told me that she had never been in the States.

'To pass to another witness. Mrs Hubbard had told us that lying in bed she was unable to see whether the communicating door was bolted or not, and so asked Miss Ohlsson to see for her. Now, though her statement would have been perfectly true if she had been occupying compartments Nos. 2, 4, 12, or any *even* number – where the bolt is directly under the handle of the door – in the *uneven* numbers, such as compartment No. 3, the bolt is well *above* the handle and could not therefore be masked by the sponge-bag in the least. I was forced to the conclusion that Mrs Hubbard was inventing an incident that had never occurred.

'And here let me say just a word or two about *times*. To my mind, the really interesting point about the dented watch was the place where it was found – in Ratchett's pyjama pocket, a singularly uncomfortable and unlikely place to keep one's watch, especially as there is a watch "hook" provided just by the head of the bed. I felt sure, therefore, that the watch had been deliberately placed in the pocket and faked. The crime, then, was not committed at a quarter-past one.

'Was it, then, committed earlier? To be exact, at twenty-three minutes to one? My friend M. Bouc advanced as an argument in favour of it the loud cry which awoke me from sleep. But if Ratchett were heavily drugged *he could not have cried out*. If he had been capable of crying out he would have been capable of making some kind of a struggle to defend himself, and there were no signs of any such struggle.

'I remembered that MacQueen had called attention, not once but twice (and the second time in a very blatant manner), to the fact that Ratchett could speak no French. I came to the conclusion that the whole business at twenty-three minutes to one was a comedy played for my benefit! Anyone might see through the watch business – it is a common enough device in detective stories. They assumed that I *should* see through it and that, pluming myself on my own cleverness, I would go on to assume that since

Ratchett spoke no French the voice I heard at twenty-three minutes to one could not be his, and that Ratchett must be already dead. But I am convinced that at twenty-three minutes to one Ratchett was still lying in his drugged sleep.

'But the device has succeeded! I have opened my door and looked out. I have actually heard the French phrase used. If I am so unbelievably dense as not to realize the significance of that phrase, it must be brought to my attention. If necessary MacQueen can come right out in the open. He can say, "Excuse me, M. Poirot, *that can't have been Mr Ratchett speaking*. He can't speak French."

'Now when was the real time of the crime? And who killed him?

'In my opinion, and this is only an opinion, Ratchett was killed at some time very close upon two o'clock, the latest hour the doctor gives us as possible.

'As to who killed him—'

He paused, looking at his audience. He could not complain of any lack of attention. Every eye was fixed upon him. In the stillness you could have heard a pin drop.

He went on slowly: 'I was particularly struck by the extraordinary difficulty of proving a case against any one person on the train and on the rather curious coincidence that in each case the testimony giving an alibi came from what I might describe as an "unlikely" person. Thus Mr MacQueen and Colonel Arbuthnot provided alibis for each other – two persons between whom it seemed most unlikely there should be any prior acquaintanceship. The same thing happened with the English valet and the Italian, with the Swedish lady and the English girl. I said to myself, "This is extraordinary – they cannot *all* be in it!"

'And then, messieurs, I saw light. They *were* all in it. For so many people connected with the Armstrong case to be travelling by the same train by a coincidence was not only unlikely, it was *impossible*. It must be not chance, but *design*. I remembered a remark of Colonel Arbuthnot's about trial by jury. A jury is composed of twelve people – there were twelve passengers – Ratchett was stabbed twelve times. And the thing that had worried me all along – the extraordinary crowd travelling in the Stamboul–Calais coach at a slack time of year – was explained.

'Ratchett had escaped justice in America. There was no question as to his guilt. I visualized a self-appointed jury of twelve people who condemned him to death and were forced by the exigencies of the case to be their own executioners. And immediately, on that assumption, the whole case fell into beautiful shining order.

'I saw it as a perfect mosaic, each person playing his or her allotted part. It was so arranged that if suspicion should fall on any one person, the evidence of one or more of the others would clear the accused person and confuse the issue. Hardman's evidence was necessary in case some outsider should be suspected of the crime and be unable to prove an alibi. The passengers in the Stamboul carriage were in no danger. Every minute detail of their evidence was worked out beforehand. The whole thing was a very cleverly planned jigsaw puzzle, so arranged that every fresh piece of knowledge that came to light made the solution of the whole more difficult. As my friend M. Bouc remarked, the case seemed fantastically impossible! That was exactly the impression intended to be conveyed.

'Did this solution explain everything? Yes, it did. The nature of the wounds – each inflicted by a different person. The artificial threatening letters – artificial since they were unreal, written only to be produced as evidence. (Doubtless there were real letters, warning Ratchett of his fate, which MacQueen destroyed, substituting for them these others.) Then Hardman's story of being called in by Ratchett – a lie, of course, from beginning to end – the description of the mythical "small dark man with a womanish voice", a convenient description, since it had the merit of not incriminating any of the actual *wagon lit* conductors and would apply equally well to a man or a woman.

'The idea of stabbing is at first sight a curious one, but on reflection nothing would fit the circumstances so well. A dagger was a weapon that could be used by everyone – strong or weak – and it made no noise. I fancy, though I may be wrong, that each person in turn entered Ratchett's darkened compartment through that of Mrs Hubbard – and struck! They themselves would never know which blow actually killed him.

'The final letter which Ratchett had probably found on his pillow was carefully burnt. With no clue pointing to the Armstrong case, there would be absolutely no reason for suspecting any of the passengers on the train. It would be put down as an outside job, and the "small dark man with the womanish voice" would actually have been seen by one or more of the passengers leaving the train at Brod.

'I do not know exactly what happened when the conspirators discovered that that part of their plan was impossible owing to the accident to the train. There was, I imagine, a hasty consultation, and then they decided to go through with it. It was true that now one and all of the passengers were bound to come under suspicion, but that possibility had already been foreseen and provided for. The only additional thing to be done was to confuse the issue even further. Two so-called "clues" were dropped in the dead man's compartment – one incriminating Colonel Arbuthnot (who had the strongest alibi and whose connection with the Armstrong family was probably the hardest to prove) and the second clue, the handkerchief, incriminating Princess Dragomiroff, who by virtue of her social position, her particularly frail physique and the alibi given her by her maid and the conductor, was practically in an unassailable position. Further to confuse the issue, a "red herring" was drawn across the trail – the mythical woman in the red kimono. Again I am to bear witness to this woman's existence. There is a heavy bang at my door. I get up and look out – and see the scarlet kimono disappearing in the distance. A judicious selection of people – the conductor, Miss Debenham and MacQueen – will also have seen her. It was, I think, someone with a sense of humour who thoughtfully placed the scarlet kimono on the top of my suitcase whilst I was interviewing people in the dining-car. Where the garment came from in the first place I do not know. I suspect it is the property of Countess Andrenyi, since her luggage contained only a chiffon negligée so elaborate as to be more a tea gown than a dressing-gown.

'When MacQueen first learned that the letter which had been so carefully burnt had in part escaped destruction, and that the word "Armstrong" was exactly the word remaining, he must at once have communicated his news to the others. It was at this minute that the position of Countess Antrenyi became acute and her husband immediately took steps to alter the passport. It was their second piece of bad luck!

'They one and all agreed to deny utterly any connection with the Armstrong family. They knew I had no immediate means of finding out the truth, and they did not believe that I should go into the matter unless my suspicions were aroused against one particular person.

'Now there was one further point to consider. Allowing that my theory of the crime was the correct one, and I believe that it *must* be the correct one, then obviously the *wagon lit* conductor himself must be privy to the plot. But, if so, that gave us thirteen persons, not twelve. Instead of the usual formula, "Of so many people one is guilty," I was faced with the problem that of thirteen persons one and one only was innocent. Which was that person?

'I came to a very odd conclusion. I came to the conclusion that the person who had taken no part in the crime was the person who would be considered the most likely to do so. I refer to Countess Andrenyi. I was impressed by the earnestness of her husband when he swore to me solemnly on his honour that his wife never left her compartment that night. I decided that Count Andrenyi took, so to speak, his wife's place.

'If so, then Pierre Michel was definitely one of the twelve. But how could one explain his complicity? He was a decent man who had been many years in the employ of the Company – not the kind of man who could be bribed to assist in a crime. Then Pierre Michel must be involved in the Armstrong case. But that seemed very improbable. Then I remembered that the dead nursery-maid was French. Supposing that that unfortunate girl had been Pierre Michel's daughter. That would explain everything – it would also explain the place chosen for the staging of the crime. Were there any others whose part in the drama was not clear? Colonel Arbuthnot I put down as a friend of the Armstrongs. They had probably been through the war together. The maid, Hildegarde Schmidt, I could guess her place in the Armstrong household. I am, perhaps, over-greedy, but I sense a good cook instinctively. I laid a trap for her – she fell into it. I said I knew she was a good cook. She answered, "Yes, indeed, all my ladies have said so." But if you are employed as a *lady's-maid* your employers seldom have a chance of learning whether or not you are a good cook.

'Then there was Hardman. He seemed quite definitely not to belong to the the Armstrong household. I could only imagine that he had been in love with the French girl. I spoke to him of the charm of foreign women – and again I obtained the reaction I was looking for. Sudden tears came into his eyes, which he pretended were dazzled by the snow.

'There remains, Mrs Hubbard. Now Mrs Hubbard, let me say, played the most important part in the drama. By occupying the compartment communicating with that of Ratchett she was more open to suspicion that anyone else. In the nature of things she could not have an alibi to fall back upon. To play the part she played – the perfectly natural, slightly ridiculous American fond mother – an artist was needed. But there *was* an artist connected with the Armstrong family – Mrs Armstrong's mother – Linda Arden, the actress . . .'

He stopped.

Then, in a soft rich dreamy voice, quite unlike the one she had used all the journey, Mrs Hubbard said: 'I always fancied myself in comedy parts.'

She went on still dreamily: 'That slip about the sponge-bag was silly. It shows you should always rehearse properly. We tried it on the way out – I was in an even-number compartment then, I suppose. I never thought of the bolts being in different places.'

She shifted her position a little and looked straight at Poirot.

'You know all about it, M. Poirot. You're a very wonderful man. But even you can't quite imagine what it was like – that awful day in New York. I was just crazy with grief – so were the servants – and Colonel Arbuthnot was there, too. He was John Armstrong's best friend.'

'He saved my life in the war,' said Arbuthnot.

'We decided then and there – perhaps we were mad – I don't know – that the sentence of death that Cassetti had escaped had got to be carried out. There were twelve of us – or rather eleven – Susanne's father was over in France, of course. First we thought we'd draw lots as to who should do it, but in the end we decided on this way. It was the chauffeur, Antonio, who suggested it. Mary worked out all the details later with Hector MacQueen. He'd always adored Sonia – my daughter – and it was he who explained to us exactly how Cassetti's money had managed to get him off.

'It took a long time to perfect our plan. We had first to track Ratchett down. Hardman managed that in the end. Then we had to try to get Masterman and Hector into his employment – or at any rate one of them. Well, we managed that. Then we had a consultation with Susanne's father. Colonel Arbuthnot was very keen on having twelve of us. He seemed to think it made it more in order. He didn't like the stabbing idea much, but he agreed that it did solve most of our difficulties. Well, Susanne's father was willing. Susanne was his only child. We knew from Hector that Ratchett would be coming back from the East sooner or later by the Orient Express. With Pierre Michel actually working on that train, the chance was too good to be missed. Besides, it would be a good way of not incriminating any outsiders.

'My daughter's husband had to know, of course, and he insisted on coming on the train with her. Hector wangled it so that Ratchett selected the right day for travelling when Michel would be on duty. We meant to engage every carriage in the Stamboul–Calais coach, but unfortunately there was one carriage we couldn't get. It was reserved long beforehand for a director of the company. Mr Harris, of course, was a myth. But it would have been awkward to have any stranger in Hector's compartment. And then, at the last minute, *you* came . . .'

She stopped.

'Well,' she said. 'You know everything now, M. Poirot. What are you going to do about it? If it must all come out, can't you lay the blame upon me and me only? I would have stabbed that man twelve times willingly. It wasn't only that he was responsible for my daughter's death and her child's, and that of the other child who might have been alive and happy now. It was more than that. There had been other children before Daisy – there might be others in the future. Society had condemned him; we were only carrying out the sentence. But it's unnecessary to bring all these others into it. All these good faithful souls – and poor Michel – and Mary and Colonel Arbuthnot – they love each other . . .'

Her voice was wonderful echoing through the crowded space – that deep, emotional, heart-stirring voice that had thrilled many a New York audience.

Poirot looked at his friend.

'You are a director of the company, M. Bouc,' he said. 'What do you say?'

M. Bouc cleared his throat.

'In my opinion, M. Poirot,' he said, 'the first theory you put forward was the correct one – decidedly so. I suggest that that is the solution we offer to the Yugoslavian police when they arrive. You agree, doctor?'

'Certainly I agree,' said Dr Constantine. 'As regards the medical evidence, I think – er – that I made one or two fantastic suggestions.'

'Then,' said Poirot, 'having placed my solution before you, I have the honour to retire from the case . . .'

CARDS ON THE TABLE

I

MR SHAITANA

'My dear M. Poirot!'

It was a soft purring voice – a voice used deliberately as an instrument – nothing impulsive or unpremeditated about it.

Hercule Poirot swung round.

He bowed.

He shook hands ceremoniously.

There was something in his eye that was unusual. One would have said that this chance encounter awakened in him an emotion that he seldom had occasion to feel.

'My dear Mr Shaitana,' he said.

They both paused. They were like duellists *en garde*.

Around them a well-dressed languid London crowd eddied mildly. Voices drawled or murmured.

'Darling – exquisite!'

'Simply divine, aren't they, my dear?'

It was the exhibition of snuff-boxes at Wessex House. Admission one guinea, in aid of the London hospitals.

'My dear man,' said Mr Shaitana, 'how nice to see you! Not hanging or guillotining much just at present? Slack season in the criminal world? Or is there to be a robbery here this afternoon – that would be too delicious.'

'Alas, Monsieur,' said Poirot. 'I am here in a purely private capacity.'

Mr Shaitana was diverted for a moment by a lovely young thing with tight poodle curls up one side of her head and three cornucopias in black straw on the other.

He said: 'My *dear – why* didn't you come to my party? It really was a marvellous party! Quite a lot of people actually *spoke* to me! One woman even said "How do you do," and "Goodbye" and "Thank you so much" – but of course she came from a Garden City, poor dear!'

While the lovely young thing made a suitable reply, Poirot allowed himself a good study of the hirsute adornment on Mr Shaitana's upper lip.

A fine moustache – a *very* fine moustache – the only moustache in London, perhaps, that could compete with that of M. Hercule Poirot.

'But it is *not* so luxuriant,' he murmured to himself. 'No, decidedly it is inferior in every respect. *Tout de même*, it catches the eye.'

The whole of Mr Shaitana's person caught the eye – it was designed to do so. He deliberately attempted a Mephistophelian effect. He was tall and thin, his face was long and melancholy, his eyebrows were heavily accented and jet black, he wore a moustache with stiff waxed ends and a tiny black imperial. His clothes were works of art – of exquisite cut – but with a suggestion of the bizarre.

Every healthy Englishman who saw him longed earnestly and fervently to kick him! They said, with a singular lack of originality, 'There's that damned Dago, Shaitana!'

Their wives, daughters, sisters, aunts, mothers, and even grandmothers said, varying the idiom according to their generation, words to this effect: 'I know, my dear. Of course, he is *too* terrible. But *so* rich! And such marvellous parties! And he's always got something amusing and spiteful to tell you about people.'

Whether Mr Shaitana was an Argentine, or a Portuguese, or a Greek, or some other nationality rightly despised by the insular Briton, nobody knew.

But three facts were quite certain: he existed richly and beautifully in a super flat in Park Lane; he gave wonderful parties – large parties, small parties, *macabre* parties, respectable parties and definitely 'queer' parties; he was a man of whom nearly everybody was a little afraid.

Why this last was so can hardly be stated in definite words. There was a feeling, perhaps, that he knew a little too much about everybody. And there was a feeling, too, that his sense of humour was a curious one.

People nearly always felt that it would be better not to risk offending Mr Shaitana.

It was his humour this afternoon to bait that ridiculous-looking little man, Hercule Poirot.

'So even a policeman needs recreation?' he said. 'You study the art in your old age, M. Poirot.'

Poirot smiled good-humouredly.

'I see,' he said, 'that you yourself have lent three snuff-boxes to the exhibition.'

Mr Shaitana waved a deprecating hand.

'One picks up trifles here and there. You must come to my flat one day. I have some interesting pieces. I do not confine myself to any particular period or class of object.'

'Your tastes are catholic,' said Poirot smiling.

'As you say.'

Suddenly Mr Shaitana's eyes danced, the corners of his lips curled up, his eyebrows assumed a fantastic tilt.

'I could even show you objects in your own line, M. Poirot!'

'You have then a private "black museum"?'

'Bah!' Mr Shaitana snapped disdainful fingers. 'The cup used by the Brighton murderer, the jemmy of a celebrated burglar — absurd childishness! I should never burden myself with rubbish like that. I collect only the best objects of their kind.'

'And what do you consider the best objects, artistically speaking, in crime?' inquired Poirot.

Mr Shaitana leaned forward and laid two fingers on Poirot's shoulder. He hissed his words dramatically.

'The human beings who commit them, M. Poirot.'

Poirot's eyebrows rose a trifle.

'Aha, I have startled you,' said Shaitana. 'My dear, dear man, you and I look on these things as from poles apart! For you crime is a matter of routine: a murder, an investigation, a clue, and ultimately (for you are undoubtedly an able fellow) a conviction. Such banalities would not interest me! I am not interested in poor specimens of any kind. And the caught murderer is necessarily one of the failures. He is second-rate. No, I look on the matter from the artistic point of view. I collect only the best!'

'The best being—?' asked Poirot.

'My dear fellow — *the ones who have got away with it*! The successes! The criminals who lead an agreeable life which no breath of suspicion has ever touched. Admit that it is an amusing hobby.'

'It was another word I was thinking of — not "amusing".'

'An idea!' cried Shaitana, paying no attention to Poirot. 'A little dinner! A dinner to meet my exhibits! Really that is a most amusing thought. I cannot think why it has never occurred to me before. Yes — yes, I see it all — I see it exactly . . . You must give me a little time — not next week — let us say the week after next. You are free? What day shall we say?'

'Any day of the week after next would suit me,' said Poirot with a bow.

'Good — then let us say Friday. Friday the 18th, that will be. I will write it down at once in my little book. Really, the idea pleases me enormously.'

'I am not quite sure if it pleases me,' said Poirot slowly. 'I do not

181

mean that I am insensible to the kindness of your invitation – no – not that—'

Shaitana interrupted him.

'But it shocks your *bourgeois* sensibilities? My dear fellow, you *must* free yourself from the limitations of the policeman mentality.'

Poirot said slowly: 'It is true that I have a thoroughly *bourgeois* attitude to murder.'

'But, my dear, *why*? A stupid, bungled, butchering business – yes, I agree with you. But murder can be an *art*! A murderer can be an artist.'

'Oh, I admit it.'

'Well then?' Mr Shaitana asked.

'But he is still a murderer!'

'Surely, my dear M. Poirot, to do a thing supremely well is a *justification*! You want, very unimaginatively, to take every murderer, handcuff him, shut him up, and eventually break his neck for him in the early hours of the morning. In my opinion a really successful murderer should be granted a pension out of the public funds and asked out to dinner!'

Poirot shrugged his shoulders.

'I am not as insensitive to art in crime as you think. I can admire the perfect murderer – I can also admire a tiger – that splendid tawny-striped beast. But I will admire him from outside his cage. I will not go inside. That is to say, not unless it is my duty to do so. For you see, Mr Shaitana, the tiger might spring . . .'

Mr Shaitana laughed.

'I see. And the murderer?'

'Might murder,' said Poirot gravely.

'My dear fellow – what an alarmist you are! Then you will not come to meet my collection of – tigers?'

'On the contrary, I shall be enchanted.'

'How brave!'

'You do not quite understand me, Mr Shaitana. My words were in the nature of a warning. You asked me just now to admit that your idea of a collection of murderers was amusing. I said I could think of another word other than "amusing". That word was "dangerous". I fancy, Mr Shaitana, that your hobby might be a dangerous one!'

Mr Shaitana laughed, a very Mephistophelian laugh.

He said: 'I may expect you, then, on the 18th?'

Poirot gave a little bow.

'You may expect me on the 18th. *Mille remerciments*.'

'I shall arrange a little party,' mused Shaitana. 'Do not forget. Eight o'clock.'

He moved away. Poirot stood a minute or two looking after him.

He shook his head slowly and thoughtfully.

— 2 —

DINNER AT MR SHAITANA'S

THE door of Mr Shaitana's flat opened noiselessly. A grey-haired butler drew it back to let Poirot enter. He closed it equally noiselessly and deftly relieved the guest of his overcoat and hat.

He murmured in a low expressionless voice: 'What name shall I say?'

'M. Hercule Poirot.'

There was a little hum of talk that eddied out into the hall as the butler opened a door and announced: 'M. Hercule Poirot.'

Sherry glass in hand, Shaitana came forward to meet him. He was, as usual, immaculately dressed. The Mephistophelian suggestion was heightened tonight, the eyebrows seemed accentuated in their mocking twist.

'Let me introduce you – do you know Mrs Oliver?'

The showman in him enjoyed the little start of surprise that Poirot gave.

Mrs Ariadne Oliver was extremely well known as one of the foremost writers of detective and other sensational stories. She wrote chatty (if not particularly grammatical) articles on *The Tendency of the Criminal, Famous Crimes Passionnels, Murder for Love v. Murder for Gain*. She was also a hot-headed feminist, and when any murder of importance was occupying space in the press there was sure to be an interview with Mrs Oliver, and it was mentioned that Mrs Oliver had said, 'Now if a *woman* were the head of Scotland Yard!' She was an earnest believer in woman's intuition.

For the rest she was an agreeable woman of middle-age, handsome in a rather untidy fashion with fine eyes, substantial shoulders and a large quantity of rebellious grey hair with which she was continually experimenting. One day her appearance would be highly intellectual – a brow with the hair scraped back from it and coiled in a large bun at the neck – on another Mrs Oliver would suddenly appear with Madonna loops, or large masses of slightly untidy curls. On this particular evening Mrs Oliver was trying out a fringe.

She greeted Poirot, whom she had met before at a literary dinner, in an agreeable bass voice.

'And Superintendent Battle you doubtless know,' said Mr Shaitana.

A big, square, wooden-faced man moved forward. Not only did an onlooker feel that Superintendent Battle was carved out of wood – he also managed to convey the impression that the wood in question was the timber out of a battleship.

Superintendent Battle was supposed to be Scotland Yard's best representative. He always looked stolid and rather stupid.

'I know M. Poirot,' said Superintendent Battle.

And his wooden face creased into a smile and then returned to its former unexpressiveness.

'Colonel Race,' went on Mr Shaitana.

Poirot had not previously met Colonel Race, but he knew something about him. A dark, handsome, deeply bronzed man of fifty, he was usually to be found in some outpost of empire – especially if there were trouble brewing. "Secret Service" is a melo-dramatic term, but it described pretty accurately to the lay mind the nature and scope of Colonel Race's activities.

Poirot had by now taken in and appreciated the particular essence of his host's humorous intentions.

'Our other guests are late,' said Mr Shaitana. 'My fault, perhaps. I believe I told them 8.15.'

But at that moment the door opened and the butler announced: 'Dr Roberts.'

The man who came in did so with a kind of parody of a brisk bedside manner. He was a cheerful, highly coloured individual of middle-age. Small twinkling eyes, a touch of baldness, a tendency to *embonpoint* and a general air of a well-scrubbed and disinfected medical practitioner. His manner was cheerful and confident. You felt that his diagnosis would be correct and his treatments agreeable and practical – 'a little champagne in convalescence perhaps'. A man of the world!

'Not late, I hope?' said Dr Roberts genially.

He shook hands with his host and was introduced to the others. He seemed particularly gratified at meeting Battle.

'Why, you're one of the big noises at Scotland Yard, aren't you? This *is* interesting! Too bad to make you talk shop but I warn you I shall have a try at it. Always been interested in crime. Bad thing for a doctor, perhaps. Mustn't say so to my nervous patients – ha ha!'

Again the door opened.

'Mrs Lorrimer.'

Mrs Lorrimer was a well-dressed woman of sixty. She had finely cut features, beautifully arranged grey hair, and a clear, incisive voice.

'I hope I'm not late,' she said, advancing to her host.

She turned from him to greet Dr Roberts, with whom she was acquainted.

The butler announced: 'Major Despard.'

Major Despard was a tall, lean, handsome man, his face slightly marred by a scar on the temple. Introductions completed, he gravitated naturally to the side of Colonel Race – and the two men were soon talking sport and comparing their experiences on safari.

For the last time the door opened and the butler announced: 'Miss Meredith.'

A girl in her early twenties entered. She was of medium height and pretty. Brown curls clustered in her neck, her grey eyes were large and wide apart. Her face was powdered but not made up. Her voice was slow and rather shy.

She said: 'Oh dear, am I the last?'

Mr Shaitana descended to her with sherry and an ornate and complimentary reply. His introductions were formal and almost ceremonious.

Miss Meredith was left sipping her sherry by Poirot's side.

'Our friend is very punctilious,' said Poirot with a smile.

The girl agreed.

'I know. People rather dispense with introductions nowadays. They just say "I expect you know everybody" and leave it at that.'

'Whether you do or you don't?'

'Whether you do or don't. Sometimes it makes it awkward – but I think this is more awe-inspiring.'

She hesitated and then said: 'Is that Mrs Oliver, the novelist?'

Mrs Oliver's bass voice rose powerfully at that minute, speaking to Dr Roberts.

'You can't get away from a woman's instinct, Doctor. Women know these things.'

Forgetting that she no longer had a brow she endeavoured to sweep her hair back from it but was foiled by the fringe.

'That is Mrs Oliver,' said Poirot.

'The one who wrote *The Body in the Library*?'

'That identical one.'

Miss Meredith frowned a little.

'And that wooden-looking man – a *superintendent* did Mr Shaitana say?'

'From Scotland Yard.'

'And you?'

'And me?'

'I know all about you, M. Poirot. It was you who really solved the A.B.C. crimes.'

'Mademoiselle, you cover me with confusion.'

Miss Meredith drew her brows together.

'Mr Shaitana,' she began and then stopped. 'Mr Shaitana—'

Poirot said quietly: 'One might say he was "crime-minded". It seems so. Doubtless he wishes to hear us dispute ourselves. He is already egging on Mrs Oliver and Dr Roberts. They are now discussing untraceable poisons.'

Miss Meredith gave a little gasp as she said: 'What a queer man he is!'

'Dr Roberts?'

'No, Mr Shaitana.'

She shivered a little and said: 'There's always something a little frightening about him, I think. You never know what would strike him as amusing. It might – it might be something *cruel*.'

'Such as fox-hunting, eh?'

Miss Meredith threw him a reproachful glance.

'I meant – oh! something *oriental*!'

'He has perhaps the tortuous mind,' admitted Poirot.

'Torturer's?'

'No, no, tortuous, I said.'

'I don't think I like him frightfully,' confided Miss Meredith, her voice dropping.

'You will like his dinner, though,' Poirot assured her. 'He has a marvellous cook.'

She looked at him doubtfully and then laughed.

'Why,' she exclaimed, 'I believe you are quite human.'

'But certainly I am human!'

'You see,' said Miss Meredith, 'all these celebrities are rather intimidating.'

'Mademoiselle, you should not be intimidated – you should be thrilled! You should have all ready your autograph book and your fountain-pen.'

'Well, you see, I'm not really terribly interested in crime. I don't think women are: it's always men who read detective stories.'

Hercule Poirot sighed affectedly.

'Alas!' he murmured. 'What would I not give at this minute to be even the most minor of film stars!'

The butler threw the door open.

'Dinner is served,' he murmured.

Poirot's prognostication was amply justified. The dinner was delicious and its serving perfection. Subdued light, polished wood, the blue gleam of Irish glass. In the dimness, at the head of the table, Mr Shaitana looked more than ever diabolical.

He apologized gracefully for the uneven number of the sexes.

Mrs Lorrimer was on his right hand, Mrs Oliver on his left. Miss Meredith was between Superintendent Battle and Major Despard. Poirot was between Mrs Lorrimer and Dr Roberts.

The latter murmured facetiously to him.

'You're not going to be allowed to monopolise the only pretty girl all the evening. You French fellows, you don't waste your time, do you?'

'I happen to be Belgian,' murmured Poirot.

'Same thing where the ladies are concerned, I expect, my boy,' said the doctor cheerfully.

Then, dropping the facetiousness, and adopting a professional tone, he began to talk to Colonel Race on his other side about the latest developments in the treatment of sleeping sickness.

Mrs Lorrimer turned to Poirot and began to talk of the latest plays. Her judgments were sound and her criticisms apt. They drifted on to books and then to world politics. He found her a well-informed and thoroughly intelligent woman.

On the opposite side of the table Mrs Oliver was asking Major Despard if he knew of any unheard-of out-of-the-way poisons.

'Well, there's *curare*.'

'My *dear* man, *vieux jeu*! That's been done hundreds of times. I mean something *new*!'

Major Despard said dryly: 'Primitive tribes are rather old-fashioned. They stick to the good old stuff their grandfathers and great-grandfathers used before them.'

'Very tiresome of them,' said Mrs Oliver. 'I should have thought they were always experimenting with pounding up herbs and things. Such a chance for explorers, I always think. They could come home and kill off all their rich old uncles with some new drug that no one's ever heard of.'

'You should go to civilisation, not to the wilds, for that,' said Despard. 'In the modern laboratory, for instance. Cultures of innocent-looking germs that will produce bona fide diseases.'

'That wouldn't do for *my* public,' said Mrs Oliver. 'Besides, one is so apt to get the names wrong – staphylococcus and streptococcus and all those things – so difficult for my secretary and anyway rather dull, don't you think so? What do *you* think, Superintendent Battle?'

'In real life people don't bother about being too subtle, Mrs

Oliver,' said the superintendent. 'They usually stick to arsenic because it's nice and handy to get hold of.'

'Nonsense,' said Mrs Oliver. 'That's simply because there are lots of crimes you people at Scotland Yard never find out. Now if you had a woman there—'

'As a matter of fact we have—'

'Yes, those dreadful policewomen in funny hats who bother people in parks. I mean a woman at the head of things. Women *know* about crime.'

'They're usually very successful criminals,' said Superintendent Battle. 'Keep their heads well. It's amazing how they'll brazen things out.'

Mr Shaitana laughed gently.

'Poison is a woman's weapon,' he said. 'There must be many secret women poisoners – never found out.'

'Of course there are,' said Mrs Oliver happily, helping herself lavishly to a *mousse of foie gras*.

'A doctor, too, has opportunities,' went on Mr Shaitana thoughtfully.

'I protest,' cried Dr Roberts. 'When we poison our patients it's entirely by accident.' He laughed heartily.

'But if I were to commit a crime,' went on Mr Shaitana.

He stopped, something in that pause compelled attention.

All faces were turned to him.

'I should make it very simple, I think. There's always accident – a shooting accident, for instance – or the domestic kind of accident.'

Then he shrugged his shoulders and picked up his wine-glass.

'But who am I to pronounce – with so many experts present . . .?'

He drank. The candlelight threw a red shade from the wine on to his face with its waxed moustache, its little imperial, its fantastic eyebrows . . .

There was a momentary silence.

Mrs Oliver said: 'Is it twenty to or twenty past? An angel passing. . . . My feet aren't crossed – it must be a black angel!'

— 3 —

A GAME OF BRIDGE

WHEN the company returned to the drawing-room a bridge table had been set out. Coffee was handed round.

'Who plays bridge?' asked Mr Shaitana. 'Mrs Lorrimer, I know. And Dr Roberts. Do you play, Miss Meredith?'

'Yes. I'm not frightfully good, though.'

'Excellent. And Major Despard? Good. Supposing you four play here.'

'Thank goodness there's to be bridge,' said Mrs Lorrimer in an aside to Poirot. 'I'm one of the worst bridge fiends that ever lived. It's growing on me. I simply will *not* go out to dinner now if there's no bridge afterwards! I just fall asleep. I'm ashamed of myself, but there it is.'

They cut for partners. Mrs Lorrimer was partnered with Anne Meredith against Major Despard and Dr Roberts.

'Women against men,' said Mrs Lorrimer as she took her seat and began shuffling the cards in an expert manner. 'The blue cards, don't you think, partner? I'm a forcing two.'

'Mind you win,' said Mrs Oliver, her feminist feelings rising. 'Show the men they can't have it all their own way.'

'They haven't got a hope, the poor dears,' said Dr Roberts cheerfully as he started shuffling the other pack. 'Your deal, I think, Mrs Lorrimer.'

Major Despard sat down rather slowly. He was looking at Anne Meredith as though he had just made the discovery that she was remarkably pretty.

'Cut, please,' said Mrs Lorrimer impatiently. And with a start of apology he cut the pack she was presenting to him.

Mrs Lorrimer began to deal with a practised hand.

'There is another bridge table in the other room,' said Mr Shaitana.

He crossed to a second door and the other four followed him into a small, comfortably furnished smoking-room where a second bridge table was set ready.

'We must cut out,' said Colonel Race.

Mr Shaitana shook his head.

'I do not play,' he said. 'Bridge is not one of the games that amuse me.'

The others protested that they would much rather not play, but he overruled them firmly and in the end they sat down: Poirot and Mrs Oliver against Battle and Race.

Mr Shaitana watched them for a little while, smiled in a Mephistophelian manner as he observed on what hand Mrs Oliver declared two no trumps, and then went noiselessly through into the other room.

There they were well down to it, their faces serious, the bids coming quickly. 'One heart.' 'Pass.' 'Three clubs.' 'Three spades.' 'Four diamonds.' 'Double.' 'Four hearts.'

Mr Shaitana stood watching a moment, smiling to himself.

Then he crossed the room and sat down in a big chair by the fireplace. A tray of drinks had been brought in and placed on an adjacent table. The firelight gleamed on the crystal stoppers.

Always an artist in lighting, Mr Shaitana had simulated the appearance of a merely firelit room. A small shaded lamp at his elbow gave him light to read by if he so desired. Discreet flood-lighting gave the room a subdued glow. A slightly stronger light shone over the bridge table, from whence the monotonous ejacu-lations continued.

'One no trump' – clear and decisive – Mrs Lorrimer.

'Three hearts' – an aggressive note in the voice – Dr Roberts.

'No bid' – a quiet voice – Anne Meredith's.

A slight pause always before Despard's voice came. Not so much a slow thinker as a man who liked to be sure before he spoke.

'Four hearts.'

'Double.'

His face lit up by the flickering firelight, Mr Shaitana smiled.

He smiled and he went on smiling. His eyelids flickered a little . . .

His party was amusing him.

'Five diamonds. Game and rubber,' said Colonel Race.

'Good for you, partner,' he said to Poirot. 'I didn't think you'd do it. Lucky they didn't lead a spade.'

'Wouldn't have made much difference, I expect,' said Superin-tendent Battle, a man of gentle magnanimity.

He had called spades. His partner, Mrs Oliver, had a spade, but 'something had told her' to lead a club – with disastrous results.

Colonel Race looked at his watch.

'Ten-past-twelve. Time for another?'

'You'll excuse me,' said Superintendent Battle. 'But I'm by way of being an "early-to-bed" man.'

'I, too,' said Hercule Poirot.

'We'd better add up,' said Race.

The result of the evening's five rubbers was an overwhelming victory for the male sex. Mrs Oliver had lost three pounds and seven shillings to the other three. The biggest winner was Colonel Race.

Mrs Oliver, though a bad bridge player, was a sporting loser. She paid up cheerfully.

'Everything went wrong for me tonight,' she said. 'It is like that sometimes. I held the most beautiful card yesterday. A hundred and fifty honours three times running.'

She rose and gathered up her embroidered evening bag, just refraining in time from stroking her hair off her brow.

'I suppose our host is next door,' she said.

She went through the communicating door, the others behind her.

Mr Shaitana was in his chair by the fire. The bridge players were absorbed in their game.

'Double five clubs,' Mrs Lorrimer was saying in her cool, incisive voice.

'Five no trumps.'

'Double five no trumps.'

Mrs Oliver came up to the bridge table. This was likely to be an exciting hand.

Superintendent Battle came with her.

Colonel Race went towards Mr Shaitana, Poirot behind him.

'Got to be going, Shaitana,' said Race.

Mr Shaitana did not answer. His head had fallen forward, and he seemed to be asleep. Race gave a momentary whimsical glance at Poirot and went a little nearer. Suddenly he uttered a muffled ejaculation, bent forward. Poirot was beside him in a minute, he, too, looking where Colonel Race was pointing – something that might have been a particularly ornate shirt stud – but was not . . .

Poirot bent, raised one of Mr Shaitana's hands, then let it fall. He met Race's inquiring glance and nodded. The latter raised his voice.

'Superintendent Battle, just a minute.'

The superintendent came over to them. Mrs Oliver continued to watch the play of five no trumps doubled.

Superintendent Battle, despite his appearance of stolidity, was a very quick man. His eyebrows went up and he said in a low voice as he joined them: 'Something wrong?'

With a nod Colonel Race indicated the silent figure in the chair.

As Battle bent over it, Poirot looked thoughtfully at what he could see of Mr Shaitana's face. Rather a silly face it looked now, the mouth drooping open – the devilish expression lacking . . .

Hercule Poirot shook his head.

Superintendent Battle straightened himself. He had examined, without touching, the thing which looked like an extra stud in Mr Shaitana's shirt – and it was not an extra stud. He had raised the limp hand and let it fall.

Now he stood up, unemotional, capable, soldierly – prepared to take charge efficiently of the situation.

'Just a minute, please,' he said.

And the raised voice was his official voice, so different that all the heads at the bridge table turned to him, and Anne Meredith's hand remained poised over an ace of spades in dummy.

'I'm sorry to tell you all,' he said, 'that our host, Mr Shaitana, is dead.'

Mrs Lorrimer and Dr Roberts rose to their feet. Despard stared and frowned. Anne Meredith gave a little gasp.

'Are you sure, man?'

Dr Roberts, his professional instincts aroused, came briskly across the floor with a bounding medical 'in-at-the-death' step.

Without seeming to, the bulk of Superintendent Battle impeded his progress.

'Just a minute, Dr Roberts. Can you tell me first who's been in and out of this room this evening?'

Roberts stared at him.

'In and out? I don't understand you. Nobody has.'

The superintendent transferred his gaze.

'Is that right, Mrs Lorrimer?'

'Quite right.'

'Not the butler nor any of the servants?'

'No. The butler brought in that tray as we sat down to bridge. He has not been in since.'

Superintendent Battle looked at Despard.

Despard nodded in agreement.

Anne said rather breathlessly, 'Yes – yes, that's right.'

'What's all this, man?' said Roberts impatiently. 'Just let me examine him; may be just a fainting fit.'

'It isn't a fainting fit, and I'm sorry – but *nobody's going to touch him until the divisional surgeon comes. Mr Shaitana's been murdered, ladies and gentlemen.*'

'Murdered?' A horrified incredulous sigh from Anne.

A stare – a very blank stare – from Despard.

A sharp incisive 'Murdered?' from Mrs Lorrimer.

A 'Good God!' from Dr Roberts.

Superintendent Battle nodded his head slowly. He looked rather like a Chinese porcelain mandarin. His expression was quite blank.

'Stabbed,' he said. 'That's the way of it. Stabbed.'

Then he shot out a question: 'Any of you leave the bridge table during the evening?'

He saw four expressions break up – waver. He saw fear – comprehension – indignation – dismay – horror; but he saw nothing definitely helpful.

'Well?'

There was a pause, and then Major Despard said quietly (he had risen now and was standing like a soldier on parade, his narrow, intelligent face turned to Battle): 'I think every one of us, at one time or another, moved from the bridge table – either to get drinks or to put wood on the fire. I did both. When I went to the fire Shaitana was asleep in the chair.'

'Asleep?'

'I thought so – yes.'

'He may have been,' said Battle. 'Or he may have been dead then. We'll go into that presently. I'll ask you now to go into the room next door.' He turned to the quiet figure at his elbow: 'Colonel Race, perhaps you'll go with them?'

Race gave a quick nod of comprehension.

'Right, Superintendent.'

The four bridge players went slowly through the doorway.

Mrs Oliver sat down in a chair at the far end of the room and began to sob quietly.

Battle took up the telephone receiver and spoke. Then he said: 'The local police will be round immediately. Orders from head-quarters are that I'm to take on the case. Divisional surgeon will be here almost at once. How long should you say he's been dead, M. Poirot? I'd say well over an hour myself.'

'I agree. Alas, that one cannot be more exact – that one cannot say, "This man has been dead one hour, twenty-five minutes and forty seconds." '

Battle nodded absently.

'He was sitting right in front of the fire. That makes a slight difference. Over an hour – not more than two and a half: that's what our doctor will say, I'll be bound. And nobody heard anything and nobody saw anything. Amazing! What a desperate chance to take. He might have cried out.'

'But he did not. The murderer's luck held. As you say, *mon ami*, it was a very desperate business.'

'Any idea, M. Poirot, as to motive? Anything of that kind?'

Poirot said slowly: 'Yes, I have something to say on that score. Tell me, Mr Shaitana – he did not give you any hint of what kind of a party you were coming to tonight?'

Superintendent Battle looked at him curiously.

'No, M. Poirot. He didn't say anything at all. Why?'

A bell whirred in the distance and a knocker was plied.

'That's our people,' said Superintendent Battle. 'I'll go and let 'em in. We'll have your story presently. Must get on with the routine work.'

Poirot nodded.

Battle left the room.

Mrs Oliver continued to sob.

Poirot went over to the bridge table. Without touching anything, he examined the scores. He shook his head once or twice.

'The stupid little man! Oh, the stupid little man,' murmured Hercule Poirot. 'To dress up as the devil and try to frighten people. *Quel enfantillage!*'

The door opened. The divisional surgeon came in, bag in hand. He was followed by the divisional inspector, talking to Battle. A camera man came next. There was a constable in the hall.

The routine of the detection of crime had begun.

— 4 —

FIRST MURDERER?

HERCULE POIROT, Mrs Oliver, Colonel Race and Superintendent Battle sat round the dining-room table.

It was an hour later. The body had been examined, photographed and removed. A fingerprint expert had been and gone.

Superintendent Battle looked at Poirot.

'Before I have those four in, I want to hear what you've got to tell me. According to you there was something behind this party tonight?'

Very deliberately and carefully Poirot retold the conversation he had held with Shaitana at Wessex House.

Superintendent Battle pursed his lips. He very nearly whistled.

'Exhibits – eh? Murderers all alive – oh! And you think he *meant* it? You don't think he was pulling your leg?'

Poirot shook his head.

'Oh, no, he meant it. Shaitana was a man who prided himself on his Mephistophelian attitude to life. He was a man of great vanity. He was also a stupid man – that is why he is dead.'

'I get you,' said Superintendent Battle, following things out in his mind. 'A party of eight and himself. Four "sleuths", so to speak – and four murderers!'

'It's impossible!' cried Mrs Oliver. 'Absolutely impossible. None of those people can be *criminals*.'

Superintendent Battle shook his head thoughtfully.

'I wouldn't be so sure of that, Mrs Oliver. Murderers look and behave very much like everybody else. Nice, quiet, well-behaved, reasonable folk very often.'

'In that case, it's Dr Roberts,' said Mrs Oliver firmly. 'I felt instinctively that there was something wrong with that man as soon as I saw him. My instincts never lie.'

Battle turned to Colonel Race.

'What do you think, sir?'

Race shrugged his shoulders. He took the question as referring to Poirot's statement and not to Mrs Oliver's suspicions.

'It could be,' he said. 'It could be. It shows that Shaitana was right in *one* case at least! After all, he can only have *suspected* that these people were murderers – he can't have been *sure*. He *may* have been right in all four cases, he may have been right in only one case – but he was right in *one* case; his death proved that.'

'One of them got the wind up. Think that's it, M. Poirot?'

Poirot nodded.

'The late Mr Shaitana had a reputation,' he said. 'He had a dangerous sense of humour, and was reputed to be merciless. The victim thought that Shaitana was giving himself an evening's amusement, leading up to a moment when he'd hand the victim over to the police – *you*! He (or she) must have thought that Shaitana had definite evidence.'

'Had he?'

Poirot shrugged his shoulders.

'That we shall never know.'

'Dr Roberts!' repeated Mrs Oliver firmly. 'Such a hearty man. Murderers are often hearty – as a disguise! If I were you, Superintendent Battle, I should arrest him at once.'

'I dare say we would if there was a woman at the head of

Scotland Yard,' said Superintendent Battle, a momentary twinkle showing in his unemotional eye. 'But, you see, mere men being in charge, we've got to be careful. We've got to get there slowly.'

'Oh, men – men,' sighed Mrs Oliver, and began to compose newspaper articles in her head.

'Better have them in now,' said Superintendent Battle. 'It won't do to keep them hanging about too long.'

Colonel Race half rose.

'If you'd like us to go—'

Superintendent Battle hesitated a minute as he caught Mrs Oliver's eloquent eye. He was well aware of Colonel Race's official position, and Poirot had worked with the police on many occasions. For Mrs Oliver to remain was decidedly stretching a point. But Battle was a kindly man. He remembered that Mrs Oliver had lost three pounds and seven shillings at bridge, and that she had been a cheerful loser.

'You can all stay,' he said, 'as far as I'm concerned. But no interruptions, please' (he looked at Mrs Oliver) 'and there mustn't be a hint of what M. Poirot has just told us. That was Shaitana's little secret, and to all intents and purposes it died with him. Understand?'

'Perfectly,' said Mrs Oliver.

Battle strode to the door and called the constable who was on duty in the hall.

'Go to the little smoking-room. You'll find Anderson there with the four guests. Ask Dr Roberts if he'll be so good as to step this way.'

'I should have kept him to the end,' said Mrs Oliver. 'In a book, I mean,' she added apologetically.

'Real life's a bit different,' said Battle.

'I know,' said Mrs Oliver. 'Badly constructed.'

Dr Roberts entered with the springiness of his step slightly subdued.

'I say, Battle,' he said. 'This is the devil of a business! Excuse me, Mrs Oliver, but it is. Professionally speaking, I could hardly have believed it! To stab a man with three other people a few yards away.' He shook his head. 'Whew! I wouldn't like to have done it!' A slight smile twitched up the corners of his mouth. 'What can I say or do to convince you that I *didn't* do it?'

'Well, there's motive, Dr Roberts.'

The doctor nodded his head emphatically.

'That's all clear. I hadn't the shadow of a motive for doing away with poor Shaitana. I didn't even know him very well. He amused me – he was such a fantastic fellow. Touch of the Oriental about him. Naturally, you'll investigate my relations with him closely – I expect that. I'm not a fool. But you won't find anything. I'd no reason for killing Shaitana, and I didn't kill him.'

Superintendent Battle nodded woodenly.

'That's all right, Dr Roberts. I've got to investigate, as you know. You're a sensible man. Now, can you tell me anything about the other three people?'

'I'm afraid I don't know very much. Despard and Miss Meredith I met for the first time tonight. I knew *of* Despard before – read his travel book, and a jolly good yarn it is.'

'Did you know that he and Mr Shaitana were acquainted?'

'No. Shaitana never mentioned him to me. As I say, I'd heard of him, but never met him. Miss Meredith I've never seen before. Mrs Lorrimer I know slightly.'

'What do you know about her?'

Roberts shrugged his shoulders.

'She's a widow. Moderately well off. Intelligent, well-bred woman – first-class bridge player. That's where I've met her, as a matter of fact – playing bridge.'

'And Mr Shaitana never mentioned her, either?'

'No.'

'H'm – that doesn't help us much. Now, Dr Roberts, perhaps you'll be so kind as to tax your memory carefully and tell me how often you yourself left your seat at the bridge table, and all you can remember about the movements of the others.'

Dr Roberts took a few minutes to think.

'It's difficult,' he said frankly. 'I can remember my own movements, more or less. I got up three times – that is, on three occasions when I was dummy I left my seat and made myself useful. Once I went over and put wood on the fire. Once I brought drinks to the two ladies. Once I poured out a whisky and soda for myself.'

'Can you remember the times?'

'I could only say very roughly. We began to play about nine-thirty, I imagine. I should say it was about an hour later that I stoked the fire, quite a short time after that I fetched the drinks (next hand but one, I think), and perhaps half-past eleven when I got myself a whisky and soda – but those times are quite approximate. I couldn't answer for their being correct.'

'The table with the drinks was beyond Mr Shaitana's chair?'

'Yes. That's to say, I passed quite near him three times.'

'And each time, to the best of your belief, he was asleep?'

197

'That's what I thought the first time. The second time I didn't even look at him. Third time I rather fancy the thought just passed through my mind: "How the beggar does sleep." But I didn't really look closely at him.'

'Very good. Now, when did your fellow-players leave their seats?'

Dr Roberts frowned.

'Difficult – very difficult. Despard went and fetched an extra ash-tray, I think. And he went for a drink. That was before me, for I remember he asked me if I'd have one, and I said I wasn't quite ready.'

'And the ladies?'

'Mrs Lorrimer went over to the fire once. Poked it, I think. I rather fancy she spoke to Shaitana, but I don't know. I was playing a rather tricky No Trump at the time.'

'And Miss Meredith?'

'She certainly left the table once. Came round and looked at my hand – I was her partner at the time. Then she looked at the other people's hands, and then she wandered round the room. I don't know what she was doing exactly. I wasn't paying attention.'

Superintendent Battle said thoughtfully: 'As you were sitting at the bridge table, no one's chair was directly facing the fireplace?'

'No, sort of sideways-on, and there was a big cabinet between – Chinese piece, very handsome. I can see, of course, that it would be perfectly *possible* to stab the old boy. After all, when you're playing bridge, you're playing bridge. You're not looking round you and noticing what is going on. The only person who's likely to be doing that is dummy. And in this case—'

'In this case, undoubtedly, dummy was the murderer,' said Superintendent Battle.

'All the same,' said Dr Roberts, 'it wanted nerve, you know. After all, who is to say that somebody won't look up just at the critical moment?'

'Yes,' said Battle. 'It was a big risk. The motive must have been a strong one. I wish we knew what it was,' he added with unblushing mendacity.

'You'll find out, I expect,' said Roberts. 'You'll go through his papers, and all that sort of thing. There will probably be a clue.'

'We'll hope so,' said Superintendent Battle gloomily.

He shot a keen glance at the other.

'I wonder if you'd oblige me, Dr Roberts, by giving me a personal opinion – as man to man?'

'Certainly.'

'Which do you fancy yourself of the three?'

Dr Roberts shrugged his shoulders.

'That's easy. Off-hand, I'd say Despard. The man's got plenty of nerve; he's used to a dangerous life where you've got to act quickly. He wouldn't mind taking a risk. It doesn't seem to me likely the women are in on this. Take a bit of strength, I should imagine.'

'Not so much as you might think. Take a look at this.'

Rather like a conjurer, Battle suddenly produced a long thin instrument of gleaming metal with a small round jewelled head.

Dr Roberts leaned forward, took it, and examined it with rich professional appreciation. He tried the point and whistled.

'What a tool! What a tool! Absolutely made for murder, this little toy. Go in like butter – absolutely like butter. Brought it with him, I suppose.'

Battle shook his head.

'No. It was Mr Shaitana's. It lay on the table near the door with a good many other knick-knacks.'

'So the murderer helped himself. A bit of luck finding a tool like that.'

'Well, that's one way of looking at it,' said Battle slowly.

'Well, of course, it wasn't luck for Shaitana, poor fellow.'

'I didn't mean that, Dr Roberts. I meant that there was another angle of looking at the business. It occurs to me that it was noticing this weapon that put the idea of murder into our criminal's mind.'

'You mean it was a sudden inspiration – that the murder wasn't premeditated? He conceived the idea after he got here? Er – anything to suggest that idea to you?'

'He glanced at him searchingly.

'It's just an idea,' said Superintendent Battle stolidly.

'Well, it might be so, of course,' said Dr Roberts slowly.

Superintendent Battle cleared his throat.

'Well, I won't keep you any longer, Doctor. Thank you for your help. Perhaps you'll leave your address.'

'Certainly. 200 Gloucester Terrace, W.2. Telephone number Bayswater 23896.'

'Thank you. I may have to call upon you shortly.'

'Delighted to see you any time. Hope there won't be too much in the papers. I don't want my nervous patients upset.'

'Superintendent Battle looked round at Poirot.

'Excuse me, M. Poirot. If you'd like to ask any questions, I'm sure the doctor wouldn't mind.'

'Of course not. Of course not. Great admirer of yours, M. Poirot. Little grey cells – order and method. I know all about it. I feel sure you'll think of something most intriguing to ask me.'

Hercule Poirot spread out his hands in his most foreign manner.

'No, no. I just like to get all the details clear in my mind. For instance, how many rubbers did you play?'

'Three,' said Roberts promptly. 'We'd got to one game all, in the fourth rubber, when you came in.'

'And who played with who?'

'First rubber, Despard and I against the ladies. They beat us, God bless 'em. Walkover; we never held a card.

'Second rubber, Miss Meredith and I against Despard and Mrs Lorrimer. Third rubber, Mrs Lorrimer and I against Miss Meredith and Despard. We cut each time, but it worked out like a pivot. Fourth rubber, Miss Meredith and I again.'

'Who won and who lost?'

'Mrs Lorrimer won every rubber. Miss Meredith won the first and lost the next two. I was a bit up and Miss Meredith and Despard must have been down.'

Poirot said, smiling, 'The good superintendent has asked you your opinion of your companions as candidates for murder. I now ask you for your opinion of them as bridge players.'

'Mrs Lorrimer's first class,' Dr Roberts replied promptly. 'I'll bet she makes a good income a year out of bridge. Despard's a good player, too – what I call a *sound* player – long-headed chap. Miss Meredith you might describe as quite a safe player. She doesn't make mistakes, but she isn't brilliant.'

'And you yourself, doctor?'

Roberts' eyes twinkled.

'I overcall my hand a bit, or so they say. But I've always found it pays.'

Poirot smiled.

Dr Roberts rose.

'Anything more?'

Poirot shook his head.

'Well, good night, then. Good night, Mrs Oliver. You ought to get some copy out of this. Better than your untraceable poisons, eh?'

Dr Roberts left the room, his bearing springy once more. Mrs Oliver said bitterly as the door closed behind him: 'Copy! Copy, indeed! People are so unintelligent. I could invent a better murder *any* day than anything *real*. I'm *never* at a loss for a plot. And the people who read my books *like* untraceable poisons!'

SECOND MURDERER?

Mrs Lorrimer came into the dining-room like a gentlewoman. She looked a little pale, but composed.

'I'm sorry to have to bother you,' Superintendent Battle began.

'You must do your duty, of course,' said Mrs Lorrimer quietly. 'It is, I agree, an unpleasant position in which to be placed, but there is no good shirking it. I quite realize that one of the four people in that room must be guilty. Naturally, I can't expect you to take my word that I am not the person.'

She accepted the chair that Colonel Race offered her and sat down opposite the superintendent. Her intelligent grey eyes met his. She waited attentively.

'You knew Mr Shaitana well?' began the superintendent.

'Not very well. I have known him over a period of some years, but never intimately.'

'Where did you meet him?'

'At a hotel in Egypt – the Winter Palace at Luxor, I think.'

'What did you think of him?'

Mrs Lorrimer shrugged her shoulders slightly.

'I thought him – I may as well say so – rather a charlatan.'

'You had – excuse me for asking – no motive for wishing him out of the way?'

Mrs Lorrimer looked slightly amused.

'Really, Superintendent Battle, do you think I should admit it if I had?'

'You might,' said Battle. 'A really intelligent person might know that a thing was bound to come out.'

Mrs Lorrimer inclined her head thoughtfully.

'There is that, of course. No, Superintendent Battle, I had no motive for wishing Mr Shaitana out of the way. It is really a matter of indifference to me whether he is alive or dead. I thought him a *poseur*, and rather theatrical, and sometimes he irritated me. That is – or rather was – my attitude towards him.'

'That is that, then. Now, Mrs Lorrimer, can you tell me anything about your three companions?'

'I'm afraid not. Major Despard and Miss Meredith I met for the first time tonight. Both of them seem charming people. Dr Roberts I know slightly. He's a very popular doctor, I believe.'

'He is not your own doctor?'

'Oh, no.'

'Now, Mrs Lorrimer, can you tell me how often you got up from your seat tonight and will you also describe the movements of the other three?'

Mrs Lorrimer did not take any time to think.

'I thought you would probably ask me that. I have been trying to think it out. I got up once myself when I was dummy. I went over to the fire. Mr Shaitana was alive then. I mentioned to him how nice it was to see a wood fire.'

'And he answered?'

'That he hated radiators.'

'Did anyone overhear your conversation?'

'I don't think so. I lowered my voice, not to interrupt the players.' She added dryly: 'In fact you have only my word for it that Mr Shaitana *was* alive and spoke to me.'

Superintendent Battle made no protest. He went on with his quiet methodical questioning.

'What time was that?'

'I should think we had been playing a little over an hour.'

'What about the others?'

'Dr Roberts got me a drink. He also got himself one – that was later. Major Despard also went to get a drink – at about 11.15, I should say.'

'Only once?'

'No – twice, I think. The men moved about a fair amount – but I didn't notice what they did. Miss Meredith left her seat once only, I think. She went round to look at her partner's hand.'

'But she remained near the bridge table?'

'I couldn't say at all. She may have moved away.'

Battle nodded.

'It's all very vague,' he grumbled.

'I am sorry.'

Once again Battle did his conjuring trick and produced the long delicate stiletto.

'Will you look at this, Mrs Lorrimer?'

Mrs Lorrimer took it without emotion.

'Have you ever seen that before?'

'Never.'

'Yet it was lying on a table in the drawing-room.'

'I didn't notice it.'

'You realize, perhaps, Mrs Lorrimer, that with a weapon like that a woman could do the trick just as easily as a man.'

'I suppose she could,' said Mrs Lorrimer quietly.

She leaned forward and handed the dainty little thing back to him.

'But all the same,' said Superintendent Battle, 'the woman would have to be pretty desperate. It was a long chance to take.'

He waited a minute, but Mrs Lorrimer did not speak.

'Do you know anything of the relations between the other three and Mr Shaitana?'

She shook her head.

'Nothing at all.'

'Would you care to give me an opinion as to which of them you consider the most likely person?'

Mrs Lorrimer drew herself up stiffly.

'I should not care to do anything of the kind. I consider that a most improper question.'

The superintendent looked like an abashed little boy who had been reprimanded by his grandmother.

'Address, please,' he mumbled, drawing his notebook towards him.

'111 Cheyne Lane, Chelsea.'

'Telephone number?'

'Chelsea 45632.'

Mrs Lorrimer rose.

'Anything you want to ask, M. Poirot?' said Battle hurriedly.

Mrs Lorrimer paused, her head slightly inclined.

'Would it be a *proper* question, Madame, to ask you your opinion of your companions, not as potential murderers but as bridge players?'

Mrs Lorrimer answered coldly: 'I have no objection to answering that – if it bears upon the matter at issue in any way – though I fail to see how it can.'

'I will be the judge of that. Your answer, if you please, Madame.'

In the tone of a patient adult humouring an idiot child, Mrs Lorrimer replied: 'Major Despard is a good sound player. Dr Roberts overcalls, but plays his hand brilliantly. Miss Meredith is quite a nice little player, but a bit too cautious. Anything more?'

In his turn doing a conjuring trick, Poirot produced four crumpled bridge scores.

'These scores, Madame, is one of these yours?'

She examined them.

'This is my writing. It is the score of the third rubber.'

'And this score?'

'That must be Major Despard's. He cancels as he goes.'

'And this one?'

'Miss Meredith's. The first rubber.'

'So this unfinished one is Dr Roberts'?'

'Yes.'

'Thank you, Madame, I think that is all.'

Mrs Lorrimer turned to Mrs Oliver.

'Good night, Mrs Oliver. Good night, Colonel Race.'

Then, having shaken hands with all four of them, she went out.

— 6 —

THIRD MURDERER?

'DIDN'T get any extra change out of her,' commented Battle. 'Put me in my place, too. She's the old-fashioned kind, full of consideration for others, but arrogant as the devil! I can't believe she did it, but you never know! She's got plenty of resolution. What's the idea of the bridge scores, M. Poirot?'

Poirot spread them out on the table.

'They are illuminating, do you not think? What do we want in this case? A clue to character. And a clue not to one character, but to four characters. And this is where we are most likely to find it – in these scribbled figures. Here is the first rubber, you see – a tame business, soon over. Small neat figures – careful addition and subtraction – that is Miss Meredith's score. She was playing with Mrs Lorrimer. They had the cards, and they won.

'In this next one it is not so easy to follow the play, since it is kept in the cancellation style. But it tells us perhaps something about Major Despard – a man who likes the whole time to know at a glance where he stands. The figures are small and full character.

'This next score is Mrs Lorrimer's – she and Dr Roberts against the other two – a Homeric combat – figures mounting up above the line each side. Overcalling on the doctor's part, and they go down; but, since they are both first-class players, they never go down very much. If the doctor's overcalling induces rash bidding on the other side there is the chance seized of doubling. See – these figures here are doubled tricks gone down. A characteristic handwriting, graceful, very legible, firm.

'Here is the last score – the unfinished rubber. I collected one score in each person's handwriting, you see. Figures rather flamboyant. Not such high scores as the preceding rubber. That is probably because the doctor was playing with Miss Meredith, and she is a timid player. His calling would make her more so!

'You think, perhaps, that they are foolish, these questions that I ask? But it is not so. I want to get at the characters of these four players, and when it is only about bridge I ask, everyone is ready and willing to speak.'

'I never think your questions foolish, M. Poirot,' said Battle. 'I've seen too much of your work. Everyone's got their own ways of working. I know that. I give my inspectors a free hand always. Everyone's got to find out for themselves what method suits them best. But we'd better not discuss that now. We'll have the girl in.'

Anne Meredith was upset. She stopped in the doorway. Her breath came unevenly.

Superintendent Battle was immediately fatherly. He rose, set a chair for her at a slightly different angle.

'Sit down, Miss Meredith, sit down. Now, don't be alarmed. I know all this seems rather dreadful, but it's not so bad really.'

'I don't think anything could be worse,' said the girl in a low voice. 'It's so awful – so *awful* – to think that *one* of us – that one of *us*—'

'You let me do the thinking,' said Battle kindly. 'Now, then, Miss Meredith, suppose we have your address first of all.'

'Wendon Cottage, Wallingford.'

'No address in town?'

'No, I'm staying at my club for a day or two.'

'And your club is?'

'Ladies' Naval and Military.'

'Good. Now, then, Miss Meredith, how well did you know Mr Shaitana?'

'I didn't know him well at all. I always thought he was a most frightening man.'

'Why?'

'Oh, well, he *was*! That awful smile! And a way he had of bending over you. As though he might bite you.'

'Had you known him long?'

'About nine months. I met him in Switzerland during the winter sports.'

'I should never have thought he went in for winter sports,' said Battle, surprised.

'He only skated. He was a marvellous skater. Lots of figures and tricks.'

'Yes, that sounds more like him. And did you see much of him after that?'

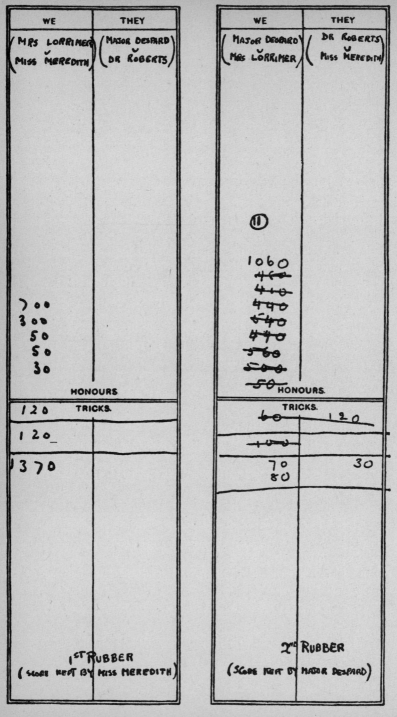

WE	THEY
(MRS LORRIMER)	(MAJOR DESPARD)
(MISS MEREDITH)	(DR ROBERTS)
700	
300	
50	
50	
30	

HONOURS

120	TRICKS.
120	
370	

1ST RUBBER
(SCORE KEPT BY MISS MEREDITH)

WE	THEY
(MAJOR DESPARD)	(DR ROBERTS)
(MRS LORRIMER)	(MISS MEREDITH)
⑪	
1060	
460	
410	
440	
540	
440	
560	
200	
50	

HONOURS.

TRICKS.	
60	120
100	
70	30
80	

2ND RUBBER
(SCORE KEPT BY MAJOR DESPARD)

WE	THEY
(Dr Roberts Mrs Lorrimer)	(Major Despard Miss Meredith)

WE	THEY
500	
1500	
100	200
100	100
350	200
500	100
200	100
200	50
30	50
HONOURS.	50
TRICKS.	30
	120
100	
280	
3810	1000

(28)

3RD RUBBER

(SCORE KEPT BY MRS LORRIMER)

WE	THEY
(Dr Roberts Miss Meredith)	(Major Despard Mrs Lorrimer)

WE	THEY
50	
100	
100	100
50	50
200	100
50	50
60 HONOURS.	50
TRICKS.	
30	70

4TH RUBBER

(UNFINISHED)

(SCORE KEPT BY DR ROBERTS)

'Well – a fair amount. He asked me to parties and things like that. They were rather fun.'

'But you didn't like him himself?'

'No, I thought he was a shivery kind of man.'

Battle said gently: 'But you'd no special reason for being afraid of him?'

Anne Meredith raised wide limpid eyes to his.

'Special reason? Oh, no.'

'That's all right, then. Now about tonight. Did you leave your seat at all?'

'I don't think so. Oh, yes, I may have done once. I went round to look at the others' hands.'

'But you stayed by the bridge table all the time?'

'Yes.'

'Quite sure, Miss Meredith?'

The girl's cheeks flamed suddenly.

'No – no, I think I walked about.'

'Right. You'll excuse me, Miss Meredith, but try and speak the truth. I know you're nervous, and when one's nervous one's apt to – well, to say the thing the way you want it to be. But that doesn't really pay in the end. You walked about. Did you walk over in the direction of Mr Shaitana?'

The girl was silent for a minute, then she said: 'Honestly – *honestly* – I don't remember.'

'Well, we'll leave it that you may have done. Know anything about the other three?'

The girl shook her head.

'I've never seen any of them before.'

'What do you think of them? Any likely murderers amongst them?'

'I can't believe it. I just can't believe it. It couldn't be Major Despard. And I don't believe it could be the doctor – after all, a doctor could kill anyone in much easier ways. A drug – something like that.'

'Then, if it's anyone, you think it's Mrs Lorrimer.'

'Oh, I *don't*. I'm sure she wouldn't. She's so charming – and so kind to play bridge with. She's so good herself, and yet she doesn't make one feel nervous, or point out one's mistakes.'

'Yet you left her name to the last,' said Battle.

'Only because stabbing seems somehow more like a woman.'

Battle did his conjuring trick. Anne Meredith shrank back.

'Oh, horrible. Must I – take it?'

'I'd rather you did.'

He watched her as she took the stiletto gingerly, her face contracted with repulsion.

'With this tiny thing – with this—'

'Go in like butter,' said Battle with gusto. 'A child could do it.'

'You mean – you mean' – wide, terrified eyes fixed themselves on his face – 'that *I* might have done it? But I didn't. Oh, I didn't. Why should I?'

'That's just the question we'd like to know,' said Battle. 'What's the motive? Why did anyone want to kill Shaitana? He was a picturesque person, but he wasn't dangerous, as far as I can make out.'

Was there a slight indrawing of her breath – a sudden lifting of her breast?

'Not a blackmailer, for instance, or anything of that sort?' went on Battle. 'And anyway, Miss Meredith, you don't look the sort of girl who's got a lot of guilty secrets.'

For the first time she smiled, reassured by his geniality.

'No, indeed I haven't. I haven't got any secrets at all.'

'Then don't you worry, Miss Meredith. We shall have to come round and ask you a few more questions, I expect, but it will be all a matter of routine.'

He got up.

'Now off you go. My constable will get you a taxi; and don't you lie awake worrying yourself. Take a couple of aspirins.'

He ushered her out. As he came back Colonel Race said in a low, amused voice: 'Battle, what a really accomplished liar you are! Your fatherly air was unsurpassed.'

'No good dallying about with her, Colonel Race. Either the poor kid is dead scared – in which case it's cruelty, and I'm not a cruel man; I never have been – or she's a highly accomplished little actress, and we shouldn't get any further if we were to keep her here half the night.'

Mrs Oliver gave a sigh and ran her hands freely through her fringe until it stood upright and gave her a wholly drunken appearance.

'Do you know,' she said, 'I rather believe now that she did it! It's lucky it's not in a book. They don't really like the young and beautiful girl to have done it. All the same, I rather think she did. What do *you* think, M. Poirot?'

'Me, I have just made a discovery.'

'In the bridge scores again?'

'Yes. Miss Anne Meredith turns her score over, draws lines and uses the back.'

209

'And what does that mean?'

'It means she has the habit of poverty or else is of a naturally economical turn of mind.'

'She's expensively dressed,' said Mrs Oliver.

'Send in Major Despard,' said Superintendent Battle.

— 7 —

FOURTH MURDERER?

DESPARD entered the room with a quick springing step – a step that reminded Poirot of something or someone.

'I'm sorry to have kept you waiting all this while, Major Despard,' said Battle. 'But I wanted to let the ladies get away as soon as possible.'

'Don't apologize. I understand.'

He sat down and looked inquiringly at the superintendent.

'How well did you know Mr Shaitana?' began the latter.

'I've met him twice,' said Despard crisply.

'Only twice?'

'That's all.'

'On what occasions?'

'About a month ago we were both dining at the same house. Then he asked me to a cocktail party a week later.'

'A cocktail party here?'

'Yes.'

'Where did it take place – this room or the drawing-room?'

'In all the rooms.'

'See this little thing lying about?'

Battle once more produced the stiletto.

Major Despard's lip twisted slightly.

'No,' he said. 'I didn't mark it down on that occasion for future use.'

'There's no need to go ahead of what I say, Major Despard.'

'I beg your pardon. The inference was fairly obvious.'

There was a moment's pause, then Battle resumed his inquiries.

'Had you any motive for disliking Mr Shaitana?'

'Every motive.'

'Eh?' The superintendent sounded startled.

'For disliking him – not for killing him,' said Despard. 'I hadn't the least wish to kill him, but I would thoroughly have enjoyed kicking him. A pity. It's too late now.'

'Why did you want to kick him, Major Despard?'

'Because he was the sort of Dago who needed kicking badly. He used to make the toe of my boot fairly itch.'

'Know anything about him – to his discredit, I mean?'

'He was too well dressed – he wore his hair too long – and he smelt of scent.'

'Yet you accepted his invitation to dinner,' Battle pointed out.

'If I were only to dine in houses where I thoroughly approved of my host I'm afraid I shouldn't dine out very much, Superintendent Battle,' said Despard dryly.

'You like society, but you don't approve of it?' suggested the other.

'I like it for very short periods. To come back from the wilds to lighted rooms and women in lovely clothes, to dancing and good food and laughter – yes, I enjoy that – for a time. And then the insincerity of it all sickens me, and I want to be off again.'

'It must be a dangerous sort of life that you lead, Major Despard, wandering about in these wild places.'

Despard shrugged his shoulders. He smiled slightly.

'Mr Shaitana didn't lead a dangerous life – but he is dead, and I am alive!'

'He may have led a more dangerous life than you think,' said Battle meaningly.

'What do you mean?'

'The late Mr Shaitana was a bit of a nosey parker,' said Battle. The other leaned forward.

'You mean that he meddled with other people's lives – that he discovered – what?'

'I really meant that perhaps he was the sort of man who meddled – er – well, with women.'

Major Despard leant back in his chair. He laughed, an amused but indifferent laugh.

'I don't think women would take a mountebank like that seriously.'

'What's your theory of who killed him, Major Despard?'

'Well, I know I didn't. Little Miss Meredith didn't. I can't imagine Mrs Lorrimer doing so – she reminds me of one of my more God-fearing aunts. That leaves the medical gentleman.'

'Can you describe your own and other people's movements this evening?'

211

'I got up twice – once for an ash-tray, and I also poked the fire – and once for a drink—'

'At what times?'

'I couldn't say. First time might have been about half-past ten, the second time eleven, but that's pure guesswork. Mrs Lorrimer went over to the fire once and said something to Shaitana. I didn't actually hear him answer, but, then, I wasn't paying attention. I couldn't swear he didn't. Miss Meredith wandered about the room a bit, but I don't think she went over near the fireplace. Roberts was always jumping up and down – three or four times at least.'

'I'll ask you M. Poirot's question,' said Battle with a smile. 'What did you think of them as bridge players?'

'Miss Meredith's quite a good player. Roberts overcalls his hand disgracefully. He deserves to go down more than he does. Mrs Lorrimer's damned good.'

Battle turned to Poirot.

'Anything else, M. Poirot?'

Poirot shook his head.

Despard gave his address as the Albany, wished them good night and left the room.

As he closed the door behind him, Poirot made a slight movement.

'What is it?' demanded Battle.

'Nothing,' said Poirot. 'It just occurred to me that he walked like a tiger – yes, just so – lithe, easy, does the tiger move along.'

'H'm!' said Battle. 'Now, then' – his eye glanced round at his three companions – '*which of 'em did it?*'

— 8 —

WHICH OF THEM?

BATTLE looked from one face to another. Only one person answered his question. Mrs Oliver, never averse to giving her views, rushed into speech.

'The girl or the doctor,' she said.

Battle looked questioningly at the other two. But both the men were unwilling to make a pronouncement. Race shook his head. Poirot carefully smoothed his crumpled bridge scores.

'One of 'em did it,' said Battle musingly. 'One of 'em's lying like hell. But which? It's not easy – no, it's not easy.'

He was silent for a minute or two, then he said: 'If we're to go by what they *say*, the medico thinks Despard did it, Despard thinks the medico did it, the girl thinks Mrs Lorrimer did it – and Mrs Lorrimer won't say! Nothing very illuminating there.'

'Perhaps not,' said Poirot.

Battle shot him a quick glance.

'You think there is?'

Poirot waved an airy hand.

'A *nuance* – nothing more! Nothing to go upon.'

Battle continued: 'You two gentlemen won't say what you think—'

'No evidence,' said Race curtly.

'Oh, you *men*!' sighed Mrs Oliver, despising such reticence.

'Let's look at the rough possibilities,' said Battle. He considered a minute. 'I put the doctor first, I think. Specious sort of customer. Would know the right spot to shove the dagger in. But there's not much more than that to it. Then take Despard. There's a man with any amount of nerve. A man accustomed to quick decisions and a man who's quite at home doing dangerous things. Mrs Lorrimer? She's got any amount of nerve, too, and she's the sort of woman who might have a secret in her life. She looks as though she's known trouble. On the other hand, I'd say she's what I call a high-principled woman – sort of woman who might be head-mistress of a girls' school. It isn't easy to think of her sticking a knife into anyone. In fact, I don't think she did. And lastly, there's little Miss Meredith. We don't know anything about her. She seems an ordinary, good-looking, rather shy girl. But one doesn't know, as I say, anything about her.'

'We know that Shaitana believed she had committed murder,' said Poirot.

'The angelic face masking the demon,' mused Mrs Oliver.

'This getting us anywhere, Battle?' asked Colonel Race.

'Unprofitable speculation, you think, sir? Well, there's bound to be speculation in a case like this.'

'Isn't it better to find out something about these people?'

Battle smiled.

'Oh, we shall be hard at work on that. I think you could help us there.'

'Certainly. How?'

'As regards Major Despard. He's been abroad a lot – in South America, in East Africa, in South Africa – you've means of knowing those parts. You could get information about him.'

213

Race nodded.

'It shall be done. I'll get all available data.'

'Oh,' cried Mrs Oliver. 'I've got a plan. There are four of us – four sleuths, as you might say – and four of *them*! How would it be if we each took one. Backed our fancy! Colonel Race takes Major Despard, Superintendent Battle takes Dr Roberts, I'll take Anne Meredith, and M. Poirot takes Mrs Lorrimer. Each of us to follow our own line!'

Superintendent Battle shook his head decisively.

'Couldn't quite do that, Mrs Oliver. This is official, you see. I'm in charge. I've got to investigate *all* lines. Besides, it's all very well to say back your fancy. Two of us might want to back the same horse! Colonel Race hasn't said he suspects Major Despard. And M. Poirot mayn't be putting his money on Mrs Lorrimer.'

Mrs Oliver sighed.

'It was such a good plan,' she sighed regretfully. 'So *neat*.' Then she cheered up a little. 'But you don't mind me doing a little investigating on my own, do you?'

'No,' said Superintendent Battle slowly. 'I can't say I object to that. In fact, it's out of my power to object. Having been at this party tonight, you're naturally free to do anything your own curiosity or interest suggests. But I'd like to point out to you, Mrs Oliver, that you'd better be a little careful.'

'Discretion itself,' said Mrs Oliver. 'I shan't breathe a word of – of anything—' she ended a little lamely.

'I do not think that was quite Superintendent Battle's meaning,' said Hercule Poirot. 'He meant that you will be dealing with a person who has already, to the best of our belief, killed twice. A person, therefore, who will not hesitate to kill a third time – if he considers it necessary.'

Mrs Oliver looked at him thoughtfully. Then she smiled – an agreeable engaging smile, rather like that of an impudent small child.

"YOU HAVE BEEN WARNED," she quoted. 'Thank you, M. Poirot. I'll watch my step. But I'm not going to be out of this.'

Poirot bowed gracefully.

'Permit me to say – you are the sport, Madame.'

'I presume,' said Mrs Oliver, sitting up very straight and speaking in a business-like committee-meeting manner, 'that all information we receive will be pooled – that is, that we will not keep any knowledge to ourselves. Our own deductions and impressions, of course, we are entitled to keep up our sleeves.'

Superintendent Battle sighed.

'This isn't a detective story, Mrs Oliver,' he said.

Race said: 'Naturally, all information must be handed over to the police.'

Having said this in his most 'Orderly Room' voice, he added with a slight twinkle in his eye: 'I'm sure you'll play fair, Mrs Oliver – the stained glove, the fingerprint on the tooth-glass, the fragment of burnt paper – you'll turn them over to Battle here.'

'You may laugh,' said Mrs Oliver. 'But a woman's intuition—'

She nodded her head with decision.

Race rose to his feet.

'I'll have Despard looked up for you. It may take a little time. Anything else I can do?'

'I don't think so, thank you, sir. You've no hints? I'd value anything of that kind.'

'H'm. Well – I'd keep a special lookout for shooting or poison or accidents, but I expect you're on to that already.'

'I'd made a note of that – yes, sir.'

'Good man, Battle. You don't need me to teach you your job. Good night, Mrs Oliver. Good night, M. Poirot.'

And, with a final nod to Battle, Colonel Race left the room.

'Who is he?' asked Mrs Oliver.

'Very fine army record,' said Battle. 'Travelled a lot, too. Not many parts of the world he doesn't know about.'

'Secret Service, I suppose,' said Mrs Oliver. 'You can't tell me so – I know; but he wouldn't have been asked otherwise this evening. The four murderers and the four sleuths – Scotland Yard, Secret Service, Private, Fiction. A clever idea.'

Poirot shook his head.

'You are in error, Madame. It was a very *stupid* idea. The tiger was alarmed – and the tiger sprang.'

'The tiger? Why the tiger?'

'By the tiger I mean the murderer,' said Poirot.

Battle said bluntly: 'What's *your* idea of the right line to take, M. Poirot? That's one question. And I'd also like to know what you think of the psychology of these four people. You're rather hot on that.'

Still smoothing his bridge scores, Poirot said: 'You are right – psychology is very important. We know the *kind* of murder that has been committed, the *way* it was committed. If we have a person who from the psychological point of view could not have committed that particular type of murder, then we can dismiss that person from our calculations.

'We know *something* about these people. We have our own impression of them, we know the line that each has elected to take, and we know something about their minds and their characters from what we have learned about them as card players and from the study of their handwriting and of these scores. But alas! it is not too easy to give a definite pronouncement. This murder required audacity and nerve – a person who was willing to take a risk.

'Well, we have Dr Roberts – a bluffer – an overcaller of his hand – a man with complete confidence in his own powers to pull off a risky thing. His psychology fits very well with the crime. One might say, then, that that automatically wipes out Miss Meredith. She is timid, frightened of overcalling her hand, careful, economical, prudent and lacking in self-confidence. The last type of person to carry out a bold and risky *coup*. But a timid person will murder out of fear. A frightened nervous person can be made desperate, can turn like a rat at bay if driven into a corner. If Miss Meredith had committed a crime in the past, and if she believed that Mr Shaitana knew the circumstances of that crime and was about to deliver her up to justice she would be wild with terror – she would stick at nothing to save herself. It would be the same result, though brought about through a different reaction – not cool nerve and daring, but desperate panic.

'Then take Major Despard – a cool, resourceful man willing to try a long shot if he believed it absolutely necessary. He would weigh the pros and cons and might decide that there was a sporting chance in his favour – and he is the type of man to prefer action to inaction, and a man who would never shrink from taking the dangerous way if he believed there was a reasonable chance of success. Finally, there is Mrs Lorrimer, an elderly woman, but a woman in full possession of her wits and faculties. A cool woman. A woman with a mathematical brain. She has probably the best brain of the four. I confess that if Mrs Lorrimer committed a crime, I should expect it to be a *premeditated* crime. I can see her planning a crime slowly and carefully, making sure that there were no flaws in her scheme. For that reason she seems to me slightly more unlikely than the other three. She is, however, the most dominating personality, and whatever she undertook she would probably carry through without a flaw. She is a thoroughly efficient woman.'

He paused.

'So, you see, that does not help us much. No – there is only one way in this crime. We must go back into the past.'

Battle sighed.

'You've said it,' he murmured.

'In the opinion of Mr Shaitana, each of those four people had committed murder. Had he evidence? Or was it a guess? We cannot tell. It is unlikely, I think, that he could have had actual evidence in all four cases—'

'I agree with you there,' said Battle, nodding his head. 'That would be a bit too much of a coincidence.'

'I suggest that it might come about this way – murder or a certain form of murder is mentioned, and Mr Shaitana surprised a look on someone's face. He was very quick – very sensitive to expression. It amuses him to experiment – to probe gently in the course of apparently aimless conversation – he is alert to notice a wince, a reservation, a desire to turn the conversation. Oh, it is easily done. If you suspect a certain secret, nothing is easier than to confirm your suspicion. Every time a word goes home you notice it – *if you are watching for such a thing.*'

'It's the sort of game would have amused our late friend,' said Battle, nodding.

'We may assume, then, that such was the procedure in one or more cases. He may have come across a piece of actual evidence in another case and followed it up. I doubt whether, in any of the cases, he had sufficient actual knowledge with which, for instance, to have gone to the police.'

'Or it mayn't have been the kind of case,' said Battle. 'Often enough there's a fishy business – we suspect foul play, but we can't ever prove it. Anyway, the course is clear. We've got to go through the records of all these people – and note any deaths that may be significant. I expect you noticed, just as the Colonel did, what Shaitana said at dinner.'

'The black angel,' murmured Mrs Oliver.

'A neat little reference to poison, to accidents, to a doctor's opportunities, to shooting accidents. I shouldn't be surprised if he signed his death-warrant when he said those words.'

'It was a nasty sort of pause,' said Mrs Oliver.

'Yes,' said Poirot. 'Those words went home to one person at least – that person probably thought that Shaitana knew far more than he really did. That listener thought that they were the prelude to the end – that the party was a dramatic entertainment arranged by Shaitana leading up to arrest for murder as its climax! Yes, as you say, he signed his death-warrant when he baited his guests with these words.'

There was a moment's silence.

'This will be a long business,' said Battle with a sigh. 'We can't find out all we want in a moment – and we've got to be careful. We don't want any of the four to suspect what we're doing. All our questioning and so on must seem to have to do with *this* murder. There mustn't be a suspicion that we've got any idea of the motive for the crime. And the devil of it is we've got to check up on four possible murders in the past, not one.'

Poirot demurred.

'Our friend Mr Shaitana was not infallible,' he said. 'He may – it is just possible – have made a mistake.'

'About all four?'

'No – he was more intelligent than that.'

'Call it fifty-fifty?'

'Not even that. For me, I say one in four.'

'One innocent and three guilty? That's bad enough. And the devil of it is, even if we get at the truth it mayn't help us. Even if somebody did push their great-aunt down the stairs in 1912, it won't be much use to us in 1937.'

'Yes, yes, it will be of use to us,' Poirot encouraged him. 'You know that. You know it as well as I do.'

Battle nodded slowly.

'I know what you mean,' he said. 'Same hallmark.'

'Do you mean,' said Mrs Oliver, 'that the former victim will have been stabbed with a dagger too?'

'Not quite as crude as that, Mrs Oliver,' said Battle, turning to her. 'But I don't doubt it will be essentially the same *type* of crime. The *details* may be different, but the essentials underlying them will be the same. It's odd, but a criminal gives himself away every time by that.'

'Man is an unoriginal animal,' said Hercule Poirot.

'Women,' said Mrs Oliver, 'are capable of infinite variation. I should never commit the same type of murder twice running.'

'Don't you ever write the same plot twice running?' asked Battle.

'The Lotus Murder,' murmured Poirot, 'The Clue of the Candle Wax.'

Mrs Oliver turned on him, her eyes beaming appreciation.

'That's clever of you – that's really very clever of you. Because, of course, those two are exactly the same plot – but nobody else has seen it. One is stolen papers at an informal week-end party of the Cabinet, and the other's a murder in Borneo in a rubber planter's bungalow.'

'But the essential point on which the story turns is the same,' said Poirot. 'One of your neatest tricks. The rubber planter arranges his own murder – the Cabinet Minister arranges the robbery of his own papers. At the last minute the third person steps in and turns deception into reality.'

'I enjoyed your last, Mrs Oliver,' said Superintendent Battle kindly. 'The one where all the Chief Constables were shot simultaneously. You just slipped up once or twice on official details. I know you're keen on accuracy, so I wondered if—'

Mrs Oliver interrupted him.

'As a matter of fact I don't care two pins about accuracy. Who is accurate? Nobody nowadays. If a reporter writes that a beautiful girl of twenty-two dies by turning on the gas after looking out over the sea and kissing her favourite labrador, Bob, goodbye, does anybody make a fuss because the girl was twenty-six, the room faced inland, and the dog was a Sealyham terrier called Bonnie? If a journalist can do that sort of thing, I don't see that it matters if I mix up police ranks and say a revolver when I mean an automatic, and a dictograph when I mean a phonograph, and use a poison that just allows you to gasp one dying sentence and no more. What really matters is plenty of *bodies*! If the thing's getting a little dull, some more blood cheers it up. Somebody is going to tell something – and then they're killed first! That always goes down well. It comes in all my books – camouflaged different ways, of course. And people *like* untraceable poisons, and idiotic police inspectors and girls tied up in cellars with sewer gas or water pouring in (such a troublesome way of killing anyone really) and a hero who can dispose of anything from three to seven villains single-handed. I've written thirty-two books by now – and of course they're all exactly the same really, as M. Poirot seems to have noticed – but nobody else has – and I only regret one thing – making my detective a Finn. I don't really know anything about Finns and I'm always getting letters from Finland pointing out something impossible that he's said or done. They seem to read detective stories a good deal in Finland. I suppose it's the long winters with no daylight. In Bulgaria and Roumania they don't seem to read at all. I'd have done better to have made him a Bulgar.'

She broke off.

'I'm so sorry. I'm talking shop. And this is a real murder.' Her face lit up. 'What a good idea it would be if *none* of them had murdered him. If he'd asked them all, and then quietly committed suicide just for the fun of making a schemozzle.'

Poirot nodded approvingly.

'An admirable solution. So neat. So ironic. But, alas, Mr Shaitana was not that sort of man. He was very fond of life.'

'I don't think he was really a nice man,' said Mrs Oliver slowly.

'He was not nice, no,' said Poirot. 'But he was alive – and now he is dead, and as I told him once, I have a *bourgeois* attitude to murder. I disapprove of it.'

He added softly: 'And so – I am prepared to go inside the tiger's cage . . .'

— 9 —

DR ROBERTS

'GOOD morning, Superintendent Battle.'

Dr Roberts rose from his chair and offered a large pink hand smelling of a mixture of good soap and faint carbolic.

'How are things going?' he went on.

Superintendent Battle glanced round the comfortable consulting-room before answering.

'Well, Dr Roberts, strictly speaking, they're not going. They're standing still.'

'There's been nothing much in the papers, I've been glad to see.'

'*Sudden death of the well-known Mr Shaitana at an evening party in his own house.* It's left at that for the moment. We've had the autopsy – I brought a report of the findings along – thought it might interest you—'

'That's very kind of you – it would – h'm – h'm. Yes, very interesting.'

He handed it back.

'And we've interviewed Mr Shaitana's solicitor. We know the terms of his will. Nothing of interest there. He has relatives in Syria, it seems. And then, of course, we've been through all his private papers.'

Was it fancy or did that broad, clean-shaven countenance look a little strained – a little wooden?

'And?' said Dr Roberts.

'Nothing,' said Superintendent Battle, watching him.

There wasn't a sigh of relief. Nothing so blatant as that. But the doctor's figure seemed to relax just a shade more comfortably in his chair.

'And so you've come to me?'

'And so, as you say, I've come to you.'

The doctor's eyebrows rose a little and his shrewd eyes looked into Battle's.

'Want to go through *my* private papers – eh?'

'That was my idea.'

'Got a search-warrant?'

'No.'

'Well, you could get one easily enough, I suppose. I'm not going to make difficulties. It's not very pleasant being suspected of murder, but I suppose I can't blame you for what's obviously your duty.'

'Thank you, sir,' said Superintendent Battle with real gratitude. 'I appreciate your attitude, if I may say so, very much. I hope all the others will be as reasonable, I'm sure.'

'What can't be cured must be endured,' said the doctor good-humouredly.

He went on: 'I've finished seeing my patients here. I'm just off on my rounds. I'll leave you my keys and just say a word to my secretary and you can rootle to your heart's content.'

'That's all very nice and pleasant, I'm sure,' said Battle. 'I'd like to ask you a few more questions before you go.'

'About the other night? Really, I told you all I know.'

'No, not about the other night. About yourself.'

'Well, man, ask away. What do you want to know?'

'I'd just like a rough sketch of your career, Dr Roberts. Birth, marriage, and so on.'

'It will get me into practice for *Who's Who*,' said the doctor dryly. 'My career's a perfectly straightforward one. I'm a Shropshire man, born at Ludlow. My father was in practice there. He died when I was fifteen. I was educated at Shrewsbury and went in for medicine like my father before me. I'm a St Christopher's man – but you'll have all the medical details already, I expect.'

'I looked you up, yes, sir. You an only child or have you any brothers or sisters?'

'I'm an only child. Both my parents are dead and I'm unmarried. Will that do to get on with? I came into partnership here with Dr Emery. He retired about fifteen years ago. Lives in Ireland. I'll give you his address if you like. I live here with a cook, a parlourmaid and a housemaid. My secretary comes in daily. I make a good income and I only kill a reasonable number of my patients. How's that?'

Superintendent Battle grinned.

'That's fairly comprehensive, Dr Roberts. I'm glad you've got a sense of humour. Now I'm going to ask you one more thing.'

'I'm a strictly moral man, Superintendent.'

'Oh, that wasn't my meaning. No, I was just going to ask you if you'd give me the names of four friends – people who've known you intimately for a number of years. Kind of references, if you know what I mean.'

'Yes, I think so. Let me see now. You'd prefer people who are actually in London now?'

'It would make it a bit easier, but it doesn't really matter.'

The doctor thought for a minute or two, then with his fountain-pen he scribbled four names and addresses on a sheet of paper and pushed it across the desk to Battle.

'Will those do? They're the best I can think of on the spur of the moment.'

Battle read carefully, nodded his head in satisfaction and put the sheet of paper away in an inner pocket.

'It's just a question of elimination,' he said. 'The sooner I can get one person eliminated and go on to the next the better it is for everyone concerned. I've got to make perfectly certain that you weren't on bad terms with the late Mr Shaitana, that you had no private connections or business dealings with him, that there was no question of his having injured you at any time and your bearing resentment. *I* may believe you when you say you only knew him slightly – but it isn't a question of *my* belief. I've got to say I've made *sure*.'

'Oh, I understand perfectly. You've got to think everybody's a liar till he's proved he's speaking the truth. Here are my keys, Superintendent. That's the drawers of the desk – that's the bureau – that little one's the key of the poison cupboard. Be sure you lock it up again. Perhaps I'd better just have a word with my secretary.'

He pressed a button on his desk.

Almost immediately the door opened and a competent-looking young woman appeared.

'You rang, Doctor?'

'This is Miss Burgess – Superintendent Battle from Scotland Yard.'

Miss Burgess turned a cool gaze on Battle. It seemed to say: 'Dear me, what sort of an animal is this?'

'I should be glad, Miss Burgess, if you will answer any questions Superintendent Battle may put to you, and give him any help he may need.'

'Certainly, if you say so, Doctor.'

'Well,' said Roberts, rising, 'I'll be off. Did you put the morphia in my case? I shall need it for the Lockhaert case.'

He bustled out, still talking, and Miss Burgess followed him.

She returned a minute or two later to say: 'Will you press the button when you want me, Superintendent Battle?'

Superintendent Battle thanked her and said he would do so. Then he set to work.

His search was careful and methodical, though he had no great hopes of finding anything of importance. Roberts' ready acquiescence dispelled the chance of that. Roberts was no fool. He would realize that a search would be bound to come and he would make provisions accordingly. There was, however, a faint chance that Battle might come across a hint of the information he was really after, since Roberts would not know the real object of his search.

Superintendent Battle opened and shut drawers, rifled pigeon-holes, glanced through a cheque-book, estimated the unpaid bills – noted what those same bills were for, scrutinized Roberts' pass-book, ran through his case-notes and generally left no written document unturned. The result was meagre in the extreme. He next took a look through the poison cupboard, noted the wholesale firms with which the doctor dealt, and the system of checking, relocked the cupboard and passed on to the bureau. The contents of the latter were of a more personal nature, but Battle found nothing germane to his search. He shook his head, sat down in the doctor's chair and pressed the desk button.

Miss Burgess appeared with commendable promptitude.

Superintendent Battle asked her politely to be seated and then sat studying her for a moment, before he decided which way to tackle her. He had sensed immediately her hostility and he was uncertain whether to provoke her into unguarded speech by increasing that hostility or whether to try a softer method of approach.

'I suppose you know what all this is about, Miss Burgess?' he said at last.

'Dr Roberts told me,' said Miss Burgess shortly.

'The whole thing's rather delicate,' said Superintendent Battle.

'Is it?' said Miss Burgess.

'Well, it's rather a nasty business. Four people are under suspicion and one of them must have done it. What I want to know is whether you've ever seen this Mr Shaitana.'

'Never.'

'Ever heard Dr Roberts speak of him?'

'Never – no, I am wrong. About a week ago Dr Roberts told me to enter up a dinner appointment in his engagement-book. Mr Shaitana, 8.15, on the 18th.'

'And that is the first you ever heard of this Mr Shaitana?'

'Yes.'

'Never seen his name in the papers? He was often in the fashionable news.'

'I've got better things to do than reading the fashionable news.'

'I expect you have. Oh, I expect you have,' said the superintendent mildly.

'Well,' he went on. 'There it is. All four of these people will only admit to knowing Mr Shaitana slightly. But one of them knew him well enough to kill him. It's my job to find out which of them it was.'

There was an unhelpful pause. Miss Burgess seemed quite uninterested in the performance of Superintendent Battle's job. It was her job to obey her employer's orders and sit here listening to what Superintendent Battle chose to say and answer any direct questions he might choose to put to her.

'You know, Miss Burgess' – the superintendent found it uphill work but he persevered – 'I doubt if you appreciate half the difficulties of our job. People say things, for instance. Well, we mayn't believe a word of it, but we've got to take notice of it all the same. It's particularly noticeable in a case of this kind. I don't want to say anything against your sex but there's no doubt that a woman, when she's rattled, is apt to lash out with her tongue a bit. She makes unfounded accusations, hints this, that and the other, and rakes up all sorts of old scandals that have probably nothing whatever to do with the case.'

'Do you mean,' demanded Miss Burgess, 'that one of these other people have been saying things against the doctor?'

'Not exactly *said* anything,' said Battle cautiously. 'But all the same, I'm bound to take notice. Suspicious circumstances about the death of a patient. Probably all a lot of nonsense. I'm ashamed to bother the doctor with it.'

'I suppose someone's got hold of that story about Mrs Graves,' said Miss Burgess wrathfully. 'The way people talk about things they know nothing whatever about is disgraceful. Lots of old ladies get like that – they think everybody is poisoning them – their relations and their servants and even their doctors. Mrs Graves had had three doctors before she came to Dr Roberts and then when she got the same fancies about him he was quite willing for her to have Dr Lee instead. It's the only thing to do in these cases, he said. And after Dr Lee she had Dr Steele, and then Dr Farmer – until she died, poor old thing.'

'You'd be surprised the way the smallest thing starts a story,' said Battle. 'Whenever a doctor benefits by the death of a patient somebody has something ill-natured to say. And yet why shouldn't a grateful patient leave a little something, or even a big something, to her medical attendant.'

'It's the relations,' said Miss Burgess. 'I always think there's nothing like death for bringing out the meanness of human nature. Squabbling over who's to have what before the body's cold. Luckily, Dr Roberts has never had any trouble of that kind. He always says he hopes his patients won't leave him anything. I believe he once had a legacy of fifty pounds and he's had two walking-sticks and a gold watch, but nothing else.'

'It's a difficult life, that of a professional man,' said Battle with a sigh. 'He's always open to blackmail. The most innocent occurrences lend themselves sometimes to a scandalous appearance. A doctor's got to avoid even the appearance of evil – that means he's got to have his wits about him good and sharp.'

'A lot of what you say is true,' said Miss Burgess. 'Doctors have a difficult time with hysterical women.'

'Hysterical women. That's right. I thought, in my own mind, that that was all it amounted to.'

'I suppose you mean that dreadful Mrs Craddock?'

Battle pretended to think.

'Let me see, was it three years ago? No, more.'

'Four or five, I think. She was a *most* unbalanced woman! I was glad when she went abroad and so was Dr Roberts. She told her husband the most frightful lies – they always do, of course. Poor man, he wasn't quite himself – he'd begun to be ill. He died of anthrax, you know, an infected shaving-brush.'

'I'd forgotten that,' said Battle untruthfully.

'And then she went abroad and died not long afterwards. But I always thought she was a nasty type of woman – man-mad, you know.'

'I know the kind,' said Battle. 'Very dangerous, they are. A doctor's got to give them a wide berth. Whereabouts did she die abroad? I seem to remember . . .'

'Egypt, I think it was. She got blood-poisoning – some native infection.'

'Another thing that must be difficult for a doctor,' said Battle, making a conversational leap, 'is when he suspects that one of his patients is being poisoned by one of their relatives. What's he to do? He's got to be sure – or else hold his tongue. And if he's done the latter, then it's awkward for him if there's talk of foul play afterwards. I wonder if any case of that kind has ever come Dr Roberts' way?'

'I really don't think it has,' said Miss Burgess, considering. 'I've never heard of anything like that.'

'From the statistical point of view, it would be interesting to know how many deaths occur among a doctor's practice per year. For instance now, you've been with Dr Roberts some years—'

'Seven.'

'Seven. Well, how many deaths have there been in that time, off-hand?'

'Really, it's difficult to say.' Miss Burgess gave herself up to calculation. She was by now quite thawed and unsuspicious. 'Seven, eight – of course, I can't remember exactly – I shouldn't say more than thirty in the time.'

'Then I fancy Dr Roberts must be a better doctor than most,' said Battle genially. 'I suppose, too, most of his patients are upper-class. They can afford to take care of themselves.'

'He's a very popular doctor. He's so good at diagnosis.'

Battle sighed and rose to his feet.

'I'm afraid I've been wandering from my duty, which is to find out a connection between the doctor and this Mr Shaitana. You're quite sure he wasn't a patient of the doctor's?'

'Quite sure.'

'Under another name, perhaps?' Battle handed her a photograph. 'Recognize him at all?'

'What a very theatrical-looking person. No, I've never seen him here at any time.'

'Well, that's that.' Battle sighed. 'I'm much obliged to the doctor, I'm sure, for being so pleasant about everything. Tell him so from me, will you? Tell him I'm passing on to No. 2. Goodbye, Miss Burgess, and thank you for your help.'

He shook hands and departed. Walking along the street he took a small note-book from his pocket and made a couple of entries in it under the letter R.

Mrs Graves? Unlikely.
Mrs Craddock?
No legacies.
No wife. (Pity.)
Investigate deaths of patients. Difficult.

He closed the book and turned into the Lancaster Gate branch of the London & Wessex Bank.

The display of his official card brought him to a private interview with the manager.

'Good morning, sir. One of your clients is a Dr Geoffrey Roberts, I understand.'

'Quite correct, Superintendent.'

'I shall want some information about that gentleman's account going back over a period of years.'

'I will see what I can do for you.'

A complicated half-hour followed. Finally Battle, with a sigh, tucked away a sheet of pencilled figures.

'Got what you want?' inquired the bank manager curiously.

'No, I haven't. Not one suggestive lead. Thank you all the same.'

At the same moment, Dr Roberts, washing his hands in his consulting-room, said over his shoulder to Miss Burgess: 'What about our stolid sleuth, eh? Did he turn the place upside down and you inside out?'

'He didn't get much out of me, I can tell you,' said Miss Burgess, setting her lips tightly.

'My dear girl, no need to be an oyster. I told you to tell him all he wanted to know. What did he want to know, by the way?'

'Oh, he kept harping on your knowing that man Shaitana – suggested even that he might have come here as a patient under a different name. He showed me his photograph. Such a theatrical-looking man!'

'Shaitana? Oh, yes, fond of posing as a modern Mephistopheles. It went down rather well on the whole. What else did Battle ask you?'

'Really nothing very much. Except – oh, yes, somebody had been telling him some absurd nonsense about Mrs Graves – you know the way she used to go on.'

'Graves? Graves? Oh, yes, old Mrs Graves! That's rather funny!' The doctor laughed with considerable amusement. 'That's really very funny indeed.'

And in high good humour he went in to lunch.

10

DR ROBERTS (CONTINUED)

SUPERINTENDENT BATTLE was lunching with M. Hercule Poirot.

The former looked downcast, the latter sympathetic.

'Your morning, then, has not been entirely successful,' said Poirot thoughtfully.

Battle shook his head.

'It's going to be uphill work, M. Poirot.'

'What do you think of him?'

'Of the doctor? Well, frankly, I think Shaitana was right. He's a killer. Reminds me of Westaway. And of that lawyer chap in Norfolk. Same hearty, self-confident manner. Same popularity. Both of them were clever devils – so's Roberts. All the same, it doesn't follow that Roberts killed Shaitana – and as a matter of fact I don't think he did. He'd know the risk too well – better than a layman would – that Shaitana might wake and cry out. No, I don't think Roberts murdered him.'

'But you think he has murdered someone?'

'Possibly quite a lot of people. Westaway had. But it's going to be hard to get at. I've looked over his bank account – nothing suspicious there – no large sums suddenly paid in. At any rate, in the last seven years he's not had any legacy from a patient. That wipes out murder for direct gain. He's never married – that's a pity – so ideally simple for a doctor to kill his own wife. He's well-to-do, but, then, he's got a thriving practice among well-to-do people.'

'In fact he appears to lead a thoroughly blameless life – and perhaps does do so.'

'Maybe. But I prefer to believe the worst.'

He went on: 'There's the hint of a scandal over a woman – one of his patients – name of Craddock. That's worth looking up, I think. I'll get someone on to that straight away. Woman actually died out in Egypt of some local disease, so I don't think there's anything in that – but it might throw a light on his general character and morals.'

'Was there a husband?'

'Yes. Husband died of anthrax.'

'Anthrax?'

'Yes, there were a lot of cheap shaving-brushes on the market just then – some of them infected. There was a regular scandal about it.'

'Convenient,' suggested Poirot.

'That's what I thought. If her husband were threatening to kick up a row— But there, it's all conjecture. We haven't a leg to stand upon.'

'Courage, my friend. I know your patience. In the end you will have perhaps as many legs as a centipede.'

'And fall into the ditch as a result of thinking about them,' grinned Battle.

Then he asked curiously: 'What about you, M. Poirot? Going to take a hand?'

'I, too, might call on Dr Roberts.'

'Two of us in one day. That ought to put the wind up him.'

'Oh, I shall be very discreet. I shall not inquire into his past life.'

'I'd like to know just exactly what line you'll take,' said Battle curiously, 'but don't tell me unless you want to.'

'*Du tout – du tout*. I am most willing. I shall talk a little of bridge, that is all.'

'Bridge again. You harp on that, don't you, M. Poirot?'

'I find the subject very useful.'

'Well, every man to his taste. I don't deal much in these fancy approaches. They don't suit my style.'

'What is your style, Superintendent?'

The superintendent met the twinkle in Poirot's eye with an answering twinkle in his own.

'A straightforward, honest, zealous officer doing his duty in the most laborious manner – that's my style. No frills. No fancy work. Just honest perspiration. Stolid and a bit stupid – that's my ticket.'

Poirot raised his glass.

'To our respective methods – and may success crown our joint efforts.'

'I expect Colonel Race may get us something worth having about Despard,' said Battle. 'He's got a good many sources of information.'

'And Mrs Oliver?'

'Bit of a toss-up there. I rather like that woman. Talks a lot of nonsense, but she's a sport. And women get to know things about other women that men can't get at. She may spot something useful.'

They separated. Battle went back to Scotland Yard to issue

229

instructions for certain lines to be followed up. Poirot betook himself to 200 Gloucester Terrace.

Dr Roberts' eyebrows rose comically as he greeted his guest.

'Two sleuths in one day,' he asked. 'Handcuffs by this evening, I suppose?'

Poirot smiled.

'I can assure you, Dr Roberts, that my attentions are being equally divided between all four of you.'

'That's something to be thankful for, at all events. Smoke?'

'If you permit, I prefer my own.'

Poirot lighted one of his tiny Russian cigarettes.

'Well, what can I do for you?' asked Roberts.

Poirot was silent for a minute or two puffing, then he said: 'Are you a keen observer of human nature, Doctor?'

'I don't know. I suppose I am. A doctor has to be.'

'That was exactly my reasoning. I said to myself, "A doctor has always to be studying his patients – their expressions, their colour, how fast they breathe, any signs of restlessness – a doctor notices these things automatically almost without noticing he notices! Dr Roberts is the man to help me."'

'I'm willing enough to help. What's the trouble?'

Poirot produced from a neat little pocket-case three carefully folded bridge scores.

'These are the first three rubbers the other evening,' he explained. 'Here is the first one – in Miss Meredith's handwriting. Now can you tell me – with this to refresh your memory – exactly what the calling was and how each hand went?'

Roberts stared at him in astonishment.

'You're joking, M. Poirot. How can I possibly remember?'

'Can't you? I should be so very grateful if you could. Take this first rubber. The first game must have resulted in a game call in hearts or spades, or else one or other side must have gone down fifty.'

'Let me see – that was the first hand. Yes, I think they went out in spades.'

'And the next hand?'

'I suppose one or other of us went down fifty – but I can't remember which or what it was in. Really, M. Poirot, you can hardly expect me to do so.'

'Can't you remember any of the calling or the hands?'

'I got a grand slam – I remember that. It was doubled too. And I also remember going down a nasty smack – playing three no trumps, I think it was – went down a packet. But that was later on.'

'Do you remember with whom you were playing?'

'Mrs Lorrimer. She looked a bit grim, I remember. Didn't like my overcalling I expect.'

'And you can't remember any other of the hands or the calling?'

Roberts laughed.

'My dear M. Poirot, did you really expect I could? First there was the murder – enough to drive the most spectacular hands out of one's mind – and in addition I've played at least half a dozen rubbers since then.'

Poirot sat looking rather crestfallen.

'I'm sorry,' said Roberts.

'It does not matter very much,' said Poirot slowly. 'I hoped that you might remember one or two, at least, of the hands, because I thought they might be valuable landmarks in remembering other things.'

'What other things?'

'Well, you might have noticed, for instance, that your partner made a mess of playing a perfectly simple no trump, or that an opponent, say, presented you with a couple of unexpected tricks by failing to lead an obvious card.'

Dr Roberts became suddenly serious. He leaned forward in his chair.

'Ah,' he said. 'Now I see what you're driving at. Forgive me. I thought at first you were talking pure nonsense. You mean that the murder – the successful accomplishment of the murder – might have made a definite difference in the guilty party's play?'

Poirot nodded.

'You have seized the idea correctly. It would be a clue of the first excellence if you had been four players who knew each other's game well. A variation, a sudden lack of brilliance, a missed opportunity – that would have been immediately noticed. Unluckily, you were all strangers to each other. Variation in play would not be so noticeable. But think, *M. le docteur*, I beg of you to *think*. Do you remember any inequalities – any sudden glaring mistakes – in the play of anyone?'

There was silence for a minute or two, then Dr Roberts shook his head.

'It's no good. I can't help you,' he said frankly. 'I simply don't remember. All I can tell you is what I told you before: Mrs Lorrimer is a first-class player – she never made a slip that I noticed. She was brilliant from start to finish. Despard's play was uniformly good too. Rather a conventional player – that is, his bidding is strictly conventional. He never steps outside the rules. Won't take a long chance. Miss Meredith—' He hesitated.

'Yes? Miss Meredith?' Poirot prompted him.

'She did make mistakes – once or twice – I remember – towards the end of the evening, but that may simply have been because she was tired – not being a very experienced player. Her hand shook, too—'

He stopped.

'When did her hand shake?'

'When was it now? I can't remember . . . I think she was just nervous. M. Poirot, you're making me imagine things.'

'I apologize. There is another point on which I seek your help.'

'Yes?'

Poirot said slowly: 'It is difficult. I do not, you see, wish to ask you a leading question. If I say, did you notice so and so – well, I have put the thing into your head. Your answer will not be so valuable. Let me try to get at the matter another way. If you will be so kind, Dr Roberts, describe to me the contents of the room in which you played.'

Roberts looked thoroughly astonished.

'The contents of the room?'

'If you will be so good.'

'My dear fellow, I simply don't know where to begin.'

'Begin anywhere you choose.'

'Well, there was a good deal of furniture—'

'*Non, non, non*, be precise, I pray of you.'

Dr Roberts sighed.

He began facetiously after the manner of an auctioneer.

'One large settee upholstered in ivory brocade – one ditto in green ditto – four or five large chairs. Eight or nine Persian rugs – a set of twelve small gilt Empire chairs. William and Mary bureau. (I feel just like an auctioneer's clerk.) Very beautiful Chinese cabinet. Grand piano. There was other furniture but I'm afraid I didn't notice it. Six first-class Japanese prints. Two Chinese pictures on looking-glass. Five or six very beautiful snuff-boxes. Some Japanese ivory *netsuke* figures on a table by themselves. Some old silver – Charles I *tazzas*, I think. One or two pieces of Battersea enamel—'

'Bravo, bravo!' Poirot applauded.

'A couple of old English slipware birds – and, I think, a Ralph Wood figure. Then there was some Eastern stuff – intricate silverwork. Some jewellery, I don't know much about that. Some Chelsea birds, I remember. Oh, and some miniatures in a case – pretty good ones, I fancy. That's not all by a long way – but it's all I can think of for the minute.'

'It is magnificent,' said Poirot with due appreciation. 'You have the true observer's eye.'

The doctor asked curiously: 'Have I included the object you had in mind?'

'That is the interesting thing about it,' said Poirot. 'If you had mentioned the object I had in mind it would have been extremely surprising to me. As I thought, you would not mention it.'

'Why?'

Poirot twinkled.

'Perhaps – because it was not there to mention.'

Roberts stared.

'That seems to remind me of something.'

'It reminds you of Sherlock Holmes, does it not? The curious incident of the dog in the night. The dog did not howl in the night. That is the curious thing! Ah, well, I am not above stealing the tricks of others.'

'Do you know, M. Poirot, I am completely at sea as to what you are driving at.'

'That is excellent, that. In confidence, that is how I get my little effects.'

Then, as Dr Roberts still looked rather dazed, Poirot said with a smile as he rose to his feet: 'You may at least comprehend this, what you have told me is going to be very helpful to me in my next interview.'

The doctor rose also.

'I can't see how, but I'll take your word for it,' he said.

They shook hands.

Poirot went down the steps of the doctor's house, and hailed a passing taxi.

'111 Cheyne Lane, Chelsea,' he told the driver.

— I I —

MRS LORRIMER

111 CHEYNE LANE was a small house of very neat and trim appearance standing in a quiet street. The door was painted black and the steps were particularly well whitened, the brass of the knocker and handle gleamed in the afternoon sun.

The door was opened by an elderly parlourmaid with an immaculate white cap and apron.

In answer to Poirot's inquiry she said that her mistress was at home.

She preceded him up the narrow staircase.

'What name, sir?'

'M. Hercule Poirot.'

He was ushered into a drawing-room of the usual L-shape. Poirot looked about him, noting details. Good furniture, well polished, of the old family type. Shiny chintz on the chairs and settees. A few silver photograph-frames about in the old-fashioned manner. Otherwise an agreeable amount of space and light, and some really beautiful chrysanthemums arranged in a tall jar.

Mrs Lorrimer came forward to meet him. She shook hands without showing any particular surprise at seeing him, indicated a chair, took one herself and remarked favourably on the weather.

There was a pause.

'I hope, Madame,' said Hercule Poirot, 'that you will forgive this visit.'

Looking directly at him, Mrs Lorrimer asked: 'Is this a professional visit?'

'I confess it.'

'You realize, I suppose, M. Poirot, that though I shall naturally give Superintendent Battle and the official police any information and help they may require, I am by no means bound to do the same for any unofficial investigator?'

'I am quite aware of that fact, Madame. If you show me the door, me, I march to that door with complete submission.'

Mrs Lorrimer smiled very slightly.

'I am not yet prepared to go to those extremes, M. Poirot. I can give you ten minutes. At the end of that time I have to go out to a bridge party.'

'Ten minutes will be ample for my purpose. I want you to describe to me, Madame, the room in which you played bridge the other evening – the room in which Mr Shaitana was killed.'

Mrs Lorrimer's eyebrows rose.

'What an extraordinary question! I do not see the point of it.'

'Madame, if when you were playing bridge, someone were to say to you – why do you play that ace or why do you put on the knave that is taken by the queen and not the king which would take the trick? If people were to ask you such questions, the answers would be rather long and tedious, would they not?'

Mrs Lorrimer smiled slightly.

'Meaning that in this game you are the expert and I am the novice. Very well.' She reflected a minute. 'It was a large room. There were a good many things in it.'

'Can you describe some of those things?'

'There were some glass flowers – modern – rather beautiful . . . And I think there were some Chinese or Japanese pictures. And there was a bowl of tiny red tulips – amazingly early for them.'

'Anything else?'

'I'm afraid I didn't notice anything in detail.'

'The furniture – do you remember the colour of the upholstery?'

'Something silky, I think. That's all I can say.'

'Did you notice any of the small objects?'

'I'm afraid not. There were so many. I know it struck me as quite a collector's room.'

There was silence for a minute. Mrs Lorrimer said with a faint smile: 'I'm afraid I have not been very helpful.'

'There is something else.' He produced the bridge scores. 'Here are the first three rubbers played. I wondered if you could help me with the aid of these scores to reconstruct the hands.'

'Let me see.' Mrs Lorrimer looked interested. She bent over the scores.

'That was the first rubber. Miss Meredith and I were playing against the two men. The first game was played in four spades. We made it and an over trick. Then the next hand was left at two diamonds and Dr Roberts went down one trick on it. There was quite a lot of bidding on the third hand, I remember. Miss Meredith passed. Major Despard went a heart. I passed. Dr Roberts gave a jump bid of three clubs. Miss Meredith went three spades. Major Despard bid four diamonds. I doubled. Dr Roberts took it into four hearts. They went down one.'

'*Epatant*,' said Poirot. 'What a memory!'

Mrs Lorrimer went on, disregarding him: 'On the next hand Major Despard passed and I bid a no trump. Dr Roberts bid three hearts. My partner said nothing. Despard put his partner to four. I doubled and they went down two tricks. Then I dealt and we went out on a four-spade call.'

She took up the next score.

'It is difficult, that,' said Poirot. 'Major Despard scores in the cancellation manner.'

'I rather fancy both sides went down fifty to start with – then Dr Roberts went down to five diamonds and we doubled and got him down three tricks. Then we made three clubs, but immediately after the others went game in spades. We made the second game in five clubs. Then we went down a hundred. The others made one heart, we made two no trumps and we finally won the rubber with a four-club call.'

She picked up the next score.

'This rubber was rather a battle, I remember. It started tamely. Major Despard and Miss Meredith made a one-heart call. Then we went down a couple of fifties trying for four hearts and four spades. Then the others made game in spades – no use trying to stop them. We went down three hands running after that but undoubled. Then we won the second game in no trumps. Then a battle royal started. Each side went down in turn. Dr Roberts overcalled but though he went down badly once or twice, his calling paid, for more than once he frightened Miss Meredith out of bidding her hand. Then he bid an original two spade, I gave him three diamonds, he bid four no trumps, I bid five spades and he suddenly jumped to seven diamonds. We were doubled, of course. He had no business to make such a call. By a kind of miracle we got it. I never thought we should when I saw his hand go down. If the others led a heart we would have been three tricks down. As it was they led the king of clubs and we got it. It was really very exciting.'

'*Je crois bien* – a grand slam vulnerable doubled. It causes the emotions, that! Me, I admit it, I have not the nerve to go for the slams. I content myself with the game.'

'Oh, but you shouldn't,' said Mrs Lorrimer with energy. 'You must play the game properly.'

'Take risks, you mean?'

'There is no risk if the bidding is correct. It should be a mathematical certainty. Unfortunately, few people really bid well. They know the opening bids but later they lose their heads. They cannot distinguish between a hand with winning cards in it and a hand without losing cards – but I mustn't give you a lecture on bridge, or on the losing count, M. Poirot.'

'It would improve my play, I am sure, Madame.'

Mrs Lorrimer resumed her study of the score.

'After that excitement the next hands were rather tame. Have you the fourth score there? Ah, yes. A ding-dong battle – neither side able to score below.'

'It is often like that as the evening wears on?'

'Yes, one starts tamely and then the cards get worked up.'

Poirot collected the scores and made a little bow.

'Madame, I congratulate you. Your card memory is magnificent – but magnificent! You remember, one might say, every card that was played!

236

'I believe I do.'

'Memory is a wonderful gift. With it the past is never the past –
I should imagine, Madame, that to you the past unrolls itself,
every incident clear as yesterday. Is that so?'

She looked at him quickly. Her eyes were wide and dark.

It was only for a moment, then she had resumed her woman-
of-the-world manner, but Hercule Poirot did not doubt. That shot
had gone home.

Mrs Lorrimer rose.

'I'm afraid I shall have to leave now. I am sorry – but I really
mustn't be late.'

'Of course not – of course not. I apologize for trespassing on
your time.'

'I'm sorry I haven't been able to help you more.'

'But you have helped me,' said Hercule Poirot.

'I hardly think so.'

She spoke with decision.

'But yes. You have told me something I wanted to know.'

She asked no question as to what that something was.

He held out his hand.

'Thank you, Madame, for your forbearance.'

As she shook hands with him she said: 'You are an extraordinary man, M. Poirot.'

'I am as the good God made me, Madame.'

'We are all that, I suppose.'

'Not all, Madame. Some of us have tried to improve on His
pattern. Mr Shaitana, for instance.'

'In what way do you mean?'

'He had a very pretty taste in *objets de virtu* and *bric-à-brac* – he
should have been content with that. Instead, he collected other
things.'

'What sort of things?'

'Well – shall we say – sensations?'

'And don't you think that was *dans son caractère*?'

Poirot shook his head gravely.

'He played the part of the devil too successfully. But he was not
the devil. *Au fond*, he was a stupid man. And so – he died.'

'Because he was stupid?'

'It is the sin that is never forgiven and always punished,
Madame.'

There was a silence. Then Poirot said: 'I take my departure. A
thousand thanks for your amiability, Madame. I will not come
again unless you send for me.'

Her eyebrows rose.

'Dear me, M. Poirot, why should I send for you?'

'You might. It is just an idea. If so, I will come. Remember that.'

He bowed once more and left the room.

In the street he said to himself: 'I am right . . . I am sure I am right . . . It *must* be that!'

— 12 —

ANNE MEREDITH

Mrs Oliver extricated herself from the driving-seat of her little two-seater with some difficulty. To begin with, the makers of modern motor-cars assume that only a pair of sylph-like knees will ever be under the steering-wheel. It is also the fashion to sit low. That being so, for a middle-aged woman of generous proportions it requires a good deal of superhuman wriggling to get out from under the steering-wheel. In the second place, the seat next to the driving-seat was encumbered by several maps, a handbag, three novels and a large bag of apples. Mrs Oliver was partial to apples and had indeed been known to eat as many as five pounds straight off whilst composing the complicated plot of *The Death in the Drain Pipe* – coming to herself with a start and an incipient stomach-ache an hour and ten minutes after she was due at an important luncheon party given in her honour.

With a final determined heave and a sharp shove with the knee against a recalcitrant door, Mrs Oliver arrived a little too suddenly on the sidewalk outside the gate of Wendon Cottage, showering apple cores freely round her as she did so.

She gave a deep sigh, pushed back her country hat to an unfashionable angle, looked down with approval at the tweeds she had remembered to put on, frowned a little when she saw that she had absent-mindedly retained her London high-heeled patent-leather shoes, and pushing open the gate of Wendon Cottage walked up the flagged path to the front door. She rang the bell and executed a cheerful little rat-a-tat-tat on the knocker – a quaint conceit in the form of a toad's head.

As nothing happened she repeated the performance.

After a further pause of a minute and a half, Mrs Oliver stepped briskly round the side of the house on a voyage of exploration.

There was a small old-fashioned garden with Michaelmas daisies and straggling chrysanthemums behind the cottage, and beyond it a field. Beyond the field was the river. For an October day the sun was warm.

Two girls were just crossing the field in the direction of the cottage. As they came through the gate into the garden, the foremost of the two stopped dead.

Mrs Oliver came forward.

'How do you do, Miss Meredith? You remember me, don't you?'

'Oh – oh, of course.' Anne Meredith extended her hand hurriedly. Her eyes looked wide and startled. Then she pulled herself together.

'This is my friend who lives with me – Miss Dawes. Rhoda, this is Mrs Oliver.'

The other girl was tall, dark, and vigorous-looking. She said excitedly: 'Oh, are you *the* Mrs Oliver? Ariadne Oliver?'

'I am,' said Mrs Oliver, and she added to Anne, 'Now let us sit down somewhere, my dear, because I've got a lot to say to you.'

'Of course. And we'll have tea—'

'Tea can wait,' said Mrs Oliver.

Anne led the way to a little group of deck and basket chairs, all rather dilapidated. Mrs Oliver chose the strongest-looking with some care, having had various unfortunate experiences with flimsy summer furniture.

'Now, my dear,' she said briskly. 'Don't let's beat about the bush. About this murder the other evening. We've got to get busy and do something.'

'Do something?' queried Anne.

'Naturally,' said Mrs Oliver. 'I don't know what *you* think, but I haven't the least doubt who did it. That doctor. What was his name? Roberts. That's it! Roberts. A Welsh name! I never trust the Welsh! I had a Welsh nurse and she took me to Harrogate one day and went home having forgotten all about me. Very unstable. But never mind about her. Roberts did it – that's the point and we must put our heads together and prove he did.'

Rhoda Dawes laughed suddenly – then she blushed.

'I beg your pardon. But you're – you're so different from what I would have imagined.'

'A disappointment, I expect,' said Mrs Oliver serenely. 'I'm used to that. Never mind. What we must do is prove that Roberts did it!'

'How can we?' said Anne.

'Oh, don't be so defeatist, Anne,' cried Rhoda Dawes. 'I think

239

Mrs Oliver's splendid. Of course, she knows all about these things. She'll do just as Sven Hjerson does.'

Blushing slightly at the name of her celebrated Finnish detective, Mrs Oliver said: 'It's got to be done, and I'll tell you why, child. You don't want people thinking *you* did it?'

'Why should they?' asked Anne, her colour rising.

'You know what people are!' said Mrs Oliver. 'The three who didn't do it will come in for just as much suspicion as the one who did.'

Anne Meredith said slowly: 'I still don't quite see why you came to *me*, Mrs Oliver.'

'Because in my opinion the other two don't matter! Mrs Lorrimer is one of those women who play bridge at bridge clubs all day. Women like that *must* be made of armour-plating – they can look after themselves all right! And anyway she's old. It wouldn't matter if anyone thought she'd done it. A girl's different. She's got her life in front of her.'

'And Major Despard?' asked Anne.

'Pah!' said Mrs Oliver. 'He's a man! I never worry about men. Men can look after themselves. Do it remarkably well, if you ask me. Besides, Major Despard enjoys a dangerous life. He's getting his fun at home instead of on the Irrawaddy – or do I mean the Limpopo? You know what I mean – that yellow African river that men like so much. No, I'm not worrying my head about either of those two.'

'It's very kind of you,' said Anne slowly.

'It was a beastly thing to happen,' said Rhoda. 'It's broken Anne up, Mrs Oliver. She's awfully sensitive. And I think you're quite right. It would be ever so much better to do something than just to sit here thinking about it all.'

'Of course it would,' said Mrs Oliver. 'To tell you the truth, a real murder has never come my way before. And, to continue telling the truth, I don't believe real murder is very much in my line. I'm so used to loading the dice – if you understand what I mean. But I wasn't going to be out of it and let those three men have all the fun to themselves. I've always said that if a woman were the head of Scotland Yard—'

'Yes?' said Rhoda, leaning forward with parted lips. 'If you were head of Scotland Yard, what would you do?'

'I should arrest Dr Roberts straight away—'

'Yes?'

'However, I'm not the head of Scotland Yard,' said Mrs Oliver, retreating from dangerous ground. 'I'm a private individual—'

'Oh, you're not that,' said Rhoda, confusedly complimentary.

'Here we are,' continued Mrs Oliver, 'three private individuals – all women. Let us see what we can do by putting our heads together.'

Anne Meredith nodded thoughtfully. Then she said: 'Why do you think Dr Roberts did it?'

'He's that sort of man,' replied Mrs Oliver promptly.

'Don't you think, though—?' Anne hesitated. 'Wouldn't a doctor—? I mean, something like poison would be so much easier for him.'

'Not at all. Poison – drugs of any kind would point straight to a doctor. Look how they are always leaving cases of dangerous drugs in cars all over London and getting them stolen. No, just because he *was* a doctor he'd take special care not to use anything of a medical kind.'

'I see,' said Anne doubtfully.

Then she said: 'But why do you think he wanted to kill Mr Shaitana? Have you any idea?'

'Idea? I've got any amount of ideas. In fact, that's just the difficulty. It always is my difficulty. I can never think of even one plot at a time. I always think of at least five, and then it's agony to decide between them. I can think of six beautiful reasons for the murder. The trouble is I've no earthly means of knowing which is right. To begin with, perhaps Shaitana was a moneylender. He had a very oily look. Roberts was in his clutches, and killed him because he couldn't get the money to repay the loan. Or perhaps Shaitana ruined his daughter or his sister. Or perhaps Roberts is a bigamist, and Shaitana knew it. Or possibly Roberts married Shaitana's second cousin, and will inherit all Shaitana's money through her. Or— How many have I got to?'

'Four,' said Rhoda.

'Or – and this is a really good one – suppose Shaitana knew some secrets in Roberts' past. Perhaps you didn't notice, my dear, but Shaitana said something rather peculiar at dinner – just before a rather queer pause.'

Anne stooped to tickle a caterpillar. She said, 'I don't think I remember.'

'What did he say?' asked Rhoda.

'Something about – what was it? – an accident and poison. Don't you remember?'

Anne's left hand tightened on the basketwork of her chair.

'I do remember something of the kind,' she said composedly.

Rhoda said suddenly, 'Darling, you ought to have a coat. It's not summer, remember. Go and get one.'

Anne shook her head.

'I'm quite warm.'

But she gave a queer little shiver as she spoke.

'You see my theory,' went on Mrs Oliver. 'I dare say one of the doctor's patients poisoned himself by accident; but, of course, really, it was the doctor's own doing. I dare say he's murdered lots of people that way.'

A sudden colour came into Anne's cheeks. She said, 'Do doctors usually want to murder their patients wholesale? Wouldn't it have rather a regrettable effect on their practice?'

'There would be a reason, of course,' said Mrs Oliver vaguely.

'I think the idea is absurd,' said Anne crisply. 'Absolutely absurdly melodramatic.'

'Oh, Anne!' cried Rhoda in an agony of apology. She looked at Mrs Oliver. Her eyes, rather like those of an intelligent spaniel, seemed to be trying to say something. 'Try and understand. Try and understand,' those eyes said.

'I think it's a splendid idea, Mrs Oliver,' Rhoda said earnestly. 'And a doctor could get hold of something quite untraceable, couldn't he?'

'Oh!' exclaimed Anne.

The other two turned to look at her.

'I remember something else,' she said. 'Mr Shaitana said something about a doctor's opportunities in a laboratory. He must have meant something by that.'

'It wasn't Mr Shaitana who said that.' Mrs Oliver shook her head. 'It was Major Despard.'

A footfall on the garden walk made her turn her head.

'Well!' she exclaimed. 'Talk of the devil!'

Major Despard had just come round the corner of the house.

— 13 —

SECOND VISITOR

AT the sight of Mrs Oliver, Major Despard looked slightly taken aback. Under his tan his face flushed a rich brick-red. Embarrassment made him jerky. He made for Anne.

'I apologize, Miss Meredith,' he said. 'Been ringing your bell. Nothing happened. Was passing this way. Thought I might just look you up.'

'I'm so sorry you've been ringing,' said Anne. 'We haven't got a maid – only a woman who comes in the mornings.'

She introduced him to Rhoda.

Rhoda said briskly: 'Let's have some tea. It's getting chilly. We'd better go in.'

They all went into the house. Rhoda disappeared into the kitchen. Mrs Oliver said: 'This is quite a coincidence – our all meeting here.'

Despard said slowly, 'Yes.'

His eyes rested on her thoughtfully – appraising eyes.

'I've been telling Miss Meredith,' said Mrs Oliver, who was thoroughly enjoying herself, 'that we ought to have a plan of campaign. About the murder, I mean. Of course, that doctor did it. Don't you agree with me?'

'Couldn't say. Very little to go on.'

Mrs Oliver put on her 'How like a man!' expression.

A certain air of constraint had settled over the three. Mrs Oliver sensed it quickly enough. When Rhoda brought in tea she rose and said she must be getting back to town. No, it was ever so kind of them, but she wouldn't have any tea.

'I'm going to leave you my card,' she said. 'Here it is, with my address on it. Come and see me when you come up to town, and we'll talk everything over and see if we can't think of something ingenious to get to the bottom of things.'

'I'll come out to the gate with you,' said Rhoda.

Just as they were walking down the path to the front gate, Anne Meredith ran out of the house and overtook them.

'I've been thinking things over,' she said.

Her pale face looked unusually resolute.

'Yes, my dear?'

'It's extraordinarily kind of you, Mrs Oliver, to have taken all this trouble. But I'd really rather not do anything at all. I mean – it was all so horrible. I just want to forget about it.'

'My dear child, the question is, will you be *allowed* to forget about it?'

'Oh, I quite understand that the police won't let it drop. They'll probably come here and ask me a lot more questions. I'm prepared for that. But privately, I mean, I don't want to think about it – or be reminded of it in any way. I dare say I'm a coward, but that's how I feel about it.'

'Oh, Anne!' cried Rhoda Dawes.

'I can understand your feeling, but I'm not at all sure that you're wise,' said Mrs Oliver. 'Left to themselves, the police will probably never find out the truth.'

Anne Meredith shrugged her shoulders.

'Does that really matter?'

'Matter?' cried Rhoda. 'Of course it matters. It *does* matter, doesn't it, Mrs Oliver?'

'I should certainly say so,' said Mrs Oliver dryly.

'I don't agree,' said Anne obstinately. 'Nobody who knows me would ever think I'd done it. I don't see any reason for interfering. It's the business of the police to get at the truth.'

'Oh, Anne, you *are* spiritless,' said Rhoda.

'That's how I feel, anyway,' said Anne. She held out her hand. 'Thank you very much, Mrs Oliver. It's very good of you to have bothered.'

'Of course, if you feel that way, there's nothing more to be said,' said Mrs Oliver cheerfully. 'I, at any rate, shall not let the grass grow under my feet. Goodbye, my dear. Look me up in London if you change your mind.'

She climbed into the car, started it, and drove off, waving a cheerful hand at the two girls.

Rhoda suddenly made a dash after the car and leapt on the running-board.

'What you said – about looking you up in London,' she said breathlessly. 'Did you only mean Anne, or did you mean me, too?'

Mrs Oliver applied the brake.

'I meant both of you, of course.'

'Oh, thank you. Don't stop. I – perhaps I might come one day. There's something— No, don't stop. I can jump off.'

She did so and, waving a hand, ran back to the gate, where Anne was standing.

'What on earth—?' began Anne.

'Isn't she a duck?' asked Rhoda enthusiastically. 'I do like her. She had on odd stockings, did you notice? I'm sure she's frightfully clever. She must be – to write all those books. What fun if she found out the truth when the police and everyone were baffled.'

'Why did she come here?' asked Anne.

Rhoda's eyes opened wide.

'Darling – she told you—'

Anne made an impatient gesture.

'We must go in. I forgot. I've left him all alone.'

'Major Despard? Anne, he's frightfully good-looking, isn't he?'

'I suppose he is.'

They walked up the path together.

Major Despard was standing by the mantelpiece, teacup in hand.

He cut short Anne's apologies for leaving him.

'Miss Meredith, I want to explain why I've butted in like this.'

'Oh – but—'

'I said that I happened to be passing – that wasn't strictly true. I came here on purpose.'

'How did you know my address?' asked Anne slowly.

'I got it from Superintendent Battle.'

He saw her shrink slightly at the name.

He went on quickly: 'Battle's on his way here now. I happened to see him at Paddington. I got my car out and came down here. I knew I could beat the train easily.'

'But why?'

Despard hesitated just for a minute.

'I may have been presumptuous – but I had the impression that you were, perhaps, what is called "alone in the world".'

'She's got me,' said Rhoda.

Despard shot a quick glance at her, rather liking the gallant boyish figure that leant against the mantelpiece and was following his words so intensely. They were an attractive pair, these two.

'I'm sure she couldn't have a more devoted friend than you, Miss Dawes,' he said courteously, 'but it occurred to me that, in the peculiar circumstances, the advice of someone with a good dash of worldly wisdom might not be amiss. Frankly, the situation is this: Miss Meredith is under suspicion of having committed murder. The same applies to me and to the two other people who were in the room last night. Such a situation is not agreeable – and it has its own peculiar difficulties and dangers which someone as young and inexperienced as you are, Miss Meredith, might not recognize. In my opinion, you ought to put yourself in the hands of a thoroughly good solicitor. Perhaps you have already done so?'

Anne Meredith shook her head.

'I never thought of it.'

'Exactly as I suspected. Have you got a good man – a London man, for choice?'

Again Anne shook her head.

'I've hardly ever needed a solicitor.'

'There's Mr Bury,' said Rhoda. 'But he's about a hundred and two, and quite gaga.'

'If you'll allow me to advise you, Miss Meredith, I recommend your going to Mr Myherne, my own solicitor. Jacobs, Peel & Jacobs is the actual name of the firm. They're first-class people, and they know all the ropes.'

Anne had got paler. She sat down.

'Is it really necessary?' she asked in a low voice.

'I should say emphatically so. There are all sorts of legal pitfalls.'

'Are these people very – expensive?'

'That doesn't matter a bit,' said Rhoda. 'That will be *quite* all right, Major Despard. I think everything you say is quite true. Anne ought to be protected.'

'Their charges will, I think, be quite reasonable,' said Despard. He added seriously: 'I really do think it's a wise course, Miss Meredith.'

'Very well,' said Anne slowly. 'I'll do it if you think so.'

'Good.'

Rhoda said warmly: 'I think it's awfully nice of you, Major Despard. Really frightfully nice.'

Anne said, 'Thank you.'

She hesitated, and then said: 'Did you say Superintendent Battle was coming here?'

'Yes. You mustn't be alarmed by that. It's inevitable.'

'Oh, I know. As a matter of fact, I've been expecting him.'

Rhoda said impulsively: 'Poor darling – it's nearly killing her, this business. It's such a shame – so frightfully unfair.'

Despard said: 'I agree – it's a pretty beastly business – dragging a young girl into an affair of this kind. If anyone wanted to stick a knife into Shaitana, they ought to have chosen some other place or time.'

Rhoda asked squarely: 'Who do you think did it? Dr Roberts or that Mrs Lorrimer?'

A very faint smile stirred Despard's moustache.

'May have done it myself, for all you know.'

'Oh, no,' cried Rhoda. 'Anne and I know *you* didn't do it.'

He looked at them both with kindly eyes.

A nice pair of kids. Touchingly full of faith and trust. A timid little creature, the Meredith girl. Never mind, Myherne would see her through. The other was a fighter. He doubted if she would have crumpled up in the same way if she'd been in her friend's place. Nice girls. He'd like to know more about them.

These thoughts passed through his mind. Aloud he said: 'Never take anything for granted, Miss Dawes. I don't set as much value on human life as most people do. All this hysterical fuss about road deaths, for instance. Man is always in danger – from traffic, from germs, from a hundred and one things. As well be killed one way as another. The moment you begin being careful of yourself – adopting as your motto "Safety First" – you might as well be dead, in my opinion.'

'Oh, I do agree with you,' cried Rhoda. 'I think one ought to live frightfully dangerously – if one gets the chance, that is. But life, on the whole, is terribly tame.'

'It has its moments.'

'Yes, for *you*. You go to out-of-the-way places and get mauled by tigers and shoot things and jiggers bury themselves in your toes and insects sting you, and everything's terribly uncomfortable but frightfully thrilling.'

'Well, Miss Meredith has had her thrill, too. I don't suppose it often happens that you've actually *been in the room* while a murder was committed—'

'Oh, don't!' cried Anne.

He said quickly: 'I'm sorry.'

But Rhoda said with a sigh: 'Of course it was awful – but it was exciting, too! I don't think Anne appreciates that side of it. You know, I think that Mrs Oliver is thrilled to the core to have been there that night.'

'Mrs—? Oh, your fat friend who writes the books about the unpronounceable Finn. Is she trying her hand at detection in real life?'

'She wants to.'

'Well, let's wish her luck. It would be amusing if she put one over on Battle and Co.'

'What is Superintendent Battle like?' asked Rhoda curiously.

Major Despard said gravely: 'He's an extraordinarily astute man. A man of remarkable ability.'

'Oh!' said Rhoda. 'Anne said he looked rather stupid.'

'That, I should imagine, is part of Battle's stock-in-trade. But we mustn't make any mistakes. Battle's no fool.'

He rose.

'Well, I must be off. There's just one other thing I'd like to say.'

Anne had risen also.

'Yes?' she said as she held out her hand.

Despard paused a minute, picking his words carefully. He took her hand and retained it in his. He looked straight into the wide, beautiful grey eyes.

'Don't be offended with me,' he said. 'I just want to say this: It's humanly possible that there may be some feature of your acquaintanceship with Shaitana that you don't want to come out. If so – don't be angry, please' (he felt the instinctive pull of her hand) – 'you are perfectly within your rights in refusing to answer any questions Battle may ask unless your solicitor is present.'

Anne tore her hand away. Her eyes opened, their grey darkening with anger.

'There's nothing – *nothing*! I hardly knew the beastly man.'

'Sorry,' said Major Despard. 'Thought I ought to mention it.'

'It's quite true,' said Rhoda. 'Anne barely knew him. She didn't like him much, but he gave frightfully good parties.'

'That,' said Major Despard grimly, 'seems to have been the only justification for the late Mr Shaitana's existence.'

Anne said in a cold voice: 'Superintendent Battle can ask me anything he likes. I've nothing to hide – *nothing*.'

Despard said very gently: 'Please forgive me.'

She looked at him. Her anger dwindled. She smiled – it was a very sweet smile.

'It's all right,' she said. 'You meant it kindly, I know.'

She held out her hand again. He took it and said: 'We're in the same boat, you know. We ought to be pals . . .'

It was Anne who went with him to the gate. When she came back Rhoda was staring out of the window and whistling. She turned as her friend entered the room.

'He's frightfully attractive, Anne.'

'He's nice, isn't he?'

'A great deal more than nice . . . I've got an absolute passion for him. Why wasn't I at that damned dinner instead of you? I'd have enjoyed the excitement – the net closing round me – the shadow of the scaffold—'

'No, you wouldn't. You're talking nonsense, Rhoda.'

Anne's voice was sharp. Then it softened as she said: 'It was nice of him to come all this way – for a stranger – a girl he's only met once.'

'Oh, he fell for you. Obviously. Men don't do purely disinterested kindnesses. He wouldn't have come toddling down if you'd been cross-eyed and covered with pimples!'

'Don't you think so?'

'I do not, my good idiot. Mrs Oliver's a *much* more disinterested party.'

'I don't like her,' said Anne abruptly. 'I had a sort of feeling about her . . . I wonder what she really came for?'

'The usual suspicions of your own sex. I dare say Major Despard had an axe to grind, if it comes to that.'

'I'm sure he hadn't,' cried Anne hotly.

Then she blushed as Rhoda Dawes laughed.

14

THIRD VISITOR

SUPERINTENDENT BATTLE arrived at Wallingford about six o'clock. It was his intention to learn as much as he could from innocent local gossip before interviewing Miss Anne Meredith.

It was not difficult to glean such information as there was. Without committing himself definitely to any statement, the superintendent nevertheless gave several different impressions of his rank and calling in life.

At least two people would have said confidently that he was a London builder come down to see about a new wing to be added to the cottage, from another you would have learned that he was 'one of these weekenders wanting to take a furnished cottage', and two more would have said they knew positively, and for a fact, that he was the representative of a hardcourt tennis firm.

The information that the superintendent gathered was entirely favourable.

'Wendon Cottage? Yes, that's right – on the Marlbury Road. You can't miss it. Yes, two young ladies. Miss Dawes and Miss Meredith. Very nice young ladies, too. The quiet kind.

'Here for years? Oh, no, not that long. Just over two years. September quarter they came in. Mr Pickersgill they bought it from. Never used it much, he didn't, after his wife died.'

Superintendent Battle's informant had never heard they came from Northumberland. London, *he* thought they came from. Popular in the neighbourhood, though some people were old-fashioned and didn't think two young ladies ought to be living alone. But very quiet, they were. None of this cocktail-drinking week-end lot. Miss Rhoda, she was the dashing one. Miss Meredith was the quiet one. Yes, it was Miss Dawes what paid the bills. She was the one had got the money.

The superintendent's researches at last led him inevitably to Mrs Astwell – who 'did' for the ladies at Wendon Cottage.

Mrs Astwell was a loquacious lady.

'Well, no, sir. I hardly think they'd want to sell. Not so soon. They only got in two years ago. I've done for them from the beginning, yes, sir. Eight o'clock till twelve – those are my hours. Very nice, lively young ladies, always ready for a joke or a bit of fun. Not stuck-up at all.'

'Well, of course, I couldn't say if it's the same Miss Dawes *you* knew, sir – the same *family*, I mean. It's my fancy her home's in Devonshire. She gets the cream sent her now and again, and says it reminds her of home; so I think it must be.

'As you say, sir, it's sad for so many young ladies having to earn their livings nowadays. These young ladies aren't what you'd call rich, but they have a very pleasant life. It's Miss Dawes has got the money, of course. Miss Anne's her companion, in a manner of speaking, I suppose you might say. The cottage belongs to Miss Dawes.

'I couldn't really say what part Miss Anne comes from. I've heard her mention the Isle of Wight, and I know she doesn't like the North of England; and she and Miss Rhoda were together in Devonshire, because I've heard them joke about the hills and talk about the pretty coves and beaches.'

The flow went on. Every now and then Superintendent Battle made a mental note. Later, a cryptic word or two was jotted down in his little book.

At half-past eight that evening he walked up the path to the door of Wendon Cottage.

It was opened to him by a tall, dark girl wearing a frock of orange cretonne.

'Miss Meredith live here?' inquired Superintendent Battle.

He looked very wooden and soldierly.

'Yes, she does.'

'I'd like to speak to her, please. Superintendent Battle.'

He was immediately favoured with a piercing stare.

'Come in,' said Rhoda Dawes, drawing back from the doorway.

Anne Meredith was sitting in a cosy chair by the fire, sipping coffee. She was wearing embroidered crêpe-de-chine pyjamas.

'It's Superintendent Battle,' said Rhoda, ushering in the guest.

Anne rose and came forward with outstretched hand.

'A bit late for a call,' said Battle. 'But I wanted to find you in, and it's been a fine day.'

Anne smiled.

'Will you have some coffee, Superintendent? Rhoda, fetch another cup.'

'Well, it's very kind of you, Miss Meredith.'

'We think we make rather good coffee,' said Anne.

She indicated a chair, and Superintendent Battle sat down. Rhoda brought a cup, and Anne poured out his coffee. The fire crackled and the flowers in the vases made an agreeable impression upon the superintendent.

It was a pleasant homey atmosphere. Anne seemed self-possessed and at her ease, and the other girl continued to stare at him with devouring interest.

'We've been expecting you,' said Anne.

Her tone was almost reproachful. 'Why have you neglected me?' it seemed to say.

'Sorry, Miss Meredith. I've had a lot of routine work to do.'

'Satisfactory?'

'Not particularly. But it all has to be done. I've turned Dr Roberts inside out, so to speak. And the same for Mrs Lorrimer. And now I've come to do the same for you, Miss Meredith.'

Anne smiled.

'I'm ready.'

'What about Major Despard?' asked Rhoda.

'Oh, he won't be overlooked. I can promise you that,' said Battle.

He set down his coffee-cup and looked towards Anne. She sat up a little straighter in her chair.

'I'm quite ready, Superintendent. What do you want to know?'

'Well, roughly, all about yourself, Miss Meredith.'

'I'm quite a respectable person,' said Anne, smiling.

'She's led a blameless life, too,' said Rhoda. 'I can answer for that.'

'Well, that's very nice,' said Superintendent Battle cheerfully. 'You've known Miss Meredith a long time, then?'

'We were at school together,' said Rhoda. 'What ages ago it seems, doesn't it, Anne?'

'So long ago, you can hardly remember it, I suppose,' said Battle with a chuckle. 'Now, then, Miss Meredith, I'm afraid I'm going to be rather like those forms you fill up for passports.'

'I was born—' began Anne.

'Of poor but honest parents,' Rhoda put in.

Superintendent Battle held up a slightly reproving hand.

'Now, now, young lady,' he said.

'Rhoda, darling,' said Anne gravely. 'It's serious, this.'

'Sorry,' said Rhoda.

'Now, Miss Meredith, you were born – where?'

'At Quetta, in India.'

'Ah, yes. Your people were Army folk?'

'Yes – my father was Major John Meredith. My mother died when I was eleven. Father retired when I was fifteen and went to live in Cheltenham. He died when I was eighteen and left practically no money.'

Battle nodded his head sympathetically.

'Bit of a shock to you, I expect.'

'It was, rather. I always knew that we weren't well off, but to find there was practically nothing – well, that's different.'

'What did you do, Miss Meredith?'

'I had to take a job. I hadn't been particularly well educated and I wasn't clever. I didn't know typing or shorthand, or anything. A friend in Cheltenham found me a job with friends of hers – two small boys home in the holidays, and general help in the house.'

'Name, please?'

'That was Mrs Eldon, The Larches, Ventnor. I stayed there for two years, and then the Eldons went abroad. Then I went to a Mrs Deering.'

'My aunt,' put in Rhoda.

'Yes, Rhoda got me the job. I was very happy. Rhoda used to come and stay sometimes, and we had great fun.'

'What were you there – companion?'

'Yes – it amounted to that.'

'More like under-gardener,' said Rhoda.

She explained: 'My Aunt Emily is just mad on gardening. Anne spent most of her time weeding or putting in bulbs.'

'And you left Mrs Deering?'

'Her health got worse, and she had to have a regular nurse.'

'She's got cancer,' said Rhoda. 'Poor darling, she has to have morphia and things like that.'

'She had been very kind to me. I was very sorry to go,' went on Anne.

'I was looking about for a cottage,' said Rhoda, 'and wanting someone to share it with me. Daddy's married again – not my sort at all. I asked Anne to come here with me, and she's been here ever since.'

'Well, that certainly seems a most blameless life,' said Battle. 'Let's just get the dates clear. You were with Mrs Eldon two years, you say. By the way, what is her address now?'

'She's in Palestine. Her husband has some Government appointment out there – I'm not sure what.'

'Ah, well, I can soon find out. And after that you went to Mrs Deering?'

'I was with her three years,' said Anne quickly. 'Her address is Marsh Dene, Little Hembury, Devon.'

'I see,' said Battle. 'So you are now twenty-five, Miss Meredith. Now, there's just one thing more – the name and address of a couple of people in Cheltenham who knew you and your father.'

Anne supplied him with these.

'Now, about this trip to Switzerland – where you met Mr Shaitana. Did you go alone there – or was Miss Dawes here with you?'

'We went out together. We joined some other people. There was a party of eight.'

'Tell me about your meeting with Mr Shaitana.'

Anne crinkled her brows.

'There's really nothing to tell. He was just there. We knew him in the way you do know people in a hotel. He got first prize at the fancy-dress ball. He went as Mephistopheles.'

Superintendent Battle sighed.

'Yes, that always was his favourite effect.'

'He really was marvellous,' said Rhoda. 'He hardly had to make up at all.'

The superintendent looked from one girl to the other.

'Which of you two young ladies knew him best?'

Anne hesitated. It was Rhoda who answered.

'Both the same to begin with. Awfully little, that is. You see, our crowd was the ski-ing lot, and we were off doing runs most days and dancing together in the evenings. But then Shaitana seemed to take rather a fancy to Anne. You know, went out of his way to pay her compliments, and all that. We ragged her about it, rather.'

'I just think he did it to annoy me,' said Anne. 'Because I didn't like him. I think it amused him to make me feel embarrassed.'

Rhoda said, laughing: 'We told Anne it would be a nice rich marriage for her. She got simply wild with us.'

'Perhaps,' said Battle, 'you'd give me the names of the other people in your party?'

'You aren't what I'd call a trustful man,' said Rhoda. 'Do you think that every word we're telling you is downright lies?'

Superintendent Battle twinkled.

'I'm going to make quite sure it isn't, anyway,' he said.

'You *are* suspicious,' said Rhoda.

She scribbled some names on a piece of paper and gave it to him.

Battle rose.

'Well, thank you very much, Miss Meredith,' he said. 'As Miss Dawes says, you seem to have led a particularly blameless life. I don't think you need worry much. It's odd the way Mr Shaitana's manner changed to you. You'll excuse my asking, but he didn't ask you to marry him – or – er – pester you with attentions of another kind?'

'He didn't try to seduce her,' said Rhoda helpfully. 'If that's what you mean.'

Anne was blushing.

'Nothing of the kind,' she said. 'He was always most polite and – and – formal. It was just his elaborate manners that made me uncomfortable.'

'And little things he said or hinted?'

'Yes – at least – no. He never hinted things.'

'Sorry. These lady-killers do sometimes. Well, goodnight, Miss Meredith. Thank you very much. Excellent coffee. Goodnight, Miss Dawes.'

'There,' said Rhoda as Anne came back into the room after shutting the front door after Battle. 'That's over, and not so very terrible. He's a nice fatherly man, and he evidently doesn't suspect you in the least. It was all ever so much better than I expected.'

Anne sank down with a sigh.

'It was really quite easy,' she said. 'It was silly of me to work myself up so. I thought he'd try to brow-beat me – like K.C.s on the stage.'

'He looks sensible,' said Rhoda. 'He'd know well enough you're not a murdering kind of female.'

She hesitated and then said: 'I say, Anne, you didn't mention being at Croftways. Did you forget?'

Anne said slowly: 'I didn't think it counted. I was only there a few months. And there's no one to ask about me there. I can write and tell him if you think it matters; but I'm sure it doesn't. Let's leave it.'

'Right, if you say so.'

Rhoda rose and turned on the wireless.

A raucous voice said: 'You have just heard the Black Nubians play "Why Do You Tell Me Lies, Baby?"'

15

MAJOR DESPARD

MAJOR DESPARD came out of the Albany, turned sharply into Regent Street and jumped on a bus.

It was the quiet time of day – the top of the bus had very few seats occupied. Despard made his way forward and sat down on the front seat.

He had jumped on the bus while it was going. Now it came to a halt, took up passengers and made its way once more up Regent Street.

A second traveller climbed the steps, made his way forward and sat down in the front seat on the other side.

Despard did not notice the new-comer, but after a few minutes a tentative voice murmured: 'It is a good view of London, is it not, that one gets from the top of a bus?'

Despard turned his head. He looked puzzled for a moment, then his face cleared.

'I beg your pardon, M. Poirot. I didn't see it was you. Yes, as you say, one has a good bird's eye view of the world from here. It was better, though, in the old days, when there wasn't all this caged-in glass business.'

Poirot sighed.

'*Tout de même*, it was not always agreeable in the wet weather when the inside was full. And there is much wet weather in this country.'

'Rain? Rain never did any harm to anyone.'

'You are in error,' said Poirot. 'It leads often to a *fluxion de poitrine*.'

Despard smiled.

'I see you belong to the well-wrapped-up school, M. Poirot.'

Poirot was indeed well equipped against any treachery of an autumn day. He wore a greatcoat and a muffler.

'Rather odd, running into you like this,' said Despard.

He did not see the smile that the muffler concealed. There was nothing odd in this encounter. Having ascertained a likely hour for Despard to leave his rooms, Poirot had been waiting for him. He had prudently not risked leaping on the bus, but he had trotted after it to its next stopping-place and boarded it there.

'True. We have not seen each other since the evening at Mr Shaitana's,' he replied.

'Aren't you taking a hand in that business?' asked Despard.

Poirot scratched his ear delicately.

'I reflect,' he said. 'I reflect a good deal. To run to and fro, to make the investigations, that, no. It does not suit my age, my temperament, or my figure.'

Despard said unexpectedly: 'Reflect, eh? Well, you might do worse. There's too much rushing about nowadays. If people sat tight and thought about a thing before they tackled it, there'd be less mess-ups than there are.'

'Is that your procedure in life, Major Despard?'

'Usually,' said the other simply. 'Get your bearings, figure out your route, weigh up the pros and cons, make your decision – and stick to it.'

His mouth set grimly.

'And, after that, nothing will turn you from your path, eh?' asked Poirot.

'Oh, I don't say that. No use in being pig-headed over things. If you've made a mistake, admit it.'

'But I imagine that you do not often make a mistake, Major Despard.'

'We all make mistakes, M. Poirot.'

'Some of us,' said Poirot with a certain coldness, possibly due to the pronoun the other had used, 'make fewer than others.'

Despard looked at him, smiled slightly and said: 'Don't you ever have failure, M. Poirot?'

'The last time was twenty-eight years ago,' said Poirot with dignity. 'And even then, there were circumstances – but no matter.'

'That seems a pretty good record,' said Despard.

He added: 'What about Shaitana's death? That doesn't count, I suppose, since it isn't officially your business.'

'It is not my business – no. But, all the same, it offends my *amour propre*. I consider it an impertinence, you comprehend, for a murder to be committed under my very nose – by someone who mocks himself at my ability to solve it!'

'Not under *your* nose only,' said Despard dryly. 'Under the nose of the Criminal Investigation Department also.'

'That was probably a bad mistake,' said Poirot gravely. 'The good square Superintendent Battle, he may look wooden, but he is not wooden in the head – not at all.'

'I agree,' said Despard. 'That stolidity is a pose. He's a very clever and able officer.'

'And I think he is very active in the case.'

'Oh, he's active enough. See a nice quiet soldierly-looking fellow on one of the back seats?'

Poirot looked over his shoulder.

'There is no one here now but ourselves.'

'Oh, well, he's inside, then. He never loses me. Very efficient fellow. Varies his appearance, too, from time to time. Quite artistic about it.'

'Ah, but that would not deceive you. You have the very quick and accurate eye.'

'I never forget a face – even a black one – and that's a lot more than most people can say.'

'You are just the person I need,' said Poirot. 'What a chance, meeting you today! I need someone with a good eye and a good memory. *Malheureusement* the two seldom go together. I have asked the Dr Roberts a question, without result, and the same with Madame Lorrimer. Now, I will try you and see if I get what I want. Cast your mind back to the room in which you played cards at Mr Shaitana's, and tell me what you remember of it.'

Despard looked puzzled.

'I don't quite understand.'

'Give me a description of the room – the furnishings – the objects in it.'

'I don't know that I'm much of a hand at that sort of thing,' said Despard slowly. 'It was a rotten sort of room – to my mind. Not a man's room at all. A lot of brocade and silk and stuff. Sort of room a fellow like Shaitana would have.'

'But to particularise—'

Despard shook his head.

'Afraid I didn't notice . . . He'd got some good rugs. Two Bokharas and three or four really good Persian ones, including a Hamadan and a Tabriz. Rather a good eland head – no, that was in the hall. From Rowland Ward's, I expect.'

'You do not think that the late Mr Shaitana was one to go out and shoot wild beasts?'

'Not he. Never potted anything but sitting game, I'll bet. What else was there? I'm sorry to fail you, but I really can't help much. Any amount of knick-knacks lying about. Tables were thick with them. Only thing I noticed was a rather jolly idol. Easter Island, I should say. Highly polished wood. You don't see many of them. There was some Malay stuff, too. No, I'm afraid I can't help you.'

'No matter,' said Poirot, looking slightly crestfallen.

He went on: 'Do you know, Mrs Lorrimer, she has the most amazing card memory! She could tell me the bidding and play of nearly every hand. It was astonishing.'

Despard shrugged his shoulders.

'Some women are like that. Because they play pretty well all day long, I suppose.'

'You could not do it, eh?'

The other shook his head.

'I just remember a couple of hands. One where I could have got game in diamonds – and Roberts bluffed me out of it. Went down himself, but we didn't double him, worse luck. I remember a no trumper, too. Tricky business – every card wrong. We went down a couple – lucky not to have gone down more.'

'Do you play much bridge, Major Despard?'

'No, I'm not a regular player. It's a good game, though.'

'You prefer it to poker?'

'I do personally. Poker's too much of a gamble.'

Poirot said thoughtfully: 'I do not think Mr Shaitana played any game – any card game, that is.'

'There's only one game that Shaitana played consistently,' said Despard grimly.

'And that?'

'A lowdown game.'

Poirot was silent for a minute, then he said: 'Is it that you *know* that? Or do you just *think* it?'

Despard went brick red.

'Meaning one oughtn't to say things without giving chapter and verse? I suppose that's true. Well, it's accurate enough. I happen to *know*. On the other hand, I'm not prepared to give chapter and verse. Such information as I've got came to me privately.'

'Meaning a woman or women are concerned?'

'Yes. Shaitana, like the dirty dog he was, preferred to deal with women.'

'You think he was a blackmailer? That is interesting.'

Despard shook his head.

'No, no, you've misunderstood me. In a way, Shaitana was a blackmailer, but not the common or garden sort. He wasn't after money. He was a spiritual blackmailer, if there can be such a thing.'

'And he got out of it – what?'

'He got a kick out of it. That's the only way I can put it. He got a thrill out of seeing people quail and flinch. I suppose it made him feel less of a louse and more of a man. And it's a very effective pose with women. He'd only got to hint that he knew everything – and they'd start telling him a lot of things that perhaps he didn't know. That would tickle his sense of humour. Then he'd strut about in his Mephistophelian attitude of "I know everything! I am the great Shaitana!" The man was an ape!'

'So you think that he frightened Miss Meredith that way,' said Poirot slowly.

'Miss Meredith?' Despard stared. 'I wasn't thinking of her. She isn't the kind to be afraid of a man like Shaitana.'

'*Pardon*. You meant Mrs Lorrimer.'

'No, no, no. You misunderstand me. I was speaking generally. It wouldn't be easy to frighten Mrs Lorrimer. And she's not the kind of woman who you can imagine having a guilty secret. No, I was not thinking of anyone in particular. '

'It was the general method to which you referred?'

'Exactly.'

'There is no doubt,' said Poirot slowly, 'that what you call a Dago often has a very clever understanding of women. He knows how to approach them. He worms secrets out of them—'

He paused.

Despard broke in impatiently: 'It's absurd. The man was a mountebank – nothing really dangerous about him. And yet women were afraid of him. Ridiculously so.'

He started up suddenly.

'Hallo, I've overshot the mark. Got too interested in what we were discussing. Goodbye, M. Poirot. Look down and you'll see my faithful shadow leave the bus when I do.'

He hurried to the back and down the steps. The conductor's bell jangled. But a double pull sounded before it had time to stop.

Looking down to the street below, Poirot noticed Despard striding back along the pavement. He did not trouble to pick out the following figure. Something else was interesting him.

'No one in particular,' he murmured to himself. 'Now, I wonder.'

THE EVIDENCE OF ELSIE BATT

Sergeant O'Connor was unkindly nicknamed by his colleagues at the Yard: 'The maidservant's prayer.'

There was no doubt that he was an extremely handsome man. Tall, erect, broad-shouldered, it was less the regularity of his features than the roguish and daredevil spark in his eye which made him so irresistible to the fair sex. It was indubitable that Sergeant O'Connor got results, and got them quickly.

So rapid was he, that only four days after the murder of Mr Shaitana, Sergeant O'Connor was sitting in the three-and-sixpenny seats at the *Willy Nilly Revue* side by side with Miss Elsie Batt, late parlourmaid to Mrs Craddock of 117 North Audley Street.

Having laid his line of approach carefully, Sergeant O'Connor was just launching the great offensive.

'Reminds me,' he was saying, 'of the way one of my old governors used to carry on. Name of Craddock. He was an odd cuss, if you like.'

'Craddock,' said Elsie. 'I was with some Craddocks once.'

'Well, that's funny. Wonder whether they were the same?'

'Lived in North Audley Street, they did,' said Elsie.

'My lot were going to London when I left them,' said O'Connor promptly. 'Yes, I believe it *was* North Audley Street. Mrs Craddock was rather a one for the gents.'

Elsie tossed her head.

'I'd no patience with her. Always finding fault and grumbling. Nothing you did right.'

'Her husband got some of it, too, didn't he?'

'She was always complaining he neglected her – that he didn't understand her. And she was always saying how bad her health was and gasping and groaning. Not ill at all, if you ask *me*.'

O'Connor slapped his knee.

'Got it. Wasn't there something about her and some doctor? A bit too thick or something?'

'You mean Dr Roberts? He was a nice gentleman, he was.'

'You girls, you're all alike,' said Sergeant O'Connor. 'The moment a man's a bad lot, all the girls stick up for him. I know his kind.'

'No, you don't, and you're all wrong about him. There wasn't anything of that kind about him. Wasn't his fault, was it, if Mrs Craddock was always sending for him? What's a doctor to do? If you ask me, he didn't think nothing of her at all, except as a patient. It was all her doing. Wouldn't leave him alone, she wouldn't.'

'That's all very well, Elsie. Don't mind me calling you Elsie, do you? Feel as though I'd known you all my life.'

'Well, you haven't! Elsie, indeed.'

She tossed her head.

'Oh, very well, Miss Batt.' He gave her a glance. 'As I was saying, that's all very well, but the husband, he cut up rough, all the same, didn't he?'

'He was a bit ratty one day,' admitted Elsie. 'But, if you ask me, he was ill at the time. He died just after, you know.'

'I remember – died of something queer, didn't he?'

'Something Japanese, it was – all from a new shaving-brush he'd got. Seems awful, doesn't it, that they're not more careful? I've not fancied anything Japanese since.'

'Buy British, that's my motto,' said Sergeant O'Connor sententiously. 'And you were saying he and the doctor had a row?'

Elsie nodded, enjoying herself as she re-lived past scandals.

'Hammer and tongs, they went at it,' she said. 'At least, the master did. Dr Roberts was ever so quiet. Just said, "Nonsense." And, "What have you got into your head?"'

'This was at the house, I suppose?'

'Yes. She'd sent for him. And then she and the master had words, and in the middle of it Dr Roberts arrived, and the master went for him.'

'What did he say exactly?'

'Well, of course, I wasn't supposed to hear. It was all in the missus's bedroom. I thought something was up, so I got the dustpan and did the stairs. I wasn't going to miss anything.'

Sergeant O'Connor heartily concurred in this sentiment, reflecting how fortunate it was that Elsie was being approached unofficially. On interrogation by Sergeant O'Connor of the Police, she would have virtuously protested that she had not overheard anything at all.

'As I say,' went on Elsie, 'Dr Roberts, he was very quiet – the master was doing all the shouting.'

'What was he saying?' asked O'Connor, for the second time approaching the vital point.

'Abusing of him proper,' said Elsie with relish.

'How do you mean?'

Would the girl never come to actual words and phrases?

'Well, I didn't understand a lot of it,' admitted Elsie. 'There were a lot of long words, "unprofessional conduct", and "taking advantage", and things like that – and I heard him say he'd get Dr Roberts struck off the – medical register, would it be? Something like that.'

'That's right,' said O'Connor. 'Complain to the Medical Council.'

'Yes, he said something like that. And the missus was going on in sort of hysterics, saying, 'You never cared for me. You neglected me. You left me alone." And I heard her say that Dr Roberts had been an angel of goodness to her.

'And then the doctor, he came through into the dressing-room with the master and shut the door of the bedroom – I heard it – and he said quite plain: "My good man, don't you realize your wife's hysterical? She doesn't know what she's saying. To tell you the truth, it's been a very difficult and trying case, and I'd have thrown it up long ago if I'd thought it was con – con" – some long word; oh, yes, "consistent" – that was it – "consistent with my duty." That's what he said. He said something about not over-stepping a boundary, too – something between doctor and patient.

'He got the master quietened a bit, and then he said: "You'll be late at your office, you know. You'd better be off. Just think things over quietly. I think you'll realize that the whole business is a mare's nest. I'll just wash my hands here before I go on to my next case. Now, you think it over, my dear fellow. I can assure you that the whole thing arises out of your wife's disordered imagination." And the master, he said, "I don't know what to think."

'And he come out – and, of course, I was brushing hard – but he never even noticed me. I thought afterwards he looked ill. The doctor, he was whistling quite cheerily and washing his hands in the dressing-room, where there was hot and cold laid on. And presently he came out, too, with his bag, and he spoke to me very nicely and cheerily, as he always did, and he went down the stairs, quite cheerful and gay and his usual self. So, you see, I'm quite sure as he hadn't done anything wrong. It was all her.'

'And then Craddock got this anthrax?'

'Yes, I think he'd got it already. The mistress, she nursed him very devoted, but he died. Lovely wreaths there was at the funeral.'

'And afterwards? Did Dr Roberts come to the house again?'

'No, he didn't, Nosey! You've got some grudge against him. I tell you there was nothing in it. If there were, he'd have married her when the master was dead, wouldn't he? And he never did. No such fool. He'd taken her measure all right. She used to ring him up, though, but somehow he was never in. And then she sold the house, and we all got our notices, and she went abroad to Egypt.'

'And you didn't see Dr Roberts in all that time?'

'No. *She* did, because she went to him to have this – what do you call it? – 'noculation against the typhoid fever. She came back with her arm ever so sore with it. If you ask me, he made it clear to her then that there was nothing doing. She didn't ring him up no more, and she went off very cheerful with a lovely lot of new clothes – all light colours, although it was the middle of winter, but she said it would be all sunshine and hot out there.'

'That's right,' said Sergeant O'Connor. 'It's too hot sometimes, I've heard. She died out there. You know that, I suppose?'

'No, indeed I didn't. Well, fancy that! She may have been worse than I thought, poor soul.'

She added with a sigh: 'I wonder what they did with all that lovely lot of clothes. They're blacks out there, so they couldn't wear them.'

'You'd have looked a treat in them, I expect,' said Sergeant O'Connor.

'Impudence,' said Elsie.

'Well, you won't have my impudence much longer,' said Sergeant O'Connor. 'I've got to go away on business for my firm.'

'You going for long?'

'May be going abroad,' said the Sergeant.

Elsie's face fell.

Though unacquainted with Lord Byron's famous poem, 'I never loved a dear gazelle', etc., its sentiments were at that moment hers. She thought to herself: 'Funny how all the really attractive ones never come to anything. Oh, well, there's always Fred.'

Which is gratifying, since it shows that the sudden incursion of Sergeant O'Connor into Elsie's life did not affect it permanently. Fred may even have been the gainer!

THE EVIDENCE OF RHODA DAWES

RHODA DAWES came out of Debenham's and stood meditatively upon the pavement. Indecision was written all over her face. It was an expressive face; each fleeting emotion showed itself in a quickly varying expression.

Quite plainly at this moment Rhoda's face said, 'Shall I or shan't I? I'd like to . . . But perhaps I'd better not . . .'

The commissionaire said, 'Taxi, miss?' to her, hopefully.

Rhoda shook her head.

A stout woman carrying parcels, with an eager 'shopping early for Christmas' expression on her face, cannoned into her severely, but still Rhoda stood stockstill, trying to make up her mind.

Chaotic odds and ends of thoughts flashed through her mind.

'After all, why shouldn't I? She asked me to – but perhaps it's just a thing she stays to everyone . . . She doesn't mean it to be taken seriously . . . Well, after all, Anne didn't want me. She made it quite clear she'd rather go with Major Despard to the solicitor man alone . . . And why shouldn't she? I mean, three *is* a crowd . . . And it isn't really any business of mine . . . It isn't as though I particularly *wanted* to see Major Despard . . . He is nice, though . . . I think he must have fallen for Anne. Men don't take a lot of trouble unless they have . . . I mean, it's never just kindness . . .'

A messenger boy bumped into Rhoda and said, 'Beg pardon, miss,' in a reproachful tone.

'Oh dear,' thought Rhoda. 'I can't go on standing here all day. Just because I'm such an idiot that I can't make up my mind . . . I think that coat and skirt's going to be awfully nice. I wonder if brown would have been more useful than green? No, I don't think so. Well, come on, shall I go, or shan't I? Half-past three – it's quite a good time – I mean, it doesn't look as though I'm cadging a meal or anything. I might just go and look, anyway.'

She plunged across the road, turned to the right, and then to the left, up Harley Street, finally pausing by the block of flats always airily described by Mrs Oliver as 'all among the nursing homes'.

'Well, she can't eat me,' thought Rhoda, and plunged boldly into the building.

Mrs Oliver's flat was on the top floor. A uniformed attendant whisked her up in a lift and decanted her on a smart new mat outside a bright green door.

'This is awful,' thought Rhoda. 'Worse than dentists. I must go through with it now, though.'

Pink with embarrassment, she pushed the bell.

The door was opened by an elderly maid.

'Is – could I – is Mrs Oliver at home?' asked Rhoda.

The maid drew back, Rhoda entered; she was shown into a very untidy drawing-room. The maid said: 'What name shall I say, please?'

'Oh – er – Miss Dawes – Miss Rhoda Dawes.'

The maid withdrew. After what seemed to Rhoda about a hundred years, but was really exactly a minute and forty-five seconds, the maid returned.

'Will you step this way, miss?'

Pinker than ever, Rhoda followed her. Along a passage, round a corner, a door was opened. Nervously she entered into what seemed at first to her startled eyes to be an African forest!

Birds – masses of birds, parrots, macaws, birds unknown to ornithology – twined themselves in and out of what seemed to be a primeval forest. In the middle of this riot of bird and vegetable life, Rhoda perceived a battered kitchen table with a typewriter on it, masses of typescript littered all over the floor and Mrs Oliver, her hair in wild confusion, rising from a somewhat rickety-looking chair.

'My dear, how nice to see you,' said Mrs Oliver, holding out a carbon-stained hand and trying with her other hand to smooth her hair, a quite impossible proceeding.

A paper bag, touched by her elbow, fell from the desk, and apples rolled energetically all over the floor.

'Never mind, my dear, don't bother, someone will pick them up sometime.'

Rather breathless, Rhoda rose from a stooping position with five apples in her grasp.

'Oh, thank you – no, I shouldn't put them back in the bag. I think it's got a hole in it. Put them on the mantelpiece. That's right. Now, then, sit down and let's talk.'

Rhoda accepted a second battered chair and focused her eyes on her hostess.

'I say, I'm terribly sorry. Am I interrupting, or anything?' she asked breathlessly.

'Well, you are and you aren't,' said Mrs Oliver. 'I *am* working, as you see. But that dreadful Finn of mine has got himself terribly tangled up. He did some awfully clever deduction with a dish of French beans, and now he's just detected deadly poison in the sage-and-onion stuffing of the Michaelmas goose, and I've just remembered that French beans are over by Michaelmas.'

Thrilled by this peep into the inner world of creative detective fiction, Rhoda said breathlessly, 'They might be tinned.'

'They might, of course,' said Mrs Oliver doubtfully. 'But it would rather spoil the point. I'm always getting tangled up in horticulture and things like that. People write to me and say I've got the wrong flowers all out together. As though it mattered – and, anyway, they are all out together in a London shop.'

'Of course it doesn't matter,' said Rhoda loyally. 'Oh, Mrs Oliver, it must be marvellous to write.'

Mrs Oliver rubbed her forehead with a carbonny finger and said: 'Why?'

'Oh,' said Rhoda, a little taken aback. 'Because it must. It must be wonderful just to sit down and write off a whole book.'

'It doesn't happen exactly like that,' said Mrs Oliver. 'One actually has to *think*, you know. And thinking is always a bore. And you have to plan things. And then one gets stuck every now and then, and you feel you'll never get out of the mess – but you do! Writing's not particularly enjoyable. It's hard work, like everything else.'

'It doesn't seem like work,' said Rhoda.

'Not to *you*,' said Mrs Oliver, 'because you don't have to do it! It feels very like work to me. Some days I can only keep going by repeating over and over to myself the amount of money I might get for my next serial rights. That spurs you on, you know. So does your bank-book when you see how much overdrawn you are.'

'I never imagined you actually typed your books yourself,' said Rhoda. 'I thought you'd have a secretary.'

'I did have a secretary, and I used to try and dictate to her, but she was so competent that it used to depress me. I felt she knew so much more about English and grammar and full stops and semi-colons than I did, that it gave me a kind of inferiority complex. Then I tried having a thoroughly incompetent secretary, but, of course, that didn't answer very well, either.'

'It must be so wonderful to be able to think of things,' said Rhoda.

'I can always think of things,' said Mrs Oliver happily. 'What is so tiring is writing them down. I always think I've finished, and then when I count up I find I've only written thirty thousand words instead of sixty thousand, and so then I have to throw in another murder and get the heroine kidnapped again. It's all very boring.'

Rhoda did not answer. She was staring at Mrs Oliver with the reverence felt by youth for celebrity – slightly tinged by disappointment.

'Do you like the wall-paper?' asked Mrs Oliver, waving an airy hand. 'I'm frightfully fond of birds. The foliage is supposed to be tropical. It makes me feel it's a hot day, even when it's freezing. I can't do anything unless I feel very, very warm. But Sven Hjerson breaks the ice on his bath every morning!'

'I think it's all marvellous,' said Rhoda. 'And it's awfully nice of you to say I'm not interrupting you.'

'We'll have some coffee and toast,' said Mrs Oliver. 'Very black coffee and very hot toast. I can always eat that any time.'

She went to the door, opened it and shouted. Then she returned and said: 'What brings you to town – shopping?'

'Yes, I've been doing some shopping.'

'Is Miss Meredith up, too?'

'Yes, she's gone with Major Despard to a solicitor.'

'Solicitor, eh?'

Mrs Oliver's brows rose inquiringly.

'Yes. You see, Major Despard told her she ought to have one. He's been awfully kind – he really has.'

'I was kind, too,' said Mrs Oliver, 'but it didn't seem to go down very well, did it? In fact, I think your friend rather resented my coming.'

'Oh, she didn't – really she didn't.' Rhoda wriggled on her chair in a paroxysm of embarrassment. 'That's really one reason why I wanted to come today – to explain. You see, I saw you had got it all wrong. She did seem very ungracious, but it wasn't that, really. I mean, it wasn't your coming. It was something you said.'

'Something I *said*?'

'Yes. You couldn't tell, of course. It was just unfortunate.'

'What did I say?'

'I don't expect you remember, even. It was just the way you put it. You said something about an accident and poison.'

'Did I?'

'I knew you'd probably not remember. Yes. You see, Anne had a ghastly experience once. She was in a house where a woman took some poison – hat paint, I think it was – by mistake for something else. And she died. And, of course, it was an awful shock to Anne. She can't bear thinking of it or speaking of it. And your saying that

267

reminded her, of course, and she dried up and got all stiff and queer like she does. And I saw you noticed it. And I couldn't say anything in front of her. But I did want you to know that it wasn't what you thought. She wasn't ungrateful.'

Mrs Oliver looked at Rhoda's flushed eager face. She said slowly: 'I see.'

'Anne's awfully sensitive,' said Rhoda. 'And she's bad about – well, facing things. If anything's upset her, she'd just rather not talk about it, although that isn't any good, really – at least, I don't think so. Things are there just the same – whether you talk about them or not. It's only running away from them to pretend they don't exist. I'd rather have it all out, however painful it would be.'

'Ah,' said Mrs Oliver quietly. 'But you, my dear, are a soldier. Your Anne isn't.'

Rhoda flushed.

Mrs Oliver smiled.

'Anne's a darling.'

She said, 'I didn't say she wasn't. I only said she hadn't got your particular brand of courage.'

She sighed, then said rather unexpectedly to the girl: 'Do you believe in the value of truth, my dear, or don't you?'

'Of course I believe in the truth,' said Rhoda, staring.

'Yes, you say that – but perhaps you haven't thought about it. The truth hurts sometimes – and destroys one's illusions.'

'I'd rather have it, all the same,' said Rhoda.

'So would I. But I don't know that we're wise.'

Rhoda said earnestly: 'Don't tell Anne, will you, what I've told you? She wouldn't like it.'

'I certainly shouldn't dream of doing any such thing. Was this long ago?'

'About four years ago. It's odd, isn't it, how the same things happen again and again to people. I had an aunt who was always in shipwrecks. And here's Anne mixed up in two sudden deaths – only, of course, this one's much worse. Murder's rather awful, isn't it?'

'Yes, it is.'

The black coffee and the hot buttered toast appeared at this minute.

Rhoda ate and drank with childish gusto. It was very exciting to her thus to be sharing an intimate meal with a celebrity.

When they had finished she rose and said: 'I do hope I haven't interrupted you too terribly. Would you mind – I mean, would it bother you awfully – if I sent one of your books to you, would you sign it for me?'

Mrs Oliver laughed.

'Oh, I can do better than that for you.' She opened a cupboard at the far end of the room. 'Which would you like? I rather fancy *The Affair of the Second Goldfish* myself. It's not quite such frightful tripe as the rest.'

A little shocked at hearing an authoress thus describe the children of her pen, Rhoda accepted eagerly. Mrs Oliver took the book, opened it, inscribed her name with a superlative flourish and handed it to Rhoda.

'There you are.'

'Thank you very much. I have enjoyed myself. Sure you didn't mind my coming?'

'I wanted you to,' said Mrs Oliver.

She added after a moment's pause: 'You're a nice child. Good-bye. Take care of yourself my dear.'

'Now, why did I say that?' she murmured to herself as the door closed behind her guest.

She shook her head, ruffled her hair, and returned to the masterly dealings of Sven Hjerson with the sage-and-onion stuffing.

— 18 —

TEA INTERLUDE

MRS LORRIMER came out of a certain door in Harley Street.

She stood for a minute at the top of the steps, and then she descended them slowly.

There was a curious expression on her face – a mingling of grim determination and of strange indecision. She bent her brows a little, as though to concentrate on some all-absorbing problem.

It was just then that she caught sight of Anne Meredith on the opposite pavement.

Anne was standing staring up at a big block of flats just on the corner.

Mrs Lorrimer hesitated a moment, then she crossed the road.

'How do you do, Miss Meredith?'

Anne started and turned.

'Oh, how do you do?'

'Still in London?' said Mrs Lorrimer.

'No. I've only come up for the day. To do some legal business.'

Her eyes were still straying back to the big block of flats.

Mrs Lorrimer said: 'Is anything the matter?'

Anne started guiltily.

'The matter? Oh, no, what should be the matter?'

'You were looking as though you had something on your mind.'

'I haven't – well, at least I have, but it's nothing important, something quite silly.' She laughed a little.

She went on: 'It's only that I thought I saw my friend – the girl I live with – go in there, and I wondered if she'd gone to see Mrs Oliver.'

'Is that where Mrs Oliver lives? I didn't know.'

'Yes. She came to see us the other day and she gave us her address and asked us to come and see her. I wondered if it was Rhoda I saw or not.'

'Do you want to go up and see?'

'No, I'd rather not do that.'

'Come and have tea with me,' said Mrs Lorrimer. 'There is a shop quite near here that I know.'

'It's very kind of you,' said Anne, hesitating.

Side by side they walked down the street and turned into a side street. In a small pastrycook's they were served with tea and muffins.

They did not talk much. Each of them seemed to find the other's silence restful.

Anne asked suddenly: 'Has Mrs Oliver been to see you?'

Mrs Lorrimer shook her head.

'No one has been to see me except M. Poirot.'

'I didn't mean—' began Anne.

'Didn't you? I think you did,' said Mrs Lorrimer.

The girl looked up – a quick, frightened glance. Something she saw in Mrs Lorrimer's face seemed to reassure her.

'He hasn't been to see me,' she said slowly.

There was a pause.

'Hasn't Superintendent Battle been to see you?' asked Anne.

'Oh, yes, of course,' said Mrs Lorrimer.

Anne said hesitatingly: 'What sort of things did he ask you?'

Mrs Lorrimer sighed wearily.

'The usual things, I suppose. Routine inquiries. He was very pleasant over it all.'

'I suppose he interviewed everyone.'

'I should think so.'

There was another pause.

Anne said: 'Mrs Lorrimer, do you think – they will ever find out who did it?'

Her eyes were bent on her plate. She did not see the curious expression in the older woman's eyes as she watched the downcast head.

Mrs Lorrimer said quietly: 'I don't know . . .'

Anne murmured: 'It's not – very nice, is it?'

There was that same curious appraising and yet sympathetic look on Mrs Lorrimer's face, as she asked: 'How old are you, Anne Meredith?'

'I – I?' the girl stammered. 'I'm twenty-five.'

'And I am sixty-three,' said Mrs Lorrimer.

She went on slowly: 'Most of your life is in front of you . . .'

Anne shivered.

'I might be run over by a bus on the way home,' she said.

'Yes, that is true. And I – might not.'

She said it in an odd way. Anne looked at her in astonishment.

'Life is a difficult business,' said Mrs Lorrimer. 'You'll know that when you come to my age. It needs infinite courage and a lot of endurance. And in the end one wonders: "Was it worth while?" '

'Oh, *don't*,' said Anne.

Mrs Lorrimer laughed, her old competent self again.

'It's rather cheap to say gloomy things about life,' she said.

She called the waitress and settled the bill.

As they got to the shop door a taxi crawled past, and Mrs Lorrimer hailed it.

'Can I give you a lift?' she asked. 'I am going south of the park.'

Anne's face had lighted up.

'No, thank you. I see my friend turning the corner. Thank you so much, Mrs Lorrimer. Goodbye.'

'Goodbye. Good luck,' said the older woman.

She drove away and Anne hurried forward.

Rhoda's face lit up when she saw her friend, then changed to a slightly guilty expression.

'Rhoda, have you been to see Mrs Oliver?' demanded Anne.

'Well, as a matter of fact, I have.'

'And I just caught you.'

'I don't know what you mean by "caught". Let's go down here and take a bus. You'd gone off on your own ploys with the boyfriend. I thought at least he'd give you tea.'

Anne was silent for a minute – a voice ringing in her ears.

'Can't we pick up your friend somewhere and all have tea together?'

And her own answer – hurried, without taking time to think: 'Thanks awfully, but we've got to go out to tea together with some people.'

A lie – and such a silly lie. The stupid way one said the first thing that came into one's head instead of just taking a minute or two to think. Perfectly easy to have said: 'Thanks, but my friend has got to go out to tea.' That is, if you didn't, as she hadn't, wanted to have Rhoda too.

Rather odd, that, the way she hadn't wanted Rhoda. She had wanted, definitely, to keep Despard to herself. She had felt jealous. Jealous of Rhoda. Rhoda was so bright, so ready to talk, so full of enthusiasm and life. The other evening Major Despard had looked as though he thought Rhoda nice. But it was her, Anne Meredith, he had come down to see. Rhoda was like that. She didn't mean it, but she reduced you to the background. No, definitely she hadn't wanted Rhoda there.

But she had managed it very stupidly, getting flurried like that. If she'd managed better, she might be sitting now having tea with Major Despard at his club or somewhere.

She felt definitely annoyed with Rhoda. Rhoda was a nuisance. And what had she been doing going to see Mrs Oliver?

Out loud she said: 'Why did you go and see Mrs Oliver?'

'Well, she asked us to.'

'Yes, but I didn't suppose she really meant it. I expect she always has to say that.'

'She did mean it. She was awfully nice – couldn't have been nicer. She gave me one of her books. Look.'

Rhoda flourished her prize.

Anne said suspiciously: 'What did you talk about? Not me?'

'Listen to the conceit of the girl!'

'No, but did you? Did you talk about the – the murder?'

'We talked about her murders. She's writing one where there's poison in the sage and onions. She was frightfully human – and said writing was awfully hard work and said how she got into tangles with plots, and we had black coffee and hot buttered toast,' finished Rhoda in a triumphant burst.

Then she added: 'Oh, Anne, you want your tea.'

'No, I don't. I've had it. With Mrs Lorrimer.'

'Mrs Lorrimer? Isn't that the one – the one who was there?'
Anne nodded.

'Where did you come across her? Did you go and see her?'

'No. I ran across her in Harley Street.'

'What was she like?'

Anne said slowly: 'I don't know. She was – rather queer. Not at all like the other night.'

'Do you still think she did it?' asked Rhoda.

Anne was silent for a minute or two. Then she said: 'I don't know. Don't let's talk of it, Rhoda! You know how I hate talking of things.'

'All right, darling. What was the solicitor like? Very dry and legal?'

'Rather alert and Jewish.'

'Sounds all right.' She waited a little and then said: 'How was Major Despard?'

'Very kind.'

'He's fallen for you, Anne. I'm sure he has.'

'Rhoda, don't talk nonsense.'

'Well, you'll see.'

Rhoda began humming to herself. She thought: 'Of course he's fallen for her. Anne's awfully pretty. But a bit wishy-washy . . . She'll never go on treks with him. Why, she'd scream if she saw a snake . . . Men always do take fancies to unsuitable women.'

Then she said aloud.

'That bus will take us to Paddington. We'll just catch the 4.48.'

— 19 —

CONSULTATION

THE telephone rang in Poirot's room and a respectful voice spoke.

'Sergeant O'Connor. Superintendent Battle's compliments and would it be convenient for Mr Hercule Poirot to come to Scotland Yard at 11.30?'

Poirot replied in the affirmative and Sergeant O'Connor rang off.

It was 11.30 to the minute when Poirot descended from his taxi at the door of New Scotland Yard – to be at once seized upon by Mrs Oliver.

'M. Poirot. How splendid! Will you come to my rescue?'

'*Enchanté*, Madame. What can I do?'

'Pay my taxi for me. I don't know how it happened but I brought out the bag I keep my going-abroad money in and the man simply won't take francs or liras or marks!'

Poirot gallantly produced some loose change, and he and Mrs Oliver went inside the building together.

They were taken to Superintendent Battle's own room. The superintendent was sitting behind a table and looking more wooden than ever. 'Just like a piece of modern sculpture,' whispered Mrs Oliver to Poirot.

Battle rose and shook hands with them both and they sat down.

'I thought it was about time for a little meeting,' said Battle. 'You'd like to hear how I've got on, and I'd like to hear how you've got on. We're just waiting for Colonel Race and then—'

But at that moment the door opened and the colonel appeared.

'Sorry I'm late, Battle. How do you do, Mrs Oliver. Hallo, M. Poirot. Very sorry if I've kept you waiting. But I'm off tomorrow and had a lot of things to see to.'

'Where are you going to?' asked Mrs Oliver.

'A little shooting trip – Baluchistan way.'

Poirot said, smiling ironically: 'A little trouble, is there not, in that part of the world? You will have to be careful.'

'I mean to be,' said Race gravely – but his eyes twinkled.

'Got anything for us, sir?' asked Battle.

'I've got you your information re Despard. Here it is—'

He pushed over a sheaf of papers.

'There's a mass of dates and places there. Most of it quite irrelevant, I should imagine. Nothing against him. He's a stout fellow. Record quite unblemished. Strict disciplinarian. Liked and trusted by the natives everywhere. One of their cumbrous names for him in Africa, where they go in for such things, is "The man who keeps his mouth shut and judges fairly". General opinion of the white races that Despard is a Pukka Sahib. Fine shot. Cool head. Generally long-sighted and dependable.'

Unmoved by this eulogy, Battle asked: 'Any sudden deaths connected with him?'

'I laid special stress on that point. There's one fine rescue to his credit. Pal of his was being mauled by a lion.'

Battle sighed.

'It's not rescues I want.'

'You're a persistent fellow, Battle. There's only one incident I've been able to rake up that might suit your book. Trip into the interior in South America. Despard accompanied Professor Luxmore, the celebrated botanist, and his wife. The professor died of fever and was buried somewhere up the Amazon.'

'Fever – eh?'

'Fever. But I'll play fair with you. One of the native bearers (who was sacked for stealing, incidentally) had a story that the professor didn't die of fever, but was shot. The rumour was never taken seriously.'

'About time it was, perhaps.'

Race shook his head.

'I've given you the facts. You asked for them and you're entitled to them, but I'd lay long odds against its being Despard who did the dirty work the other evening. He's a white man, Battle.'

'Incapable of murder, you mean?'

Colonel Race hesitated.

'Incapable of what I'd call murder – yes,' he said.

'But not incapable of killing a man for what would seem to him good and sufficient reasons, is that it?

'If so, they *would* be good and sufficient reasons!'

Battle shook his head.

'You can't have human beings judging other human beings and taking the law into their own hands.'

'It happens, Battle – it happens.'

'It shouldn't happen – that's my point. What do you say, M. Poirot?'

'I agree with you, Battle. I have always disapproved of murder.'

'What a delightfully droll way of putting it,' said Mrs Oliver. 'Rather as though it were fox-hunting or killing ospreys for hats. Don't you think there are people who ought to be murdered?'

'That, very possibly.'

'Well, then!'

'You do not comprehend. It is not the victim who concerns me so much. It is the effect on the character of the slayer.'

'What about war?'

'In war you do not exercise the right of private judgment. *That* is what is so dangerous. Once a man is imbued with the idea that he knows who ought to be allowed to live and who ought not – then he is half-way to becoming the most dangerous killer there is – the arrogant criminal who kills not for profit – but for an idea. He has usurped the functions of *le bon Dieu*.'

Colonel Race rose: 'I'm sorry I can't stop with you. Too much to do. I'd like to see the end of this business. Shouldn't be surprised if there never was an end. Even if you find out who did it, it's going to be next to impossible to prove. I've given you the facts you wanted, but in my opinion Despard's not the man. I don't believe he's ever committed murder. Shaitana may have heard some garbled rumour of Professor Luxmore's death, but I don't believe there's more to it than that. Despard's a white man, and I don't believe he's ever been a murderer. That's my opinion. And I know something of men.'

'What's Mrs Luxmore like?' asked Battle.

'She lives in London, so you can see for yourself. You'll find the address among those papers. Somewhere in South Kensington. But I repeat, Despard isn't the man.'

Colonel Race left the room, stepping with the springy noiseless tread of a hunter.

Battle nodded his head thoughtfully as the door closed behind him.

'He's probably right,' he said. 'He knows men, Colonel Race does. But, all the same, one can't take anything for granted.'

He looked through the mass of documents Race had deposited on the table, occasionally making a pencil note on the pad beside him.

'Well, Superintendent Battle,' said Mrs Oliver. 'Aren't you going to tell us what you have been doing?'

He looked up and smiled, a slow smile that creased his wooden face from side to side.

'This is all very irregular, Mrs Oliver. I hope you realize that.'

'Nonsense,' said Mrs Oliver. 'I don't suppose for a moment you'll tell us anything you don't want to.'

Battle shook his head.

'No,' he said decidedly. 'Cards on the table. That's the motto for this business. I mean to play fair.'

Mrs Oliver hitched her chair nearer.

'Tell us,' she begged.

Superintendent Battle said slowly: 'First of all, I'll say this. As far as the actual murder of Mr Shaitana goes, I'm not a penny the wiser. There's no hint nor clue of any kind to be found in his papers. As for the four others, I've had them shadowed, naturally, but without any tangible result. That was only to be expected. No, as M. Poirot said, there's only one hope – the past. Find out what crime exactly (if any, that is to say – after all, Shaitana may have been talking through his hat to make an impression on M. Poirot)

276

these people have committed – and it may tell you who committed this crime.'

'Well, have you found out anything?'

'I've got a line on one of them.'

'Which?'

'Dr Roberts.'

Mrs Oliver looked at him with thrilled expectation.

'As M. Poirot here knows, I tried out all kinds of theories. I established the fact pretty clearly that none of his immediate family had met with a sudden death. I've explored every alley as well as I could, and the whole thing boils down to one possibility – and rather an outside possibility at that. A few years ago Roberts must have been guilty of indiscretion, at least, with one of his lady patients. There may have been nothing in it – probably wasn't. But the woman was the hysterical, emotional kind who likes to make a scene, and either the husband got wind of what was going on, or his wife "confessed". Anyway, the fat was in the fire as far as the doctor was concerned. Enraged husband threatening to report him to the General Medical Council – which would probably have meant the ruin of his professional career.'

'What happened?' demanded Mrs Oliver breathlessly.

'Apparently Roberts managed to calm down the irate gentleman temporarily – and he died of anthrax almost immediately afterwards.'

'Anthrax? But that's a cattle disease!'

The superintendent grinned.

'Quite right, Mrs Oliver. It isn't the untraceable arrow poison of the South American Indian! You may remember that there was rather a scare about infected shaving-brushes of cheap make about that time. Craddock's shaving-brush was proved to have been the cause of infection.'

'Did Dr Roberts attend him?'

'Oh, no. Too canny for that. Dare say Craddock wouldn't have wanted him in any case. The only evidence I've got – and that's precious little – is that among the doctor's patients there *was* a case of anthrax at the time.'

'You mean the doctor infected the shaving-brush?'

'That's the big idea. And, mind you, it's only an idea. Nothing whatever to go on. Pure conjecture. But it could be.'

'He didn't marry Mrs Craddock afterwards?'

'Oh, dear me, no, I imagine the affection was always on the lady's side. She tended to cut up rough, I hear, but suddenly went off to Egypt quite happily for the winter. She died there. A case of some obscure blood-poisoning. It's got a long name, but I don't expect it would convey much to you. Most uncommon in this country, fairly common amongst the natives in Egypt.'

'So the doctor couldn't have poisoned her?'

'I don't know,' said Battle slowly. 'I've been chatting to a bacteriologist friend of mine – awfully difficult to get straight answers out of these people. They never can say yes or no. It's always "that might be possible under certain conditions" – "it would depend on the pathological condition of the recipient" – "such cases have been known" – "a lot depends on individual idiosyncrasy" – all that sort of stuff. But as far as I could pin my friend down I got at this – the germ, or germs, I suppose, might have been introduced into the blood before leaving England. The symptoms would not make their appearance for some time to come.'

Poirot asked: 'Was Mrs Craddock inoculated for typhoid before going to Egypt? Most people are, I fancy.'

'Good for you, M. Poirot.'

'And Dr Roberts did the inoculation?'

'That's right. There you are again – we can't prove anything. She had the usual two inoculations – and they may have been typhoid inoculations for all we know. Or one of them may have been typhoid inoculation and the other – something else. We don't know. We never shall know. The whole thing is pure hypothesis. All we can say is: it might be.'

Poirot nodded thoughtfully.

'It agrees very well with some remarks made to me by Mr Shaitana. He was exalting the successful murderer – the man against whom his crime could never be brought home.'

'How did Mr Shaitana know about it, then?' asked Mrs Oliver.

Poirot shrugged his shoulders.

'That we shall never learn. He himself was in Egypt at one time. We know that, because he met Mrs Lorrimer there. He may have heard some local doctor comment on curious features of Mrs Craddock's case – a wonder as to how the infection arose. At some other time he may have heard gossip about Roberts and Mrs Craddock. He might have amused himself by making some cryptic remark to the doctor and noted the startled awareness in his eye – all that one can never know. Some people have an uncanny gift of divining secrets. Mr Shaitana was one of those people. All that does not concern us. We have only to say – he guessed. Did he guess right?'

'Well, I think he did,' said Battle. 'I've a feeling that our

278

cheerful, genial doctor wouldn't be too scrupulous. I've known one or two like him – wonderful how certain types resemble each other. In my opinion he's a killer all right. He killed Craddock. He may have killed Mrs Craddock if she was beginning to be a nuisance and cause a scandal. *But did he kill Shaitana?* That's the real question. And, comparing the crimes, I rather doubt it. In the case of the Craddocks he used medical methods each time. The deaths appeared to be due to natural causes. In my opinion, if he had killed Shaitana, he would have done so in a medical way. He'd have used the germ and not the knife.'

'I never thought it was him,' said Mrs Oliver. 'Not for a minute. He's too obvious, somehow.'

'Exit Roberts,' murmured Poirot. 'And the others?'

Battle made a gesture of impatience.

'I've pretty well drawn blank. Mrs Lorrimer's been a widow for twenty years now. She lived in London most of the time, occasionally going abroad in the winter. Civilized places – the Riviera, Egypt, that sort of thing. Can't find any mysterious deaths associated with her. She seems to have led a perfectly normal, respectable life – the life of a woman of the world. Everyone seems to respect her and to have the highest opinion of her character. The worst that they can say about her is that she doesn't suffer fools gladly! I don't mind admitting I've been beaten all along the line there. And yet there must be *something*! Shaitana thought there was.'

He sighed in a dispirited manner.

'Then there's Miss Meredith. I've got her history taped out quite clearly. Usual sort of story. Army officer's daughter. Left with very little money. Had to earn her living. Not properly trained for anything. I've checked up on her early days at Cheltenham. All quite straightforward. Everyone very sorry for the poor little thing. She went first to some people in the Isle of Wight – kind of nursery-governess and mother's-help. The woman she was with is out in Palestine but I've talked with her sister and she says Mrs Eldon liked the girl very much. Certainly no mysterious deaths nor anything of that kind.

'When Mrs Eldon went abroad, Miss Meredith went to Devonshire and took a post as companion to an aunt of a school friend. The school friend is the girl she is living with now – Miss Rhoda Dawes. She was there over two years until Miss Dawes got too ill and had to have a regular trained nurse. Cancer, I gather. She's alive still, but very vague. Kept under morphia a good deal, I imagine. I had an interview with her. She remembered "Anne", said she was a nice child. I also talked to a neighbour of hers who would be better able to remember the happenings of the last few years. No deaths in the parish except one or two of the older villagers, with whom, as far as I can make out, Anne Meredith never came into contact.

'Since then there's been Switzerland. Thought I might get on the track of some fatal accident there, but nothing doing. And there's nothing in Wallingford either.'

'So Anne Meredith is acquitted?' asked Poirot.

Battle hesitated.

'I wouldn't say that. There's *something* . . . There's a scared look about her that can't quite be accounted for by panic over Shaitana. She's too watchful. Too much on the alert. I'd swear there was *something*. But there it is – she's led a perfectly blameless life.'

Mrs Oliver took a deep breath – a breath of pure enjoyment.

'And yet,' she said, 'Anne Meredith was in the house when a woman took poison by mistake and died.'

She had nothing to complain of in the effect her words produced.

Superintendent Battle spun round in his chair and stared at her in amazement.

'Is this true, Mrs Oliver? How do you know?'

'I've been sleuthing,' said Mrs Oliver. 'I get on with girls. I went down to see those two and told them a cock-and-bull story about suspecting Dr Roberts. The Rhoda girl was friendly – oh, and rather impressed by thinking I was a celebrity. The little Meredith hated my coming and showed it quite plainly. She was suspicious. Why should she be if she hadn't got anything to hide? I asked either of them to come and see me in London. The Rhoda girl did. And she blurted the whole thing out. How Anne had been rude to me the other day because something I'd said had reminded her of a painful incident, and then she went on to describe the incident.'

'Did she say when and where it happened?'

'Three years ago in Devonshire.'

The superintendent muttered something under his breath and scribbled on his pad. His wooden calm was shaken.

Mrs Oliver sat enjoying her triumph. It was a moment of great sweetness to her.

Battle recovered his temper.

'I take off my hat to you, Mrs Oliver,' he said. 'You've put one over on us this time. That is very valuable information. And it just shows how easily you can miss a thing.'

He frowned a little.

'She can't have been there – wherever it was – long. A couple of months at most. It must have been between the Isle of Wight and going to Miss Dawes. Yes, that could be it right enough. Naturally Mrs Eldon's sister only remembers she went off to a place in Devonshire – she doesn't remember exactly who or where.'

'Tell me,' said Poirot, 'was this Mrs Eldon an untidy woman?'

Battle bent a curious gaze upon him.

'It's odd your saying that, M. Poirot. I don't see how you could have known. The sister was rather a precise party. In talking I remember her saying "My sister is so dreadfully untidy and slapdash." But how did *you* know?'

'Because she needed a mother's-help,' said Mrs Oliver.

Poirot shook his head.

'No, no, it was not that. It is of no moment. I was only curious. Continue, Superintendent Battle.'

'In the same way,' went on Battle, 'I took it for granted that she went to Miss Dawes straight from the Isle of Wight. She's sly, that girl. She deceived me all right. Lying the whole time.'

'Lying is not always a sign of guilt,' said Poirot.

'I know that, M. Poirot. There's the natural liar. I should say she was one, as a matter of fact. Always says the thing that sounds best. But all the same it's a pretty grave risk to take, suppressing facts like that.'

'She wouldn't know you had any idea of past crimes,' said Mrs Oliver.

'That's all the more reason for not suppressing that little piece of information. It must have been accepted as a bona fide case of accidental death, so she'd nothing to fear – *unless she were guilty.*'

'Unless she were guilty of the Devonshire death, yes,' said Poirot.

Battle turned to him.

'Oh, I know. Even if that accidental death turns out to be not so accidental, *it doesn't follow that she killed Shaitana*. But these other murders are murders too. I want to be able to bring home a crime to the person responsible for it.'

'According to Mr Shaitana, that is impossible,' remarked Poirot.

'It is in Roberts' case. It remains to be seen if it is in Miss Meredith's. I shall go down to Devon tomorrow.'

'Will you know where to go?' asked Mrs Oliver. 'I didn't like to ask Rhoda for more details.'

'No, that was wise of you. I shan't have much difficulty. There must have been an inquest. I shall find it in the coroner's records.

That's routine police work. They'll have it all taped out for me by tomorrow morning.'

'What about Major Despard?' asked Mrs Oliver. 'Have you found out anything about him?'

'I've been waiting for Colonel Race's report. I've had him shadowed, of course. One rather interesting thing, he went down to see Miss Meredith at Wallingford. You remember he said he'd never met her until the other night.'

'But she is a very pretty girl,' murmured Poirot.

Battle laughed.

'Yes, I expect that's all there is to it. By the way, Despard's taking no chances. He's already consulted a solicitor. That looks as though he's expecting trouble.'

'He is a man who looks ahead,' said Poirot. 'He is a man who prepares for every contingency.'

'And therefore not the kind of man to stick a knife into a man in a hurry,' said Battle with a sigh.

'Not unless it was the only way,' said Poirot. 'He can act quickly, remember.'

Battle looked across the table at him.

'Now, M. Poirot, what about your cards? Haven't seen your hand down on the table yet.'

Poirot smiled.

'There is so little in it. You think I conceal facts from you? It is not so. I have not learned many facts. I have talked with Dr Roberts, with Mrs Lorrimer, with Major Despard (I have still to talk to Miss Meredith) and what have I learnt? This! That Dr Roberts is a keen observer, that Mrs Lorrimer on the other hand has a most remarkable power of concentration but is, in consequence, almost blind to her surroundings. But she is fond of flowers. Despard notices only those things which appeal to him – rugs, trophies of sport. He has neither what I call the outward vision (seeing details all around you – what is called "an observant person") nor the inner vision – concentration, the focusing of the mind on one object. He has a purposefully limited vision. He sees only what blends and harmonises with the bent of his mind.'

'So those are what you call facts – eh?' said Battle curiously.

'They *are* facts. Very small fry – perhaps.'

'What about Miss Meredith?'

'I have left her to the end. But I shall question her too as to what she remembers in that room.'

'It's an odd method of approach,' said Battle thoughtfully.

'Purely psychological. Suppose they're leading you up the garden path?'

Poirot shook his head with a smile.

'No, that would be impossible. Whether they try to hinder or to help, they necessarily reveal their *type of mind*.'

'There's something in it, no doubt,' said Battle thoughtfully. 'I couldn't work that way myself, though.'

Poirot said, still smiling: 'I feel I have done very little in comparison with you and with Mrs Oliver – and with Colonel Race. My cards, that I place on the table, are very low ones.'

Battle twinkled at him.

'As to that, M. Poirot, the two of trumps is a low card, but it can take any one of three aces. All the same, I'm going to ask you to do a practical job of work.'

'And that is?'

'I want you to interview Professor Luxmore's widow.'

'And why do you not do that yourself?'

'Because, as I said just now, I'm off to Devonshire.'

'Why do you not do that yourself?' repeated Poirot.

'Won't be put off, will you? Well, I'll speak the truth. I think you'll get more out of her than I shall.'

'My methods being less straightforward?'

'You can put it that way if you like,' said Battle, grinning. 'I've heard Inspector Japp say that you've got a tortuous mind.'

'Like the late Mr Shaitana?'

'You think he would have been able to get things out of her?'

Poirot said slowly: 'I rather think he *did* get things out of her!'

'What makes you think so?' asked Battle sharply.

'A chance remark of Major Despard's.'

'Gave himself away, did he? That sounds unlike him.'

'Oh, my dear friend, it is impossible *not* to give oneself away – unless one never opens one's mouth! Speech is the deadliest of revealers.'

'Even if people tell lies?' asked Mrs Oliver.

'Yes, Madame, because it can be seen at once that you tell *a certain kind of lie*.'

'You make me feel quite uncomfortable,' said Mrs Oliver, getting up.

Superintendent Battle accompanied her to the door and shook her warmly by the hand.

'You've been the goods, Mrs Oliver,' he said. 'You're a much better detective than that long lanky Laplander of yours.'

'Finn,' corrected Mrs Oliver. 'Of course he's idiotic. But people like him. Goodbye.'

'I, too, must depart,' said Poirot.

Battle scribbled an address on a piece of paper and shoved it into Poirot's hand.

'There you are. Go and tackle her.'

Poirot smiled.

'And what do you want me to find out?'

'The truth about Professor Luxmore's death.'

'*Mon cher* Battle! Does anybody know the truth about anything?'

'I'm going to about this business in Devonshire,' said the superintendent with decision.

Poirot murmured: 'I wonder.'

— 20 —

THE EVIDENCE OF MRS LUXMORE

THE maid who opened the door at Mrs Luxmore's South Kensington address looked at Hercule Poirot with deep disapproval. She showed no disposition to admit him into the house.

Unperturbed, Poirot gave her a card.

'Give that to your mistress. I think she will see me.'

It was one of his more ostentatious cards. The words 'Private Detective' were printed in one corner. He had had them specially engraved for the purpose of obtaining interviews with the so-called fair sex. Nearly every woman, whether conscious of innocence or not, was anxious to have a look at a private detective and find out what he wanted.

Left ignominiously on the mat, Poirot studied the door-knocker with intense disgust at its unpolished condition.

'Ah! for some Brasso and a rag,' he murmured to himself.

Breathing excitedly the maid returned and Poirot was bidden to enter.

He was shown into a room on the first floor – a rather dark room smelling of stale flowers and unemptied ashtrays. There were large quantities of silk cushions of exotic colours all in need of cleaning. The walls were emerald green and the ceiling was of pseudo-copper.

A tall, rather handsome woman was standing by the mantelpiece. She came forward and spoke in a deep husky voice.

'M. Hercule Poirot?'

Poirot bowed. His manner was not quite his own. He was not only foreign but ornately foreign. His gestures were positively baroque. Faintly, very faintly, it was the manner of the late Mr Shaitana.

'What did you want to see me about?'

Again Poirot bowed.

'If I might be seated? It will take a little time—'

She waved him impatiently to a chair and sat down herself on the edge of a sofa.

'Yes? Well?'

'It is, Madame, that I make the inquiries – the private inquiries, you understand?'

The more deliberate his approach, the greater her eagerness.

'Yes – yes?'

'I make inquiries into the death of the late Professor Luxmore.'

She gave a gasp. Her dismay was evident.

'But why? What do you mean? What has it got to do with you?'

Poirot watched her carefully before proceeding.

'There is, you comprehend, a book being written. A life of your eminent husband. The writer, naturally, is anxious to get all his facts exact. As to your husband's death for instance—'

She broke in at once: 'My husband died of fever – on the Amazon.'

Poirot leaned back in his chair. Slowly, very, very slowly, he shook his head to and fro – a maddening, monotonous motion.

'Madame, Madame—' he protested.

'But I know! I was there at the time.'

'Ah, yes, certainly. You were *there*. Yes, my information says so.'

She cried out: 'What information?'

Eyeing her closely Poirot said: 'Information supplied to me by the late Mr Shaitana.'

She shrank back as though flicked with a whip.

'Shaitana?' she muttered.

'A man,' said Poirot, 'possessed of vast stores of knowledge. A remarkable man. That man knew many secrets.'

'I suppose he did,' she murmured, passing a tongue over her dry lips.

Poirot leaned forward. He achieved a little tap on her knee.

'He knew, for instance, that your husband did not die of fever.'

She stared at him. Her eyes looked wild and desperate.

He leaned back and watched the effect of his words.

She pulled herself together with an effort.

'I don't – I don't know what you mean.'

It was very unconvincingly said.

'Madame,' said Poirot, 'I will come out into the open. I will,' he smiled, 'place my cards upon the table. Your husband did not die of a fever. *He died of a bullet!*'

'Oh!' she cried.

She covered her face with her hands. She rocked herself to and fro. She was in terrible distress. But somewhere, in some remote fibre of her being, she was enjoying her own emotions. Poirot was quite sure of that.

'And therefore,' said Poirot in a matter-of-fact tone, 'you might just as well tell me the whole story.'

She uncovered her face and said: 'It wasn't in the least the way you think.'

Again Poirot leaned forward – again he tapped her knee.

'You misunderstand me – you misunderstand me utterly,' he said. 'I know very well that it was not you who shot him. It was Major Despard. But you were the cause.'

'I don't know. I don't know. I suppose I was. It was all too terrible. There is a sort of fatality that pursues me.'

'Ah, how true that is,' cried Poirot. 'How often have I not seen it? There are some women like that. Wherever they go, tragedies follow in their wake. It is not their fault. These things happen in spite of themselves.'

Mrs Luxmore drew a deep breath.

'You understand. I see you understand. It all happened so naturally.'

'You travelled together into the interior, did you not?'

'Yes. My husband was writing a book on various rare plants. Major Despard was introduced to us as a man who knew the conditions and would arrange the necessary expedition. My husband liked him very much. We started.'

There was a pause. Poirot allowed it to continue for about a minute and a half and then murmured as though to himself.

'Yes, one can picture it. The winding river – the tropical night – the hum of the insects – the strong soldierly man – the beautiful woman . . .'

Mrs Luxmore sighed.

'My husband was, of course, years older than I was. I married as a mere child before I knew what I was doing . . .'

Poirot shook his head sadly.

'I know. I know. How often does that not occur?'

'Neither of us would admit what was happening,' went on Mrs Luxmore. 'John Despard never said anything. He was the soul of honour.'

'But a woman always knows,' prompted Poirot.

'How right you are . . Yes, a woman knows . . . But I never showed him that I knew. We were Major Despard and Mrs Luxmore to each other right up to the end . . . We were both determined to play the game.'

She was silent, lost in admiration of that noble attitude.

'True,' murmured Poirot. 'One must play the cricket. As one of your poets so finely says, "I could not love thee, dear, so much, loved I not cricket more."'

'"Honour,"' corrected Mrs Luxmore with a slight frown.

'Of course – of course – "honour". "Loved I not honour more."'

'Those words might have been written for us,' murmured Mrs Luxmore. 'No matter what it cost us, we were both determined never to say the fatal word. And then—'

'And then—' prompted Poirot.

'That ghastly night.' Mrs Luxmore shuddered.

'Yes?'

'I suppose they must have quarrelled – John and Timothy, I mean. I came out of my tent . . . I came out of my tent . . .'

'Yes – yes?'

Mrs Luxmore's eyes were wide and dark. She was seeing the scene as though it were being repeated in front of her.

'I came out of my tent,' she repeated. 'John and Timothy were— Oh!' She shuddered. 'I can't remember it all clearly. I came between them . . . I said "No – no, it isn't *true*!" Timothy wouldn't listen. He was threatening John. John had to fire – in self-defence. Ah!' She gave a cry and covered her face with her hands. 'He was dead – stone dead – shot through the heart.'

'A terrible moment for you, Madame.'

'I shall never forget it. John was noble. He was all for giving himself up. I refused to hear of it. We argued all night. "For my sake," I kept saying. He saw that in the end. Naturally he couldn't let me suffer. The awful publicity. Think of the headlines. *Two Men and a Woman in the Jungle. Primeval Passions.*

'I put it all to John. In the end he gave in. The boys had seen and heard nothing. Timothy had been having a bout of fever. We said he had died of it. We buried him there beside the Amazon.'

A deep, tortured sigh shook her form.

'And then – back to civilization – and to part for ever.'

'Was it necessary, Madame?'

'Yes, yes. Timothy dead stood between us just as Timothy alive had done – more so. We said goodbye to each other – for ever. I meet John Despard sometimes – out in the world. We smile, we speak politely – no one would ever guess that there was anything between us. But I see in his eyes – and he in mine – that we will never forget . . .'

There was a long pause. Poirot paid tribute to the curtain by not breaking the silence.

Mrs Luxmore took out a vanity case and powdered her nose – the spell was broken.

'What a tragedy,' said Poirot, but in a more everyday tone.

'You can see, M. Poirot,' said Mrs Luxmore earnestly, 'that the truth must never be told.'

'It would be painful—'

'It would be impossible. This friend, this writer – surely he would not wish to blight the life of a perfectly innocent woman?'

'Or even to hang a perfectly innocent man?' murmured Poirot.

'You see it like that? I am so glad. He *was* innocent. A *crime passionnel* is not really a crime. And in any case it was in self-defence. He *had* to shoot. So you do understand, M. Poirot, that the world must continue to think Timothy died of fever?'

Poirot murmured.

'Writers are sometimes curiously callous.'

'Your friend is a woman-hater? He wants to make us suffer? But you must not allow that. I shall not allow it. If necessary I shall take the blame on myself. I shall say *I* shot Timothy.'

She had risen to her feet. Her head was thrown back.

Poirot also rose.

'Madame,' he said as he took her hand, 'such splendid self-sacrifice is unnecessary. I will do my best so that the true facts shall never be known.'

A sweet womanly smile stole over Mrs Luxmore's face. She raised her hand slightly, so that Poirot, whether he had meant to do so or not, was forced to kiss it.

'An unhappy woman thanks you, M. Poirot,' she said.

It was the last word of a persecuted queen to a favoured courtier – clearly an exit line. Poirot duly made his exit.

Once out in the street, he drew a long breath of fresh air.

MAJOR DESPARD

'*Quelle femme,*' murmured Hercule Poirot. '*Ce pauvre Despard! Ce qu'il a du souffrir! Quel voyage épouvantable!*'

Suddenly he began to laugh.

He was now walking along the Brompton Road. He paused, took out his watch, and made a calculation.

'But, yes, I have the time. In any case to wait will do him no harm. I can now attend to the other little matter. What was it that my friend in the English police force used to sing – how many years – forty years ago? "A little piece of sugar for the bird."'

Humming a long-forgotten tune, Hercule Poirot entered a sumptuous-looking shop mainly devoted to the clothing and general embellishment of women and made his way to the stocking counter.

Selecting a sympathetic-looking and not too haughty damsel he made known his requirements.

'Silk stockings? Oh, yes, we have a very nice line here. Guaranteed pure silk.'

Poirot waved them away. He waxed eloquent once more.

'French silk stockings? With the duty, you know, they are very expensive.'

A fresh lot of boxes was produced.

'Very nice, Mademoiselle, but I had something of a finer texture still in mind.'

'These are a hundred gauge. Of course, we have some extra-fine, but I'm afraid they come out at about thirty-five shillings a pair. And no durability, of course. Just like cobwebs.'

'*C'est ça. C'est ça, exactement.*'

A prolonged absence of the young lady this time.

She returned at last.

'I'm afraid they are actually thirty-seven and sixpence a pair. But beautiful, aren't they?'

She slid them tenderly from a gauzy envelope – the finest, gauziest wisps of stockings.

'*En fin* – that is it exactly!'

'Lovely, aren't they? How many pairs, sir?'

'I want – let me see, nineteen pairs.'

The young lady very nearly fell down behind the counter, but long training in scornfulness just kept her erect.

'There would be a reduction on two dozen,' she said faintly.

'No, I want nineteen pairs. Of slightly different colours, please.'

The girl sorted them out obediently, packed them up and made out the bill.

As Poirot departed with his purchase, the next girl at the counter said: 'Wonder who the lucky girl is. Must be a nasty old man. Oh, well, she seems to be stringing him along good and proper. Stockings at thirty-seven and sixpence indeed!'

Unaware of the low estimate formed by the young ladies of Messrs Harvey Robinson's upon his character, Poirot was trotting homewards.

He had been in for about half an hour when he heard the door-bell ring. A few minutes later Major Despard entered the room.

He was obviously keeping his temper with difficulty.

'What the devil did you want to go and see Mrs Luxmore for?' he asked.

Poirot smiled.

'I wished, you see, for the true story of Professor Luxmore's death.'

'True story? Do you think that woman's capable of telling the truth about anything?' demanded Despard wrathfully.

'*Eh bien*, I did wonder now and then,' admitted Poirot.

'I should think you did. That woman's crazy.'

Poirot demurred.

'Not at all. She is a romantic woman, that is all.'

'Romantic be damned. She's an out-and-out liar. I sometimes think she even believes her own lies.'

'It is quite possible.'

'She's an appalling woman. I had the hell of a time with her out there.'

'That also I can well believe.'

Despard sat down abruptly.

'Look here, M. Poirot, I'm going to tell you the truth.'

'You mean you are going to give me your version of the story?'

'My version will be the true version.'

Poirot did not reply.

Despard went on dryly: 'I quite realize that I can't claim any merit in coming out with this now. I'm telling the truth because it's the only thing to be done at this stage. Whether you believe me or not is up to you. I've no kind of proof that my story is the correct one.'

He paused for a minute and then began.

'I arranged the trip for the Luxmores. He was a nice old boy, quite batty about mosses and plants and things. She was a – well, she was what you've no doubt observed her to be! That trip was a nightmare. I didn't care a damn for the woman – rather disliked her, as a matter of fact. She was the intense, soulful kind that always makes me feel prickly with embarrassment. Everything went all right for the first fortnight. Then we all had a go of fever. She and I had it slightly. Old Luxmore was pretty bad. One night – now you've got to listen to this carefully – I was sitting outside my tent. Suddenly I saw Luxmore in the distance staggering off into the bush by the river. He was absolutely delirious and quite unconscious of what he was doing. In another minute he would be in the river – and at that particular spot it would have been the end of him. No chance of a rescue. There wasn't time to rush after him – only one thing to be done. My rifle was beside me as usual. I snatched it up. I'm a pretty accurate shot. I was quite sure I could bring the old boy down – get him in the leg. And then, just as I fired, that idiotic fool of a woman flung herself from somewhere upon me, yelping out, "Don't shoot. For God's sake, don't shoot." She caught my arm and jerked it ever so slightly just as the rifle went off – with the result that the bullet got him in the back and killed him dead!

'I can tell you that was a pretty ghastly moment. And that damned fool of a woman still didn't understand what she'd done. Instead of realizing that she'd been responsible for her husband's death, she firmly believed that I'd been trying to shoot the old boy in cold blood – for love of her, if you please! We had the devil of a scene – she insisting that we should say he'd died of fever. I was sorry for her – especially as I saw she didn't realize what she'd done. But she'd have to realize it if the truth came out! And then her complete certainty that I was head over heels in love with her gave me a bit of a jar. It was going to be a pretty kettle of fish if she went about giving that out. In the end I agreed to do what she wanted – partly for the sake of peace, I'll admit. After all, it didn't seem to matter much. Fever or accident. And I didn't want to drag a woman through a lot of unpleasantness – even if she was a damned fool. I gave it out next day that the professor was dead of fever and we buried him. The bearers knew the truth, of course, but they were all devoted to me and I knew that what I said they'd swear to if need be. We buried poor old Luxmore and got back to civilization. Since then I've spent a good deal of time dodging the woman.'

He paused, then said quietly: 'That's my story, M. Poirot.'

Poirot said slowly: 'It was to that incident that Mr Shaitana referred, or so you thought, at dinner that night?'

Despard nodded.

'He must have heard it from Mrs Luxmore. Easy enough to get the story out of her. That sort of thing would have amused him.'

'It might have been a dangerous story – to you – in the hands of a man like Shaitana.'

Despard shrugged his shoulders.

'I wasn't afraid of Shaitana.'

Poirot didn't answer.

Despard said quietly: 'That again you have to take my word for. It's true enough, I suppose, that I had a kind of motive for Shaitana's death. Well, the truth's out now – take it or leave it.'

Poirot held out a hand.

'I will take it, Major Despard. I have no doubt at all that things in South America happened exactly as you have described.'

Despard's face lit up.

'Thanks,' he said laconically.

And he clasped Poirot's hand warmly.

— 22 —

EVIDENCE FROM COMBEACRE

SUPERINTENDENT BATTLE was in the police station of Combeacre.

Inspector Harper, rather red in the face, talked in a slow, pleasing Devonshire voice.

'That's how it was, sir. Seemed all as right as rain. The doctor was satisfied. Everyone was satisfied. Why not?'

'Just give me the facts about the two bottles again. I want to get it quite clear.'

'Syrup of figs – that's what the bottle was. She took it regular, it seems. Then there was this hat paint she'd been using – or, rather, the young lady, her companion, had been using for her. Brightening up a garden hat. There was a good deal left over, and the bottle broke, and Mrs Benson herself said, "Put it in that old bottle – the syrup of figs bottle." That's all right. The servants heard her. The young lady, Miss Meredith, and the housemaid

and the parlourmaid – they all agree on that. The paint was put
into the old syrup of figs bottle and it was put on the top shelf in the
bathroom with other odds and ends.'

'Not re-labelled?'

'No. Careless, of course; the coroner commented on that.'

'Go on.'

'On this particular night the deceased went into the bathroom,
took down a syrup of figs bottle, poured herself out a good dose
and drank it. Realized what she'd done and they sent off at once
for the doctor. He was out on a case and it was some time before
they could get at him. They did all they could, but she died.'

'She herself believed it to be an accident?'

'Oh, yes – everyone thought so. It seems clear the bottles must
have got mixed up somehow. It was suggested the housemaid did
it when she dusted, but she swears she didn't.'

Superintendent Battle was silent – thinking. Such an easy
business. A bottle taken down from an upper shelf, put in place of
the other. So difficult to trace a mistake like that to its source.
Handled it with gloves, possibly, and, anyway, the last prints
would be those of Mrs Benson herself. Yes, so easy – so simple.
But, all the same, murder! The perfect crime.

But why? That still puzzled him – why?

'This young lady-companion, this Miss Meredith, she didn't
come into money at Mrs Benson's death?' he asked.

Inspector Harper shook his head.

'No. She'd only been there about six weeks. Difficult place, I
should imagine. Young ladies didn't stay long as a rule.'

Battle was still puzzled. Young ladies didn't stay long. A
difficult woman, evidently. But if Anne Meredith had been
unhappy, she could have left as her predecessors had done. No
need to kill – unless it were sheer unreasoning vindictiveness. He
shook his head. That suggestion did not ring true.

'Who did get Mrs Benson's money?'

'I couldn't say, sir, nephews and nieces, I believe. But it
wouldn't be very much – not when it was divided up, and I heard
as how most of her income was one of these annuities.'

Nothing there then. But Mrs Benson had died. And Anne
Meredith had not told him that she had been at Combeacre.

It was all profoundly unsatisfactory.

He made diligent and painstaking inquiries. The doctor was
quite clear and emphatic. No reason to believe it was anything but
an accident. Miss – couldn't remember her name – nice girl but
rather helpless – had been very upset and distressed. There was

293

the vicar. He remembered Mrs Benson's last companion – a modest-looking girl. Always came to church with Mrs Benson. Mrs Benson had been – not difficult – but a trifle severe toward young people. She was the rigid type of Christian.

Battle tried one or two other people but learned nothing of value. Anne Meredith was hardly remembered. She had lived among them a few months – that was all – and her personality was not sufficiently vivid to make a lasting impression. 'A nice little thing' seemed to be the accepted description.

Mrs Benson loomed out a little more clearly. A self-righteous grenadier of a woman, working her companions hard and changing her servants often. A disagreeable woman – but that was all.

Nevertheless Superintendent Battle left Devonshire under the firm impression that, for some reason unknown, Anne Meredith had deliberately murdered her employer.

— 23 —

THE EVIDENCE OF A PAIR
OF SILK STOCKINGS

As SUPERINTENDENT Battle's train rushed eastwards through England, Anne Meredith and Rhoda Dawes were in Hercule Poirot's sitting-room.

Anne had been unwilling to accept the invitation that had reached her by the morning's post, but Rhoda's counsel had prevailed.

'Anne – you're a coward – yes, a coward. It's no good going on being an ostrich, burying your head in the sand. There's been a murder and you're one of the suspects – the least likely one perhaps—'

'That would be the worst,' said Anne with a touch of humour. 'It's always the least likely person who did it.'

'But you are one,' continued Rhoda, undisturbed by the interruption. 'And so it's no use putting your nose in the air as though murder was a nasty smell and nothing to do with you.'

'It *is* nothing to do with me,' Anne persisted. 'I mean, I'm quite willing to answer any questions the police want to ask me, but this man, this Hercule Poirot, he's an outsider.'

'And what will he think if you hedge and try to get out of it? He'll think you're bursting with guilt.'

'I'm certainly not bursting with guilt,' said Anne coldly.

'Darling, I know that. You couldn't murder anybody if you tried. But horrible suspicious foreigners don't know that. I think we ought to go nicely to his house. Otherwise he'll come down here and try to worm things out of the servants.'

'We haven't got any servants.'

'We've got Mother Astwell. She can wag a tongue with anybody! Come on, Anne, let's go. It will be rather fun really.'

'I don't see why he wants to see me.' Anne was obstinate.

'To put one over on the official police, of course,' said Rhoda impatiently. 'They always do – the amateurs, I mean. They make out that Scotland Yard are all boots and brainlessness.'

'Do you think this man Poirot is clever?'

'He doesn't look a Sherlock,' said Rhoda. 'I expect he has been quite good in his day. He's gaga now, of course. He must be at least sixty. Oh, come on, Anne, let's go and see the old boy. He may tell us dreadful things about the others.'

'All right,' said Anne, and added, 'You do *enjoy* all this so, Rhoda.'

'I suppose because it isn't my funeral,' said Rhoda. 'You were a noodle, Anne, not just to have looked up at the right minute. If only you had, you could live like a duchess for the rest of your life on blackmail.'

So it came about that at three o'clock of that same afternoon, Rhoda Dawes and Anne Meredith sat primly on their chairs in Poirot's neat room and sipped blackberry *sirop* (which they disliked very much but were too polite to refuse) from old-fashioned glasses.

'It was most amiable of you to accede to my request, Mademoiselle,' Poirot was saying.

'I'm sure I shall be glad to help you in any way I can,' murmured Anne vaguely.

'It is a little matter of memory.'

'Memory?'

'Yes, I have already put these questions to Mrs Lorrimer, to Dr Roberts and to Major Despard. None of them, alas, have given me the response that I hoped for.'

Anne continued to look at him inquiringly.

'I want you, Mademoiselle, to cast your mind back to that evening in the drawing-room of Mr Shaitana.'

A weary shadow passed over Anne's face. Was she never to be free of that nightmare?

Poirot noticed the expression.

'I know, Mademoiselle, I know,' he said kindly. '*C'est pénible, n'est ce pas?* That is very natural. You, so young as you are, to be brought in contact with horror for the first time. Probably you have never known or seen a violent death.'

Rhoda's feet shifted a little uncomfortably on the floor.

'Well?' said Anne.

'Cast your mind back. I want you to tell me what you remember of that room.'

Anne stared at him suspiciously.

'I don't understand.'

'But, yes. The chairs, the tables, the ornaments, the wallpaper, the curtains, the fire-irons. You saw them all. Can you not, then, describe them?'

'Oh, I see.' Anne hesitated, frowning. 'It's difficult. I don't really think I remember. I couldn't say what the wallpaper was like. I think the walls were painted – some inconspicuous colour. There were rugs on the floor. There was a piano.' She shook her head. 'I really couldn't tell you any more.'

'But you are not trying, Mademoiselle. You must remember some object, some ornament, some piece of *bric-à-brac?*'

'There was a case of Egyptian jewellery, I remember,' said Anne slowly. 'Over by the window.'

'Oh, yes, at the extreme other end of the room from the table on which lay the little dagger.'

Anne looked at him.

'I never heard which table that was on.'

'*Pas si bête,*' commented Poirot to himself. 'But, then, no more is Hercule Poirot! If she knew me better she would realize I would never lay a *piège* as gross as that!'

Aloud he said: 'A case of Egyptian jewellery, you say?'

Anne answered with some enthusiasm.

'Yes – some of it was lovely. Blues and red. Enamel. One or two lovely rings. And scarabs – but I don't like them so much.'

'He was a great collector, Mr Shaitana,' murmured Poirot.

'Yes, he must have been,' Anne agreed. 'The room was full of stuff. One couldn't begin to look at it all.'

'So that you cannot mention anything else that particularly struck your notice?'

Anne smiled a little as she said:

'Only a vase of chrysanthemums that badly wanted their water changed.'

'Ah, yes, servants are not always too particular about that.'

Poirot was silent for a moment or two.

Anne asked timidly: 'I'm afraid I didn't notice – whatever it is you wanted me to notice.'

Poirot smiled kindly.

'It does not matter, *mon enfant*. It was, indeed, an outside chance. Tell me, have you seen the good Major Despard lately?'

He saw the delicate pink colour come up in the girl's face. She replied: 'He said he would come and see us again quite soon.'

Rhoda said impetuously: '*He* didn't do it, anyway! Anne and I are quite sure of that.'

Poirot twinkled at them.

'How fortunate – to have convinced two such charming young ladies of one's innocence.'

'Oh dear,' thought Rhoda. 'He's going to be French, and it does embarrass me so.'

She got up and began examining some etchings on the wall.

'These are awfully good,' she said.

'They are not bad,' said Poirot.

He hesitated, looking at Anne.

'Mademoiselle,' he said at last. 'I wonder if I might ask you to do me a great favour – oh, nothing to do with the murder. This is an entirely private and personal matter.'

Anne looked a little surprised. Poirot went on speaking in a slightly embarrassed manner.

'It is, you understand, that Christmas is coming on. I have to buy presents for many nieces and grand-nieces. And it is a little difficult to choose what young ladies like in this present time. My tastes, alas, are rather old-fashioned.'

'Yes?' said Anne kindly.

'Silk stockings, now – are silk stockings a welcome present to receive?'

'Yes, indeed. It's always nice to be given stockings.'

'You relieve my mind. I will ask my favour. I have obtained some different colours. There are, I think, about fifteen or sixteen pairs. Would you be so amiable as to look through them and set aside half a dozen pairs that seem to you the most desirable?'

'Certainly I will,' said Anne, rising, with a laugh.

Poirot directed her towards a table in an alcove – a table whose contents were strangely at variance, had she but known it, with the well-known order and neatness of Hercule Poirot. There were stockings piled up in untidy heaps – some fur-lined gloves – calendars and boxes of bonbons.

'I send off my parcels very much *à l'avance*,' Poirot explained.

'See, Mademoiselle, here are the stockings. Select me, I pray of you, six pairs.'

He turned, intercepting Rhoda, who was following him.

'As for Mademoiselle here, I have a little treat for her – a treat that would be no treat for you, I fancy, Mademoiselle Meredith.'

'What is it?' cried Rhoda.

He lowered his voice.

'A knife, Mademoiselle, with which twelve people once stabbed a man. It was given me as a souvenir by the Compagnie Internationale des Wagons Lits.'

'Horrible!' cried Anne.

'Ooh! Let me see,' said Rhoda.

Poirot led her through into the other room, talking as he went.

'It was given me by the Compagnie Internationale des Wagons Lits because—'

They passed out of the room.

They returned three minutes later. Anne came towards them.

'I think these six are the nicest, M. Poirot. Both these are very good evening shades, and this lighter colour would be nice when summer comes and it's daylight in the evening.'

'*Mille remercîments, Mademoiselle.*'

He offered them more *sirop*, which they refused, and finally accompanied them to the door, still talking genially.

When they had finally departed he returned to the room and went straight to the littered table. The pile of stockings still lay in a confused heap. Poirot counted the six selected pairs and then went on to count the others.

He had bought nineteen pairs. There were now only seventeen.

He nodded his head slowly.

— 24 —

ELIMINATION OF THREE MURDERERS?

ON ARRIVAL in London, Superintendent Battle came straight to Poirot. Anne and Rhoda had then been gone an hour or more.

Without more ado, the superintendent recounted the result of his researches in Devonshire.

'We're on to it – not a doubt of it,' he finished. 'That's what

Shaitana was aiming at – with his "domestic accident" business. But what gets me is the motive. Why did she want to kill the woman?'

'I think I can help you there, my friend.'

'Go ahead, M. Poirot.'

'This afternoon I conducted a little experiment. I induced Mademoiselle and her friend to come here. I put to them my usual questions as to what there was in the room that night.'

Battle looked at him curiously.

'You're very keen on that question.'

'Yes, it's useful. It tells me a good deal. Mademoiselle Meredith was suspicious – very suspicious. She takes nothing for granted, that young lady. So that good dog, Hercule Poirot, he does one of his best tricks. He lays a clumsy amateurish trap. Mademoiselle mentions a case of jewellery. I say was not that at the opposite end of the room from the table with the dagger. Mademoiselle does not fall into the trap. She avoids it cleverly. And after that she is pleased with herself, and her vigilance relaxes. So that is the object of this visit – to get her to admit that she knew where the dagger was, and that she noticed it! Her spirits rise when she has, as she thinks, defeated me. She talked quite freely about the jewellery. She has noticed many details of it. There is nothing else in the room that she remembers – except that a vase of chrysanthemums needed its water changing.'

'Well?' said Battle.

'Well, it is significant, that. Suppose we knew nothing about this girl. Her words would give us a clue to her character. She notices flowers. She is, then, fond of flowers? No, since she does not mention a very big bowl of early tulips which would at once have attracted the attention of a flower lover. No, it is the paid companion who speaks – the girl whose duty it has been to put fresh water in the vases – and, allied to that, there is a girl who loves and notices jewellery. Is not that, at least, suggestive?'

'Ah,' said Battle. 'I'm beginning to see what you're driving at.'

'Precisely. As I told you the other day, I place my cards on the table. When you recounted her history the other day, and Mrs Oliver made her startling announcement, my mind went at once to an important point. The murder could not have been committed for gain, since Miss Meredith had still to earn her living after it happened. Why, then? I considered Miss Meredith's temperament as it appeared superficially. A rather timid young girl, poor, but well-dressed, fond of pretty things . . . The temperament, is it not, of a *thief*, rather than a murderer? And I asked immediately if Mrs Eldon had been a tidy woman. You replied that, no, she had not been tidy. I formed a hypothesis. Supposing that Anne Meredith was a girl with a weak streak in her character – the kind of girl who takes little things from the big shops. Supposing that, poor, and yet loving pretty things, she helped herself once or twice to things from her employer. A brooch, perhaps, an odd half-crown or two, a string of beads. Mrs Eldon, careless, untidy, would put down these disappearances to her own carelessness. She would not suspect her gentle little mother's-help. But, now, suppose a different type of employer – an employer who *did* notice – accused Anne Meredith of theft. That would be a possible motive for murder. As I said the other evening, Miss Meredith would only commit a murder through fear. She knows that her employer will be able to prove the theft. There is only one thing that can save her: her employer must die. And so she changes the bottles, and Mrs Benson dies – ironically enough convinced that the mistake is her own, and not suspecting for a minute that the cowed, frightened girl has had a hand in it.'

'It's possible,' said Superintendent Battle. 'It's only a hypothesis, but it's possible.'

'It is a little more than possible, my friend – it is also probable. For this afternoon I laid a little trap nicely baited – the real trap – after the sham one had been circumvented. If what I suspect is true, Anne Meredith will never, never be able to resist a really expensive pair of stockings! I ask her to aid me. I let her know carefully that I am not sure exactly how many stockings there are, I go out of the room, leaving her alone – and the result, my friend, is that I have now seventeen pairs of stockings, instead of nineteen, and that two pairs have gone away in Anne Meredith's handbag.'

'Whew!' Superintendent Battle whistled. 'What a risk to take, though.'

'*Pas du tout*. What does she think I suspect her of? Murder. What is the risk, then, in stealing a pair, or two pairs, of silk stockings? I am not looking for a thief. And, besides, the thief, or the kleptomaniac, is always the same – convinced that she can get away with it.'

Battle nodded his head.

'That's true enough. Incredibly stupid. The pitcher goes to the well time after time. Well, I think between us we've arrived fairly clearly at the truth. Anne Meredith was caught stealing. Anne Meredith changed a bottle from one shelf to another. We know that was murder – but I'm damned if we could ever prove it. Successful crime No. 2. Roberts gets away with it. Anne Meredith gets away with it. But what about Shaitana? Did Anne Meredith kill Shaitana?'

He remained silent for a moment or two, then he shook his head.

'It doesn't work out right,' he said reluctantly. 'She's not one to take a risk. Change a couple of bottles, yes. She knew no one could fasten that on her. It was absolutely safe – because anyone might have done it! Of course, it mightn't have worked. Mrs Benson might have noticed before she drank the stuff, or she mightn't have died from it. It was what I call a *hopeful* kind of murder. It might work or it mightn't. Actually, it did. But Shaitana was a very different pair of shoes. That was deliberate, audacious, purposeful murder.'

Poirot nodded his head.

'I agree with you. The two types of crime are not the same.'

Battle rubbed his nose.

'So that seems to wipe her out as far as he's concerned. Roberts and the girl, both crossed off our list. What about Despard? Any luck with the Luxmore woman?'

Poirot narrated his adventures of the preceding afternoon.

Battle grinned.

'I know that type. You can't disentangle what they remember from what they invent.'

Poirot went on. He described Despard's visit, and the story the latter had told.

'Believe him?' Battle asked abruptly.

'Yes, I do.'

Battle sighed.

'So do I. Not the type to shoot a man because he wanted the man's wife. Anyway, what's wrong with the divorce court? Everyone flocks there. And he's not a professional man; it wouldn't ruin him, or anything like that. No, I'm of the opinion that our late lamented Mr Shaitana struck a snag there. Murderer No. 3 wasn't a murderer, after all.'

He looked at Poirot.

'That leaves—?'

'Mrs Lorrimer,' said Poirot.

The telephone rang. Poirot got up and answered it. He spoke a few words, waited, spoke again. Then he hung up the receiver and returned to Battle.

301

His face was very grave.

'That was Mrs Lorrimer speaking,' he said. 'She wants me to come round and see her – now.'

He and Battle looked at each other. The latter shook his head slowly.

'Am I wrong?' he said. 'Or were you expecting something of the kind?'

'I wondered,' said Hercule Poirot. 'That was all. I wondered.'

'You'd better get along,' said Battle. 'Perhaps you'll manage to get at the truth at last.'

— 25 —

MRS LORRIMER SPEAKS

THE DAY was not a bright one, and Mrs Lorrimer's room seemed rather dark and cheerless. She herself had a grey look, and seemed much older than she had done on the occasion of Poirot's last visit.

She greeted him with her usual smiling assurance.

'It is very nice of you to come so promptly, M. Poirot. You are a busy man, I know.'

'At your service, Madame,' said Poirot with a little bow.

Mrs Lorrimer pressed the bell by the fireplace.

'We will have tea brought in. I don't know what you feel about it, but I always think it's a mistake to rush straight into confidences without any decent paving of the way.'

'There are to be confidences, then, Madame?'

Mrs Lorrimer did not answer, for at that moment her maid answered the bell. When she had received the order and gone again, Mrs Lorrimer said dryly: 'You said, if you remember, when you were last here, that you would come if I sent for you. You had an idea, I think, of the reason that should prompt me to send.'

There was no more just then. Tea was brought. Mrs Lorrimer dispensed it, talking intelligently on various topics of the day.

Taking advantage of a pause, Poirot remarked: 'I hear you and little Mademoiselle Meredith had tea together the other day.'

'We did. You have seen her lately?'

'This very afternoon.'

'She is in London, then, or have you been down to Wallingford?'

'No. She and her friend were so amiable as to pay me a visit.'

'Ah, the friend. I have not met her.'

Poirot said, smiling a little: 'This murder – it has made for a *rapprochement*. You and Mademoiselle Meredith have tea together. Major Despard, he, too, cultivates Miss Meredith's acquaintance. The Dr Roberts, he is perhaps the only one out of it.'

'I saw him out at bridge the other day,' said Mrs Lorrimer. 'He seemed quite his usual cheerful self.'

'As fond of bridge as ever?'

'Yes – still making the most outrageous bids – and very often getting away with it.'

She was silent for a moment or two, then said: 'Have you seen Superintendent Battle lately?'

'Also this afternoon. He was with me when you telephoned.'

Shading her face from the fire with one hand, Mrs Lorrimer asked: 'How is he getting on?'

Poirot said gravely: 'He is not very rapid, the good Battle. He gets there slowly, but he does get there in the end, Madame.'

'I wonder.' Her lips curved in a faintly ironical smile.

She went on: 'He has paid me quite a lot of attention. He has delved, I think, into my past history right back to my girlhood. He has interviewed my friends, and chatted to my servants – the ones I have now and the ones who have been with me in former years. What he hoped to find I do not know, but he certainly did not find it. He might as well have accepted what I told him. It was the truth. I knew Mr Shaitana very slightly. I met him at Luxor, as I said, and our acquaintanceship was never more than an acquaintanceship. Superintendent Battle will not be able to get away from these facts.'

'Perhaps not,' said Poirot.

'And you, M. Poirot? Have not you made any inquiries?'

'About you, Madame?'

'That is what I meant.'

Slowly the little man shook his head.

'It would have been of no avail.'

'Just exactly what do you mean by that, M. Poirot?'

'I will be quite frank, Madame. I have realized from the beginning that, of the four persons in Mr Shaitana's room that night, the one with the best brains, with the coolest, most logical head, was you, Madame. If I had to lay money on the chance of one of those four planning a murder and getting away with it successfully, it is on you that I should place my money.'

Mrs Lorrimer's brows rose.

'Am I expected to feel flattered?' she asked dryly.

Poirot went on, without paying any attention to her interruption.

'For a crime to be successful, it is usually necessary to think every detail of it out beforehand. All possible contingencies must be taken into account. The *timing* must be accurate. The *placing* must be scrupulously correct. Dr Roberts might bungle a crime through haste and over-confidence; Major Despard would probably be too prudent to commit one; Miss Meredith might lose her head and give herself away. You, Madame, would do none of these things. You would be clear-headed and cool, you are sufficiently resolute of character, and could be sufficiently obsessed with an idea to the extent of overruling prudence, you are not the kind of woman to lose her head.'

Mrs Lorrimer sat silent for a minute or two, a curious smile playing round her lips. At last she said: 'So that is what you think of me, M. Poirot. That I am the kind of woman to commit an ideal murder.'

'At least you have the amiability not to resent the idea.'

'I find it very interesting. So it is your idea that I am the only person who could successfully have murdered Shaitana?'

Poirot said slowly: 'There is a difficulty there, Madame.'

'Really? Do tell me.'

'You may have noticed that I said just now a phrase something like this: "For a crime to be successful it is usually necessary to plan every detail of it carefully beforehand." "Usually" is the word to which I want to draw your attention. For there *is* another type of successful crime. Have you ever said suddenly to anyone, "Throw a stone and see if you can hit that tree," and the person obeys quickly, without thinking – and surprisingly often he *does* hit the tree? But when he comes to repeat the throw it is not so easy – for he has begun to *think*. "So hard – no harder – a little more to the right – to the left." The first was an almost unconscious action, the body obeying the mind as the body of an animal does. *Eh bien*, Madame, there is a type of crime like that – a crime committed on the spur of the moment – an inspiration – a flash of genius – without time to pause or think. And that, Madame, was the kind of crime that killed Mr Shaitana. A sudden dire necessity, a flash of inspiration, rapid execution.'

He shook his head.

'And that, Madame, is not your type of crime at all. If you killed Mr Shaitana, it should have been a premeditated crime.'

'I see.' Her hand waved softly to and fro, keeping the heat of the fire from her face. 'And, of course, it wasn't a premeditated crime, so I couldn't have killed him – eh, M. Poirot?'

Poirot bowed.

'That is right, Madame.'

'And yet—' She leaned forward, her waving hand stopped. '*I did kill Shaitana, M. Poirot . . .*'

— 26 —

THE TRUTH

THERE was a pause – a very long pause.

The room was growing dark. The firelight leaped and flickered.

Mrs Lorrimer and Hercule Poirot looked not at each other, but at the fire. It was as though time was momentarily in abeyance.

Then Hercule Poirot sighed and stirred.

'So it was that – all the time . . . *Why* did you kill him, Madame?'

'I think you know why, M. Poirot.'

'Because he knew something about you – something that had happened long ago?'

'Yes.'

'And that something was – another death, Madame?'

She bowed her head.

Poirot said gently: 'Why did you tell me? What made you send for me today?'

'You told me once that I should do so some day.'

'Yes – that is, I hoped . . . I knew, Madame, that there was only one way of learning the truth as far as you were concerned – and that was by your own free will. If you did not choose to speak, you would not do so, and you would never give yourself away. But there was a chance – that you yourself might *wish* to speak.'

Mrs Lorrimer nodded.

'It was clever of you to foresee that – the weariness – the loneliness—'

Her voice died away.

Poirot looked at her curiously.

'So it has been like that? Yes, I can understand it might be . . .'

'Alone – quite alone,' said Mrs Lorrimer. 'No one knows what that means unless they have lived, as I have lived, with the knowledge of what one has done.'

Poirot said gently: 'Is it an impertinence, Madame, or may I be permitted to offer my sympathy?'

She bent her head a little.

'Thank you, M. Poirot.'

There was another pause, then Poirot said, speaking in a slightly brisker tone: 'Am I to understand, Madame, that you took the words Mr Shaitana spoke at dinner as a direct menace aimed at you?'

She nodded.

'I realized at once that he was speaking so that one person should understand him. That person was myself. The reference to a woman's weapon being poison was meant for me. He *knew*. I had suspected it once before. He had brought the conversation round to a certain famous trial, and I saw his eyes watching me. There was a kind of uncanny knowledge in them. But, of course, that night I was quite sure.'

'And you were sure, too, of his future intentions?'

Mrs Lorrimer said dryly: 'It was hardly likely that the presence of Superintendent Battle and yourself was an accident. I took it that Shaitana was going to advertise his own cleverness by pointing out to you both that he had discovered something that no one else had suspected.'

'How soon did you make up your mind to act, Madame?'

Mrs Lorrimer hesitated a little.

'It is difficult to remember exactly when the idea came into my mind,' she said. 'I had noticed the dagger before going in to dinner. When we returned to the drawing-room I picked it up and slipped it into my sleeve. No one saw me do it. I made sure of that.'

'It would be dexterously done, I have no doubt, Madame.'

'I made up my mind then exactly what I was going to do. I had only to carry it out. It was risky, perhaps, but I considered that it was worth trying.'

'That is your coolness, your successful weighing of chances, coming into play. Yes, I see that.'

'We started to play bridge,' continued Mrs Lorrimer. Her voice was cool and unemotional. 'At last an opportunity arose. I was dummy. I strolled across the room to the fireplace. Shaitana had dozed off to sleep. I looked over at the others. They were all intent on the game. I leant over and – and did it—'

Her voice shook just a little, but instantly it regained its cool aloofness.

'I spoke to him. It came into my head that that would make a kind of alibi for me. I made some remark about the fire, and then

306

pretended he had answered me and went on again, saying something like: "I agree with you. I do not like radiators, either." '

'He did not cry out at all?'

'No. I think he made a little grunt – that was all. It might have been taken for words from a distance.'

'And then?'

'And then I went back to the bridge table. The last trick was just being played.'

'And you sat down and resumed play?'

'Yes.'

'With sufficient interest in the game to be able to tell me nearly all the calling and the hands two days later?'

'Yes,' said Mrs Lorrimer simply.

'*Epatant!*' said Hercule Poirot.

He leaned back in his chair. He nodded his head several times. Then, by way of a change, he shook it.

'But there is still something, Madame, that I do not understand.'

'Yes?'

'It seems to me that there is some factor I have missed. You are a woman who considers and weighs everything carefully. You decide that, for a certain reason, you will run an enormous risk. You do run it – successfully. And then, not two weeks later, you change your mind. Frankly, Madame, that does not seem to me to ring true.'

A queer little smile twisted her lips.

'You are quite right, M. Poirot, there is one factor that you do not know. Did Miss Meredith tell you where she met me the other day?'

'It was, I think she said, near Mrs Oliver's flat.'

'I believe that is so. But I meant the actual name of the street. Anne Meredith met me in Harley Street.'

'Ah!' He looked at her attentively. 'I begin to see.'

'Yes, I thought you would. I had been to see a specialist there. He told me what I already half suspected.'

Her smile widened. It was no longer twisted and bitter. It was suddenly sweet.

'I shall not play very much more bridge, M. Poirot. Oh, he didn't say so in so many words. He wrapped up the truth a little. With great care, etc., etc., I might live several years. But I shall not take any great care. I am not that kind of a woman.'

'Yes, yes, I begin to understand,' said Poirot.

'It made a difference, you see. A month – two months, perhaps

– not more. And then, just as I left the specialist, I saw Miss Meredith. I asked her to have tea with me.'

She paused, then went on: 'I am not, after all, a wholly wicked woman. All the time we were having tea I was thinking. By my action the other evening I had not only deprived the man Shaitana of life (that was done, and could not be undone), I had also, to a varying degree, affected unfavourably the lives of three other people. Because of what I had done, Dr Roberts, Major Despard and Anne Meredith, none of whom had injured me in any way, were passing through a very grave ordeal, and might even be in danger. That, at least, I could undo. I don't know that I felt particularly moved by the plight of either Dr Roberts or Major Despard – although both of them had presumably a much longer span of life in front of them than I had. They were men, and could, to a certain extent, look after themselves. But when I looked at Anne Meredith—'

She hesitated, then continued slowly: 'Anne Meredith was only a girl. She had the whole of her life in front of her. This miserable business might ruin that life . . .

'I didn't like the thought of that . . .

'And then, M. Poirot, with these ideas growing in my mind, I realized that what you had hinted had come true. I was not going to be able to keep silence. This afternoon I rang you up . . .'

Minutes passed.

Hercule Poirot leaned forward. He stared, deliberately stared through the gathering gloom, at Mrs Lorrimer. She returned that intent gaze quietly and without any nervousness.

He said at last: 'Mrs Lorrimer, are you sure – are you *positive* (you will tell me the truth, will you not?) – *that the murder of Mr Shaitana was not premeditated*? Is it not a fact that you planned the crime *beforehand* – that you went to that dinner with the murder already all mapped out in your mind?'

Mrs Lorrimer stared at him for a moment, then she shook her head sharply.

'No,' she said.

'You did not plan the murder beforehand?'

'Certainly not.'

'Then – then . . . Oh, you are lying to me – you must be lying! . . .'

Mrs Lorrimer's voice cut into the air like ice.

'Really, M. Poirot, you forget yourself.'

The little man sprang to his feet. He paced up and down the room, muttering to himself, uttering ejaculations.

Suddenly he said: 'Permit me?'

And, going to the switch, he turned on the electric lights.

He came back, sat down in his chair, placed both hands on his knees and stared straight at his hostess.

'The question is,' he said, 'can Hercule Poirot possibly be wrong?'

'No one can always be right,' said Mrs Lorrimer coldly.

'I am,' said Poirot. 'Always I am right. It is so invariable that it startles me. But now it looks, it very much looks, as though I am wrong. And that upsets me. Presumably, you know what you are saying. It is your murder! Fantastic, then, that Hercule Poirot should know better than you do how you committed it.'

'Fantastic and very absurd,' said Mrs Lorrimer still more coldly.

'I am, then, mad. Decidedly I am mad. No – *sacré nom d'un petit bonhomme* – I am *not* mad! I am right. I *must* be right. I am willing to believe that you killed Mr Shaitana – *but you cannot have killed him in the way you say you did.* No one can do a thing that is not *dans son caractère*!'

He paused. Mrs Lorrimer drew in an angry breath and bit her lips. She was about to speak, but Poirot forestalled her.

'Either the killing of Shaitana was planned beforehand – *or you did not kill him at all!*'

'I really believe you *are* mad, M. Poirot. If I am willing to admit I committed the crime, I should not be likely to lie about the way I did it. What would be the point of such a thing?'

Poirot got up again and took one turn round the room. When he came back to his seat his manner had changed. He was gentle and kindly.

'You did not kill Shaitana,' he said softly. 'I see that now. I see everything. Harley Street. And little Anne Meredith standing forlorn on the pavement. I see, too, another girl – a very long time ago, a girl who has gone through life always alone – terribly alone. Yes, I see all that. But one thing I do not see – why are you so certain that Anne Meredith did it?'

'Really, M. Poirot—'

'Absolutely useless to protest – to lie further to me, Madame. *I tell you, I know the truth.* I know the very emotions that swept over you that day in Harley Street. You would not have done it for Major Despard, *non plus*. You would not have done it for Dr Roberts – oh, no! But Anne Meredith is different. You have compassion for her, *because she has done what you once did.* You do not know even – or so I imagine – what *reason* she had for the crime. But you are quite sure she did it. You were sure that first evening – the evening it happened – when Superintendent Battle invited you to give your views on the case. Yes, I know it all, you see. It is quite useless to lie further to me. You see that, do you not?'

He paused for an answer, but none came. He nodded his head in satisfaction.

'Yes, you are sensible. That is good. It is a very noble action that you perform there, Madame, to take the blame on yourself and to let this child escape.'

'You forget,' said Mrs Lorrimer in a dry voice, 'I am not an innocent woman. Years ago, M. Poirot, I killed my husband . . .'

There was a moment's silence.

'I see,' said Poirot. 'It is justice. After all, only justice. You have the logical mind. You are willing to suffer for the act you committed. Murder is murder – it does not matter who the victim is. Madame, you have courage, and you have clear-sightedness. But I ask of you once more: *How can you be so sure?* How do you *know* that it was Anne Meredith who killed Mr Shaitana?'

A deep sigh broke from Mrs Lorrimer. Her last resistance had gone down before Poirot's insistence. She answered his question quite simply like a child.

'Because,' she said, 'I saw her.'

— 27 —

THE EYE-WITNESS

SUDDENLY Poirot laughed. He could not help it. His head went back, and his high Gallic laugh filled the room.

'*Pardon, Madame,*' he said, wiping his eyes. 'I could not help it. Here we argue and we reason! We ask questions! We invoke the psychology – and all the time *there was an eye-witness of the crime*. Tell me, I pray of you.'

'It was fairly late in the evening. Anne Meredith was dummy. She got up and looked over her partner's hand, and then she moved about the room. The hand wasn't very interesting – the conclusion was inevitable. I didn't need to concentrate on the cards. Just as we got to the last three tricks I looked over towards the fireplace. Anne Meredith was bent over Mr Shaitana. As I

310

watched, she straightened herself – her hand had been actually on his breast – a gesture which awakened my surprise. She straightened herself, and I saw her face and her quick look over towards us. Guilt and fear – that is what I saw on her face. Of course, I didn't know what had happened then. I only wondered what on earth the girl could have been doing. Later – I knew.'

Poirot nodded.

'But *she* did not know that you knew. *She* did not know that you had seen her?'

'Poor child,' said Mrs Lorrimer. 'Young, frightened – her way to make in the world. Do you wonder that I – well, held my tongue?'

'No, no, I do not wonder.'

'Especially knowing that I – that I myself—' She finished the sentence with a shrug. 'It was certainly not my place to stand accuser. It was up to the police.'

'Quite so – but today you have gone further than that.'

Mrs Lorrimer said grimly: 'I've never been a very soft-hearted or compassionate woman, but I suppose these qualities grow upon one in one's old age. I assure you, I'm not often actuated by pity.'

'It is not always a very safe guide, Madame. Mademoiselle Anne is young, she is fragile, she looks timid and frightened – oh, yes, she seems a very worthy subject for compassion. But I, *I do not agree.* Shall I tell you, Madame, why Miss Anne Meredith killed Mr Shaitana? It was because he knew that she had previously killed an elderly lady to whom she was companion – because that lady had found her out in a petty theft.'

Mrs Lorrimer looked a little startled.

'Is that true, M. Poirot?'

'I have no doubt of it, whatsoever. She is so soft – so gentle – one would say. Pah! She is dangerous, Madame, that little Mademoiselle Anne! Where her own safety, her own comfort, is concerned, she will strike wildly – treacherously. With Mademoiselle Anne *those two crimes will not be the end*. She will gain confidence from them . . .'

Mrs Lorrimer said sharply: 'What you say is horrible, M. Poirot. Horrible!'

Poirot rose.

'Madame, I will now take my leave. Reflect on what I have said.'

Mrs Lorrimer was looking a little uncertain of herself. She said with an attempt at her old manner: 'If it suits me, M. Poirot, I shall deny this whole conversation. You have no witnesses, remember. What I have just told you that I saw on that fatal evening is – well, private between ourselves.'

Poirot said gravely.

'Nothing shall be done without your consent, Madame. And be at peace; I have my own methods. Now that I know what I am driving at—'

He took her hand and raised it to his lips.

'Permit me to tell you, Madame, that you are a most remarkable woman. All my homage and respects. Yes, indeed, a woman in a thousand. Why, you have not even done what nine hundred and ninety-nine women out of a thousand could not have resisted doing.'

'What is that?'

'Told me just why you killed your husband – and how entirely justified such a proceeding really was.'

Mrs Lorrimer drew herself up.

'Really, M. Poirot,' she said stiffly. 'My reasons were entirely my own business.'

'*Magnifique!*' said Poirot, and, once more raising her hand to his lips, he left the room.

It was cold outside the house, and he looked up and down for a taxi, but there was none in sight.

He began to walk in the direction of King's Road.

As he walked he was thinking hard. Occasionally he nodded his head; once he shook it.

He looked back over his shoulder. Someone was going up the steps of Mrs Lorrimer's house. In figure it looked very like Anne Meredith. He hesitated for a minute, wondering whether to turn back or not, but in the end he went on.

On arrival at home, he found that Battle had gone without leaving any message.

He proceeded to ring the superintendent up.

'Hallo.' Battle's voice came through. 'Got anything?'

'*Je crois bien. Mon ami*, we must get after the Meredith girl – and quickly.'

'I'm getting after her – but why quickly?'

'Because, my friend, she may be dangerous.'

Battle was silent for a minute or two. Then he said: 'I know what you mean. But there's no one . . . Oh, well, we mustn't take chances. As a matter of fact, I've written her. Official note, saying I'm calling to see her tomorrow. I thought it might be a good thing to get her rattled.'

312

'It is a possibility, at least. I may accompany you?'

'Naturally. Honoured to have your company, M. Poirot.'

Poirot hung up the receiver with a thoughtful face.

His mind was not quite at rest. He sat for a long time in front of his fire, frowning to himself. At last, putting his fears and doubts aside, he went to bed.

'We will see in the morning,' he murmured.

But of what the morning would bring he had no idea.

— 28 —

SUICIDE

THE SUMMONS came by telephone at the moment when Poirot was sitting down to his morning coffee and rolls.

He lifted the telephone receiver, and Battle's voice spoke: 'That M. Poirot?'

'Yes, it is I. *Qu'est ce qu'il y a?*'

The mere inflection of the superintendent's voice had told him that something had happened. His own vague misgivings came back to him.

'But quickly, my friend, tell me.'

'It's Mrs Lorrimer.'

'Lorrimer — yes?'

'What the devil did you say to her — or did she say to you — yesterday? You never told me anything; in fact, you let me think that the Meredith girl was the one we were after.'

Poirot said quietly: 'What has happened?'

'Suicide.'

'Mrs Lorrimer has committed suicide?'

'That's right. It seems she has been very depressed and unlike herself lately. Her doctor had ordered her some sleeping stuff. Last night she took an overdose.'

Poirot drew a deep breath.

'There is no question of — accident?'

'Not the least. It's all cut and dried. She wrote to the three of them.'

'Which three?'

'The other three. Roberts, Despard and Miss Meredith. All fair

313

and square – no beating about the bush. Just wrote that she would like them to know that she was taking a short-cut out of all the mess – that it was she who had killed Shaitana – and that she apologized – apologized! – to all three of them for the incon- venience and annoyance they had suffered. Perfectly calm, business-like letter. Absolutely typical of the woman. She was a cool customer all right.'

For a minute or two Poirot did not answer.

So this was Mrs Lorrimer's final word. She had determined, after all, to shield Anne Meredith. A quick painless death instead of a protracted painful one, and her last action an altruistic one – the saving of the girl with whom she felt a secret bond of sympathy. The whole thing planned and carried out with quite ruthless efficiency – a suicide carefully announced to the three interested parties. What a woman! His admiration quickened. It was like her – like her clear-cut determination, her insistence on what she had decided being carried out.

He had thought to have convinced her – but evidently she had preferred her own judgment. A woman of very strong will.

Battle's voice cut into his meditations.

'What the devil did you say to her yesterday? You must have put the wind up her, and this is the result. But you implied that the result of your interview was definite suspicion of the Meredith girl.'

Poirot was silent a minute or two. He felt that, dead, Mrs Lorrimer constrained him to her will, as she could not have done if she were living.

He said at last slowly: 'I was in error . . .'

They were unaccustomed words on his tongue, and he did not like them.

'You made a mistake, eh?' said Battle. 'All the same, she must have thought you were on to her. It's a bad business – letting her slip through our fingers like this.'

'You could not have proved anything against her,' said Poirot.

'No – I suppose that's true . . . Perhaps it's all for the best. You – er – didn't mean this to happen, M. Poirot?'

Poirot's disclaimer was indignant. Then he said: 'Tell me exactly what has occurred.'

'Roberts opened his letters just before eight o'clock. He lost no time, dashed off at once in his car, leaving his parlourmaid to communicate with us, which she did. He got to the house to find that Mrs Lorrimer hadn't been called yet, rushed up to her bedroom – but it was too late. He tried artificial respiration, but there was nothing doing. Our divisional surgeon arrived soon after and confirmed his treatment.'

'What was the sleeping stuff?'

'Veronal, I think. One of the barbituric group, at any rate. There was a bottle of tablets by her bed.'

'What about the other two? Did they not try to communicate with you?'

'Despard is out of town. He hasn't had this morning's post.'

'And – Miss Meredith?'

'I've just rung her up.'

'*Eh bien?*'

'She had just opened the letter a few moments before my call came through. Post is later there.'

'What was her reaction?'

'A perfectly proper attitude. Intense relief decently veiled. Shocked and grieved – that sort of thing.'

Poirot paused a moment, then he said: 'Where are you now, my friend?'

'At Cheyne Lane.'

'*Bien.* I will come round immediately.'

In the hall at Cheyne Lane he found Dr Roberts on the point of departure. The doctor's usual florid manner was rather in abeyance this morning. He looked pale and shaken.

'Nasty business this, M. Poirot. I can't say I'm not relieved – from my own point of view – but, to tell you the truth, it's a bit of a shock. I never really thought for a minute that it was Mrs Lorrimer who stabbed Shaitana. It's been the greatest surprise to me.'

'I, too, am surprised.'

'Quiet, well-bred, self-contained woman. Can't imagine her doing a violent thing like that. What was the motive, I wonder? Oh, well, we shall never know now. I confess I'm curious, though.'

'It must take a load off your mind – this occurrence.'

'Oh, it does, undoubtedly. It would be hypocrisy not to admit it. It's not very pleasant to have a suspicion of murder hanging over you. As for the poor woman herself – well, it was undoubtedly the best way out.'

'So she thought herself.'

Roberts nodded.

'Conscience, I suppose,' he said as he let himself out of the house.

Poirot shook his head thoughtfully. The doctor had misread the situation. It was not remorse that had made Mrs Lorrimer take her life.

On his way upstairs he paused to say a few words of comfort to the elderly parlourmaid, who was weeping quietly.

'It's so dreadful, sir. So very dreadful. We were all so fond of her. And you having tea with her yesterday so nice and quiet. And now today she's gone. I shall never forget this morning – never as long as I live. The gentleman pealing at the bell. Rang three times, he did, before I could get to it. And, "Where's your mistress?" he shot out at me. I was so flustered, I couldn't hardly answer. You see, we never went in to the mistress till she rang – that was her orders. And I just couldn't get out anything. And the doctor, he says, "Where's her room?" and ran up the stairs, and me behind him, and I showed him the door, and he rushes in, not so much as knocking, and takes one look at her lying there, and, "Too late," he says. She was dead, sir. But he sent me for brandy and hot water, and he tried desperate to bring her back, but it couldn't be done. And then the police coming and all – it isn't – it isn't – decent, sir. Mrs Lorrimer wouldn't have liked it. And why the police? It's none of their business, surely, even if an accident has occurred and the poor mistress did take an overdose by mistake.'

Poirot did not reply to her question.

He said: 'Last night, was your mistress quite as usual? Did she seem upset or worried at all?'

'No, I don't think so, sir. She was tired – and I think she was in pain. She hasn't been well lately, sir.'

'No, I know.'

The sympathy in his tone made the woman go on.

'She was never one for complaining, sir, but both cook and I had been worried about her for some time. She couldn't do as much as she used to do, and things tired her. I think, perhaps, the young lady coming after you left was a bit too much for her.'

With his foot on the stairs, Poirot turned back.

'The young lady? Did a young lady come here yesterday evening?'

'Yes, sir. Just after you left, it was. Miss Meredith, her name was.'

'Did she stay long?'

'About an hour, sir.'

Poirot was silent for a minute or two, then he said: 'And afterwards?'

'The mistress went to bed. She had dinner in bed. She said she was tired.'

Again Poirot was silent; then he said: 'Do you know if your mistress wrote any letters yesterday evening?'

'Do you mean after she went to bed? I don't think so, sir.'

'But you are not sure?'

'There were some letters on the hall table ready to be posted, sir. We always took them last thing before shutting up. But I think they had been lying there since earlier in the day.'

'How many were there?'

'Two or three – I'm not quite sure, sir. Three, I think.'

'You – or cook – whoever posted them – did not happen to notice to whom they were addressed? Do not be offended at my question. It is of the utmost importance.'

'I went to the post myself with them, sir. I noticed the top one – it was to Fortnum & Mason's. I couldn't say as to the others.'

The woman's tone was earnest and sincere.

'Are you sure there were not more than three letters?'

'Yes, sir, I'm quite certain of that.'

Poirot nodded his head gravely. Once more he started up the staircase. Then he said: 'You knew, I take it, that your mistress took medicine to make her sleep?'

'Oh, yes, sir, it was the doctor's orders. Dr Lang.'

'Where was this sleeping medicine kept?'

'In the little cupboard in the mistress's room.'

Poirot did not ask any further questions. He went upstairs. His face was very grave.

On the upper landing Battle greeted him. The superintendent looked worried and harassed.

'I'm glad you've come, M. Poirot. Let me introduce you to Dr Davidson.'

The divisional surgeon shook hands. He was a tall, melancholy man.

'The luck was against us,' he said. 'An hour or two earlier, and we might have saved her.'

'H'm,' said Battle. 'I mustn't say so officially, but I'm not sorry. She was a – well, she was a lady. I don't know what her reasons were for killing Shaitana, but she may just conceivably have been justified.'

'In any case,' said Poirot, 'it is doubtful if she would have lived to stand her trial. She was a very ill woman.'

The surgeon nodded in agreement.

'I should say you were quite right. Well, perhaps it is all for the best.'

He started down the stairs.

Battle moved after him.

'One minute, Doctor.'

Poirot, his hand on the bedroom door, murmured, 'I may enter – yes?'

Battle nodded over his shoulder. 'Quite all right. 'We're through.' Poirot passed into the room, closing the door behind him . . .

He went over to the bed and stood looking down at the quiet, dead face.

He was very disturbed.

Had the dead woman gone to the grave in a last determined effort to save a young girl from death and disgrace – or was there a different, a more sinister explanation?

There were certain facts . . .

Suddenly he bent down, examining a dark, discoloured bruise on the dead woman's arm.

He straightened himself up again. There was a strange, cat-like gleam in his eyes that certain close associates of his would have recognized.

He left the room quickly and went downstairs. Battle and a subordinate were at the telephone. The latter laid down the receiver and said: 'He hasn't come back, sir.'

Battle said: 'Despard. I've been trying to get him. There's a letter for him with the Chelsea postmark all right.'

Poirot asked an irrelevant question.

'Had Dr Roberts had his breakfast when he came here?'

Battle stared.

'No,' he said, 'I remember he mentioned that he'd come out without it.'

'Then he will be at his house now. We can get him.'

'But why—?'

But Poirot was already busy at the dial. Then he spoke: 'Dr Roberts? It is Dr Roberts speaking? *Mais oui*, it is Poirot here. Just one question. Are you well acquainted with the handwriting of Mrs Lorrimer?'

'Mrs Lorrimer's handwriting? I – no, I don't know that I'd ever seen it before.'

'*Je vous remercie.*'

Poirot laid down the receiver quickly.

Battle was staring at him.

'What's the big idea, M. Poirot?' he asked quietly.

Poirot took him by the arm.

'Listen, my friend. A few minutes after I left this house

yesterday Anne Meredith arrived. I actually saw her going up the steps, though I was not quite sure of her identity at the time. Immediately after Anne Meredith left Mrs Lorrimer went to bed. As far as the maid knows, *she did not write any letters then.* And, for reasons which you will understand when I recount to you our interview, *I do not believe that she wrote those three letters before my visit.* When did she write them, then?'

'After the servants had gone to bed?' suggested Battle. 'She got up and posted them herself.'

'That is possible, yes, but there is another possibility – *that she did not write them at all.*'

Battle whistled.

'My God, you mean—'

The telephone trilled. The sergeant picked up the receiver. He listened a minute, then turned to Battle.

'Sergeant O'Connor speaking from Despard's flat, sir. There's reason to believe that Despard's down at Wallingford-on-Thames.'

Poirot caught Battle by the arm.

'Quickly, my friend. We, too, must go to Wallingford. I tell you, I am not easy in my mind. This may not be the end. I tell you again, my friend, this young lady, she is dangerous.'

— 29 —

ACCIDENT

'ANNE,' said Rhoda.

'Mmm?'

'No, really, Anne, don't answer with half your mind on a crossword puzzle. I want you to attend to me.'

'I am attending.'

Anne sat bolt upright and put down the paper.

'That's better. Look here, Anne.' Rhoda hesitated. 'About this man coming.'

'Superintendent Battle?'

'Yes. Anne, I wish you'd tell him – about being at the Bensons'.'

Anne's voice grew rather cold.

'Nonsense. Why should I?'

319

'Because – well, it might look – as though you'd been keeping something back. I'm sure it would be better to mention it.'

'I can't very well now,' said Anne coldly.

'I wish you had in the first place.'

'Well, it's too late to bother about that now.'

'Yes.' Rhoda did not sound convinced.

Anne said rather irritably: 'In any case, I can't see *why*. It's got nothing to do with all this.'

'No, of course not.'

'I was only there about two months. He only wants these things as – well – references. Two months doesn't count.'

'No, I know. I expect I'm being foolish, but it does worry me rather. I feel you ought to mention it. You see, if it came out some other way, it might look rather bad – your keeping dark about it, I mean.'

'I don't see how it can come out. Nobody knows but you.'

'N-no?'

Anne pounced on the slight hesitation in Rhoda's voice.

'Why, who does know?'

'Well, everyone at Combeacre,' said Rhoda after a moment's pause.

'Oh, that!' Anne dismissed it with a shrug. 'The superintendent isn't likely to come up against anyone from there. It would be an extraordinary coincidence if he did.'

'Coincidences happen.'

'Rhoda, you're being extraordinary about this. Fuss, fuss, fuss.'

'I'm terribly sorry, darling. Only you know what the police might be like if they thought you were – well – hiding things.'

'They won't know. Who's to tell them? Nobody knows but you.'

It was the second time she had said those words. At this second repetition her voice changed a little – something queer and speculative came into it.

'Oh, dear, I wish you would,' sighed Rhoda unhappily.

She looked guiltily at Anne, but Anne was not looking at her. She was sitting with a frown on her face, as though working out some calculation.

'Rather fun, Major Despard turning up,' said Rhoda.

'What? Oh, yes.'

'Anne, he *is* attractive. If you don't want him, *do, do, do* hand him over to me!'

'Don't be absurd, Rhoda. He doesn't care tuppence for me.'

'Then why does he keep on turning up? Of course he's keen on you. You're just the sort of distressed damsel that he'd enjoy rescuing. You look so beautifully helpless, Anne.'

'He's equally pleasant to both of us.'

'That's only his niceness. But, if you don't want him, I could do the sympathetic friend act – console his broken heart, etc., etc., and in the end I might get him. Who knows?' Rhoda concluded inelegantly.

'I'm sure you're quite welcome to him, my dear,' said Anne, laughing.

'He's got such a lovely back to his neck,' sighed Rhoda. 'Very brick red and muscular.'

'Darling, must you be so mawkish?'

'Do you like him, Anne?'

'Yes, very much.'

'Aren't we prim and sedate? I think he likes me a little – not as much as you, but a little.'

'Oh, but he does like you,' said Anne.

Again there was an unusual note in her voice, but Rhoda did not hear it.

'What time is our sleuth coming?' she asked.

'Twelve,' said Anne. She was silent for a minute or two, then she said, 'It's only half-past ten now. Let's go out on the river.'

'But isn't – didn't – didn't Despard say he'd come round about eleven?'

'Why should we wait in for him? We can leave a message with Mrs Astwell which way we've gone, and he can follow us along the towpath.'

'In fact, don't make yourself cheap, dear, as mother always said!' laughed Rhoda. 'Come on, then.'

She went out of the room and through the garden door. Anne followed her.

Major Despard called at Wendon Cottage about ten minutes later. He was before his time, he knew, so he was a little surprised to find both girls had already gone out.

He went through the garden and across the fields and turned to the right along the towpath.

Mrs Astwell remained a minute or two looking after him, instead of getting on with her morning chores.

'Sweet on one or other of 'em, he is,' she observed to herself. 'I think it's Miss Anne, but I'm not certain. He don't give away much by his face. Treats 'em both alike. I'm not sure they ain't both sweet on him, too. If so, they won't be such dear friends so much longer. Nothing like a gentleman for coming between two young ladies.'

Pleasurably excited by the prospect of assisting at a budding romance, Mrs Astwell turned indoors to her task of washing up the breakfast things, when once again the door-bell rang.

'Drat that door,' said Mrs Astwell. 'Do it on purpose, they do. Parcel, I suppose. Or might be a telegram.'

She moved slowly to the front door.

Two gentlemen stood there, a small foreign gentleman and an exceedingly English, big, burly gentleman. The latter she had seen before, she remembered.

'Miss Meredith at home?' asked the big man.

Mrs Astwell shook her head.

'Just gone out.'

'Really? Which way? We didn't meet her.'

Mrs Astwell, secretly studying the amazing moustache of the other gentleman and deciding that they looked an unlikely pair to be friends, volunteered further information.

'Gone out on the river,' she explained.

The other gentleman broke in: 'And the other lady? Miss Dawes?'

'They've both gone.'

'Ah, thank you,' said Battle. 'Let me see, which way does one get to the river?'

'First turning to the left, down the lane,' Mrs Astwell replied promptly. 'When you get to the towpath, go right. I heard them say that's the way they were going,' she added helpfully. 'Not above a quarter of an hour ago. You'll soon catch 'em up.'

'And I wonder,' she added to herself as she unwillingly closed the front door, having stared inquisitively at their retreating backs, 'who you two may be. Can't place you, somehow.'

Mrs Astwell returned to the kitchen sink, and Battle and Poirot duly took the first turning to the left – a straggling lane which soon ended abruptly at the towpath.

Poirot was hurrying along, and Battle eyed him curiously.

'Anything the matter, M. Poirot? You seem in a mighty hurry.'

'It is true. I am uneasy, my friend.'

'Anything particular?'

Poirot shook his head.

'No. But there are possibilities. You never know . . .'

'You've something in your head,' said Battle. 'You were urgent that we should come down here this morning without losing a moment – and, my word, you made Constable Turner step on the gas! What are you afraid of? The girl's shot her bolt.'

Poirot was silent.

'What are you afraid of?' Battle repeated.

'What is one always afraid of in these cases?'

Battle nodded.

'You're quite right. I wonder—'

'You wonder what, my friend?'

Battle said slowly: 'I'm wondering if Miss Meredith knows that her friend told Mrs Oliver a certain fact.'

Poirot nodded his head in vigorous appreciation.

'Hurry, my friend,' he said.

They hastened along the river bank. There was no craft visible on the water's surface, but presently they rounded a bend and Poirot suddenly stopped dead. Battle's quick eyes saw also.

'Major Despard,' he said.

Despard was about two hundred yards ahead of them, striding along the river bank.

A little farther on the two girls were in view in a punt on the water. Rhoda punting – Anne lying and laughing up at her. Neither of them were looking towards the bank.

And then – *it happened*. Anne's hand outstretched, Rhoda's stagger, her plunge overboard – her desperate grasp at Anne's sleeve – the rocking boat – then an overturned punt and two girls struggling in the water.

'See it?' cried Battle as he started to run. 'Little Meredith caught her round the ankle and tipped her in. My God, that's her fourth murder!'

They were both running hard. But someone was ahead of them. It was clear that neither girl could swim, but Despard had run quickly along the path to the nearest point, and now he plunged in and swam towards them.

'*Mon Dieu*, this is interesting,' cried Poirot. He caught at Battle's arm. 'Which of them will he go for first?'

The two girls were not together. About twelve yards separated them.

Despard swam powerfully towards them – there was no check in his stroke. He was making straight for Rhoda.

Battle, in his turn, reached the nearest bank and went in. Despard had just brought Rhoda successfully to shore. He hauled her up, flung her down and plunged in again, swimming towards the spot where Anne had just gone under.

323

'Be careful', called Battle. 'Weeds.'

He and Battle got to the spot at the same time, but Anne had gone under before they reached her.

They got her at last and between them towed her to the shore.

Rhoda was being ministered to by Poirot. She was sitting up now, her breath coming unevenly.

Despard and Battle laid Anne Meredith down.

'Artificial respiration,' said Battle. 'Only thing to do. But I'm afraid she's gone.'

He set to work methodically. Poirot stood by, ready to relieve him.

Despard dropped down by Rhoda.

'Are you all right?' he asked hoarsely.

She said slowly: 'You saved me. You saved *me* . . .' She held out her hands to him, and as he took them she burst suddenly into tears.

He said, 'Rhoda . . .'

Their hands clung together . . .

He had a sudden vision – of African scrub, and Rhoda, laughing and adventurous, by his side . . .

— 30 —

MURDER

'Do you mean to say,' said Rhoda incredulously, 'that Anne *meant* to push me in? I know it *felt* like it. And she knew I can't swim. But – but was it *deliberate*?'

'It was quite deliberate,' said Poirot.

They were driving through the outskirts of London.

'But – but – why?'

Poirot did not reply for a minute or two. He thought he knew one of the motives that had led Anne to act as she had done, and that motive was sitting next to Rhoda at the minute.

Superintendent Battle coughed.

'You'll have to prepare yourself, Miss Dawes, for a bit of a shock. This Mrs Benson your friend lived with, her death wasn't quite the accident that it appeared – at least, so we've reason to suppose.'

'What *do* you mean?'

'We believe,' said Poirot, 'that Anne Meredith changed two bottles.'

'Oh, no – no, how horrible! It's *impossible*. Anne? Why should she?'

'She had her reasons,' said Superintendent Battle. 'But the point is, Miss Dawes, that, as far as Miss Meredith knew, *you were the only person who could give us a clue to that incident*. You didn't tell her, I suppose, that you'd mentioned it to Mrs Oliver?'

Rhoda said slowly: 'No. I thought she'd be annoyed with me.'

'She would. Very annoyed,' said Battle grimly. 'But she thought that the only danger could come from *you*, and that's why she decided to – er – eliminate you.'

'Eliminate? *Me?* Oh, how beastly! It *can't* be all true.'

'Well, she's dead now,' said Superintendent Battle, 'so we might as well leave it at that; but she wasn't a nice friend for you to have, Miss Dawes – and that's a fact.'

The car drew up in front of a door.

'We'll go in to M. Poirot's,' said Superintendent Battle, 'and have a bit of a talk about it all.'

In Poirot's sitting-room they were welcomed by Mrs Oliver, who was entertaining Dr Roberts. They were drinking sherry. Mrs Oliver was wearing one of the new horsy hats and a velvet dress with a bow on the chest on which reposed a large piece of apple core.

'Come in, come in,' said Mrs Oliver hospitably and quite as though it were her house and not Poirot's. 'As soon as I got your telephone call I rang up Dr Roberts, and we came round here. And all his patients are dying, but he doesn't care. They're probably getting better, really. We want to hear all about everything.'

'Yes, indeed, I'm thoroughly fogged,' said Roberts.

'*Eh bien,*' said Poirot. 'The case is ended. The murderer of Mr Shaitana is found at last.'

'So Mrs Oliver told me. That pretty little thing, Anne Meredith. I can hardly believe it. A most unbelievable murderess.'

'She was a murderess all right,' said Battle. 'Three murders to her credit – and not her fault that she didn't get away with a fourth one.'

'Incredible!' murmured Roberts.

'Not at all,' said Mrs Oliver. 'Least likely person. It seems to work out in real life just the same as in books.'

'It's been an amazing day,' said Roberts. 'First Mrs Lorrimer's letter. I suppose that was a forgery, eh?'

'Precisely. A forgery written in triplicate.'

'She wrote one to herself, too?'

'Naturally. The forgery was quite skilful – it would not deceive an expert, of course – but, then, it was highly unlikely that an expert would have been called in. All the evidence pointed to Mrs Lorrimer's having committed suicide.'

'You will excuse my curiosity, M. Poirot, but what made you suspect that she had not committed suicide?'

'A little conversation that I had with a maidservant at Cheyne Lane.'

'She told you of Anne Meredith's visit the former evening?'

'That among other things. And then, you see, I had already come to a conclusion in my own mind as to the identity of the guilty person – that is, the person who killed Mr Shaitana. That person was not Mrs Lorrimer.'

'What made you suspect Miss Meredith?'

Poirot raised his hand.

'A little minute. Let me approach this matter in my own way. Let me, that is to say, eliminate. The murderer of Mr Shaitana was not Mrs Lorrimer, nor was it Major Despard, and, curiously enough, it was not Anne Meredith . . .'

He leaned forward. His voice purred, soft and catlike.

'You see, Dr Roberts, *you were the person who killed Mr Shaitana*. And you also killed Mrs Lorrimer . . .'

There was at least three minutes' silence. Then Roberts laughed a rather menacing laugh.

'Are you quite mad, M. Poirot? I certainly did not murder Mr Shaitana, and I could not possibly have murdered Mrs Lorrimer. My dear Battle' – he turned to the Scotland Yard man – are *you* standing for this?'

'I think you'd better listen to what M. Poirot has to say,' said Battle quietly.

Poirot said: 'It is true that though I have known for some time that you – and only you – could have killed Shaitana, it would not be an easy matter to prove it. But Mrs Lorrimer's case is quite different.' He leaned forward. 'It is not a case of my knowing. It is much simpler than that – for we have *an eye-witness who saw you do it*.'

Roberts grew very quiet. His eyes glittered. He said sharply: 'You are talking rubbish!'

'Oh, no, I am not. It was early in the morning. You bluffed your

326

way into Mrs Lorrimer's room, where she was still heavily asleep under the influence of the drug she had taken the night before. You bluff again – pretend to see at a glance that she is dead! You pack the parlourmaid off for brandy – hot water – all the rest of it. You are left alone in the room. The maid has only had the barest peep. And then what happens?

'You may not be aware of the fact, Dr Roberts, *but certain firms of window-cleaners specialize in early-morning work.* A window cleaner with his ladder arrived at the same time as you did. He placed his ladder against the side of the house and began his work. The first window he tackled was that of Mrs Lorrimer's room. When, however, he saw what was going on, he quickly retired to another window, *but he had seen something first.* He shall tell us his own story.'

Poirot stepped lightly across the floor, turned a door handle, called: 'Come in, Stephens,' and returned.

A big awkward-looking man with red hair entered. In his hand he held a uniformed hat bearing the legend 'Chelsea Window Cleaners' Association' which he twirled awkwardly.

Poirot said: 'Is there anybody you recognize in this room?'

The man looked round, then gave a bashful nod of the head towards Dr Roberts.

'Him,' he said.

'Tell us when you saw him last and what he was doing.'

'This morning it was. Eight o'clock job at a lady's house in Cheyne Lane. I started on the windows there. Lady was in bed. Looked ill, she did. She was just turning her head round on the pillow. This gent I took to be a doctor. He shoved her sleeve up and jabbed something into her arm just about there—' He gestured. 'She just dropped back on the pillow again. I thought I'd better hop it to another window, so I did. Hope I didn't do wrong in any way?'

'You did admirably, my friend,' said Poirot.

He said quietly: '*Eh bien*, Dr Roberts?'

'A – a simple restorative –' stammered Roberts. 'A last hope of bringing her round. It's monstrous—'

Poirot interrupted him.

'A simple restorative? – N-methyl-cyclo-hexenyl-methyl-malonyl urea,' said Poirot. He rolled out the syllables unctuously. 'Known more simply as Evipan. Used as an anaesthetic for short operations. Injected intravenously in large doses it produces instant unconsciousness. It is dangerous to use it after Veronal or any barbiturates have been given. I noticed the bruised place on her arm where something had obviously been injected into a vein.

A hint to the police surgeon and the drug was easily discovered by no less a person than Sir Charles Imphrey, the Home Office Analyst.'

'That about cooks your goose, I think,' said Superintendent Battle. 'No need to prove the Shaitana business, though, of course, if necessary we can bring a further charge as to the murder of Mr Charles Craddock – and possibly his wife also.'

The mention of those two names finished Roberts. He leaned back in his chair.

'I throw in my hand,' he said. 'You've got me! I suppose that sly devil Shaitana put you wise before you came that evening. And I thought I'd settled his hash so nicely.'

'It isn't Shaitana you've got to thank,' said Battle. 'The honours lie with M. Poirot here.'

He went to the door and two men entered.

Superintendent Battle's voice became official as he made the formal arrest.

As the door closed behind the accused man Mrs Oliver said happily, if not quite truthfully: 'I always *said* he did it!'

— 31 —

CARDS ON THE TABLE

It was Poirot's moment, every face was turned to his in eager anticipation.

'You are very kind,' he said, smiling. 'You know, I think, that I enjoy my little lecture. I am a prosy old fellow.

'This case, to my mind, has been one of the most interesting cases I have ever come across. There was *nothing*, you see, to go upon. There were four people, one of whom *must* have committed the crime, but which of the four? Was there anything to tell one? In the material sense – no. There were no tangible clues – no fingerprints – no incriminating papers or documents. There were only – the people themselves.

'And one tangible clue – the bridge scores.

'You may remember that from the beginning I showed a particular interest in those scores. They told me something about the various people who had kept them and they did more. They

328

gave me one valuable hint. I noticed at once, in the third rubber, the figure of 1500 above the line. That figure could only represent one thing – a call of grand slam. Now if a person were to make up their minds to commit a crime under these somewhat unusual circumstances (that is, during a rubber game of bridge) that person was clearly running two serious risks. The first was that the victim might cry out and the second was that even if the victim did not cry out some one of the other three might chance to look up at the psychological moment and *actually witness the deed*.

'Now as to the first risk, nothing could be done about it. It was a matter of a gambler's luck. But something could be done about the second. It stands to reason that during an interesting or an exciting hand the attention of the three players would be wholly on the game, whereas during a dull hand they were more likely to be looking about them. Now a bid of grand slam is always exciting. It is very often (as in this case it was) doubled. Every one of the three players is playing with close attention – the declarer to get his contract, the adversaries to discard correctly and to get him down. It was, then, a distinct possibility that the murder was committed during this particular hand and I determined to find out, if I could, exactly how the bidding had gone. I soon discovered that dummy during this particular hand had been Dr Roberts. I bore that in mind and approached the matter from my second angle – psychological probability. Of the four suspects Mrs Lorrimer struck me as by far the most likely to plan and carry out a successful murder – but I could not see her as committing any crime that had to be improvised on the spur of the moment. On the other hand her manner that first evening puzzled me. It suggested either that she had committed the murder herself or that she knew who had committed it. Miss Meredith, Major Despard and Dr Roberts were all psychological possibilities, though, as I have already mentioned, each of them would have committed the crime from an entirely different *angle*.

'I next made a second test. I got everyone in turn to tell me just what they remembered of the room. From that I got some very valuable information. First of all, by far the most likely person to have noticed the dagger was Dr Roberts. He was a natural observer of trifles of all kinds – what is called an observant man. Of the bridge hands, however, he remembered practically nothing at all. I did not expect him to remember much, but his complete forgetfulness looked as though he had had something else on his mind all the evening. Again, you see, Dr Roberts was indicated.

'Mrs Lorrimer I found to have a marvellous card memory, and I could well imagine that with any one of her powers of concentration a murder could easily be committed close at hand and she would never notice anything. She gave me a valuable piece of information. The grand slam was bid by Dr Roberts (quite unjustifiably) – and he bid it in her suit, not his own, so that she necessarily played the hand.

'The third test, the test on which Superintendent Battle and I built a good deal, was the discovery of the earlier murders so as to establish a similarity of method. Well, the credit for those discoveries belongs to Superintendent Battle, to Mrs Oliver and to Colonel Race. Discussing the matter with my friend Battle, he confessed himself disappointed because there were no points of similarity between any of the three earlier crimes and that of the murder of Mr Shaitana. But actually that was not true. The two murders attributed to Dr Roberts, when examined closely, *and from the psychological point of view and not the material one*, proved to be *almost exactly the same*. They, too, had been what I might describe as *public* murders. A shaving-brush boldly infected in the victim's own dressing-room while the doctor officially washes his hands after a visit. The murder of Mrs Craddock under cover of a typhoid inoculation. Again done quite openly – in the sight of the world, as you might say. And the reaction of the man is the same. Pushed into a corner, he seizes a chance and acts at once – sheer bold audacious bluff – exactly like his play at bridge. As at bridge, so in the murder of Shaitana, he took a long chance and played his cards well. The blow was perfectly struck and at exactly the right moment.

'Now just at the moment that I had decided quite definitely that Roberts was the man, Mrs Lorrimer asked me to come and see her – and quite convincingly accused herself of the crime! I nearly believed her! For a minute or two I *did* believe her – and then my little grey cells reasserted their mastery. It could not be – so it was not!

'But what she told me was more difficult still.

'She assured me that she had actually *seen* Anne Meredith commit the crime.

'It was not till the following morning – when I stood by a dead woman's bed – that I saw how I could still be right and Mrs Lorrimer still have spoken the truth.

'Anne Meredith went over to the fireplace – *and saw that Mr Shaitana was dead*! She stopped over him – perhaps stretched out her hand to the gleaming head of the jewelled pin.

'Her lips part to call out, but she does not call out. She

remembers Shaitana's talk at dinner. Perhaps he has left some record. She, Anne Meredith, has a motive for desiring his death. Everyone will say that she has killed him. She dare not call out. Trembling with fear and apprehension she goes back to her seat.

'So Mrs Lorrimer is right, since she, as she thought, saw the crime committed – but I am right too, for actually she did not see it.

'If Roberts had held his hand at this point, I doubt if we could have ever brought his crimes home to him. We *might* have done so – by a mixture of bluff and various ingenious devices. I would at any rate have *tried*.

'But he lost his nerve and once again overbid his hand. And this time the cards lay wrong for him and he came down heavily.

'No doubt he was uneasy. He knew that Battle was nosing about. He foresaw the present situation going on indefinitely, the police still searching – and perhaps, by some miracle, coming on traces of his former crimes. He hit upon the brilliant idea of making Mrs Lorrimer the scapegoat for the party. His practised eye guessed, no doubt, that she was ill and that her life could not be very much prolonged. How natural in those circumstances for her to choose a quick way out and, before taking it, confess to the crime! So he manages to get a sample of her handwriting – forges three indentical letters and arrives at the house hot-foot in the morning with his story of the letter he has just received. His parlourmaid quite correctly is instructed to ring up the police. All he needs is a start. And he gets it. By the time the police surgeon arrives it is all over. Dr Roberts is ready with his story of artificial respiration that has failed. It is all perfectly plausible – perfectly straightforward.

'In all this he has no idea of throwing suspicion on Anne Meredith. He does not even know of her visit the night before. It is suicide and security only that he is aiming at.

'It is in fact an awkward moment for him when I ask if he is acquainted with Mrs Lorrimer's handwriting. If the forgery has been detected he must save himself by saying that he has never seen her handwriting. His mind works quickly, but not quickly enough.

'From Wallingford I telephone to Mrs Oliver. She plays her part by lulling his suspicions and bringing him here. And then when he is congratulating himself that all is well, though not exactly in the way he has planned, the blow falls. Hercule Poirot springs! And so – the gambler will gather in no more tricks. He has thrown his cards upon the table. *C'est fini*.'

There was silence. Rhoda broke it with a sigh.

'What amazing luck that window cleaner happened to be there,' she said.

'Luck? Luck? That was not luck, Mademoiselle. That was the grey cells of Hercule Poirot. And that reminds me—'

He went to the door.

'Come in – come in, my dear fellow. You acted your part *à merveille*.'

He returned accompanied by the window cleaner, who now held his red hair in his hand and who looked somehow a very different person.

'My friend Mr Gerald Hemmingway, a very promising young actor.'

'Then there was no window cleaner?' cried Rhoda. 'Nobody saw him?'

'I saw,' said Poirot. 'With the eyes of the mind one can see more than with the eyes of the body. One leans back and closes the eyes—'

Despard said cheerfully: 'Let's stab him, Rhoda, and see if his ghost can come back and find out who did it.'

HERCULE POIROT'S CHRISTMAS

— I —

DECEMBER 22ND

STEPHEN pulled up the collar of his coat as he walked briskly along the platform. Overhead a dim fog clouded the station. Large engines hissed superbly, throwing off clouds of steam into the cold raw air. Everything was dirty and smoke-grimed.

Stephen thought with revulsion: 'What a foul country – what a foul city!'

His first excited reaction to London, its shops, its restaurants, its well-dressed, attractive women, had faded. He saw it now as a glittering rhinestone in a dingy setting.

Supposing he were back in South Africa now . . . He felt a quick pang of homesickness. Sunshine – blue skies – gardens of flowers – cool blue flowers – hedges of plumbago – blue convolvulus clinging to every little shanty.

And here – dirt, grime and endless, incessant crowds – moving, hurrying – jostling. Busy ants running industriously about their ant-hill.

For a moment he thought: 'I wish I hadn't come . . .'

Then he remembered his purpose and his lips set back in a grim line. No, by hell, he'd go on with it! He'd planned this for years. He'd always meant to do – what he was going to do. Yes, he'd go on with it!

That momentary reluctance, that sudden questioning of himself: 'Why? Is it worth it? Why dwell on the past? Why not wipe out the whole thing?' – all that was only weakness. He was not a boy – to be turned this way and that by the whim of the moment. He was a man of forty, assured, purposeful. He would go on with it. He would do what he had come to England to do.

He got on the train and passed along the corridor looking for a place. He had waved aside a porter and was carrying his own raw-hide suitcase. He looked into carriage after carriage. The train was full. It was only three days before Christmas. Stephen Farr looked distastefully at the crowded carriages.

People! Incessant, innumerable people! And all so – so – what was the word? – so *drab*-looking! So alike, so horribly alike! Those that hadn't got faces like sheep had faces like rabbits, he thought. Some of them chattered and fussed. Some, heavily middle-aged men, grunted. More like pigs, those. Even the girls, slender, egg-faced, scarlet-lipped, were of a depressing uniformity.

He thought with a sudden longing of open veldt, sunbaked and lonely . . .

And then, suddenly, he caught his breath, looking into a carriage. This girl was different. Black hair, rich creamy pallor – eyes with the depth and darkness of night in them. The sad proud eyes of the south . . . It was all wrong that this girl should be sitting in this train among these dull, drab-looking people – all wrong that she should be going into the dreary midlands of England. She should have been on a balcony, a rose between her lips, a piece of black lace draping her proud head, and there should have been dust and heat and the smell of blood – the smell of the bull-ring – in the air . . . She should be somewhere splendid, not squeezed into the corner of a third-class carriage.

He was an observant man. He did not fail to note the shabbiness of her little black coat and skirt, the cheap quality of her fabric gloves, the flimsy shoes and the defiant note of a flame-red handbag. Nevertheless, splendour was the quality he associated with her. She *was* splendid, fine, exotic . . .

What the hell was she doing in this country of fogs and chills and hurrying industrious ants?

He thought: 'I've got to know who she is and what she's doing here . . . I've got to know . . .'

II

Pilar sat squeezed up against the window and thought how very odd the English smelt . . . It was what had struck her so far most forcibly about England – the difference of smell. There was no garlic and no dust and very little perfume. In this carriage now there was a smell of cold stuffiness – the sulphur smell of the trains – the smell of soap and another very unpleasant smell – it came, she thought, from the fur collar of the stout woman sitting beside her. Pilar sniffed delicately, imbibing the odour of mothballs reluctantly. It was a funny scent to choose to put on yourself, she thought.

A whistle blew, a stentorian voice cried out something and the train jerked slowly out of the station. They had started. She was on her way . . .

Her heart beat a little faster. Would it be all right? Would she be able to accomplish what she had set out to do? Surely – surely – she had thought it all out so carefully . . . She was prepared for every eventuality. Oh, yes, she would succeed – she must succeed . . .

The curve of Pilar's red mouth turned upwards. It was suddenly cruel, that mouth. Cruel and greedy – like the mouth of a child or a kitten – a mouth that knew only its own desires and that was as yet unaware of pity.

She looked round her with the frank curiosity of a child. All these people, seven of them – how funny they were, the English! They all seemed so rich, so prosperous – their clothes – their boots. Oh! undoubtedly England was a very rich country as she had always heard. But they were not at all gay – no, decidedly not gay.

That was a handsome man standing in the corridor . . . Pilar thought he was very handsome. She liked his deeply bronzed face and his high-bridged nose and his square shoulders. More quickly than any English girl, Pilar had seen that the man admired her. She had not looked at him once directly, but she knew perfectly how often he had looked at her and exactly how he had looked.

She registered the facts without much interest or emotion. She came from a country where men looked at women as a matter of course and did not disguise the fact unduly. She wondered if he was an Englishman and decided that he was not.

'He is too alive, too real, to be English,' Pilar decided. 'And yet he is fair. He may be perhaps Americano.' He was, she thought, rather like the actors she had seen in Wild West films.

An attendant pushed his way along the corridor.

'First lunch, please. First lunch. Take your seats for first lunch.'

The seven occupants of Pilar's carriage all held tickets for the first lunch. They rose in a body and the carriage was suddenly deserted and peaceful.

Pilar quickly pulled up the window which had been let down a couple of inches at the top by a militant-looking, grey-haired lady in the opposite corner. Then she sprawled comfortably back on her seat and peered out of the window at the northern suburbs of London. She did not turn her head at the sound of the door sliding back. It was the man from the corridor, and Pilar knew, of course, that he had entered the carriage on purpose to talk to her.

She continued to look pensively out of the window.

Stephen Farr said: 'Would you like the window down at all?'

Pilar replied demurely: 'On the contrary. I have just shut it.'

She spoke English perfectly, but with a slight accent.

During the pause that ensued, Stephen thought: 'A delicious voice. It has the sun in it . . . It is warm like a summer night . . .'

Pilar thought: 'I like his voice. It is big and strong. He is attractive – yes, he is attractive.'

Stephen said: 'The train is very full.'

'Oh, yes, indeed. The people go away from London, I suppose, because it is so black there.'

Pilar had not been brought up to believe that it was a crime to talk to strange men in trains. She could take care of herself as well as any girl, but she had no rigid taboos.

If Stephen had been brought up in England he might have felt ill at ease at entering into conversation with a young girl. But Stephen was a friendly soul who found it perfectly natural to talk to anyone if he felt like it.

He smiled without any self-consciousness and said: 'London's rather a terrible place, isn't it?'

'Oh, yes. I do not like it at all.'

'No more do I.'

Pilar said: 'You are not English, no?'

'I'm British, but I come from South Africa.'

'Oh, I see, that explains it.'

'Have you just come from abroad?'

Pilar nodded. 'I come from Spain.'

Stephen was interested.

'From Spain, do you? You're Spanish, then?'

'I am half-Spanish. My mother was English. That is why I talk English so well.'

'What about this war business?' asked Stephen.

'It is terrible, yes – very sad. There has been damage done, quite a lot – yes.'

'Which side are you on?'

Pilar's politics seemed to be rather vague. In the village where she came from, she explained, nobody had paid very much attention to the war. 'It has not been near us, you understand. The mayor, he is, of course, an officer of the government, so he is for the government, and the priest is for General Franco – but most of the people are busy with the vines and the land, they have not time to go into these questions.'

'So there wasn't any fighting round you?'

Pilar said that there had not been. 'But, then, I drove in a car,' she explained, 'all across the country and there was much destruction. And I saw a bomb drop and it blew up a car – yes, and another destroyed a house. It was very exciting!'

Stephen Farr smiled a faintly twisted smile.

'So that's how it seemed to you?'

'It was a nuisance, too,' explained Pilar. 'Because I wanted to get on, and the driver of my car, he was killed.'

Stephen said, watching her: 'That didn't upset you?'

Pilar's great dark eyes opened very wide. 'Everyone must die! That is so, is it not? If it comes quickly from the sky – bouff – like that, it is as well as any other way. One is alive for a time – yes, and then one is dead. That is what happens in this world.'

Stephen Farr laughed.

'I don't think you are a pacifist.'

'You do not think I am what?' Pilar seemed puzzled by a word which had not previously entered her vocabulary.

'Do you forgive your enemies, señorita?'

Pilar shook her head.

'I have no enemies. But if I had—'

'Well?'

He was watching her, fascinated anew by the sweet, cruel upward-curving mouth.

Pilar said gravely: 'If I had an enemy – if anyone hated me and I hated them – then I would cut my enemy's throat like *this* . . .'

She made a graphic gesture.

It was so swift and so crude that Stephen Farr was momentarily taken aback. He said: 'You are a bloodthirsty young woman!'

Pilar asked in a matter-of-fact tone: 'What would you do to your enemy?'

He started – stared at her, then laughed aloud.

'I wonder—' he said. 'I wonder!'

Pilar said disapprovingly: 'But surely – you know?'

He checked his laughter, drew in his breath and said in a low voice: 'Yes, I know . . .'

Then, with a rapid change of manner, he asked: 'What made you come to England?'

Pilar replied with a certain demureness.

'I am going to stay with my relations – with my English relations.'

'I see.'

He leaned back in his seat, studying her – wondering what these English relations of whom she spoke were like – wondering what they would make of this Spanish stranger . . . trying to picture her in the midst of some sober British family at Christmas-time.

Pilar asked: 'Is it nice, South Africa, yes?'

He began to talk to her about South Africa. She listened with the pleased attention of a child hearing a story. He enjoyed her naïve but shrewd questions and amused himself by making a kind of exaggerated fairy story of it all.

The return of the proper occupants of the carriage put an end to this diversion. He rose, smiled into her eyes, and made his way out again into the corridor.

As he stood for a minute in the doorway, to allow an elderly lady to come in, his eyes fell on the label of Pilar's obviously foreign straw case. He read the name with interest – *Miss Pilar Estravados* – then as his eye caught the address it widened to incredulity and some other feeling – *Gorston Hall, Longdale, Addlesfield.*

He half-turned, staring at the girl with a new expression – puzzled, resentful, suspicious . . . He went out into the corridor and stood there smoking a cigarette and frowning to himself . . .

III

In the big blue and gold drawing-room at Gorston Hall, Alfred Lee and Lydia, his wife, sat discussing their plans for Christmas. Alfred was a squarely built man of middle-age with a gentle face and mild brown eyes. His voice when he spoke was quiet and precise with a very clear enunciation. His head was sunk into his shoulders and he gave a curious impression of inertia. Lydia, his wife, was an energetic, lean greyhound of a woman. She was amazingly thin, but all her movements had a swift, startled grace about them.

There was no beauty in her careless, haggard face, but it had distinction. Her voice was charming.

Alfred said: 'Father insists! There's nothing else to it.'

Lydia controlled a sudden impatient movement. She said: 'Must you always give in to him?'

'He's a very old man, my dear—'

'Oh, I know – I know!'

'He expects to have his own way.'

Lydia said dryly: 'Naturally, since he has always had it! But some time or other, Alfred, you will have to make a stand.'

'What do you mean, Lydia?'

He stared at her, so palpably upset and startled that for a moment she bit her lip and seemed doubtful whether to go on.

Alfred Lee repeated: 'What do you mean, Lydia?'

She shrugged her thin, graceful shoulders.

She said, trying to choose her words cautiously: 'Your father is – inclined to be – tyrannical—'

'He's old.'

'And will grow older. And consequently more tyrannical. Where will it end? Already he dictates our lives to us completely. We can't make a plan of our own! If we do, it is always liable to be upset.'

Alfred said: 'Father expects to come first. He is very good to us, remember.'

'Oh! Good to us!'

'*Very* good to us.'

Alfred spoke with a trace of sternness.

Lydia said calmly: 'You mean financially?'

'Yes. His own wants are very simple. But he never grudges us money. You can spend what you like on dress and on this house, and the bills are paid without a murmur. He gave us a new car only last week.'

'As far as money goes, your father is very generous, I admit,' said Lydia. 'But in return he expects us to behave like slaves.'

'Slaves?'

'That's the word I used. You *are* his slave, Alfred. If we have planned to go away and Father suddenly wishes us not to go, you cancel the arrangements and remain without a murmur! If the whim takes him to send us away, we go . . . We have no lives of our own – no independence.'

Her husband said distressfully: 'I wish you wouldn't talk like this, Lydia. It is very ungrateful. My father has done everything for us . . .'

She bit off a retort that was on her lips. She shrugged those thin, graceful shoulders once more.

Alfred said: 'You know, Lydia, the old man is very fond of you—'

His wife said clearly and distinctly: 'I am not at all fond of him.'

'Lydia, it distresses me to hear you say things like that. It is so unkind—'

'Perhaps. But sometimes a compulsion comes over one to speak the truth.'

'If Father guessed—'

'Your father knows perfectly well that I do not like him! It amuses him, I think.'

'Really, Lydia, I am sure you are wrong there. He has often told me how charming your manner to him is.'

'Naturally I've always been polite. I always shall be. I'm just letting you know what my real feelings are. I dislike your father, Alfred. I think he is a malicious and tyrannical old man. He bullies you and presumes on your affection for him. You ought to have stood up to him years ago.'

Alfred said sharply: 'That will do, Lydia. Please don't say any more.'

She sighed.

'I'm sorry. Perhaps I was wrong . . . Let's talk of our Christmas arrangements. Do you think your brother David will really come?'

'Why not?'

She shook her head doubtfully.

'David is – queer. He's not been inside the house for years, remember. He was so devoted to your mother – he's got some feeling about this place.'

'David always got on Father's nerves,' said Alfred, 'with his music and his dreamy ways. Father was, perhaps, a bit hard on him sometimes. But I think David and Hilda will come all right. Christmas time, you know.'

'Peace and goodwill,' said Lydia. Her delicate mouth curved ironically. 'I wonder! George and Magdalene are coming. They said they would probably arrive tomorrow. I'm afraid Magdalene will be frightfully bored.'

Alfred said with some slight annoyance: 'Why my brother George ever married a girl twenty years younger than himself I can't think! George was always a fool!'

'He's very successful in his career,' said Lydia. 'His constituents like him. I believe Magdalene works quite hard politically for him.'

Alfred said slowly: 'I don't think I like her very much. She is very good-looking – but I sometimes think she is like one of those beautiful pears one gets – they have a rosy flush and a rather waxen appearance—' He shook his head.

'And they're bad inside?' said Lydia. 'How funny you should say that, Alfred!'

'Why funny?'

She answered: 'Because – usually – you are such a gentle soul. You hardly ever say an unkind thing about anyone. I get annoyed with you sometimes because you're not sufficiently – oh, what shall I say? – sufficiently suspicious – not worldly enough!'

Her husband smiled.

'The world, I always think, is as you yourself make it.'

Lydia said sharply: 'No! Evil is not only in one's mind. Evil

exists! *You* seem to have no consciousness of the evil in the world. I
have. I can feel it. I've always felt it – here in this house—' She bit
her lip and turned away.

Alfred said: 'Lydia—'

But she raised a quick admonitory hand, her eyes looking past
him at something over his shoulder. Alfred turned.

A dark man with a smooth face was standing there deferentially.

Lydia said sharply: 'What is it, Horbury?'

Horbury's voice was low, a mere deferential murmur.

'It's Mr Lee, Madam. He asked me to tell you that there would
be two more guests arriving for Christmas, and would you have
rooms prepared for them.'

Lydia said: 'Two more guests?'

Horbury said smoothly: 'Yes, Madam, another gentleman and
a young lady.'

Alfred said wonderingly: 'A young lady?'

'That's what Mr Lee said, sir.'

Lydia said quickly: 'I will go up and see him—'

Horbury made one little step, it was a mere ghost of a
movement but it stopped Lydia's rapid progress automatically.

'Excuse me, madam, but Mr Lee is having his afternoon sleep.
He asked specially that he should not be disturbed.'

'I see,' said Alfred. 'Of course we won't disturb him.'

'Thank you, sir.' Horbury withdrew.

Lydia said vehemently: 'How I dislike that man! He creeps
about the house like a cat! One never hears him going or coming.'

'I don't like him very much, either. But he knows his job. It's not
easy to get a good male nurse-attendant. And Father likes him,
that's the main thing.'

'Yes, that's the main thing, as you say. Alfred, what is this
about a young lady? What young lady?'

Her husband shook his head.

'I can't imagine. I can't even think of anyone it might be likely
to be.'

They stared at each other. Then Lydia said, with a sudden twist
of her expressive mouth: 'Do you know what I think, Alfred?'

'What?'

'I think your father has been bored lately. I think he is planning
a little Christmas diversion for himself.'

'By introducing two strangers into a family gathering?'

'Oh, I don't know what the details are – but I do fancy that your
father is preparing to – amuse himself.'

343

'I hope he *will* get some pleasure out of it,' said Alfred gravely. 'Poor old chap, tied by the leg, an invalid – after the adventurous life he has led.'

Lydia said slowly: 'After the – adventurous life he has led.'

The pause she made before the adjective gave it some special though obscure significance. Alfred seemed to feel it. He flushed and looked unhappy.

She cried out suddenly: 'How he ever had a son like you, I can't imagine! You two are poles apart. And he fascinates you – you simply worship him!'

Alfred said with a trace of vexation: 'Aren't you going a little far, Lydia? It's natural, I should say, for a son to love his father. It would be very unnatural not to do so.'

Lydia said: 'In that case, most of the members of this family are – unnatural! Oh, don't let's argue! I apologize. I've hurt your feelings, I know. Believe me, Alfred, I really didn't mean to do that. I admire you enormously for your – your –*fidelity*. Loyalty is such a rare virtue in these days. Let us say, shall we, that I am jealous? Women are supposed to be jealous of their mothers-in-law – why not, then, of their fathers-in-law?'

He put a gentle arm round her.

'Your tongue runs away with you, Lydia. There's no reason for you to be jealous.'

She gave him a quick remorseful kiss, a delicate caress on the tip of his ear.

'I know. All the same, Alfred, I don't believe I should have been in the least jealous of your mother. I wish I'd known her.'

He sighed.

'She was a poor creature,' he said.

His wife looked at him interestedly.

'So that's how she struck you . . . as a poor creature . . . That's interesting.'

He said dreamily: 'I remember her as nearly always ill . . . Often in tears. . . .' He shook his head. 'She had no spirit.'

Still staring at him, she murmured very softly: 'How odd . . .'

But as he turned a questioning glance on her she shook her head quickly and changed the subject.

'Since we are not allowed to know who our mysterious guests are I shall go out and finish my garden.'

'It's very cold, my dear, a biting wind.'

'I'll wrap up warmly.'

She left the room. Alfred Lee, left alone, stood for some minutes motionless, frowning a little to himself, then he walked over to the big window at the end of the room. Outside was a terrace running the whole length of the house. Here, after a minute or two, he saw Lydia emerge, carrying a flat basket. She was wearing a big blanket coat. She set down the basket and began to work at a square stone sink slightly raised above the ground level.

Her husband watched for some time. At last he went out of the room, fetched himself a coat and muffler, and emerged on to the terrace by a side door. As he walked along he passed various other sinks arranged as miniature gardens, all the products of Lydia's agile fingers.

One represented a desert scene with smooth yellow sand, a little clump of green palm trees in coloured tin, and a procession of camels with one or two little Arab figures. Some primitive mud houses had been constructed of plasticine. There was an Italian garden with terraces and formal beds with flowers in coloured sealing-wax. There was an Arctic one, too, with clumps of green glass for icebergs, and a little cluster of penguins. Next came a Japanese garden with a couple of beautiful little stunted trees, looking-glass arranged for water, and bridges modelled out of plasticine.

He came at last to stand beside her where she was at work. She had laid down blue paper and covered it over with glass. Round this were lumps of rock piled up. At the moment she was pouring out coarse pebbles from a little bag and forming them into a beach. Between the rocks were some small cactuses.

Lydia was murmuring to herself: 'Yes, that's exactly right – exactly what I want.'

Alfred said: 'What's this latest work of art?'

She started, for she had not heard him come up.

'This? Oh, it's the Dead Sea, Alfred. Do you like it?'

He said: 'It's rather arid, isn't it? Oughtn't there to be more vegetation?'

She shook her head.

'It's my idea of the Dead Sea. It *is* dead, you see—'

'It's not so attractive as some of the others.'

'It's not meant to be specially attractive.'

Footsteps sounded on the terrace. An elderly butler, white-haired and slightly bowed, was coming towards them.

'Mrs George Lee on the telephone, madam. She says will it be convenient if she and Mr George arrive by the five-twenty tomorrow?'

'Yes, tell her that will be quite all right.'

'Thank you, madam.'

345

The butler hurried away. Lydia looked after him with a softened expression on her face.

'Dear old Tressilian. What a standby he is! I can't imagine what we should do without him.'

Alfred agreed.

'He's one of the old school. He's been with us nearly forty years. He's devoted to us all.'

Lydia nodded.

'Yes. He's like the faithful old retainers of fiction. I believe he'd lie himself blue in the face if it was necessary to protect one of the family!'

Alfred said: 'I believe he would . . . Yes, I believe he would.'

Lydia smoothed over the last bit of her shingle.

'There,' she said. 'That's ready.'

'Ready?' Alfred looked puzzled.

She laughed.

'For Christmas, silly! For this sentimental family Christmas we're going to have.'

IV

David was reading the letter. Once he screwed it up into a ball and thrust it away from him. Then, reaching for it, he smoothed it out and read it again.

Quietly, without saying anything, his wife, Hilda, watched him. She noted the jerking muscle (or was it a nerve?) in his temple, the slight tremor of the long delicate hands, the nervous spasmodic movements of his whole body. When he pushed aside the lock of fair hair that always tended to stray down over his forehead and looked across at her with appealing blue eyes she was ready.

'Hilda, what shall we do about it?'

Hilda hesitated a minute before speaking. She had heard the appeal in his voice. She knew how dependent he was upon her – had always been ever since their marriage – knew that she could probably influence his decision finally and decisively. But for just that reason she was chary of pronouncing anything too final.

She said, and her voice had the calm, soothing quality that can be heard in the voice of an experienced nannie in a nursery: 'It depends on how you feel about it, David.'

A broad woman, Hilda, not beautiful, but with a certain

346

magnetic quality. Something about her like a Dutch picture. Something warming and endearing in the sound of her voice. Something strong about her – the vital hidden strength that appeals to weakness. An over-stout dumpy middle-aged woman – not clever – not brilliant – but with *something* about her that you couldn't pass over. Force! Hilda Lee had force!

David got up and began pacing up and down. His hair was practically untouched by grey. He was strangely boyish-looking. His face had the mild quality of a Burne-Jones knight. It was, somehow, not very real . . .

He said, and his voice was wistful: 'You know how I feel about it, Hilda. You must.'

'I'm not sure.'

'But I've told you – I've told you again and again! How I hate it all – the house and the country round and everything! It brings back nothing but misery. I hated every moment that I spent there! When I think of it – of all that *she* suffered – my mother . . .'

His wife nodded sympathetically.

'She was so sweet, Hilda, and so patient. Lying there, often in pain, but bearing it – enduring everything. And when I think of my father' – his face darkened – 'bringing all that misery into her life – humiliating her – boasting of his love affairs – constantly unfaithful to her and never troubling to conceal it.'

Hilda Lee said: 'She should not have put up with it. She should have left him.'

He said with a touch of reproof: 'She was too good to do that. She thought it was her duty to remain. Besides, it was her home – where else should she go?'

'She could have made a life of her own.'

David said fretfully: 'Not in those days! You don't understand. Women didn't behave like that. They put up with things. They endured patiently. She had us to consider. Even if she divorced my father, what would have happened? He would probably have married again. There might have been a second family. *Our* interests might have gone to the wall. She had to think of all those considerations.'

Hilda did not answer.

David went on: 'No, she did right. She was a saint! She endured to the end – uncomplainingly.'

Hilda said: 'Not quite uncomplainingly or you would not know so much, David!'

He said softly, his face lighting up: 'Yes – she told me things . . . She knew how I loved her. When she died—'

347

He stopped. He ran his hands through his hair.

'Hilda, it was awful – horrible! The desolation! She was quite young still, she *needn't* have died. *He* killed her – my father! He was responsible for her dying. He broke her heart. I decided then that I'd not go on living under his roof. I broke away – got away from it all.'

Hilda nodded.

'You were very wise,' she said. 'It was the right thing to do.'

David said: 'Father wanted me to go into the works. That would have meant living at home. I couldn't have stood that. I can't think how Alfred stands it – how he has stood it all these years.'

'Did he never rebel against it?' asked Hilda with some interest. 'I thought you told me something about his having given up some other career.'

David nodded.

'Alfred was going into the Army. Father arranged it all. Alfred, the eldest, was to go into some cavalry regiment, Harry was to go into the works, so was I. George was to enter politics.'

'And it didn't work out like that?'

David shook his head.

'Harry broke all that up! He was always frightfully wild. Got into debt – and all sorts of other troubles. Finally he went off one day with several hundred pounds that didn't belong to him, leaving a note behind him saying an office stool didn't suit him and he was going to see the world.'

'And you never heard any more of him?'

'Oh, yes, we did!' David laughed. 'We heard quite often! He was always cabling for money from all over the world. He usually got it, too!'

'And Alfred?'

'Father made him chuck up the Army and come back and go into the works.'

'Did he mind?'

'Very much to begin with. He hated it. But Father could always twist Alfred round his little finger. He's absolutely under Father's thumb still, I believe.'

'And you – escaped!' said Hilda.

'Yes. I went to London and studied painting. Father told me plainly that if I went off on a fool's errand like that I'd get a small allowance from him during his lifetime and nothing when he died. I said I didn't care. He called me a young fool, and that was that! I've never seen him since.'

Hilda said gently: 'And you haven't regretted it?'

'No, indeed. I realize I shan't ever get anywhere with my art. I shall never be a great artist – but we're happy enough in this cottage – we've got everything we want – all the essentials. And if I die, well, my life's insured for you.'

He paused and then said: 'And now – *this*!'

He struck the letter with his open hand.

'I am sorry your father ever wrote that letter, if it upsets you so much,' said Hilda.

David went on as though he had not heard her.

'Asking me to bring my wife for Christmas, expressing a hope that we may be all together for Christmas; a united family! What can it mean?'

Hilda said: 'Need it mean anything more than it says?'

He looked at her questioningly.

'I mean,' she said, smiling, 'that your father is growing old. He's beginning to feel sentimental about family ties. That does happen, you know.'

'I suppose it does,' said David slowly.

'He's an old man and he's lonely.'

He gave her a quick look.

'You want me to go, don't you, Hilda?'

She said slowly: 'It seems a pity – not to answer an appeal. I'm old-fashioned, I dare say, but why not have peace and goodwill at Christmas-time?'

'After all I've told you?'

'I know, dear, I know. But all that's in the *past*. It's all done and finished with.'

'Not for me.'

'No, *because you won't let it die*. You keep the past alive in your own mind.'

'I can't forget.'

'You *won't* forget – that's what you mean, David.'

His mouth set in a firm line.

'We're like that, we Lees. We remember things for years – brood about them, keep memory green.'

Hilda said with a touch of impatience: 'Is that anything to be proud of? I do not think so!'

He looked thoughtfully at her, a touch of reserve in his manner.

He said: 'You don't attach much value to loyalty, then – loyalty to a memory?'

Hilda said: 'I believe the *present* matters – not the past! The past must go. If we seek to keep the past alive, we end, I think, by

349

distorting it. We see it in exaggerated terms – a false perspective.'

'I can remember every word and every incident of those days perfectly,' said David passionately.

'Yes, but you *shouldn't*, my dear! It isn't natural to do so! You're applying the judgment of a boy to those days instead of looking back on them with the more temperate outlook of a man.'

'What difference would that make?' demanded David.

Hilda hesitated. She was aware of unwisdom in going on, and yet there were things she badly wanted to say.

'I think,' she said, 'that you're seeing your father as a *bogy*! You're exalting him into a kind of personification of evil. Probably, if you were to see him now, you would realize that he was only a very ordinary man; a man, perhaps, whose passions ran away with him, a man whose life was far from blameless, but nevertheless merely a *man* – not a kind of inhuman monster!'

'You don't understand! His treatment of my mother—'

Hilda said gravely: 'There is a certain kind of meekness – of submission – that brings out the worst in a man – whereas that same man, faced by spirit and determination, might be a different creature!'

'So you say it was her fault—'

Hilda interrupted him.

'No, of course I don't! I've no doubt your father treated your mother very badly indeed, but marriage is an extraordinary thing – and I doubt if any outsider – even a child of the marriage – has the right to judge. Besides, all this resentment on your part now cannot help your mother. It is all *gone* – it is behind you! What is left now is an old man, in feeble health, asking his son to come home for Christmas.'

'And you want me to go?'

Hilda hesitated, then she suddenly made up her mind. 'Yes,' she said, 'I do. I want you to go and lay the bogy once and for all.'

V

George Lee, MP for Westeringham, was a somewhat corpulent gentleman of forty-one. His eyes were pale blue and slightly prominent with a suspicious expression, he had a heavy jowl, and a slow pedantic utterance.

He said now in a weighty manner: 'I have told you, Magdalene, that I think it my *duty* to go.'

His wife shrugged her shoulders impatiently.

She was a slender creature, a platinum blonde with plucked eyebrows and a smooth egg-like face. It could, on occasions, look quite blank and devoid of any expression whatever. She was looking like that now.

'Darling,' she said, 'it will be perfectly grim, I am sure of it.'

'Moreover,' said George Lee, and his face lit up as an attractive idea occurred to him, 'it will enable us to save considerably. Christmas is always an expensive time. We can put the servants on board wages.'

'Oh, well!' said Magdalene. 'After all, Christmas is pretty grim anywhere!'

'I suppose,' said George, pursuing his own line of thought, 'they will expect to have a Christmas dinner? A nice piece of beef, perhaps, instead of a turkey.'

'Who? The servants? Oh, George, don't fuss so. You're always worrying about money.'

'Somebody has to worry,' said George.

'Yes, but it's absurd to pinch and scrape in all these little ways. Why don't you make your father give you some more money?'

'He always gives me a very handsome allowance.'

'It's awful to be completely dependent on your father, as you are! He ought to settle some money on you outright.'

'That's not his way of doing things.'

Magdalene looked at him. Her hazel eyes were suddenly sharp and keen. The expressionless egg-like face showed sudden meaning.

'He's frightfully rich, isn't he, George? A kind of millionaire, isn't he?'

'A millionaire twice over, I believe.'

Magdalene gave an envious sigh.

'How did he make it all? South Africa, wasn't it?'

'Yes, he made a big fortune there in his early days, mainly diamonds.'

'Thrilling!' said Magdalene.

'Then he came to England and started in business and his fortune has actually doubled or trebled itself, I believe.'

'What will happen when he dies?' asked Magdalene.

'Father's never said much on the subject. Of course one can't exactly *ask*. I should imagine that the bulk of his money will go to Alfred and myself. Alfred, of course, will get the larger share.'

'You've got other brothers, haven't you?'

'Yes, there's my brother David. I don't fancy *he* will get much.

He went off to do art or some tomfoolery of that kind. I believe Father warned him that he would cut him out of his will and David said he didn't care.'

'How silly!' said Magdalene with scorn.

'There was my sister Jennifer, too. She went off with a foreigner – a Spanish artist – one of David's friends. But she died just over a year ago. She left a daughter, I believe. Father might leave a little money to her, but nothing much. And of course there's Harry—'

He stopped, slightly embarrassed.

'Harry?' said Magdalene, surprised. 'Who is Harry?'

'Ah – er – my brother.'

'I never knew you had another brother.'

'My dear, he wasn't a great – er – credit – to us. We don't mention him. His behaviour was disgraceful. We haven't heard anything of him for some years now. He's probably dead.'

Magdalene laughed suddenly.

'What is it? What are you laughing at?'

Magdalene said: 'I was only thinking how funny it was that you – *you*, George – should have a disreputable brother! You're so very respectable.'

'I should hope so,' said George coldly.

Her eyes narrowed.

'Your father isn't – very respectable, George.'

'Really, Magdalene!'

'Sometimes the things he says make me feel quite uncomfortable.'

George said: 'Really, Magdalene, you surprise me. Does – er – does Lydia feel the same?'

'He doesn't say the same kind of things to Lydia,' said Magdalene. She added angrily: '*No*, he never says them to *her*. I can't think why not.'

George glanced at her quickly and then glanced away.

'Oh, well,' he said vaguely. 'One must make allowances. At Father's age – and with his health being so bad—'

He paused. His wife asked: 'Is he really – pretty ill?'

'Oh, I wouldn't say *that*. He's remarkably tough. All the same, since he wants to have his family round him at Christmas, I think we are quite right to go. It may be his last Christmas.'

She said sharply: 'You *say* that, George, but really, I suppose, he may live for years?'

Slightly taken aback, her husband stammered: 'Yes – yes, of course he may.'

Magdalene turned away.

'Oh, well,' she said, 'I suppose we're doing the right thing by going.'

'I have no doubt about it.'

'But I hate it! Alfred's so dull, and Lydia snubs me.'

'Nonsense.'

'She does. And I hate that beastly manservant.'

'Old Tressilian?'

'No, Horbury. Sneaking round like a cat and smirking.'

'Really, Magdalene, I can't see that Horbury can affect you in any way!'

'He just gets on my nerves, that's all. But don't let's bother. We've got to go, I can see that. Won't do to offend the old man.'

'No – no, that's just the point. About the servants' Christmas dinner—'

'Not now, George, some other time. I'll just ring up Lydia and tell her that we'll come by the five-twenty tomorrow.'

Magdalene left the room precipitately. After telephoning she went up to her own room and sat down in front of the desk. She let down the flap and rummaged in its various pigeon-holes. Cascades of bills came tumbling out. Magdalene sorted through them, trying to arrange them in some kind of order. Finally, with an impatient sigh, she bundled them up and thrust them back whence they had come. She passed a hand over her smooth platinum head.

'What on earth am I to do?' she murmured.

VI

On the first floor of Gorston Hall a long passage led to a big room overlooking the front drive. It was a room furnished in the more flamboyant of old-fashioned styles. It had heavy brocaded wallpaper, rich leather arm-chairs, large vases embossed with dragons, sculptures in bronze . . . Everything in it was magnificent, costly and solid.

'In a big grandfather arm-chair, the biggest and most imposing of all the chairs , sat the thin, shrivelled figure of an old man. His long claw-like hands rested on the arms of the chair. A gold-mounted stick was by his side. He wore an old shabby blue dressing-gown. On his feet were carpet slippers. His hair was white and the skin of his face was yellow.

A shabby, insignificant figure, one might have thought. But the nose, aquiline and proud, and the eyes, dark and intensely alive, might cause an observer to alter his opinion. Here was fire and life and vigour.

Old Simeon Lee cackled to himself, a sudden, high cackle of amusement.

He said: 'You gave my message to Mrs Alfred, hey?'

Horbury was standing beside his chair. He replied in his soft deferential voice: 'Yes, sir.'

'Exactly in the words I told you? Exactly, mind?'

'Yes, sir. I didn't make a mistake, sir.'

'No – you don't make mistakes. You'd better not make mistakes, either – or you'll regret it! And what did she say, Horbury? What did Mr Alfred say?'

Quietly, unemotionally, Horbury repeated what had passed. The old man cackled again and rubbed his hands together.

'Splendid . . . First-rate . . . They'll have been thinking and wondering – all the afternoon! Splendid! I'll have 'em up now. Go and get them.'

'Yes, sir.'

Horbury walked noiselessly across the room and went out.

'And, Horbury—'

The old man looked round, then cursed to himself.

'Fellow moves like a cat. Never know where he is.'

He sat quite still in his chair, his fingers caressing his chin, till there was a tap on the door, and Alfred and Lydia came in.

'Ah, there you are, there you are. Sit here, Lydia, my dear, by me. What a nice colour you've got.'

'I've been out in the cold. It makes one's cheeks burn afterwards.'

Alfred said: 'How are you, Father? Did you have a good rest this afternoon?'

'First-rate – first-rate. Dreamt about the old days! That was before I settled down and became a pillar of society.'

He cackled with sudden laughter.

His daughter-in-law sat silently smiling with polite attention.

Alfred said: 'What's this, Father, about two extra being expected for Christmas?'

'Ah, that! Yes, I must tell you about that. It's going to be a grand Christmas for me this year – a grand Christmas. Let me see, George is coming and Magdalene—'

Lydia said: 'Yes, they are arriving tomorrow by the five-twenty.'

Old Simeon said: 'Poor stick, George! Nothing but a gasbag! Still, he *is* my son.'

Alfred said: 'His constituents like him.'

Simeon cackled again.

'They probably think he's honest. Honest! There never was a Lee who was honest yet.'

'Oh, come now, Father.'

'I except you, my boy. I except you.'

'And David?' asked Lydia.

'David, now. I'm curious to see the boy after all these years. He was a namby-pamby youngster. Wonder what his wife is like? At any rate, *he* hasn't married a girl twenty years younger than himself, like that fool George!'

'Hilda wrote a very nice letter,' said Lydia. 'I've just had a wire from her confirming it and saying they are definitely arriving tomorrow.'

Her father-in-law looked at her, a keen, penetrating glance. He laughed.

'I never get any change out of you, Lydia,' he said. 'I'll say this for you, Lydia, you're a well-bred woman. Breeding tells. I know that well enough. A funny thing, though, heredity. There's only one of you that's taken after me – only one out of all the litter.'

His eyes danced.

'Now guess who's coming for Christmas. I'll give you three guesses and I'll bet you a fiver you won't get the answer.'

He looked from one face to the other. Alfred said frowning: 'Horbury said you expected a young lady.'

'That intrigued you – yes, I dare say it did. Pilar will be arriving any minute now. I gave orders for the car to go and meet her.'

Alfred said sharply: '*Pilar?*'

Simeon said: 'Pilar Estravados. Jennifer's girl. My Granddaughter. I wonder what she'll be like.'

Alfred cried out: 'Good heavens, Father, you never told me . . .'

The old man was grinning.

'No, I thought I'd keep it a secret! Got Charlton to write out and fix things.'

Alfred repeated, his tone hurt and reproachful: 'You never told me . . .'

His father said, still grinning wickedly: 'It would have spoilt the surprise! Wonder what it will be like to have young blood under this roof again? I never saw Estravados. Wonder which the girl takes after – her mother or her father?'

'Do you really think it's wise, Father?' began Alfred. 'Taking everything into consideration—'

The old man interrupted him.

'Safety – safety – you play for safety too much, Alfred! Always have! That hasn't been my way! Do what you want and be damned to it! That's what I say! The girl's my granddaughter – the only grandchild in the family! I don't care what her father was or what he did! She's my flesh and blood! And she's coming to live here in my house.'

Lydia said sharply: 'She's coming to *live* here?'

He darted a quick look at her. 'Do you object?'

She shook her head. She said smiling: 'I couldn't very well object to your asking someone to your own house, could I? No, I was wondering about – her.'

'About her – what d'you mean?'

'Whether she would be happy here.'

Old Simeon flung up his head.

'She's not got a penny in the world. She ought to be thankful!'

Lydia shrugged her shoulders.

Simeon turned to Alfred: 'You see? It's going to be a grand Christmas! All my children round me. *All* my children! There, Alfred, there's your clue. Now guess who the other visitor is.'

Alfred stared at him.

'All my children! Guess, boy! *Harry*, of course! Your brother Harry!'

Alfred had gone very pale. He stammered: 'Harry – not Harry—'

'Harry himself!'

'But we thought he was dead!'

'Not he!'

'You – you're having him back here? After everything?'

'The prodigal son, eh? You're right. The fatted calf! We must kill the fatted calf, Alfred. We must give him a grand welcome.'

Alfred said: 'He treated you – all of us – disgracefully. He—'

'No need to recite his crimes! It's a long list. But Christmas, you'll remember, is the season of forgiveness! We'll welcome the prodigal home.'

Alfred rose. He murmured: 'This has been – rather a shock. I never dreamt that Harry would ever come inside these walls again.'

Simeon leaned forward.

You never liked Harry, did you?' he said softly.

'After the way he behaved to you—'

Simeon cackled. He said: 'Ah, but bygones must be bygones. That's the spirit for Christmas, isn't it, Lydia?'

Lydia, too, had gone pale. She said dryly: 'I see that you have thought a good deal about Christmas this year.'

'I want my family round me. Peace and goodwill. I'm an old man. Are you going, my dear?'

Alfred had hurried out. Lydia paused a moment before following him.

Simeon nodded his head after the retreating figure.

'It's upset him. He and Harry never got on. Harry used to jeer at Alfred. Called him Old Slow and Sure.'

Lydia's lips parted. She was about to speak, then, as she saw the old man's eager expression, she checked herself. Her self-control, she saw, disappointed him. The perception of that fact enabled her to say: 'The hare and the tortoise. Ah, well, the tortoise wins the race.'

'Not always,' said Simeon. 'Not always, my dear Lydia.'

She said, still smiling: 'Excuse me, I must go after Alfred. Sudden excitements always upset him.'

Simeon cackled.

'Yes, Alfred doesn't like changes. He always was a regular sobersides.'

Lydia said: 'Alfred is very devoted to *you*.'

'That seems odd to you, doesn't it?'

'Sometimes,' said Lydia, 'it does.'

She left the room. Simeon looked after her.

He chuckled softly and rubbed his palms together.

'Lots of fun,' he said. 'Lots of fun still. I'm going to enjoy this Christmas.'

With an effort he pulled himself upright and, with the help of his stick, shuffled across the room.

He went to a big safe that stood at the corner of the room. He twirled the handle of the combination. The door came open and, with shaking fingers, he felt inside.

He lifted out a small wash-leather bag and, opening it, let a stream of uncut diamonds pass through his fingers.

'Well, my beauties, well . . . Still the same – still my old friends. Those were good days – good days . . . They shan't carve you and cut you about, my friends. *You* shan't hang round the necks of women or sit on their fingers or hang on their ears. You're *mine*! My old friends! We know a thing or two, you and I. I'm old, they say, and ill, but I'm not done for! Lots of life in the old dog yet. And there's still some fun to be got out of life. Still some fun—'

DECEMBER 23RD

TRESSILIAN went to answer the doorbell. It had been an unusually aggressive peal, and now, before he could make his slow way across the hall, it pealed out again.

Tressilian flushed. An ill-mannered, impatient way of ringing the bell at a gentleman's house! If it was a fresh lot of those carol singers he'd give them a piece of his mind.

Through the frosted glass of the upper half of the door he saw a silhouette – a big man in a slouch hat. He opened the door. As he had thought – a cheap, flashy stranger – nasty pattern of suit he was wearing – loud! Some impudent begging fellow!

'Blessed if it isn't Tressilian,' said the stranger. 'How are you, Tressilian?'

Tressilian stared – took a deep breath – stared again. That bold arrogant jaw, the high-bridged nose, the rollicking eye. Yes, they had all been there twenty years ago. More subdued then . . .

He said with a gasp: 'Mr Harry!'

Harry Lee laughed.

'Looks as though I'd given you quite a shock. Why? I'm expected, aren't I?'

'Yes, indeed, sir. Certainly, sir.'

'Then why the surprise act?' Harry stepped back a foot or two and looked up at the house – a good solid mass of red brick, unimaginative but solid.

'Just the same ugly old mansion,' he remarked. 'Still standing, though, that's the main thing. How's my father, Tressilian?'

'He's somewhat of an invalid, sir. Keeps his room, and can't get about much. But he's wonderfully well, considering.'

'The old sinner!'

Harry Lee came inside, let Tressilian remove his scarf and take the somewhat theatrical hat.

'How's my dear brother Alfred, Tressilian?'

'He's very well, sir.'

Harry grinned.

'Looking forward to seeing me? Eh?'

'I expect so, sir.'

'I don't! Quite the contrary. I bet it's given him a nasty jolt, my turning up! Alfred and I never did get on. Ever read your Bible, Tressilian?'

'Why, yes, sir, sometimes, sir.

'Remember the tale of the prodigal's return? The good brother didn't like it, remember? Didn't like it at all! Good old stay-at-home Alfred doesn't like it, either, I bet.'

Tressilian remained silent, looking down his nose. His stiffened back expressed protest. Harry clapped him on the shoulder.

'Lead on, old son,' he said. 'The fatted calf awaits me! Lead me right to it.'

Tressilian murmured: 'If you will come this way into the drawing-room, sir. I am not quite sure where everyone is . . . They were unable to send to meet you, sir, not knowing the time of your arrival.'

Harry nodded. He followed Tressilian along the hall, turning his head to look about him as he went.

'All the old exhibits in their place, I see,' he remarked. 'I don't believe anything has changed since I went away all those years ago.'

He followed Tressilian into the drawing-room. The old man murmured: 'I will see if I can find Mr or Mrs Alfred,' and hurried out.

Harry Lee had marched into the room and had then stopped, staring at the figure who was seated on one of the window-sills. His eyes roamed incredulously over the black hair and the creamy exotic pallor.

'Good Lord!' he said. 'Are you my father's seventh and most beautiful wife?'

Pilar slipped down and came towards him.

'I am Pilar Estravados,' she announced. 'And you must be my Uncle Harry, my mother's brother.'

Harry said, staring: 'So that's who you are! Jenny's daughter.'

Pilar said: 'Why did you ask me if I was your father's seventh wife? Has he really had six wives?'

Harry laughed.

'No, I believe he's only had one official one. Well – Pil – what's your name?'

'Pilar, yes.'

'Well, Pilar, it really gives me quite a turn to see something like you blooming in this mausoleum.'

'This – maus – please?'

'This museum of stuffed dummies! I always thought this house was lousy! Now I see it again I think it's lousier than ever!'

Pilar said in a shocked voice: 'Oh, no, it is very handsome here! The furniture is good and the carpets – thick carpets everywhere –

and there are lots of ornaments. Everything is very good quality and very, very rich!'

'You're right there,' said Harry, grinning. He looked at her with amusement. 'You know, I can't help getting a kick out of seeing you in the midst—'

He broke off as Lydia came rapidly into the room.

She came straight to him.

'How d'you do, Harry? I'm Lydia – Alfred's wife.'

'How de do, Lydia.' He shook hands, examining her intelligent mobile face in a swift glance and approving mentally of the way she walked – very few women moved well.

Lydia in her turn took stock of him.

She thought: 'He looks a frightful tough – attractive, though. I wouldn't trust him an inch . . .'

She said, smiling: 'How does it look after all these years? Quite different, or very much the same?'

'Pretty much the same.' He looked round him. 'This room's been done over.'

'Oh, many times.'

He said: 'I meant by you. You've made it – different.'

'Yes, I expect so . . .'

He grinned at her, a sudden impish grin that reminded her with a start of the old man upstairs.

'It's got more class about it now! I remember hearing that old Alfred had married a girl whose people came over with the Conqueror.'

Lydia smiled. She said: 'I believe they did. But they've rather run to seed since those days.'

Harry said: 'How's old Alfred? Just the same blessed old stick-in-the-mud as ever?'

'I've no idea whether you will find him changed or not.'

'How are the others? Scattered all over England?'

'No – they're all here for Christmas, you know.'

Harry's eyes opened.

'Regular Christmas family reunion.' What's the matter with the old man? He used not to give a damn for sentiment. Don't remember his caring much for his family, either. He must have changed!'

'Perhaps.' Lydia's voice was dry.

Pilar was staring, her big eyes wide and interested.

Harry said: 'How's old George? Still the same skinflint? How he used to howl if he had to part with a halfpenny of his pocket-money!'

Lydia said: 'George is in Parliament. He's Member for Westeringham.'

'What? Popeye in Parliament? Lord, that's good.'

Harry threw back his head and laughed.

It was rich stentorian laughter – it sounded uncontrolled and brutal in the confined space of the room. Pilar drew in her breath with a gasp. Lydia flinched a little.

Then, at a movement behind him, Harry broke off his laugh and turned sharply. He had not heard anyone coming in, but Alfred was standing there quietly. He was looking at Harry with an odd expression on his face.

Harry stood a minute, then a slow smile crept to his lips. He advanced a step.

'Why,' he said, 'it's Alfred!'

Alfred nodded.

'Hallo, Harry,' he said.

They stood staring at each other. Lydia caught her breath. She thought: 'How absurd! Like two dogs – looking at each other . . .'

Pilar's gaze widened even further. She thought to herself: 'How silly they look standing there . . . Why do they not embrace? No, of course the English do not do that. But they might *say* something. Why do they just *look*?'

Harry said at last: 'Well, well. Feels funny to be here again!'

'I expect so – yes. A good many years since you – got out.'

Harry threw up his head. He drew his finger along the line of his jaw. It was a gesture that was habitual with him. It expressed belligerence.

'Yes,' he said. 'I'm glad I have come' – he paused to bring out the word with greater significance – '*home* . . .'

II

'I've been, I suppose, a very wicked man,' said Simeon Lee.

He was leaning back in his chair. His chin was raised and with one finger he was stroking his jaw reflectively. In front of him a big fire glowed and danced. Beside it sat Pilar, a little screen of papier-mâché held in her hand. With it she shielded her face from the blaze. Occasionally she fanned herself with it, using her wrist in a supple gesture. Simeon looked at her with satisfaction.

He went on talking, perhaps more to himself than to the girl, and stimulated by the fact of her presence.

'Yes,' he said. 'I've been a wicked man. What do you say to that, Pilar?'

Pilar shrugged her shoulders. She said: 'All men are wicked. The nuns say so. That is why one has to pray for them.'

'Ah, but I've been more wicked than most.' Simeon laughed. 'I don't regret it, you know. No, I don't regret anything. I've enjoyed myself . . . every minute! They say you repent when you get old. That's bunkum. I don't repent. And, as I tell you, I've done most things . . . all the good old sins! I've cheated and stolen and lied . . . Lord, yes! And women – always women! Someone told me the other day of an Arab chief who had a bodyguard of forty of his sons – all roughly the same age! Aha! Forty! I don't know about forty, but I bet I could produce a very fair bodyguard if I went about looking for the brats! Hey, Pilar, what do you think of that? Shocked?'

Pilar stared.

'No, why should I be shocked? Men always desire women. My father, too. That is why wives are so often unhappy and why they go to church and pray.'

Old Simeon was frowning.

'I made Adelaide unhappy,' he said. He spoke almost under his breath, to himself. 'Lord, what a woman! Pink and white and pretty as they make 'em when I married her! And afterwards? Always wailing and weeping. It rouses the devil in a man when his wife is always crying . . . She'd no guts, that's what was the matter with Adelaide. If she'd stood up to me! But she never did – not once. I believed when I married her that I was going to be able to settle down, raise a family – cut loose from the old life . . .'

His voice died away. He stared – stared into the glowing heart of the fire.

'Raise a family . . . God, what a family!' He gave a sudden shrill pipe of angry laughter. 'Look at 'em – look at 'em! Not a child among them – to carry on! What's the matter with them? Haven't they got any of my blood in their veins? Not a son among 'em, legitimate or illegitimate. Alfred, for instance – heavens above, how bored I get with Alfred! Looking at me with his dog's eyes. Ready to do anything I ask. Lord, what a fool! His wife, now – Lydia – I like Lydia. She's got spirit. She doesn't like me, though. No, she doesn't like me. But she has to put up with me for that nincompoop Alfred's sake.' He looked over at the girl by the fire. 'Pilar – remember – nothing is so boring as devotion.'

She smiled at him. He went on, warmed by the presence of her youth and strong femininity.

'George? What's George? A stick! A stuffed codfish! A pompous windbag with no brains and no guts – and mean about money as well! David? David always was a fool – a fool and a dreamer. His mother's boy, that was always David. Only sensible thing he ever did was to marry that solid comfortable-looking woman.' He brought down his hand with a bang on the edge of his chair. 'Harry's the best of 'em! Poor old Harry, the wrong 'un! But at any rate he's *alive*.'

Pilar agreed.

'Yes, he is nice. He laughs – laughs out loud – and throws his head back. Oh, yes, I like him very much.'

The old man looked at her.

'You do, do you, Pilar? Harry always had a way with the girls. Takes after me there.' He began to laugh, a slow wheezy chuckle. 'I've had a good life – a very good life. Plenty of everything.'

Pilar said: 'In Spain we have a proverb. It is like this: "*Take what you like and pay for it, says God*."'

Simeon beat an appreciative hand on the arm of his chair.

'That's good. That's the stuff. Take what you like . . . I've done that – all my life – taken what I wanted . . .'

Pilar said, her voice high and clear, and suddenly arresting: 'And you have paid for it?'

Simeon stopped laughing to himself. He sat up and stared at her. He said: 'What's that you say?'

'I said, have you paid for it, Grandfather?'

Simeon Lee said slowly: 'I – don't know . . .'

Then, beating his fist on the arm of the chair, he cried out with sudden anger: 'What makes you say that, girl? What makes you say that?'

Pilar said: 'I – wondered.'

Her hand, holding the screen, was arrested. Her eyes were dark and mysterious. She sat, her head thrown back, conscious of herself, of her womanhood.

Simeon said: 'You devil's brat . . .'

She said softly: 'But you like me, Grandfather. You like me to sit here with you.'

Simeon said: 'Yes, I like it. It's a long time since I've seen anything so young and beautiful . . . It does me good, warms my old bones . . . And you're my own flesh and blood . . . Good for Jennifer, she turned out to be the best of the bunch after all!'

Pilar sat there smiling.

'Mind you, you don't fool me,' said Simeon. 'I know why you sit here so patiently and listen to me droning on. It's money – it's all money . . . Or do you pretend you love your old grandfather?'

Pilar said: 'No, I do not love you. But I like you. I like you very much. You must believe that, for it is true. I think you have been wicked, but I like that, too. You are more real than the other people in this house. And you have interesting things to say. You have travelled and you have led a life of adventure. If I were a man I would like be that, too.'

Simeon nodded.

'Yes, I believe you would . . . We've gipsy blood in us, so it's always been said. It hasn't shown much in my children – except Harry – but I think it's come out in you. I can be patient, mind you, when it's necessary. I waited once fifteen years to get even with a man who'd done me an injury. That's another characteristic of the Lees – they don't forget! They'll avenge a wrong if they have to wait years to do it. A man swindled me. I waited fifteen years till I saw my chance – then I struck. I ruined him. Cleaned him right out!'

He laughed softly.

Pilar said: 'That was in South Africa?'

'Yes. A grand country.'

'You have been back there, yes?'

'I went back last five years after I married. That was the last time.'

'But before that? You were there for many years?'

'Yes.'

'Tell me about it.'

He began to talk. Pilar, shielding her face, listened.

His voice slowed, wearied. He said: 'Wait, I'll show you something.'

He pulled himself carefully to his feet. Then, with his stick, he limped slowly across the room. He opened the big safe. Turning, he beckoned her to him.

'There, look at these. Feel them, let them run through your fingers.'

He looked into her wondering face and laughed.

'Do you know what they are? Diamonds, child, diamonds.'

Pilar's eyes opened. She said as she bent over: 'But they are little pebbles, that is all.'

Simeon laughed.

'They are uncut diamonds. That is how they are found – like this.'

Pilar asked incredulously: 'And if they were cut they would be real diamonds?'

'Certainly.'

'They would flash and sparkle?'

'Flash and sparkle.'

Pilar said childishly: 'O-o-o, I cannot believe it!'

He was amused.

'It's quite true.'

'They are valuable?'

'Fairly valuable. Difficult to say before they are cut. Anyway, this little lot is worth several thousands of pounds.'

Pilar said with a space between each word: 'Several – thousands – of – pounds?'

'Say nine or ten thousands – they're biggish stones, you see.'

Pilar asked, her eyes opening: 'But why do you not sell them, then?'

'Because I like to have them here.'

'But all that money?'

'I don't need the money.'

'Oh – I see.' Pilar looked impressed.

She said: 'But why do you not have them cut and made beautiful?'

'Because I prefer them like this.' His face was set in a grim line. He turned away and began speaking to himself. 'They take me back – the touch of them, the feel of them through my fingers . . . It all comes back to me, the sunshine, and the smell of the veldt, the oxen – old Eb – all the boys – the evenings . . .'

There was a soft tap on the door.

Simeon said: 'Put 'em back in the safe and bang it to.'

Then he called: 'Come in.'

Horbury came in, soft and deferential.

He said: 'Tea is ready downstairs.'

III

Hilda said: 'So there you are, David. I've been looking for you everywhere. Don't let's stay in this room, it's so frightfully cold.'

David did not answer for a minute. He was standing looking at a chair, a low chair with faded satin upholstery. He said abruptly: 'That's her chair . . . the chair she always sat in . . . just the same – it's just the same. Only faded, of course.'

A little frown creased Hilda's forehead. She said: 'I see. Do let's come out of here, David. It's frightfully cold.'

David took no notice. Looking round, he said: 'She sat in here mostly. I remember sitting on that stool there while she read to me. *Jack the Giant Killer* – that was it – *Jack the Giant Killer*. I must have been six years old then.'

Hilda put a firm hand through his arm.

'Come back to the drawing-room, dear. There's no heating in this room.'

He turned obediently, but she felt a little shiver go through him.

'Just the same,' he murmured. 'Just the same. As though time had stood still.'

Hilda looked worried. She said in a cheerful determined voice: 'I wonder where the others are. It must be nearly tea-time.'

David disengaged his arm and opened another door.

'There used to be a piano in here . . . Oh, yes, here it is! I wonder if it's in tune.'

He sat down and opened the lid, running his hands lightly over the keys.

'Yes, it's evidently kept tuned.'

He began to play. His touch was good, the melody flowed out from under this fingers.

Hilda asked: 'What is that? I seem to know it, and I can't quite remember.'

He said: 'I haven't played it for years. *She* used to play it. One of Mendelssohn's "Songs Without Words".'

The sweet, over-sweet melody filled the room. Hilda said: 'Play some Mozart, do.'

David shook his head. He began another Mendelssohn.

Then suddenly he brought his hands down upon the keys in a harsh discord. He got up. He was trembling all over. Hilda went to him.

She said: 'David – David.'

He said: 'It's nothing – it's nothing . . .'

IV

The bell pealed aggressively. Tressilian rose from his seat in the pantry and went slowly out along to the door.

The bell pealed again. Tressilian frowned. Through the frosted glass of the door he saw the silhouette of a man wearing a slouch hat.

Tressilian passed a hand over his forehead. Something worried him. It was as though everything was happening twice.

Surely this had happened before. Surely—

He drew back the latch and opened the door.

Then the spell broke. The man standing there said: 'Is this where Mr Simeon Lee lives?'

'Yes, sir.'

'I'd like to see him, please.'

A faint echo of memory awoke in Tressilian. It was an intonation of voice that he remembered from the old days when Mr Lee was first in England.

Tressilian shook his head dubiously.

'Mr Lee is an invalid, sir. He doesn't see many people now. If you—'

The stranger interrupted.

He drew out an envelope and handed it to the butler.

'Please give this to Mr Lee.'

'Yes, sir.'

v

Simeon Lee took the envelope. He drew out the single sheet of paper it held. He looked surprised. His eyebrows rose, but he smiled.

'By all that's wonderful!' he said.

Then to the butler: 'Show Mr Farr up here, Tressilian.'

'Yes, sir.'

Simeon said: 'I was just thinking of old Ebenezer Farr. He was my partner out there in Kimberley. Now here's his son come along!'

Tressilian reappeared. He announced: 'Mr Farr.'

Stephen Farr came in with a trace of nervousness. He disguised it by putting on a little extra swagger. He said – and just for the moment his South African accent was more marked than usual: 'Mr Lee?'

'I'm glad to see you. So you're Eb's boy?'

Stephen Farr grinned rather sheepishly.

He said: 'My first visit to the old country. Father always told me to look you up if I did come.'

'Quite right.' The old man looked round. 'This is my granddaughter, Pilar Estravados.'

'How do you do?' said Pilar demurely.

Stephen Farr thought with a touch of admiration: 'Cool little devil. She was surprised to see me, but it only showed for a flash.'

He said, rather heavily: 'I'm very pleased to make your acquaintance, Miss Estravados.'

'Thank you,' said Pilar.

Simeon Lee said: 'Sit down and tell me all about yourself. Are you in England for long?'

'Oh, I shan't hurry myself now I've really got here!'

He laughed, throwing his head back.

Simeon Lee said: 'Quite right. You must stay here with us for a while.'

'Oh, look here, sir. I can't butt in like that. It's only two days to Christmas.'

'You must spend Christmas with us – unless you've got other plans?'

'Well, no, I haven't, but I don't like—'

Simeon said: 'That's settled.' He turned his head.

'Pilar?'

'Yes, Grandfather.'

'Go and tell Lydia we shall have another guest. Ask her to come up here.'

Pilar left the room. Stephen's eyes followed her. Simeon noted the fact with amusement.

He said: 'You've come straight here from South Africa?'

'Pretty well.'

They began to talk of that country.

Lydia entered a few minutes later.

Simeon said: 'This is Stephen Farr, son of my old friend and partner, Ebenezer Farr. He's going to be with us for Christmas if you can find room for him.'

Lydia smiled.

'Of course.' Her eyes took in the stranger's appearance. His bronzed face and blue eyes and the easy backward tilt of his head.

'My daughter-in-law,' said Simeon.

Stephen said: 'I feel rather embarrassed – butting in on a family party like this.'

'You're one of the family, my boy,' said Simeon. 'Think of yourself as that.'

'You're too kind, sir.'

Pilar re-entered the room. She sat down quietly by the fire and picked up the hand screen. She used it as a fan, slowly tilting her wrist to and fro. Her eyes were demure and downcast.

— 3 —

DECEMBER 24TH

'Do you really want me to stay on here, Father?' asked Harry. He tilted his head back. 'I'm stirring up rather a hornets' nest, you know.'

'What do you mean?' asked Simeon sharply.

'Brother Alfred,' said Harry. 'Good brother Alfred! He, if I may say so, resents my presence here.'

'The devil he does!' snapped Simeon. 'I'm master in this house.'

'All the same, sir, I expect you're pretty dependent on Alfred. I don't want to upset—'

'You'll do as I tell you,' snapped his father.

Harry yawned.

'Don't know that I shall be able to stick a stay-at-home life. Pretty stifling to a fellow who's knocked about the world.'

His father said: 'You'd better marry and settle down.'

Harry said: 'Who shall I marry? Pity one can't marry one's niece. Young Pilar is devilish attractive.'

'You've noticed that?'

'Talking of settling down, fat George has done well for himself as far as looks go. Who was she?'

Simeon shrugged his shoulders.

'How should I know? George picked her up at a mannequin parade, I believe. She says her father was a retired naval officer.'

Harry said: 'Probably a second mate on a coasting steamer. George will have a bit of trouble with her if he's not careful.'

'George,' said Simeon Lee, 'is a fool.'

Harry said: 'What did she marry him for – his money?'

Simeon shrugged his shoulders.

Harry said: 'Well, you think that you can square Alfred all right?'

'We'll soon settle that,' said Simeon grimly.

He touched a bell that stood on a table near him.

Horbury appeared promptly. Simeon said: 'Ask Mr Alfred to come here.'

Horbury went out and Harry drawled: 'That fellow listens at doors!'

Simeon shrugged his shoulders.

'Probably.'

Alfred hurried in. His face twitched when he saw his brother. Ignoring Harry, he said pointedly: 'You wanted me, Father?'

'Yes, sit down. I was just thinking we must reorganize things a bit now that we have two more people living in the house.'

'*Two?*'

'Pilar will make her home here, naturally. And Harry is home for good.'

Alfred said: 'Harry is coming to live here?'

'Why not, old boy?' said Harry.

Alfred turned sharply to him.

'I should think that you yourself would see that!'

'Well, sorry – but I don't.'

'After everything that has happened? The disgraceful way you behaved. The scandal—'

Harry waved an easy hand.

'All that's in the past, old boy.'

'You behaved abominably to Father, after all he'd done for you.'

'Look here, Alfred, it strikes me that's Father's business, not yours. If he's willing to forgive and forget—'

'I'm willing,' said Simeon. 'Harry's my son, after all, you know, Alfred.'

'Yes, but – I resent it – for Father's sake.'

Simeon said: 'Harry's coming here! I wish it.' He laid a hand gently on the latter's shoulder. 'I'm very fond of Harry.'

Alfred got up and left the room. His face was white. Harry rose, too, and went after him, laughing.

Simeon sat chuckling to himself. Then he started and looked round. 'Who the devil's that? Oh, it's you, Horbury. Don't creep about that way.'

'I beg your pardon, sir.'

'Never mind. Listen, I've got some orders for you. I want everybody to come up here after lunch – *everybody*.'

'Yes, sir.'

'There's something else. When they come, you come with them. And when you get half-way along the passage *raise your voice so that I can hear*. Any pretext will do. Understand?'

'Yes, sir.'

Horbury went downstairs. He said to Tressilian: 'If you ask me, we *are* going to have a Merry Christmas.'

Tressilian said sharply: 'What d'you mean?'

'You wait and see, Mr Tressilian. It's Christmas Eve today, and a nice Christmas spirit abroad – I don't think!'

They came into the room and paused at the doorway. Simeon was speaking into the telephone. He waved a hand to them.

'Sit down, all of you. I shan't be a minute.'

He went on speaking into the telephone.

'Is that Charlton, Hodgkins & Bruce? Is that you, Charlton? Simeon Lee speaking. Yes, isn't it? . . . Yes . . . No, I wanted you to make a new will for me . . . Yes, it's some time since I made the other . . . Circumstances have altered . . . Oh, no, no hurry. Don't want you to spoil your Christmas. Say Boxing Day or the day after. Come along, and I'll tell you what I want done. No, that's quite all right. I shan't be dying just yet.'

He replaced the receiver, then looked round at the eight members of his family. He cackled and said: 'You're all looking very glum. What is the matter?'

Alfred said: 'You sent for us . . .'

Simeon said quickly: Oh, sorry – nothing portentous about it. Did you think it was a family council? No, I'm just rather tired today, that's all. None of you need come up after dinner. I shall go to bed. I want to be fresh for Christmas Day.'

He grinned at them. George said earnestly: 'Of course . . . of course . . .'

Simeon said: 'Grand old institution, Christmas. Promotes solidarity of family feeling. What do *you* think, Magdalene, my dear?'

Magdalene Lee jumped. Her rather silly little mouth flew open and then shut itself. She said: 'Oh – oh, *yes!*'

Simeon said: 'Let me see, you lived with a retired naval officer' – he paused – 'your *father*. Don't suppose you made much of Christmas. It needs a big family for that!'

'Well – well – yes, perhaps it does.'

Simeon's eyes slid past her.

'Don't want to talk of anything unpleasant at this time of year, but, you know, George, I'm afraid I'll have to cut down your allowance a bit. My establishment here is going to cost me a bit more to run in future.'

George got very red.

'But look here, Father, you can't do that!'

Simeon said softly: 'Oh, can't I!'

'My expenses are very heavy already. Very heavy. As it is, I don't know how I make both ends meet. It needs the most rigorous economy.'

'Let your wife do a bit more of it,' said Simeon. 'Women are good at that sort of thing. They often think of economies where a man would never have dreamt of them. And a clever woman can make her own clothes. My wife, I remember, was clever with her needle. About all she *was* clever with – a good woman, but deadly dull—'

David sprang up. His father said: 'Sit down, boy, you'll knock something over—'

David said: 'My mother—'

Simeon said: 'Your mother had the brains of a louse! And it seems to me she's transmitted those brains to her children.' He raised himself up suddenly. A red spot appeared in each cheek. His voice came high and shrill. 'You're not worth a penny piece, any of you! I'm sick of you all! You're not *men*! You're weaklings – a set of namby-pamby weaklings. Pilar's worth any two of you put together! I'll swear to heaven I've got a better son somewhere in the world than any of you, even if you are born the right side of the blanket!'

'Here, Father, hold hard,' cried Harry.

He had jumped up and stood there, a frown on his usually good-humoured face. Simeon snapped: 'The same goes for *you*! What have *you* ever done? Whined to me for money from all over the world! I tell you I'm sick of the sight of you all! Get out!'

He leaned back in his chair, panting a little.

Slowly, one by one, his family went out. George was red and indignant. Magdalene looked frightened. David was pale and quivering. Harry blustered out of the room. Alfred went like a man in a dream. Lydia followed him with her head held high. Only Hilda paused in the doorway and came slowly back.

She stood over him, and he started when he opened his eyes and found her standing there. There was something menacing in the solid way she stood there quite immovably.

He said irritably: 'What is it?'

Hilda said: 'When your letter came I believed what you said – that you wanted your family round you for Christmas. I persuaded David to come.'

Simeon said: 'Well, what of it?'

Hilda said slowly: 'You *did* want your family round you – but not for the purpose you said! You wanted them here, didn't you, in order to set them all by the ears? God help you, it's your idea of *fun*!'

Simeon chuckled. He said: 'I always had rather a specialised sense of humour. I don't expect anyone else to appreciate the joke. *I'm* enjoying it!'

She said nothing. A vague feeling of apprehension came over Simeon Lee. He said sharply: 'What are you thinking about?'

Hilda Lee said slowly: 'I'm afraid . . .'

Simeon said: 'You're afraid – of me?'

Hilda said: 'Not *of* you. I'm afraid – *for* you!'

Like a judge who has delivered sentence, she turned away. She marched, slowly and heavily, out of the room . . .

Simeon sat staring at the door.

Then he got to his feet and made his way over to the safe. He murmured: 'Let's have a look at my beauties.'

III

The doorbell rang about a quarter to eight. Tressilian went to answer it. He returned to his pantry to find Horbury there, picking up the coffee-cups off the tray and looking at the mark on them.

'Who was it?' said Horbury.

'Superintendent of police – Mr Sugden – mind what you're doing!'

Horbury had dropped one of the cups with a crash.

'Look at that now,' lamented Tressilian. 'Eleven years I've had the washing up of those and never one broken, and now you come along touching things you've no business to touch, and look what happens!'

'I'm sorry, Mr Tressilian. I am indeed,' the other apologized. His face was covered with perspiration. 'I don't know how it happened. Did you say a superintendent of police had called?'

'Yes – Mr Sugden.'

The valet passed a tongue over pale lips.

'What – what did he want?'

'Collecting for the police orphanage.'

'Oh!' The valet straightened his shoulders. In a more natural voice he said: 'Did he get anything?'

'I took up the book to old Mr Lee, and he told me to fetch the superintendent up and to put the sherry on the table.'

'Nothing but begging, this time of year,' said Horbury. 'The old devil's generous, I will say that for him, in spite of his other failings.'

Tressilian said with dignity: 'Mr Lee has always been an open-handed gentleman.'

Horbury nodded.

'It's the best thing about him! Well, I'll be off now.'

'Going to the pictures?'

'I expect so. Ta-ta, Mr Tressilian.'

He went through the door that led to the servants' hall.

Tressilian looked up at the clock hanging on the wall.

He went into the dining-room and laid the rolls in the napkins.

Then, after assuring himself that everything was as it should be, he sounded the gong in the hall.

As the last note died away the police superintendent came down the stairs. Superintendent Sugden was a large handsome man. He wore a tightly buttoned blue suit and moved with a sense of his own importance.

He said affably: 'I rather think we shall have a frost tonight. Good thing: the weather's been very unseasonable lately.

Tressilian said, shaking his head: 'The damp affects my rheumatism.'

The superintendent said that rheumatism was a painful complaint, and Tressilian let him out by the front door.

The old butler refastened the door and came back slowly into the hall. He passed his hand over his eyes and sighed. Then he straightened his back as he saw Lydia pass into the drawing-room. George Lee was just coming down the stairs.

Tressilian hovered ready. When the last guest, Magdalene, had entered the drawing-room, he made his own appearance, murmuring: 'Dinner is served.'

In his way Tressilian was a connoisseur of ladies' dress. He always noted and criticised the gowns of the ladies as he circled round the table, decanter in hand.

Mrs Alfred, he noted, had got on her new flowered black and white taffeta. A bold design, very striking, but she could carry it off, though many ladies couldn't. The dress Mrs George had on was a model, he was pretty sure of that. Must have cost a pretty penny. He wondered how Mr George would like paying for it! Mr George didn't like spending money – he never had. Mrs David now: a nice lady, but didn't have any idea of how to dress. For her figure, plain black velvet would have been the best. Figured velvet, and crimson at that, was a bad choice. Miss Pilar, now, it didn't matter what she wore, with her figure and her hair she looked well in anything. A flimsy cheap little white gown it was, though. Still, Mr Lee would soon see to that! Taken to her wonderful, he had. Always was the same way when a gentleman was elderly. A young face could do anything with him!

'Hock or claret?' murmured Tressilian in a deferential whisper in Mrs George's ear. Out of the tail of his eye he noted that Walter, the footman, was handing the vegetables before the gravy again – after all he had been told!

Tressilian went round with the soufflé. It struck him, now that his interest in the ladies' toilettes and his misgivings over Walter's deficiencies were a thing of the past, that everyone was very silent tonight. At least, not exactly *silent*: Mr Harry was talking enough for twenty – no, not Mr Harry, the South African gentleman. And the others were talking, too, but only, as it were, in spasms. There was something a little – queer about them.

Mr Alfred, for instance, he looked downright ill. As though he had had a shock or something. Quite dazed he looked and just turning over the food on his plate without eating it. The mistress, she was worried about him. Tressilian could see that. Kept looking down the table towards him – not noticeably, of course, just quietly. Mr George was very red in the face – gobbling his food, he was, without tasting it. He'd get a stroke one day if he wasn't careful. Mrs George wasn't eating. Slimming, as likely as not. Miss Pilar seemed to be enjoying her food all right and talking and laughing up at the South African gentleman. Properly taken with her, he was. Didn't seem to be anything on *their* minds!

Mr David? Tressilian felt worried about Mr David. Just like his mother, he was, to look at. And remarkably young-looking still. But nervy; there, he'd knocked over his glass.

Tressilian whisked it away, mopped up the stream deftly. It was all over. Mr David hardly seemed to notice what he had done, just sat staring in front of him with a white face.

Thinking of white faces, funny the way Horbury had looked in the pantry just now when he'd heard a police officer had come to the house . . . almost as though—

Tressilian's mind stopped with a jerk. Walter had dropped a pear off the dish he was handing. Footmen were no good nowadays! They might be stable-boys, the way they went on!

He went round with the port. Mr Harry seemed a bit distrait tonight. Kept looking at Mr Alfred. Never had been any love lost between those two, not even as boys. Mr Harry, of course, had always been his father's favourite, and that had rankled with Mr Alfred. Mr Lee had never cared for Mr Alfred much. A pity, when Mr Alfred always seemed so devoted to his father.

There, Mrs Alfred was getting up now. She swept round the table. Very nice that design on the taffeta; that cape suited her. A very graceful lady.

He went out to the pantry, closing the dining-room door on the gentlemen with their port.

He took the coffee-tray into the drawing-room. The four ladies were sitting there rather uncomfortably, he thought. They were not talking. He handed round the coffee in silence.

He went out again. As he went into his pantry he heard the dining-room door open. David Lee came out and went along the hall to the drawing-room.

Tressilian went back into his pantry. He read the Riot Act to Walter. Walter was nearly, if not quite, impertinent!

Tressilian, alone in his pantry, sat down rather wearily.

He had a feeling of depression. Christmas Eve, and all this strain and tension . . . He didn't like it!

With an effort he roused himself. He went to the drawing-room and collected the coffee-cups. The room was empty except for Lydia, who was standing half-concealed by the window curtain at the far end of the room. She was standing there looking out into the night.

From next door the piano sounded.

Mr David was playing. But why, Tressilian asked himself, did Mr David play the 'Dead March'? For that's what it was. Oh, indeed things were very wrong.

He went slowly along the hall and back into his pantry.

It was then he first heard the noise from overhead: a crashing of china, the overthrowing of furniture, a series of cracks and bumps.

'Good gracious!' thought Tressilian. 'Whatever is the master doing? What's happening up there?'

And then, clear and high, came a scream – a horrible high wailing scream that died away in a choke or gurgle.

Tressilian stood there a moment paralysed, then he ran out into the hall and up the broad staircase. Others were with him. That scream had been heard all over the house.

They raced up the stairs and round the bend, past a recess with statues gleaming white and eerie, and along the straight passage to Simeon Lee's door. Mr Farr was there already and Mrs David. She was leaning back against the wall and he was twisting at the door handle.

'The door's locked,' he was saying. 'The door's locked!'

Harry Lee pushed past and wrested it from him. He, too, turned and twisted at the handle.

'Father,' he shouted. 'Father, let us in.'

He held up his hand and in the silence they all listened. There was no answer. No sound from inside the room.

The front-door bell rang, but no one paid any attention to it.

Stephen Farr said: 'We've got to break the door down. It's the only way.'

Harry said: 'That's going to be a tough job. These doors are good solid stuff. Come on, Alfred.'

They heaved and strained. Finally they went and got an oak bench and used it as a battering-ram. The door gave at last. Its hinges splintered and the door sank shuddering from its frame.

For a minute they stood there huddled together, looking in. What they saw was a sight that no one of them ever forgot. . . .

There had clearly been a terrific struggle. Heavy furniture was overturned. China vases lay splintered on the floor. In the middle of the hearthrug in front of the blazing fire lay Simeon Lee in a great pool of blood . . . Blood was splashed all round. The place was like a shambles.

There was a long shuddering sigh, and then two voices spoke in turn. Strangely enough, the words they uttered were both quotations.

David Lee said: *'The mills of God grind slowly . . .'*

Lydia's voice came like a fluttering whisper: *'Who would have thought the old man to have had so much blood in him?'*

IV

Superintendent Sugden had rung the bell three times. Finally, in desperation, he pounded on the knocker.

A scared Walter at length opened the door.

'Oo-er,' he said. A look of relief came over his face. 'I was just ringing up the police.'

'What for?' said Superintendent Sugden sharply. 'What's going on here?'

Walter whispered: 'It's old Mr Lee. *He's been done in . . .*'

The superintendent pushed past him and ran up the stairs. He came into the room without anyone being aware of his entrance. As he entered he saw Pilar bend forward and pick up something from the floor. He saw David Lee standing with his hands over his eyes.

He saw the others huddled into a little group. Alfred Lee alone had stepped near his father's body. He stood now quite close, looking down. His face was blank.

George Lee was saying importantly: 'Nothing must be touched

– remember that – *nothing* – till the police arrive. That is *most* important!'

'Excuse me,' said Sugden.

He pushed his way forward, gently thrusting the ladies aside. Alfred Lee recognized him.

'Ah,' he said. 'It's you, Superintendent Sugden. You've got here very quickly.'

'Yes, Mr Lee.' Superintendent Sugden did not waste time on explanations. 'What's all this?'

'My father,' said Alfred Lee, 'has been killed – *murdered* . . .' His voice broke.

Magdalene began suddenly to sob hysterically.

Superintendent Sugden held up a large official hand. He said authoritatively: 'Will everybody kindly leave the room except Mr Lee and – er – Mr George Lee?

They moved slowly towards the door, reluctantly, like sheep. Superintendent Sugden intercepted Pilar suddenly.

'Excuse me, miss,' he said pleasantly. 'Nothing must be touched or disturbed.'

She stared at him. Stephen Farr said impatiently: 'Of course not. She understands that.'

Superintendent Sugden said, still in the same pleasant manner: 'You picked up something from the floor just now.'

Pilar's eyes opened. She stared and said incredulously: '*I* did?'

Superintendent Sugden was still pleasant. His voice was just a little firmer.

'Yes, I saw you . . .'

'Oh!'

'So please give it to me. It's in your hand now.'

Slowly Pilar unclosed her hand. There lay in it a wisp of rubber and a small object made of wood. Superintendent Sugden took them, enclosed them in an envelope and put them away in his breast pocket. He said: 'Thank you.'

He turned away. Just for a minute Stephen Farr's eyes showed a startled respect. It was as though he had under-estimated the large handsome superintendent.

They went slowly out of the room. Behind them they heard the superintendent's voice saying officially: And now, if you please . . .'

V

'Nothing like a wood fire,' said Colonel Johnson as he threw on an additional log and then drew his chair nearer to the blaze. 'Help yourself,' he added, hospitably calling attention to the tantalus and siphon that stood near his guest's elbow.

The guest raised a polite hand in negation. Cautiously he edged his own chair nearer to the blazing logs, though he was of the opinion that the opportunity for roasting the soles of one's feet (like some mediæval torture) did not offset the cold draught that swirled round the back of the shoulders.

Colonel Johnson, chief constable of Middleshire, might be of the opinion that nothing could beat a wood fire, but Hercule Poirot was of opinion that central heating could and did every time!

'Amazing business, that Cartwright case,' remarked the host reminiscently. 'Amazing man! Enormous charm of manner. Why, when he came here with you, he had us all eating out of his hand.'

He shook his head.

'We'll never have anything like that case!' he said. 'Nicotine poisoning is rare, fortunately.'

'There was a time when you would have considered all poisoning un-English,' suggested Hercule Poirot. 'A device of foreigners! Unsportsmanlike!'

'I hardly think we could say that,' said the chief constable. 'Plenty of poisoning by arsenic – probably a good deal more than has ever been suspected.'

'Always an awkward business, a poisoning case,' said Johnson. 'Conflicting testimony of the experts – then doctors are usually so extremely cautious in what they say. Always a difficult case to take to a jury. No, if one *must* have murder (which heaven forbid!) give me a straightforward case. Something where there's no ambiguity about the cause of death.'

Poirot nodded.

'The bullet wound, the cut throat, the crushed-in skull? It is there your preference lies?'

'Oh, don't call it preference, my dear fellow. Don't harbour the idea that I *like* murder cases! Hope I never have another. Anyway, we ought to be safe enough during your visit.'

Poirot began modestly: 'My reputation—'

But Johnson had gone on.

'Christmas-time,' he said. 'Peace, goodwill—and all that kind of thing. Goodwill all round.'

Hercule Poirot leaned back in his chair. He joined his fingertips. He studied his host thoughtfully.

He murmured: 'It is, then, your opinion that Christmas-time is an unlikely season for crime?'

'That's what I said.'

'Why?'

'Why?' Johnson was thrown slightly out of his stride. 'Well, as I've just said – season of good cheer, and all that!'

Hercule Poirot murmured: 'The British, they are so sentimental!'

Johnson said stoutly: 'What if we are? What if we do like the old ways, the old traditional festivities? What's the harm?'

'There is no harm. It is all most charming! But let us for a moment examine *facts*. You have said that Christmas is a season of good cheer. That means, does it not, a lot of eating and drinking? It means, in fact, the *over-eating*! And with the over-eating there comes the indigestion! And with the indigestion there comes the irritability!'

'Crimes,' said Colonel Johnson, 'are not committed from irritability.'

'I am not so sure! Take another point. There is, at Christmas, a spirit of goodwill. It is, as you say, "the thing to do". Old quarrels are patched up, those who have disagreed consent to agree once more, even if it is only temporarily.'

Johnson nodded.

'Bury the hatchet, that's right.'

Poirot pursued his theme: 'And families now, families who have been separated throughout the year, assemble once more together. Now under these conditions, my friend, you must admit that there will occur a great amount of *strain*. People who do not *feel* amiable are putting great pressure on themselves to *appear* amiable! There is at Christmas-time a great deal of *hypocrisy*, honourable hypocrisy, hypocrisy undertaken *pour le bon motif, c'est entendu,* but nevertheless hypocrisy!'

'Well, I shouldn't put it quite like that myself,' said Colonel Johnson doubtfully.

Poirot beamed upon him.

'No, no. It is *I* who am putting it like that, not *you*. I am pointing out to you that under these conditions – mental strain, physical *malaise* – it is highly probable that dislikes that were before merely mild and disagreements that were trivial might suddenly assume a more serious character. The result of pretending to be a more amiable, a more forgiving, a more high-minded person than one really is has sooner or later the effect of causing one to behave as a more disagreeable, a more ruthless and an altogether more unpleasant person than is actually the case! If you dam the stream of natural behaviour, *mon ami*, sooner or later the dam bursts and a cataclysm occurs!'

Colonel Johnson looked at him doubtfully.

'Never know when you're serious and when you're pulling my leg,' he grumbled.

Poirot smiled at him.

'I am not serious! Not in the least am I serious! But, all the same, it is true what I say – artificial conditions bring about their natural reaction.'

Colonel Johnson's manservant entered the room.

'Superintendent Sugden on the phone, sir.'

'Right. I'll come.'

With a word of apology the chief constable left the room.

He returned some three minutes later. His face was grave and perturbed.

'Damn it all!' he said. 'Case of murder! On Christmas Eve, too!'

Poirot's eyebrows rose.

'It is that definitely – murder, I mean?'

'Eh? Oh, no other solution possible! Perfectly clear case. Murder – and a brutal murder at that!'

'Who is the victim?'

'Old Simeon Lee. One of the richest men we've got! Made his money in South Africa originally. Gold – no, diamonds, I believe. He sunk an immense fortune in manufacturing some particular gadget of mining machinery. His own invention, I believe. Anyway, it's paid him hand over fist! They say he's a millionaire twice over.'

Poirot said: 'He was well liked, yes?'

Johnson said slowly: 'Don't think anyone liked him. Queer sort of chap. He's been an invalid for some years now. I don't know very much about him myself. But of course he is one of the big figures of the county.'

'So this case, it will make a big stir?'

'Yes, I must get over to Longdale as fast as I can.'

He hesitated, looking at his guest. Poirot answered the unspoken question: 'You would like that I should accompany you?'

Johnson said awkwardly: 'Seems a shame to ask you. But, well, you know how it is! Superintendent Sugden is a good man, none better, painstaking, careful, thoroughly sound – but – well, he's not an *imaginative* chap in any way. Should like very much, as you are here, benefit of your advice.'

He halted a little over the end part of his speech, making it somewhat telegraphic in style. Poirot responded quickly.

'I shall be delighted. You can count on me to assist you in any way I can. We must not hurt the feelings of the good superintendent. It will be his case – not mine. I am only the unofficial consultant.'

Colonel Johnson said warmly: 'You're a good fellow, Poirot.'

With those words of commendation, the two men started out.

VI

It was a constable who opened the front door to them and saluted. Behind him, Superintendent Sugden advanced down the hall and said: 'Glad you've got here, sir. Shall we come into this room here on the left – Mr Lee's study? I'd like to run over the main outlines. The whole thing's a rum business.'

He ushered them into a small room on the left of the hall. There was a telephone there and a big desk covered with papers. The walls were lined with bookcases.

The chief constable said: 'Sugden, this is M. Hercule Poirot. You may have heard of him. Just happened to be staying with me. Superintendent Sugden.'

Poirot made a little bow and looked the other man over. He saw a tall man with square shoulders and a military bearing who had an aquiline nose, a pugnacious jaw and a large flourishing chestnut-coloured moustache. Sugden stared hard at Hercule Poirot after acknowledging the introduction. Hercule Poirot stared hard at Superintendent Sugden's moustache. Its luxuriance seemed to fascinate him.

The superintendent said: 'Of course I have heard of you, M. Poirot. You were in this part of the world some years ago, if I remember rightly. Death of Sir Bartholomew Strange. Poisoning case. Nicotine. Not my district, but of course I heard all about it.'

Colonel Johnson said impatiently: 'Now, then, Sugden, let's have the facts. A clear case, you said.'

'Yes, sir, it's murder right enough – not a doubt of that. Mr Lee's throat was cut – jugular vein severed, I understand from the doctor. But there's something very odd about the whole matter.'

'You mean—?'

'I'd like you to hear my story first, sir. These are the circumstances: This afternoon, about five o'clock, I was rung up by Mr Lee at Addlesfield police station. He sounded a bit odd over the phone – asked me to come and see him at eight o'clock this evening – made a special point of the time. Moreover, he instructed me to say to the butler that I was collecting subscriptions for some police charity.'

The chief constable looked up sharply.

'Wanted some plausible pretext to get you into the house?'

'That's right, sir. Well, naturally, Mr Lee is an important person, and I acceded to his request. I got here a little before eight o'clock, and represented myself as seeking subscriptions for the police orphanage. The butler went away and returned to tell me that Mr Lee would see me. Thereupon he showed me up to Mr Lee's room, which is situated on the first floor, immediately over the dining-room.'

Superintendent Sugden paused, drew a breath and then proceeded in a somewhat official manner with his report.

'Mr Lee was seated in a chair by the fireplace. He was wearing a dressing-gown. When the butler had left the room and closed the door, Mr Lee asked me to sit near him. He then said rather hesitatingly that he wanted to give me particulars of a robbery. I asked him what had been taken. He replied that he had reason to believe that diamonds (uncut diamonds, I think he said) to the value of several thousand pounds had been stolen from his safe.'

'Diamonds, eh?' said the chief constable.

'Yes, sir. I asked him various routine questions, but his manner was very uncertain and his replies were somewhat vague in character. At last he said, "You must understand, Superintendent, that I may be mistaken in this matter." I said, "I do not quite understand, sir. Either the diamonds are missing or they are not missing – one or the other." He replied, "The diamonds are certainly missing, but it is just possible, Superintendent, that their disappearance may be simply a rather foolish kind of practical joke." Well, that seemed odd to me, but I said nothing. He went on: "It is difficult for me to explain in detail, but what it amounts to is this: So far as I can see, only two persons can possibly have the stones. One of those persons might have done it as a joke. If the other person took them, then they have definitely been stolen." I said, "What exactly do you want me to do, sir?" He said quickly, "I want you, Superintendent, to return here in about an hour – no, make it a little more than that – say nine-fifteen. At that time I shall be able to tell you definitely whether I have been robbed or

383

not." I was a little mystified, but I agreed and went away.'

Colonel Johnson commented: 'Curious – very curious. What do you say, Poirot?'

Hercule Poirot said: 'May I ask, Superintendent, what conclusions you yourself drew?'

The superintendent stroked his jaw as he replied carefully: 'Well, various ideas occurred to me but, on the whole, I figured it out this way: There was no question of any practical joke. The diamonds had been stolen all right. But the old gentlemen wasn't sure who'd done it. It's my opinion that he was speaking the truth when he said that it might have been one of two people – and of those two people one was a servant and the other was a *member of the family*.'

Poirot nodded appreciatively.

'*Très bien*. Yes, that explains his attitude very well.'

'Hence his desire that I should return later. In the interval he meant to have an interview with the person in question. He would tell them that he had already spoken of the matter to the police but that, if restitution were promptly made, he could hush the matter up.'

Colonel Johnson said: 'And if the suspect didn't respond?'

'In that case, he meant to place the investigation in our hands.'

Colonel Johnson frowned and twisted his moustache. He demurred.

'Why not take that course *before* calling you in?'

'No, no, sir.' The superintendent shook his head. 'Don't you see, if he had done that, it might have been bluff. It wouldn't have been half so convincing. The person might say to himself, "The old man won't call the police in, no matter what he suspects!" But if the old gentleman says to him, "I've *already spoken to the police*, the superintendent has only just left," then the thief asks the butler, say, and the butler confirms that. He says, "Yes, the superintendent was here just before dinner." Then the thief is convinced the old gentleman means business and it's up to him to cough up the stones.'

'H'm, yes, I see that,' said Colonel Johnson. 'Any idea, Sugden, who this "member of the family" might be?'

'No, sir.'

'No indication whatsoever?'

'None.'

Johnson shook his head. Then he said: 'Well, let's get on with it.'

Superintendent Sugden resumed his official manner.

'I returned to the house, sir, at nine-fifteen precisely. Just as I was about to ring the front-door bell, I heard a scream from inside the house, and then a confused sound of shouts and a general commotion. I rang several times and also used the knocker. It was three or four minutes before the door was answered. When the footman at last opened it I could see that something momentous had occurred. He was shaking all over and looked as though he was about to faint. He gasped out that Mr Lee had been murdered. I ran hastily upstairs. I found Mr Lee's room in a state of wild confusion. There had evidently been a severe struggle. Mr Lee himself was lying in front of the fire with his throat cut in a pool of blood.'

The chief constable said sharply: 'He couldn't have done it himself?'

Sugden shook his head.

'Impossible, sir. For one thing, there were the chairs and tables overturned, and the broken crockery and ornaments, and then there was no sign of the razor or knife with which the crime had been committed.'

The chief constable said thoughtfully: 'Yes, that seems conclusive. Anyone in the room?'

'Most of the family were there, sir. Just standing round.'

Colonel Johnson said sharply: 'Any ideas, Sugden?'

The superintendent said slowly: 'It's a bad business, sir. It looks to me as though one of them must have done it. I don't see how anyone from outside could have done it and got away in time.'

'What about the window? Closed or open?'

'There are two windows in the room, sir. One was closed and locked. The other was open a few inches at the bottom – but it was fixed in that position by a burglar screw and, moreover, I've tried it and it's stuck fast – hasn't been opened for years, I should say. Also the wall outside is quite smooth and unbroken – no ivy or creepers. I don't see how anyone could have left that way.'

'How many doors in the room?'

'Just one. The room is at the end of a passage. That door was locked on the inside. When they heard the noise of the struggle and the old man's dying scream, and rushed upstairs, they had to break down the door to get in.'

Johnson said sharply: 'And who was in the room?'

Superintendent Sugden replied gravely: 'Nobody was in the room, sir, except the old man who had been killed not more than a few minutes previously.'

Colonel Johnson stared at Sugden for some minutes before he spluttered: 'Do you mean to tell me, Superintendent, that this is one of those damned cases you get in detective stories where a man is killed in a locked room by some apparently supernatural agency?'

A very faint smile agitated the superintendent's moustache as he replied gravely: 'I do not think it's quite as bad as that, sir.'

Colonel Johnson said: 'Suicide. It must be suicide!'

'Where's the weapon, if so? No, sir, suicide won't do.'

'Then how did the murderer escape? By the window?' Sugden shook his head.

'I'll take my oath he didn't do that.'

'But the door was locked, you say, on the inside?'

The superintendent nodded. He drew a key from his pocket and laid it on the table.

'No fingerprints,' he announced. 'But just look at that key, sir. Take a look at it with that magnifying glass there.'

Poirot bent forward. He and Johnson examined the key together. The chief constable uttered an exclamation.

'By Jove, I get you. Those faint scratches on the end of the barrel. You see 'em, Poirot?'

'But, yes, I see. That means, does it not, that the key was turned from outside the door – turned by means of a special implement that went through the keyhole and gripped the barrel – possibly an ordinary pair of pliers would do it.'

The superintendent nodded.

'It can be done all right.'

Poirot said: 'The idea being, then, that the death would be thought to be suicide, since the door was locked and no one was in the room?'

'That was the idea, M. Poirot, not a doubt of it, I should say.'

Poirot shook his head doubtfully.

'But the disorder in the room! As you say, that by itself wiped out the idea of suicide. Surely the murderer would first of all have set the room to rights.'

Superintendent Sugden said: 'But he hadn't *time*, M. Poirot. That's the whole point. He hadn't time. Let's say he counted on catching the old gentleman unawares. Well, that didn't come off. There was a struggle – a struggle heard plainly in the room underneath; and, what's more, the old gentleman called out for help. Everyone came rushing up. The murderer's only got time to nip out of the room and turn the key from the outside.'

'That is true,' Poirot admitted. 'Your murderer, he may have made the bungle. But why, oh why, did he not at least leave the weapon? For naturally, if there is no weapon, it cannot be suicide! That was an error most grave.'

Superintendent Sugden said stolidly: 'Criminals usually make mistakes. That's our experience.'

Poirot gave a light sigh. He murmured: 'But, all the same, in spite of his mistakes, he has escaped, this criminal.'

'I don't think he has exactly *escaped*.'

'You mean he is in the house still?'

'I don't see where else he can be. It was an inside job.'

'But, *tout de même*,' Poirot pointed out gently, 'he has escaped to this extent: *You do not know who he is*.'

Superintendent Sugden said gently but firmly: 'I rather fancy that we soon shall. We haven't done any questioning of the household yet.'

Colonel Johnson cut in: 'Look here, Sugden, one thing strikes me. Whoever turned that key from the outside must have had some knowledge of the job. That's to say, he probably had had criminal experience. These sort of tools aren't easy to manage.'

'You mean it was a professional job, sir?'

'That's what I mean.'

'It does seem like it,' the other admitted. 'Following that up, it looks as though there were a professional thief among the servants. That would explain the diamonds being taken and the murder would follow on logically from that.'

'Well, anything wrong with that theory?'

'It's what I thought myself to begin with. But it's difficult. There are eight servants in the house; six of them are women and, of those six, five have been here for four years and more. Then there's the butler and the footman. The butler has been here for close on forty years – bit of a record that, I should say. The footman's local, son of the gardener, and brought up here. Don't see very well how he can be a professional. The only other person is Mr Lee's valet-attendant. He's comparatively new, but he was out of the house – still is – went out just before eight o'clock.'

Colonel Johnson said: 'Have you got a list of just who exactly was in the house?'

'Yes, sir. I got it from the butler.' He took out his note-book. 'Shall I read it to you?'

'Please, Sugden.'

'Mr and Mrs Alfred Lee. Mr George Lee, MP, and his wife. Mr Henry Lee. Mr and Mrs David Lee. Miss' – the superintendent paused a little, taking the words carefully – 'Pilar' – he pro-

nounced it like a piece of architecture – 'Estravados. Mr Stephen
Farr. Then for the servants: Edward Tressilian, butler. Walter
Champion, footman. Emily Reeves, cook. Queenie Jones, kitchenmaid. Gladys Spent, head housemaid. Grace Best, second housemaid. Beatrice Moscombe, third housemaid. Joan Kench, between-
maid. Sydney Horbury, valet-attendant.'

'That's the lot. eh?'

'That's the lot, sir.'

'Any idea where everybody was at the time of the murder?'

'Only roughly. As I told you, I haven't questioned anybody yet.
According to Tressilian, the gentlemen were in the dining-room
still. The ladies had gone to the drawing-room. Tressilian had
served coffee. According to his statement, he had just got back to
his pantry when he heard a noise upstairs. It was followed by a
scream. He ran out into the hall and upstairs in the wake of the
others.'

Colonel Johnson said: 'How many of the family live in the
house, and who are just staying here?'

'Mr and Mrs Alfred Lee live here. The others are just visiting.'
Johnson nodded.

'Where are they all?'

'I asked them to stay in the drawing-room until I was ready to
take their statements.'

'I see. Well, we'd better go upstairs and take a look at the
doings.'

The superintendent led the way up the broad stairs and along
the passage.

As he entered the room where the crime had taken place,
Johnson drew a deep breath.

'Pretty horrible,' he commented.

He stood for a minute studying the overturned chairs, the
smashed china, and the blood-bespattered débris.

A thin elderly man stood up from where he had been kneeling
by the body and gave a nod.

'Evening, Johnson,' he said. 'Bit of a shambles, eh?'

'I should say it was. Got anything for us, Doctor?'

The doctor shrugged his shoulders. He grinned.

'I'll let you have the scientific language at the inquest! Nothing
complicated about it. Throat cut like a pig. He bled to death in
less than a minute. No sign of the weapon.'

Poirot went across the room to the windows. As the superintendent had said, one was shut and bolted. The other was open about
four inches at the bottom. A thick patent screw of the kind known

many years ago as an anti-burglar screw secured it in that position.

Sugden said: 'According to the butler, that window was never shut, wet or fine. There's a linoleum mat underneath it in case rain beat in, but it didn't much, as the overhanging roof protects it.'

Poirot nodded.

He came back to the body and stared down at the old man.

The lips were drawn back from the bloodless gums in something that looked like a snarl. The fingers were curved like claws.

Poirot said: 'He does not seem a strong man, no.'

The doctor said: 'He was pretty tough, I believe. He'd survived several pretty bad illnesses that would have killed most men.'

Poirot said: 'I do not mean that. I mean, he was not big, not strong physically.'

'No, he's frail enough.'

Poirot turned from the dead man. He bent to examine an overturned chair, a big chair of mahogany. Beside it was a round mahogany table and the fragments of a big china lamp. Two other smaller chairs lay nearby, also the smashed fragments of a decanter and two glasses, a heavy glass paperwieght, unbroken; some miscellaneous books, a big Japanese vase smashed in pieces, and a bronze statuette of a naked girl completed the débris.

Poirot bent over all these exhibits, studying them gravely, but without touching them. He frowned to himself as though perplexed.

The chief constable said: 'Anything strike you, Poirot?'

Hercule Poirot sighed. He murmured: 'Such a frail shrunken old man – and yet – all this.'

Johnson looked puzzled. He turned away and said to the sergeant, who was busy at his work: 'What about prints?'

'Plenty of them, sir, all over the room.'

'What about the safe?'

'No good. Only prints on that are those of the old gentleman himself.'

Johnson turned to the doctor.

'What about bloodstains?' he asked. 'Surely whoever killed him must have got blood on him.'

The doctor said doubtfully: 'Not necessarily. Bleeding was almost entirely from the jugular vein. That wouldn't spout like an artery.'

'No, no. Still, there seems a lot of blood about.'

Poirot said: 'Yes, there is a lot of blood – it strikes one, that. A lot of blood.'

Superintendent Sugden said respectfully: 'Do you – er – does that suggest anything to you, M. Poirot?'

Poirot looked about him. He shook his head perplexedly.

He said: 'There is something here – some violence . . .' He stopped a minute, then went on: 'Yes, that is it – *violence* . . . And blood – an insistence on *blood* . . . There is – how shall I put it? – there is *too much blood*. Blood on the chairs, on the tables, on the carpet . . . The blood ritual? Sacrificial blood? Is that it? Perhaps. Such a frail old man, so thin, so shrivelled, so dried up – and yet – in his death – *so much blood* . . .'

His voice died away. Superintendent Sugden, staring at him with round, startled eyes, said in an awed voice: 'Funny – that's what she said – the lady . . .'

Poirot said sharply: 'What lady? What was it she said?'

Sugden answered: 'Mrs Lee – Mrs Alfred. Stood over there by the door and half-whispered it. It didn't make sense to me.'

'What did she say?'

'Something about who would have thought the old gentleman had so much blood in him . . .'

Poirot said softly: '"*Who would have thought the old man to have had so much blood in him?*" The words of Lady Macbeth. She said that . . . Ah, this is interesting . . .'

VIII

Alfred Lee and his wife came into the small study where Poirot, Sugden and the chief constable were standing waiting. Colonel Johnson came forward.

'How do you do, Mr Lee? We've never actually met but, as you know, I'm chief constable of the county. Johnson's my name. I can't tell you how distressed I am by this.'

Alfred, his brown eyes like those of a suffering dog, said hoarsely: 'Thank you. It's terrible – quite terrible. I – this is my wife.'

Lydia said in her quiet voice: 'It has been a frightful shock to my husband – to all of us – but particularly to him.'

Her hand was on her husband's shoulder.

Colonel Johnson said: 'Won't you sit down, Mrs Lee? Let me introduce M. Hercule Poirot.'

Hercule Poirot bowed. His eyes went interestedly from husband to wife.

Lydia's hands pressed gently on Alfred's shoulder.

'Sit down, Alfred.'

Alfred sat. He murmured: 'Hercule Poirot. Now, who – who—?'

He passed his hand in a dazed fashion over his forehead.

Lydia Lee said: 'Colonel Johnson will want to ask you a lot of questions, Alfred.'

The chief constable looked at her with approval. He was thankful that Mrs Alfred Lee was turning out to be such a sensible and competent woman.

Alfred said: 'Of course. Of course . . .'

Johnson said to himself: 'Shock seems to have knocked him out completely. Hope he can pull himself together a bit.'

Aloud he said: 'I've got a list here of everybody who was in the house tonight. Perhaps you'll tell me, Mr Lee, if it is correct.'

He made a slight gesture to Sugden and the latter pulled out his note-book and once more recited the list of names.

The businesslike procedure seemed to restore Alfred Lee to something more like his normal self. He had regained command of himself, his eyes no longer looked dazed and staring. When Sugden finished, he nodded in agreement.

'That's quite right,' he said.

'Do you mind telling me a little more about your guests? Mr and Mrs George Lee and Mr and Mrs David Lee are, I gather, relatives?'

'They are my two younger brothers and their wives.'

'They are staying here only?'

'Yes, they came to us for Christmas.'

'Mr Henry Lee is also a brother?'

'Yes.'

'And your two other guests? Miss Estravados and Mr Farr?'

'Miss Estravados is my niece. Mr Farr is the son of my father's one-time partner in South Africa.'

'Ah, an old friend.'

Lydia intervened.

'No, actually we have never seen him before.'

'I see. But you invited him to stay with you for Christmas?'

Alfred hesitated, then looked towards his wife. She said clearly: 'Mr Farr turned up quite unexpectedly yesterday. He happened to be in the neighbourhood and came to call upon my father-in-law. When my father-in-law found he was the son of his old friend and partner, he insisted on his remaining with us for Christmas.'

Colonel Johnson said: 'I see. That explains the household. As regards the servants, Mrs Lee, do you consider them all trustworthy?'

Lydia considered for a moment before replying. Then she said: 'Yes. I am quite sure they are all thoroughly reliable. They have mostly been with us for many years. Tressilian, the butler, has been here since my husband was a young child. The only newcomers are the between-maid, Joan, and the nurse-valet who attended on my father-in-law.'

'What about them?'

'Joan is rather a silly little thing. That is the worst that can be said of her. I know very little about Horbury. He has been here just over a year. He was quite competent at his job and my father-in-law seemed satisfied with him.'

Poirot said acutely: 'But you, Madame, were not so satisfied?'

Lydia shrugged her shoulders slightly.

'It was nothing to do with me.'

'But you are the mistress of the house, Madame. The servants are your concern?'

'Oh, yes, of course. But Horbury was my father-in-law's personal attendant. He did not come under my jurisdiction.'

'I see.'

Colonel Johnson said: 'We come now to the events of tonight. I'm afraid this will be painful for you, Mr Lee, but I would like your account of what happened.'

Alfred said in a low voice: 'Of course.'

Colonel Johnson said, prompting him: 'When, for instance, did you last see your father?'

A slight spasm of pain crossed Alfred's face as he replied in a low voice: 'It was after tea. I was with him for a short time. Finally I said goodnight to him and left him at – let me see – about a quarter to six.'

Poirot observed: 'You said goodnight to him? You did not, then, expect to see him again that evening?'

'No. My father's supper, a light meal, was always brought to him at seven. After that he sometimes went to bed early or sometimes sat up in his chair, but he did not expect to see any members of the family again unless he specially sent for them.'

'Did he often send for them?'

'Sometimes. If he felt like it.'

'But it was not the ordinary procedure?'

'No.'

'Go on, please, Mr Lee.'

Alfred continued: 'We had our dinner at eight o'clock. Dinner was over and my wife and the other ladies had gone into the drawing-room.' His voice faltered. His eyes began to stare again. 'We were sitting there – at the table . . . Suddenly there was the most astounding noise overhead. Chairs overturning, furniture crashing, breaking glass and china, and then— Oh, God' – he shuddered – 'I can hear it still – my father screamed – a horrible, long-drawn scream – the scream of a man in mortal agony . . .'

He raised shaking hands to cover his face. Lydia stretched out her hand and touched his sleeve. Colonel Johnson said gently: 'And then?'

Alfred said in a broken voice: 'I think – just for a moment we were *stunned*. Then we sprang up and went out of the door and up the stairs to my father's room. The door was locked. We couldn't get in. It had to be broken open. Then, when we did get in, we saw—'

His voice died away.

Johnson said quickly: 'There's no need to go into that part of it, Mr Lee. To go back a little, to the time you were in the dining-room. Who was there with you when you heard the cry?'

'Who was there? Why, we were all— No, let me see. My brother was there – my brother Harry.'

'Nobody else?'

'No one else.'

'Where were the other gentlemen?'

Alfred sighed and frowned in an effort of remembrance.

'Let me see – it seems so long ago – yes, like years – what did happen? Oh, of course, George had gone to telephone. Then we began to talk of family matters, and Stephen Farr said something about seeing we wanted to discuss things, and he took himself off. He did it very nicely and tactfully.'

'And your brother David?'

Alfred frowned.

'David? Wasn't he there? No, of course, he wasn't. I don't quite know when he slipped away.'

Poirot said gently: 'So you had the family matters to discuss?'

'Er – yes.'

'That is to say, you had matters to discuss with *one* member of your family?'

Lydia said: 'What do you mean, M. Poirot?'

He turned quickly to her.

'Madame, your husband says that Mr Farr left them because

393

he saw they had affairs of the family to discuss. But it was not a *conseil de famille*, since Mr David was not there and Mr George was not there. It was, then, a discussion between two members of the family only.'

Lydia said: 'My brother-in-law, Harry, had been abroad for a great number of years. It was natural that he and my husband should have things to talk over.'

'Ah! I see. It was like that.'

She shot him a quick glance, then turned her eyes away.

Johnson said: 'Well, that seems clear enough. Did you notice anyone else as you ran upstairs to your father's room?'

'I – really I don't know. I think so. We all came from different directions. But I'm afraid I didn't notice – I was so alarmed. That terrible cry . . .'

Colonel Johnson passed quickly to another subject.

'Thank you, Mr Lee. Now, there is another point. I understand that your father had some valuable diamonds in his possession.'

Alfred looked rather surprised.

'Yes,' he said. 'That is so.'

'Where did he keep them?'

'In the safe in his room.'

'Can you describe them at all?'

'They were rough diamonds – that is, uncut stones.'

'Why did your father have them there?'

'It was a whim of his. They were stones he had brought with him from South Africa. He never had them cut. He just liked keeping them in his possession. As I say, it was a whim of his.'

'I see,' said the chief constable.

From his tone it was plain that he did not see. He went on: 'Were they of much value?'

'My father estimated their value at about ten thousand pounds.'

'In fact, they were very valuable stones?'

'Yes.'

'It seems a curious idea to keep such stones in a bedroom safe.'

Lydia interposed.

'My father-in-law, Colonel Johnson, was a somewhat curious man. His ideas were not the conventional ones. It definitely gave him pleasure to handle those stones.'

'They recalled, perhaps, the past to him,' said Poirot.

She gave him a quick appreciative look.

'Yes,' she said. 'I think they did.'

'Were they insured?' asked the chief constable.

'I think not.'

Johnson leaned forward. He asked quietly: 'Did you know, Mr Lee, that those stones had been stolen?'

'What?' Alfred Lee stared at him.

'Your father said nothing to you of their disappearance?'

'Not a word.'

'You did not know that he had sent for Superintendent Sugden here and had reported the loss to him?'

'I hadn't the faintest idea of such a thing!'

The chief constable transferred his gaze.

'What about you, Mrs Lee?'

Lydia shook her head.

'I heard nothing about it.'

'As far as you knew, the stones were still in the safe?'

'Yes.'

She hesitated and then asked: 'Is that why he was killed? For the sake of those stones?'

Colonel Johnson said: 'That is what we are going to find out!'

He went on: 'Have you any idea, Mrs Lee, who could have engineered such a theft?'

She shook her head

'No, indeed. I am sure the servants are all honest. In any case, it would be very difficult for them to get at the safe. My father-in-law was always in his room. He never came downstairs.'

'Who attended to the room?'

'Horbury. He made the bed and dusted. The second housemaid went in to do the grate and lay the fire every morning, otherwise Horbury did everything.'

Poirot said: 'So Horbury would be the person with the best opportunity?'

'Yes.'

'Do you think that it was he who stole the diamonds, then?'

'It is possible, I suppose . . . He had the best opportunity. Oh, I don't know what to think.'

Colonel Johnson said: 'Your husband has given us his account of the evening. Will you do the same, Mrs Lee? When did you last see your father-in-law?'

'We were all up in his room this afternoon – before tea. That was the last time I saw him.'

'You did not see him later to bid him goodnight?'

'No.'

Poirot said: 'Do you usually go and say goodnight to him?'

Lydia said sharply: 'No.'

The chief constable went on: 'Where were you when the crime took place?'

'In the drawing-room.'

'You heard the noise of the struggle?'

'I think I heard something heavy fall. Of course my father-in-law's room is over the dining-room, not the drawing-room, so I shouldn't hear so much.'

'But you heard the cry?'

Lydia shuddered.

'Yes, I heard that . . . It was horrible – like – like a soul in hell. I knew at once something dreadful had happened. I hurried out and followed my husband and Harry up the stairs.'

'Who else was in the drawing-room at the time?'

Lydia frowned.

'Really – I can't remember. David was next door in the music-room, playing Mendelssohn. I think Hilda had gone to join him.'

'And the other two ladies?'

Lydia said slowly: 'Magdalene went to telephone. I can't remember whether she had come back or not. I don't know where Pilar was.'

Poirot said gently: 'In fact, you may have been quite alone in the drawing-room?'

'Yes – yes – as a matter of fact, I believe I was.'

Colonel Johnson said: 'About these diamonds. We ought, I think, to make quite sure about them. Do you know the combination of your father's safe, Mr Lee? I see it is of a somewhat old-fashioned pattern.'

'You will find it written down in a small note-book he carried in the pocket of his dressing-gown.'

'Good. We will go and look presently. It will be better, perhaps, if we interview the other members of the house-party first. The ladies may want to get to bed.'

Lydia stood up.

'Come, Alfred.' She turned to them. 'Shall I send them in to you?'

'One by one, if you wouldn't mind, Mrs Lee.'

'Certainly.'

She moved towards the door. Alfred followed her.

Suddenly, at the last moment, he swung round.

'Of course,' he said. He came quickly back to Poirot. 'You are Hercule Poirot! I don't know where my wits have been. I should have realized at once.'

He spoke quickly, in a low, excited voice.

'It's an absolute godsend your being here! You must find out the truth, M. Poirot. Spare no expense! I will be responsible for any expense. *But find out* . . . My poor father – killed by someone – killed with the utmost brutality! You *must* find out, M. Poirot. My father has got to be avenged.'

Poirot answered quietly: 'I can assure you, Mr Lee, that I am prepared to do my utmost to assist Colonel Johnson and Superintendent Sugden.'

Alfred Lee said: 'I want you work for *me*. My father has got to be avenged.'

He began to tremble violently. Lydia had come back. She went up to him and drew his arm through hers.

'Come, Alfred,' she said. 'We must get the others.'

Her eyes met Poirot's. They were eyes that kept their own secrets. They did not waver.

Poirot said softly: *'Who would have thought the old man—'*

She interrupted him: 'Stop! Don't say that!'

Poirot murmured: *'You* said it, Madame.'

She breathed softly: 'I know . . . I remember . . . It was – so horrible.'

Then she went abruptly out of the room, her husband beside her.

IX

George Lee was solemn and correct.

'A terrible business,' he said, shaking his head. 'A terrible, terrible business. I can only believe that it must – er – have been the work of a *lunatic*!'

Colonel Johnson said politely: 'That is your theory?'

'Yes. Yes, indeed. A homicidal maniac. Escaped, perhaps, from some mental home in the vicinity.'

Superintendent Sugden put in: 'And how do you suggest this – er – lunatic gained admittance to the house, Mr Lee? And how did he leave it?'

George shook his head.

'That,' he said firmly, 'is for the police to discover.'

Sugden said: 'We made the round of the house at once. All windows were closed and barred. The side door was locked, so was the front door. Nobody could have left by the kitchen premises without being seen by the kitchen staff.'

George Lee cried: 'But that's absurd! You'll be saying next that my father was never murdered at all!'

'He was murdered all right,' said Superintendent Sugden. 'There's no doubt about that.'

The chief constable cleared his throat and took up the questioning.

'Just where were you, Mr Lee, at the time of the crime?'

'I was in the dining-room. It was just after dinner. No, I was, I think, in this room. I had just finished telephoning.'

'You had been telephoning?'

'Yes. I had put a call through to the Conservative agent in Westeringham – my constituency. Some urgent matters.'

'And it was after that that you heard the scream?'

George Lee gave a slight shiver.

'Yes, very unpleasant. It – er – froze my marrow. It died away in a kind of choke or gurgle.'

He took out a handkerchief and wiped his forehead where the perspiration had broken out.

'Terrible business,' he muttered.

'And then you hurried upstairs?'

'Yes.'

'Did you see your brothers, Mr Alfred and Mr Harry Lee?'

'No, they must have gone up just ahead of me, I think.'

'When did you last see your father, Mr Lee?'

'This afternoon. We were all up there.'

'You did not see him after that?'

'No.'

The chief constable paused, then he said: 'Were you aware that your father kept a quantity of valuable uncut diamonds in the safe in his bedroom?'

George Lee nodded.

'A most unwise procedure,' he said pompously. 'I often told him so. He might have been murdered for them – I mean – that is to say—'

Colonel Johnson cut in: 'Are you aware that these stones have disappeared?'

George's jaw dropped. His protuberant eyes stared.

'Then he *was* murdered for them?'

The chief constable said slowly: 'He was aware of their loss and reported it to the police some hours before his death.'

George said: 'But, then – I don't understand – I—'

Hercule Poirot said gently: 'We, too, do not understand . . .'

Harry Lee came into the room with a swagger. For a moment
Poirot stared at him, frowning. He had a feeling that somewhere
he had seen this man before. He noted the features: the high-
bridged nose, the arrogant poise of the head, the line of the jaw;
and he realized that, though Harry was a big man and his father
had been a man of merely middle height, yet there had been a
good deal of resemblance between them.

He noted something else, too. For all his swagger, Harry Lee
was nervous. He was carrying it off with a swing, but the anxiety
underneath was real enough.

'Well, gentlemen,' he said. 'What can I tell you?'

Colonel Johnson said: 'We shall be gald of any light you can
throw on the events of this evening.'

Harry Lee shook his head.

'I don't know anything at all. It's all pretty horrible and utterly
unexpected.'

Poirot said: 'You have recently returned from abroad, I think,
Mr Lee?'

Harry turned to him quickly.

'Yes. Landed in England a week ago.'

Poirot said: 'You had been away a long time?'

Harry Lee lifted up his chin and laughed.

'You might as well hear straight away – someone will soon tell
you! I'm the prodigal son, gentlemen! It's nearly twenty years
since I last set foot in this house.'

'But you returned – now. Will you tell us why?' asked Poirot.

With the same appearance of frankness Harry answered readily
enough.

'It's the good old parable still. I got tired of the husks that the
swine do eat – or don't eat, I forget which. I thought to myself that
the fatted calf would be a welcome exchange. I had a letter from
my father suggesting that I come home. I obeyed the summons
and came. That's all.'

Poirot said: 'You came for a short visit – or a long one?'

Harry said: 'I came home – for good!'

'Your father was willing?'

'The old man was delighted.' He laughed again. The corners of
his eyes crinkled engagingly. 'Pretty boring for the old man living
here with Alfred! Alfred's a dull stick – very worthy and all that,
but poor company. My father had been a bit of a rip in his time.
He was looking forward to my company.'

'And your brother and his wife, were they pleased that you were to live here?'

Poirot asked the question with a slight lifting of his eyebrows.

'Alfred? Alfred was livid with rage. Don't know about Lydia. She was probably annoyed on Alfred's behalf. But I've no doubt she'd be quite pleased in the end. I like Lydia. She's a delightful woman. I should have got on with Lydia. But Alfred was quite another pair of shoes.' He laughed again. 'Alfred's always been as jealous as hell of me. He's always been the good dutiful stay-at-home stick-in-the-mud son. And what was he going to get for it in the end? What the good boy of the family always gets – a kick in the pants. Take it from me, gentlemen, virtue doesn't pay.' He looked from one face to another.

'Hope you're not shocked by my frankness. But, after all, it's the truth you're after. You'll drag out all the family dirty linen into the light of day in the end. I might as well display mine straight away. I'm not particularly broken-hearted by my father's death – after all, I hadn't seen the old devil since I was a boy – but nevertheless he was my father and he was murdered. I'm all out for revenge on the murderer.' He stroked his jawbone, watching them. 'We're rather hot on revenge in our family. None of the Lees forgets easily. I mean to make sure that my father's murderer is caught and hanged.'

'I think you can trust us to do our best in that line, Mr Lee,' said Sugden.

'If you don't I shall take the law into my own hands,' said Harry Lee.

The chief constable said sharply: 'Have you any ideas on the subject of the murderer's identity, then, Mr Lee?'

Harry shook his head.

'No,' he said slowly. 'No – I haven't. You know it's rather a jolt. Because I've been thinking about it – and I don't see that it can have been an outside job . . .'

'Ah,' said Sugden, nodding his head.

'And if so,' said Harry Lee, 'then someone here in the house killed him . . . But who the devil could have done it? Can't suspect the servants. Tressilian has been here since the year one. The half-witted footman? Not on your life. Horbury, now, he's a cool customer, but Tressilian tells me he was out at the pictures. So what do you come to? Passing over Stephen Farr (and why the devil should Stephen Farr come all the way from South Africa and murder a total stranger?) there's only the family. And for the life of me I can't see one of us doing it. Alfred? He adored Father.

George? He hasn't got the guts. David? David's always been a moon dreamer. He'd faint if he saw his own finger bleed. The wives? Women don't go and slit a man's throat in cold blood. So who did? Blessed if I know. But it's damned disturbing.'

Colonel Johnson cleared his throat – an official habit of his – and said: 'When did you last see your father this evening?'

'After tea. He'd just had a row with Alfred – about your humble servant. The old man was no end bucked with himself. He always liked stirring up trouble. In my opinion, that's why he kept my arrival dark from the others. Wanted to see the fur fly when I blew in unexpectedly! That's why he talked about altering his will, too.'

Poirot stirred softly. He murmured: 'So your father mentioned his will?'

'Yes – in front of the whole lot of us, watching us like a cat to see how we reacted. Just told the lawyer chap to come over and see him about it after Christmas.'

Poirot asked: 'What changes did he contemplate making?'

Harry Lee grinned: 'He didn't tell us that! Trust the old fox! I imagine – or shall we say I hoped – that the change was to the advantage of your humble servant! I should imagine I'd been cut out of any former wills. Now, I rather fancy, I was to go back. Nasty blow for the others. Pilar, too – he'd taken a fancy to her. She was in for something good, I should imagine. You haven't seen her yet? My Spanish niece. She's a beautiful creature, Pilar – with the lovely warmth of the south – and its cruelty. Wish I wasn't a mere uncle!'

'You say your father took to her?'

Harry nodded.

'She knew how to get round the old man. Sat up there with him a good deal. I bet she knew just what she was after! Well, he's dead now. No wills can be altered in Pilar's favour – nor mine, either worse luck.'

He frowned, paused a minute, and then went on with a change of tone.

'But I'm wandering from the point. You wanted to know what was the last time I saw my father. As I've told you, it was after tea – might have been a little past six. The old man was in good spirits then – a bit tired, perhaps. I went away and left him with Horbury. I never saw him again.'

'Where were you at the time of his death?'

'In the dining-room with brother Alfred. Not a very harmonious after-dinner session. We were in the middle of a pretty sharp argument when we heard the noise overhead. Sounded as though

401

ten men were wrestling up there. And then poor old Father screamed. It was like killing a pig. The sound of it paralysed Alfred. He just sat there with his jaw dropping. I fairly shook him back to life, and we started off upstairs. The door was locked. Had to break it open. Took some doing, too. How the devil that door came to be locked, I can't imagine! There was no one in the room but Father, and I'm damned if anyone could have got away through the windows.'

Superintendent Sugden said: 'The door was locked from the outside.'

'What?' Harry stared. 'But I'll swear the key was on the *inside*.'

Poirot murmured: 'So you noticed that?'

Harry Lee said sharply: 'I do notice things. It's a habit of mine.'

He looked sharply from one face to the other.

'Is there anything more you want to know, gentlemen?'

Johnson shook his head.

'Thank you, Mr Lee, not for the moment. Perhaps you will ask the next member of the family to come along?'

'Certainly I will.'

He walked to the door and went out without looking back.

The three men looked at each other.

Colonel Johnson said: 'What about it, Sugden?'

The superintendent shook his head doubtfully. He said: 'He's afraid of something. I wonder why.'

XI

Magdalene Lee paused effectively in the doorway. One long slender hand touched the burnished platinum sheen of her hair. The leaf-green velvet frock she wore clung to the delicate lines of her figure. She looked very young and a little frightened.

The three men were arrested for a moment looking at her. Johnson's eyes showed a sudden surprised admiration. Superintendent Sugden's showed no animation, merely the impatience of a man anxious to get on with his job. Hercule Poirot's eyes were deeply appreciative (as she saw) but the appreciation was not for her beauty, but for the effective use she made of it. She did not know that he was thinking to himself: '*Jolie mannequin, la petite. Mais elle a les yeux durs.*'

Colonel Johnson was thinking: 'Damned good-looking girl. George Lee will have trouble with her if he doesn't look out. Got an eye for a man all right.'

Superintendent Sugden was thinking: 'Empty-headed vain piece of goods. Hope we get through with her quickly.'

'Will you sit down, Mrs Lee? Let me see, you are—?'

'Mrs George Lee.'

She accepted the chair with a warm smile of thanks. 'After all,' the glance seemed to say, 'although you *are* a man and a police-man, you are not so dreadful after all.'

The tail-end of the smile included Poirot. Foreigners were so susceptible where women were concerned. About Superintendent Sugden she did not bother.

She murmured, twisting her hands together in pretty distress: 'It's all so terrible. I feel so frightened.'

'Come, come, Mrs Lee,' said Colonel Johnson kindly but briskly. 'It's been a shock, I know, but it's all over now. We just want an account from you of what happened this evening.'

She cried out: 'But I don't know anything about it – I don't indeed.'

For a moment the chief constable's eyes narrowed. He said gently: 'No, of course not.'

'We only arrived here yesterday. George *would* make me come here for Christmas! I wish we hadn't. I'm sure I shall never feel the same again!

'Very upsetting – yes.'

'I hardly know George's family, you see. I've only seen Mr Lee once or twice – at our wedding and once since. Of course I've seen Alfred and Lydia more often, but they're really all quite strangers to me.'

Again the wide-eyed frightened-child look. Again Hercule Poirot's eyes were appreciative – and again he thought to himself: '*Elle joue très bien la comédie, cette petite . . .*'

'Yes, yes,' said Colonel Johnson. 'Now just tell me about the last time you saw your father-in-law – Mr Lee – alive.'

'Oh, *that*! That was this afternoon. It was dreadful!'

Johnson said quickly: 'Dreadful? Why?'

'They were so angry!'

'Who was angry?'

'Oh, all of them . . . I don't mean George. His father didn't say anything to him. But all the others.'

'What happened exactly?'

'Well, when we got there – he asked for all of us – he was speaking into the telephone – to his lawyers about his will. And then he told Alfred he was looking very glum. I think that was because of Harry coming home to live. Alfred was very upset about that, I believe. You see, Harry did something quite dreadful. And then he said something about his wife – she's dead long ago – but she had the brains of a louse, he said, and David sprang up and looked as though he'd like to murder him— Oh!' She stopped suddenly, her eyes alarmed. 'I didn't *mean* that – I didn't mean it at all!'

Colonel Johnson said soothingly: 'Quite – quite, figure of speech, that was all.'

'Hilda, that's David's wife, quieted him down and – well, I think that's all. Mr Lee said he didn't want to see anyone again that evening. So we all went away.'

'And that was the last time you saw him?'

'Yes. Until – until—'

She shivered.

Colonel Johnson said: 'Yes, quite so. Now, where were you at the time of the crime?'

'Oh – let me see, I think I was in the drawing-room.'

'Aren't you sure?'

Magdalene's eyes flickered a little, the lids drooped over them.

She said: 'Of course! How stupid of me . . . I'd gone to telephone. One gets so mixed up.'

'You were telephoning, you say. In this room?'

'Yes, that's the only telephone except the one upstairs in my father-in-law's room.'

Superintendent Sugden said: 'Was anybody else in the room with you?'

Her eyes widened.

'Oh, no, I was quite alone.'

'Had you been here long?'

'Well – a little time. It takes some time to put a call through in the evening.'

'It was a trunk call, then?'

'Yes – to Westeringham.'

'I see.'

'And then?'

'And then there was that awful scream – and everybody running – and the door being locked and having to break it down. Oh! It was like a *nightmare*! I shall always remember it!'

'No, no.' Colonel Johnson's tone was mechanically kind. He went on: 'Did you know that your father-in-law kept a quantity of valuable diamonds in his safe?'

'No, did he?' Her tone was quite frankly thrilled. 'Real diamonds?'

Hercule Poirot said: 'Diamonds worth about ten thousand pounds.'

'Oh!' It was a soft gasping sound – holding in it the essence of feminine cupidity.

'Well,' said Colonel Johnson, 'I think that's all for the present. We needn't bother you any further, Mrs Lee.'

'Oh, thank you.'

She stood up – smiled from Johnson to Poirot – the smile of a grateful little girl, then she went out walking with her head held high and her palms a little turned outwards.

Colonel Johnson called: 'Will you ask your brother-in-law, Mr David Lee, to come here?' Closing the door after her, he came back to the table.

'Well,' he said, 'what do you think? We're getting at some of it now! You notice one thing: George Lee was telephoning when he heard the scream! His wife was telephoning when she heard it! That doesn't fit – it doesn't fit at all.'

He added: 'What do you think, Sugden?'

The superintendent said slowly: 'I don't want to speak offensively of the lady, but I should say that, though she's the kind who would be first class at getting money out of a gentleman, I don't think she's the kind who'd cut a gentleman's throat. That wouldn't be her line at all.'

'Ah, but one never knows, *mon vieux*,' murmured Poirot.

The chief constable turned round on him.

'And you, Poirot, what do you think?'

Hercule Poirot leaned forward. He straightened the blotter in front of him and flicked a minute speck of dust from a candlestick. He answered: 'I would say that the character of the late Mr Simeon Lee begins to emerge for us. It is there, I think, that the whole importance of the case lies . . . in the character of the dead man.'

Superintendent Sugden turned a puzzled face to him.

'I don't quite get you, M. Poirot,' he said. 'What exactly has the character of the deceased got to do with his murder?'

Poirot said dreamily: 'The character of the victim has always something to do with his or her murder. The frank and unsuspicious mind of Desdemona was the direct cause of her death. A more suspicious woman would have seen Iago's machinations and circumvented them much earlier. The uncleanness of Marat directly invited his end in a bath. From the temper of Mercutio's mind came his death at the sword's point.'

Colonel Johnson pulled his moustache.

'What exactly are you getting at, Poirot?'

'I am telling you that, because Simeon Lee was a certain kind of man, he set in motion certain forces, which forces in the end brought about his death.'

'You don't think the diamonds had anything to do with it, then?'

Poirot smiled at the honest perplexity in Johnson's face.

'*Mon cher*,' he said. 'It was because of Simeon Lee's peculiar character that he kept ten thousand pounds' worth of uncut diamonds in his safe! You have not there the action of every man.'

'That's very true, M. Poirot,' said Superintendent Sugden, nodding his head with the air of a man who at last sees what a fellow-conversationalist is driving it. 'He was a queer one, Mr Lee was. He kept those stones there so he could take them out and handle them and get the feeling of the past back. Depend upon it, that's why he never had them cut.'

Poirot nodded energetically.

'Precisely – precisely. I see you have great acumen, Superintendent.'

The superintendent looked a little doubtful at the compliment, but Colonel Johnson cut in: 'There's something else, Poirot. I don't know whether it has struck you—'

'*Mais oui*,' said Poirot. 'I know what you mean. Mrs George Lee, she let the cat out of the bag more than she knew! She gave us a pretty impression of that last family meeting. She indicates – oh, so naïvely – that Alfred was angry with his father – and that David looked as "though he could murder him". Both those statements I think were true. But from them we can draw our own reconstruction. What did Simeon Lee assemble his family for? Why should they have arrived in time to hear him telephoning to his lawyer? *Parbleu*, it was no error, that. He *wanted* them to hear it! The poor old one, he sits in his chair and he has lost the diversions of his younger days. So he invents a new diversion for himself. He amuses himself by playing upon the cupidity and the greed of human nature – yes, and on its emotions and its passions, too! But from that arises one further deduction. In his game of rousing the greed and emotion of his children, he would not omit anyone. He must, logically and necessarily, have had his dig at Mr George Lee as well as at the others! His wife is carefully silent about that. At her, too, he may have shot a poisoned arrow or two. We shall find out, I think, from others, what Simeon Lee had to say to George Lee and George Lee's wife—'

He broke off. The door opened and David Lee came in.

XII

David Lee had himself well in hand. His demeanour was calm
– almost unnaturally so. He came up to them, drew a chair forward and sat down, looking with grave interrogation at Colonel
Johnson.

The electric light touched the fair peak of hair that grew on his
forehead and showed up the sensitive modelling of the cheek
bones. He looked absurdly young to be the son of that shrivelled
old man who lay dead upstairs.

'Yes, gentlemen,' he said, 'what can I tell you?'

Colonel Johnson said: 'I understand, Mr Lee, that there was a
kind of family meeting held in your father's room this afternoon?'

'There was. But it was quite informal. I mean, it was not a
family council or anything of that kind.'

'What took place there?'

David Lee answered calmly: 'My father was in a difficult mood.
He was an old man and an invalid, of course; one had to make
allowances for him. He seemed to have assembled us there in
order to – well – vent his spite upon us.'

'Can you remember what he said?'

David said quietly: 'It was really all rather foolish. He said we
were no use – any of us – that there wasn't a single man in the
family! He said Pilar (that is my Spanish niece) was worth two of
any of us. He said—' David stopped.

Poirot said: 'Please, Mr Lee, the exact words, if you can.'

David said reluctantly: 'He spoke rather coarsely – said he
hoped that somewhere in the world he had better sons – even if
they were born the wrong side of the blanket . . .'

His sensitive face showed distaste for the words he was repeating. Superintendent Sugden looked up, suddenly alert. Leaning
forward, he said: 'Did your father say anything in particular to
your brother, Mr George Lee?'

'To George? I don't remember. Oh, yes, I believe he told him he
would have to cut down expenses in future; he'd have to reduce his
allowance. George was very upset, got as red as a turkey cock. He
spluttered and said he couldn't possibly manage with less. My
father said quite coolly that he'd have to. He said he'd better get
his wife to help him economise. Rather a nasty dig, that – George
has always been the economical one – saves and stints on every
penny. Magdalene, I fancy, is a bit of a spender – she has
extravagant tastes.'

Poirot said: 'So that she, too, was annoyed?'

'Yes. Besides, my father worded something else rather crude-

407

ly – mentioned her as having lived with a naval officer. Of course he really meant her father, but it sounded rather dubious. Magdalene went scarlet. I don't blame her.'

Poirot said: 'Did your father mention his late wife, your mother?'

The red blood ran in waves up David's temples. His hands clenched themselves on the table in front of him, trembling slightly.

He said in a low choked voice: 'Yes, he did. He insulted her.'

Colonel Johnson said: 'What did he say?'

David said abruptly: 'I don't remember. Just some slighting reference.'

Poirot said softly: 'Your mother has been dead some years?'

David said shortly: 'She died when I was a boy.'

'She was not – perhaps – very happy in her life here?'

David gave a scornful laugh: 'Who could be happy with a man like my father? My mother was a saint. She died a broken-hearted woman.'

Poirot went on: 'Your father was, perhaps, distressed by her death?'

David said abruptly: 'I don't know. I left home.'

He paused and then said: 'Perhaps you may not be aware of the fact that when I came on this visit I had not seen my father for nearly twenty years. So, you see, I can't tell you very much about his habits or his enemies or what went on here.'

Colonel Johnson asked: 'Did you know that your father kept a lot of valuable diamonds in the safe in his bedroom?'

David said indifferently: 'Did he? Seems a foolish sort of thing to do.'

Johnson said: 'Will you describe briefly your own movements last night?'

'Mine? Oh, I went away from the dinner-table fairly quickly. It bores me, this sitting round over port. Besides, I could see that Alfred and Harry were working up for a quarrel. I hate rows. I slipped away and went to the music-room and played the piano.'

Poirot asked: 'The music-room, it is next to the drawing-room, is it not?'

'Yes. I played there for some time – till – till the thing happened.'

'What did you hear exactly?'

'Oh! A far-off noise of furniture being overturned somewhere upstairs. And then a pretty ghastly cry.' He clenched his hands again. 'Like a soul in hell. God, it was awful!'

Johnson said: 'Were you alone in the music-room?'

'Eh? No, my wife, Hilda, was there. She'd come in from the drawing-room. We – we went up with the others.'

He added quickly and nervously: 'You don't want me, do you, to describe what – what I saw there?'

Colonel Johnson said: No, quite unnecessary. Thank you, Mr Lee, there's nothing more. You can't imagine, I suppose, who would be likely to want to murder your father?'

David Lee said recklessly: 'I should think – quite a lot of people! I don't know of anyone definite.'

He went out rapidly, shutting the door loudly behind him.

XIII

Colonel Johnson had had no time to do more than clear his throat when the door opened again and Hilda Lee came in.

Hercule Poirot looked at her with interest. He had to admit to himself that the wives these Lees had married were an interesting study. The swift intelligence and greyhound grace of Lydia, the meretricious airs and graces of Magdalene, and now the solid comfortable strength of Hilda. She was, he saw, younger than her rather dowdy style of hair-dressing and unfashionable clothes made her appear. Her mouse-brown hair was unflecked with grey and her steady hazel eyes set in the rather podgy face shone out like beacons of kindliness. She was, he thought, a nice woman.

Colonel Johnson was talking in his kindliest tone.

'. . . A great strain on all of you,' he was saying. 'I gather from your husband, Mrs Lee, that this is the first time you have been to Gorston Hall?'

She bowed her head.

'Were you previously acquainted with your father-in-law, Mr Lee?'

Hilda replied in her pleasant voice: 'No. We were married soon after David left home. He always wanted to have nothing to do with his family. Until now we have not seen any of them.'

'How, then, did this visit come about?'

'My father-in-law wrote to David. He stressed his age and his desire that all his children should be with him this Christmas.'

'And your husband responded to this appeal?'

Hilda said: 'His acceptance was, I am afraid, all my doing. I – misunderstood the situation.'

Poirot interposed. He said: 'Will you be so kind as to explain yourself a little more clearly, Madame? I think what you can tell us may be of value.'

She turned to him immediately.

She said: 'At that time I had never seen my father-in-law. I had no idea what his real motive was. I assumed that he was old and lonely and that he really wanted to be reconciled to all his children.'

'And what was his real motive, in your opinion, Madame?'

Hilda hesitated a moment. Then she said slowly: 'I have no doubt – no doubt at all – that what my father-in-law really wanted was not to promote peace but to stir up strife.'

'In what way?'

Hilda said in a low voice: 'It amused him to – to appeal to the worst instincts in human nature. There was – how can I put it? – a kind of diabolical impishness about him. He wished to set every member of the family at loggerheads with one another.'

Johnson said sharply: 'And did he succeed?'

'Oh, yes,' said Hilda Lee. 'He succeeded.'

Poirot said: 'We have been told, Madame, of a scene that took place this afternoon. It was, I think, rather a violent scene.'

She bowed her head.

'Will you describe it to us – as truthfully as possible, if you please.'

She reflected a minute.

'When we went in my father-in-law was telephoning.'

'To his lawyer, I understand?'

'Yes, he was suggesting that Mr – was it Charlton? – I don't quite remember the name – should come over as he, my father-in-law, wanted to make a new will. His old one, he said, was quite out of date.'

Poirot said: 'Think carefully, Madame. In your opinion did your father-in-law deliberately ensure that you should all overhear this conversation, or was it just by *chance* that you overheard it?'

Hilda Lee said: 'I am almost sure that he meant us to overhear.'

'With the object of fomenting doubt and suspicions among you?'

'Yes.'

'So that, really, he may not have meant to alter his will at all?'

She demurred.

'No. I think that part of it was quite genuine: He probably did wish to make a new will – but he enjoyed underlining the fact.'

'Madame,' said Poirot, 'I have no official standing and my

questions, you understand, are not perhaps those that an English officer of the law would ask. But I have a great desire to know what form you think that new will would have taken. I am asking, you perceive, not for your knowledge, but simply for your opinion. *Les femmes*, they are never slow to form an opinion, *Dieu merci*.'

Hilda Lee smiled a little.

'I don't mind saying what I think. My husband's sister Jennifer married a Spaniard, Juan Estravados. Her daughter, Pilar, has just arrived here. She is a very lovely girl – and she is, of course, the only grandchild in the family. Old Mr Lee was delighted with her. He took a tremendous fancy to her. In my opinion, he wished to leave her a considerable sum in his new will. Probably he had only left her a small portion or even nothing at all in an old one.'

'Did you know your sister-in-law at all?'

'No, I never met her. Her Spanish husband died in tragic circumstances, I believe, soon after the marriage. Jennifer herself died a year ago. Pilar was left an orphan. This is why Mr Lee sent for her to come and live with him in England.'

'And the other members of the family, did they welcome her coming?'

Hilda said quietly: 'I think they all liked her. It was very pleasant to have someone young and alive in the house.'

'And she, did she seem to like being here?'

Hilda said slowly: 'I don't know. It must seem cold and strange to a girl brought up in the south – in Spain.'

Johnson said: 'Can't be very pleasant being in Spain just at present. Now, Mrs Lee, we'd like to hear your account of the conversation this afternoon.'

Poirot murmured: 'I apologize. I have made the digressions.'

Hilda Lee said: 'After my father-in-law finished telephoning, he looked round at us and laughed, and said we all looked very glum. Then he said he was tired and should go to bed early. Nobody was to come up and see him this evening. He said he wanted to be in good form for Christmas Day. Something like that.

'Then—' Her brows knit in an effort of remembrance. 'I think he said something about its being necessary to be one of a large family to appreciate Christmas, and then he went on to speak of money. He said it would cost him more to run this house in future. He told George and Magdalene they would have to economise. Told her she ought to make her own clothes. Rather an old-fashioned idea, I'm afraid. I don't wonder it annoyed her. He said his own wife had been clever with her needle.'

Poirot said gently: 'Is that all that he said about her?'

Hilda flushed.

'He made a slighting reference to her brains. My husband was very devoted to his mother, and that upset him very much. And then suddenly Mr Lee began shouting at us all. He worked himself up about it. I can understand, of course, how he felt—'

Poirot said gently, interrupting her: 'How did he feel?'

She turned her tranquil eyes upon him.

'He was disappointed, of course,' she said. 'Because there are no grandchildren – no boys, I mean – no Lees to carry on. I can see that must have festered for a long time. And suddenly he couldn't keep it in any longer and vented his rage against his sons – saying they were a lot of namby-pamby old women – something like that. I felt sorry for him then, because I realized how his pride was hurt by it.'

'And then?'

'And then,' said Hilda slowly, 'we all went away.'

'That was the last you saw of him?'

She bowed her head.

'Where were you at the time the crime occurred?'

'I was with my husband in the music-room. He was playing to me.'

'And then?'

'We heard tables and chairs overturned upstairs, and china being broken – some terrible struggle. And then that awful scream as his throat was cut . . .'

Poirot said: 'Was it such an awful scream? Was it' – he paused – '*like a soul in hell?*'

Hilda Lee said: 'It was worse than that!'

'What do you mean, Madame?'

'It was like someone *who had no soul* . . . It was inhuman like a beast . . .'

Poirot said gravely: 'So – you have judged him, Madame?'

She raised a hand in sudden distress. Her eyes fell and she stared down at the floor.

XIV

Pilar came into the room with the wariness of an animal who suspects a trap. Her eyes went quickly from side to side. She looked not so much afraid as deeply suspicious.

Colonel Johnson rose and put a chair for her. Then he said: 'You understand English, I suppose, Miss Estravados?'

Pilar's eyes opened wide. She said: 'Of course. My mother was English. I am really very English indeed.'

A faint smile came to Colonel Johnson's lips, as his eyes took in the black gloss of her hair, the proud dark eyes, and the curling red lips. Very English! An incongruous term to apply to Pilar Estravados.

He said: 'Mr Lee was your grandfather. He sent for you to come from Spain. And you arrived a few days ago. Is that right?'

Pilar nodded.

'That is right. I had – oh, a lot of adventures getting out of Spain – there was a bomb from the air and the chauffeur he was killed – where his head had been there was all blood. And I could not drive a car, so for a long way I had to walk – and I do not like walking. I never walk. My feet were sore – but sore—'

Colonel Johnson smiled. He said: 'At any rate, you arrived here. Had your mother spoken to you of your grandfather much?'

Pilar nodded cheerfully.

'Oh, yes, she said he was an old devil.'

Hercule Poirot smiled. He said: 'And what did you think of him when you arrived, Mademoiselle?'

Pilar said: 'Of course he was very, very old. He had to sit in a chair – and his face was all dried up. But I liked him all the same. I think that when he was a young man he must have been hand-some – very handsome, like you,' said Pilar to Superintendent Sugden. Her eyes dwelt with naïve pleasure on his handsome face, which had turned brick-red at the compliment.

Colonel Johnson stifled a chuckle. It was one of the few occasions when he had seen the stolid superintendent taken aback.

'But of course,' Pilar continued regretfully, 'he could never have been so big as you.'

Hercule Poirot sighed.

'You like, then, big men, Señorita?' he inquired.

Pilar agreed enthusiastically.

'Oh, yes, I like a man to be very big, tall and the shoulders broad, and very, very strong.'

Colonel Johnson said sharply: 'Did you see much of your grandfather when you arrived here?'

Pilar said: 'Oh, yes. I went to sit with him. He told me things – that he had been a very wicked man, and all the things he did in South Africa.'

'Did he ever tell you that he had diamonds in the safe in his room?'

'Yes, he showed them to me. But they were not like diamonds – they were just like pebbles – very ugly – very ugly indeed.'

Superintendent Sugden said shortly: 'So he showed them to you, did he?'

'Yes.'

'He didn't give you any of them?'

Pilar shook her head.

'No, he did not. I thought that perhaps one day he would – if I were very nice to him and came often to sit with him. Because old gentlemen they like very much young girls.'

Colonel Johnson said: 'Do you know that those diamonds have been stolen?'

Pilar opened her eyes very wide.

'Stolen?'

'Yes, have you any idea who might have taken them?'

Pilar nodded her head.

'Oh, yes,' she said. 'It would be Horbury.'

'Horbury? You mean the valet?'

'Yes.'

'Why do you think that?'

'Because he has the face of a thief. His eyes go so, from side to side, he walks softly and listens at doors. He is like a cat. And all cats are thieves.'

'H'm,' said Colonel Johnson. 'We'll leave it at that. Now I understand that all the family were up in your grandfather's room this afternoon, and that some – er – angry words passed.'

Pilar nodded and smiled.

'Yes,' she said. 'It was great fun, Grandfather made them, oh, so angry!'

'Oh, you enjoyed it, did you?'

'Yes. I like to see people get angry. I like it very much. But here in England they do not get angry like they do in Spain. In Spain they take out their knives and they curse and shout. In England they do nothing, just get very red in the face and shut up their mouths tight.'

'Do you remember what was said?'

Pilar seemed rather doubtful.

'I am not sure. Grandfather said they were no good – that they had not got any children. He said I was better than any of them. He liked me, very much.'

'Did he say anything about money or a will?'

'A will – no, I don't think so. I don't remember.'

'What happened?'

'They all went away – except Hilda – the fat one, David's wife, she stayed behind.'

'Oh, she did, did she?'

'Yes. David looked very funny. He was all shaking and, oh, so white. He looked as though he might be sick.'

'And what then?'

'Then I went and found Stephen. We danced to the gramophone.'

'Stephen Farr?'

'Yes. He is from South Africa – he is the son of grandfather's partner. He is very handsome, too. Very brown and big, and he has nice eyes.'

Johnson asked: 'Where were you when the crime occurred?'

'You ask where I was?'

'Yes.'

'I had gone into the drawing-room with Lydia. And then I went up to my room and did my face. I was going to dance again with Stephen. And then, far away, I heard a scream and everyone was running, so I went too. And they were trying to break down grandfather's door. Harry did it with Stephen; they are both big strong men.'

'Yes?'

'And then – crash – down it went – and we all looked in. Oh, such a sight – everything smashed and knocked over, and Grandfather lying in a lot of blood, and his throat was cut like *this*' – she made a vivid dramatic gesture at her own neck – 'right up under his ear.'

She paused, having obviously enjoyed her narrative.

Johnson said: 'The blood didn't make you feel ill?'

She stared.

'No, why should it? There is usually blood when people are killed. There was, oh, so much blood everywhere!'

Poirot said: 'Did anyone say anything?'

Pilar said: 'David said such a funny thing – what was it? Oh, yes. "The mills of God" – that is what he said' – she repeated it with emphasis on each word – "*The mills* – of – God—*"* What does that mean? Mills are what make flour, are they not?'

Colonel Johnson said: 'Well, I don't think there is anything more just now, Miss Estravados.'

Pilar got up obediently. She flashed a quick charming smile at each man in turn.

'I will go now, then.' She went out.

Colonel Johnson said: "*The mills of God grind slowly, but they grind exceeding small.*" And David Lee said that!'

415

XV

As the door opened once more, Colonel Johnson looked up. For a moment he took the entering figure to be that of Harry Lee, but as Stephen Farr advanced into the room he saw his error.

'Sit down, Mr Farr,' he said.

Stephen sat. His eyes – cool intelligent eyes – went from one to the other of the three men. He said: 'I'm afraid I shan't be much use to you. But please ask me anything that you think may help. Perhaps I'd better explain, to start with, who I am. My father, Ebenezer Farr, was Simeon Lee's partner in South Africa in the old days. I'm talking of over forty years ago.'

He paused.

'My dad talked to me a lot about Simeon Lee – what a personality he was. He and Dad cleaned up a good bit together. Simeon Lee went home with a fortune and my father didn't do badly, either. My father always told me that when I came to this country I was to look up Mr Lee. I said once that it was a long time ago and that he'd probably not know who I was, but Dad scoffed at the idea. He said, "When two men have been through what Simeon and I went through, they don't forget." Well, my father died a couple of years ago. This year I came over to England for the first time, and I thought I'd act on Dad's advice and look up Mr Lee.'

With a slight smile he went on: 'I was just a little nervous when I came along here, but I needn't have been. Mr Lee gave me a warm welcome and absolutely insisted that I should stay with the family over Christmas. I was afraid I was butting in, but he wouldn't hear of a refusal.'

He added rather shyly: 'They were all very nice to me – Mr and Mrs Alfred Lee couldn't have been nicer. I'm terribly sorry for them that all this should come upon them.'

'How long have you been here, Mr Farr?'

'Since yesterday.'

'Did you see Mr Lee today at all?'

'Yes. I had a chat with him this morning. He was in good spirits then and anxious to hear about a lot of people and places.'

'That was the last time you saw him?'

'Yes.'

'Did he mention to you that he kept a quantity of uncut diamonds in his safe?'

'No.'

He added before the other could speak; 'Do you mean that this business was murder *and* robbery?'

416

'We're not sure yet,' said Johnson. 'Now to come to the events of this evening, will you tell me, in your own words, what you were doing?'

'Certainly. After the ladies left the dining-room I stayed and had a glass of port. Then I realized that the Lees had family business they wanted to discuss and that my being there was hampering them so I excused myself and left them.'

'And what did you do then?'

Stephen Farr leaned back in his chair. His forefinger caressed his jaw. He said rather woodenly: 'I – er – went along to a big room with a parquet floor – kind of ballroom, I fancy. There's a gramophone there and dance records. I put some records on.'

Poirot said: 'It was possible, perhaps, that someone might join you there?'

A very faint smile curved Stephen Farr's lips. He answered: 'It was possible, yes. One always hopes.'

And he grinned outright.

Poirot said: 'Señorita Estravados is very beautiful.'

Stephen answered: 'She's easily the best thing to look at that I've seen since I came to England.'

'Did Miss Estravados join you?' asked Colonel Johnson.

Stephen shook his head.

'I was still there when I heard the rumpus. I came out into the hall and ran hell for leather to see what was the matter. I helped Harry Lee to break the door down.'

'And that's all you have to tell us?'

'Absolutely all, I'm afraid.'

Hercule Poirot leaned forward. He said softly: 'But I think, Mr Farr, that you could tell us a good deal if you liked.'

Farr said sharply: 'What d'you mean?'

'You can tell us something that is very important in this case – the character of Mr Lee. You say that your father talked much of him to you. What manner of a man was it that he described to you?'

Stephen Farr said slowly: 'I think I see what you're driving at. What was Simeon Lee like in his young days? Well – you want me to be frank, I suppose?'

'If you please.'

'Well, to begin with, I don't think that Simeon Lee was a highly moral member of society. I don't mean that he was exactly a crook, but he sailed pretty near the wind. His morals were nothing to boast about, anyway. He had charm, though, a good deal of it. And he was fantastically generous. No one with a hard-luck story

HERCULE POIROT'S CHRISTMAS

ever appealed to him in vain. He drank a bit, but not over-much, was attractive to women, and had a sense of humour. All the same, he had a queer revengeful streak in him. Talk of the elephant never forgets and you talk of Simeon Lee. My father told me several cases where Lee waited years to get even with someone who'd done him a nasty turn.'

Superintendent Sugden said: 'Two might play at that game. You've no knowledge, I suppose, Mr Farr, of anyone who Simeon Lee had done a bad turn to out there? Nothing out of the past that could explain the crime committed here this evening?'

Stephen Farr shook his head.

'He had enemies, of course, must have had, being the man he was. But I know of no specific case. Besides,' his eyes narrowed, 'I understand (as a matter of fact, I've been questioning Tressilian) there have been no strangers in or near the house this evening.'

Hercule Poirot said: '*With the exception of yourself, Mr Farr.*'

Stephen Farr swung round upon him.

'Oh, so that's it? Suspicious stranger within the gates! Well, you won't find anything of that kind. No back history of Simeon Lee doing Ebenezer Farr down, and Eb's son coming over to revenge his dad! No,' he shook his head, 'Simeon and Ebenezer had nothing against each other. I came here, as I've told you, out of sheer curiosity. And, moreover, I should imagine a gramophone is as good an alibi as anything else. I never stopped putting on records – somebody must have heard them. One record wouldn't give me time to race away upstairs – these passages are a mile long, anyway – slit an old man's throat, wash off the blood, and get back again before the others came rushing up. The idea's farcical!'

Colonel Johnson said: 'We're not making any insinuations against you, Mr Farr.'

Stephen Farr said: 'I didn't care much for the tone of M. Poirot's voice.'

'That,' said Hercule Poirot, 'is unfortunate!'

He smiled benignly at the other.

Stephen Farr looked angrily at him.

Colonel Johnson interposed quickly: 'Thank you, Mr Farr. That will be all for the present. You will not, of course, leave this house.'

Stephen Farr nodded. He got up and left the room, walking with a freely swinging stride.

As the door closed behind him, Johnson said: 'There goes X, the unknown quantity. His story seems straightforward enough.

All the same, he's the dark horse. He *might* have pinched those diamonds – might have come here with a bogus story just to gain admittance. You'd better get his fingerprints, Sugden, and see if he's known.'

'I've already got them,' said the superintendent with a dry smile.

'Good man. You don't overlook much. I suppose you're on to all the obvious lines?'

Superintendent Sugden checked off on his fingers.

'Check up on those telephone calls – times, etc. Check up on Horbury. What time he left, who saw him go. Check up all entrances and exits. Check up on staff generally. Check up financial position of members of family. Get on to the lawyers and check up on will. Search house for the weapon and for bloodstains on clothing – also possibly diamonds hidden somewhere.'

'That covers everything, I think,' said Colonel Johnson approvingly. 'Can you suggest anything, M. Poirot?'

Poirot shook his head. He said: 'I find the superintendent admirably thorough.'

Sugden said gloomily: 'It won't be any joke looking through this house for the missing diamonds. Never saw so many ornaments and knick-knacks in my life.'

'The hiding-places are certainly abundant,' Poirot agreed.

'And there's really nothing you would suggest, Poirot?'

The chief constable looked a little disappointed – rather like a man whose dog has refused to do its trick.

Poirot said: 'You will permit that I take a line of my own?'

'Certainly – certainly,' said Johnson at the same moment as Superintendent Sugden said rather suspiciously: 'What line?'

'I would like,' said Hercule Poirot, 'to converse – very often – very frequently – with members of the family.'

'You mean you'd like to have another shot at questioning them?' asked the colonel, a little puzzled.

'No, no, not to question – to converse!'

'Why?' asked Sugden.

Hercule Poirot waved an emphatic hand.

'In conversation, points arise! If a human being converses much, it is impossible for him to avoid the truth!'

Sugden said: 'Then you think someone is lying?'

Poirot sighed.

'*Mon cher*, everyone lies – in parts like the egg of the English curate. It is profitable to separate the harmless lies from the vital ones.'

Colonel Johnson said sharply: 'All the same, it's incredible, you know. Here's a particularly crude and brutal murder – and whom have we as suspects? Alfred Lee and his wife – both charming, well-bred, quiet people. George Lee, who's a Member of Parliament and the essence of respectability. His wife? She's just an ordinary modern lovely. David Lee seems a gentle creature and we've got his brother Harry's word for it that he can't stand the sight of blood. His wife seems a nice sensible woman – quite commonplace. Remains the Spanish niece and the man from South Africa. Spanish beauties have hot tempers, but I don't see that attractive creature slitting the old man's neck in cold blood, especially as from what has come out she had every reason to keep him alive – at any rate until he had signed a new will. Stephen Farr's a possibility – that is to say, he may be a professional crook and have come here after the diamonds. The old man discovered the loss and Farr slit his throat to keep him quiet. That could have been so – that gramophone alibi isn't too good.'

Poirot shook his head.

'My dear friend,' he said. 'Compare the physique of Mr Stephen Farr and old Simeon Lee. If Farr decided to kill the old man he could have done it in a minute – Simeon Lee couldn't possibly have put up that fight against him. Can one believe that that frail old man and that magnificent specimen of humanity struggled for some minutes overturning chairs and breaking china? To imagine such a thing is fantastic!'

Colonel Johnson's eyes narrowed.

'You mean,' he said, 'that it was a *weak* man who killed Simeon Lee?'

'Or a woman!' said the superintendent.

XVI

Colonel Johnson looked at his watch.

'Nothing much more that I can do here. You've got things well in hand, Sugden. Oh, just one thing. We ought to see the butler fellow. I know you've questioned him, but we know a bit more about things now. It's important to get confirmation of just where everybody says he was at the time of the murder.'

Tressilian came in slowly. The chief constable told him to sit down.

'Thank you, sir. I will, if you don't mind. I've been feeling very queer – very queer indeed. My legs, sir, and my head.'

Poirot said gently: 'You have had the shock, yes.'

The butler shuddered. 'Such – such a violent thing to happen. In this house! Where everything has always gone on so quietly.'

Poirot said: 'It was a well-ordered house, yes? But not a happy one?'

'I wouldn't like to say that, sir.'

'In the old days when all the family was at home, it was happy then?'

Tressilian said slowly: 'It wasn't perhaps what one would call very harmonious, sir.'

'The late Mrs Lee was somewhat of an invalid, was she not?'

'Yes, sir, very poorly she was.'

'Were her children fond of her?'

'Mr David, he was devoted to her. More like a daughter than a son. And after she died he broke away, couldn't face living here any longer.'

Poirot said: 'And Mr Harry? What was he like?'

'Always rather a wild young gentleman, sir, but good-hearted. Oh dear, gave me quite a turn, it did, when the bell rang – and then again, so impatient like – and I opened the door and there was a strange man, and then Mr Harry's voice said, "Hallo, Tressilian. Still here, eh?" Just the same as ever.'

Poirot said sympathetically: 'It must have been the strange feeling, yes, indeed.'

Tressilian said, a little pink flush showing in his cheek: 'It seems sometimes, sir, as though the past isn't the past! I believe there's been a play on in London about something like that. There's something in it, sir – there really is. There's a feeling comes over you – as though you'd done everything before. It just seems to me as though the bell rings and I go to answer it and there's Mr Harry – even if it should be Mr Farr or some other person – I'm just saying to myself – *but I've done this before* . . .'

Poirot said: 'That is very interesting – very interesting.'

Tressilian looked at him gratefully.

Johnson, somewhat impatient, cleared his throat and took charge of the conversation.

'Just want to get various times checked correctly,' he said. 'Now, when the noise upstairs started, I understand that only Mr Alfred Lee and Mr Harry Lee were in the dining-room. Is that so?'

'I really couldn't tell you, sir. All the gentlemen were there when I served coffee to them – but that would be about a quarter of an hour earlier.'

'Mr George Lee was telephoning. Can you confirm that?'

'I think somebody did telephone, sir. The bell rings in my

pantry, and when anybody takes off the receiver to call a number, there's just a faint noise on the bell. I do remember hearing that, but I didn't pay attention to it.'

'You don't know exactly when it was?'

'I couldn't say, sir. It was after I had taken coffee to the gentlemen, that is all I can say.'

'Do you know where any of the ladies were at the time I mentioned?'

'Mrs Alfred was in the drawing-room, sir, when I went for the coffee tray. That was just a minute or two before I heard the cry upstairs.'

Poirot asked: 'What was she doing?'

'She was standing by the far window, sir. She was holding the curtain a little back and looking out.'

'And none of the other ladies was in the room?'

'No, sir.'

'Do you know where they were?'

'I couldn't say at all, sir.'

'You don't know where anyone else was?'

'Mr David, I think, was playing in the music-room next door to the drawing-room.'

'You heard him playing?'

'Yes, sir.' Again the old man shivered. 'It was like a sign, sir, so I felt afterwards. It was the "Dead March" he was playing. Even at the time, I remember, it gave me the creeps.'

'It is curious, yes,' said Poirot.

'Now, about this fellow, Horbury, the valet,' said the chief constable. 'Are you definitely prepared to swear that he was out of the house by eight o'clock?'

'Oh, yes, sir. It was just after Mr Sugden here arrived. I remember particular because he broke a coffee-cup.'

Poirot said: 'Horbury broke a coffee-cup?'

'Yes, sir – one of the old Worcester ones. Eleven years I've washed them up and never one broken till this evening.'

Poirot said: 'What was Horbury doing with the coffee-cups?'

'Well, of course, sir, he'd no business to have been handling them at all. He was just holding one up, admiring it like, and I happened to mention that Mr Sugden had called, and he dropped it.'

Poirot said: 'Did you say "Mr Sugden" or did you mention the word "police"?'

Tressilian looked a little startled.

'Now I come to think of it, sir, I mentioned that the police superintendent had called.'

'And Horbury dropped the coffee-cup,' said Poirot.

'Seems suggestive, that,' said the chief constable. 'Did Horbury ask any questions about the superintendent's visit?'

'Yes, sir, asked what he wanted here. I said he'd come collecting for the police orphanage and had gone up to Mr Lee.'

'Did Horbury seem relieved when you said that?'

'Do you know, sir, now you mention it, he certainly did. His manner changed at once. Said Mr Lee was a good old chap and free with his money – rather disrespectfully he spoke – and then he went off.'

'Which way?'

'Out through the door to the servants' hall.'

Sugden interposed: 'All that's OK, sir. He passed through the kitchen, where the cook and the kitchenmaid saw him, and out through the back door.'

'Now listen, Tressilian, and think carefully. Is there any means by which Horbury could return to the house without anyone seeing him?'

The old man shook his head.

'I don't see how he could have done so, sir. All the doors are locked on the inside.'

'Supposing he had had a key?'

'The doors are bolted as well.'

'How does he get in when he comes?'

'He has a key of the back door, sir. All the servants come in that way.'

'He *could* have returned that way, then?'

'Not without passing through the kitchen, sir. And the kitchen would be occupied till well after half-past nine or a quarter to ten.'

Colonel Johnson said: 'That seems conclusive. Thank you, Tressilian.'

The old man got up and with a bow left the room. He returned, however, a minute or two later.

'Horbury has just returned, sir. Would you like to see him now?'

'Yes, please, send him in at once.'

XVII

Sydney Horbury did not present a very prepossessing appearance. He came into the room and stood rubbing his hands together and darting quick looks from one person to another. His manner was unctuous.

Johnson said: 'You're Sydney Horbury?'

'Yes, sir.'

'Valet-attendant to the late Mr Lee?'

'Yes, sir. It's terrible, isn't it? You could have knocked me down with a feather when I heard from Gladys. Poor old gentleman—'

Johnson cut him short.

'Just answer my questions, please.'

'Yes, sir, certainly, sir.'

'What time did you go out tonight, and where have you been?'

'I left the house just before eight, sir. I went to the Superb, sir, just five minutes' walk away. *Love in Old Seville* was the picture, sir.'

'Anyone who saw you there?'

'The young lady in the box office, sir, she knows me. And the commissionaire at the door, he knows me too. And – er – as a matter of fact, I was with a young lady, sir. I met her there by appointment.'

'Oh, you did, did you? What's her name?'

'Doris Buckle, sir. She works in the Combined Dairies, sir, 23, Markham Road.'

'Good. We'll look into that. Did you come straight home?'

'I saw my young lady home first, sir. Then I came straight back. You'll find it's quite all right, sir. I didn't have anything to do with this. I was—'

Colonel Johnson said curtly: 'Nobody's accusing you of having anything to do with it.'

'No, sir, of course not, sir. But it's not very pleasant when a murder happens in a house.'

'Nobody said it was. Now, then, how long had you been in Mr Lee's service?'

'Just over a year, sir.'

'Did you like your place here?'

'Yes, sir. I was quite satisfied. The pay was good. Mr Lee was rather difficult sometimes, but of course I'm used to attending on invalids.'

'You've had previous experience?'

'Oh, yes, sir. I was with Major West and with the Honourable Jasper Finch—'

'You can give all those particulars to Sugden later. What I want to know is this: At what time did you last see Mr Lee this evening?'

'It was about half-past seven, sir. Mr Lee had a light supper brought to him every evening at seven o'clock. I then prepared him for bed. After that he would sit in front of the fire in his dressing-gown till he felt like going to bed.'

'What time was that usually?'

'It varied, sir. Sometimes he would go to bed as early as eight o'clock – that's if he felt tired. Sometimes he would sit up till eleven or after.'

'What did he do when he did want to go to bed?'

'Usually he rang for me, sir.'

'And you assisted him to bed?'

'Yes, sir.'

'But this was your evening out. Did you always have Fridays?'

'Yes, sir. Friday was my regular day.'

'What happened, then, when Mr Lee wanted to go to bed?'

'He would ring his bell and either Tressilian or Walter would see to him.'

'He was not helpless? He could move about?'

'Yes, sir, but not very easily. Rheumatoid arthritis was what he suffered from, sir. He was worse some days than others.'

'Did he never go into another room in the daytime?'

'No, sir. He preferred to be in just the one room. Mr Lee wasn't luxurious in his tastes. It was a big room with plenty of air and light in it.'

'Mr Lee had his supper at seven, you say?'

'Yes, sir. I took the tray away and put out the sherry and two glasses on the bureau.'

'Why did you do that?'

'Mr Lee's orders.'

'Was that usual?'

'Sometimes. It was the rule that none of the family came to see Mr Lee in the evening unless he invited them. Some evenings he liked to be alone. Other evenings he'd send down and ask Mr Alfred, or Mrs Alfred, or both of them, to come up after dinner.'

'But, as far as you know, he had not done so on this occasion? That is, he had not sent a message to any member of the family requesting their presence?'

'He hadn't sent any message by *me*, sir.'

'So that he wasn't expecting any of the family?'

'He might have asked one of them personally, sir.'

'Of course.'

Horbury continued: 'I saw that everything was in order, wished Mr Lee goodnight and left the room.'

Poirot asked: 'Did you make up the fire before you left the room?'

The valet hesitated.

'It wasn't necessary, sir. It was well built up.'

'Could Mr Lee have done that himself?'

'Oh, no, sir. I expect Mr Harry Lee had done it.'

'Mr Harry Lee was with him when you came in before supper?'

'Yes, sir. He went away when I came.'

'What was the relationship between the two as far as you could judge?'

'Mr Harry Lee seemed in very good spirits, sir. Throwing back his head and laughing a good deal.'

'And Mr Lee?'

'He was quiet and rather thoughtful.'

'I see. Now, there's something more I want to know, Horbury: What can you tell us about the diamonds Mr Lee kept in his safe?'

'Diamonds, sir? I never saw any diamonds.'

'Mr Lee kept a quantity of uncut stones there. You must have seen him handling them.'

'Those funny little pebbles, sir? Yes, I did see him with them once or twice. But I didn't know they were dismonds. He was showing them to the foreign young lady only yesterday – or was it the day before?'

Colonel Johnson said abruptly: 'These stones have been stolen.'

Horbury cried out: 'I hope you don't think, sir, that *I* had anything to do with it!'

'I'm not making any accusations,' said Johnson. 'Now, then, is there anything you can tell us that has any bearing on this matter?'

'The diamonds, sir? Or the murder?'

'Both.'

Horbury considered. He passed his tongue over his pale lips. At last he looked up with eyes that were a shade furtive.

'I don't think there's anything, sir.'

Poirot said softly: 'Nothing you've overheard, say, in the course of your duties, which might be helpful?'

The valet's eyelids flickered a little.

'No, sir, I don't think so, sir. There was a little awkwardness between Mr Lee and – and some members of his family.'

'Which members?'

'I gathered there was a little trouble over Mr Harry Lee's return. Mr Alfred Lee resented it. I understand he and his father had a few words about it – but that was all there was to it. Mr Lee didn't accuse him for a minute of having taken any diamonds. And I'm sure Mr Alfred wouldn't do such a thing.'

Poirot said quickly: 'His interview with Mr Alfred was *after* he had discovered the loss of the diamonds, was it not, though?'

'Yes, sir.'

Poirot leaned forward.

'I thought, Horbury,' he said softly, *'that you did not know of the theft of the diamonds until we informed you of it just now.* How, then, do you know that Mr Lee had discovered his loss *before* he had this conversation with his son?'

Horbury turned brick red.

'No use lying. Out with it,' said Sugden. 'When did you know?'

Horbury said sullenly: 'I heard him telephoning to someone about it.'

'You weren't in the room?'

'No, outside the door. Couldn't hear much – only a word or two.'

'What did you hear exactly?' asked Poirot sweetly.

'I heard the words "robbery" and "diamonds", and I heard him say, "I don't know who to suspect" – and I heard him say something about this evening at eight o'clock.'

Superintendent Sugden nodded.

'That was to me he was speaking, my lad. About five-ten, was it?'

'That's right, sir.'

'And when you went into his room afterwards, did he look upset?'

'Just a bit, sir. Seemed absent-minded and worried.'

'So much so that you got the wind up – eh?'

'Look here, Mr Sugden, I won't have you saying things like that. Never touched any diamonds, I didn't, and you can't prove I did. I'm not a thief.'

Superintendent Sugden, unimpressed, said: 'That remains to be seen.' He glanced questioningly at the chief constable, received a nod, and went on: 'That'll do for you, my lad. Shan't want you again tonight.'

Horbury went out gratefully in haste.

Sugden said appreciatively: 'Pretty bit of work, M. Poirot. You trapped him as neatly as I've ever seen it done. He may be the thief or he may not, but he's certainly a first-class liar!'

'An unprepossessing person,' said Poirot.

'Nasty bit of goods,' agreed Johnson. 'Question is, what do we think of his evidence?'

Sugden summarized the position neatly.

'Seems to me there are three possibilities: (1) Horbury's a thief *and* a murderer. (2) Horbury's a thief, but *not* a murderer. (3) Horbury's an innocent man. Certain amount of evidence for (1). He overheard telephone call and knew the theft had been discovered. Gathered from old man's manner that he was suspected. Made his plans accordingly. Went out ostentatiously at eight o'clock and cooked up an alibi. Easy enough to slip out of a cinema and return there unnoticed. He'd have to be pretty sure of the girl, though, that she wouldn't give him away. I'll see what I can get out of her tomorrow.'

'How, then, did he manage to re-enter the house?' asked Poirot.

'That's more difficult,' Sugden admitted. 'But there might be ways. Say one of the women servants unlocked a side door for him.'

Poirot raised his eyebrows quizzically.

'He places, then, his life at the mercy of two women? With *one* woman it would be taking a big risk; with *two – eh bien*, I find the risk fantastic!'

Sugden said: 'Some criminals think they can get away with anything!'

He went on: 'Let's take (2). Horbury pinched those diamonds. He took 'em out of the house tonight and has possibly passed them on to some accomplice. That's quite easy going and highly probable. Now we've got to admit that somebody else chose this night to murder Mr Lee. That somebody being quite unaware of the diamond complication. It's possible, of course, but it's a bit of a coincidence.

'Possibility (3) – Horbury's innocent. Somebody else both took the diamonds and murdered the old gentleman. There it is; it's up to us to get at the truth.'

Colonel Johnson yawned. He looked again at his watch and got up.

'Well,' he said, 'I think we'll call it a night, eh? Better just have a look in the safe before we go. Odd thing if those wretched diamonds were there all the time.'

But the diamonds were not in the safe. They found the combination where Alfred Lee had told them, in the small note-book taken from the dressing-gown pocket of the dead man. In the safe they found an empty chamois leather bag. Among the papers the safe contained only one was of interest.

It was a will dated some fifteen years previously. After various legacies and bequests, the provisions were simple enough. Half Simeon Lee's fortune went to Alfred Lee. The other half was to be divided in equal shares between his remaining children: Harry, George, David and Jennifer.

— 4 —

DECEMBER 25TH

In the bright sun of Christmas noon, Poirot walked in the gardens of Gorston Hall. The Hall itself was a large solidly built house with no special architectural pretensions.

Here, on the south side, was a broad terrace flanked with a hedge of clipped yew. Little plants grew in the interstices of the stone flags and at intervals along the terrace there were stone sinks arranged as miniature gardens.

Poirot surveyed them with benign approval. He murmured to himself: *'C'est bien imaginé, ça!'*

In the distance he caught sight of two figures going towards an ornamental sheet of water some three hundred yards away. Pilar was easily recognizable as one of the figures, and he thought at first the other was Stephen Farr, then he saw that the man with Pilar was Harry Lee. Harry seemed very attentive to his attractive niece. At intervals he flung his head back and laughed, then bent once more attentively towards her.

'Assuredly, there is one who does not mourn,' Poirot murmured to himself.

A soft sound behind him made him turn. Magdalene Lee was standing there. She, too, was looking at the retreating figures of the man and girl. She turned her head and smiled enchantingly at Poirot. She said: 'It's such a glorious sunny day! One can hardly believe in all the horrors of last night, can one, M. Poirot?'

'It is difficult, truly, Madame.'

Magdalene sighed.

'I've never been mixed up in tragedy before. I've – I've really only just grown up. I stayed a child too long, I think . . . That's not a good thing to do.'

Again she sighed. She said: 'Pilar, now, seems so extraordinarily self-possessed . . . I suppose it's the Spanish blood. It's all very odd, isn't it?'

'What is odd, Madame?'

'The way she turned up here, out of the blue!'

Poirot said: 'I have learned that Mr Lee had been searching for her for some time. He had been in correspondence with the consulate in Madrid and with the vice-consul at Aliquara, where her mother died.'

'He was very secretive about it all,' said Magdalene. 'Alfred knew nothing about it. No more did Lydia.'

'Ah!' said Poirot.

Magdalene came a little nearer to him. He could smell the delicate perfume she used.

'You know, M. Poirot, there's some story connected with Jennifer's husband, Estravados. He died quite soon after the marriage, and there's some mystery about it. Alfred and Lydia know. I believe it was something – rather disgraceful . . .'

'That,' said Poirot, 'is indeed sad.'

Magdalene said: 'My husband feels – and I agree with him – that the family ought to have been told more about the girl's antecedents. After all, if her father was a *criminal*—'

She paused, but Hercule Poirot said nothing. He seemed to be admiring such beauties of nature as could be seen in the winter season in the grounds of Gorston Hall.

Magdalene said: 'I can't help feeling that the manner of my father-in-law's death was somehow *significant*. It – it was so very *un-English*.'

Hercule Poirot turned slowly. His grave eyes met hers in innocent inquiry.

'Ah,' he said. 'The Spanish touch, you think?'

'Well, they *are* cruel, aren't they?' Magdalene spoke with an effect of childish appeal. 'All those bull-fights and things!'

Hercule Poirot said pleasantly: 'You are saying that in your opinion Señorita Estravados cut her grandfather's throat?'

'Oh, no, M. Poirot!' Magdalene was vehement. She was shocked. 'I never said anything of the kind! Indeed I didn't!'

'Well,' said Poirot. 'Perhaps you did not.'

'But I *do* think that she is – well, a suspicious person. The furtive way she picked up something from the floor of that room last night, for instance.'

A different note crept into Hercule Poirot's voice. He said sharply: 'She picked up something from the floor last night?'

Magdalene nodded. Her childish mouth curved spitefully.

'Yes, as soon as we got into the room. She gave a quick glance round to see if anyone was looking, and then pounced on it. But the superintendent man saw her, I'm glad to say, and made her give it up.'

'What was it that she picked up, do you know, Madame?'

'No. I wasn't near enough to see.' Magdalene's voice held regret. 'It was something quite small.'

Poirot frowned to himself.

'It is interesting, that,' he murmured to himself.

Magdalene said quickly: 'Yes, I thought you ought to know about it. After all, we don't know *anything* about Pilar's upbringing and what her life has been like. Alfred is always so unsuspicious and dear Lydia is so casual.' Then she murmured: 'Perhaps I'd better go and see if I can help Lydia in any way. There may be letters to write.'

She left him with a smile of satisfied malice on her lips.

Poirot remained lost in thought on the terrace.

II

To him there came Superintendent Sugden. The police super-intendent looked gloomy. He said: 'Good morning, M. Poirot. Doesn't seem quite the right thing to say Merry Christmas, does it?'

'*Mon cher collègue*, I certainly do not observe any traces of merriment on your countenance. If you had said "Merry Christmas" I should not have replied "Many of them!"'

'I don't want another one like this one, and that's a fact,' said Sugden.

'You have made the progress, yes?'

'I've checked up on a good many points. Horbury's alibi is holding water all right. The commissionaire at the cinema saw him go in with the girl, and saw him come out with her at the end of the performance, and seems pretty positive he didn't leave, and couldn't have left and returned during the performance. The girl swears quite definitely he was with her in the cinema all the time.'

Poirot's eyebrows rose.

'I hardly see, then, what more there is to say.'

431

The cynical Sugden said: 'Well, one never knows with girls! Lie themselves black in the face for the sake of a man.'

'That does credit to their hearts,' said Hercule Poirot.

Sugden growled.

'That's a foreign way of looking at it. It's defeating the ends of justice.'

Hercule Poirot said: 'Justice is a very strange thing. Have you ever reflected on it?'

Sugden stared at him. He said: 'You're a queer one, M. Poirot.'

'Not at all. I know a logical train of thought. But we will not enter into a dispute on the question. It is your belief, then, that this *demoiselle* from the milk shop is not speaking the truth?'

Sugden shook his head.

'No,' he said, 'it's not like that at all. As a matter of fact, I think she *is* telling the truth. She's a simple kind of girl, and I think if she was telling me a pack of lies I'd spot it.'

Poirot said: 'You have the experience, yes?'

'That's just it, M. Poirot. One does know, more or less, after a lifetime of taking down statements, when a person's lying and when they're not. No, I think the girl's evidence is genuine and, if so, Horbury *couldn't* have murdered old Mr Lee, and that brings us right back to the people in the house.'

He drew a deep breath.

'One of 'em did it, M. Poirot. One of 'em did it. But *which*?'

'You have no new idea?'

'Yes, I've had a certain amount of luck over the telephone calls. Mr George Lee put through a call to Westeringham at two minutes to nine. That call lasted under six minutes.'

'Aha!'

'As you say! Moreover, *no other call* was put through – to Westeringham or anywhere else.'

'Very interesting,' said Poirot, with approval. 'Mr George Lee says he has just finished telephoning when he hears the noise overhead – but actually he had finished telephoning nearly *ten minutes before that*. Where was he in those ten minutes? Mrs George Lee says that *she* was telephoning – but actually she never put through a call at all. Where was *she*?'

Sugden said: 'I saw you talking to her, M. Poirot?'

His voice held a question, but Poirot replied: 'You are in error!'

'Eh?'

'*I* was not talking to her – *she* was talking to *me*!'

'Oh—' Sugden seemed to be about to brush the distinction aside impatiently; then, as its significance sank in, he said: 'She was talking to *you*, you say?'

432

'Most definitely. She came out here for that purpose.'

'What did she have to say?'

'She wished to stress certain points: the un-English character of the crime – the possibly undesirable antecedents of Miss Estravados on the paternal side – the fact that Miss Estravados had furtively picked up something from the floor last night.'

'She told you that, did she?' said Sugden with interest.

'Yes. What was it that the señorita picked up?'

Sugden sighed.

'I could give you three hundred guesses! I'll show it to you. It's the sort of thing that solves the whole mystery in detective stories! If you can make anything out of it, I'll retire from the police force!'

'Show it me.'

Sugden took an envelope from his pocket and tilted its contents on to the palm of his hand. A faint grin showed on his face.

'There you are. What do you make of it?'

On the superintendent's broad palm lay a little triangular piece of pink rubber and a small wooden peg.

His grin broadened as Poirot picked up the articles and frowned over them.

'Make anything of them, M. Poirot?'

'This little piece of stuff might have been cut from a sponge-bag.'

'It was. It comes from a sponge-bag in Mr Lee's room. Somebody with sharp scissors just cut a small triangular piece out of it. Mr Lee may have done it himself, for all I know. But it beats me *why* he should do it. Horbury can't throw any light on the matter. As for the peg, it's about the size of a cribbage peg, but they're usually made of ivory. This is just rough wood – whittled out of a bit of deal, I should say.'

'Most remarkable,' murmured Poirot.

'Keep 'em if you like,' said Sugden kindly. '*I* don't want them.'

'*Mon ami*, I would not deprive you of them!'

'They don't mean anything at all to you?'

'I must confess – nothing whatever!'

'Splendid!' said Sugden with heavy sarcasm, returning them to his pocket. 'We *are* getting on!'

Poirot said: 'Mrs George Lee, she recounts that the young lady stopped and picked these *bagatelles* up in a furtive manner. Should you say that that was true?'

Sugden considered the point.

'N-o,' he said hesitatingly. 'I shouldn't quite go as far as that. She didn't look guilty – nothing of that kind – but she did set about it rather – well, quickly and quietly – if you know what I mean.

And she didn't know I'd seen her do it! That I'm sure of. She jumped when I rounded on her.'

Poirot said thoughtfully: 'Then there *was* a reason? But what conceivable reason could there have been? That little piece of rubber is quite fresh. It has not been used for anything. It can have no meaning whatsoever; and yet—'

Sugden said impatiently: 'Well, you can worry about it if you like, M. Poirot. I've got other things to think about.'

Poirot asked: 'The case stands – where, in your opinion?'

Sugden took out his note-book.

'Let's get down to *facts*. To begin with, there are the people who *couldn't* have done it. Let's get them out of the way first—'

'They are—?'

'Alfred and Harry Lee. They've got a definite alibi. Also Mrs Alfred Lee, since Tressilian saw her in the drawing-room only about a minute before the row started upstairs. Those three are clear. Now for the others. Here's a list. I've put it this way for clearness.'

He handed the book to Poirot.

At the time of the crime

George Lee	*was ?*
Mrs George Lee	*was ?*
David Lee	*was playing piano in music-room (confirmed by his wife)*
Mrs David Lee	*was in music-room (confirmed by husband)*
Miss Estravados	*was in her bedroom (no confirmation)*
Stephen Farr	*was in ballroom playing gramophone (confirmed by three of staff who could hear the music in servants' hall).*

Poirot said, handing back the list: 'And therefore?'

'And therefore,' said Sugden, 'George Lee could have killed the old man. Mrs George Lee could have killed him. Pilar Estravados could have killed him; and *either Mr or Mrs David Lee could have killed him,* but not *both*.'

'You do not, then, accept that alibi?'

Superintendent Sugden shook his head emphatically.

'Not on your life! Husband and wife – devoted to each other! They may be in it together or, if one of them did it, the other is ready to swear to an alibi. I look at it this way: *Someone* was in the music-room playing the piano. It *may* have been David Lee. It probably *was*, since he was an acknowledged musician, but there's nothing to say his wife was there too *except her word and his*. In the same way, it *may* have been Hilda who was playing that piano while David Lee crept upstairs and killed his father! No, it's an absolutely different case from the two brothers in the dining-room. Alfred Lee and Harry Lee don't love each other. Neither of them would perjure himself for the other's sake.'

'What about Stephen Farr?'

'He's a possible suspect because that gramophone alibi is a bit thin. On the other hand, it's the sort of alibi that's really sounder than a good cast-iron dyed-in-the-wool alibi which, ten to one, has been faked up beforehand!'

Poirot bowed his head thoughtfully.

'I know what you mean. It is the alibi of a man *who did not know that he would be called upon to provide such a thing.*'

'Exactly! And anyway, somehow, I don't believe a stranger was mixed up in this thing.'

Poirot said quickly: 'I agree with you. It is here a *family* affair. It is a poison that works in the blood – it is intimate – it is deep-seated. There is here, I think, *hate* and *knowledge* . . .'

He waved his hands.

'I do not know – it is difficult!'

Superintendent Sugden had waited respectfully, but without being much impressed. He said: 'Quite so, M. Poirot. But we'll get at it, never fear, with elimination and logic. We've got the *possibilities* now – the people with *opportunity*.

'George Lee, Magdalene Lee, David Lee, Hilda Lee, Pilar Estravados, and I'll add Stephen Farr. Now we come to *motive*. Who had a *motive* for putting old Mr Lee out of the way? There again we can wash out certain people. Miss Estravados, for one. I gather that as the will stands now, she doesn't get anything at all. If Simeon Lee had died before her mother, her mother's share would have come down to her (unless her mother willed it other-wise), but as Jennifer Estravados predeceased Simeon Lee, that particular legacy reverts to the other members of the family. So it was definitely to Miss Estravados' interests to keep the old man alive. He'd taken a fancy to her; it's pretty certain he'd have left her a good slice of money when he made a new will. She had everything to lose and nothing to gain by his murder. You agree to that?'

'Perfectly.'

'There remains, of course, the possibility that she cut his throat in the heat of a quarrel, but that seems extremely unlikely to me.

To begin with, they were on the best of terms, and she hadn't been here long enough to bear him a grudge about anything. It therefore seems highly unlikely that Miss Estravados has anything to do with the crime – except that you might argue that to cut a man's throat is an un-English sort of thing to do, as your friend Mrs George puts it.'

'Do not call her *my* friend,' said Poirot hastily. 'Or I shall speak of *your* friend Miss Estravados, who finds you such a handsome man!'

He had the pleasure of seeing the superintendent's official poise upset again. The police officer turned crimson. Poirot looked at him with malicious amusement.

He said, and there was a wistful note in his voice: 'It is true that your moustache is superb . . . Tell me, do you use for it a special *pomade?*'

'*Pomade?* Good Lord, no!'

'What do you use?'

'Use? Nothing at all. It – it just *grows.*'

Poirot sighed.

'You are favoured by nature.' He caressed his own luxuriant black moustache, then sighed. 'However expensive the preparation,' he murmured, 'to restore the natural colour does somewhat impoverish the quality of the hair.'

Superintendent Sugden, uninterested in hairdressing problems, was continuing in a stolid manner: 'Considering the *motive* for the crime, I should say that we can probably wash out Mr Stephen Farr. It's just possible that there was some hanky-panky between his father and Mr Lee and the former suffered, but I doubt it. Farr's manner was too easy and assured when he mentioned that subject. He was quite confident – and I don't think he was acting. No, I don't think we'll find anything there.'

'I do not think you will,' said Poirot.

'And there's one other person with a motive for keeping old Mr Lee alive – his son Harry. It's true that he benefits under the will, but I don't believe *he was aware of the fact.* Certainly couldn't have been *sure* of it! The general impression seemed to be that Harry had been definitely cut out of his share of the inheritance at the time he cut loose. But now he was on the point of coming back into favour! It was all to his advantage that his father should make a new will. He wouldn't be such a fool as to kill him now. Actually, as we know, he *couldn't* have done it. You see, we're getting on; we're clearing quite a lot of people out of the way.'

'How true. Very soon there will be nobody left!'

Sugden grinned.

'We're not going as fast as that! We've got George Lee and his wife, and David Lee and Mrs David. They all benefit by the death, and George Lee, from all I can make out, is grasping about money. Moreover, his father was threatening to cut down supplies. So we've got George Lee with motive *and* opportunity!'

'Continue,' said Poirot.

'And we've got Mrs George! As fond of money as a cat is fond of cream; and I'd be prepared to bet she's heavily in debt at the minute! She was jealous of the Spanish girl. She was quick to spot that the other was gaining an ascendancy over the old man. She'd heard him say that he was sending for the lawyer. So she struck quickly. You could make out a case.'

'Possibly.'

'Then there's David Lee and his wife. They inherit under the present will, but I don't believe, somehow, that the money motive would be particularly strong in their case.'

'No?'

'No, David Lee seems to be a bit of a dreamer – not a mercenary type. But he's – well, he's *odd*. As I see it, there are three possible motives for this murder: There's the diamond complication, there's the will, and there's – well – just plain *hate*.'

'Ah, you see that, do you?'

Sugden said: 'Naturally. It's been present in my mind all along. *If* David Lee killed his father, I don't think it was for money. And if he was the criminal it might explain the – well, the blood-letting!'

Poirot looked at him appreciatively.

'Yes, I wondered when you would take that into consideration. *So much blood* – that is what Mrs Alfred said. It takes one back to ancient rituals – to blood sacrifice, to the anointing with the blood of the sacrifice . . .'

Sugden said, frowning: 'You mean whoever did it was mad?'

'*Mon cher* – there are all sorts of deep instincts in man of which he himself is unaware. The craving for blood – the demand for sacrifice!'

Sugden said doubtfully: 'David Lee looks a quiet, harmless fellow.'

Poirot said: 'You do not understand the psychology. David Lee is a man who lives in the past – a man in whom the memory of his mother is still very much alive. He kept away from his father for many years because he could not forgive his father's treatment of his mother. He came here, let us suppose, to forgive. *But he may not*

437

have been able to forgive . . . We do know one thing – that when David Lee stood by his father's dead body, some part of him was appeased and satisfied. *"The mills of God grind slowly, yet they grind exceeding small."* Retribution! Payment! The wrong wiped out by expiation!'

Sugden gave a sudden shudder. He said: 'Don't talk like that, M. Poirot. You give me quite a turn. It may be that it's as you say. If so, Mrs David knows – and means to shield him all she knows how. I can imagine her doing that. On the other hand, I can't imagine her being a murderess. She's such a comfortable common-place sort of woman.'

Poirot looked at him curiously,

'So she strikes you like that?' he murmured.

'Well, yes – a homely body, if you know what I mean!'

'Oh, I know what you mean perfectly!'

Sugden looked at him.

'Come, now, M. Poirot, you've got ideas about the case. Let's have them.'

Poirot said slowly: 'I have ideas, yes, but they are rather nebulous. Let me first hear your summing-up of the case.'

'Well, it's as I said – three possible motives: hate, gain, and this diamond complication. Take the facts chronologically.

'3.30. Family gathering. Telephone conversation to lawyer overheard by all the family. Then the old man lets loose on his family, tells them where they all get off. They slink out like a lot of scared rabbits.'

'Hilda Lee remained behind,' said Poirot.

'So she did. But not for long. Then about six Alfred has an interview with his father – unpleasant interview. Harry is to be reinstated. Alfred isn't pleased. Alfred, of course, *ought* to be our principal suspect. He had by far the strongest motive. However, to get on, Harry comes along next. Is in boisterous spirits. Has got the old man just where he wants him. But *before* those two interviews Simeon Lee has discovered the loss of the diamonds and has telephoned to me. He doesn't mention his loss to either of his two sons. Why? In my opinion because he was quite sure neither of them had anything to do with it. Neither of them were under suspicion. I believe, as I've said all along, that the old man suspected Horbury and *one other person*. And I'm pretty sure of what he meant to do. Remember, he said definitely he didn't want anyone to come and sit with him that evening. Why? Because he was preparing the way for two things: First, my visit, and, second, *the visit of that other suspected person.* He did ask *someone* to come and see him immediately after dinner. Now who was that person likely to be? Might have been George Lee. Much more likely to have been his wife. And there's another person who comes back into the picture here – Pilar Estravados. He's shown her the diamonds. He'd told her their value. How do we know that girl isn't a thief? Remember these mysterious hints about the disgraceful behaviour of her father. Perhaps *he* was a professional thief and finally went to prison for it.'

Poirot said slowly: 'And so, as you say, Pilar Estravados comes back into the picture . . .'

'Yes – as a *thief.* No other way. She *may* have lost her head when she was found out. She *may* have flown at her grandfather and attacked him.'

Poirot said slowly: 'It is possible – yes . . .'

Superintendent Sugden looked at him keenly.

'But that's not *your* idea? Come, M. Poirot, what *is* your idea?'

Poirot said: 'I go back always to the same thing: *the character of the dead man.* What manner of a man was Simeon Lee?'

'There isn't much mystery about that,' said Sugden, staring.

'Tell me, then. That is to say, tell me from the local point of view what was known of the man.'

Superintendent Sugden drew a doubtful finger along his jawbone. He looked perplexed. He said: 'I'm not a local man myself. I come from Reeveshire, over the border – next county. But of course old Mr Lee was a well-known figure in these parts. I know all about him by hearsay.'

'Yes? And that hearsay was – what?'

Sugden said: 'Well, he was a sharp customer; there weren't many who could get the better of him. But he was generous with his money. Open-handed as they make 'em. Beats me how Mr George Lee can be the exact opposite, and he his father's son.'

'Ah! But there are two distinct strains in the family. Alfred, George, and David resemble – superficially at least – their mother's side of the family. I have been looking at some portraits in the gallery this morning.'

'He was hot-tempered,' continued Superintendent Sugden, 'and of course he had a bad reputation with women – that was in his younger days. He's been an invalid for many years now. But even there he always behaved generously. If there was trouble, he always paid up handsomely and got the girl married off as often as not. He may have been a bad lot, but he wasn't mean. He treated his wife badly, ran after other women, and neglected her. She died of a broken heart, so they say. It's a convenient term, but I believe she was really very unhappy, poor lady. She was always sickly and never went about much. There's no doubt that Mr Lee was an odd character. Had a revengeful streak in him, too. If anyone did him a nasty turn he always paid it back, so they say, and didn't mind how long he had to wait to do it.'

'"The mills of God grind slowly, yet they grind exceeding small,"' murmured Poirot.

Superintendent Sugden said heavily: 'Mills of the devil, more likely! Nothing saintly about Simeon Lee. The kind of man you might say had sold his soul to the devil and enjoyed the bargain! And he was proud, too, proud as Lucifer.'

'Proud as Lucifer!' said Poirot. 'It is suggestive, what you say there.'

Superintendent Sugden said, looking puzzled: 'You don't mean that he was murdered because he was proud?'

'I mean,' said Poirot, 'that there is such a thing as inheritance. Simeon Lee transmitted that pride to his sons—'

He broke off. Hilda Lee had come out of the house and was standing looking along the terrace.

III

'I wanted to find you, M. Poirot.'

Superintendent Sugden had excused himself and gone back into the house. Looking after him, Hilda said: 'I didn't know he was with you. I thought he was with Pilar. He seems a nice man, quite considerate.'

Her voice was pleasant, a low, soothing cadence to it.

Poirot asked: 'You wanted to see me, you say?'

She inclined her head.

'Yes, I think you can help me.'

'I shall be delighted to do so, Madame.'

She said: 'You are a very intelligent man, M. Poirot. I saw that last night. There are things which you will, I think, find out quite easily. I want you to understand my husband.'

'Yes, Madame?'

'I shouldn't talk like this to Superintendent Sugden. He wouldn't understand. But you will.'

Poirot bowed. 'You honour me, Madame.'

Hilda went calmly on: 'My husband, for many years, ever since I married him, has been what I can describe as a mental cripple.'

'Ah!'

'When one suffers some great hurt physically, it causes shock and pain, but slowly it mends, the flesh heals, the bone knits. There may be, perhaps, a little weakness, a slight scar, but nothing more. My husband, M. Poirot, suffered a great hurt *mentally* at his most susceptible age. He adored his mother and he saw her die. He believed that his father was morally responsible for that death. From that shock he has never quite recovered. His resentment against his father never died down. It was I who persuaded David to come here this Christmas to be reconciled to his father. I wanted it – for *his* sake – I wanted that mental wound to heal. I realize now that coming here was a mistake. Simeon Lee amused himself by probing into that old wound. It was – a very dangerous thing to do . . .'

Poirot said: 'Are you telling me, Madame, that your husband killed his father?'

'I am telling you, M. Poirot, that he easily *might* have done so . . . And I will also tell you this – that he did *not*! When Simeon Lee was killed, his son was playing the "Dead March". The wish to kill was in his heart. It passed out through his fingers and died in waves of sound – that is the truth.'

Poirot was silent for a minute or two, then he said: 'And you, Madame, what is your verdict on that past drama?'

'You mean the death of Simeon Lee's wife?'

'Yes.'

Hilda said slowly: 'I know enough of life to know that you can never judge any case on its outside merits. To all seeming, Simeon Lee was entirely to blame and his wife was abominably treated. At the same time, I honestly believe that there is a kind of meekness, a predisposition to martyrdom which does arouse the worst instincts in men of a certain type. Simeon Lee would have admired, I think, spirit and force of character. He was merely irritated by patience and tears.'

Poirot nodded. He said: 'Your husband said last night: "My mother never complained." Is that true?'

Hilda Lee said impatiently: 'Of course it isn't! She complained the whole time to David! She laid the whole burden of her unhappiness on his shoulders. He was too young – far too young to bear all she gave him to bear!'

Poirot looked thoughtfully at her. She flushed under his gaze and bit her lip.

He said: 'I see.'

She said sharply: 'What do you see?'

441

He answered: 'I see that you have had to be a mother to your husband when you would have preferred to be a wife.'

She turned away.

At that moment David Lee came out of the house and along the terrace towards them. He said, and his voice had a clear joyful note in it: 'Hilda, isn't it a glorious day? Almost like spring instead of winter.'

He came nearer. His head was thrown back, a lock of fair hair fell across his forehead, his blue eyes shone. He looked amazingly young and boyish. There was about him a youthful eagerness, a carefree radiance. Hercule Poirot caught his breath . . .

David said: 'Let's go down to the lake, Hilda.'

She smiled, put her arm through his, and they moved off together.

As Poirot watched them go, he saw her turn and give him a rapid glance. He caught a momentary glimpse of swift anxiety – or was it, he wondered, fear?

Slowly Hercule Poirot walked to the other end of the terrace. He murmured to himself: 'As I have always said, me, I am the father confessor! And, since women come to confession more frequently than men, it is women who have come to me this morning. Will there, I wonder, be another very shortly?'

As he turned at the end of the terrace and paced back again, he knew that his question was answered. Lydia Lee was coming towards him.

IV

Lydia said: 'Good morning, M. Poirot. Tressilian told me I should find you out here with Harry; but I am glad to find you alone. My husband has been speaking about you. I know he is very anxious to talk to you.'

'Ah! Yes? Shall I go and see him now?'

'Not just yet. He got hardly any sleep last night. In the end I gave him a strong sleeping draught. He is still asleep, and I don't want to disturb him.'

'I quite understand. That was very wise. I could see last night that the shock had been very great.'

She said seriously: 'You see, M. Poirot, he really *cared* – much more than the others.'

'I understand.'

She asked: 'Have you – has the superintendent – any idea of who can have done this awful thing?'

Poirot said deliberately: 'We have certain ideas, Madame, as to who did *not* do it.'

Lydia said, almost impatiently: 'It's like a nightmare – so fantastic – I can't believe it's *real*!'

She added: 'What about Horbury? Was he really at the cinema, as he said?'

'Yes, Madame, his story has been checked. He was speaking the truth.'

Lydia stopped and plucked at a bit of yew. Her face went a little paler. She said: 'But that's *awful*! It only leaves – the family!'

'Exactly.'

'M. Poirot, I *can't* believe it!'

'Madame, you *can* and you *do* believe it!'

She seemed about to protest. Then suddenly she smiled ruefully.

She said: 'What a hypocrite one is!'

He nodded.

'If you were to be frank with me, Madame,' he said, 'you would admit that to you it seems quite natural that one of his family should murder your father-in-law.'

Lydia said sharply: 'That's really a fantastic thing to say, M. Poirot!'

'Yes, it is. But your father-in-law was a fantastic person!'

Lydia said: 'Poor old man. I can feel sorry for him now. When he was alive, he just annoyed me unspeakably!'

Poirot said: 'So I should imagine!'

He bent over one of the stone sinks.

'They are very ingenious, these. Very pleasing.'

'I'm glad you like them. It's one of my hobbies. Do you like this Arctic one with the penguins and the ice?'

'Charming. And this – what is this?'

'Oh, that's the Dead Sea – or going to be. It isn't finished yet. You mustn't look at it. Now this one is supposed to be Piana in Corsica. The rocks there, you know, are quite pink and too lovely where they go down into the blue sea. This desert scene is rather fun, don't you think?'

She led him along. When they had reached the farther end she glanced at her wrist-watch.

'I must go and see if Alfred is awake.'

When she had gone Poirot went slowly back again to the garden representing the Dead Sea. He looked at it with a good deal of interest. Then he scooped up a few of the pebbles and let them run through his fingers.

Suddenly his face changed. He held up the pebbles close to his face.

'Sapristi!' he said. 'This is a surprise! Now what exactly does this mean?'

— 5 —

DECEMBER 26TH

THE chief constable and Superintendent Sugden stared at Poirot incredulously. The latter returned a stream of small pebbles carefully into a small cardboard box and pushed it across to the chief constable.

'Oh, yes,' he said. 'It is the diamonds all right.'

'And you found them where, did you say? In the garden?'

'In one of the small gardens constructed by Mrs Alfred Lee.'

'Mrs Alfred?' Sugden shook his head. 'Doesn't seem likely.'

Poirot said: 'You mean, I suppose, that you do not consider it likely that Mrs Alfred cut her father-in-law's throat?'

Sugden said quickly: 'We know she didn't do that. I meant it seemed unlikely that she pinched these diamonds.'

Poirot said: 'One would not easily believe her a thief – no.'

Sugden said: 'Anybody could have hidden them there.'

'That is true. It was convenient that in that particular garden – the Dead Sea as it represents – there happened to be pebbles very similar in shape and appearance.'

Sugden said: 'You mean she fixed it like that beforehand? Ready?'

Colonel Johnson said warmly: 'I don't believe it for a moment. Not for a moment. Why should she take the diamonds in the first place?'

'Well, as to that . . .' Sugden said slowly.

Poirot nipped in quickly: 'There is a possible answer to that. She took the diamonds to suggest a motive for the murder. That is to say, she knew that murder was going to be done though she herself took no active part in it.'

Johnson frowned.

'That won't hold water for a minute. You're making her out to be an accomplice – but whose accomplice would she be likely to be? Only her husband's. But, as we know that he, too, had nothing to do with the murder, the whole theory falls to the ground.'

Sugden stroked his jaw reflectively.

'Yes,' he said, 'that's so. No, if Mrs Lee took the diamonds – and it's a big *if* – it was just plain robbery, and it's true she might have prepared that garden specially as a hiding-place for them till the hue and cry had died down. Another possibility is that of *coincidence*. That garden, with its similarity of pebbles, struck the thief, whoever he or she was, as an ideal hiding-place.'

Poirot said: 'That is quite possible. I am always prepared to admit *one* coincidence.'

Superintendent Sugden shook his head dubiously.

Poirot said: 'What is your opinion, Superintendent?'

The superintendent said cautiously: 'Mrs Lee's a very nice lady. Doesn't seem likely that she'd be mixed up in any business that was fishy. But, of course, one never knows.'

Colonel Johnson said testily: 'In any case, whatever the truth is about the diamonds, her being mixed up in the murder is out of the question. The butler saw her in the drawing-room at the actual time of the crime. You remember that, Poirot?'

Poirot said: 'I had not forgotten that.'

The chief constable turned to his subordinate.

'We'd better get on. What have you to report? Anything fresh?'

'Yes, sir. I've got hold of some new information. To start with – Horbury. There's a reason why he might be scared of the police.'

'Robbery? Eh?'

'No, sir. Extorting money under threats. Modified blackmail. The case couldn't be proved so he got off, but I rather fancy he's got away with a thing or two in that line. Having a guilty con- science, he probably thought we were on to something of that kind when Tressilian mentioned a police officer last night and it made him get the wind up.'

The chief constable said:

'H'm! So much for Horbury. What else?'

The superintendent coughed.

'Er – Mrs George Lee, sir. We've got a line on her before her marriage. Was living with a Commander Jones. Passed as his daughter – but she *wasn't* his daughter . . . I think, from what we've been told, that old Mr Lee summed her up pretty correctly – he was smart where women were concerned, knew a bad lot when he saw one – and was just amusing himself by taking a shot in the dark. *And* he got her on the raw!'

Colonel Johnson said thoughtfully: 'That gives her another

possible motive – apart from the money angle. She may have thought he knew something definite and was going to give her away to her husband. That telephone story of hers is pretty fishy. She *didn't* telephone.'

Sugden suggested: 'Why not have them in together, sir, and get at that telephone business straight? See what we get.'

Colonel Johnson said: 'Good idea.'

He rang the bell. Tressilian answered it.

'Ask Mr and Mrs George Lee to come here.'

'Very good, sir.'

As the old man turned away, Poirot said: 'The date on that wall calendar, has it remained like it is since the murder?'

Tressilian turned back.

'Which calendar, sir?'

'The one on the wall over there.'

The three men were sitting once more in Alfred Lee's small sitting-room. The calendar in question was a large one with tear-off leaves, a bold date on each leaf.

Tressilian peered across the room, then shuffled slowly across till he was a foot or two away.

He said: 'Excuse me, sir, it has been torn off. It's the twenty-sixth today.

'Ah, pardon. Who would have been the person to tear it off?'

'Mr Lee does, sir, every morning. Mr Alfred, he's a very methodical gentleman.'

'I see. Thank you.'

Tressilian went out. Sugden said, puzzled: 'Is there anything fishy about that calendar, M. Poirot? Have I missed something there?'

With a shrug of his shoulders Poirot said: 'The calendar is of no importance. It was just a little experiment I was making.'

Colonel Johnson said: 'Inquest tomorrow. There'll be an adjournment, of course.'

Sugden said: 'Yes, sir, I've seen the coroner and it's all arranged for.'

II

George Lee came into the room, accompanied by his wife.

Colonel Johnson said: 'Good morning. Sit down, will you?

There are a few questions I want to ask both of you. Something I'm not quite clear about.'

'I shall be glad to give you any assistance I can,' said George, somewhat pompously.

Magdalene said faintly: 'Of course!'

The chief constable gave a slight nod to Sugden. The latter said: 'About those telephone calls on the night of the crime. You put through a call to Westeringham, I think you said, Mr Lee?'

George said coldly: 'Yes, I did. To my agent in the constituency. I can refer you to him and—'

Superintendent Sugden held up his hand to stem the flow.

'Quite so – quite so, Mr Lee. We're not disputing that point. Your call went through at 8.59 exactly.'

'Well – I – er – couldn't say as to the exact time.'

'Ah,' said Sugden. 'But we can! We always check up on these things very carefully. Very carefully indeed. The call was put through at 8.59 and it was terminated at 9.4. Your father, Mr Lee, was killed about 9.15. I must ask you once more for an account of your movements.'

'I've told you – I was telephoning!'

'No, Mr Lee, you weren't.'

'Nonsense – you must have made a mistake! Well, I may, perhaps, have just finished telephoning – I think I debated making another call – was just considering whether it was – er – worth – the expense – when I heard the noise upstairs.'

'You would hardly debate whether or not to make a telephone call for ten minutes.'

George went purple. He began to splutter.

'What do you mean? What the devil do you mean? Damned impudence! Are you doubting my word? Doubting the word of a man of my position. I – er – why should I have to account for every minute of my time?'

Superintendent Sugden said with a stolidness that Poirot admired: 'It's usual.'

George turned angrily on the chief constable.

'Colonel Johnson. Do you countenance this – this unprecedented attitude?'

The chief constable said crisply: 'In a murder case, Mr Lee, these questions must be asked – *and answered*.'

'I have answered them! I had finished telephoning and was – er – debating a further call!'

'You were in this room when the alarm was raised upstairs?'

'I was – yes, I was.'

Johnson turned to Magdalene.

'I think, Mrs Lee,' he said, 'that you stated that *you* were telephoning when the alarm broke out, and that at the time you were alone in this room?'

Magdalene was flustered. She caught her breath, looked sideways at George – at Sugden, then appealingly at Colonel Johnson. She said: 'Oh, really – I don't know – I don't remember what I said . . . I was so *upset* . . .'

Sugden said: 'We've got it all written down, you know.'

She turned her batteries on him – wide appealing eyes – quivering mouth. But she met in return the rigid aloofness of a man of stern respectability who didn't approve of her type.

She said uncertainly: 'I – I – of course I telephoned. I can't be quite sure just *when*—'

She stopped.

George said: 'What's all this? Where did you telephone from? Not in here.'

Superintendent Sugden said: 'I suggest, Mrs Lee, that *you didn't telephone at all*. In that case, where were you and what were you doing?'

Magdalene glanced distractedly about her and burst into tears. She sobbed: 'George, don't let them bully me! You know that if anyone frightens me and thunders questions at me I can't remember anything *at all*! I – I don't know *what* I was saying that night – it was all so horrible – and I was so upset – and they're being so beastly to me . . .'

She jumped up and ran sobbing out of the room.

Springing up, George Lee blustered: 'What d'you mean? I won't have my wife bullied and frightened out of her life! She's very sensitive. It's disgraceful! I shall have a question asked in the House about the disgraceful bullying methods of the police. It's absolutely disgraceful!'

He strode out of the room and banged the door.

Superintendent Sugden threw his head back and laughed.

He said: 'We've got them going properly! Now we'll see!'

Johnson said frowning: 'Extraordinary business! Looks fishy. We must get a further statement out of her.'

Sugden said easily: 'Oh! She'll be back in a minute or two. When she's decided what to say. Eh, M. Poirot?'

Poirot, who had been sitting in a dream, gave a start.

'Pardon!'

'I said she'll be back.'

'Probably – yes, possibly – oh, yes!'

Sugden said, staring at him: 'What's the matter, M. Poirot? Seen a ghost?'

Poirot said slowly: 'You know – I am not sure that I have not done *just exactly that*.'

Colonel Johnson said impatiently: 'Well, Sugden, anything else?'

Sugden said: 'I've been trying to check up on the order in which everyone arrived on the scene of the murder. It's quite clear what must have happened. After the murder when the victim's dying cry had given the alarm, the murderer slipped out, locked the door with pliers, or something of that kind, and a moment or two later became one of the people hurrying *to* the scene of the crime. Unfortunately it's not easy to check exactly whom everyone had seen because people's memories aren't very accurate on a point like that. Tressilian says he saw Harry and Alfred Lee cross the hall from the dining-room and race upstairs. That lets them out, but we don't suspect them anyway. As far as I can make out, Miss Estravados got there late – one of the last. The general idea seems to be that Farr, Mrs George, and Mrs David were the first. Each of those three says one of the others was just ahead of them. That's what's so difficult: you can't distinguish between a deliberate lie and a genuine haziness of recollection. Everybody ran there – that's agreed – but in what order they ran isn't so easy to get at.'

Poirot said slowly: 'You think that important?'

Sugden said: 'It's the time element. The time, remember, was incredibly short.'

Poirot said: 'I agree with you that the time element is very important in this case.'

Sugden went on: 'What makes it more difficult is that there are two staircases. There's the main one in the hall here about equidistant from the dining-room and the drawing-room doors. Then there's one the other end of the house. Stephen Farr came up by the latter. Miss Estravados came along the upper landing from that end of the house (her room is right the other end). The others say they went up by this one.'

Poirot said: 'It is a confusion, yes.'

The door opened and Magdalene came quickly in. She was breathing fast and had a bright spot of colour in each cheek. She came up to the table and said quietly: 'My husband thinks I'm lying down. I slipped out of my room quietly. Colonel Johnson,'

449

she appealed to him with wide, distressed eyes, 'if I tell you the truth you *will* keep quiet about it, won't you? I mean, you don't have to make *everything* public?'

Colonel Johnson said: 'You mean, I take it, Mrs Lee, something that has no connection with the crime?'

'Yes, no connection at all. Just something in my – my private life.'

The chief constable said: 'You'd better make a clean breast of it, Mrs Lee, and leave us to judge.'

Magdalene said, her eyes swimming: 'Yes, I will trust you. I know I can. You look so kind. You see, it's like this. There's somebody—' She stopped.

'Yes, Mrs Lee?'

'I wanted to telephone to somebody last night – a man – a friend of mine, and I didn't want George to know about it. I know it was very wrong of me – but, well, it was like that. So I went to telephone after dinner when I thought George would be safely in the dining-room. But when I got here I heard him telephoning, so I waited.'

'Where did you wait, Madame?' asked Poirot.

'There's a place for coats and things behind the stairs. It's dark there. I slipped back there, where I could see George come out from this room. But he didn't come out, and then all the noise happened and Mr Lee screamed, and I ran upstairs.'

'So your husband did not leave this room until the moment of the murder?'

'No.'

The chief constable said: 'And you yourself from nine o'clock to nine-fifteen were waiting in the recess behind the stairs?'

'Yes, but I couldn't *say* so, you see! They'd want to know what I was doing there. It's been very, very awkward for me, you *do* see that, *don't* you?'

Johnson said dryly: 'It was certainly awkward.'

She smiled at him sweetly.

'I'm *so* relieved to have told you the truth. And you *won't* tell my husband, will you? No, I'm sure you won't! I can trust you, all of you.'

She included them all in her final pleading look, then she slipped quickly out of the room.

Colonel Johnson drew a deep breath.

'Well,' he said. 'It *might* be like that! It's a perfectly plausible story. On the other hand—'

'It might not,' finished Sugden. 'That's just it. We don't know.'

III

Lydia Lee stood by the window of the drawing-room looking out. Her figure was half hidden by the heavy window curtains. A sound in the room made her turn with a start to see Hercule Poirot standing by the door.

She said: 'You startled me, M. Poirot.'

'I apologize, Madame. I walk softly.'

She said: 'I thought it was Horbury.'

Hercule Poirot nodded.

'It is true, he steps softly, that one – like a cat – or a *thief*.'

He paused a minute, watching her.

Her face showed nothing, but she made a slight grimace of distaste as she said: 'I have never cared for that man. I shall be glad to get rid of him.'

'I think you will be wise to do so, Madame.'

She looked at him quickly. She said: 'What do you mean? Do you know anything against him?'

Poirot said: 'He is a man who collects secrets – and uses them to his advantage.'

She said sharply: 'Do you think he knows anything – about the murder?'

Poirot shrugged his shoulders. He said: 'He has quiet feet and long ears. He may have overheard something that he is keeping to himself.'

Lydia said clearly: 'Do you mean that he may try to blackmail one of us?'

'It is within the bounds of possibility. But that is not what I came here to say.'

'What did you come to say?'

Poirot said slowly: 'I have been talking with Mr Alfred Lee. He has made to me a proposition, and I wished to discuss it with you before accepting or declining it. But I was so struck by the picture you made – the charming pattern of your jumper against the deep red of the curtains – that I paused to admire.'

Lydia said sharply: 'Really, M. Poirot, must we waste time in compliments?'

'I beg your pardon, Madame. So few English ladies understand *la toilette*. The dress you were wearing the first night I saw you, its bold but simple pattern, it had grace – distinction.'

Lydia said impatiently: 'What was it you wanted to see me about?'

Poirot became grave.

'Just this, Madame. Your husband, he wishes me to take up the investigation very seriously. He demands that I stay here, in the house, and do my utmost to get to the bottom of the matter.'

Lydia said sharply: 'Well?'

Poirot said slowly: 'I should not wish to accept an invitation that was not endorsed by the lady of the house.'

She said coldly: 'Naturally I endorse my husband's invitation.'

'Yes, Madame, but I need more than that. Do you really *want* me to come here?'

'Why not?'

'Let us be more frank. What I ask you is this: Do you want the truth to come out, or not?'

'Naturally.'

Poirot sighed.

'Must you return me these conventional replies?'

Lydia said: 'I am a conventional woman.'

Then she bit her lip, hesitated, and said: 'Perhaps it is better to speak frankly. Of course I understand you! The position is not a pleasant one. My father-in-law has been brutally murdered, and unless a case can be made out against the most likely suspect – Horbury – for robbery and murder – and it seems that it cannot – then it comes to this – *one of his own family killed him*. To bring that person to justice will mean bringing shame and disgrace on us all . . . If I am to speak honestly I must say that I do *not* want this to happen.'

Poirot said: 'You are content for the murderer to escape unpunished?'

'There are probably several undiscovered murderers at large in the world.'

'That I grant you.'

'Does one more matter, then?'

Poirot said: 'And what about the other members of the family? The innocent?'

She stared.

'What about them?'

'Do you realize that, if it turns out as you hope, *no one will ever know*. The shadow will remain on all alike . . .'

She said uncertainly: 'I hadn't thought of that.'

Poirot said: '*No one will ever know who the guilty person is* . . .'

He added softly: 'Unless *you* already know, Madame?'

She cried out: 'You have no business to say that! It's not true! Oh, if only it could be a stranger – not a member of the family.'

Poirot said: 'It might be both.'

She stared at him.

'What do you mean?'

'It might be a member of the family – and, at the same time, a stranger . . . You do not see what I mean? *Eh bien,* it is an idea that has occurred to the mind of Hercule Poirot.'

He looked at her.

'Well, Madame, what am I to say to Mr Lee?'

Lydia raised her hands and let them fall in a sudden helpless gesture.

She said: 'Of course – you must accept.'

IV

Pilar stood in the centre of the music-room. She stood very straight, her eyes darting from side to side like an animal who fears an attack.

She said: 'I want to get away from here!'

Stephen Farr said gently: 'You're not the only one who feels like that. But they won't let us go, my dear.'

'You mean – the police?'

'Yes.'

Pilar said very seriously: 'It is not nice to be mixed up with the police. It is a thing that should not happen to respectable people.'

Stephen said with a faint smile: 'Meaning yourself?'

Pilar said: 'No, I mean Alfred and Lydia and David and George and Hilda and – yes – Magdalene, too.'

Stephen lit a cigarette. He puffed at it for a moment or two before saying: 'Why the exception?'

'What is that, please?'

Stephen said: 'Why leave out brother Harry?'

Pilar laughed, her teeth showing white and even.

'Oh, Harry is different! I think he knows very well what it is to be mixed up with the police.'

'Perhaps you are right. He certainly is a little too picturesque to blend well into the domestic picture.'

He went on: 'Do you like your English relations, Pilar?'

Pilar said doubtfully: 'They are kind – they are all very kind. But they do not laugh much, they are not gay.'

'My dear girl, there's just been a murder in the house!'

'Y-es,' said Pilar doubtfully.

'A murder,' said Stephen instructively, 'is not such an everyday occurrence as your nonchalance seems to imply. In England they take their murders seriously, whatever they may do in Spain.'

Pilar said: 'You are laughing at me . . .'

Stephen said: 'You're wrong. I'm not in a laughing mood.'

Pilar looked at him and said: 'Because you, too, wish to get away from here?'

'Yes.'

'And the big, handsome policeman will not let you go?'

'I haven't asked him. But, if I did, I've no doubt he'd say no. I've got to watch my step, Pilar, and be very careful.'

'That is tiresome,' said Pilar, nodding her head.

'It's just a little bit more than tiresome, my dear. Then there's that lunatic foreigner prowling about. I don't suppose he's any good but he makes me feel jumpy.'

Pilar was frowning. She said: 'My grandfather was very, very rich, was he not?'

'I should imagine so.'

'Where does his money go to now? To Alfred and the others?'

'Depends on his will.'

Pilar said thoughtfully: 'He might have left me some money, but I am afraid that perhaps he did not.'

Stephen said kindly: 'You'll be all right. After all, you're one of the family. You belong here. They'll have to look after you.'

Pilar said with a sigh: 'I – belong here. It is funny, that. And yet it is not funny at all.'

'I can see that you mightn't find it very humorous.'

Pilar sighed again. She said: 'Do you think if we put on the gramophone we could dance?'

Stephen said dubiously: 'It wouldn't look any too good. This is a house of mourning, you callous Spanish baggage.'

Pilar said, her big eyes opening very wide: 'But I do not feel sad at all. Because I did not really know my grandfather and, though I liked to talk to him, I do not want to cry and be unhappy because he is dead. It is very silly to pretend.'

Stephen said: 'You're adorable!'

Pilar said coaxingly: 'We could put some stockings and some gloves in the gramophone, and then it would not make much noise, and no one would hear.'

'Come along, then, temptress.'

She laughed happily and ran out of the room, going along towards the ballroom at the far end of the house.

Then, as she reached the side passage which led to the garden door, she stopped dead. Stephen caught up with her and stopped also.

Hercule Poirot had unhooked a portrait from the wall and was studying it by the light from the terrace. He looked up and saw them.

'Aha!' he said. 'You arrive at an opportune moment.'

Pilar said: 'What are you doing?'

She came and stood beside him.

Poirot said gravely: 'I am studying something very important, the face of Simeon Lee when he was a young man.'

'Oh, is that my grandfather?'

'Yes, Mademoiselle.'

She stared at the painted face. She said slowly: 'How different – how very different . . . He was so old, so shrivelled up. Here he is like Harry, like Harry might have been ten years ago.'

Hercule Poirot nodded.

'Yes, Mademoiselle. Harry Lee is very much the son of his father. Now here—' He led her a little way along the gallery. 'Here is Madame, your grandmother – a long gentle face, very blonde hair, mild blue eyes.'

Pilar said: 'Like David.'

Stephen said: 'Just a look of Alfred, too.'

Poirot said: 'The heredity, it is very interesting. Mr Lee and his wife were diametrically opposite types. On the whole, the children of the marriage took after the mother. See here, Mademoiselle.'

He pointed to a picture of a girl of nineteen or so, with hair like spun gold and wide, laughing blue eyes. The colouring was that of Simeon Lee's wife, but there was a spirit, a vivacity that those mild blue eyes and placid features had never known.

'Oh!' said Pilar.

The colour came up in her face.

Her hand went to her neck. She drew out a locket on a long gold chain. She pressed the catch and it flew open. The same laughing face looked up at Poirot.

'My mother,' said Pilar.

Poirot nodded. On the opposite side of the locket was the portrait of a man. He was young and handsome, with black hair and dark blue eyes.

Poirot said: 'Your father?'

Pilar said: 'Yes, my father. He is very beautiful, is he not?'

'Yes, indeed. Few Spaniards have blue eyes, have they, señorita?'

'Sometimes, in the north. Besides, my father's mother was Irish.'

Poirot said thoughtfully: 'So you have Spanish blood, and Irish and English, and a touch of gypsy, too. Do you know what I think, Mademoiselle? With that inheritance, you should make a bad enemy.'

Stephen said, laughing: 'Remember what you said in the train, Pilar? That your way of dealing with your enemies would be to cut their throats. Oh!'

He stopped – suddenly realizing the import of his words.

Hercule Poirot was quick to lead the conversation away. He said: 'Ah, yes, there was something, señorita, I had to ask you. Your passport. It is needed by my friend the superintendent. There are, you know, police regulations – very stupid, very tiresome, but necessary – for a foreigner in this country. And of course, by law, you are a foreigner.'

Pilar's eyebrows rose.

'My passport? Yes, I will get it. It is in my room.'

Poirot said apologetically as he walked by her side: 'I am most sorry to trouble you. I am indeed.'

They had reached the end of the long gallery. Here was a flight of stairs. Pilar ran up and Poirot followed. Stephen came, too. Pilar's bedroom was just at the head of the stairs.

She said as she reached the door: 'I will get it for you.'

She went in. Poirot and Stephen Farr remained waiting outside.

Stephen said remorsefully: 'Damn silly of me to say a thing like that. I don't think she noticed, though, do you?'

Poirot did not answer. He held his head a little on one side as though listening.

He said: 'The English are extraordinarily fond of fresh air. Miss Estravados must have inherited that characteristic.'

Stephen said, staring: 'Why?'

Poirot said softly: 'Because though it is today extremely cold – the black frost you call it (not like yesterday so mild and sunny) – Miss Estravados has just flung up her lower window-sash. Amazing to love so much the fresh air.'

Suddenly there was an exclamation in Spanish from inside the room and Pilar reappeared laughingly dismayed.

'Ah!' she cried. 'But I am stupid – and clumsy. My little case it was on the window-sill, and I was sorting through it so quickly and very stupidly I knock my passport out of the window. It is down on the flower-bed below. I will get it.'

'I'll get it,' said Stephen, but Pilar had flown past him and cried back over her shoulder: 'No, it was my stupidity. You go to the drawing-room with M. Poirot and I will bring it to you there.'

Stephen Farr seemed inclined to go after her, but Poirot's hand fell gently on his arm and Poirot's voice said: 'Let us go this way.'

They went along the first-floor corridor towards the other end of the house until they got to the head of the main staircase. Here Poirot said: 'Let us not go down for a minute. If you will come with me to the room of the crime there is something I want to ask you.'

They went along the corridor which led to Simeon Lee's room. On their left they passed an alcove which contained two marble statues, stalwart nymphs clasping their draperies in an agony of Victorian propriety.

Stephen Farr glanced at them and murmured: 'Pretty frightful by daylight. I thought there were three of them when I came along the other night, but thank goodness there are only two!'

'They are not what is admired nowadays,' admitted Poirot. 'But no doubt they cost much money in their time. They look better by night, I think.'

'Yes, one sees only a white glimmering figure.'

Poirot murmured: 'All cats are grey in the dark!'

They found Superintendent Sugden in the room. He was kneeling by the safe and examining it with a magnifying glass. He looked up as they entered.

'This was opened with the key all right,' he said. 'By someone who knew the combination. No sign of anything else.'

Poirot went up to him, drew him aside, and whispered something. The superintendent nodded and left the room.

Poirot turned to Stephen Farr, who was standing staring at the arm-chair in which Simeon Lee always sat. His brows were drawn together and the veins showed in his forehead. Poirot looked at him for a minute or two in silence, then he said: 'You have the memories – yes?'

Stephen said slowly: 'Two days ago he sat there alive – and now . . .'

Then, shaking off his absorption, he said: 'Yes, M. Poirot, you brought me here to ask me something?'

'Ah, yes. You were, I think, the first person to arrive on the scene that night?'

'Was I? I don't remember. No, I think one of the ladies was here before me.'

'Which lady?'

'One of the wives – George's wife or David's – I know they were both here pretty soon.'

'You did not hear the scream, I think you said?'

457

'I don't think I did. I can't quite remember. Somebody did cry out but that may have been someone downstairs.'

Poirot said: 'You did not hear a noise like this?'

He threw his head back and suddenly gave vent to a piercing yell.

It was so unexpected that Stephen started backwards and nearly fell over. He said angrily: 'For the Lord's sake, do you want to scare the whole house? No, I didn't hear anything in the least like that! You'll have the whole place by the ears again! They'll think another murder has happened!'

Poirot looked crestfallen. He murmured: 'True . . . it was foolish . . . We must go at once.'

He hurried out of the room. Lydia and Alfred were at the foot of the stairs peering up – George came out of the library to join them, and Pilar came running, a passport held in her hand.

Poirot cried: 'It is nothing – nothing. Do not be alarmed. A little experiment that I make. That was all.'

Alfred looked annoyed and George indignant. Poirot left Stephen to explain and he hurriedly slipped away along the passage to the other end of the house.

At the end of the passage Superintendent Sugden came quietly out of Pilar's door and met Poirot.

'*Eh bien?*' asked Poirot.

The superintendent shook his head.

'Not a sound.'

His eyes met Poirot's appreciatively and he nodded.

v

Alfred Lee said: 'Then you accept, M. Poirot?'

His hand, as it went to his mouth, shook slightly. His mild brown eyes were alight with a new and feverish expression. He stammered slightly in his speech. Lydia, standing silently by, looked at him with some anxiety.

Alfred said: 'You don't know – you c-c-can't imagine – what it m-m-means to me . . . My father's murderer *must* be f-f-found.'

Poirot said: 'Since you have assured me that you have reflected long and carefully – yes, I accept. But you comprehend, Mr Lee, there can be no drawing back. I am not the dog one sets on to hunt and then recalls because you do not like the game he puts up!'

'Of course . . . of course . . . Everything is ready. Your bedroom is prepared. Stay as long as you like—'

Poirot said gravely: 'It will not be long.'

'Eh? What's that?'

'I said it will not be long. There is in this crime such a restricted circle that it cannot possibly take long to arrive at the truth. Already, I think, the end draws near.'

Alfred stared at him. 'Impossible!' he said.

'Not at all. The facts all point more or less clearly in one direction. There is just some irrelevant matter to be cleared out of the way. When that is done the truth will appear.'

Alfred said incredulously: 'You mean you *know*?'

Poirot smiled. 'Oh, yes,' he said. 'I know.'

Alfred said: 'My father – my father—' He turned away.

Poirot said briskly: 'There are, Mr Lee, two requests that I have to make.'

Alfred said in a muffled voice: 'Anything – anything.'

'Then, in the first place, I would like the portrait of Mr Lee as a young man placed in the bedroom you are good enough to allot to me.'

Alfred and Lydia stared at him.

The former said: 'My father's portrait – but why?'

Poirot said with a wave of the hand: 'It will – how shall I say? – inspire me.'

Lydia said sharply: 'Do you propose, M. Poirot, to solve a crime by clairvoyance?'

'Let us say, Madame, that I intend to use not only the eyes of the body, but the eyes of the mind.'

She shrugged her shoulders.

Poirot continued: 'Next, Mr Lee, I should like to know of the true circumstances attending the death of your sister's husband, Juan Estravados.'

Lydia said: 'Is that necessary?'

'I want all the facts, Madame.'

Alfred said: 'Juan Estravados, as the result of a quarrel about a woman, killed another man in a café.'

'How did he kill him?'

Alfred looked appealingly at Lydia. She said evenly: 'He stabbed him. Juan Estravados was not condemned to death, as there had been provocation. He was sentenced to a term of imprisonment and died in prison.'

'Does his daughter know about her father?'

'I think not.'

Alfred said: 'No, Jennifer never told her.'

'Thank you.'

Lydia said: 'You don't think that Pilar—? Oh, it's absurd!'

Poirot said: 'Now, Mr Lee, will you give me some facts about your brother, Mr Harry Lee?'

'What do you want to know?'

'I understand that he was considered somewhat of a disgrace to the family. Why?'

Lydia said: 'It is so long ago . . .'

Alfred said, the colour coming up in his face: 'If you want to know, M. Poirot, he stole a large sum of money by forging my father's name to a cheque. Naturally my father didn't prosecute. Harry's always been crooked. He's been in trouble all over the world. Always cabling for money to get out of a scrape. He's been in and out of goal here, there and everywhere.'

Lydia said: 'You don't really *know* all this, Alfred.'

Alfred said angrily, his hands shaking: 'Harry's no good – no good whatever! He never has been!'

Poirot said: 'There is, I see, no love lost between you?'

Alfred said: 'He victimised my father – victimised him shamefully!'

Lydia sighed – a quick, impatient sigh. Poirot heard it and gave her a sharp glance.

She said: 'If only those diamonds could be found. I'm sure the solution lies there.'

Poirot said: '*They have been found, Madame.*'

'What?'

Poirot said gently: 'They were found in your little garden of the Dead Sea . . .'

Lydia cried: 'In my garden? How – how extraordinary!'

Poirot said softly: 'Is it not, Madame?'

— 6 —

DECEMBER 27TH

ALFRED LEE said with a sigh: 'That was better than I feared!'

They had just returned from the inquest.

Mr Charlton, an old-fashioned type of solicitor with a cautious blue eye, had been present and had returned with them. He said: 'Ah – I told you the proceedings would be purely formal – purely formal – there was bound to be an adjournment – to enable the police to gather up additional evidence.'

George Lee said vexedly: 'It is all most unpleasant – really *most* unpleasant – a terrible position in which to be placed! I myself am quite convinced that this crime was done by a maniac who somehow or other gained admittance to the house.

'That man Sugden is as obstinate as a mule. Colonel Johnson should enlist the aid of Scotland Yard. These local police are no good. Thick-headed. What about this man Horbury, for instance? I hear his past is definitely unsatisfactory but the police do nothing whatever about it.'

Mr Charlton said: 'Ah – I believe the man Horbury has a satisfactory alibi covering the period of time in question. The police have accepted it.'

'Why should they?' George fumed. 'If I were they, I should accept such an alibi with reserve – with great reserve. Naturally, a criminal always provides himself with an alibi! It is the duty of the police to break down the alibi – that is, if they know their job.'

'Well, well,' said Mr Charlton. 'I don't think it's quite our business to teach the police their jobs, eh? Pretty competent body of men on the whole.'

George shook his head darkly.

'Scotland Yard should be called in. I'm not at all satisfied with Superintendent Sugden – he may be painstaking, but he is certainly far from brilliant.'

Mr Charlton said: 'I don't agree with you, you know. Sugden's a good man. Doesn't throw his weight about, but he gets there.'

Lydia said: 'I'm sure the police are doing their best. Mr Charlton, will you have a glass of sherry?'

Mr Charlton thanked her politely, but declined. Then, clearing his throat, he proceeded to the reading of the will, all members of the family being assembled.

He read it with a certain relish, lingering over its more obscure phraseology, and savouring its legal technicalities.

He came to the end, took off his glasses, wiped them, and looked round on the assembled company inquiringly.

Harry Lee said: 'All this legal stuff's a bit hard to follow. Give us the bare bones of it, will you?'

'Really,' said Mr Charlton. 'It's a perfectly simple will.'

Harry said: 'My God, what's a difficult will like, then?'

Mr Charlton rebuked him with a cold glance. He said: 'The main provisions of the will are quite simple. Half Mr Lee's property goes to his son, Mr Alfred Lee, the remainder is divided between his other children.'

Harry laughed unpleasantly. He said: 'As usual, Alfred's struck lucky! Half my father's fortune! Lucky dog, aren't you, Alfred?'

Alfred flushed. Lydia said sharply: 'Alfred was a loyal and devoted son to his father. He's managed the works for years and has had all the responsibility.'

Harry said: 'Oh, yes. Alfred was always the good boy.'

Alfred said sharply: 'You may consider *yourself* lucky, I think, Harry, that my father left you anything at all!'

Harry laughed, throwing his head back. He said: 'You'd have liked it better if he'd cut me right out, wouldn't you? You've always disliked me.'

Mr Charlton coughed. He was used – only too well used – to the painful scenes that succeeded the reading of a will. He was anxious to get away before the usual family quarrel got too well under way.

He murmured: 'I think – er – that is all that I need – er—'

Harry said sharply: 'What about Pilar?'

Mr Charlton coughed again, this time apologetically.

'Er – Miss Estravados is not mentioned in the will.'

Harry said: 'Doesn't she get her mother's share?'

Mr Charlton explained.

'Señora Estravados, if she had lived, would of course have received an equal share with the rest of you; but, as she is dead, the portion that would have been hers goes back into the estate to be shared out between you.'

Pilar said slowly in her rich southern voice: 'Then – I – have – nothing?'

Lydia said quickly: 'My dear, the family will see to that, of course.'

George Lee said: 'You will be able to make your home here with Alfred – eh, Alfred? We – er – you are our niece – it is our duty to look after you.'

Hilda said: 'We shall always be glad to have Pilar with us.'

Harry said: 'She ought to have her proper share. She ought to have Jennifer's whack.'

Mr Charlton murmured:

'Must really – er – be going. Goodbye, Mrs Lee – anything I can do – er – consult me at any time . . .'

He escaped quickly. His experience enabled him to predict that all the ingredients for a family row were present.

As the door shut behind him Lydia said in her clear voice: 'I agree with Harry. I think Pilar is entitled to a definite share. This will was made many years before Jennifer's death.'

'Nonsense,' said George. 'Very slipshod and illegal way of thinking, Lydia. The law's the law. We must abide by it.'

Magdalene said: 'It's hard luck, of course, and we're all very sorry for Pilar, but George is right. As he says, the law is the law.'

Lydia got up. She took Pilar by the hand.

'My dear,' she said. 'This must be very unpleasant for you. Will you please leave us while we discuss the question?'

She led the girl to the door.

'Don't worry, Pilar, dear,' she said. 'Leave it to me.'

Pilar went slowly out of the room. Lydia shut the door behind her and turned back.

There was a moment's pause while everyone drew breath and in another moment the battle was in full swing.

Harry said: 'You've always been a damned skinflint, George.'

George retorted: 'At any rate, I've not been a sponge and a rotter!'

'You've been just as much of a sponge as I have! You've battened on Father all these years.'

'You seem to forget that I hold a responsible and arduous position which—'

Harry said: 'Responsible and arduous my foot! You're only an inflated gasbag!'

Magdalene screamed: 'How dare you?'

Hilda's calm voice, slightly raised, said: 'Couldn't we just discuss this *quietly*?'

Lydia threw her a grateful glance.

David said with sudden violence: 'Must we have all this disgraceful fuss over *money*!'

Magdalene said venomously to him: 'It's all very well to be so high-minded. You're not going to refuse your legacy, are you? *You* want money just as much as the rest of us do! All this unworldliness is just a pose!'

David said in a strangled voice: 'You think I ought to refuse it? I wonder—'

Hilda said sharply: 'Of course you oughtn't. Must we all behave like children? Alfred, you're the head of the family—'

Alfred seemed to wake out of a dream. He said: 'I beg your pardon. All of you shouting at once. It – it confuses me.'

Lydia said: 'As Hilda has just pointed out, why must we behave like greedy children? Let us discuss this thing quietly and sanely and' – she added this quickly – 'one at a time. Alfred shall speak first because he is the eldest. What do you think, Alfred, we should do about Pilar?'

He said slowly: 'She must make her home here, certainly. And we should make her an allowance. I do not see that she has any legal claim to the money which would have gone to her mother. She's not a Lee, remember. She's a Spanish subject.'

'No legal claim, no,' said Lydia. 'But I think she has a *moral* claim. As I see it, your father, although his daughter had married a Spaniard against his wishes, recognized her to have an equal claim upon him. George, Harry, David, and Jennifer were to share equally. Jennifer only died last year. I am sure that when he sent for Mr Charlton he meant to make ample provision for Pilar in a new will. He would have allotted her at least her mother's share. It is possible that he might have done much more than that. She was the only grandchild, remember. I think the least *we* can do is to endeavour to remedy an injustice that your father himself was preparing to remedy.'

Alfred said warmly: 'Well put, Lydia! I was wrong. I agree with you that Pilar must be given Jennifer's share of my father's fortune.'

Lydia said: 'Your turn, Harry.'

Harry said: 'As you know, I agree. I think Lydia has put the case very well, and I'd like to say I admire her for it.'

Lydia said: 'George?'

George was red in the face. He spluttered: 'Certainly not! Whole thing's preposterous! Give her a home and a decent dress allowance. Quite enough for her!'

'Then you refuse to co-operate?' asked Alfred.

'Yes, I do.'

'And he's quite right,' said Magdalene. 'It's disgraceful to suggest he should do anything of the kind! Considering that George is the *only* member of the family who has done *anything* in the world, I think it's a shame his father left him so little!'

Lydia said: 'David?'

David said vaguely: 'Oh, I think you're right. It's a pity there's got to be so much ugliness and disputing about it all.'

Hilda said: 'You're quite right, Lydia. It's only justice!'

Harry looked round. He said: 'Well, that's clear. Of the family, Alfred, myself and David are in favour of the motion. George is against it. The ayes have it.'

George said sharply: 'There is no question of ayes or noes. My share of my father's estate is mine absolutely. I shall not part with a penny of it.'

'No, indeed,' said Magdalene.

Lydia said sharply: 'If you like to stand out, that is your business. The rest of us will make up your share of the total.'

She looked round for assent and the others nodded.

Harry said: 'Alfred's got the lion's share. He ought to stand most of the racket.'

Alfred said: 'I see that your original disinterested suggestion will soon break down.'

Hilda said firmly: 'Don't let's start again! Lydia shall tell Pilar what we've decided. We can settle details later.' She added in the hope of making a diversion, 'I wonder where Mr Farr is, and M. Poirot?'

Alfred said: 'We dropped Poirot in the village on our way to the inquest. He said he had an important purchase to make.'

Harry said: 'Why didn't *he* go the inquest? Surely he ought to have done!'

Lydia said: 'Perhaps he knew it was not going to be important. Who's that out there in the garden? Superintendent Sugden, or Mr Farr?'

The efforts of the two women were successful. The family conclave broke up.

Lydia said to Hilda privately: 'Thank you, Hilda. It was nice of you to back me up. You know, you really *have* been a comfort in all this.'

Hilda said thoughtfully: 'Queer how money upsets people.'

The others had all left the room. The two women were alone.

Lydia said: 'Yes – even Harry – although it was his suggestion! And my poor Alfred – he is so British – he doesn't really like Lee money going to a Spanish subject.'

Hilda said, smiling: 'Do you think we women are more unworldly?'

Lydia said with a shrug of her graceful shoulders: 'Well, you know, it isn't really our money – not our *own*! That may make a difference.'

Hilda said thoughtfully: 'She is a strange child – Pilar, I mean. I wonder what will become of her?'

Lydia sighed.

'I'm glad that she will be independent. To live here, to be given a home and a dress allowance, would not, I think, be very satisfactory to her. She's too proud and, I think, too – too – alien.'

She added musingly: 'I once brought some beautiful blue lapis home from Egypt. Out there, against the sun and the sand, it was a glorious colour – a brilliant warm blue. But when I got it home the blue of it hardly showed any more. It was just a dull, darkish string of beads.'

Hilda said: 'Yes, I see . . .'

Lydia said gently: 'I am so glad to come to know you and David at last. I'm glad you both came here.'

Hilda sighed: 'How often I've wished in the last few days that we hadn't!'

'I know. You must have done . . . But, you know, Hilda, the shock hasn't affected David nearly as badly as it might have done. I mean, he is so sensitive that it might have upset him completely. Actually, since the murder, he's seemed ever so much better—'

Hilda looked slightly disturbed. She said: 'So you've noticed that? It's rather dreadful in a way . . . But oh, Lydia, it's undoubtedly so!'

She was silent a minute recollecting words that her husband had spoken only the night before. He had said to her, eagerly, his fair hair tossed back from his forehead: 'Hilda, you remember in *Tosca* – when Scarpia is dead and Tosca lights the candles at his head and feet? Do you remember what she says: "*Now* I can forgive him . . ." That is what I feel – about Father. I see now that all these years I couldn't forgive him, and yet I really wanted to . . . But now – *now* – there's no rancour any more. It's all wiped away. And I feel – oh, I feel as though a great load had been lifted from my back.'

She had said, striving to fight back a sudden fear: 'Because he's dead?'

He had answered quickly, stammering in his eagerness: 'No, no, you don't understand. Not because *he* is dead, but because my childish stupid hate of him is dead . . .'

Hilda thought of those words now.

She would have liked to repeat them to the woman at her side, but she felt instinctively that it was wiser not.

She followed Lydia out of the drawing-room into the hall.

Magdalene was there, standing by the hall table with a little parcel in her hand. She jumped when she saw them. She said: 'Oh, this must be M. Poirot's important purchase. I saw him put it down here just now. I wonder what it is.'

She looked from one to the other of them, giggling a little, but her eyes were sharp and anxious, belying the affected gaiety of her words.

Lydia's eyebrows rose. She said: 'I must go and wash before lunch.'

Magdalene said, still with that affectation of childishness, but unable to keep the desperate note out of her voice: 'I must just *peep*!'

She unrolled the piece of paper and gave a sharp exclamation. She stared at the thing in her hand.

Lydia stopped and Hilda too. Both women stared.

Magdalene said in a puzzled voice: 'It's a false moustache. But – but – why—?'

Hilda said doubtfully: 'Disguise? But—'

Lydia finished the sentence for her.

'But M. Poirot has a very fine moustache of his own!'

Magdalene was wrapping the parcel up again. She said: 'I don't understand. It's – it's *mad*. *Why* does M. Poirot buy a false moustache?'

II

When Pilar left the drawing-room she walked slowly along the hall. Stephen Farr was coming in through the garden door. He said: 'Well? Is the family conclave over? Has the will been read?'

Pilar said, her breath coming fast: 'I have got nothing – at all! It was a will made many years ago. My grandfather left money to my mother, but because she is dead it does not go to me but goes back to *them*.'

Stephen said: 'That seems rather hard lines.'

Pilar said: 'If that old man had lived, he would have made another will. He would have left money to *me* – a lot of money! Perhaps in time he would have left me *all* the money!'

Stephen said, smiling: 'That wouldn't have been very fair, either, would it?'

'Why not? He would have liked me best, that is all.'

Stephen said: 'What a greedy child you are. A real little gold-digger.'

Pilar said soberly: 'The world is very cruel to women. They must do what they can for themselves – while they are young. When they are old and ugly no one will help them.'

Stephen said slowly: 'That's more true than I like to think. But it isn't *quite* true. Alfred Lee, for instance, was genuinely fond of his father in spite of the old man being thoroughly trying and exacting.'

Pilar's chin went up.

'Alfred,' she said, 'is rather a fool.'

Stephen laughed.

Then he said: 'Well, don't worry, lovely Pilar. The Lees are bound to look after you, you know.'

Pilar said disconsolately: 'It will not be very amusing, that.'

Stephen said slowly: 'No, I'm afraid it won't. I can't see you living here, Pilar. Would you like to come to South Africa?'

Pilar nodded.

Stephen said: 'There's sun there, and space. There's hard work, too. Are you good at work, Pilar?'

Pilar said doubtfully: 'I do not know.'

He said: 'You'd rather sit on a balcony and eat sweets all day long? And grow enormously fat and have three double chins?'

Pilar laughed and Stephen said: 'That's better. I've made you laugh.'

Pilar said: 'I thought I should laugh this Christmas! In books I have read that an English Christmas is very gay, that one eats burning raisins and there is a plum pudding all in flames, and something that is called a Yule Log.'

Stephen said: 'Ah, but you must have a Christmas uncomplicated by murder. Come in here a minute. Lydia took me in here yesterday. It's her store-room.'

He led her into a small room little bigger than a cupboard.

'Look, Pilar, boxes and boxes of crackers, and preserved fruits and oranges and dates and nuts. And here—'

'Oh!' Pilar clasped her hands. 'They are pretty, these gold and silver balls.'

'Those were to hang on a tree, with presents for the servants. And here are little snowmen all glittering with frost to put on the dinner table. And here are balloons of every colour all ready to blow up!'

'Oh!' Pilar's eyes shone. 'Oh! Can we blow one up? Lydia would not mind. I do love balloons.'

Stephen said: 'Baby! Here, which will you have?'

Pilar said: 'I will have a red one.'

They selected their balloons and blew, their cheeks distended. Pilar stopped blowing to laugh, and her balloon went down again.

She said: 'You look so funny – blowing – with your cheeks puffed out.'

Her laugh rang out. Then she fell to, blowing industriously. They tied up their balloons carefully and began to play with them, patting them upwards, sending them to and fro.

Pilar said: 'Out in the hall there would be more room.'

They were sending the balloons to each other, and laughing, when Poirot came along the hall. He regarded them indulgently.

'So you play *les jeux d'enfants*? It is pretty, that!'

Pilar said breathlessly: 'Mine is the red one. It is bigger than his. Much bigger. If we took it outside, it would go right up in the sky.'

'Let's send them up and wish,' said Stephen.

'Oh, yes, that is a good idea.'

Pilar ran to the garden door, Stephen followed. Poirot came behind, still looking indulgent.

'I will wish for a great deal of money,' announced Pilar.

She stood on tiptoe, holding the string of the balloon. It tugged gently as a puff of wind came. Pilar let go and it floated along, taken by the breeze.

Stephen laughed.

'You mustn't tell your wish.'

'No? Why not?'

'Because it doesn't come true. Now I'm going to wish.'

He released his balloon. But he was not so lucky. It floated sideways, caught on a holly bush and expired with a bang.

Pilar ran to it.

She announced tragically: 'It is gone . . .'

Then, as she stirred the little wisp of rubber with her toe, she said: 'So that was what I picked up in Grandfather's room. He, too, had had a balloon, only his was a pink one.'

Poirot gave a sharp exclamation. Pilar turned inquiringly.

Poirot said: 'It is nothing. I stabbed – no, stubbed – the toe.'

He wheeled round and looked at the house.

He said: 'So many windows! A house, Mademoiselle, has its eyes – and its ears. It is indeed regrettable that the English are so fond of open windows.'

Lydia came out on the terrace. She said: 'Lunch is just ready. Pilar, my dear, everything has been settled quite satisfactorily. Alfred will explain the exact details to you after lunch. Shall we come in?'

They went into the house. Poirot came last. He was looking grave.

III

Lunch was over.

As they came out of the dining-room, Alfred said to Pilar: 'Will you come into my room? There is something I want to talk over with you.'

He led her across the hall and into his study, shutting the door

469

after him. The others went on into the drawing-room. Only Hercule Poirot remained in the hall looking thoughtfully at the closed study door.

He was aware suddenly of the old butler hovering uneasily near him.

Poirot said: 'Yes, Tressilian, what is it?'

The old man seemed troubled. He said: 'I wanted to speak to Mr Lee. But I don't like to disturb him now.'

Poirot said: 'Something has occurred?'

Tressilian said slowly: 'It's such a queer thing. It doesn't make sense.'

'Tell me,' said Hercule Poirot.

Tressilian hesitated. Then he said: 'Well, it's this, sir. You may have noticed that each side of the front door there was a cannon ball. Big heavy stone things. Well, sir, *one of them's gone.*'

Hercule Poirot's eyebrows rose. He said: 'Since when?'

'They were both there this morning, sir. I'll take my oath on that.'

'Let me see.'

Together they went outside the front door. Poirot bent and examined the remaining cannon ball. When he straightened himself, his face was very grave.

Tressilian quavered: 'Who'd want to steal a thing like that, sir? It doesn't make *sense.*'

Poirot said: 'I do not like it. I do not like it at all . . .'

Tressilian was watching him anxiously. He said slowly: 'What's come to the house, sir? Ever since the master was murdered it doesn't seem like the same place. I feel the whole time as though I was going about in a dream. I mix things up, and I sometimes feel I can't trust my own eyes.'

Hercule Poirot shook his head. He said: 'You are wrong. Your own eyes are just what you must trust.'

Tressilian said, shaking his head: 'My sight's bad – I can't see like I used to do. I get things mixed up – and people. I'm getting too old for my work.'

Hercule Poirot clapped him on the shoulder and said: 'Courage.'

'Thank you, sir. You mean it kindly, I know. But there it is, I am too old. I'm always going back to the old days and the old faces. Miss Jenny and Master David and Master Alfred. I'm always seeing them as young gentlemen and ladies. Ever since that night when Mr Harry came home—'

Poirot nodded.

470

'Yes,' he said, 'that is what I thought. You said just now "Ever since the master was murdered" – but it began before that. *It is ever since Mr Harry came home*, is it not, that things have altered and seemed unreal?'

The butler said: 'You're quite right, sir. It *was* then. Mr Harry always brought trouble into the house, even in the old days.'

His eyes wandered back to the empty stone base.

'Who can have taken it, sir?' he whispered. 'And why? It's – it's like a madhouse.'

Hercule Poirot said: 'It is not madness I am afraid of. It is sanity! Somebody, Tressilian, is in great danger.'

He turned and re-entered the house.

At that moment Pilar came out from the study. A red spot shone on either cheek. She held her head high and her eyes glittered.

As Poirot came up to her, she suddenly stamped her foot and said: 'I will not take it.'

Poirot raised his eyebrows. He said: 'What is it that you will not take, Mademoiselle?'

Pilar said: 'Alfred has just told me that I am to have my mother's share of the money my grandfather left.'

'Well?'

'I could not get it by law, he said. But he and Lydia and the others consider it should be mine. They say it is a matter of justice. And so they will hand it over to me.'

Poirot said again: 'Well?'

Pilar stamped once more with her foot.

'Do you not understand? They are giving it to me – *giving* it to me.'

'Need that hurt your pride? Since what they say is true – that it should in justice be yours?'

Pilar said: 'You do not understand . . .'

Poirot said: 'On the contrary – I understand very well.'

'Oh!' She turned away pettishly.

There was a ring at the bell. Poirot glanced over his shoulder. He saw the silhouette of Superintendent Sugden outside the door. He said hurriedly to Pilar: 'Where are you going?'

She said sulkily: 'To the drawing-room. To the others.'

Poirot said quickly: 'Good. Stay with them there. Do not wander about the house alone, especially after dark. Be on your guard. You are in great danger, Mademoiselle. You will never be in greater danger than you are today.'

He turned away from her and went to meet Sugden.

The latter waited till Tressilian had gone back into his pantry.

Then he shoved a cable form under Poirot's nose.

'Now we've got it!' he said. 'Read that. It's from the South African Police.'

The cable said: *'Ebenezer Farr's only son died two years ago.'*

Sugden said: 'So now we know! Funny – I was on a different tack altogether . . .'

IV

Pilar marched into the drawing-room, her head held high.

She went straight up to Lydia, who was sitting in the window with some knitting.

Pilar said: 'Lydia, I have come to tell you that I will not take that money. I am going away – at once . . .'

Lydia looked astonished. She laid down her knitting. She said: 'My dear child, Alfred must have explained very badly! It is not in the least a matter of charity, if that is what you feel. Really, it is not a question of kindness or generosity on our part. It is a plain matter of right and wrong. In the ordinary course of events your mother would have inherited this money, and you would have come into it from her. It is your right – your blood right. It is a matter, not of charity, but of *justice!*'

Pilar said fiercely: 'And that is why I cannot do it – not when you speak like that – not when you are like that! I enjoyed coming here. It was fun! It was an adventure, but now you have spoilt it all! I am going away now, at once – you will never be bothered by me again . . .'

Tears choked her voice. She turned and ran blindly out of the room.

Lydia stared. She said helplessly: 'I'd no idea she would take it like that!'

Hilda said: 'The child seems quite upset.'

George cleared his throat and said portentously: 'Er – as I pointed out this morning – the principle involved is wrong. Pilar has the wit to see that for herself. She refuses to accept charity—'

Lydia said sharply: 'It is *not* charity. It is her right!'

George said: 'She does not seem to think so!'

Superintendent Sugden and Hercule Poirot came in. The former looked round and asked: 'Where's Mr Farr? I want a word with him.'

472

Before anyone had time to answer, Hercule Poirot said sharply: 'Where is the Señorita Estravados?'

George Lee said with a trace of malicious satisfaction: 'Going to clear out, so she says. Apparently she has had enough of her English relations.'

Poirot wheeled round.

He said to Sugden: 'Come!'

As the two men emerged into the hall, there was the sound of a heavy crash and a far-away shriek.

Poirot cried: 'Quick . . . Come . . .'

They raced along the hall and up the far staircase. The door of Pilar's room was open and a man stood in the doorway. He turned his head as they ran up. It was Stephen Farr.

He said: 'She's alive . . .'

Pilar stood crouched against the wall of her room. She was staring at the floor where a big stone cannon ball was lying.

She said breathlessly: 'It was on top of my door, balanced there. It would have crashed down on my head when I came in, but my skirt caught on a nail and jerked me back just as I was coming in.'

Poirot knelt down and examined the nail. On it was a thread of purple tweed. He looked up and nodded gravely.

'That nail, Mademoiselle,' he said, 'saved your life.'

The superintendent said, bewildered: 'Look here, what's the meaning of all this?'

Pilar said: 'Someone tried to kill me!'

She nodded her head several times.

Superintendent Sugden glanced up at the door.

'Booby trap,' he said. 'An old-fashioned booby trap – and its purpose was murder! That's the second murder planned in this house. But this time it didn't come off!'

Stephen Farr said huskily: 'Thank God you're safe.'

Pilar flung out her hands in a wide, appealing gesture.

'*Madre de Dios!*' she cried. 'Why should anyone wish to kill *me*? What have I done?'

Hercule Poirot said slowly: 'You should rather ask, Mademoiselle, *What do I know?*'

She stared.

'Know? I do not know anything.'

Hercule Poirot said: 'That is where you are wrong. Tell me, Mademoiselle Pilar, where were you at the time of the murder? You were not in this room.'

'I was. I have told you so!'

Superintendent Sugden said with deceptive mildness: 'Yes, but you weren't speaking the truth when you said that, you know. You told us you heard your grandfather scream – you couldn't have heard that if you were in here – M. Poirot and I tested that yesterday.'

'Oh!' Pilar caught her breath.

Poirot said: 'You were somewhere very much nearer his room. I will tell you where I think you were, Mademoiselle. You were in the recess with the statues quite close to your grandfather's door.'

Pilar said, startled: 'Oh . . . How did you know?'

Poirot said with a faint smile: 'Mr Farr saw you there.'

Stephen said sharply: 'I did not. That's an absolute lie!'

Poirot said: 'I ask your pardon, Mr Farr, but you *did* see her. Remember your impression that there were *three* statues in that recess, not *two*. Only one person wore a white dress that night, Mademoiselle Estravados. *She* was the third white figure you saw. That is so, is it not, Mademoiselle?'

Pilar said, after a moment's hesitation: 'Yes, it is true.'

Poirot said gently: 'Now tell us, Mademoiselle, the whole truth. *Why* were you there?'

Pilar said: 'I left the drawing-room after dinner and I thought I would go and see my grandfather. I thought he would be pleased. But when I turned into the passage I saw someone else was there at his door. I did not want to be seen because I knew my grandfather had said he did not want to see anyone that night. I slipped into the recess in case the person at the door turned round.

'Then, all at once, I heard the most horrible sounds, tables – chairs' – she waved her hands – 'everything falling and crashing. I did not move. I do not know why. I was frightened. And then there was a terrible scream' – she crossed herself – 'and my heart it stopped beating, and I said, "*Someone is dead* . . ."'

'And then?'

'And then people began coming running along the passage and I came out at the end and joined them.'

Superintendent Sugden said sharply: 'You said nothing of all this when we first questioned you. Why not?'

Pilar shook her head. She said, with an air of wisdom: 'It is not good to tell too much to the police. I thought, you see, that if I said I was near there you might think that *I* had killed him. So I said I was in my room.'

Sugden said sharply: 'If you tell deliberate lies, all that it ends in is that you're bound to come under suspicion.'

Stephen Farr said: 'Pilar?'

'Yes?'

'*Who did you see standing at the door* when you turned into the passage? Tell us.'

Sugden said: 'Yes, tell us.'

For a moment the girl hesitated. Her eyes opened, then narrowed. She said slowly: 'I don't know who it was. It was too dimly lit to see. *But it was a woman* . . .'

V

Superintendent Sugden looked round at the circle of faces. He said, with something as near irritation as he had yet shown: 'This is very irregular, M. Poirot.'

Poirot said: 'It is a little idea of mine. I wish to share with everyone the knowledge that I have acquired. I shall then invite their co-operation, and so we shall get at the truth.'

Sugden murmured under his breath: 'Monkey tricks.'

He leaned back in his chair. Poirot said: 'To begin with, you have, I think, an explanation to ask of Mr Farr.'

Sugden's mouth tightened.

'I should have chosen a less public moment,' he said. 'However, I've no objection.' He handed the cable to Stephen Farr. 'Now, Mr *Farr*, as you call yourself, perhaps you can explain *this*?'

Stephen Farr took it. Raising his eyebrows, he read it slowly out loud. Then, with a bow, he handed it back to the superintendent.

'Yes,' he said. 'It's pretty damning, isn't it?'

Sugden said: 'Is that all you've got to say about it? You quite understand there is no obligation on you to make a statement—'

Stephen Farr interrupted. He said: 'You needn't caution me, Superintendent. I can see it trembling on your tongue! Yes, I'll give you an explanation. It's not a very good one, but it's the truth.'

He paused. Then he began: 'I'm not Ebenezer Farr's son. But I knew both father and son quite well. Now try and put yourself in my place. (My name is Stephen Grant, by the way.) I arrived in this country for the first time in my life. I was disappointed. Everything and everybody seemed drab and lifeless. Then I was travelling by train and I saw a girl. I've got to say it straight out: I fell for that girl! She was the loveliest and most unlikely creature in the world! I talked to her for a while in the train and I made up my mind then and there not to lose sight of her. As I was leaving the compartment I caught sight of the label on her suitcase. Her name meant nothing to me, but the address to which she was travelling did. I'd heard of Gorston Hall, and I knew all about its owner. He was Ebenezer Farr's one-time partner and old Eb often talked about him and said what a personality he was.

'Well, the idea came to me to go to Gorston Hall and pretend I was Eb's son. He had died, as this cable says, two years ago, but I remembered old Eb saying that he had not heard from Simeon Lee now for many years, and I judged that Lee would not know of the death of Eb's son. Anyway, I felt it was worth trying.'

Sugden said: 'You didn't try it on at once, though. You stayed in the King's Arms at Addlesfield for two days.'

Stephen said: 'I was thinking it over – whether to try it or not. At last I made up my mind I would. It appealed to me as a bit of an adventure. Well, it worked like a charm! The old man greeted me in the friendliest manner and at once asked me to come and stay in the house. I accepted. There you are, Superintendent, there's my explanation. If you don't fancy it, cast your mind back to your courting days and see if you don't remember some bit of foolishness you indulged in then. As for my real name, as I say, it's Stephen Grant. You can cable South Africa and check up on me, but I'll tell you this: you'll find I'm a perfectly respectable citizen. I'm not a crook or a jewel thief.'

Poirot said softly: 'I never believed you were.'

Superintendent Sugden stroked his jaw cautiously. He said: 'I'll have to check up on that story. What I'd like to know is this: Why didn't you come clean after the murder instead of telling us a pack of lies?'

Stephen said disarmingly: 'Because I was a fool! I thought I could get away with it! I thought it would look fishy if I admitted to being here under a false name. If I hadn't been a complete idiot I would have realized you were bound to cable to Jo'burg.'

Sugden said: 'Well, Mr Farr – er – Grant – I'm not saying I disbelieve your story. It will be proved or disproved soon enough.'

He looked across inquiringly at Poirot. The latter said: 'I think Miss Estravados has something to say.'

Pilar had gone very white. She said, in a breathless voice: 'It is true. I would never have told you, but for Lydia and the money. To come here and pretend and cheat and act – that was fun, but when Lydia said the money was mine, and that it was only justice, that was different; it was not fun any longer.'

Alfred Lee said with a puzzled face: 'I do not understand, my dear, what you are talking about.'

Pilar said: 'You think I am your niece, Pilar Estravados? But that is not so! Pilar was killed when I was travelling with her in a car in Spain. A bomb came and it hit the car and she was killed, but I was not touched. I did not know her very well, but she had told me all about herself and how her grandfather had sent for her to go to England and that he was very rich. And I had no money at all and I did not know where to go or what to do. And I thought suddenly: "Why should not I take Pilar's passport, and go to England and become very rich?"' Her face lit up with its sudden wide smile. 'Oh, it was fun wondering if I could get away with it! Our faces on the photograph were not unlike. But when they wanted my passport here I opened the window and threw it out and ran down to get it, and then I rubbed some earth just over the face a little because at a barrier travelling they do not look very closely, but here they might—'

Alfred Lee said angrily: 'Do you mean to say that you represented yourself to my father as his granddaughter, and played on his affection for you?'

Pilar nodded. She said complacently: 'Yes, I saw at once I could make him like me very much.'

George Lee broke out: 'Preposterous!' he spluttered. 'Criminal! Attempting to get money by false pretences.'

Harry Lee said: 'She didn't get any from *you*, old boy! Pilar, I'm on your side! I've got a profound admiration for your daring. And, thank goodness, I'm not your uncle any more! That gives me a much freer hand.'

Pilar said to Poirot: '*You* knew? When did you know?'

Poirot smiled: 'Mademoiselle, if you have studied the laws of Mendel you would know that two blue-eyed people are not likely to have a brown-eyed child. Your mother was, I was sure, a most chaste and respectable lady. It followed, then, that you were not Pilar Estravados at all. When you did your trick with the passport, I was quite sure of it. It was ingenious, but not, you understand, quite ingenious enough.'

Superintendent Sugden said unpleasantly: 'The whole thing's not quite ingenious enough.'

Pilar stared at him. She said: 'I don't understand . . .'

Sugden said: 'You've told us a story – but I think there's a good deal more you haven't told.'

Stephen said: 'You leave her alone!'

Superintendent Sugden took no notice. He went on: 'You've told us that you went up to your grandfather's room after dinner. You said it was an impulse on your part. I'm going to suggest something else. It was you who stole those diamonds. You'd handled them. On occasion, perhaps, you'd put them away in the safe and the old man hadn't watched you do it! When he found the stones were missing, he saw at once that only two people could have taken them. One was Horbury, who might have got to know the combination and have crept in and stolen them during the night. The other person was *you*.

'Well, Mr Lee at once took measures. He rang me up and had me come to see him. Then he sent word to you to come and see him immediately after dinner. You did so and he accused you of the theft. You denied it; he pressed the charge. I don't know what happened next – perhaps he tumbled to the fact that you weren't his granddaughter, but a very clever little professional thief. Anyway, the game was up, exposure loomed over you, and you slashed at him with a knife. There was a struggle and he screamed. You were properly up against it then. You hurried out of the room, turned the key from the outside and then, knowing you could not get away, before the others came, *you slipped into the recess by the statues*.'

Pilar cried shrilly: 'It is not true! It is not true! I did not steal the diamonds! I did not kill him. I swear it by the Blessed Virgin.'

Sugden said sharply: '*Then who did?* You say you saw a figure standing outside Mr Lee's door. According to your story, *that person must have been the murderer. No one else* passed the recess! But we've only *your* word for it *that there was a figure there at all*. In other words, *you made that up* to exculpate yourself!'

George Lee said sharply: 'Of course she's guilty! It's clear enough! I always *said* an outsider killed my father! Preposterous nonsense to pretend one of his family would do a thing like that! It – it wouldn't be natural!'

Poirot stirred in his seat. He said: 'I disagree with you. Taking into consideration the character of Simeon Lee, it would be a very natural thing to happen.'

'Eh?' George's jaw dropped. He stared at Poirot.

Poirot went on: 'And, in my opinion, that very thing *did* happen. Simeon Lee was killed by his own flesh and blood, for what seemed to the murderer a very good and sufficient reason.'

George cried: 'One of us? I deny—'

Poirot's voice broke in hard as steel.

'There is a case against every person here. We will, Mr George Lee, begin with the case against *you*. *You* had no love for your father! You kept on good terms with him for the sake of money. On the day of his death *he threatened to cut down your allowance*. You knew that on his death you would probably inherit a very substantial sum. There is the motive. After dinner you went, as you say, to telephone. You *did* telephone – but the call lasted only *five minutes*. After that you could easily have gone to your father's room, chatted with him, and then attacked him and killed him. You left the room and turned the key from outside, for you hoped the affair would be put down to a burglar. You omitted, in your panic, to make sure that the window was fully open so as to support the burglar theory. That was stupid; but you are, if you will pardon my saying so, rather a stupid man!

'However,' said Poirot, after a brief pause during which George tried to speak and failed, 'many stupid men have been criminals!'

He turned his eyes on Magdalene.

'Madame, too, she also had a motive. She is, I think, in debt, and the tone of certain of your father's remarks may – have caused her uneasiness. She, too, has no alibi. She went to telephone, but she did *not* telephone, and we have *only her word* for what she did do . . .

'Then,' he paused, 'there is Mr David Lee. We have heard, not once but many times, of the revengeful tempers and long memories that went with the Lee blood. Mr David Lee did not forget or forgive the way his father had treated his mother. A final jibe directed at the dead lady may have been the last straw. David Lee is said to have been playing the piano at the time of the murder. By a coincidence he was playing the "Dead March". But suppose *somebody else* was playing that "Dead March", somebody who knew what he was going to do, and who approved his action?'

Hilda Lee said quietly: 'That is an infamous suggestion.'

Poirot turned to her. 'I will offer you another, Madame. It was *your* hand that did the deed. It was *you* who crept upstairs to execute judgment on a man you considered beyond human forgiveness. You are of those, Madame, who can be terrible in anger . . .'

Hilda said: 'I did not kill him.'

Superintendent Sugden said brusquely: 'M. Poirot's quite right. There is a possible case against everyone except Mr Alfred Lee, Mr Harry Lee, and Mrs Alfred Lee.'

Poirot said gently: 'I should not even except those three . . .'

The superintendent protested: 'Oh, come now, M. Poirot!'

Lydia Lee said: 'And what is the case against me, M. Poirot?'

She smiled a little as she spoke, her brows raised ironically.

Poirot bowed. He said: 'Your motive, Madame, I pass over. It is sufficiently obvious. As to the rest, you were wearing last night a flowered taffeta dress of a very distinctive pattern with a cape. I will remind you of the fact that Tressilian, the butler, is short-sighted. Objects at a distance are dim and vague to him. I will also point out that your drawing-room is big and lighted by heavily shaded lamps. On that night, a minute or two before the cries were heard, Tressilian came into the drawing-room to take away the coffee-cups. He saw you, *as he thought,* in a familiar attitude by the far window half concealed by the heavy curtains.'

Lydia Lee said: 'He did see me.'

Poirot went on: 'I suggest that it is possible that *what Tressilian saw was the cape of your dress,* arranged to show by the window curtain, as though you yourself were standing there.'

Lydia said: 'I was standing there . . .'

Alfred said: 'How dare you suggest—?'

Harry interrupted him.

'Let him go on, Alfred. It's our turn next. How do you suggest that dear Alfred killed his beloved father since we were both together in the dining-room at the time?'

Poirot beamed at him.

'That,' he said, 'is very simple. An alibi gains in force accordingly as it is unwillingly given. You and your brother are on bad terms. It is well known. *You* jibe at *him* in public. *He* has not a good word to say for *you!* But, *supposing that were all part of a very clever plot.* Supposing that Alfred Lee is tired of dancing attendance upon an exacting taskmaster. Supposing that you and he have got together some time ago. Your plan is laid. You come home. Alfred appears to resent your presence. He shows jealousy and dislike of you. You show contempt for him. And then comes the night of the murder you have so cleverly planned together. One of you remains in the dining-room, talking and perhaps quarrelling aloud as though two people were there. *The other goes upstairs and commits the crime . . .*'

Alfred sprang to his feet.

'You devil!' he said. His voice was inarticulate.

Sugden was staring at Poirot. He said: 'Do you really mean—?'

Poirot said, with a sudden ring of authority in his voice: 'I have had to show you the *possibilities*! These are the things that *might* have happened! Which of them actually *did* we can only tell by passing from the outside appearance to the inside reality . . .'

He paused and then said slowly: 'We must come back, as I said before, to the character of Simeon Lee himself . . .'

There was a momentary pause. Strangely enough, all indignation and all rancour had died down. Hercule Poirot held his audience under the spell of his personality. They watched him, fascinated, as he began slowly to speak.

'It is all there, you see. The dead man is the focus and centre of the mystery! We must probe deep into the heart and mind of Simeon Lee and see what we find there. For a man does not live and die to himself alone. That which he has he hands on – to those who come after him . . .

'What had Simeon Lee to bequeath to his sons and daughter? Pride, to begin with – a pride which, in the old man, was frustrated in his disappointment over his children. Then there was the quality of patience. We have been told that Simeon Lee waited patiently for years in order to revenge himself upon someone who had done him an injury. We see that that aspect of his temperament was inherited by the son who resembled him least in face. David Lee also could remember and continue to harbour resentment through long years. In *face*, Harry Lee was the only one of his children who closely resembled him. That resemblance is quite striking when we examine the portrait of Simeon Lee as a young man. There is the same high-bridged aquiline nose, the long sharp line of the jaw, the backward poise of the head. I think, too, that Harry inherited many of his father's mannerisms – that habit, for instance, of throwing back his head and laughing, and another habit of drawing his finger along the line of his jaw.

'Bearing all these things in mind, and being convinced that the murder was committed by a person closely connected with the dead man, I studied the family from the psychological standpoint. That is, I tried to decide which of them were *psychologically possible criminals*. *And*, in my judgment, only two persons qualified in that respect. They were Alfred Lee and Hilda Lee, David's wife. David himself I rejected as a possible murderer. I do not think a person of his delicate susceptibilities could have faced the actual blood-shed of a cut throat. George Lee and his wife I likewise rejected. Whatever their desires, I did not think they had the temperament to take a *risk*. They were both essentially cautious. Mrs Alfred Lee I felt sure was quite incapable of an act of violence. She has too much irony in her nature. About Harry Lee I hesitated. He has a certain coarse truculence of aspect, but I was nearly sure that Harry Lee, in spite of his bluff and his bluster, was essentially a weakling. That, I now know, was also his father's opinion. Harry, he said, was worth no more than the rest. That left me with two people I have already mentioned. Alfred Lee was a person capable of a great deal of selfless devotion. He was a man who had controlled and subordinated himself to the will of another for many years. It was always possible under these conditions for something to snap. Moreover, he might quite possibly have harboured a secret grudge against his father which might gradually have grown in force through never being expressed in any way. It is the quietest and meekest people who are often capable of the most sudden and unexpected violence for the reason that when their control does snap it does so entirely! The other person I considered was capable of the crime was Hilda Lee. She is the kind of individual who is capable, on occasions, of taking the law into her own hands – though never through selfish motives. Such people judge and also execute. Many Old Testament characters are of this type. Jael and Judith, for example.

'And now, having got so far, I examined the circumstances of the crime itself. And the first thing that arises – that strikes one in the face, as it were – is the extraordinary conditions under which that crime took place! Take your minds back to that room where Simeon Lee lay dead. If you remember, there was both a heavy table and a heavy chair overturned, a lamp, crockery, glasses, etc. But the chair and the table were especially surprising. They were of solid mahogany. It was hard to see how *any* struggle between that frail old man and his opponent could result in so much solid furniture being overturned and knocked down. The whole thing seemed *unreal*. And yet surely no one in their senses would stage such an effect if it had not really occurred – unless possibly Simeon Lee had been killed by a powerful man and the idea was to suggest that the assailant was a woman or somebody of weak physique.

'But such an idea was unconvincing in the extreme, since the noise of the furniture would give the alarm and the murderer would thereby have very little time to make his exit. It would surely be to *anyone's* advantage to cut Simeon Lee's throat as *quietly* as possible.

'Another extraordinary point was the turning of the key in the lock from the outside. Again, there seemed no *reason* for such a proceeding. It could not suggest suicide, since nothing in the death itself accorded with suicide. It was not to suggest escape through the windows – for those windows were so arranged that escape that way was impossible! Moreover, once again, it involved *time*. Time which *must* be precious to the murderer!

'There was one other incomprehensible thing – a piece of

rubber cut from Simeon Lee's spongebag and a small wooden peg shown to me by Superintendent Sugden. These had been picked up from the floor by one of the persons who first entered that room. There again – *these things did not make sense*! They meant exactly nothing at all! Yet they had been there.

'The crime, you perceive, is becoming increasingly incomprehensible. It has no order, no method – *enfin*, it is not *reasonable*.

'And now we come to a further difficulty. Superintendent Sugden was sent for by the dead man; a robbery was reported to him, and he was asked to return an hour and a half later. *Why?* If it is because Simeon Lee suspected his granddaughter or some other member of the family, why does he not ask Superintendent Sugden to wait downstairs while he has his interview straight away with the suspected party? With the superintendent actually in the house, his lever over the guilty person would have been much stronger.

'So now we arrive at the point where not only the behaviour of the murderer is extraordinary, but the behaviour of Simeon Lee also is extraordinary!

'And I say to myself: "This thing is all wrong!" Why? Because we are looking at it *from the wrong angle*. We are looking at it *from the angle that the murderer wants us to look at it* . . .

'We have three things that do not make sense: the struggle, the turned key, and the snip of rubber. But there *must* be some way of looking at those three things which *would* make sense! And I empty my mind blank and forget the circumstances of the crime and take these things *on their own merits*. I say – *a struggle*. What does *that* suggest? Violence – breaking – noise . . . *The Key? Why* does one turn a key? So that no one shall enter? But the key did not prevent that, since the door was broken down almost immediately. To keep someone *in*? To keep someone *out*? *A snip of rubber?* I say to myself: "A little piece of a spongebag is a little piece of a spongebag, and that is all!"

'So you would say there is nothing there – and yet that is not strictly true, for three impressions remain: Noise – seclusion – blankness . . .

'Do they fit with either of my two possibles? No, they do not. To both Alfred Lee and Hilda Lee a *quiet* murder would have been infinitely preferable, to have wasted time in locking the door from the outside is absurd, and the little piece of spongebag means yet once more – nothing at all!

'And yet I have very strongly the feeling that there is nothing absurd about this crime – that it is, on the contrary, very well planned and admirably executed. That it has, in fact, *succeeded*! Therefore that everything that has happened was *meant* . . .

'And then, going over it again, I got my first glimmer of light . . .

'Blood – *so much blood* – blood everywhere . . . An insistence on blood – fresh, wet, gleaming blood . . . So much blood – *too much blood* . . .

'And a second thought comes with that. This is a crime of *blood* – it is *in* the blood. *It is Simeon Lee's own blood that rises up against him* . . .'

Hercule Poirot leaned forward.

'The two most valuable clues in this case were uttered quite unconsciously by two different people. The first was when Mrs Alfred Lee quoted a line from *Macbeth*: "*Who would have thought the old man to have had so much blood in him?*" The other was a phrase uttered by Tressilian, the butler. He described how he felt dazed and things seemed to be happening that had happened before. It was a very simple occurrence that gave him that strange feeling. He heard a ring at the bell and went to open the door to Harry Lee, and the next day he did the same thing to Stephen Farr.

'Now *why* did he have that feeling? Look at Harry Lee and Stephen Farr *and you will see why*. They are astoundingly alike! *That* was why *opening the door to Stephen Farr was just like opening the door to Harry Lee*. It might almost have been the same man standing there. And then, only today, Tressilian mentioned that he was always getting muddled between people. No wonder! Stephen Farr has a high-bridged nose, a habit of throwing his head back when he laughs, and a trick of stroking his jaw with his forefinger. Look long and earnestly at the portrait of Simeon Lee as a young man and you see *not only Harry Lee, but Stephen Farr* . . .'

Stephen moved. His chair creaked. Poirot said: 'Remember that outburst of Simeon Lee, his tirade against his family. He said, you remember it, that he would swear he had better sons *born the wrong side of the blanket*. We are back again at the character of Simeon Lee. Simeon Lee, who was successful with women and who broke his wife's heart! Simeon Lee, who boasted to Pilar that he might have a bodyguard of sons almost the same age! So I came to this conclusion: Simeon Lee had not only his legitimate family in the house, *but an unacknowledged and unrecognized son of his own blood.*'

Stephen got to his feet. Poirot said: 'That was your real reason, wasn't it? Not that pretty romance of the girl you met in the train!

You were coming here *before you met her.* Coming to see *what kind of a man your father was . . .*'

Stephen had gone dead white. He said, and his voice was broken and husky: 'Yes, I've always wondered . . . Mother spoke about him sometimes. It grew into a kind of obsession with me – to see what he was like! I made a bit of money and I came to England. I wasn't going to let him know who I was. I pretended to be old Eb's son. I came here for one reason only – to see the man who was my father . . .'

Superintendent Sugden said in almost a whisper: 'Lord, I've been blind . . . I can see it now. Twice I've taken you for Mr Harry Lee and then seen my mistake, and yet I never guessed!'

He turned on Pilar.

'That was it, wasn't it? It was Stephen Farr you saw standing outside that door? You hesitated, I remember, and looked at him before you said it was a woman. It was Farr you saw, *and you weren't going to give him away.*'

There was a gentle rustle. Hilda Lee's deep voice spoke: 'No,' she said. 'You're wrong. It was *I* whom Pilar saw . . .'

Poirot said: 'You, Madame? Yes, I thought so . . .'

Hilda said quietly: 'Self-preservation is a curious thing. I wouldn't believe I could be such a coward. To keep silence just because I was afraid!'

Poirot said: 'You will tell us now?'

She nodded.

'I was with David in the music-room. He was playing. He was in a very queer mood. I was a little frightened and I felt my responsibility very keenly because it was I who had insisted on coming here. David began to play the "Dead March", and suddenly I made up my mind. However odd it might seem, I determined that we would both leave at once – that night. I went quietly out of the music-room and upstairs. I meant to go to old Mr Lee and tell him quite plainly why we were going. I went along the corridor to his room and knocked on the door. There was no answer. I knocked again a little louder. There was still no answer. Then I tried the door handle. The door was locked. And then, as I stood hesitating, *I heard a sound inside the room—*'

She stopped.

'You won't believe me, but it's true! *Someone was in there –* assaulting Mr Lee. I heard tables and chairs overturned and the crash of glass and china, and then I heard that one last horrible cry that died away to nothing – and then silence.

'I stood there paralysed! I couldn't move! And then Mr Farr came running along and Magdalene and all the others and Mr Farr and Harry began to batter on the door. It went down and we saw the room, *and there was no one in it* – except Mr Lee lying dead in all that blood.'

Her quiet voice rose higher. She cried: '*There was no one else there – no one*, you understand! And *no one had come out of the room* . . .'

VII

Superintendent Sugden drew a deep breath. He said: 'Either I'm going mad or everybody else is! What you've said, Mrs Lee, is just plumb impossible. It's crazy!'

Hilda Lee cried: 'I tell you I heard them fighting in there, and I heard the old man scream when his throat was cut – and no one came out and no one was in the room!'

Hercule Poirot said: 'And all this time you have said nothing.'

Hilda Lee's face was white, but she said steadily: 'No, because if I told you what had happened, there's only one thing you could say or think – that it was *I* who killed him . . .'

Poirot shook his head.

'No,' he said. 'You did not kill him. His son killed him.'

Stephen Farr said: 'I swear before God I never touched him!'

'Not you,' said Poirot. 'He had other sons!'

Harry said: 'What the hell—?'

George stared. David drew his hand across his eyes. Alfred blinked twice.

Poirot said: 'The very first night I was here – the night of the murder – I saw a ghost. *It was the ghost of the dead man.* When I first saw Harry Lee I was puzzled. I felt I had seen him before. Then I noted his features carefully and I realized how like his father he was, and I told myself that that was what caused the feeling of familiarity.

'But yesterday a man sitting opposite me threw back his head and laughed – *and I knew who it was Harry Lee reminded me of.* And I traced again, in another face, the features of the dead man.

'No wonder poor old Tressilian felt confused when he had answered the door not to two, but to *three* men who resembled each other closely. No wonder he confessed to getting muddled about people when there were three men in the house who, at a little distance, could pass for each other! The same build, the same gestures (one in particular, a trick of stroking the jaw), the same habit of laughing with the head thrown back, the same distinctive high-bridged nose. Yet the similarity was not always easy to see – *for the third man had a moustache.*'

He leaned forward.

'One forgets sometimes that police officers are men, that they have wives and children, mothers' – he paused – 'and *fathers . . .* Remember Simeon Lee's local reputation: a man who broke his wife's heart because of his affairs with women. A son born the wrong side of the blanket may inherit many things. He may inherit his father's features and even his gestures. He may inherit his pride and his patience and his revengeful spirit!'

His voice rose.

'All your life, Sugden, you've resented the wrong your father did you. I think you determined long ago to kill him. You come from the next county, not very far away. Doubtless your mother, with the money Simeon Lee so generously gave her, was able to find a husband who would stand father to her child. Easy for you to enter the Middleshire police force and wait your opportunity. A police superintendent has a grand opportunity of committing a murder and getting away with it.'

Sugden's face had gone white as paper.

He said: 'You're mad! I was outside the house when he was killed.'

Poirot shook his head.

'No, you killed him before you left the house the first time. No one saw him alive after you left. It was all so easy for you. Simeon Lee expected you, yes, *but he never sent for you.* It was *you* who rang him up and spoke vaguely about an attempt at robbery. You said you would call upon him just before eight that night and would pretend to be collecting for a police charity. Simeon Lee had no suspicions. He did not know you were his son. You came and told him a tale of substituted diamonds. He opened the safe to show you that the real diamonds were safe in his possession. You apologized, came back to the hearth with him and, catching him unawares, you cut his throat, holding your hand over his mouth so that he shouldn't cry out. Child's play to a man of your powerful physique.

'Then you set the scene. You took the diamonds. You piled up tables and chairs, lamps and glasses, and twined a very thin rope or cord which you had brought in coiled round your body, in and out between them. You had with you a bottle of some freshly killed animal's blood to which you had added a quantity of sodium citrate. You sprinkled this about freely and added more sodium citrate to the pool of blood which flowed from Simeon Lee's wound. You made up the fire so that the body should keep its warmth. Then you passed the two ends of the cord out through the narrow slit at the bottom of the window and let them hang down the wall. You left the room and turned the key from the outside. That was vital, *since no one must, by any chance, enter that room.*

'Then you went out and hid the diamonds in the stone sink garden. If, sooner or later, they were discovered there, they would only focus suspicion more strongly where you wanted it: on the members of Simeon Lee's legitimate family. A little before nine-fifteen you returned and, going up to the wall underneath the window, you pulled on the cord. That dislodged the carefully piled-up structure you had arranged. Furniture and china fell with a crash. You pulled on one end of the cord and re-wound it round your body under your coat and waistcoat.

'You had one further device!'

He turned to the others.

'Do you remember, all of you, how each of you described the dying scream of Mr Lee in a different way? You, Mr Lee, described it as the cry of a man in mortal agony. Your wife and David Lee both used the expression "a soul in hell". Mrs David Lee, on the contrary, said it was the cry of someone who had *no* soul. She said it was inhuman, like a beast. It was Harry Lee who came nearest to the truth. He said it sounded like killing a pig.

'Do you know those long pink bladders that are sold at fairs with faces painted on them called "Dying Pigs"? As the air rushes out they give forth an inhuman wail. That, Sugden, was your final touch. You arranged one of those in the room. The mouth of it was stopped up with a peg, but that peg was connected to the cord. When you pulled on the cord the peg came out and the pig began to deflate. On top of the falling furniture came the scream of the "Dying Pig".'

He turned once more to the others.

'You see now what it was that Pilar Estravados picked up? The superintendent had hoped to get there in time to retrieve that little wisp of rubber before anyone noticed it. However, he took it from Pilar quickly enough in his most official manner. But remember, *he never mentioned that incident to anyone.* In itself, that was a singularly suspicious fact. I heard of it from Magdalene Lee and tackled him about it. He was prepared for that eventuality. He had snipped a piece from Mr Lee's rubber spongebag and produced that, together with a wooden peg. Superficially it answered to the same description – a fragment of rubber and a piece of wood. It meant, as I realized at the time, absolutely nothing! But, fool that I was, I did not at once say: "This means nothing, *so it cannot have been there, and Superintendent Sugden is lying* . . ." No, I foolishly went on trying to find an explanation for it. It was not until Mademoiselle Estravados was playing with a balloon that burst, and she cried out that it must have been a burst balloon she picked up in Simeon Lee's room, that I saw the truth.

'You see now how everything fits in? The improbable struggle, *which is necessary to establish a false time of death*; the locked door – so that nobody shall find the body too soon; the dying man's scream. The crime is now logical and reasonable.

'But from the moment that Pilar Estravados cried aloud her discovery about the balloon she was a source of danger to the murderer. And if that remark had been heard by him from the house (which it well might, for her voice was high and clear and the windows were open) she herself was in considerable danger. Already she had given the murderer one very nasty moment. She had said, speaking of old Mr Lee, "He must have been very good-looking when he was young." And had added, speaking directly to Sugden: "*Like you.*" She meant that literally, and Sugden knew it. No wonder Sugden went purple in the face and nearly choked. It was so unexpected and so deadly dangerous. He hoped, after that, to fix the guilt on her, but it proved unexpectedly difficult, since, as the old man's portionless granddaughter, she had obviously no motive for the crime. Later, when he overheard from the house her clear, high voice calling out its remark about the balloon, he decided on desperate measures. He set that booby trap when we were at lunch. Luckily, almost by a miracle, it failed . . .'

There was dead silence. Then Sugden said quietly: 'When were you sure?'

Poirot said: 'I was not quite sure till I brought home a false moustache and tried it on Simeon Lee's picture. Then – the face that looked at me was yours.'

Sugden said: 'God rot his soul in hell! I'm glad I did it!'

— 7 —

DECEMBER 28TH

LYDIA LEE said: 'Pilar, I think you had better stay with us until we can arrange something definite for you.'

Pilar said meekly: 'You are very good, Lydia. You are nice. You forgive people quite easily without making a fuss about it.'

Lydia said, smiling: 'I still call you Pilar, though I suppose your name is something else.'

'Yes, I am really Conchita Lopez.'

'Conchita is a pretty name, too.'

'You are really almost too nice, Lydia. But you don't need to be bothered by me. I am going to marry Stephen, and we are going to South Africa.'

Lydia said, smiling: 'Well, that rounds off things very nicely.'

Pilar said timidly: 'Since you have been so kind, do you think, Lydia, that one day we might come back and stay with you – perhaps for Christmas – and then we could have the crackers and the burning raisins and those shiny things on a tree and the little snowmen?'

'Certainly, you shall come and have a real English Christmas.'

'That will be lovely. You see, Lydia, I feel that this year it was not a nice Christmas at all.'

Lydia caught her breath. She said: 'No, it was not a nice Christmas . . .'

II

Harry said: 'Well, goodbye, Alfred. Don't suppose you'll be troubled by seeing much of me. I'm off to Hawaii. Always meant to live there if I had a bit of money.'

Alfred said: 'Goodbye, Harry. I expect you'll enjoy yourself. I hope so.'

Harry said rather awkwardly: 'Sorry I riled you so much, old man. Rotten sense of humour I've got. Can't help trying to pull a fellow's leg.'

Alfred said with an effort: 'Suppose I must learn to take a joke.'

Harry said with relief: 'Well – so long.'

490

III

Alfred said: 'David, Lydia and I have decided to sell up this place. I thought perhaps you'd like some of the things that were our mother's – her chair and that footstool. You were always her favourite.'

David hesitated a minute. Then he said slowly: 'Thanks for the thought, Alfred, but do you know, I don't think I will. I don't want anything out of the house. I feel it's better to break with the past altogether.'

Alfred said: 'Yes, I understand. Maybe you're right.'

IV

George said: 'Well, goodbye, Alfred. Goodbye, Lydia. What a terrible time we have been through. There's the trial coming on, too. I suppose the whole disgraceful story is bound to come out – Sugden being – er – my father's son. One couldn't arrange for it to be put to him, I suppose, that it would be better if he pleaded advanced communist views and dislike of my father as a capitalist – something of that kind?'

Lydia said: 'My dear George, do you really imagine that a man like Sugden would tell lies to soothe *our* feelings?'

George said: 'Er – perhaps not. No, I see your point. All the same, the man must be mad. Well, goodbye again.'

Magdalene said: '*Goodbye*. Next year do let's all go to the Riviera or somewhere for Christmas and be really gay.'

George said: 'Depends on the Exchange.'

Magdalene said: 'Darling, don't be *mean*.'

V

Alfred came out on the terrace. Lydia was bending over a stone sink. She straightened up when she saw him.

He said with a sigh: 'Well – they've all gone.'

Lydia said: 'Yes – what a blessing.'

'It is, rather.'

Alfred said: 'You'll be glad to leave here.'

She asked: 'Will you mind very much?'

'No, I shall be glad. There are so many interesting things we can do together. To live on here would be to be constantly reminded of that nightmare. Thank God it's all over!'

Lydia said: 'Thanks to Hercule Poirot.'

'Yes. You know, it was really amazing the way everything fell into place when he explained it.'

'I know. Like when you finish a jig-saw puzzle and all the queer-shaped bits you swear won't fit in anywhere find their places quite naturally.'

Alfred said: 'There's one little thing that never fitted in. What *was* George doing *after* he telephoned. Why wouldn't he say?'

'Don't you know? I knew all the time. He was having a look through your papers on your desk.'

'Oh! No, Lydia, no one would do a thing like that!'

'George would. He's frightfully curious about money matters. But of course he couldn't say so. He'd have had to be actually in the dock before he'd have owned up to that.'

Alfred said: 'Are you making another garden?'

'Yes.'

'What is it this time?'

'I think,' said Lydia, 'it's an attempt at the Garden of Eden. A new version – without any serpent – and Adam and Eve are definitely middle-aged.'

Alfred said gently: 'Dear Lydia, how patient you have been all these years. You have been very good to me.'

Lydia said: 'But, you see, Alfred, I love you . . .'

VI

Colonel Johnson said: 'God bless my soul!' Then he said: 'Upon my word!' And finally, once more: 'God bless my soul!'

He leaned back in his chair and stared at Poirot. He said plaintively: 'My best man! What's the police coming to?'

Poirot said: 'Even policemen have private lives! Sugden was a very proud man.'

Colonel Johnson shook his head.

To relieve his feelings he kicked at the logs in the grate. He said jerkily: 'I always say – nothing like a wood fire.'

Hercule Poirot, conscious of the draughts round his neck, thought to himself: '*Pour moi*, every time the central heating . . .'

492

FIVE
LITTLE PIGS

INTRODUCTION

CARLA LEMARCHANT

HERCULE POIROT looked with interest and appreciation at the young woman who was being ushered into the room.

There had been nothing distinctive in the letter she had written. It had been a mere request for an appointment, with no hint of what lay behind that request. It had been brief and business-like. Only the firmness of the handwriting had indicated that Carla Lemarchant was a young woman.

And now here she was in the flesh – a tall, slender young woman in her early twenties. The kind of young woman that one definitely looked at twice. Her clothes were good: an expensive well-cut coat and skirt and luxurious furs. Her head was well poised on her shoulders, she had a square brow, a sensitively cut nose and a determined chin. She looked very much alive. It was her aliveness, more than her beauty, which struck the predominant note.

Before her entrance, Hercule Poirot had been feeling old; now he felt rejuvenated – alive – keen!

As he came forward to greet her, he was aware of her dark grey eyes studying him attentively. She was very earnest in that scrutiny.

She sat down and accepted the cigarette that he offered her. After it was lit she sat for a minute or two smoking, still looking at him with that earnest, thoughtful gaze.

Poirot said gently: 'Yes, it has to be decided, does it not?'

She started. 'I beg your pardon?'

Her voice was attractive, with a faint, agreeable huskiness in it.

'You are making up your mind, are you not, whether I am a mere mountebank, or the man you need?'

She smiled. She said: 'Well, yes – something of that kind. You see, M. Poirot, you – you don't look exactly the way I pictured you.'

'And I am old, am I not? Older than you imagined?'

'Yes, that, too.' She hesitated. 'I'm being frank, you see. I want – I've got to have – the best.'

'Rest assured,' said Hercule Poirot. 'I *am* the best!'

Carla said: 'You're not modest . . . All the same, I'm inclined to take you at your word.'

Poirot said placidly: 'One does not, you know, employ merely the muscles. I do not need to bend and measure the footprints and pick up the cigarette ends and examine the bent blades of grass. It is enough for me to sit back in my chair and *think*. It is this' – he tapped his egg-shaped head – '*this* that functions!'

'I know,' said Carla Lemarchant. 'That's why I've come to you. I want you, you see, to do something fantastic!'

'That,' said Hercule Poirot, 'promises well!'

He looked at her in encouragement.

Carla Lemarchant drew a deep breath.

'My name,' she said, 'isn't Carla. It's Caroline. The same as my mother's. I was called after her.' She paused. 'And, though I've always gone by the name of Lemarchant, my real name is Crale.'

Hercule Poirot's forehead creased a moment perplexedly. He murmured: 'Crale – I seem to remember . . .'

She said: 'My father was a painter – rather a well-known painter. Some people say he was a great painter. *I* think he was.'

Hercule Poirot said: 'Amyas Crale?'

'Yes.' She paused, then she went on: 'And my mother, Caroline Crale, was tried for murdering him!'

'Aha,' said Hercule Poirot. 'I remember now – but only vaguely. I was abroad at the time. It was a long time ago.'

'Sixteen years,' said the girl.

Her face was very white now and her eyes two burning lights.

She said: 'Do you understand? *She was tried and convicted* . . . She wasn't hanged because they felt that there were extenuating circumstances – so the sentence was commuted to penal servitude for life. But she died only a year after the trial. You see? It's all over – done – finished with . . .'

Poirot said quietly: 'And so?'

The girl called Carla Lemarchant pressed her hands together. She spoke slowly and haltingly but with an odd, pointed emphasis.

She said: 'You've got to understand – exactly – where I come in. I was five years old at the time it – happened. Too young to know anything about it. I remember my mother and my father, of course, and I remember leaving home suddenly – being taken to the country. I remember the pigs and a nice fat farmer's wife – and everybody being very kind – and I remember, quite clearly, the funny way they used to look at me – everybody – a sort of furtive look. I knew, of course – children do – that there was something wrong – but I didn't know what.

'And then I went on a ship – it was exciting – it went on for days, and then I was in Canada and Uncle Simon met me, and I lived in Montreal with him and with Aunt Louise, and when I asked about Mummy and Daddy they said they'd be coming soon. And then – and then I think I forgot – only I sort of knew that they were dead without remembering anyone actually telling me so. Because by that time, you see, I didn't think about them any more. I was very happy, you know. Uncle Simon and Aunt Louise were sweet to me, and I went to school and had a lot of friends, and I'd quite forgotten that I'd ever had another name, not Lemarchant. Aunt Louise, you see, told me that that was my name in Canada and that seemed quite sensible to me at the time – it was just my Canadian name – but, as I say, I forgot in the end that I'd ever had any other.'

She flung up her defiant chin. She said: 'Look at me. You'd say – wouldn't you? – if you met me: "There goes a girl who's got nothing to worry about!" I'm well off, I've got splendid health, I'm sufficiently good to look at, I can enjoy life. At twenty, there wasn't a girl anywhere I'd have changed places with.

'But already, you know, I'd begun to ask questions. About my own mother and father. Who they were and what they did. I'd have been bound to find out in the end—

'As it was, they told me the truth. When I was twenty-one. They had to then, because, for one thing, I came into my own money. And, then, you see, there was the letter. The letter my mother left for me when she died.'

Her expression changed, dimmed. Her eyes were no longer two burning points, they were dark dim pools. She said: 'That's when I learnt the truth. That my mother had been convicted of murder. It was – rather horrible.'

She paused.

'There's something else I must tell you. I was engaged to be married. They said we must wait – that we couldn't be married until I was twenty-one. When I knew, I understood why.'

Poirot stirred and spoke for the first time. He said: 'And what was your fiancé's reaction?'

'John? John didn't care. He said it made no difference – not to him. He and I were John and Carla – and the past didn't matter.'

She leaned forward.

'We're still engaged. But, all the same, you know, it *does* matter. It matters to me. And it matters to John, too . . . It isn't the past

497

that matters to us – it's the future.' She clenched her hands. 'We want children, you see. We both want children. And we don't want to watch our children growing up and be afraid.'

Poirot said: 'Do you realize that amongst everyone's ancestors there has been violence and evil?'

'You don't understand. That's so, of course. But, then, one doesn't usually know about it. We do. It's very near to us. And sometimes – I've seen John just look at me. Such a quick glance – just a flash. Supposing we were married and we'd quarrelled – and I saw him look at me and – and *wonder*?'

Hercule Poirot said: 'How was your father killed?

Carla's voice came clear and firm.

'He was poisoned.'

Hercule Poirot said: 'I see.'

There was a silence.

Then the girl said in a calm, matter-of-fact voice: 'Thank goodness you're sensible. You see that it does matter – and what it involves. You don't try and patch it up and trot out consoling phrases.'

'I understand very well,' said Poirot. 'What I do not understand is what you want of *me*?'

Carla Lemarchant said simply: 'I want to marry John! And I mean to marry John! And I want to have at least two girls and two boys. And you're going to make that possible!'

'You mean – you want me to talk to your fiancé? Ah, no, it is idiocy what I say there! It is something quite different that you are suggesting. Tell me what is in your mind.'

'Listen, M. Poirot. Get this – and get it clearly. I'm hiring you to investigate a case of murder.'

'Do you mean—?'

'Yes, I do mean. A case of murder is a case of murder whether it happened yesterday or sixteen years ago.'

'But my dear young lady—'

'Wait, M. Poirot. You haven't got it all yet. There's a very important point.'

'Yes?'

'My mother was innocent,' said Carla Lemarchant.

Hercule Poirot rubbed his nose. He murmured: 'Well, naturally – I comprehend that—'

'It isn't sentiment. There's her letter. She left it for me before she died. It was to be given to me when I was twenty-one. She left it for that one reason – that I should be quite sure. That's all that was in it. That she hadn't done it – that she was innocent – that I could be sure of that always.'

Hercule Poirot looked thoughtfully at the young vital face staring so earnestly at him. He said slowly: *'Tout de même—'*

Carla smiled.

'No, Mother wasn't like that! You're thinking that it might be a lie – a sentimental lie?' She leaned forward earnestly. 'Listen, M. Poirot, there are some things that children know quite well. I can remember my mother – a patchy remembrance, of course, but I remember quite well the *sort* of person she was. She didn't tell lies – kind lies. If a thing was going to hurt she always told you so. Dentists, or thorns in your finger – all that sort of thing. Truth was a – a natural impulse to her. I wasn't, I don't think, especially fond of her – but I trusted her. I *still* trust her! If she says she didn't kill my father, then she didn't kill him! She wasn't the sort of person who would solemnly write down a lie when she knew she was dying.'

Slowly, almost reluctantly, Hercule Poirot bowed his head.

Carla went on: 'That's why it's all right for *me* marrying John. *I* know it's all right. *But he doesn't.* He feels that naturally I would think my mother was innocent. It's got to be cleared up, M. Poirot. And *you're* going to do it!'

Hercule Poirot said slowly: 'Granted that what you say is true, Mademoiselle, sixteen years have gone by!'

Carla Lemarchant said: 'Oh, of course it's going to be *difficult*! Nobody but *you* could do it!'

Hercule Poirot's eyes twinkled slightly. He said: 'You give me the best butter – *hein?*'

Carla said: 'I've heard about you. The things you've done. The *way* you have done them. It's psychology that interests you, isn't it? Well, that doesn't change with time. The tangible things are gone – the cigarette-end and the footprints and the bent blades of grass. You can't look for those any more. But you can go over all the facts of the case, and perhaps talk to the people who were there at the time – they're all alive still – and then – and then, as you said just now, you can lie back in your chair and *think. And you'll know what really happened . . .'*

Hercule Poirot rose to his feet. One hand caressed his moustache. He said: 'Mademoiselle, I am honoured! I will justify your faith in me. I will investigate your case of murder. I will search back into the events of sixteen years ago and I will find out the truth.'

Carla got up. Her eyes were shining. But she only said: 'Good.'
Hercule Poirot shook an eloquent forefinger.

'One little moment. I have said I will find out the truth. I do not, you understand, have the bias. I do not accept your assurance of your mother's innocence. If she was guilty – *eh bien*, what then?'

Carla's proud head went back. She said: 'I'm her daughter. I want the *truth*!'

Hercule Poirot said: '*En avant*, then. Though it is not that that I should say. On the contrary. *En arrière* . . .'

PART I

— I —

COUNSEL FOR THE DEFENCE

'Do I remember the Crale case?'. asked Sir Montague Depleach. 'Certainly I do. Remember it very well. Most attractive woman. But unbalanced, of course. No self-control.'

He glanced sideways at Poirot.

'What makes you ask me about it?'

'I am interested.'

'Not really tactful of you, my dear man,' said Depleach, showing his teeth in his sudden famous 'wolf's smile', which had been reputed to have such a terrifying effect upon witnesses. 'Not one of my successes, you know. I didn't get her off.'

'I know that.'

Sir Montague shrugged his shoulders. He said: 'Of course I hadn't quite as much experience then as I have now. All the same, I think I did all that could humanly be done. One can't do much without *co-operation*. We *did* get it commuted to penal servitude. Provocation, you know. Lots of respectable wives and mothers got up a petition. There was a lot of sympathy for her.'

He leaned back, stretching his long legs. His face took on a judicial, appraising look.

'If she'd shot him, you know, or even knifed him – I'd have gone all out for manslaughter. But poison – no, you can't play tricks with that. It's tricky – very tricky.'

'What was the defence?' asked Hercule Poirot.

He knew because he had already read the newspaper files, but he saw no harm in playing the complete ignorant to Sir Montague.

'Oh, suicide. Only thing you *could* go for. But it didn't go down well. Crale simply wasn't that kind of man! You never met him, I suppose? No? Well, he was a great blustering, vivid sort of chap. Great womaniser, beer drinker – all the rest of it. Went in for the lusts of the flesh and enjoyed them. You can't persuade a jury that a man like that is going to sit down and quietly do away with

501

himself. It just doesn't fit. No, I was afraid I was up against a losing proposition from the first. And she wouldn't play up! I knew we'd lost as soon as she went into the box. No fight in her at all. But there it is – if you *don't* put your client into the box, the jury draw their own conclusions.'

Poirot said: 'Is that what you meant when you said just now that one cannot do much without co-operation?'

'Absolutely, my dear fellow. We're not magicians, you know. Half the battle is the impression the accused makes on the jury. I've known juries time and again bring in verdicts dead against the judge's summing up. " 'E did it, all right" – that's the point of view. Or "*He* never did a thing like that – don't tell me!" Caroline Crale didn't even *try* to put up a fight.'

'Why was that?'

Sir Montague shrugged his shoulders.

'Don't ask me. Of course, she was fond of the fellow. Broke her all up when she came to and realized what she'd done. Don't believe she ever rallied from the shock.'

'So in your opinion she was guilty?'

Depleach looked rather startled. He said: 'Er – well, I thought we were taking that for granted.'

'Did she ever admit to you that she was guilty?'

Depleach looked shocked.

'Of course not – of course not. We have our code, you know. Innocence is always – er – assumed. If you're so interested, it's a pity you can't get hold of old Mayhew. Mayhews were the solicitors who briefed me. Old Mayhew could have told you more than I can. But there – he's joined the great majority. There's young George Mayhew, of course, but he was only a boy at the time. It's a long time ago, you know.'

'Yes, I know. It is unfortunate for me that you remember so much. You have a remarkable memory.'

Depleach looked pleased. He murmured: 'Oh, well, one remembers the main headings, you know. Especially when it's a capital charge. And, of course, the Crale case got a lot of publicity from the press. Lot of sex interest and all that. The girl in the case was pretty striking. Hard-boiled piece of goods, I thought.'

'You will forgive me if I seem too insistent,' said Poirot, 'but I repeat once more, you had no doubt of Caroline Crale's guilt?'

Depleach shrugged his shoulders. He said: 'Frankly – as man to man – I don't think there's much doubt about it. Oh, yes, she did it all right.'

'What was the evidence against her?'

'Very damning indeed. First of all there was motive. She and Crale had led a kind of cat-and-dog life for years – interminable rows. He was always getting mixed up with some woman or other. Couldn't help it. He was that kind of man. She stood it pretty well on the whole. Made allowances for him on the score of temperament – and the man really was a first-class painter, you know. His stuffs's gone up enormously in price – enormously. Don't care for that style of painting myself – ugly forceful stuff; but it's *good* – no doubt of that.

'Well, as I say, there had been trouble about women from time to time. Mrs Crale wasn't the meek kind who suffers in silence. There were rows all right. But he always came back to her in the end. These affairs of his blew over. But this final affair was rather different. It was a girl, you see – and quite a young girl. She was only twenty.

'Elsa Greer, that was her name. She was the only daughter of some Yorkshire manufacturer. She'd got money and determination, and she knew what she wanted. What she wanted was Amyas Crale. She got him to paint her – he didn't paint regular society portraits, "Mrs Blinkety Blank in pink satin and pearls", but he painted figures. I don't know that most women would have cared to be painted by him – he didn't spare them! But he painted the Greer girl, and he ended by falling for her good and proper. He was getting on for forty, you know, and he'd been married a good many years. He was just ripe for making a fool of himself over some chit of a girl. Elsa Greer was the girl. He was crazy about her, and his idea was to get a divorce from his wife and marry Elsa.

'Caroline Crale wasn't standing for that. She threatened him. She was overheard by two people to say that if he didn't give the girl up she'd kill him. And she meant it all right! The day before it happened, they'd been having tea with a neighbour. He was by way of dabbling in herbs and home-brewed medicines. Amongst his patent brews was one of coniine – spotted hemlock. There was some talk about it and its deadly properties.

'The next day he noticed that half the contents of the bottle had gone. Got the wind up about it. They found an almost empty bottle of it in Mrs Crale's room, hidden away at the bottom of a drawer.'

Hercule Poirot moved uncomfortably. He said: 'Somebody else might have put it there.'

'Oh, she admitted to the police she'd taken it. Very unwise, of course, but she didn't have a solicitor to advise her at that stage. When they asked her about it, she admitted quite frankly that she had taken it.'

'For what reason?'

'She made out that she'd taken it with the idea of doing herself in. She couldn't explain how the bottle came to be empty – nor how it was that there were only her fingerprints on it. That part of it was pretty damaging. She contended, you see, that Amyas Crale had committed suicide. But, if he'd taken the coniine from the bottle she'd hidden in her room, *his* fingerprints would have been on the bottle as well as hers.'

'It was given him in beer, was it not?'

'Yes. She got out the bottle from the refrigerator and took it down herself to where he was painting in the garden. She poured it out and gave it to him and watched him drink it. Everyone went up to lunch and left him – he often didn't come in to meals. Afterwards she and the governess found him there dead. Her story was that the beer *she* gave him was all right. Our theory was that he suddenly felt so worried and remorseful that he slipped the poison in himself. All poppycock – he wasn't that kind of man! And the fingerprint evidence was the most damning of all.'

'They found her fingerprints on the bottle?'

'No, they didn't – they found only *his* – and they were phoney ones. She was alone with the body, you see, while the governess went to call up a doctor. And what she must have done was to wipe the bottle and glass and then press his fingers on them. She wanted to pretend, you see, that she'd never even handled the stuff. Well, that didn't work. Old Rudolph, who was prosecuting, had a lot of fun with that – proved quite definitely by demonstration in court that a man *couldn't* hold a bottle with his fingers in that position! Of course *we* did our best to prove that he *could* – that his hands would take up a contorted attitude when he was dying – but frankly our stuff wasn't very convincing.'

Hercule Poirot said: 'The coniine in the bottle must have been put there before she took it down to the garden.'

'There was no coniine in the bottle at all. Only in the glass.'

He paused – his large handsome face suddenly altered – he turned his head sharply. 'Hallo,' he said. 'Now, then, Poirot, *what are you driving at?*'

Poirot said: '*If* Caroline Crale was innocent, how did that coniine get into the beer? The defence said at the time that Amyas Crale himself put it there. But you say to me that that was in the highest degree unlikely – and for my part I agree with you. He was not that kind of man. Then, if Caroline Crale did not do it, *someone else did.*'

Depleach said with almost a splutter: 'Oh, damn it all, man, you can't flog a dead horse. It's all over and done with years ago. Of course she did it. You'd know that well enough if you'd seen her at the time. It was written all over her! I even fancy that the verdict was a relief to her. She wasn't frightened. No nerves at all. Just wanted to get through the trial and have it over. A very brave woman, really . . .'

'And yet,' said Hercule Poirot, 'when she died she left a letter to be given to her daughter in which she swore solemnly that she was innocent.'

'I dare say she did,' said Sir Montague Depleach. 'You or I would have done the same in her place.'

'Her daughter says she was not that kind of woman.'

'The daughter says— Pah! What does *she* know about it? My dear Poirot, the daughter was a mere infant at the time of the trial. What was she – four – five? They changed her name and sent her out of England somewhere to some relatives. What can *she* know or remember?'

'Children know people very well sometimes.'

'Maybe they do. But that doesn't follow in this case. Naturally the girl wants to believe her mother didn't do it. Let her believe it. It doesn't do any harm.'

'But unfortunately she demands proof.'

'Proof that Caroline Crale didn't kill her husband?'

'Yes.'

'Well' said Depleach. 'She won't get it.'

'You think not?'

The famous KC looked thoughtfully at his companion.

'I've always thought you were an honest man, Poirot. What are you doing? Trying to make money by playing on a girl's natural affections?'

'You do not know the girl. She is an unusual girl. A girl of great force of character.'

'Yes, I should imagine the daughter of Amyas and Caroline Crale might be that. What does she want?'

'She wants the truth.'

'H'm – I'm afraid she'll find the truth unpalatable. Honestly, Poirot, I don't think there's any doubt about it. She killed him.'

'You will forgive me, my friend, but I must satisfy myself on that point.'

'Well, I don't know what more you can do. You can read up the

505

newspaper accounts of the trial. Humphrey Rudolph appeared for the Crown. He's dead. Let me see, who was his junior? Young Fogg, I think. Yes, Fogg. You can have a chat with him. And then there are the people who were there at the time. Don't suppose they'll enjoy your butting in and raking the whole thing up, but I dare say you'll get what you want out of them. You're a plausible devil.'

'Ah, yes, the people concerned. That is very important. You remember, perhaps, who they were?'

Depleach considered.

'Let me see – it's a long time ago. There were only five people who were really in it, so to speak – I'm not counting the servants – a couple of faithful old things, scared-looking creatures – they didn't know anything about anything. No one could suspect them.'

'There are five people, you say. Tell me about them.'

'Well, there was Philip Blake. He was Crale's greatest friend – had known him all his life. He was staying in the house at the time. *He's* alive. I see him now and again on the links. Lives at St George's Hill. Stockbroker. Plays the markets and gets away with it. Successful man, running to fat a bit.'

'Yes. And who next?'

'Then there was Blake's elder brother. Country squire – stay-at-home sort of chap.'

A jingle ran through Poirot's head. He repressed it. He must *not* always be thinking of nursery rhymes. It seemed an obsession with him lately. And yet the jingle persisted.

'This little pig went to market, this little pig stayed at home . . .'

He murmured: 'He stayed at home – yes?'

'He's the fellow I was telling you about – messed about with drugs – and herbs – bit of a chemist. His hobby. What was his name now? Literary sort of name – I've got it. Meredith. Meredith Blake. Don't know whether he's alive or not.'

'And who next?'

'Next? Well, there's the cause of all the trouble. The girl in the case. Elsa Greer.'

'This little pig ate roast beef,' murmured Poirot.

Depleach stared at him.

'They've fed her meat all right,' he said. 'She's been a go-getter. She's had three husbands since then. In and out of the divorce court as easy as you please. And every time she makes a change it's for the better. Lady Dittisham – that's who she is now. Open any *Tatler* and you're sure to find her.'

'And the other two?'

'There was the governess woman. I don't remember her name. Nice capable woman. Thompson – Jones – something like that. And there was the child. Caroline Crale's half-sister. She must have been about fifteen. She's made rather a name for herself. Digs up things and goes trekking to the back of beyond. Warren – that's her name. Angela Warren. Rather an alarming young woman nowadays. I met her the other day.'

'She is not, then, the little pig who cried *Wee Wee Wee*?'

Sir Montague Depleach looked at him rather oddly. He said dryly: 'She's had something to cry *Wee Wee* about in her life! She's disfigured, you know. Got a bad scar down one side of her face. She— Oh, well, you'll hear all about it, I dare say.'

Poirot stood up. He said: 'I thank you. You have been very kind. If Mrs Crale did *not* kill her husband—'

Depleach interrupted him: 'But she did, old boy, she did. Take my word for it.'

Poirot continued without taking any notice of the interruption.

'Then it seems logical to suppose that one of these five people must have done so.'

'One of them *could* have done it, I suppose,' said Depleach, doubtfully. 'But I don't see why any of them *should*. No reason at all! In fact, I'm quite sure none of them *did* do it. Do get this bee out of your bonnet, old boy!'

But Hercule Poirot only smiled and shook his head.

— 2 —

COUNSEL FOR THE PROSECUTION

'GUILTY as Hell,' said Mr Fogg succinctly.

Hercule Poirot looked meditatively at the thin clear-cut face of the barrister.

Quentin Fogg, KC, was a very different type from Montague Depleach. Depleach had force, magnetism, an overbearing and slightly bullying personality. He got his effects by a rapid and dramatic change of manner. Handsome, urbane, charming one minute – then an almost magical transformation, lips back,'snarling smile – out for your blood.

Quentin Fogg was thin, pale, singularly lacking in what is called personality. His questions were quiet and unemotional – but steadily persistent. If Depleach was like a rapier, Fogg was like an auger. He bored steadily. He had never reached spectacular fame, but he was known as a first-class man on law. He usually won his cases.

Hercule Poirot eyed him meditatively.

'So that,' he said, 'was how it struck you?'

Fogg nodded. He said: 'You should have seen her in the box. Old Humpie Rudolph (he was leading, you know) simply made mincemeat of her. Mincemeat!'

He paused and then said unexpectedly: 'On the whole, you know, it was rather too much of a good thing.'

'I am not sure,' said Hercule Poirot, 'that I quite understand you?'

Fogg drew his delicately marked brows together. His sensitive hand stroked his bare upper lip. He said: 'How shall I put it? It's a very English point of view. "Shooting the sitting bird" describes it best. Is that intelligible to you?'

'It is, as you say, a very English point of view, but I think I understand you. In the Central Criminal Court, as on the playing-fields of Eton, and in the hunting country, the Englishman likes the victim to have a sporting chance.'

'That's it, exactly. Well, in this case, the accused *didn't* have a chance. Humpie Rudolph did as he liked with her. It started with her examination by Depleach. She stood up there, you know – as docile as a little girl at a party, answering Depleach's questions with the answers she'd learnt off by heart. Quite docile, word perfect – and absolutely unconvincing! She'd been told what to say and she said it. It wasn't Depleach's fault. That old mountebank played his part perfectly – but in any scene that needs two actors one alone can't carry it. She didn't play up to him. It made the worst possible effect on the jury. And then old Humpie got up. I expect you've seen him? He's a great loss. Hitching his gown up, swaying back on his feet – and then – straight off the mark!

'As I tell you, he made mincemeat of her! Led up to this and that – and she fell into the pitfall every time. He got her to admit the absurdities of her own statements, he got her to contradict herself, she floundered in deeper and deeper. And then he wound up with his usual stuff. Very compelling – very convinced: "I suggest to you, Mrs Crale, that this story of yours about stealing coniine in order to commit suicide is a tissue of falsehood. I suggest that you took it in order to administer it to your husband, who was about to leave you for another woman, and that you *did* deliberately administer it to him." And she looked at him – such a pretty creature – graceful, delicate – and she said: "Oh, no – no, I didn't." It was the flattest thing you ever heard – the most unconvincing. I saw old Depleach squirm in his seat. He knew it was all up then.'

Fogg paused a minute – then he went on: 'And yet – I don't know. It some ways it was the cleverest thing she could have done! It appealed to chivalry – to that queer chivalry closely allied to blood sports which makes most foreigners think us such almighty humbugs! The jury felt – the whole court felt – that she hadn't got a chance. She couldn't even fight for herself. She certainly couldn't put up any kind of a show against a great big clever brute like old Humpie. That weak, unconvincing "*Oh, no* – no, I didn't" it was pathetic – simply pathetic. She was done for!

'Yes, in a way it was the best thing she could have done. The jury were only out just over half an hour. They brought her in: Guilty with a recommendation to mercy.

'Actually, you know, she made a good contrast to the other woman in the case. The girl. The jury were unsympathetic to *her* from the start. She never turned a hair. Very good-looking, hard-boiled, modern. To the women in the court she stood for a type – type of the home-breaker. Homes weren't safe when girls like that were wandering abroad. Girls damn full of sex and contemptuous of the rights of wives and mothers. She didn't spare herself, I will say. She was honest. Admirably honest. She'd fallen in love with Amyas Crale and he with her, and she'd no scruples at all about taking him away from his wife and child.

'I admired her in a way. She had guts. Depleach put in some nasty stuff in cross-examination and she stood up well to it. But the court was unsympathetic. And the judge didn't like her. Old Avis, it was. Been a bit of a rip himself when young – but he's very hot on morality when he's presiding in his robes. His summing up against Caroline Crale was mildness itself. He couldn't deny the facts but he threw out pretty strong hints as to provocation and all that.'

Hercule Poirot asked: 'He did not support the suicide theory of the defence?'

Fogg shook his head.

'*That* never really had a leg to stand upon. Mind you, I don't say Depleach didn't do his best with it. He was magnificent. He painted a most moving picture of a great-hearted, pleasure-loving, temperamental man, suddenly overtaken by a passion for a lovely young girl, conscience-stricken, yet unable to resist. Then his recoil, his disgust with himself, his remorse for the way he was treating his wife and child and his sudden decision to end it all! The honourable way out. I can tell you, it was a most moving performance; Depleach's voice brought tears to your eyes. You saw the poor wretch torn by his passions and his essential decency. The effect was terrific. Only – when it was all over – and the spell was broken, you couldn't quite square that mythical figure with Amyas Crale. Everybody knew too much about Crale. He wasn't at all that kind of man. And Depleach hadn't been able to get hold of any evidence to show that he was. I should say Crale came as near as possible to being a man without even a rudimentary conscience. He was a ruthless, selfish, good-tempered, happy egoist. Any ethics he had would have applied to painting. He wouldn't I'm convinced, have painted a sloppy, bad picture – no matter what the inducement. But, for the rest, he was a full-blooded man and he loved life – he had a zest for it. Sucide? Not he!'

'Not, perhaps, a very good defence to have chosen?'

Fogg shrugged his thin shoulders. He said: 'What else was there? Couldn't sit back and plead that there was no case for the jury – that the prosecution had got to prove their case against the accused. There was a great deal too much proof. She'd handled the poison – admitted pinching it, in fact. There was means, motive, opportunity – everything.'

'One might have attempted to show that these things were artificially arranged?'

Fogg said bluntly: 'She admitted most of them. And, in any case, it's too far-fetched. You're implying, I presume, that somebody else murdered him and fixed it up to look as though she had done it.'

'You think that quite untenable?'

Fogg said slowly: 'I'm afraid I do. You're suggesting the mysterious X. Where do we look for him?'

Poirot said: 'Obviously in a close circle. There were five people, were there not, who *could* have been concerned?'

'Five? Let me see. There was the old duffer who messed about with his herb brewing. A dangerous hobby – but an amiable creature. Vague sort of person. Don't see him as X. There was the girl – she might have polished off Caroline, but certainly not Amyas. Then there was the stockbroker – Crale's best friend. That's popular in detective stories, but I don't believe in it in real life. There's no one else – oh, yes, the kid sister, but one doesn't seriously consider her. That's four.'

Hercule Poirot said: 'You forget the governess.'

'Yes, that's true. Wretched people, governesses, one never does remember them. I do recall her dimly, though. Middle-aged, plain, competent. I suppose a psychologist would say that she had a guilty passion for Crale and therefore killed him. The repressed spinster! It's no good – I just don't believe it. As far as my dim remembrance goes she wasn't the neurotic type.'

'It is a long time ago.'

'Fifteen or sixteen years, I suppose. Yes, quite that. You can't expect my memories of the case to be very acute.'

Hercule Poirot said: 'But, on the contrary, you remember it amazingly well. That astounds me. You can see it, can you not? When you talk the picture is there before your eyes.'

Fogg said slowly: 'Yes, you're right – I do see it – quite plainly.'

Poirot said: 'It would interest me, my friend, very much, if you would tell me *why*?'

'Why?' Fogg considered the question. His thin intellectual face was alert – interested. 'Yes, now *why*?'

Poirot asked: '*What* do you see so plainly? The witness? The counsel? The judge? The accused standing in the dock?'

Fogg said quietly: 'That's the reason, of course! You've put your finger on it. I shall always see *her* . . . Funny thing, romance. She had the quality of it. I don't know if she was really beautiful . . . She wasn't very young – tired-looking – circles under her eyes. But it all centred round her. The interest – the drama. And yet, half the time, *she wasn't there*. She'd gone away somewhere, quite far away – just left her body there, quiescent, attentive with the little polite smile on her lips. She was all half-tones, you know, lights and shades. And yet, with it all, she was more alive than the other – that girl with the perfect body, and the beautiful face, and the crude young strength. I admired Elsa Greer because she had guts, because she could fight, because she stood up to her tormentors and never quailed! But I admired Caroline Crale because she didn't fight, because she retreated into her world of half-lights and shadows. She was never defeated because she never gave battle.'

He paused: 'I'm only sure of one thing. She loved the man she killed. Loved him so much that half of her died with him . . .'

Mr Fogg, KC, paused and polished his glasses.

'Dear me,' he said. 'I seem to be saying some very strange things! I was quite a young man at the time, you know. Just an ambitious youngster. These things make an impression. But, all the same, I'm sure that Caroline Crale was a very remarkable woman. I shall never forget her. No – I shall never forget her . . .'

— 3 —

THE YOUNG SOLICITOR

GEORGE MAYHEW was cautious and non-committal.

He remembered the case, of course, but not at all clearly. His father had been in charge – he himself had been only nineteen at the time.

Yes, the case had made a great stir. Because of Crale being such a well-known man. His pictures were very fine – very fine indeed. Two of them were in the Tate. Not that that meant anything.

M. Poirot would excuse him, but he didn't see quite what M. Poirot's interest was in the matter. Oh, the *daughter*! Really? Indeed? Canada? He had always heard it was New Zealand.

George Mayhew became less rigid. He unbent.

A shocking thing in a girl's life. He had the deepest sympathy for her. Really it would have been better if she had never learned the truth. Still, it was no use saying that *now*.

She wanted to know? Yes, but what *was* there to know? There were the reports of the trial, of course. He himself didn't really know anything.

No, he was afraid there wasn't much doubt as to Mrs Crale's being guilty. There was a certain amount of excuse for her. These artists – difficult people to live with. With Crale, he understood, it had always been some woman or other.

And she herself had probably been the possessive type of woman. Unable to accept facts. Nowadays she'd simply have divorced him and got it over with. He added cautiously: 'Let me see – er – Lady Dittisham, I believe was the girl in the case.'

Poirot said that he believed that that was so.

'The newspapers bring it up from time to time,' said Mayhew. 'She's been in the divorce court a good deal. She's a very rich woman, as I expect you know. She was married to that explorer fellow before Dittisham. She's always more or less in the public eye. The kind of woman who likes notoriety, I should imagine.'

'Or possibly a hero worshipper,' suggested Poirot.

The idea was upsetting to George Mayhew. He accepted it dubiously.

'Well, possibly – yes, I suppose that might be so.'

He seemed to be turning the idea over in his mind.

Poirot said: 'Had your firm acted for Mrs Crale for a long period of years?'

512

George Mayhew shook his head.

'On the contrary. Jonathan & Jonathan were the Crale solicitors. Under the circumstances, however, Mr Jonathan felt that he could not very well act for Mrs Crale, and he arranged with us – with my father – to take over her case. You would do well, I think, M. Poirot, to arrange a meeting with old Mr Jonathan. He has retired from active work – he is over seventy – but he knew the Crale family intimately, and he could tell you far more than I can. Indeed, I myself can tell you nothing at all. I was a boy at the time. I don't think I was even in court.'

Poirot rose and George Mayhew, rising, too, added: 'You might like to have a word with Edmunds, our managing clerk. He was with the firm then and took a great interest in the case.'

Edmunds was a man of slow speech. His eyes gleamed with legal caution. He took his time in sizing up Poirot before he let himself be betrayed into speech. He said: 'Aye, I mind the Crale case.'

He added severely: 'It was a disgraceful business.'

His shrewd eyes rested appraisingly on Hercule Poirot.

He said: 'It's a long time since to be raking things up again.'

'A court verdict is not always an ending.'

Edmunds' square head nodded slowly.

'I'd not say that you weren't in the right of it there.'

Hercule Poirot went on: 'Mrs Crale left a daughter.'

'Aye, I mind there was a child. Sent abroad to relatives, was she not?'

Poirot went on: 'That daughter believes firmly in her mother's innocence.'

The huge bushy eyebrows of Mr Edmunds rose.

'That's the way of it, is it?'

Poirot asked: 'Is there anything you can tell me to support that belief?'

Edmunds reflected. Then, slowly, he shook his head.

'I could not conscientiously say there was. I admired Mrs Crale. Whatever else she was, she was a lady! Not like the other. A hussy – no more, no less. Bold as brass! Jumped-up trash – that's what *she* was – and showed it! Mrs Crale was quality.'

'But nonetheless a murderess?'

Edmunds frowned. He said, with more spontaneity than he had yet shown: 'That's what I used to ask myself day after day. Sitting there in the dock so calm and gentle. "I'll not believe it," I used to say to myself. But, if you take my meaning, M. Poirot, there wasn't anything else to believe. That hemlock didn't get into Mr

Crale's beer by accident. It was put there. And, if Mrs Crale
didn't put it there, who did?'

'That is the question,' said Poirot. 'Who did?'

Again those shrewd old eyes searched his face.

'So that's your idea,' said Mr Edmunds.

'What do you think yourself?'

There was a pause before the man answered. Then he said:
'There was nothing that pointed that way – nothing at all.'

Poirot said: 'You were in court during the hearing of the case?'

'Every day.'

'You heard the witnesses give evidence?'

'I did.'

'Did anything strike you about them – any abnormality, any
insincerity?'

Edmunds said bluntly: 'Was one of them lying, do you mean?
Had one of them a reason to wish Mr Crale dead? If you'll excuse
me, M. Poirot, that's a very *melodramatic* idea.'

'At least consider it,' Poirot urged.

He watched the shrewd face, the screwed-up, thoughtful eyes.
Slowly, regretfully, Edmunds shook his head.

'That Miss Greer,' he said, 'she was bitter enough, *and* vindictive! I'd say she overstepped the mark in a good deal she said, but
it was Mr Crale alive she wanted. He was no use to her dead. She
wanted Mrs Crale hanged all right – but that was because death
had snatched her man away from her. Like a baulked tigress she
was! But, as I say, it was Mr Crale alive she'd wanted. Mr Philip
Blake, *he* was against Mrs Crale, too. Prejudiced. Got his knife into
her whenever he could. But I'd say he was honest according to
his lights. He'd been Mr Crale's great friend. His brother, Mr
Meredith Blake – a bad witness, he was – vague, hesitating – never
seemed sure of his answers. I've seen many witnesses like that.
Look as though they're lying when all the time they're telling the
truth. Didn't want to say anything more than he could help, Mr
Meredith Blake didn't. Counsel got all the more out of him on that
account. One of those quiet gentlemen who get easily flustered.
The governess now, she stood up well to them. Didn't waste words
and answered pat and to the point. You couldn't have told,
listening to her, which side she was on. Got all her wits about her,
she had. The brisk kind.' He paused. 'Knew a lot more than she
ever let on about the whole thing, I shouldn't wonder.'

'I, too, should not wonder,' said Hercule Poirot.

He looked sharply at the wrinkled, shrewd face of Mr Alfred
Edmunds. It was quite bland and impassive. But Hercule Poirot
wondered if he had been vouchsafed a hint.

— 4 —

THE OLD SOLICITOR

MR CALEB JONATHAN lived in Essex. After a couretous exchange of letters, Poirot received an invitation, almost royal in character, to dine and sleep. The old gentleman was decidedly a character. After the insipidity of young George Mayhew, Mr Jonathan was like a glass of his own vintage port.

He had his own methods of approach to a subject, and it was not until well on towards midnight, when sipping a glass of fragrant old brandy, that Mr Jonathan really unbent. In oriental fashion he had appreciated Hercule Poirot's courteous refusal to rush him in any way. Now, in his own good time, he was willing to elaborate the theme of the Crale family.

'Our firm, of course, has known many generations of the Crales. I knew Amyas Crale and his father, Richard Crale, and I can remember Enoch Crale – the grandfather. Country squires, all of them, thought more of horses than human beings. They rode straight, liked women, and had no truck with ideas. They distrusted ideas. But Richard Crale's wife was cram full of ideas – more ideas than sense. She was poetical and musical – she played the harp, you know. She enjoyed poor health and looked very picturesque on her sofa. She was an admirer of Kingsley. That's why she called her son Amyas. His father scoffed at the name – but he gave in.

'Amyas Crale profited by his mixed inheritance. He got his artistic trend from his weakly mother, and his driving power and ruthless egoism from his father. All the Crales were egoists. They never by any chance saw any point of view but their own.'

Tapping with a delicate finger on the arm of his chair, the old man shot a shrewd glance at Poirot

'Correct me if I am wrong, M. Poirot, but I think you are interested in – character, shall we say?'

Poirot replied: 'That, to me, is the principal interest of all my cases.'

'I can conceive of it. To get under the skin, as it were, of your criminal. How interesting. How absorbing. Our firm, of course, have never had a criminal practice. We should not have been competent to act for Mrs Crale, even if taste had allowed. Mayhews, however, were a very adequate firm. They briefed Depleach – they didn't perhaps show much imagination there – still, he was very expensive, and, of course, exceedingly dramatic!

What they hadn't the wits to see was that Caroline would never play up in the way he wanted her to. She wasn't a dramatic woman.'

'What was she?' asked Poirot. 'It is that that I am chiefly anxious to know.'

'Yes, yes – of course. How did she come to do what she did? That is the really vital question. I knew her, you know, before she married. Caroline Spalding she was. A turbulent, unhappy creature. Very alive. Her mother was left a widow early in life and Caroline was devoted to her mother. Then the mother married again – there was another child. Yes – yes, very sad, very painful. These young, ardent, adolescent jealousies.'

'She was jealous?'

'Passionately so. There was a regrettable incident. Poor child, she blamed herself bitterly afterwards. But, you know, M. Poirot, these things happen. There is an inability to put on the brakes. It comes – it comes with maturity.'

Poirot said: 'What happened?'

'She struck the child – the baby – flung a paperweight at her. The child lost the sight of one eye and was permanently disfigured.'

Mr Jonathan sighed. He said: 'You can imagine the effect a simple question on that point had at the trial.'

He shook his head: 'It gave the impression that Caroline Crale was a woman of ungovernable temper. That was not true. No, that was not true.'

He paused and then resumed: 'Caroline Spalding came often to stay at Alderbury. She rode well, and was keen. Richard Crale was fond of her. She waited on Mrs Crale and was deft and gentle – Mrs Crale also liked her. The girl was not happy at home. She was happy at Alderbury. Diana Crale, Amyas's sister, and she were by way of being friends. Philip and Meredith Blake, boys from the adjoining estate, were frequently at Alderbury. Philip was always a nasty, money-grubbing little brute. I must confess I have always had a distaste for him. But I am told that he tells a very good story and that he has the reputation of being a staunch friend. Meredith was what my contemporaries used to call "namby-pamby". Liked botany and butterflies and observing birds and beasts. "Nature study" they call it nowadays. Ah dear – all the young people were a disappointment to their parents. None of them ran true to type – huntin', shootin', fishin'. Meredith preferred watching birds and animals to shooting or hunting them, Philip definitely preferred town to country and went into the business of money-making. Diana married a fellow who wasn't a gentleman – one of the temporary officers in the war. And Amyas, strong, handsome, virile Amyas, blossomed into being a painter, of all things in the world. It's my opinion that Richard Crale died of the shock.

'And in due course Amyas married Caroline Spalding. They'd always fought and sparred, but it was a love match all right. They were both crazy about each other. And they continued to care. But Amyas was like all the Crales, a ruthless egoist. He loved Caroline but he never once considered her in any way. He did as he pleased. It's my opinion that he was as fond of her as he could be of anybody – but she came a long way behind his art. That came first. And I should say at no time did his art give place to a woman. He had affairs with women – they stimulated him – but he left them high and dry when he'd finished with them. He wasn't a sentimental man, nor a romantic one. And he wasn't entirely a sensualist, either. The only woman he cared a button for was his own wife. And because she knew that she put up with a lot. He was a very fine painter, you know. She realized that, and respected it. He chased off in his amorous pursuits and came back again – usually with a picture to show for it.

'It might have gone on like that if it hadn't come to Elsa Greer. Elsa Greer—'

Mr Jonathan shook his head.

Poirot said: 'What of Elsa Greer?'

Mr Jonathan said unexpectedly: 'Poor child. Poor child.'

Poirot said: 'So you feel like that about her?'

Mr Jonathan said: 'Maybe it is because I am an old man, but I find, M. Poirot, that there is something about the defencelessness of youth that moves me to tears. Youth is so vulnerable. It is so ruthless – so sure. So generous and so demanding.'

Getting up, he crossed to the bookcase. Taking out a volume he opened it, turned the pages, and then read out:

' "If that thy bent of love be honourable,
The purpose marriage, send me word tomorrow
By one that I'll procure to come to thee,
Where and what time thou wilt perform the rite,
And all my fortunes at thy foot I'll lay,
And follow thee, my lord, throughout the world."

'There speaks love allied to youth, in Juliet's words. No reticence, no holding back, no so-called maiden modesty. It is the courage, the insistence, the ruthless force of youth. Shakespeare knew youth. Juliet singles out Romeo. Desdemona claims Othello. They have no doubts, the young, no fear, no pride.'

Poirot said thoughtfully: 'So to you Elsa Greer spoke in the words of Juliet?'

'Yes. She was a spoiled child of fortune – young, lovely, rich. She found her mate and claimed him – no young Romeo: a married, middle-aged painter. Elsa Greer had no code to restrain her, she had the code of modernity: *"Take what you want – we shall only live once!"* '

He sighed, leaned back, and again tapped gently on the arm of his chair.

'A predatory Juliet. Young, ruthless, but horribly vulnerable! Staking everything on the one audacious throw. And seemingly she won . . . and then – at the last moment – death steps in – and the living, ardent, joyous Elsa died also. There was left only a vindictive, cold, hard woman, hating with all her soul the woman whose hand had done this thing.'

His voice changed: 'Dear, dear. Pray forgive this little lapse into melodrama. A crude young woman – with a crude outlook on life. Not, I think, an interesting character. *Rose-white youth, passionate, pale*, etc. Take that away and what remains? Only a somewhat mediocre young woman seeking for another life-sized hero to put on an empty pedestal.'

Poirot said: 'If Amyas Crale had not been a famous painter—'

Mr Jonathan agreed quickly. He said: 'Quite – quite. You have taken the point admirably. The Elsas of this world are hero-worshippers. A man must have *done* something, must *be* somebody . . . Caroline Crale, now, could have recognized quality in a bank clerk or an insurance agent! Caroline loved Amyas Crale the man, not Amyas the painter. Caroline Crale was not crude – Elsa Greer was.'

He added: 'But she was young and beautiful and to my mind infinitely pathetic.'

Hercule Poirot went to bed thoughtful. He was fascinated by the problem of personality.

To Edmunds, the clerk, Elsa Greer was a hussy – no more, no less.

To old Mr Jonathan she was the eternal Juliet.

And Caroline Crale?

Each person had seen her differently. Montague Depleach had despised her as a defeatist – a quitter. To young Fogg she had represented romance. Edmunds saw her simply as a 'lady'. Mr Jonathan had called her a stormy, turbulent creature.

How would he, Hercule Poirot, have seen her?

On the answer to that question depended, he felt, the success of his quest.

So far, not one of the people he had seen had doubted that, whatever else she was, Caroline Crale was also a murderess.

— 5 —

THE POLICE SUPERINTENDENT

Ex-Superintendent Hale pulled thoughtfully at his pipe.

He said: 'This is a funny fancy of yours, M. Poirot.'

'It is, perhaps, a little unusual,' Poirot agreed cautiously.

'You see,' said Hale, 'it's all such a long time ago.'

Hercule Poirot foresaw that he was going to get a little tired of that particular phrase. He said mildly: 'That adds to the difficulty, of course.'

'Raking up the past,' mused the other. 'If there were an *object* in it, now . . .'

'There is an object.'

'What is it?'

'One can enjoy the pursuit of truth for its own sake. I do. And you must not forget the young lady.'

Hale nodded.

'Yes, I see *her* side of it. But – you'll excuse me, M. Poirot – you're an ingenious man. You could cook her up a tale.'

Poirot replied: 'You do not know the young lady.'

'Oh, come now – a man of your experience!'

Poirot drew himself up.

'I may be, *mon cher,* an artistic and competent liar – you seem to think so. But it is not my idea of ethical conduct. I have my standards.'

'Sorry, M. Poirot. I didn't mean to hurt your feelings. But it would be all in a good cause, so to speak.'

'Oh, I wonder, would it really?'

Hale said slowly: 'It's tough luck on a happy innocent girl

who's just going to get married to find that her mother was a murderess. If I were you, I'd go to her and say that, after all, suicide was what it was. Say the case was mishandled by Depleach. Say that there's no doubt in *your* mind that Crale poisoned himself!'

'But there is every doubt in my mind! I do not believe for one minute that Crale poisoned himself. Do you consider it even reasonably possible yourself?'

Slowly Hale shook his head.

'You see? No, it is the truth I must have – not a plausible – or not very plausible – lie.'

Hale turned and looked at Poirot. His square, rather red face grew a little redder and even appeared to get a little squarer. He said: 'You talk about the *truth*. I'd like to make it plain to you that we think we *got* the truth in the Crale case.'

Poirot said quickly: 'That pronouncement from you means a great deal. I know you for what you are, an honest and capable man. Now tell me this: Was there no doubt at any time in your mind as to the guilt of Mrs Crale?'

The superintendent's answer came promptly.

'No doubt at all, M. Poirot. The circumstances pointed to her straight away, and every single fact that we uncovered supported that view.'

'You can give me an outline of the evidence against her?'

'I can. When I received your letter I looked up the case.' He picked up a small notebook. 'i've jotted down all the salient facts here.'

'Thank you, my friend. I am all eagerness to hear.'

Hale cleared his throat. A slight official intonation made itself heard in his voice.

He said: 'At two forty-five on the afternoon of September 18th, Inspector Conway was rung up by Dr Andrew Faussett. Dr Faussett stated that Mr Amyas Crale of Alderbury had died suddenly and that in consequence of the circumstances of that death and also of a statement made to him by a Mr Blake, a guest staying in the house, he considered that it was a case for the police.

'Inspector Conway, in company with a sergeant and the police surgeon, came over to Alderbury straight away. Dr Faussett was there and took him to where the body of Mr Crale had not been disturbed.

'Mr Crale had been painting in a small enclosed garden, known as the battery garden from the fact that it overlooked the sea and had some miniature cannon placed in embattlements. It

was situated at about four minutes' walk from the house. Mr
Crale had not come up to the house for lunch as he wanted to get
certain effects of light on the stone – and the sun would have been
wrong for this later. He had, therefore, remained alone in the
battery garden, painting. This was stated not to be an unusual
occurrence. Mr Crale took very little notice of meal times. Sometimes a sandwich would be sent down to him, but more often he
preferred to remain undisturbed. The last people to see him alive
were Miss Elsa Greer (staying in the house) and Mr Meredith
Blake (a near neighbour). These two went up together to the
house and went with the rest of the household in to lunch. After
lunch, coffee was served on the terrace. Mrs Crale finished
drinking her coffee and then observed that she would "go down
and see how Amyas was getting on". Miss Cecilia Williams,
governess, got up and accompanied her. She was looking for a
pullover belonging to her pupil, Miss Angela Warren, sister of
Mrs Crale, which the latter had mislaid and she thought it
possible it might have been left down on the beach.

'These two started off together. The path led downwards,
through some woods, until it emerged at the door leading into the
battery garden. You could either go into the battery garden or you
could continue on the same path, which led down to the seashore.

'Miss Williams continued on down and Mrs Crale went into the
battery garden. Almost at once, however, Mrs Crale screamed
and Miss Williams hurried back. Mr Crale was reclining on a seat
and he was dead.

'At Mrs Crale's urgent request Miss Williams left the battery
garden and hurried up to the house to telephone for a doctor. On
her way, however, she met Mr Meredith Blake and entrusted her
errand to him, herself returning to Mrs Crale, whom she felt might
be in need of someone. Dr Faussett arrived on the scene a quarter
of an hour later. He saw at once that Mr Crale had been dead for
some time – he placed the probable time of death at between one
and two o'clock. There was nothing to show what had caused
death. There was no sign of any wound and Mr Crale's attitude
was a perfectly natural one. Nevertheless, Dr Faussett, who was
well acquainted with Mr Crale's state of health, and who knew
positively that there was no disease or weakness of any kind, was
inclined to take a grave view of the situation. It was at this point
that Mr Philip Blake made a certain statement to Dr Faussett.'

Inspector Hale paused, drew a deep breath and passed, as it
were, to Chapter Two.

'Subsequently Mr Blake repeated this statement to Inspector

Conway. It was to this effect: He had that morning received a telephone message from his brother, Mr Meredith Blake (who lived at Handcross Manor, a mile and a half away). Mr Meredith Blake was an amateur chemist – or perhaps "herbalist" would describe it best. On entering his laboratory that morning, Mr Meredith Blake had been startled to note that a bottle containing a preparation of hemlock, which had been quite full the day before, was now nearly empty. Worried and alarmed by this fact he had rung up his brother to ask his advice as to what he should do about it. Mr Philip Blake had urged his brother to come over to Alderbury at once and they would talk the matter over. He himself walked part way to meet his brother and they had come up to the house together. They had come to no decision as to what course to adopt and had left the matter in order to consult again after lunch.

'As a result of further inquiries, Inspector Conway ascertained the following facts: On the preceding afternoon five people had walked over from Alderbury to tea at Handcross Manor. There were Mr and Mrs Crale, Miss Angela Warren, Miss Elsa Greer and Mr Philip Blake. During the time spent there, Mr Meredith Blake had given quite a dissertation on his hobby and had taken the party into his little laboratory and "shown them round". In the course of this tour, he had mentioned certain specific drugs – one of which was coniine, the active principle of the spotted hemlock. He had explained its properties, had lamented the fact that it had now disappeared from the pharmacopœia and boasted that he had known small doses of it to be very efficacious in whooping cough and asthma. Later he had mentioned its lethal properties and had actually read to his guests some passage from a Greek author describing its effects.'

Superintendent Hale paused, refilled his pipe and passed on to Chapter Three.

'Colonel Frere, the chief constable, put the case into my hands. The result of the autopsy put the matter beyond any doubt. Coniine, I understand, leaves no definite post-mortem appearances, but the doctors knew what to look for, and an ample amount of the drug was recovered. The doctor was of the opinion that it had been administered two or three hours before death. In front of Mr Crale, on the table, there had been an empty glass and an empty beer-bottle. The dregs of both were analysed. There was no coniine in the bottle, but there was in the glass. I made inquiries and learned that, although a case of beer and glasses were

kept in a small summerhouse in the battery garden in case Mr
Crale should feel thirsty when painting, on this particular morning
Mrs Crale had brought down from the house a bottle of freshly
iced beer. Mr Crale was busy painting when she arrived and Miss
Greer was posing for him sitting on one of the battlements.

'Mrs Crale opened the beer, poured it out and put the glass into
her husband's hand as he was standing before the easel. He tossed
it off in one draught – a habit of his, I learned. Then he made a
grimace, set down the glass on the table, and said: "Everthing
tastes foul to me today!" Miss Greer upon that laughed and said:
"Liver!" Mr Crale said: "Well, at any rate, it was *cold*." '

Hale paused. Poirot said: 'At what time did this take place?'

'At about a quarter past eleven. Mr Crale continued to paint.
According to Miss Greer, he later complained of stiffness in the
limbs and grumbled that he must have got a touch of rheumatism.
But he was the type of man who hates to admit to illness of any
kind, and he undoubtedly tried not to admit that he was feeling ill.
His irritable demand that he should be left alone and the others go
up to lunch was quite characteristic of the man, I should say.'

Poirot nodded.

Hale continued.

'So Crale was left alone in the battery garden. No doubt he
dropped down on the seat and relaxed as soon as he was alone.
Muscular paralysis would then set in. No help was at hand, and
death supervened.'

Again Poirot nodded.

Hale said: 'Well, I proceeded according to routine. There
wasn't much difficulty in getting down to the facts. On the preceding day there had been a set-to between Mrs Crale and Miss
Greer. The latter had pretty insolently described some change in
the arrangement of the furniture "when I am living here". Mrs
Crale took her up, and said: "What do you mean? When *you* are
living here."

'Miss Greer replied: "Don't pretend you don't know what I
mean, Caroline. You're just like an ostrich that buries its head in
the sand. You know perfectly well that Amyas and I care for each
other and are going to be married." Mrs Crale said: "I know
nothing of the kind." Miss Greer then said: "Well, you know it
now." Whereupon, it seems, Mrs Crale turned to her husband
who had just come into the room and said: "Is it true, Amyas, that
you are going to marry Elsa?" '

Poirot said with interest: 'And what did Mr Crale say to that?'

'Apparently he turned on Miss Greer and shouted at her: "What the devil do you mean by blurting that out? Haven't you got the sense to hold your tongue?"'

'Miss Greer said: "I think Caroline ought to recognize the truth."'

'Mrs Crale said to her husband: "Is it true, Amyas?"'

'He wouldn't look at her, it seems, turned his face away and mumbled something.

'She said: "Speak out. I've got to know." Whereupon he said: "Oh, it's true enough – but I don't want to discuss it now."'

'Then he flounced out of the room again and Miss Greer said: "You see!" and went on – with something about its being no good for Mrs Crale to adopt a dog-in-the-manger attitude about it. They must all behave like rational people. She herself hoped that Caroline and Amyas would always remain good friends.'

'And what did Mrs Crale say to that?' asked Poirot curiously.

'According to the witnesses she laughed. She said: "Over my dead body, Elsa." She went to the door and Miss Greer called after her: "What do you mean?" Mrs Crale looked back and said: "I'll kill Amyas before I give him up to *you*." '

Hale paused.

'Pretty damning – eh?'

'Yes.' Poirot seemed thoughtful. 'Who overheard this scene?'

'Miss Williams was in the room and Philip Blake. Very awkward for them.'

'Their accounts of the scene agree?'

'Near enough – you never get two witnesses to remember a thing exactly alike. *You* know that just as well as I do, M. Poirot.'

Poirot nodded. He said thoughtfully: 'Yes, it will be interesting to see—' He stopped with the sentence unfinished.

Hale went on: 'I instituted a search of the house. In Mrs Crale's bedroom I found in a bottom drawer, tucked away underneath some winter stockings, a small bottle labelled "jasmine scent". It was empty. I fingerprinted it. The only prints on it were those of Mrs Crale. On analysis it was found to contain faint traces of oil of jasmine, and a strong solution of coniine hydrobromide.

'I cautioned Mrs Crale and showed her the bottle. She replied readily. She had, she said, been in a very unhappy state of mind. After listening to Mr Meredith Blake's description of the drug she had slipped back to the laboratory, had emptied out a bottle of jasmine scent which was in her bag and had filled the bottle up with coniine solution. I asked her why she had done this and she said: "I don't want to speak of certain things more than I can help, but I had received a bad shock. My husband was proposing to leave me for another woman. If that was so, I didn't want to live. That is why I took it." '

Hale paused.

Poirot said: 'After all – it is likely enough.'

'Perhaps, M. Poirot. But it doesn't square with what she was overheard to say. And then there was a further scene on the following morning. Mr Philip Blake overheard a portion of it. Miss Greer overheard a different portion of it. It took place in the library between Mr and Mrs Crale. Mr Blake was in the hall and caught a fragment or two. Miss Greer was sitting outside near the open library window and heard a good deal more.'

'And what did they hear?'

'Mr Blake heard Mrs Crale say: "You and your women. I'd like to kill you. Some day I will kill you." '

'No mention of suicide?'

'Exactly. None at all. No words like "If you do this thing, I'll kill *myself*." Miss Greer's evidence was much the same. According to her, Mr Crale said: "Do try and be reasonable about this, Caroline. I'm fond of you and will always wish you well – you and the child. But I'm going to marry Elsa. We've always agreed to leave each other free." Mrs Crale answered to that: "Very well, don't say I haven't warned you." He said: "What do you mean?" And she said: "I mean that I love you and I'm not going to lose you. I'd rather kill you than let you go to that girl." '

Poirot made a slight gesture.

'It occurs to me,' he murmured, 'that Miss Greer was singularly unwise to raise the issue. Mrs Crale could easily have refused her husband a divorce.'

'We had some evidence bearing on that point,' said Hale. 'Mrs Crale, it seems, confided partly in Mr Meredith Blake. He was an old and trusted friend. He was very distressed and managed to get a word with Mr Crale about it. This, I may say, was on the preceding afternoon. Mr Blake remonstrated delicately with his friend, said how distressed he would be if the marriage between Mr and Mrs Crale was to break up so disastrously. He also stressed the point that Miss Greer was a very young girl and that it was a very serious thing to drag a young girl through the divorce court. To this Mr Crale replied, with a chuckle (callous sort of brute he must have been): "That isn't Elsa's idea at all. *She* isn't going to appear. We shall fix it up in the usual way." '

Poirot said: 'Therefore even more imprudent of Miss Greer to have broken out the way she did.'

Superintendent Hale said: 'Oh, you know what women are! Have to get at each other's throats. It must have been a difficult situation anyhow. I can't understand Mr Crale allowing it to happen. According to Mr Meredith Blake he wanted to finish his picture. Does that make sense to you?'

'Yes, my friend, I think it does.'

'It doesn't to me. The man was asking for trouble!'

'He was probably seriously annoyed with his young woman for breaking out the way she did.'

'Oh, he was. Meredith Blake said so. If he had to finish the picture, I don't see why he couldn't have taken some photographs and worked from them. I know a chap – does water-colours of places – *he* does that.'

Poirot shook his head.

'No – I can understand Crale the artist. You must realize, my friend, that at that moment, probably, his picture was all that mattered to Crale. However much he wanted to marry the girl, the picture came first. That's why he hoped to get through her visit without its coming to an open issue. The girl, of course, didn't see it that way. With women, love always comes first.'

'Don't I know it?' said Superintendent Hale with feeling.

'Men,' continued Poirot, 'and especially artists – are different.'

'Art!' said the superintendent with scorn. 'All this talk about *art*! I never *have* understood it and I never shall! You should have seen that picture Crale was painting. All lopsided. He'd made the girl look as though she'd got toothache, and the battlements were all cock-eyed. Unpleasant-looking, the whole thing. I couldn't get it out of my mind for a long time afterwards. I even dreamt about it. And what's more it affected my eyesight – I began to see battlements and walls and things all out of drawing. Yes, and women, too!'

Poirot smiled. He said: 'Although you do not know it, you are paying a tribute to the greatness of Amyas Crale's art.'

'Nonsense. Why can't a painter paint something nice and cheerful to look at? Why go out of your way to look for ugliness?'

'Some of us, *mon cher*, see beauty in curious places.'

'The girl was a good looker, all right,' said Hale. 'Lots of make-up and next to no clothes on. It isn't decent the way these girls go about. And that was sixteen years ago, mind you. Nowadays one wouldn't think anything of it. But then – well, it shocked me. Trousers and one of those canvas shirts open at the neck – and not another thing, I should say!'

'You seem to remember these points very well,' murmured Poirot slyly.

Superintendent Hale blushed. 'I'm just passing on the impression I got,' he said austerely.

'Quite – quite,' said Poirot soothingly. He went on: 'So it would seem that the principal witnesses against Mrs Crale were Philip Blake and Elsa Greer?'

'Yes. Vehement, they were, both of them. But the governess was called by the prosecution, too, and what she said carried more weight than the other two. She was on Mrs Crale's side entirely, you see. Up in arms for her. But she was an honest woman and gave her evidence truthfully without trying to minimize it in any way.'

'And Meredith Blake?'

'He was very distressed by the whole thing, poor gentleman. As well he might be! Blamed himself for his drug brewing – and the coroner blamed him for it, too. Coniine and AE Salts come under Schedule I of the Poisons Acts. He came in for some pretty sharp censure. He was a friend of both parties, and it hit him very hard – besides being the kind of county gentleman who shrinks from notoriety and being in the public eye.'

'Did not Mrs Crale's young sister give evidence?'

'No. It wasn't necessary. She wasn't there when Mrs Crale threatened her husband, and there was nothing she could tell us that we couldn't get from someone else equally well. She saw Mrs Crale go to the refrigerator and get the iced beer out and, of course, the defence could have subpœnaed her to say that Mrs Crale took it straight down without tampering with it in any way. But that point wasn't relevant because we never claimed that the coniine was in the beer-bottle.'

'How did she manage to put it in the glass with those two looking on?'

'Well, first of all, they weren't looking on. That is to say, Mr Crale was painting – looking at his canvas and at the sitter. And Miss Greer was posed, sitting with her back almost to where Mrs Crale was standing, and her eyes looking over Mr Crale's shoulder.'

Poirot nodded.

'As I say, neither of the two was looking at Mrs Crale. She had the stuff in one of those pipette things – one used to fill fountain pens with them. We found it crushed to splinters on the path up to the house.'

Poirot murmured: 'You have an answer to everything.'

'Well, come now, M. Poirot! Without prejudice. *She* threatens to kill him. *She* takes the stuff from the laboratory. The empty bottle is found in *her* room and *nobody has handled it but her*. She deliberately takes down iced beer to him – a funny thing, anyway, when you realize that they weren't on speaking terms—'

'A very curious thing. I had already remarked on it.'

'Yes. Bit of a give-away. *Why* was she so amiable all of a sudden? He complains of the taste of the stuff – and coniine *has* a nasty taste. She arranges to find the body and she sends the other woman off to telephone. Why? So that she can wipe that bottle and glass and then press *his* fingers on it. After that she can pipe up and say that it was remorse and that he committed suicide. A likely story.'

'It was certainly not very well imagined.'

'No. If you ask me, she didn't take the trouble to *think*. She was so eaten up with hate and jealousy. All she thought of was doing him in. And then, when it's over, when she sees him there dead – well, *then*, I should say, she suddenly comes to herself and realizes that what she's done is murder – and that you can get hanged for murder. And desperately she goes bald-headed for the only thing she can think of – which is suicide.'

Poirot said: 'It is very sound what you say there – yes. Her mind might work that way.'

'In a way it was a premeditated crime and in a way it wasn't,' said Hale. 'I don't believe she really thought it out, you know. Just went on with it blindly.'

Poirot murmured: 'I wonder . . .'

Hale looked at him curiously. He said: 'Have I convinced you, M. Poirot, that it was a straightforward case?'

'Almost. Not quite. There are one or two peculiar points.'

'Can you suggest an alternative solution – that will hold water?'

Poirot said: 'What were the movements of the other people on that morning?'

'We went into them, I can assure you. We checked up on everybody. Nobody had what you could call an alibi – you can't have with poisoning. Why, there's nothing to prevent a would-be murderer from handing his victim some poison in a capsule the day before, telling him it's a specific cure for indigestion and he must take it before lunch – and then going away to the other end of England.'

'But you don't think that happened in this case?'

'Mr Crale didn't suffer from indigestion. And, in any case, I can't see that kind of thing happening. It's true that Mr Meredith Blake was given to recommending quack nostrums of his own concocting, but I don't see Mr Crale trying any of them. And, if he did, he'd probably talk and joke about it. Besides, why *should* Mr

Meredith Blake want to kill Mr Crale?' Everything goes to show that he was on very good terms with him. They all were. Mr Philip Blake was his best friend. Miss Greer was in love with him. Miss Williams disapproved of him, I imagine, very strongly – but moral disapprobation doesn't lead to poisoning. Little Miss Warren scrapped with him a lot, she was at a tiresome age – just off to school, I believe – but he was quite fond of her and she of him. She was treated, you know, with particular tenderness and consideration in that house. You may have heard why. She was badly injured when she was a child – injured by Mrs Crale in a kind of maniacal fit of rage. That rather shows, doesn't it, that she was a pretty uncontrolled sort of person? To go for a child – and maim her for life!'

'It might show,' said Poirot thoughtfully, 'that Angela Warren had good reason to bear a grudge against Caroline Crale.'

'Perhaps – but not against Amyas Crale. And, anyway, Mrs Crale was devoted to her young sister – gave her a home when her parents died, and, as I say, treated her with special affection – spoiled her badly, so they say. The girl was obviously fond of Mrs Crale. She was kept away from the trial and sheltered from it all as far as possible – Mrs Crale was very insistent about that, I believe. But the girl was terribly upset and longed to be taken to see her sister in prison. Caroline Crale wouldn't agree. She said that sort of thing might injure a girl's mentality for life. She arranged for her to go to school abroad.'

He added: 'Miss Warren's turned out a very distinguished woman. Traveller to weird places. Lectures at the Royal Geographical – all that sort of thing.'

'And no one remembers the trial?'

'Well, it's a different name for one thing. They hadn't even the same maiden name. They had the same mother but different fathers. Mrs Crale's name was Spalding.'

'This Miss Williams, was she the child's governess, or Angela Warren's?'

'Angela's. There was a nurse for the child – but she used to do a few little lessons with Miss Williams every day, I believe.'

'Where was the child at the time?'

'She'd gone with the nurse to pay a visit to her grandmother. A Lady Tressillian. A widow-lady who'd lost her own two little girls and who was devoted to this kid.'

Poirot nodded. 'I see.'

Hale continued: 'As to the movements of the other people on the day of the murder, I can give them to you.

'Miss Greer sat on the terrace near the library window after breakfast. There, as I say, she overheard the quarrel between Crale and his wife. After that she accompanied Crale down to the battery and sat for him until lunch time with a couple of breaks to ease her muscles.

'Philip Blake was in the house after breakfast, and overheard part of the quarrel. After Crale and Miss Creer went off, he read the paper until his brother telephoned him. Thereupon he went down to the shore to meet his brother. They walked together up the path again past the battery garden. Miss Greer had just gone up to the house to fetch a pullover as she felt chilly and Mrs Crale was with her husband discussing arrangements for Angela's departure to school.'

'Ah, an amicable interview.'

'Well, no, not amicable. Crale was fairly shouting at her, I understand. Annoyed at being bothered with domestic details. I suppose she wanted to get things straightened up if there *was* going to be a break.'

Poirot nodded.

Hale went on: 'The two brothers exchanged a few words with Amyas Crale. Then Miss Greer reappeared and took up her position, and Crale picked up his brush again, obviously wanting to get rid of them. They took the hint and went up to the house. It was when they were at the battery, by the way, that Amyas Crale complained all the beer down there was hot and his wife promised to send him down some iced beer.'

'Aha!'

'Exactly – aha! Sweet as sugar she was about it. They went up to the house and sat on the terrace outside. Mrs Crale and Angela Warren brought them out beer there. Later, Angela Warren went down to bathe and Philip Blake went with her.

'Meredith Blake went down to a clearing with a seat just above the battery garden. He could just see Miss Greer as she posed on the battlements and could hear her voice and Crale's as they talked. He sat there and thought over the coniine business. He was still very worried about it and didn't know quite what to do. Elsa Greer saw him and waved her hand to him. When the bell went for lunch he came down to the battery and Elsa Greer and he went back to the house together. He noticed then that Crale was looking, as he put it, "very queer", but he didn't really think anything of it at the time. Crale was the kind of man who is never ill – and so one didn't imagine he would be. On the other hand, he *did* have moods of fury and despondency according as to whether his painting was not going as he liked it. On those occasions one left him alone and said as little as possible to him. That's what these two did on this occasion.

'As to the others, the servants were busy with housework and cooking lunch. Miss Williams was in the schoolroom part of the morning correcting some exercise books. Afterwards she took some household mending to the terrace. Angela Warren spent most of the morning wandering about the garden, climbing trees and eating things – you know what a girl of fifteen is! Plums, sour apples, hard pears, etc. After that she came back to the house and, as I say, went down with Philip Blake to the beach and had a bathe before lunch.'

Superintendent Hale paused: 'Now, then,' he said belligerently, 'do you find anything phoney about that?'

Poirot said: 'Nothing at all.'

'Well, then!'

The two words expressed volumes.

'But all the same,' said Hercule Poirot. 'I am going to satisfy myself. I—'

'What are you going to do?'

'I am going to visit these five people – and from each one I am going to get his or her own story.'

Superintendent Hale sighed with a deep melancholy.

He said: 'Man, you're nuts! None of their stories is going to agree! Don't you grasp that elementary fact? No two people can remember a thing in the same order anyway. And after all this time! Why, you'll hear five accounts of five separate murders!'

'That,' said Poirot, 'is what I am counting upon. It will be very instructive.'

— 6 —

THIS LITTLE PIG WENT TO MARKET ...

PHILIP BLAKE was recognisably like the description given of him by Montague Depleach. A prosperous, shrewd, jovial-looking man – slightly running to fat.

Hercule Poirot had timed his appointment for half-past six on a Saturday afternoon. Philip Blake had just finished his eighteen holes, and he had been on his game – winning a fiver from his opponent. He was in the mood to be friendly and expansive.

Hercule Poirot explained himself and his errand. On this occasion at least he showed no undue passion for unsullied truth. It was a question, Blake gathered, of a series of books dealing with famous crimes.

Philip Blake frowned. He said: 'Good Lord, why make up these things?'

Hercule Poirot shrugged his shoulders. He was at his most foreign today. He was out to be despised but patronised.

He murmured: 'It is the public. They eat it up – yes, they eat it up.'

'Ghouls,' said Philip Blake.

But he said it good-humouredly – not with the fastidiousness and the distaste that a more sensitive man might have displayed.

Hercule Poirot said with a shrug of the shoulders: 'It is human nature. You and I, Mr Blake, who know the world, have no illusions about our fellow human beings. Not bad people, most of them, but certainly not to be idealized.'

Blake said heartily: 'I parted with my illusions long ago.'

'Instead, you tell a very good story, so I have been told.'

'Ah!' Blake's eyes twinkled. 'Heard this one?'

Poirot's laugh came at the right place. It was an edifying story, but it was funny.

Philip Blake lay back in his chair, his muscles relaxed, his eyes creased with good humour.

Hercule Poirot thought suddenly that he looked rather like a contented pig.

A pig. *This little pig went to market . . .*

What was he like, this man, this Philip Blake? A man, it would seem, without cares. Prosperous, contented. No remorseful thoughts, no uneasy twinges of conscience from the past, no haunting memories here. No, a well-fed pig who had gone to market – and fetched the full market price.

But once, perhaps, there had been more to Philip Blake. He must have been, when young, a handsome man. Eyes always a shade too small, a fraction too near together, perhaps – but otherwise a well-made, well-set-up young man. How old was he now? At a guess between fifty and sixty. Nearing forty, then, at the time of Crale's death. Less stultified, then, less sunk in the gratifications of the minute. Asking more of life, perhaps, and receiving less . . .

Poirot murmured as a mere catch-phrase: 'You comprehend my position.'

'No, really, you know, I'm hanged if I do.' The stockbroker sat upright again, his glance was at once more shrewd. 'Why *you*? Your're not a writer?'

'Not precisely – no. Actually I am a detective.'

The modesty of this remark had probably not been equalled before in Poirot's conversation.

'Of course you are. We all know that. The famous Hercule Poirot!'

But his tone held a subtly mocking note. Intrinsically, Philip Blake was too much of an Englishman to take the pretensions of a foreigner seriously.

To his cronies he would have said: 'Quaint little mountebank. Oh, well, I expect his stuff goes down with the women all right.'

And, although that derisive patronising attitude was exactly the one which Hercule Poirot had aimed at inducing, nevertheless he found himself annoyed by it.

This man, this successful man of affairs, was unimpressed by Hercule Poirot! It was a scandal.

'I am gratified,' said Poirot untruly, 'that I am so well known to you. My success, let me tell you, has been founded on the pyschology – the eternal *why* of human behaviour. That, Mr Blake, is what interests the world of crime today.

'It used to be romance. Famous crimes were retold from one angle only – the love-story connected with them. Nowadays it is very different. People read with interest that Dr Crippen murdered his wife because she was a big bouncing woman and he was little and insignificant and therefore she made him feel inferior. They read of some famous woman criminal that she killed because she'd been snubbed by her father when she was three years old. It is, as I say, the *why* of crime that interests people nowadays.'

Philip Blake said with a slight yawn: 'The *why* of most crimes is obvious enough, I should say. Usually money.

Poirot cried: 'Ah, but, my dear sir, the *why* must never be obvious. That is the whole point!'

'And that's where *you* come in?'

'And that, as you say, is where I come in! It is proposed to rewrite the stories of certain bygone crimes – from the psychological angle. Psychology in crime, it is my speciality. I have accepted the commission.'

Philip Blake grinned.

'Pretty lucrative, I suppose.'

'I hope so – I certainly hope so.'

'Congratulations. Now, perhaps, you'll tell me where *I* come in?'

'Most certainly. The Crale murder case, Monsieur.'

Philip Blake did not look startled. But he looked thoughtful. He said: 'Yes, of course, the Crale case . . .'

Hercule Poirot said anxiously: 'It is not displeasing to you, Mr Blake?'

'Oh, as to that.' Philip Blake shrugged his shoulders. 'It's no use resenting a thing that you've no power to stop. The trial of Caroline Crale is public property. Anyone can go ahead and write it up. It's no use *my* objecting. In a way – I don't mind telling you – I do dislike it a good deal. Amyas Crale was one of my best friends. I'm sorry the whole unsavoury business has to be raked up again. But these things happen.'

'You are a philosopher, Mr Blake.'

'No, no. I just know enough not to start kicking against the pricks. I dare say you'll do it less offensively than many others.'

'I hope, at least, to write with delicacy and good taste,' said Poirot.

Philip Blake gave a loud guffaw but without any real amusement. 'Makes me chuckle to hear you say that.'

'I assure you, Mr Blake, I am really interested. It is not just a matter of money with me. I genuinely want to re-create the past, to feel and see the events that took place, to see behind the obvious and to visualise the thoughts and feelings of the actors in the drama.'

Philip Blake said: 'I don't know that there was much subtlety about it. It was a pretty obvious business. Crude female jealousy, that was all there was to it.'

'It would interest me enormously, Mr Blake, if I could have your own reactions to the affair.'

Philip Blake said with sudden heat, his face deepening in colour: 'Reactions! Reactions! Don't speak so pedantically. I didn't just stand there and react! You don't seem to understand that my friend – *my friend*, I tell you – had been killed – poisoned! And that if I'd acted quicker I could have saved him.'

'How do you make that out, Mr Blake?'

'Like this. I take it that you've already read up the facts of the case?' Poirot nodded. 'Very well. Now on that morning my brother Meredith called me up. He was in a pretty good stew. One of his Hell-brews was missing – and it was a fairly deadly

534

Hell-brew. What did I do? I told him to come along and we'd talk it over. Decide what was best to be done. Decide what was best! It beats me now how I could have been such a hesitating fool! I ought to have realized that there was no time to lose. I ought to have gone to Amyas straight away and warned him. I ought to have said: "Caroline's pinched one of Meredith's patent poisons, and you and Elsa had better look out for yourselves." '

Blake got up. He strode up and down in his excitement.

'Good God, man. Do you suppose I haven't gone over it in my mind again and again? I *knew*. I had the chance to save him – and I dallied about – waiting for Meredith! Why hadn't I the sense to realize that Caroline wasn't going to have any qualms or hesitancies. She'd taken that stuff to use – and, by God, she'd use it at the very first opportunity. She wouldn't wait till Meredith discovered his loss. I knew – of course I knew – that Amyas was in deadly danger – and I did nothing!'

'I think you reproach yourself unduly, Monsieur. You had not much time—'

The other interrupted him: 'Time? I had plenty of time. Any amount of courses open to me. I could have gone to Amyas, as I say – but there was the chance, of course, that he wouldn't believe me. Amyas wasn't the sort of man who'd believe easily in his own danger. He'd have scoffed at the notion.

'And he never thoroughly understood the sort of devil Caroline was. But I could have gone to her. I could have said: "I know what you're up to. I know what you're planning to do. But, if Amyas or Elsa die of coniine poisoning, you'll be hanged by your neck!" That would have stopped her.

'Or I might have rung up the police. Oh, there were things that could have been done – and, instead, I let myself be influenced by Meredith's slow, cautious methods. "We must be sure – talk it over – make quite certain who could have taken it . . ." Damned old fool – never made a quick decision in his life! A good thing for him he was the eldest son and has an estate to live on. If he'd ever tried to *make* money, he'd have lost every penny he had.'

Poirot asked: 'You had no doubt yourself who had taken the poison?'

'Of course not. I knew at once it must be Caroline. You see, I knew Caroline very well.'

Poirot said: 'That is very interesting. I want to know, Mr Blake, what kind of a woman Caroline Crale was.'

Philip Blāke said sharply: 'She wasn't the injured innocent people thought she was at the time of the trial!'

'What was she, then?'

535

Blake sat down again. He said seriously: 'Would you really like to know?'

'I would like to know very much indeed.'

'Caroline was a rotter. She was a rotter through and through. Mind you, she had charm. She had that kind of sweetness of manner that deceives people utterly. She had a frail, helpless look about her that appealed to people's chivalry. Sometimes, when I've read a bit of history, I think Mary Queen of Scots must have been a bit like her. Always sweet and unfortunate and magnetic – and actually a cold, calculating woman, a scheming woman who planned the murder of Darnley and got away with it. Caroline was like that – a cold, calculating planner. And she had a wicked temper.

'I don't know whether they've told you – it isn't a vital point of the trial, but it shows her up – what she did to her baby sister? She was jealous, you know. Her mother had married again, and all the notice and affection went to little Angela. Caroline couldn't stand that. She tried to kill the baby with a crowbar – smash its head in. Luckily the blow wasn't fatal. But it was a pretty ghastly thing to do.'

'Yes, indeed.'

'Well, that was the real Caroline. She had to be first. That was the thing she simply could not stand – not being first. And there was a cold, egotistical devil in her that was capable of being stirred to murderous lengths.

'She appeared implusive, you know, but she was really calculating. When she stayed at Alderbury as a girl, she gave us all the once-over and made her plans. She'd no money of her own. I was never in the running – a younger son with his way to make. (Funny, that, I could probably buy up Meredith and Crale, if he'd lived, nowadays!) She considered Meredith for a bit, but she finally fixed on Amyas. Amyas would have Alderbury and, though he wouldn't have much money with it, she realized that his talent as a painter was something quite out of the way. She gambled on his being not only a genius but a financial success as well.

'And she won. Recognition came to Amyas early. He wasn't a fashionable painter exactly – but his genius was recognized and his pictures were bought. Have you seen any of his paintings? There's one here. Come and look at it.'

He led the way into the dining-room and pointed to the left-hand wall.

'There you are. That's Amyas.'

Poirot looked in silence. It came to him with fresh amazement that a man could so imbue a conventional subject with his own particular magic. A vase of roses on a polished mahogany table. That hoary old set-piece. How, then, did Amyas Crale contrive to make his roses flame and burn with a riotous, almost obscene, life? The polished wood of the table trembled and took on sentient life. How explain the excitement the picture roused? For it was exciting. The proportions of the table would have distressed Superintendent Hale, he would have complained that no known roses were precisely of that shape or colour. And afterwards he would have gone about wondering vaguely why the roses he saw were unsatisfactory, and round mahogany tables would have annoyed him for no known reason.

Poirot gave a little sigh.

He murmured: 'Yes — it is all there.'

Blake led the way back. He mumbled: 'Never have understood anything about art myself. Don't know why I like looking at that thing so much, but I do. It's — oh, damn it all, it's *good*.'

Poirot nodded emphatically.

Blake offered his guest a cigarette and lit one himself. He said: 'And that's the man — the man who painted those roses — the man who painted the "Woman with a Cocktail Shaker" — the man who painted that amazing painful "Nativity" — *that's* the man who was cut short in his prime, deprived of his vivid forceful life all because of a vindictive mean-natured woman!'

He paused: 'You'll say that I'm bitter — that I'm unduly pre-judiced against Caroline. She *had* charm — I've felt it. But I knew — I always knew — the real woman behind. And that woman, M. Poirot, was evil. She was cruel and malignant and a grabber!'

'And yet it has been told me that Mrs Crale put up with many hard things in her married life.'

'Yes, and didn't she let everybody know about it! Always the martyr! Poor old Amyas. His married life was one long hell — or rather it would have been if it hadn't been for his exceptional quality. His art, you see — he always had that. It was an escape. When he was painting he didn't care, he shook off Caroline and her nagging and all the ceaseless rows and quarrels. They were endless, you know. Not a week passed without a thundering row over one thing or another. *She* enjoyed it. Having rows stimulated her, I believe. It was an outlet. She could say all the hard bitter stinging things she wanted to say. She'd positively purr after one of those set-tos — go off looking as sleek and well-fed as a cat. But it took it all out of *him*. He wanted peace — rest — a quiet life. Of course a man like that ought never to marry – he isn't out for domesticity. A man like Crale should have affairs but no binding ties. They're bound to chafe him.'

'He confided in you?'

'Well – he knew that I was a pretty devoted pal. He let me see things. He didn't complain. He wasn't that kind of man. Sometimes he would say, "Damn all women." Or he'd say, "Never get married, old boy. Wait for hell till after this life." '

'You knew about his attachment to Miss Greer?'

'Oh, yes – at least I saw it coming on. He told me he'd met a marvellous girl. She was different, he said, from anything or anyone he'd ever met before. Not that I paid much attention to that. Amyas was always meeting one woman or other who was "different". Usually a month later he'd stare at you if you mentioned them, and wonder who you were talking about! But this Elsa Greer really was different, I realized that when I came down to Alderbury to stay. She'd got him, you know, hooked him good and proper. The poor mutt fairly ate out of her hand.'

'You did not like Elsa Greer, either?'

'No, I didn't like her. She was definitely a predatory creature. She, too, wanted to own Crale body and soul. But I think, all the same, that she'd have been better for him than Caroline. She might conceivably have let him alone once she was sure of him. Or she might have got tired of him and moved on to someone else. The best thing for Amyas would have been to be quite free of female entanglements.'

'But that, it would seem, was not to his taste?'

Philip Blake said with a sigh: 'The damned fool was always getting himself involved with some woman or other. And yet, in a way, women really meant very little to him. The only two women who really made any impression on him at all in his life were Caroline and Elsa.'

Poirot said: 'Was he fond of the child?'

'Angela? Oh, we all liked Angela. She was such a sport. She was always game for anything. What a life she led that wretched governess of hers. Yes, Amyas liked Angela all right – but sometimes she went too far and then he used to really get mad with her – and then Caroline would step in – Caro was always on Angela's side and that would finish Amyas altogether. He hated it when Caro sided with Angela against him. There was a bit of jealousy all round, you know. Amyas was jealous of the way Caro always put Angela first and would do anything for her. And Angela was jealous of Amyas and rebelled against his overbearing ways. It was his decision that she should go to school that autumn, and she was furious about it. Not, I think, because she didn't like the idea of school – she really rather wanted to go, I believe – but it was Amyas's high-handed way of settling it all that infuriated her. She played all sorts of tricks on him in revenge. Once she put ten slugs in his bed. On the whole, I think Amyas was right. It was time she got some discipline. Miss Williams was very efficient, but even she confessed that Angela was getting too much for her.'

He paused. Poirot said: 'When I asked if Amyas was fond of the child – I referred to his own child, his daughter?'

'Oh, you mean little Carla? Yes, she was a great pet. He enjoyed playing with her when he was in the mood. But his affection for her wouldn't have deterred him from marrying Elsa, if that's what you mean. He hadn't *that* kind of feeling for her.'

'Was Caroline Crale very devoted to the child?'

A kind of spasm contorted Philip's face. He said: 'I can't say that she wasn't a good mother. No, I can't say that. It's the one thing—'

'Yes, Mr Blake?'

Philip said slowly and painfully: 'It's the one thing I really – regret – in this affair. The thought of that child. Such a tragic background to her young life. They sent her abroad to Amyas's cousin and her husband. I hope – I sincerely hope – they managed to keep the truth from her.'

Poirot shook his head. He said: 'The truth, Mr Blake, has a habit of making itself known. Even after many years.'

The stockbroker murmured: 'I wonder.'

Poirot went on: 'In the interests of truth, Mr Blake, I am going to ask you to do something.'

'What is it?'

'I am going to beg that you will write me out an exact account of what happened on those days at Alderbury. That is to say, I am going to ask you to write me out a full account of the murder and its attendant circumstances.'

'But, my dear fellow, after all this time? I should be hopelessly inaccurate.'

'Not necessarily.'

'Surely.'

'No, for one thing, with the passage of time, the mind retains a hold on essentials and rejects superficial matters.'

'Oh! You mean a mere broad outline?'

'Not at all. I mean a detailed conscientious account of each event as it occurred, and every conversation you can remember.'

'And supposing I remember them wrong?'

'You can give the wording at least to the best of your reflection. There may be gaps, but that cannot be helped.'

Blake looked at him curiously.

'But what's the idea? The police files will give you the whole thing far more accurately.'

'No, Mr Blake. We are speaking now from the psychological point of view. I do not want bare *facts*. *I want your own selection of facts*. Time and your memory are responsible for that selection. There may have been things done, words spoken, that I should seek for in vain in the police files. Things and words that you never mentioned because, maybe, you judged them irrelevant, or because you preferred not to repeat them.'

Blake said sharply: 'Is this account of mine for publication?'

'Certainly not. It is for my eye only. To assist me to draw my own deductions.'

'And you won't quote from it without my consent?'

'Certainly not.'

'H'm,' said Philip Blake. 'I'm a very busy man, M. Poirot.'

'I appreciate that there will be time and trouble involved. I should be happy to agree to a – reasonable fee.'

There was a moment's pause. Then Philip Blake said suddenly: 'No, if I do it – I'll do it for nothing.'

'And you will do it?'

Philip said warningly: 'Remember, I can't vouch for the accuracy of my memory.'

'That is perfectly understood.'

'Then I think,' said Philip Blake, 'that I should *like* to do it. I feel I owe it – in a way – to Amyas Crale.'

— 7 —

THIS LITTLE PIG STAYED AT HOME

HERCULE POIROT was not a man to neglect details.

His advance towards Meredith Blake was carefully thought out. Meredith Blake was, he already felt sure, a very different proposition from Philip Blake. Rush tactics would not succeed here. The assault must be leisurely.

Hercule Poirot knew that there was only one way to penetrate the stronghold. He must approach Meredith Blake with the proper credentials. Thos credentials must be social, not professional. Fortunately, in the course of his career, Hercule Poirot had made friends in many counties. Devonshire was no exception. He sat down to review what resources he had in Devonshire. As a result he discovered two people who were acquaintances or friends of Mr Meredith Blake. He descended upon him therefore armed with two letters, one from Lady Mary Lytton-Gore, a gentle widow lady of restricted means, the most retiring of creatures; and the other from a retired admiral, whose family had been settled in the county for four generations.

Meredith Blake received Poirot in a state of some perplexity.

As he had often felt lately, things were not what they used to be. Dash it all, private detectives used to be private detectives – fellows you got to guard wedding presents at country receptions, fellows you went to – rather shamefacedly – when there was some dirty business afoot and you'd got to get the hang of it.

But here was Lady Mary Lytton-Gore writing: 'Hercule Poirot is a very old and valued friend of mine. Please do all you can to help him, won't you?' And Mary Lytton-Gore wasn't – no, decidedly she wasn't – the sort of woman you associate with private detectives and all that they stand for. And Admiral Cronshaw wrote: 'Very good chap – absolutely sound. Grateful if you will do what you can for him. Most entertaining fellow, can tell you lots of good stories.'

And now here was the man himself. Really a most impossible person – the wrong clothes – button boots! – an incredible moustache! Not his – Meredith Blake's – kind of fellow at all. Didn't look as though he'd ever hunted or shot – or even played a decent game. A foreigner.

Slightly amused, Hercule Poirot read accurately these thoughts passing through the other's head.

He had felt his own interest rising considerably as the train brought him into the West Country. He would see now, with his own eyes, the actual place where these long-past events happened.

It was here, at Handcross Manor, that two young brothers had lived and gone over to Alderbury and joked and played tennis and fraternized with a young Amyas Crale and a girl called Caroline. It was here that Meredith had started out to Alderbury on that fatal morning. That had been sixteen years ago. Hercule Poirot looked with interest at the man who was confronting him with a somewhat uneasy politeness.

Very much what he had expected. Meredith Blake resembled

superficially every other English country gentleman of straitened means and outdoor tastes.

A shabby old coat of Harris tweed, a weather-beaten, pleasant, middle-aged face with somewhat faded blue eyes, a weak mouth, half hidden by a rather straggly moustache. Poirot found Meredith Blake a great contrast to his brother. He had a hesitating manner, his mental processes were obviously leisurely. It was as though his tempo had slowed down with the years just as his brother's had accelerated.

As Poirot had already guessed, he was a man whom you could not hurry. The leisurely life of the English countryside was in his bones.

He looked, the detective thought, a good deal older than his brother, though, from what Mr Jonathan had said, it would seem that only a couple of years separated them.

Hercule Poirot prided himself on knowing how to handle an 'old school tie'. It was no moment for trying to seem English. No, one must be a foreigner – frankly a foreigner – and be magnanimously for given for the fact. 'Of course, these foreigners don't quite know the ropes. *Will* shake hands at breakfast. Still, a decent fellow really . . .'

Poirot set about creating this impression of himself. The two men talked, cautiously, of Lady Mary Lytton-Gore and of Admiral Cronshaw. Other names were mentioned. Fortunately Poirot knew someone's cousin and had met somebody else's sister-in-law. He could see a kind of warmth dawning in the squire's eye. The fellow seemed to know the right people.

Gracefully, insidiously, Poirot slid into the purpose of his visit. He was quick to counteract the inevitable recoil. This book was, alas, going to be written. Miss Crale – Miss Lemarchant, as she was now called – was anxious for him to exercise a judicious editorship. The facts, unfortunately, were public property. But much could be done in their presentation to avoid wounding susceptibilities. Poirot murmured that before now he had been able to use discreet influence to avoid certain purple passages in a book of memoirs.

Meredith Blake flushed angrily. His hand shook a little as he filled a pipe. He said, a slight stammer in his voice: 'It's – it's g-ghoulish the way they dig these things up. S-sixteen years ago. Why can't they let it be?'

Poirot shrugged his shoulders. He said: 'I agree with you. But what will you? There is a demand for such things. And anyone is at liberty to reconstruct a proved crime and to comment on it.'

'Seems disgraceful to me.'

Poirot murmured: 'Alas – we do not live in a delicate age . . . You would be surprised, Mr Blake, if you knew the unpleasant publications I have succeeded in – shall we say? – softening. I am anxious to do all I can to save Miss Crale's feelings in the matter.'

Meredith Blake murmured: 'Little Carla! That child! A grown-up woman. One can hardly believe it.'

'I know. Time flies swiftly, does it not?'

Meredith Blake sighed. He said: 'Too quickly.'

Poirot said: 'As you will have seen in the letter I handed you from Miss Crale, she is very anxious to know everything possible about the sad events of the past.'

Meredith Blake said with a touch of irritation: 'Why? Why rake up everything again? How much better to let it all be forgotten.'

'You say that, Mr Blake, because you know all the past too well. Miss Crale, remember, knows nothing. That is to say, she knows only the story as she has learnt it from the official accounts.'

Meredith Blake winced. He said: 'Yes, I forgot. Poor child. What a detestable position for her. The shock of learning the truth. And then – those soulless, callous reports of the trial.'

'The truth,' said Hercule Poirot, 'can never be done justice to in a mere legal recital. It is the things that are left out that are the things that matter. The emotions, the feelings – the characters of the actors in the drama. The extenuating circumstances—'

He paused and the other man spoke eagerly like an actor who had received his cue.

'Extenuating circumstances! That's just it. If ever there were extenuating circumstances, there were in this case. Amyas Crale was an old friend – his family and mine had been friends for generations, but one has to admit that his conduct was, frankly, outrageous. He was an artist, of course, and presumably that explains it. But there it is – he allowed a most extraordinary set of affairs to arise. The position was one that no ordinary decent man could have contemplated for a moment.'

Hercule Poirot said: 'I am interested that you should say that. It had puzzled me, that situation. Not so does a well-bred man, a man of the world, go about his affairs.'

Blake's thin, hesitating face had lit up with animation. He said: 'Yes, but the whole point is that Amyas never was an ordinary man! He was a painter, you see, and with him painting came first – really sometimes in the most extraordinary way! I don't understand these so-called artistic people myself – never have. I understood Crale a little because, of course, I'd known him all my life. His people were the same sort as my people. And in many ways Crale ran true to type – it was only where art came in that he didn't conform to the usual standards. He wasn't, you see, an amateur in any way. He was first-class – really first-class. Some people say he's a genius. They may be right. But, as a result, he was always what I should describe as unbalanced. When he was painting a picture – nothing else mattered, nothing could be allowed to get in the way. He was like a man in a dream. Completely obsessed by what he was doing. Not till the canvas was finished did he come out of this absorption and start to pick up the threads of ordinary life again.'

He looked questioningly at Poirot and the latter nodded.

'You understand, I see. Well, that explains, I think, why this particular situation arose. He was in love with this girl. He wanted to marry her. He was prepared to leave his wife and child for her. But he'd started painting her down here, and he wanted to finish that picture. Nothing else mattered to him. He didn't *see* anything else. And the fact that the situation was a perfectly impossible one for the two women concerned doesn't seem to have occurred to him.'

'Did either of them understand his point of view?'

'Oh, yes – in a way. Elsa did, I suppose. She was terrifically enthusiastic about his painting. But it was a difficult position for her – naturally. And as for Caroline—'

He stopped. Poirot said: 'For Caroline – yes, indeed.'

Meredith Blake said, speaking with a little difficulty: 'Caroline – I had always – well, I had always been very fond of Caroline. There was a time when – when I hoped to marry her. But that was soon nipped in the bud. Still, I remained, if I may say so, devoted to – to her service.'

Poirot nodded thoughtfully. That slightly old-fashioned phrase expressed, he felt, the man before him very typically. Meredith Blake was the kind of man who would give himself readily to a romantic and honourable devotion. He would serve his lady faithfully and without hope of reward. Yes, it was all very much in character.

He said, carefully weighing his words: 'You must have resented this – attitude – on *her* behalf?'

'I did. Oh, I did. I – I actually remonstrated with Crale on the subject.'

'When was this?'

'Actually the day before – before it all happened. They came

over to tea here, you know. I got Crale aside and I – I put it to him.
I even said, I remember, that it wasn't fair on either of them.'

'Ah, you said that?'

'Yes. I didn't think, you see, that he *realized*.'

'Possibly not.'

'I said to him that it was putting Caroline in a perfectly unendurable position. If he meant to marry this girl, he ought not to
have her staying in the house and – well – more or less flaunt her in
Caroline's face. It was, I said, an unendurable insult.'

Poirot asked curiously: 'What did he answer?'

Meredith Blake replied with distaste: 'He said: "Caroline must
lump it." '

Hercule Poirot's eyebrows rose.

'Not,' he said, 'a very sympathetic reply.'

'I thought it abominable. I lost my temper. I said that no doubt,
not caring for his wife, he didn't mind how much he made her
suffer, but what, I said, about the girl? Hadn't he realized it was a
pretty rotten position for *her*? His reply to that was that Elsa must
lump it, too!

'Then he went on: "You don't seem to understand, Meredith,
that this thing I'm painting is the best thing I've done. It's *good*, I
tell you. And a couple of jealous quarrelling women aren't going
to upset it – no, by hell, they're not."

'It was hopeless talking to him. I said he seemed to have taken
leave of all decency. Painting, I said, wasn't everything. He
interrupted there. He said: "Ah, but it is to *me*."

'I was still very angry. I said it was perfectly disgraceful the way
he had always treated Caroline. She had had a miserable life with
him. He said he knew that and he was sorry about it. Sorry! He
said: "I know, Merry, you don't believe that – but it's the truth.
I've given Caroline the hell of a life and she's been a saint about it.
But she did know, I think, what she might be letting herself in for.
I told her candidly the sort of damnable egoistic, loose-living kind
of chap I was."

'I put it to him then very strongly that he ought not to break up
his married life. There was the child to be considered and
everything. I said that I could understand that a girl like Elsa
could bowl a man over, but that even for her sake he ought to
break off the whole thing. She was very young. She was going into
this bald-headed, but she might regret it bitterly afterwards. I
said couldn't he pull himself together, make a clean break and go
back to his wife?'

'And what did he say?'

Blake said: 'he just looked – embarrassed. He patted me on the shoulder and said: "You're a good chap, Merry. But you're too sentimental. You wait till the picture's finished and you'll admit that I was right."

'I said: "Damn your picture." And he grinned and said all the neurotic women in England couldn't do that. Then I said that it would have been more decent to have kept the whole thing from Caroline until after the picture was finished. He said that that wasn't *his* fault. It was Elsa who had insisted on spilling the beans. I said, Why? And he said that she had had some idea that it wasn't straight otherwise. She wanted everything to be clear and above board. Well, of course, in a way, one could understand that and respect the girl for it. However badly she was behaving, she did at least want to be honest.'

'A lot of additional pain and grief is caused by honesty,' remarked Hercule Poirot.

Meredith Blake looked at him doubtfully. He did not quite like the sentiment. He sighed: 'It was a – a most unhappy time for us all.'

'The only person who does not seem to have been affected by it was Amyas Crale,' said Poirot.

'And why? Because he was a rank egoist. I remember him now. Grinning at me as he went off saying: "Don't worry, Merry. Everything's going to pan out all right!" '

'The incurable optimist,' murmured Poirot.

Meredith Blake said: 'He was the kind of man who didn't take women seriously. *I* could have told him that Caroline was desperate.'

'Did she tell you so?'

'Not in so many words. But I shall always see her face as it was that afternoon. White and strained with a kind of desperate gaiety. She talked and laughed a lot. But her eyes – there was a kind of anguished grief in them that was the most moving thing I have ever known. Such a gentle creature, too.'

Hercule Poirot looked at him for a minute or two without speaking. Clearly the man in front of him felt no incongruity in speaking thus of a woman who on the day after had deliberately killed her husband.

Meredith Blake went on. He had by now quite overcome his first suspicious hostility. Hercule Poirot had the gift of listening. To men such as Meredith Blake, the reliving of the past has a definite attraction. He spoke now almost more to himself than to his guest.

'I ought to have suspected something, I suppose. It was Caroline who turned the conversation to – to my little hobby. It was, I must confess, an enthusiasm of mine. The old English herbalists, you know, are a very interesting study. There are so many plants that were formerly used in medicine and which have now disappeared from the official pharmacopœia. And it's astonishing, really, how a simple decoction of something or other will really work wonders. No need for doctors half the time. The French understand these things – some of their *tisanes* are first-rate.' He was well away now on his hobby.

'Dandelion tea, for instance; marvellous stuff. And a decoction of hips – I saw the other day somewhere that that's coming into fashion with the medical profession again. Oh, yes, I must confess, I got a lot of pleasure out of my brews. Gathering the plants at the right time, drying them – macerating them – all the rest of it. I've even dropped to superstition sometimes and gathered my roots at the full of the moon or whatever it was the ancients advised. On that day I gave my guests, I remember, a special disquisition on the spotted hemlock. It flowers biennially. You gather the fruits when they're ripening, just before they turn yellow. Coniine, you know, is a drug that's dropped out – I don't believe there's any official preparation of it in the last pharmacopœia – but I've proved the usefulness of it in whooping cough – and in asthma, too, for that matter—'

'You talked of all this in your laboratory?'

'Yes, I showed them round – explained the various drugs to them – valerian and the way it attracts cats – one sniff at that was enough for them! Then they asked about deadly nightshade and I told them about belladonna and atropine. They were very much interested.'

'"They"? What is comprised in that word?'

Meredith Blake looked faintly surprised as though he had forgotten that his listener had no first-hand knowledge of the scene.

'Oh, the whole party. Let me see, Philip was there and Amyas, and Caroline, of course. Angela. And Elsa Greer.'

'That was all?'

'Yes – I think so. Yes, I am sure of it.' Blake looked at him curiously. 'Who else should there be?'

'I thought perhaps the governess—'

'Oh, I see. No, she wasn't there that afternoon. I believe I've forgotten her name now. Nice woman. Took her duties very seriously. Angela worried her a good deal, I think.'

'Why was that?'

'Well, she was a nice kid, but she was inclined to run wild. Always up to something or other. Put a slug or something down Amyas's back one day when he was hard at work painting. He went up in smoke. Cursed her up and down dale. It was after that that he insisted on this school idea.'

'Sending her to school?'

'Yes. I don't mean that he wasn't fond of her, but he found her a bit of a nuisance sometimes. And I think – I've always thought—'

'Yes?'

'That he was a bit jealous. Caroline, you see, was a slave of Angela. In a way, perhaps, Angela came first with her – and Amyas didn't like that. There was a reason for it, of course. I won't go into that, but—'

Poirot interrupted.

'The reason being that Caroline Crale reproached herself for an action that had disfigured the girl?'

Blake exclaimed: 'Oh, you know that? I wasn't going to mention it. All over and done with. But, yes, that was the cause of her attitude, I think. She always seemed to feel that there was nothing too much she could do – to make up, as it were.'

Poirot nodded thoughtfully. He asked: 'And Angela? Did she bear a grudge against her half-sister?'

'Oh, no, don't run away with that idea. Angela was devoted to Caroline. She never gave that old business a thought, I'm sure. It was just Caroline who couldn't forgive herself.'

'Did Angela take kindly to the idea of boarding school?'

'No, she didn't. She was furious with Amyas. Caroline took her side, but Amyas had absolutely made his mind up about it. In spite of a hot temper, Amyas was an easy man in most respects, but when he really got his back up everyone had to give in. Both Caroline and Angela knuckled under.'

'She was to go to school – when?'

'The autumn term – they were getting her kit together, I remember. I suppose, if it hadn't been for the tragedy, she would have gone off a few days later. There was some talk of her packing on the morning of that day.'

Poirot said: 'And the governess?'

'What do you mean – the governess?'

'How did she like the idea? It deprived her of a job, did it not?'

'Yes – well, I suppose it did in a way. Little Carla used to do a few lessons, but of course she was only – what? Six or thereabouts. She had a nurse. They wouldn't have kept Miss Williams on for her. Yes, that's the name – Williams. Funny how things come back to you when you talk them over.'

'Yes, indeed. You are back now, are you not, in the past? You relive the scenes – the words that people said, their gestures – the expressions on their faces?'

Meredith Blake said slowly: 'In a way – yes . . . But there are gaps, you know . . . Great chunks missed out. I remember, for instance, the shock it was to me when I first learned that Amyas was going to leave Caroline – but I can't remember whether it was he who told me or Elsa. I do remember arguing with Elsa on the subject – trying to show her, I mean, that it was a pretty rotten thing to do. And she only laughed at me in that cool way of hers and said I was old-fashioned. Well, I dare say I *am* old fashioned, but I still think I was right. Amyas had a wife and child – he ought to have stuck to them.'

'But Miss Greer thought that point of view out of date?'

'Yes. Mind you, sixteen years ago, divorce wasn't looked on quite so much as a matter of course as it is now. But Elsa was the kind of girl who went in for being modern. Her point of view was that when two people weren't happy together it was better to make a break. She said that Amyas and Caroline never stopped having rows and that it was far better for the child that she shouldn't be brought up in an atmosphere of disharmony.'

'And her argument did not impress you?'

Meredith Blake said slowly: 'I felt, all the time, that she didn't really know what she was talking about. She was rattling these things off – things she'd read in books or heard from her friends – it was like a parrot. She was – it's a queer thing to say – pathetic somehow. So young and so self-confident.' He paused. 'There is something about youth, M. Poirot, that is – that can be – terribly moving.'

Hercule Poirot said, looking at him with some interest: 'I know what you mean . . .'

Blake went on, speaking more to himself than to Poirot: 'That's partly, I think, why I tackled Crale. He was nearly twenty years older than the girl. It didn't seem fair.'

Poirot murmured: 'Alas – how seldom one makes any effect. When a person has determined on a certain course – especially when there is a woman concerned – it is not easy to turn them from it.'

Meredith Blake said: 'That is true enough.' His tone was a shade bitter. 'I certainly did no good by my interference. But, then, I am not a very convincing person. I never have been.'

Poirot threw him a quick glance. He read into that slight acerbity of tone the dissatisfaction of a sensitive man with his own lack of personality. And he acknowledged to himself the truth of what Blake had just said. Meredith Blake was not the man to persuade anyone into or out of any course. His well-meaning attempts would always be set aside – indulgently usually, without anger, but definitely set aside. They would not carry weight. He was essentially an ineffective man.

Poirot said, with an appearance of changing a painful subject: 'You still have your laboratory of medicines and cordials, yes?'

'No.'

The word came sharply – with an almost anguished rapidity Meredith Blake said, his face flushing: 'I abandoned the whole thing – dismantled it. I couldn't go on with it – how could I? – after what had happened. The whole thing, you see, might have been said to be *my* fault.

'No, no, Mr Blake, you are too sensitive.'

'But don't you see? If I hadn't collected those damned drugs. If I hadn't laid stress on them – boasted about them – forced them on those people's notice that afternoon. But I never thought – I never dreamed – how could I—?'

'How indeed?'

'But I went bumbling on about them. Pleased with my little bit of knowledge. Blind, conceited fool. I pointed out that damned coniine. I even – fool that I was – took them back into the library and read them out that passage from the Phaedo describing Socrates's death. A beautiful piece of writing – I've always admired it. But it's haunted me ever since.'

Poirot said: 'Did they find any fingerprints on the coniine-bottle?'

'Hers.'

'Caroline Crale's?'

'Yes.'

'Not yours?'

'No. I didn't handle the bottle, you see. Only pointed to it.'

'But at the same time, surely, you had handled it?'

'Oh, of course, but I gave the bottles a periodic dusting from time to time – I never allowed the servants in there, of course – and I had done that about four or five days previously.'

'You kept the room locked up?'

'Invariably.'

'When did Caroline Crale take the coniine from the bottle?'

Meredith Blake replied reluctantly: 'She was the last to leave the room. I called her, I remember, and she came hurrying out. Her cheeks were just a little pink – and her eyes were wide and excited. Oh, God, I can see her now.'

Poirot said: 'Did you have any conversation with her at all that afternoon? I mean by that, did you discuss the situation as between her and her husband at all?'

Blake said slowly in a low voice: 'Not directly. She was looking as I've told you – very upset. I said to her at a moment when we were more or less by ourselves: "Is anything the matter, my dear?" She said: "Everything's the matter . . ." I wish you could have heard the desperation in her voice. Those words were the absolute truth. There's no getting away from it – Amyas Crale was Caroline's whole world. She said: "Everything's gone – finished. I'm finished, Meredith." And then she laughed and turned to the others and was suddenly wildly and very unnaturally gay.'

Hercule Poirot nodded his head slowly. He looked very like a china mandarin. He said: 'Yes – I see it – it was like that . . .'

Merdith Blake pounded suddenly with his fist. His voice rose. It was almost a shout.

'And I'll tell you this, M. Poirot – when Caroline Crale said at the trial that she took the stuff for herself, I'll swear she was speaking the truth! There was no thought in her mind of murder at that time. I swear there wasn't. That came later.'

Hercule Poirot asked: 'Are you sure that it *did* come later?'

Blake stared. He said: 'I beg your pardon? I don't quite understand—'

Poirot said: 'I ask you whether you are sure that the thought of murder ever did come? Are you perfectly convinced in your own mind that Caroline Crale did deliberately commit murder?'

Meredith Blake's breath came unevenly. He said: 'But if not – if not – are you suggesting – well – an accident of some kind?'

'Not necessarily.'

'That's a very extraordinary thing to say.'

'Is it? You have called Caroline Crale a gentle creature. Do gentle creatures commit murder?'

'She was a gentle creature – but all the same – well, there were very violent quarrels, you know.'

'Not such a gentle creature, then?'

'But she *was*— Oh, how difficult these things are to explain.'

'I am trying to understand.'

'Caroline had a quick tongue – a vehement way of speaking. She might say, "I hate you. I wish you were dead." But it wouldn't mean – it wouldn't entail – *action*.'

'So, in your opinion, it was highly uncharacteristic of Mrs Crale to commit murder?'

'You have the most extraordinary ways of putting things, M. Poirot. I can only say that – yes – it does seem to me uncharacteristic of her. I can only explain it by realizing that the provocation was extreme. She adored her husband. Under these circumstances a woman might – well – kill.'

Poirot nodded. 'Yes, I agree . . .'

'I was dumbfounded at first. I didn't feel it *could* be true. And it wasn't true – if you know what I mean – it wasn't the real Caroline who did that.'

'But you are quite sure that – in the legal sense – Caroline Crale did do it?'

Again Meredith Blake stared at him.

'My dear man – if she didn't—'

'Well, if she didn't?'

'I can't imagine any alternative solution. Accident? Surely impossible.'

'Quite impossible, I should say.'

'And I can't believe in the suicide theory. It had to be brought forward, but it was quite unconvincing to anyone who knew Crale.'

'Quite.'

'So what remains?' asked Meredith Blake.

Poirot said coolly: 'There remains the possibility of Amyas Crale having been killed by someone else.'

'But that's absurd!'

'You think so?'

'I'm sure of it. Who would have wanted to kill him? Who *could* have killed him?'

'You are more likely to know than I am.'

'But you don't seriously believe—'

'Perhaps not. It interests me to examine the possibility. Give it your serious consideration. Tell me what you think.'

Meredith stared at him for a minute or two. Then he lowered his eyes. After a few moments he shook his head. He said: 'I can't imagine *any* possible alternative. I should like to do so. If there were any reason for suspecting anybody else, I would believe Caroline innocent. I don't want to think she did it. I couldn't believe it at first. But who else is there? Who else was there? Philip? Crale's best friend. Elsa? Ridiculous. Myself? Do I look like a murderer? A respectable governess? A couple of old faithful servants? Perhaps you'd suggest that the child Angela did it? No, M. Poirot, there's *no* alternative. *Nobody* could have killed Amyas Crale but his wife. But he drove her to it. And so, in a way, it was suicide after all, I suppose.'

'Meaning that he died by the result of his own actions, though not by his own hand?'

'Yes, it's a fanciful point of view, perhaps. But – well – cause and effect, you know.'

Hercule Poirot said: 'Have you ever reflected, Mr Blake, that the reason for murder is nearly always to be found by a study of the person murdered?'

'I hadn't exactly – yes, I suppose I see what you mean.'

Poirot said: 'Until you know exactly *what sort of a person the victim was*, you cannot begin to see the circumstances of a crime clearly.

He added: 'That is what I am seeking for – and what you and your brother have helped to give me – a reconstruction of the man Amyas Crale.'

Meredith Blake passed the main point of the remark over. His attention had been distracted by a single word. He said quickly: 'Philip?'

'Yes.'

'You have talked with him also?'

'Certainly.'

Meredith Blake said sharply: 'You should have come to me first.'

Smiling a little, Poirot made a courteous gesture.

'According to the laws of primogeniture, that is so,' he said. 'I am aware that you are the elder. But you comprehend that, as your brother lives near London, it was easier to visit him first.'

Meredith Blake was still frowning. He pulled uneasily at his lip. He repeated: 'You should have come to me first.'

This time, Poirot did not answer. He waited. And presently Meredith Blake went on: 'Philip,' he said, 'is prejudiced.'

'Yes?'

'As a matter of fact he's a mass of prejudices – always has been.' He shot a quick uneasy glance at Poirot. 'He'll have tried to put you against Caroline.'

'Does that matter, so long – after?'

Meredith Blake gave a sharp sigh.

'I know. I forget that it's so long ago – that it's all over. Caroline is beyond being harmed. But, all the same, I shouldn't like you to get a false impression.'

'And you think your brother might give me a false impression?'

'Frankly, I do. You see, there was always a certain – how shall I put it? – antagonism between him and Caroline.'

'Why?'

The question seemed to irritate Blake. He said: 'Why? How should I know *why*? These things are so. Philip always crabbed her whenever he could. He was annoyed, I think, when Amyas married her. He never went near them for over a year. And yet Amyas was almost his best friend. That was the reason really, I suppose. He didn't feel that any woman was good enough. And he probably felt that Caroline's influence would spoil their friendship.'

'And did it?'

'No, of course it didn't. Amyas was always just as fond of Philip – right up to the end. Used to twit him with being a money-grabber and with growing a corporation and being a Philistine generally. Philip didn't care. He just used to grin and say it was a good thing Amyas had one respectable friend.'

'How did your brother react to the Elsa Greer affair?'

'Do you know, I find it rather difficult to say. His attitude wasn't really easy to define. He was annoyed, I think, with Amyas for making a fool of himself over the girl. He said more than once that it wouldn't work and that Amyas would live to regret it. At the same time I have a feeling – yes, very definitely I have a feeling that he was just faintly pleased at seeing Caroline let down.'

Poirot's eyebrows rose. He said: 'He really felt like that?'

'Oh, don't misunderstand me. I wouldn't go further than to say that I believe that feeling was at the back of his mind. I don't know that he ever quite realized himself that that is what he felt. Phipil and I have nothing much in common, but there is a link, you know, between people of the same blood. One brother often knows what the other brother is thinking.'

'And after the tragedy?'

Meredith Blake shook his head. A spasm of pain crossed his face. He said: 'Poor Phil. He was terribly cut up. Just broken up by it. He'd always been devoted to Amyas, you see. There was an element of hero worship about it, I think. Amyas Crale and I are the same age. Philip was two years younger. And he looked up to Amyas always. Yes – it was a great blow to him. He was – he was terribly bitter against Caroline.'

'He, at least, had no doubts, then?'

Meredith Blake said: 'None of us had any doubts . . .'

There was a silence. Then Blake said with the irritable plaintiveness of a weak man: 'It was all over – forgotten – and now *you* come – raking it all up . . .'

554

'Not I. Caroline Crale.'

Meredith stared at him: '*Caroline?* What do you mean?'

Poirot said, watching him: 'Caroline Crale the second.'

Meredith's face relaxed.

'Ah, yes, the child. Little Carla. I – I misunderstood you for a moment.'

'You thought I meant the original Caroline Crale? You thought that it was she who would not – how shall I say it – rest easy in her grave?'

Meredith Blake shivered.

'Don't, man.'

'You know that she wrote to her daughter – the last words she ever wrote – that she was innocent?'

Meredith stared at him. He said – and his voice sounded utterly incredulous: 'Caroline wrote *that?*'

'Yes.'

Poirot paused and said: 'It surprises you?'

'It would surprise you if you'd seen her in court. Poor, hunted, defenceless creature. Not even struggling.'

'A defeatist?'

'No, no. She wasn't that. It was, I think, the knowledge that she'd killed the man she loved – or I thought it was that.'

'You are not so sure now?'

'To write a thing like that – solemnly – when she was dying.'

Poirot suggested: 'A pious lie, perhaps.'

'Perhaps.' But Meredith was dubious. 'That's not – that's not like Caroline . . .'

Hercule Poirot nodded. Carla Lemarchant had said that. Carla had only a child's obstinate memory. But Meredith Blake had known Caroline well. It was the first confirmation Poirot had got that Carla's belief was to be depended upon.

Meredith Blake looked up at him. He said slowly: 'If – *if* Caroline was innocent – why, the whole thing's madness! I don't see – any other possible solution . . .'

He turned sharply on Poirot.

'And you? What do you think?'

There was a silence.

'As yet,' said Poirot at last, 'I think nothing. I collect only impressions. What Caroline Crale was like. What Amyas Crale was like. What the other people who were there at that time were like. What happened exactly on those two days. *That* is what I need. To go over the facts laboriously one by one. Your brother is going to help me there. He is sending me an account of the events as he remembers them.'

Meredith Blake said sharply: 'You won't get much from that. Philip's a busy man. Things slip his memory once they're past and done with. Probably he'll remember things all wrong.'

'There will be gaps, of course. I realize that.'

'I tell you what—' Meredith paused abruptly, then went on, reddening a little as he spoke. 'If you like, I – I could do the same. I mean, it would be a kind of check, wouldn't it?'

Hercule Poirot said warmly: 'It would be most valuable. An idea of the first excellence!'

'Right. I will. I've got some old diaries somewhere. Mind you,' he laughed awkwardly, 'I'm not much of a hand at literary language. Even my spelling's not too good. You – you won't expect too much?'

'Ah, it is not the style I demand. Just a plain recital of everything you can remember. What everyone said, how they looked – just what happened. Never mind if it doesn't seem relevant. It all helps with the atmosphere, so to speak.'

'Yes, I can see that. It must be difficult visualizing people and places you have never seen.'

Poirot nodded.

'There is another thing I wanted to ask you. Alderbury is the adjoining property to this, is it not? Would it be possible to go there – to see with my own eyes where the tragedy occurred?'

Meredith Blake said slowly: 'I can take you over there right away. But, of course, it is a good deal changed.'

'It has not been built over?'

'No, thank goodness – not quite so bad as that. But it's a kind of hostel now – it was bought by some society. Hordes of young people come down to it in the summer and, of course, all the rooms have been cut up and partitioned into cubicles, and the grounds have been altered a good deal.'

'You must reconstruct it for me by your explanations.'

'I'll do my best. I wish you could have seen it in the old days. It was one of the loveliest properties I know.'

He led the way out through the window and began walking down a slope of lawn.

'Who was responsible for selling it?'

'The executors on behalf of the child. Everything Crale had came to her. He hadn't made a will, so I imagine that it would be divided automatically between his wife and the child. Caroline's will left what she had to the child also.'

'Nothing to her half-sister?'

'Angela had a certain amount of money of her own left by her father.'

Poirot nodded. 'I see.'

Then he uttered an exclamation: 'But where is it that you take me? This is the seashore ahead of us!'

'Ah, I must explain our geography to you. You'll see for yourself in a minute. There's a creek, you see, Camel Creek, they call it, runs inland – looks almost like a river mouth, but it isn't – it's just sea. To get to Alderbury by land you have to go right inland and round the creek, but the shortest way from one house to the other is to row across this narrow bit of the creek. Alderbury is just opposite – there, you can see the house through the trees.'

They had come out on a little beach. Opposite them was a wooded headland and a white house could just be distinguished high up amongst the trees.

Two boats were drawn up on the beach. Meredith Blake, with Poirot's somewhat awkward assistance, dragged one of them down to the water and presently they were rowing across to the other side.

'We always went this way in the old days,' Meredith explained. 'Unless, of course, there was a storm or it was raining, and then we'd take the car. But it's nearly three miles if you go round that way.'

He ran the boat neatly alongside a stone quay on the other side. He cast a disparaging eye on a collection of wooden huts and some concrete terraces.

'All new, this. Used to be a boathouse – tumbledown old place – and nothing else. And one walked along the shore and bathed off those rocks over there.'

He assisted his guest to alight, made fast the boat, and led the way up a steep path.

'Don't suppose we'll meet anyone,' he said over his shoulder. 'Nobody here in April – except for Easter. Doesn't matter if we do. I'm on good terms with my neighbours. Sun's glorious today. Might be summer. It was a wonderful day then. More like July than September. Brilliant sun – but a chilly little wind.'

The path came out of the trees and skirted an outcrop of rock. Meredith pointed up with his hand.

'That's what they called the battery. We're more or less underneath it now – skirting round it.'

They plunged into trees again and then the path took another sharp turn and they emerged by a door set in a high wall. The path itself continued to zigzag upwards, but Meredith opened the door and the two men passed through it.

For a moment Poirot was dazzled coming in from the shade outside. The battery was an artificially cleared plateau with battlements set with cannon. It gave one the impression of over-hanging the sea. There were trees above it and behind it, but on the sea side there was nothing but the dazzling blue water below.

'Attractive spot,' said Meredith. He nodded contemptuously towards a kind of pavilion set back against the back wall. 'That wasn't there, of course – only an old tumbledown shed where Amyas kept his painting muck and some bottled beer and a few deck chairs. It wasn't concreted then, either. There used to be a bench and a table – painted iron ones. That was all. Still – it hasn't changed much.'

His voice held an unsteady note.

Poirot said: 'And it was here that it happened?'

Meredith nodded.

'The bench was there – up against the shed. He was sprawled on that. He used to sprawl there sometimes when he was painting – just fling himself down and stare and stare – and then suddenly up he'd jump and start laying the paint on the canvas like mad.'

He paused.

'That's why, you know, he looked – almost natural. As though he might be asleep – just have dropped off. But his eyes were open – and he'd – just stiffened up. Stuff sort of paralyses you, you know. There isn't any pain . . . I've – I've always been glad of that . . .'

Poirot asked a thing that he already knew.

'Who found him?'

'She did. Caroline. After lunch. I and Elsa, I suppose, were the last ones to see him alive. It must have been coming on then. He – looked queer. I'd rather not talk about it. I'll write it to you. Easier that way.'

He turned abruptly and went out of the battery. Poirot followed him without speaking.

The two men went on up the zigzag path. At a higher level than the battery there was another small plateau. It was over-shadowed with trees and there was a bench there and a table.

Meredith said: 'They haven't changed this much. But the bench used not to be Ye Olde Rustic. It was just a painted iron business. A bit hard for sitting, but a lovely view.'

Poirot agreed. Through a framework of trees one looked down over the battery to the creek mouth.

'I sat up here part of the morning,' Meredith explained. 'Trees weren't quite so overgrown then. One could see the battlements of the battery quite plainly. That's where Elsa was posing, you know. Sitting on one with her head twisted round.'

He gave a slight twitch of his shoulders.

'Trees grow faster than one thinks,' he muttered. 'Oh, well, suppose I'm getting old. Come on up to the house.'

They continued to follow the path till it emerged near the house. It had been a fine old house, Georgian in style. It had been added to and on a green lawn near it were set some fifty little wooden bathing-hutches.

'Young men sleep there, girls in the house,' Meredith explained. 'I don't suppose there's anything you want to see here. All the rooms have been cut about. Used to be a little conservatory tacked on here. These people have built a loggia. Oh, well – I suppose they enjoy their holidays. Can't keep everything as it used to be – more's the pity.'

He turned away abruptly.

'We'll go down another way. It – it all comes back to me, you know. Ghosts. Ghosts everywhere.'

They returned to the quay by a somewhat longer and more rambling route. Neither of them spoke. Poirot respected his companion's mood.

When they reached Handcross Manor once more, Meredith Blake said abruptly: 'I bought that picture, you know. The one that Amyas was painting. I just couldn't stand the idea of its being sold for – well – publicity value – a lot of dirty-minded brutes gaping at it. It was a fine piece of work. Amyas said it was the best thing he'd ever done. I shouldn't be surprised if he was right. It was practically finished. He only wanted to work on it another day or so. Would – would you care to see it?'

Hercule Poirot said quickly: 'Yes, indeed.'

Blake led the way across the hall and took a key from his pocket. He unlocked a door and they went into a fair-sized, dusty-smelling room. It was closely shuttered. Blake went across to the windows and opened the wooden shutters. Then, with a little difficulty, he flung up a window and a breath of fragant spring air came wafting into the room.

Meredith said: 'That's better.'

He stood by the window inhaling the air and Poirot joined him. There was no need to ask what the room had been. The shelves were empty but there were marks upon them where bottles had stood. Against one wall was some derelict chemical apparatus and a sink. The room was thick in dust.

Meredith Blake was looking out of the window. He said: 'How easily it all comes back. Standing here, smelling the jasmine – and talking – talking – like the damned fool I was – about my precious potions and distillations!'

Absently, Poirot stretched a hand through the window. He

pulled off the spray of jasmine leaves just breaking from their woody stem.

Meredith Blake moved resolutely across the floor. On the wall was a picture covered with a dust sheet. He jerked the dust sheet away.

Poirot caught his breath. He had seen, so far, four pictures of Amyas Crale's: two at the Tate, one at a London dealer's, one the still life of roses. But now he was looking at what the artist himself had called his best picture, and Poirot realized at once what a superb artist the man had been.

The painting had an old superficial smoothness. At first sight it might have been a poster, so seemingly crude were its contrasts. A girl, a girl in a canary-yellow shirt and dark-blue slacks, sitting on a grey wall in full sunlight against a background of violent blue sea. Just the kind of subject for a poster.

But the first appearance was deceptive; there was a subtle distortion – an amazing brilliance and clarity in the light. And the girl—

Yes, here was life. All there was, all there could be of life, of youth, of sheer blazing vitality. The face was alive and the eyes . . .

So much life! Such passionate youth! That, then, was what Amyas Crale had seen in Elsa Greer, which had made him blind and deaf to the gentle creature, his wife. Elsa *was* life. Elsa *was* youth.

A superb, slim, straight creature, arrogant, her head turned, her eyes insolent with triumph. Looking at you, watching you – waiting . . .

Hercule Poirot spread out his hands. He said: 'It is great – yes, it is great—'

Meredith Blake said, a catch in his voice: 'She was so young—'

Poirot nodded. He thought to himself: 'What do most people mean when they say that? *So young*. Something innocent, something appealing, something helpless. But youth is not that! Youth is crude, youth is strong, youth is powerful – yes, and cruel! And one thing more – youth is vulnerable.'

He followed his host to the door. His interest was quickened now in Elsa Greer, whom he was to visit next. What would the years have done to that passionate, triumphant, crude child?

He looked back at the picture.

Those eyes. Watching him . . . watching him . . . telling him something . . .

Supposing he couldn't understand what they were telling him?

Would the real woman be able to tell him? Or were those eyes saying something that the real woman did not know?

Such arrogance, such triumphant anticipation.

And then Death had stepped in and taken the prey out of those eager, clutching young hands . . .

And the light had gone out of those passionately anticipating eyes. What were the eyes of Elsa Greer like now?

He went out of the room with one last look.

He thought: 'She was too much alive.'

He felt – a little – frightened . . .

— 8 —

THIS LITTLE PIG HAD ROAST BEEF

THE house in Brook Street had Darwin tulips in the window boxes. Inside the hall a great vase of white lilac sent eddies of perfume towards the open front door.

A middle-aged butler relieved Poirot of his hat and stick. A footman appeared to take them and the butler murmured deferentially: 'Will you come this way, sir?'

Poirot followed him along the hall and down three steps. A door was opened, the butler pronounced his name with every syllable correct.

Then the door closed behind him and a tall thin man got up from a chair by the fire and came towards him.

Lord Dittisham was a man just under forty. He was not only a peer of the realm, he was a poet. Two of his fantastical poetic dramas had been staged at vast expense and had had a *succès d'estime*. His forehead was rather prominent, his chin was eager, and his eyes and his mouth unexpectedly beautiful.

He said: 'Sit down, M. Poirot.'

Poirot sat down and accepted a cigarette from his host. Lord Dittisham shut the box, struck a match and held it for Poirot to light his cigarette, then he himself sat down and looked thoughtfully at his visitor.

Then he said: 'It is my wife you have come to see, I know.'

Poirot answered: 'Lady Dittisham was so kind as to give me an appointment.'

'Yes.'

There was a pause. Poirot hazarded: 'You do not, I hope, object, Lord Dittisham?'

The thin dreamy face was transformed by a sudden quick smile.

'The objections of husbands, M. Poirot, are never taken seriously in these days.'

'Then you do object?'

'No. I cannot say that. But I am, I must confess it, a little fearful of the effect upon my wife. Let me be quite frank. A great many years ago, when my wife was only a young girl, she passed through a terrible ordeal. She has, I hope, recovered from the shock. I have come to believe that she has forgotten it. Now you appear and necessarily your questions will reawaken these old memories.'

'It is regrettable,' said Hercule Poirot politely.

'I do not know quite what the result will be.'

'I can only assure you, Lord Dittisham, that I shall be as discreet as possible, and do all I can not to distress Lady Dittisham. She is, no doubt, of a delicate and nervous temperament.'

Then, suddenly and surprisingly, the other laughed. He said: 'Elsa? Elsa's as strong as a horse!'

'Then—' Poirot paused diplomatically. The situation intrigued him.

Lord Dittisham said: 'My wife is equal to any amount of shocks. I wonder if you know her reason for seeing you.'

Poirot replied placidly: 'Curiosity?'

A kind of respect showed in the other man's eyes.

'Ah, you realize that?'

Poirot said: 'It is inevitable. Women will *always* see a private detective! Men will tell him to go to the devil.'

'Some women might tell him to go to the devil, too.'

'After they have seen him – not before.'

'Perhaps.' Lord Dittisham paused. 'What is the idea behind this book?'

Hercule Poirot shrugged his shoulders.

'One resurrects the old tunes, the old stage turns, the old costumes. One resurrects, too, the old murders.'

'Faugh!' said Lord Dittisham.

'Faugh! If you like. But you will not alter human nature by saying "Faugh". Murder is a drama. The desire for drama is very strong in the human race.'

Lord Dittisham murmured: 'I know – I know . . .'

'So you see,' said Poirot, 'the book will be written. It is my part to make sure that there shall be no gross mis-statements, no tampering with the known facts.'

'The facts are public property, I should have thought.'

'Yes. But not the interpretation of them.' ·

Dittisham said sharply: 'Just what do you mean by that, M. Poirot?'

'My dear Lord Dittisham, there are many ways of regarding, for instance, a historical fact. Take an example: many books have been written on your Mary Queen of Scots, representing her as a martyr, as an unprincipled and wanton woman, as a rather simple-minded saint, as a murderess and an intriguer, or again as a victim of circumstance and fate! One can take one's choice.'

'And in this case? Crale was killed by his wife – that is, of course, undisputed. At the trial my wife came in for some, in my opinion, undeserved calumny. She had to be smuggled out of court afterwards. Public opinion was very hostile to her.'

'The English,' said Poirot, 'are a very moral people.'

Lord Dittisham said: 'Confound them, they are!'

He added – looking at Poirot: 'And you?'

'Me,' said Poirot. 'I lead a very moral life. That is not quite the same thing as having moral ideas.'

Lord Dittisham said: 'I've wondered sometimes what this Mrs Crale was really like. All this "injured wife" business – I've a feeling there was something *behind* that.'

'Your wife might know,' agreed Poirot.

'My wife,' said Lord Dittisham, 'has never mentioned the case once.'

Poirot looked at him with quickened interest. He said: 'Ah, I begin to see—'

The other said sharply: 'What do you see?'

Poirot replied with a bow: 'The creative imagination of the poet . . .'

Lord Dittisham rose and rang the bell. He said brusquely: 'My wife will be waiting for you.'

The door opened.

'You rang, my lord?'

'Take M. Poirot up to her ladyship.'

Up two flights of stairs, feet sinking into soft-pile carpets. Subdued flood-lighting. Money, money everywhere. Of taste, not so much. There had been a sombre austerity in Lord Dittisham's room. But here, in the house, there was only a solid lavishness. The best. Not necessarily the showiest, or the most startling. Merely 'expense no object', allied to a lack of imagination.

Poirot said to himself: 'Roast beef? Yes, roast beef!'

It was not a large room into which he was shown. The big drawing-room was on the first floor. This was the personal sitting-room of the mistress of the house and the mistress of the house was standing against the mantelpiece as Poirot was announced and shown in.

A phrase leapt into his startled mind and refused to be driven out.

She died young . . .

That was his thought as he looked at Elsa Dittisham, who had been Elsa Greer.

He would never have recognized her from the picture Meredith Blake had shown him. That had been, above all, a picture of youth, a picture of vitality. Here there was not youth – there might never have been youth. And yet he realized, as he had not realized from Crale's picture, that Elsa was beautiful. Yes, it was a very beautiful woman who came forward to meet him. And certainly not old. After all, what was she? Not more than thirty-six now if she had been twenty at the time of the tragedy. Her black hair was perfectly arranged round her shapely head, her features were almost classic, her make-up was exquisite.

He felt a strange pang. It was, perhaps, the fault of old Mr Jonathan, speaking of Juliet . . . No Juliet here – unless perhaps one could imagine Juliet a survivor – living on, deprived of Romeo . . . Was it not an essential part of Juliet's make-up that she should die young?

Elsa Greer had been left alive . . .

She was greeting him in a level, rather monotonous voice.

'I am so interested, M. Poirot. Sit down and tell me what you want me to do.'

He thought: 'But she isn't interested. Nothing interests her.'

Big grey eyes – like dead lakes.

Poirot became, as was his way, a little obviously foreign.

He exclaimed: 'I am confused, Madame, veritably I am confused.'

'Oh, no, why?'

'Because I realize that this – this reconstruction of a past drama must be excessively painful to you!'

She looked amused. Yes, it was amusement. Quite genuine amusement.

She said: 'I suppose my husband put that idea into your head. He saw you when you arrived. Of course, he doesn't understand in the least. He never has. I'm not at all the sensitive sort of person he imagines I am.'

The amusement was still in her voice. She said: 'My father, you know, was a mill hand. He worked his way up and made a fortune. You don't do that if you're thin-skinned. I'm the same.

Poirot thought to himself: 'Yes, that is true. A thin-skinned person would not have come to stay in Caroline Crale's house.'

Lady Dittisham said: 'What is it you want me to do?'

'You are sure, Madame, that to go over the past would not be painful to you?'

She considered a minute, and it struck Poirot suddenly that Lady Dittisham was a very frank woman. She might lie from necessity but never from choice.

Elsa Dittisham said slowly: 'No, not *painful*. In a way, I wish it were.'

'Why?'

She said impatiently: 'It's so stupid never to feel anything . . .'

And Hercule Poirot thought: 'Yes, Elsa Greer is dead . . .'

Aloud he said: 'At all events, Lady Dittisham, it makes my task very much easier.'

She said cheerfully: 'What do you want to know?'

'Have you a good memory, Madame?'

'Reasonably good, I think.'

'And you are sure it will not pain you to go over those days in detail?'

'It won't pain me at all. Things can only pain you when they are happening.'

'It is so with some people, I know.'

Lady Dittisham said: 'That's what Edward – my husband – can't understand. He thinks the trial and all that was a terrible ordeal for me.'

'Was it not?'

Elsa Dittisham said: 'No, I enjoyed it.' There was a reflective satisfied quality in her voice. She went on: 'God, how that old brute Depleach went for me. He's a devil, if you like. I enjoyed fighting him. He didn't get me down.'

She looked at Poirot with a smile.

'I hope I'm not upsetting your illusions. A girl of twenty, I ought to have been prostrated, I suppose – agonized with shame or something. I wasn't. I didn't care what they said to me. I only wanted one thing.'

'What?'

'To get her hanged, of course,' said Elsa Dittisham.

He noticed her hands – beautiful hands but with long curving nails. Predatory hands.

She said: 'You're thinking me vindictive? So I am vindictive –

565

to anyone who has injured me. That woman was to my mind the lowest kind of woman there is. She knew that Amyas cared for me – that he was going to leave her – and she killed him so that *I* shouldn't have him.'

She looked across at Poirot.

'Don't you think that's pretty mean?'

'You do not understand or sympathize with jealousy?'

'No, I don't think I do. If you've lost, you've lost. If you can't keep your husband, let him go with a good grace. It's possessiveness I don't understand.'

'You might have understood it if you had ever married him.'

'I don't think so. We weren't—' She smiled suddenly at Poirot. Her smile was, he felt, a little frightening. It was so far removed from any real feeling. 'I'd like you to get this right,' she said. 'Don't think that Amyas Crale seduced an innocent young girl. It wasn't like that at all! Of the two of us, *I* was responsible. I met him at a party and I fell for him – I knew I'd got to have him—'

A travesty, a grotesque travesty, but –

> *And all my fortunes at thy foot I'll lay*
> *And follow thee, my lord, throughout the world . . .*

'Although he was married?'

'"Trespassers will be prosecuted"? It takes more than a printed notice to keep you from reality. If he was unhappy with his wife and could be happy with me, then why not? We've only one life to live.'

'But it has been said he was happy with his wife.'

Elsa shook her head.

'No. They quarrelled like cat and dog. She nagged at him. She was – oh, she was a horrible woman!'

She got up and lit a cigarette. She said with a little smile: 'Probably I'm unfair to her. But I really *do* think she was rather hateful.'

Poirot said slowly: 'It was a great tragedy.'

'Yes, it was a great tragedy.' She turned on him suddenly; into the dead monotonous weariness of her face something came quiveringly alive.

'It killed *me*, do you understand? It killed me. Ever since there's been nothing – nothing at all.' Her voice dropped. 'Emptiness!' She waved her hands impatiently. 'Like a stuffed fish in a glass case!'

'Did Amyas Crale mean so much to you?'

566

She nodded. It was a queer confiding little nod – oddly pathetic. She said: 'I think I've always had a single-track mind.' She mused sombrely. 'I suppose – really – one ought to put a knife into oneself – like Juliet. But – but to do that is to acknowledge that you're done for – that life's beaten you.'

'And instead?'

'There ought to be everything – just the same – once one has got over it. I *did* get over it. It didn't mean anything to me any more. I thought I'd go on to the next thing.'

Yes, the next thing. Poirot saw her plainly trying so hard to fulfil that crude determination. Saw her beautiful and rich, seductive to men, seeking with greedy predatory hands to fill up a life that was empty. Hero worship – a marriage to a famous aviator – then an explorer, that big giant of a man, Arnold Stevenson – possibly not unlike Amyas Crale physically – a reversion to the creative arts: Dittisham!

Elsa Dittisham said: 'I've never been a hypocrite! There's a Spanish proverb I've always liked. *Take what you want and pay for it, says God.* Well, I've done that. I've taken what I wanted – but I've always been willing to pay the price.'

Hercule Poirot said: 'What you do not understand is that there are things that cannot be bought.'

She stared at him. She said: 'I don't mean just money.'

Poirot said: 'No, no, I understand what you mean. But it is not everything in life that has its ticket, so much. There are things that are *not for sale.*'

'Nonsense!'

He smiled very faintly. In her voice was the arrogance of the successful mill hand who had risen to riches.

Hercule Poirot felt a sudden wave of pity. He looked at the ageless, smooth face, the weary eyes, and he remembered the girl whom Amyas Crale had painted . . .

Elsa Dittisham said: 'Tell me all about this book. What is the purpose of it? Whose idea is it?'

'Oh, my dear lady, what other purpose is there but to serve up yesterday's sensation with today's sauce?'

'But *you're* not a writer?'

'No, I am an expert on crime.'

'You mean they consult you on crime books?'

'Not always. In this case, I have a commission.'

'From whom?'

'I am – what do you say? – vetting this publication on behalf of an interested party.'

'What party?'

'Miss Carla Lemarchant.'

'Who is she?'

'She is the daughter of Amyas and Caroline Crale.'

Elsa stared for a minute. Then she said: 'Oh, of course, there *was* a child. I remember. I suppose she's grown up now?'

'Yes, she is twenty-one.'

'What is she like?'

'She is tall and dark and, I think, beautiful. And she has courage and personality.'

Elsa said thoughtfully: 'I should like to see her.'

'She might not care to see you.'

Elsa looked surprised.

'Why? Oh, I see. But what nonsense! She can't possibly remember anything about it. She can't have been more than six.'

'She knows that her mother was tried for her father's murder.'

'And she thinks it's my fault?'

'It is a possible interpretation.'

Elsa shrugged her shoulders. She said: 'How stupid! If Caroline had behaved like a reasonable human being—'

'So you take no responsibility?'

'Why should I? *I've* nothing to be ashamed of. I loved him. I would have made him happy.' She looked across at Poirot. Her face broke up – suddenly, incredibly, he saw the girl of the picture. She said: 'If I could make you see. If you could see it from my side. If you knew—'

Poirot leaned forward.

'But that is what I want. See, Mr Philip Blake, who was there at the time, he is writing me a meticulous account of everything that happened. Mr Meredith Blake the same. Now if you—'

Elsa Dittisham took a deep breath. She said contemptuously: 'Those two! Philip was always stupid. Meredith used to trot round after Caroline – but he was quite a dear. But you won't have *any* real idea from *their* accounts.'

He watched her, saw the animation rising in her eyes, saw a living woman take shape from a dead one. She said quickly and almost fiercely: 'Would you like the *truth*? Oh, not for publication. But just for yourself—'

'I will undertake not to publish without your consent.'

'I'd like to write down the truth . . .' She was silent a minute or two, thinking. He saw the smooth hardness of her cheeks falter and take on a younger curve, he saw life ebbing into her as the past claimed her again.

'To go back – to write it all down . . . To show you what she was—'

Her eyes flashed. Her breast heaved passionately.

'She killed him. She killed Amyas. Amyas who wanted to live – who enjoyed living. Hate oughtn't to be stronger than love – but her hate was. And my hate for her is – I hate her – I hate her – I hate her . . .'

She came across to him. She stooped, her hand clutched at his sleeve. She said urgently: 'You must understand – you *must* – how we felt about each other. Amyas and I, I mean. There's something – I'll show you.'

She whirled across the room. She was unlocking a little desk, pulling out a drawer concealed inside a pigeon hole.

Then she was back. In her hand was a creased letter, the ink faded. She thrust it on him and Poirot had a sudden poignant memory of a child he had known who had thrust on him one of her treasures – a special shell picked up on the seashore and zealously guarded. Just so had that child stood back and watched him. Proud, afraid, keenly critical of his reception of her treasure.

He unfolded the faded sheets.

Elsa – you wonderful child! There never was anything as beautiful. And yet I'm afraid – I'm too old – a middle-aged, ugly-tempered devil with no stability in me. Don't trust me, don't believe in me– I'm no good – apart from my work. The best of me is in that. There, don't say you haven't been warned.

Hell, my lovely – I'm going to have you all the same. I'd go to the devil for you and you know it. And I'll paint a picture of you that will make the fat-headed world hold its sides and gasp! I'm crazy about you – I can't sleep – I can't eat. Elsa – Elsa – Elsa – I'm yours for ever – yours till death.

Amyas.

Sixteen years ago. Faded ink, crumbling paper. But the words still alive – still vibrating . . .

He looked across at the woman to whom they had been written.

But it was no longer a woman at whom he looked.

It was a young girl in love.

He thought again of Juliet . . .

THIS LITTLE PIG HAD NONE

'MAY I ask why, M. Poirot?'

Hercule Poirot considered his answer to the question. He was aware of a pair of very shrewd eyes watching him out of the small wizened face.

He had climbed to the top floor of the bare building and knocked on the door of No. 584 Gillespie Buildings, which had come into existence to provide what were called 'flatlets' for working women.

Here, in a small cubic space, existed Miss Cecilia Williams, in a room that was bedroom, sitting-room, dining-room, and, by judicious use of the gas ring, kitchen – a kind of cubby hole attached to it contained a quarter-length bath and the usual offices.

Meagre though these surroundings might be, Miss Williams had contrived to impress upon them her stamp of personality.

The walls were distempered an ascetic pale grey, and various reproductions hung upon them. Dante meeting Beatrice on a bridge – and that picture once described by a child as a 'blind girl sitting on an orange and called, I don't know why, "Hope"'. There were also two water-colours of Venice and a sepia copy of Botticelli's 'Primavera'. On the top of the low chest of drawers were a large quantity of faded photographs, mostly, by their style of hairdressing, dating from twenty to thirty years ago.

The square of carpet was threadbare, the furniture battered and of poor quality. It was clear to Hercule Poirot that Cecilia Williams lived very near the bone. There was no roast beef here. This was the little pig that had none.

Clear, incisive and insistent, the voice of Miss Williams repeated its demand.

'You want my recollections of the Crale case? May I ask why?'

It has been said of Hercule Poirot, by some of his friends and associates, at moments when he has maddened them most, that he prefers lies to truth and will go out of his way to gain his ends by means of elaborate false statements, rather than trust to the simple truth.

But in this case his decision was quickly made. Hercule Poirot did not come of that class of Belgian or French children who have had an English governess, but he reacted as simply and inevitably as various small boys who had been asked in their time: 'Did you

brush your teeth this morning, Harold (Richard or Anthony)?'
They considered fleetingly the possibility of a lie and instantly
rejected it, replying miserably, 'No, Miss Williams.'

For Miss Williams had what every successful child educator
must have, that mysterious quality – authority! When Miss
Williams said 'Go up and wash your hands, Joan,' or 'I expect you
to read this chapter on the Elizabethan poets and be able to
answer my questions on it,' she was invariably obeyed. It had
never entered Miss Williams's head that she would not be obeyed.

So in this case Hercule Poirot proffered no specious explanation
of a book to be written on bygone crimes. Instead he narrated
simply the circumstances in which Carla Lemarchant had sought
him out.

The small, elderly lady in the neat shabby dress listened
attentively.

She said: 'It interests me very much to have news of that child –
to know how she has turned out.'

'She is a very charming and attractive young woman, with
plenty of courage and a mind of her own.'

'Good,' said Miss Williams briefly.

'And she is, I may say, a very persistent person. She is not a
person whom it is easy to refuse or put off.'

The ex-governess nodded thoughtfully. She asked: 'Is she
artistic?'

'I think not.'

Miss Williams said dryly: 'That's one thing to be thankful for!'

The tone of the remark left Miss Williams's views as to artists in
no doubt whatever.

She added: 'From your account of her I should imagine that she
takes after her mother rather than after her father.'

'Very possibly. That you can tell me when you have seen her.
You would like to see her?'

'I should like to see her very much indeed. It is always
interesting to see how a child you have known has developed.'

'She was, I suppose, very young when you last saw her.'

'She was five and a half. A very charming child – a little over-
quiet, perhaps. Thoughtful. Given to playing her own little games
and not inviting outside co-operation. Natural and unspoilt.'

Poirot said: 'It was fortunate she was so young.'

'Yes, indeed. Had she been older the shock of the tragedy might
have had a very bad effect.'

'Nevertheless,' said Poirot, 'one feels that there *was* a handicap
– however little the child understood or was allowed to know,

there would have been an atmosphere of mystery and evasion and an abrupt uprooting. These things are not good for a child.'

Miss Williams replied thoughtfully: 'They may have been less harmful than you think.'

Poirot said: 'Before we leave the subject of Carla Lemarchant – little Carla Crale that was, there is something I would like to ask you. If anyone can explain it, I think you can.'

'Yes?'

Her voice was inquiring, non-committal.

Poirot waved his hands in an effort to express his meaning.

'There is something – a *nuance* I cannot define – but it seems to me always that the child, when I mention her, is not given her full representational value. When I mention her, the response comes always with a vague surprise, as though the person to whom I speak had forgotten altogether that there *was* a child. Now surely, Mademoiselle, that is not natural. A child, under these circumstances, is a person of importance, not in herself, but as a pivotal point. Amyas Crale may have had reasons for abandoning his wife – or for not abandoning her. But in the usual break-up of a marriage the child forms a very important point. But here the child seems to count for very little. That seems to me – strange.'

Miss Williams said quickly: 'You have put your finger on a vital point, M. Poirot. You are quite right. And that is partly why I said what I did just now – that Carla's transportation to different surroundings might have been in some respects a good thing for her. When she was older, you see, she might have suffered from a certain lack in her home life.'

She leaned forward and spoke slowly and carefully.

'Naturally, in the course of my work, I have seen a good many aspects of the parent-and-child problem. Many children – *most* children, I should say – suffer from over-attention on the part of their parents. There is too much love, too much watching over the child. It is uneasily conscious of this brooding, and seeks to free itself, to get away and be unobserved. With an only child that is particularly the case, and of course mothers are the worst offenders. The result on the marriage is often unfortunate. The husband resents coming second, seeks consolation – or, rather, flattery and attention – elsewhere, and a divorce results sooner or later. The best thing for a child, I am convinced, is to have what I should term healthy neglect on the part of both its parents. This happens naturally enough in the case of a large family of children and very little money. They are overlooked because the mother has literally no time to occupy herself with them. They realize quite well that she is fond of them, but they are not worried by too many manifestations of the fact.

'But there is another aspect. One does occasionally find a husband and wife who are so all-sufficient to each other, so wrapped up in each other, that the child of the marriage hardly seems very real to either of them. And in those circumstances I think a child comes to resent that fact, to feel defrauded and left out in the cold. You understand that I am not speaking of *neglect* in any way. Mrs Crale, for instance, was what is termed an excellent mother, always careful of Carla's welfare, of her health – playing with her at the right times and always kind and gay. But, for all that, Mrs Crale was really completely wrapped up in her husband. She existed, one might say, only in him and for him.' Miss Williams paused a minute and then said quietly: 'That, I think, is the justification for what she eventually did.'

Hercule Poirot said: 'You mean that they were more like lovers than like husband and wife?'

Miss Williams, with a slight frown of distaste for foreign phraseology, said: 'You could certainly put it that way.'

'He was as devoted to her as she was to him?'

'They were a devoted couple. But he, of course, was a man.' Miss Williams contrived to put into that last word a wholly Victorian significance.

'Men—' said Miss Williams, and stopped.

As a rich property owner says 'Bolsheviks' – as an earnest Communist says 'Capitalists' – as a good housewife says 'Black-beetles' – so did Miss Williams say 'Men'.

From her spinster's, governess's life, there rose up a blast of fierce feminism. Nobody hearing her speak could doubt that to Miss Williams Men were the Enemy!

Poirot said: 'You hold no brief for men?'

She answered dryly: 'Men have the best of this world. I hope it will not always be so.'

Hercule Poirot eyed her speculatively. He could quite easily visualize Miss Williams methodically and efficiently padlocking herself to a railing, and later hunger-striking with resolute endurance. Leaving the general for the particular, he said: 'You did not like Mr Crale?'

'I certainly did not like Mr Crale. Nor did I approve of him. If I were his wife, I should have left him. There are things that no woman should put up with.'

'But Mrs Crale did put up with them?'

'Yes.'

'You thought she was wrong?'

'Yes, I do. A woman should have a certain respect for herself and not submit to humiliation.'

'Did you ever say anything of that kind to Mrs Crale?'

'Certainly not. It was not my place to do so. I was engaged to educate Angela, not to offer unasked advice to Mrs Crale. To do so would have been most impertinent.'

'You liked Mrs Crale?'

'I was very fond of Mrs Crale.' The efficient voice softened, held warmth and feeling. 'Very fond of her and very sorry for her.'

'And your pupil – Angela Warren?'

'She was a most interesting girl – one of the most interesting pupils I have had. A really good brain. Undisciplined, quick-tempered, most difficult to manage in many ways, but really a very fine character.'

She paused and then went on: 'I always hoped that she would accomplish something worth while. And she has! You have read her book – on the Sahara? And she excavated those very interesting tombs in the Fayum! Yes, I am proud of Angela. I was not at Alderbury very long – two years and a half – but I always cherish the belief that I helped to stimulate her mind and encourage her taste for archæology.'

Poirot murmured: 'I understand that it was decided to continue her education by sending her to school. You must have resented that decision.'

'Not at all, M. Poirot. I thoroughly concurred with it.'

She paused and went on: 'Let me make the matter clear to you. Angela was a dear girl – really a very dear girl – warm-hearted and impulsive – but she was also what I call a difficult girl. That is, she was at a difficult age. There is always a moment where a girl feels unsure of herself – neither child nor woman. At one moment Angela would be sensible and mature – quite grown-up, in fact – but a minute later she would relapse into being a hoydenish child – playing mischievous tricks and being rude and losing her temper. Girls, you know, *feel* difficult at that age – they are terribly sensitive. Everything that is said to them they resent. They are annoyed at being treated like a child and then they suddenly feel shy at being treated like adults.

'Angela was in that state. She had fits of temper, would suddenly resent teasing and flare out – and then she would be sulky for days at a time, sitting about and frowning – then again she would be in wild spirits, climbing trees, rushing about with the garden boys, refusing to submit to any kind of authority.'

Miss Williams paused and went on: 'When a girl gets to that

stage, school is very helpful. She needs the stimulation of other minds – that, and the wholesome discipline of a community, help her to become a reasonable member of society. Angela's home conditions were not what I would have called ideal. Mrs Crale spoiled her, for one thing. Angela had only to appeal to her and Mrs Crale always backed her up. The result was that Angela considered she had first claim upon her sister's time and attention, and it was in these moods of hers that she used to clash with Mr Crale.

'Mr Crale naturally thought that *he* should come first – and intended to do so. He was really very fond of the girl – they were good companions and used to spar together quite amiably, but there were times when Mr Crale used suddenly to resent Mrs Crale's preoccupation with Angela. Like all men, he was a spoilt child; he expected everybody to make a fuss of *him*. Then he and Angela used to have a real set-to – and very often Mrs Crale would take Angela's side. Then he would be furious. On the other hand, if *she* supported *him*, Angela would be furious. It was on these occasions that Angela used to revert to childish ways and play some spiteful trick on him.

'He had a habit of tossing off his drinks and she once put a lot of salt into his drink. The whole thing, of course, acted as an emetic, and he was inarticulate with fury. But what really brought things to a head was when she put a lot of slugs into his bed. He had a queer aversion to slugs. He lost his temper completely and said that the girl had got to be sent away to school. He wasn't going to put up with all this petty nonsense any more.

'Angela was terribly upset – though actually she had once or twice expressed a wish herself to go to a boarding school – but she chose to make a huge grievance of it. Mrs Crale didn't want her to go but allowed herself to be persuaded – largely owing, I think, to what I said to her on the subject. I pointed out to her that it would be greatly to Angela's advantage, and that I thought it would really be a great benefit to the girl. So it was settled that she should go to Helston – a very fine school on the south coast – in the autumn term. But Mrs Crale was still unhappy about it all those holidays. And Angela kept up a grudge against Mr Crale whenever she remembered. It wasn't really serious, you understand, M. Poirot, but it made a kind of undercurrent that summer to – well – to everything *else* that was going on.'

Poirot said: 'Meaning – Elsa Greer?'

Miss Williams said sharply: 'Exactly.' And shut her lips very tight after the word.

'What was your opinion of Elsa Greer?'

'I had no opinion of her at all. A thoroughly unprincipled woman.'

'She was very young.'

'Old enough to know better. I can see no excuse for her – none at all.'

'She fell in love with him, I suppose—'

Miss Williams interrupted with a snort.

'Fell in love with him indeed. I should hope, M. Poirot, that, whatever our feelings, we can keep them in decent control. And we can certainly control our actions. That girl had absolutely no morals of any kind. It meant nothing to her that Mr Crale was a married man. She was absolutely shameless about it all – cool and determined. Possibly she may have been badly brought up – but that's the only excuse I can find for her.'

'Mr Crale's death must have been a terrible shock to her.'

'Oh, it was. And she herself was entirely to blame for it. I don't go as far as condoning murder but, all the same, M. Poirot, if ever a woman was driven to breaking-point, that woman was Caroline Crale. I tell you frankly, there were moments when I would have liked to murder them both myself. Flaunting the girl in his wife's face, listening to her having to put up with the girl's insolence – and she *was* insolent, M. Poirot. Oh, no, Amyas Crale deserved what he got. No man should treat his wife as he did and not be punished for it. His death was a just retribution.'

Hercule Poirot said: 'You feel strongly . . .'

The small woman looked at him with those indomitable grey eyes. She said: 'I feel *very strongly* about the marriage tie. Unless it is respected and upheld, a country degenerates. Mrs Crale was a devoted and faithful wife. Her husband deliberately flouted her and introduced his mistress into her home. As I say, he deserved what he got. He goaded her past endurance and I, for one, do not blame her for what she did.'

Poirot said slowly: 'He acted very badly – that I admit – but he was a great artist, remember.'

Miss Williams gave a terrific snort.

'Oh, yes, I know. That's always the excuse nowadays. An artist! An excuse for every kind of loose living, for drunkenness, for brawling, for infidelity. And what kind of an artist was Mr Crale, when all is said and done? It may be the fashion to admire his pictures for a few years. But they won't last. Why, he couldn't even draw! His perspective was terrible! Even his anatomy was quite incorrect. I know something of what I am talking about, M. Poirot. I studied painting for a time, as a girl, in Florence, and to anyone who knows and appreciates the great masters, these daubs of Mr Crale's are really ludicrous. Just splashing a few colours about on the canvas – no construction – no careful drawing. No,' she shook her head, 'don't ask me to admire Mr Crale's painting.'

'Two of them are in the Tate Gallery,' Poirot reminded her. Miss Williams sniffed.

'Possibly. So is one of Mr Epstein's statues, I believe.'

Poirot perceived that, according to Miss Williams, the last word had been said. He abandoned the subject of art.

He said: 'You were with Mrs Crale when she found the body?'

'Yes. She and I went down from the house together after lunch. Angela had left her pullover on the beach after bathing, or else in the boat. She was always very careless about her things. I parted from Mrs Crale at the door of the battery garden, but she called me back almost at once. I believe Mr Crale had been dead over an hour. He was sprawled on the bench near his easel.'

'Was she terribly upset at the discovery?'

'What exactly do you mean by that, M. Poirot?'

'I am asking you what your impressions were at the time.'

'Oh, I see. Yes, she seemed to me quite dazed. She sent me off to telephone for the doctor. After all, we couldn't be absolutely sure he was dead – it might have been a cataleptic seizure.'

'Did she suggest such a possibility?'

'I don't remember.'

'And you went and telephoned?'

Miss Williams's tone was dry and brusque.

'I had gone half up the path when I met Mr Meredith Blake. I entrusted my errand to him and returned to Mrs Crale. I thought, you see, she might have collapsed – and men are no good in a matter of that kind.'

'And had she collapsed?'

Miss Williams said dryly: 'Mrs Crale was quite in command of herself. She was quite different from Miss Greer, who made a hysterical and very unpleasant scene.'

'What kind of a scene?'

'She tried to attack Mrs Crale.'

'You mean she realized that Mrs Crale was responsible for Mr Crale's death?'

Miss Williams considered for a moment or two.

'No, she could hardly be sure of that. That – er, – terrible suspicion had not yet arisen. Miss Greer just screamed out: "It's all your doing, Caroline. You killed him. It's all your fault." She did not actually say "You've poisoned him," but I think there is no doubt that she thought so.'

'And Mrs Crale?'

Miss Williams moved restlessly.

'Must we be hypocritical, M. Poirot? I cannot tell you what Mrs Crale really felt or thought at that moment. Whether it was horror at what she had done—'

'Did it seem like that?'

'N-no, n-no, I can't say it did. Stunned, yes – and, I think, frightened. Yes, I am sure, frightened. But that is natural enough.'

Hercule Poirot said in a dissatisfied tone: 'Yes, perhaps that is natural enough . . . What view did she adopt officially to her husband's death?'

'Suicide. She said, very definitely from the first, that it must be suicide.'

'Did she say the same when she was talking to you privately, or did she put forward any other theory?'

'No. She – she – took pains to impress upon me that it must be suicide.'

Miss Williams sounded embarrassed.

'And what did you say to that?'

'Really, M. Poirot, does it matter *what* I said?'

'Yes, I think it does.'

'I don't see why—'

But, as though his expectant silence hypnotised her, she said reluctantly: 'I think I said: "Certainly, Mrs Crale. It must have been suicide." '

'Did you believe your own words?'

Miss Williams raised her head. She said firmly: 'No, I did not. But please understand, M. Poirot, that I was entirely on Mrs Crale's side, if you like to put it that way. My sympathies were with her, not with the police.'

'You would have liked to have seen her acquitted?'

Miss Williams said defiantly: 'Yes, I would.'

Poirot said: 'Then you are in sympathy with her daughter's feelings?'

'I have every sympathy with Carla.'

'Would you have any objection to writing out for me a detailed account of the tragedy?'

'You mean for her to read?'

'Yes.'

Miss Williams said slowly: 'No, I have no objection. She is quite determined to go into the matter, is she?'

'Yes. I dare say it would have been preferable if the truth had been kept from her—'

Miss Williams interrupted him: 'No. It is always better to face the truth. It is no use evading unhappiness by tampering with facts. Carla has had a shock learning the truth – now she wants to know exactly how the tragedy came about. That seems to me the right attitude for a brave young woman to take. Once she knows all about it she will be able to forget it again and go on with the business of living her own life.'

'Perhaps you are right,' said Poirot.

'I'm quite sure I'm right.'

'But, you see, there is more to it than that. She not only wants to know – she wants to prove her mother innocent.'

Miss Williams said: 'Poor child.'

'That is what you say, is it?'

Miss Williams said: 'I see now why you said that it might be better if she had never known. All the same, I think it is best as it is. To wish to find her mother innocent is a natural hope – and, hard though the actual revelation may be, I think from what you say of her that Carla is brave enough to learn the truth and not flinch from it.'

'You are sure it *is* the truth?'

'I don't understand you.'

'You see no loophole for believing that Mrs Crale was innocent?'

'I don't think that possibility has ever been seriously considered.'

'And yet she herself clung to the theory of suicide?'

Miss Williams said dryly: 'The poor woman had to say *something*.'

'Do you know that when Mrs Crale was dying she left a letter to her daughter in which she solemnly swears that she is innocent?'

Miss Williams stared.

'That was very wrong of her,' she said sharply.

'You think so?'

'Yes, I do. Oh, I dare say you are a sentimentalist like most men—'

Poirot interrupted indignantly: 'I am *not* a sentimentalist.'

'But there is such a thing as false sentiment. Why write that, a lie, at such a solemn moment? To spare your child pain? Yes, many women would do that. But I should not have thought it of Mrs Crale. She was a brave woman and a truthful woman. I should have thought it far more like her to have told her daughter not to judge.'

Poirot said with slight exasperation: 'You will not even consider, then, the possibility that what Caroline Crale wrote was the truth?'

'And yet you profess to have loved her?'

'I did love her. I had a great affection and deep sympathy for her.'

'Well, then—'

Miss Williams looked at him in a very odd way.

'You don't understand, M. Poirot. It doesn't matter my saying this now – so long afterwards. You see, I happen to *know* that Caroline Crale was guilty!'

'What?'

'It's true. Whether I did right in withholding what I knew at the time I cannot be sure – but I *did* withhold it. But you must take it from me, quite definitely, that I *know* Caroline Crale was guilty . . .'

— 10 —

THIS LITTLE PIG CRIED
'WEE WEE WEE'

ANGELA WARREN's flat overlooked Regent's Park. Here, on this spring day, a soft air wafted in through the open window and one might have had the illusion that one was in the country if it had not been for the steady menacing roar of the traffic passing below.

Poirot turned from the window as the door opened and Angela Warren came into the room.

It was not the first time he had seen her. He had availed himself of the opportunity to attend a lecture she had given at the Royal Geographical. It had been, he considered, an excellent lecture. Dry, perhaps, from the view of popular appeal. Miss Warren had an excellent delivery, she neither paused nor hesitated for a word. She did not repeat herself. The tones of her voice were clear and not unmelodious. She made no concessions to romantic appeal or love of adventure. There was very little human interest in the lecture. It was an admirable recital of concise facts, adequaely illustrated by excellent slides, and with intelligent deductions from the facts recited. Dry, precise, clear, lucid, highly technical.

The soul of Hercule Poirot approved. Here, he considered, was an orderly mind.

Now that he saw her at close quarters he realized that Angela Warren might easily have been a very handsome woman. Her features were regular, though severe. She had finely marked dark brows, clear intelligent brown eyes, a fine pale skin. She had very square shoulders and a slightly mannish walk.

There was certainly about her no suggestion of the little pig who cries '*Wee Wee*'. But on the right cheek, disfiguring and puckering the skin, was that healed scar. The right eye was slightly distorted, the corner pulled downwards by it, but no one would have realized that the sight of that eye was destroyed. It seemed to Hercule Poirot almost certain that she had lived with her disability so long that she was now completely unconscious of it. And it occurred to him that, of the five people in whom he had become interested as a result of his investigations, those who might have been said to start with the fullest advantages were not those who had actually wrested the most success and happiness from life. Elsa, who might have been said to start with all advantages – youth, beauty, riches – had done worst. She was like a flower overtaken by untimely frost – still in bud – but without life. Cecilia Williams, to outward appearances, had no assets of which to boast. Nevertheless, to Poirot's eye, there was no despondency there and no sense of failure. Miss Williams's life had been interesting to her – she was still interested in people and events. She had that enormous mental and moral advantage of a strict Victorian upbringing denied to us in these days – she had done her duty in that station of life to which it had pleased God to call her, and that assurance encased her in an armour impregnable to the slings and darts of envy, discontent and regret. She had her memories, her small pleasures, made possible by stringent economies, and sufficient health and vigour to enable her still to be interested in life.

Now, in Angela Warren – that young creature handicapped by disfigurement and its consequent humiliation, Poirot believed he saw a spirit strengthened by its necessary fight for confidence and assurance. The undisciplined schoolgirl had given place to a vital and forceful woman, a woman of considerable mental power and gifted with abundant energy to accomplish ambitious purposes. She was a woman, Poirot felt sure, both happy and successful. Her life was full and vivid and eminently enjoyable.

She was not, incidentally, the type of woman that Poirot really liked. Though admiring the clear-cut precision of her mind, she had just a sufficient *nuance* of the *femme formidable* about her to alarm him as a mere man. His taste had always been for the flamboyant and extravagant.

With Angela Warren it was easy to come to the point of his visit. There was no subterfuge. He merely recounted Carla Lemarchant's interview with him.

Angela Warren's severe face lit up appreciatively.

'Little Carla? She is over here? I would like to see her so much.'

'You have not kept in touch with her?'

'Hardly as much as I should have done. I was a schoolgirl at the time she went to Canada, and I realized, of course, that in a year or two she would have forgotten us. Of late years, an occasional present at Christmas has been the only link between us. I imagined that she would, by now, be completely immersed in the Canadian atmosphere and that her future would lie over there. Better so, in the circumstances.'

Poirot said: 'One might think so, certainly. A change of name – a change of scene. A new life. But it was not to be so easy as that.'

And he then told of Carla's engagement, the discovery she had made upon coming of age and her motives in coming to England.

Angela Warren listened quietly, her disfigured cheek resting on one hand. She betrayed no emotion during the recital, but as Poirot finished she said quietly: 'Good for Carla.'

Poirot was startled. It was the first time that he had met with this reaction. He said: 'You approve, Miss Warren?'

'Certainly. I wish her every success. Anything I can do to help, I will. I feel guilty, you know, that I haven't attempted anything myself.'

'Then you think that there is a possibility that she is right in her views?'

Angela Warren said sharply: 'Of course she's right. Caroline didn't do it. I've always known that.'

Hercule Poirot murmured: 'You surprise me very much indeed, Mademoiselle. Everybody else I have spoken to—'

She cut in sharply: 'You mustn't go by that. I've no doubt that the circumstantial evidence is overwhelming. My own conviction is based on knowledge – knowledge of my sister. I just know quite simply and definitely that Caro *couldn't* have killed anyone.'

'Can one say that with certainty of any human creature?'

'Probably not in most cases. I agree that the human animal is full of curious surprises. But in Caroline's case there were special reasons – reasons which I have a better chance of appreciating than anyone else could.'

She touched her damaged cheek.

'You see this? You've probably heard about it.' Poirot nodded. 'Caroline did that. That's why I'm sure – *I know* – that she didn't do murder.'

'It would not be a convincing argument to most people.'

'No, it would be the opposite. It was actually used in that way, I believe. As evidence that Caroline had a violent and ungovernable temper! Because she had injured me as a baby, learned men argued that she would be equally capable of poisoning an unfaithful husband.'

Poirot said: 'I, at least, appreciate the difference. A sudden fit of ungovernable rage does not lead you to first abstract a poison and then use it deliberately on the following day.'

Angela Warren waved an impatient hand.

'That's not what I mean at all. I must try and make it plain to you. Supposing that you are a person normally affectionate and of kindly disposition – but that you are also liable to intense jealousy. And supposing that, during the years of your life when control is most difficult, you do, in a fit of rage, come near to committing what is, in effect, murder. Think of the awful shock, the horror, the remorse that seizes upon you. To a sensitive person, like Caroline, that horror and remorse will never quite leave you. It never left her. I don't suppose I was consciously aware of it at the time but, looking back, I recognize it perfectly. Caro was haunted, continually haunted, by the fact that she had injured me.

'That knowledge never left her in peace. It coloured all her actions. It explained her attitude to me. Nothing was too good for me. In her eyes, I must always come first. Half the quarrels she had with Amyas were on my account. I was inclined to be jealous of him and played all kinds of tricks on him. I pinched cat stuff to put in his drink, and once I put a hedgehog in his bed. But Caroline was always on my side.'

Miss Warren paused, then she went on: 'It was very bad for me, of course. I got horribly spoilt. But that's neither here nor there. We're discussing the effect on Caroline. The result of that impulse to violence was a life-long abhorrence of any further act of the same kind. Caro was always watching herself, always in fear that something of that kind might happen again. And she took her own ways of guarding against it. One of these ways was a great extravagance of language. She felt (and, I think, psychologically quite truly) that if she were violent enough in speech she would have no temptation to violence in action. She found by experience that the method worked.

'That's why I've heard Caro say things like "I'd like to cut so

583

and so in pieces and boil him slowly in oil." And she'd say to me, or to Amyas, "If you go on annoying me I shall murder you." In the same way she quarrelled easily and violently. She recognized, I think, the impulse to violence that there was in her nature, and she deliberately gave it an outlet that way. She and Amyas used to have the most fantastic and lurid quarrels.'

Hercule Poirot nodded.

'Yes, there was evidence of that. They quarrelled like cat and dog, it was said.'

Angela Warren said: 'Exactly. That's what is so stupid and misleading about evidence. Of course Caro and Amyas quarrelled! Of course they said bitter and outrageous and cruel things to each other! What nobody appreciates is that they *enjoyed* quarrelling. But they did! Amyas enjoyed it, too. They were that kind of couple. They both of them liked drama and emotional scenes. Most men don't. They like peace. But Amyas was an artist. He liked shouting and threatening and generally being outrageous. It was like letting off steam to him. He was the kind of man who when he loses his collar stud bellows the house down. It sounds very odd, I know, but living that way with continual rows and makings-up was Amyas's and Caroline's idea of fun!'

She made an impatient gesture.

'If they'd only not hustled me away, and let me give evidence, I'd have told them that.' Then she shrugged her shoulders. 'But I don't suppose they would have believed me. And, anyway, then it wouldn't have been as clear in my mind as it is now. It was the kind of thing I knew but hadn't thought about and certainly had never dreamed of putting into words.'

She looked across at Poirot. 'You do see what I mean?'

He nodded vigorously

'I see perfectly – and I realize the absolute rightness of what you have said. There are people to whom agreement is monotony. They require the stimulant of dissension to create drama in their lives.'

'Exactly.'

'May I ask you, Miss Warren, what were your own feelings at the time?'

Angela Warren sighed.

'Mostly bewilderment and helplessness, I think. It seemed a fantastic nightmare. Caroline was arrested very soon – about three days afterwards, I think. I can still remember my indignation, my dumb fury – and, of course, my childish faith that it was just a silly mistake, that it would be all right. Caro was chiefly perturbed about *me* – she wanted me kept right away from it all as far as possible. She got Miss Williams to take me away to some relations almost at once. The police had no objection. And then, when it was decided that my evidence would not be needed, arrangements were made for me to go to school abroad.

'I hated going, of course. But it was explained to me that Caro had me terribly on her mind and that the only way I could help her was by going.'

She paused. Then she said: 'So I went to Munich. I was there when – when the verdict was given. They never let me go to see Caro. Caro wouldn't have it. That's the only time, I think, when she failed in understanding.'

'You cannot be sure of that, Miss Warren. To visit someone dearly loved in a prison might make a terrible impression on a young sensitive girl.'

'Possibly.'

Angela Warren got up. She said: 'After the verdict, when she had been condemned, my sister wrote me a letter. I have never shown it to anyone. I think I ought to show it to you now. It may help you to understand the kind of person Caroline was. If you like, you may take it to show to Carla also.'

She went to the door, then turning back she said: 'Come with me. There is a portrait of Caroline in my room.'

For a second time, Poirot stood gazing up at a portrait.

As a painting, Caroline Crale's portrait was mediocre. But Poirot looked at it with interest – it was not its artistic value that interested him.

He saw a long oval face, a gracious line of jaw and a sweet, slightly timid expression. It was a face uncertain of itself, emotional, with a withdrawn hidden beauty. It lacked the forcefulness and vitality of her daughter's face – that energy and joy of life Carla Lemarchant had doubtless inherited from her father. This was a less positive creature. Yet, looking at the painted face, Hercule Poirot understood why an imaginative man like Quentin Fogg had not been able to forget her.

Angela Warren stood at his side again – a letter in her hand.

She said quietly: 'Now that you have seen what she was like – read her letter.'

He unfolded it carefully and read what Caroline Crale had written sixteen years ago.

My darling little Angela,

You will hear bad news and you will grieve, but what I want to impress upon you is that it is all all right. I have never told you lies and I don't now when I say that I am actually happy – that I feel an essential rightness and a peace that I have never known before. It's all right, darling, it's all right. Don't look back and regret and grieve for me – go on with your life and succeed. You can, I know. It's all all right, darling, and I'm going to Amyas. I haven't the least doubt that we shall be together. I couldn't have lived without him . . . Do this one thing for me – be happy. I've told you – I'm happy. One has to pay one's debts. It's lovely to feel peaceful.

Your loving sister,

Caro

Hercule Poirot read it through twice. Then he handed it back. He said: 'That is a very beautiful letter, Mademoiselle – and a very remarkable one. A *very* remarkable one.'

'Caroline,' said Angela Warren, 'was a very remarkable person.'

'Yes, an unusual mind . . . You take it that this letter indicates innocence?'

'Of course it does!'

'It does not say so explicitly.'

'Because Caro would know that I'd never dream of her being guilty!'

'Perhaps – perhaps . . . But it might be taken another way. In the sense that she was guilty and that in expiating her crime she will find peace.'

It fitted in, he thought, with the description of her in court. And he experienced in this moment the strongest doubts he had yet felt of the course to which he had committed himself. Everything so far had pointed unswervingly to Caroline Crale's guilt. Now, even her own words testified against her.

On the other side was only the unshaken conviction of Angela Warren. Angela had known her well, undoubtedly, but might not her certainty be the fanatical loyalty of an adolescent girl, up in arms for a dearly loved sister?

As though she had read his thoughts Angela Warren said: 'No, M. Poirot – I *know* Caroline wasn't guilty.'

Poirot said briskly: 'The *bon Dieu* knows I do not want to shake you on that point. But let us be practical. You say your sister was not guilty. Very well, then, *what really happened*?'

Angela nodded thoughtfully. She said: 'That is difficult, I agree. I suppose that, as Caroline said, Amyas committed suicide.'

'Is that likely from what you know of his character?'

586

'Very unlikely.'

'But you do not say, as in the first case, that you *know* it is impossible?'

'No, because, as I said just now, most people *do* do impossible things – that is to say, things that seem out of character. But I presume, if you know them intimately, it wouldn't be out of character.'

'You knew your brother-in-law well?'

'Yes, but not like I knew Caro. It seems to me quite fantastic that Amyas should have killed himself – but I suppose he *could* have done so. In fact, he *must* have done so.'

'You cannot see any other explanation?'

Angela accepted the suggestion calmly, but not without a certain stirring of interest.

'Oh, I see what you mean . . . I've never really considered that possibility. You mean one of the other people killed him? That it was a deliberate cold-blooded murder . . .'

'It might have been, might it not?'

'Yes, it might have been . . . But it certainly seems very unlikely.'

'More unlikely than suicide?'

'That's difficult to say . . . On the face of it, there was no reason for suspecting anybody else. There isn't now when I look back . . .'

'All the same, let us consider the possibility. Who of those intimately concerned would you say was – shall we say – the most likely person?'

'Let me think. Well, I didn't kill him. And the Elsa creature certainly didn't. She was mad with rage when he died. Who else was there? Meredith Blake? He was always very devoted to Caroline, quite a tame cat about the house. I suppose that *might* give him a motive in a way. In a book he might have wanted to get Amyas out of the way so that he himself could marry Caroline. But he could have achieved that just by letting Amyas go off with Elsa and then in due time consoling Caroline. Besides, I really can't *see* Meredith as a murderer. Too mild and too cautious. Who else was there?'

Poirot suggested: 'Miss Williams? Philip Blake?'

Angela's grave face relaxed into a smile for a minute.

'Miss Williams? One can't really make oneself believe that one's governess could commit a murder! Miss Williams was always so unyielding and so full of rectitude.'

She paused a minute and then went on: 'She was devoted to

Caroline, of course. Would have done anything for her. And she hated Amyas. She was a great feminist and disliked men. Is that enough for murder? Surely not.'

'It would hardly seem so,' agreed Poirot.

Angela went on: 'Philip Blake?' She was silent for some few moments. Then she said quietly: 'I think, you know, if we're just talking of *likelihoods*, *he's* the most likely person.'

Poirot said: 'You interest me very much, Miss Warren. May I ask why you say that?'

'Nothing at all definite. But, from what I remember of him, I should say he was a person of rather limited imagination.'

'And a limited imagination predisposes you to murder?'

'It might lead you to take a crude way of settling your difficulties. Men of that type get a certain satisfaction from action of some kind or other. Murder is a very crude business, don't you think so?'

'Yes – I think you are right . . . It is definitely a point of view, that. But all the same, Miss Warren, there must be more to it than that. What motive could Philip Blake possibly have had?'

Angela Warren did not answer at once. She stood frowning down at the floor.

Hercule Poirot said: 'He was Amyas Crale's best friend, was he not?'

She nodded.

'But there is something in your mind, Miss Warren. Something that you have not yet told me. Were the two men rivals, perhaps, over the girl – over Elsa?'

Angela Warren shook her head.

'Oh, no, not Philip.'

'What is there, then?'

Angela Warren said slowly: 'Do you know the way that things suddenly come back to you – after years perhaps? I'll explain what I mean. Somebody told me a story once, when I was eleven. I saw no point in that story whatsoever. It didn't worry me – it just passed straight over my head. I don't believe I ever, as they say, thought of it again. But about two years ago, sitting in the stalls at a revue, that story came back to me, and I was so surprised that I actually said aloud, "Oh, *now* I see the point of that silly story about the rice pudding." And yet there had been no direct allusion on the same lines – only some fun sailing rather near the wind.'

Poirot said: 'I understand what you mean, Mademoiselle.'

'Then you will understand what I am going to tell you. I was once staying at a hotel. As I walked along a passage, one of the bedroom doors opened and a woman I knew came out. It was not her bedroom – and she registered the fact plainly on her face when she saw me.

'*And I knew then the meaning of the expression I had once seen on Caroline's face when at Alderbury she came out of Philip Blake's room one night.*'

She leant forward, stopping Poirot's words.

'I had no idea at the *time*, you understand. I *knew* things – girls of the age I was usually do – but I didn't connect them with reality. Caroline coming out of Philip Blake's bedroom was just Caroline coming out of Philip Blake's bedroom to me. It might have been Miss Williams's room or my room. But what I *did* notice was the expression on her face – a queer expression that I didn't know and couldn't understand. I didn't understand it until, as I have told you, the night in Paris when I saw that same expression on another woman's face.'

Poirot said slowly: 'But what you tell me, Miss Warren, is sufficiently astonishing. From Philip Blake himself I got the impression that he disliked your sister and always had done so.'

Angela said: 'I know. I can't explain it but there it is.'

Poirot nodded slowly. Already, in his interview with Philip Blake, he had felt vaguely that something did not ring true. That overdone animosity against Caroline – it had not, somehow, been natural.

And the words and phrases from his conversation with Meredith Blake came back to him. 'Very upset when Amyas married –did not go near them for over a year . . .'

Had Philip, then, always been in love with Caroline? And had his love, when she chose Amyas, turned to bitterness and hate?

Yes, Philip had been too vehement – too biased. Poirot visualized him thoughtfully – the cheerful prosperous man with his golf and his comfortable house. What had Philip Blake really felt sixteen years ago?

Angela Warren was speaking.

'I don't understand it. You see, I've no experience in love affairs – they haven't come my way. I've told you this for what it's worth in case – in case it might have a bearing on what happened.'

PART II

— I —

NARRATIVE OF PHILIP BLAKE

(Covering letter received with manuscript)

Dear M. Poirot,

I am fulfilling my promise and herewith find enclosed an account of the events relating to the death of Amyas Crale. After such a lapse of time I am bound to point out that my memories may not be strictly accurate, but I have put down what occurred to the best of my recollection.

Yours truly,

Philip Blake

Notes on Progress of Events Leading up to
Murder of Amyas Crale in Sept. 19–

My friendship with deceased dates back to a very early period. His home and mine were next door to each other in the country, and our families were friends. Amyas Crale was a little over two years older than I was. We played together as boys, in the holidays, though we were not at the same school.

From the point of view of my long knowledge of the man I feel myself particularly qualified to testify as to his character and general outlook on life. And I will say this straight away – to anyone who knew Amyas Crale well, the notion of his committing suicide is quite ridiculous. Crale would *never* have taken his own life. He was far too fond of living! The contention of the defence at the trial that Crale was obsessed by conscience, and took poison in a fit of remorse, is utterly absurd to anyone who knew the man. Crale, I should say, had very little conscience, and certainly not a morbid one. Moreover, he and his wife were on bad terms, and I don't think he would have had any scruples about breaking up what was, to him, a very unsatisfactory married life. He was prepared to look after her financial welfare and that of the child of the marriage, and I am sure would have done so generously. He was a very generous man – and altogether a warm-hearted and lovable person. Not only was he a great painter, but he was a man whose friends were devoted to him. As far as I know, he had no enemies.

I had also known Caroline Crale for many years. I knew her before her marriage, when she used to come and stay at Alderbury. She was then a somewhat neurotic girl, subject to uncontrollable outbursts of temper, not without attraction, but unquestionably a difficult person to live with.

She showed her devotion to Amyas almost immediately. He, I do not think, was really very much in love with her. But they were frequently thrown together – she was, as I say, attractive, and they eventually became engaged. Amyas Crale's best friends were rather apprehensive about the marriage, as they felt that Caroline was quite unsuited to him.

This caused a certain amount of strain in the first few years between Crale's wife and Crale's friends, but Amyas was a loyal friend and was not disposed to give up his old friends at the bidding of his wife. After a few years, he and I were on the same old terms and I was a frequent visitor at Alderbury. I may add that I stood godfather to the little girl, Carla. This proves, I think, that Amyas considered me his best friend, and it gives me authority to speak for a man who can no longer speak for himself.

To come to the actual events of which I have been asked to write, I arrived down at Alderbury (so I see by an old diary) five days before the crime. That is, on Sept. 13th. I was conscious at once of a certain tension in the atmosphere. There was also staying in the house Miss Elsa Greer, whom Amyas was painting at the time.

It was the first time I had seen Miss Greer in the flesh, but I had been aware of her existence for some time. Amyas had raved about her to me a month previously. He had met, he said, a marvellous girl. He talked about her so enthusiastically that I said to him jokingly: 'Be careful, old boy, or you'll be losing your head again.' He told me not to be a bloody fool. He was painting the girl; he'd no personal interest in her. I said: 'Tell that to the marines! I've heard you say that before.' He said: 'This time it's different.' To which I answered somewhat cynically: 'It always is!' Amyas then looked quite worried and anxious. He said: 'You don't understand. She's just a girl. Not much more than a child.' He added that she had very modern views and was absolutely free from old-fashioned prejudices. He said: 'She's honest and natural and absolutely fearless!'

I thought to myself, though I didn't say so, that Amyas had certainly got it badly this time. A few weeks later I heard comments from other people. It was said that the 'Greer girl was absolutely infatuated'. Somebody else said that it was a bit thick of Amyas considering how young the girl was, whereupon somebody else sniggered and said that Elsa Greer knew her way about all right. Further remarks were that the girl was rolling in money and had always got everything she wanted, and also that 'she was the one who was making most of the running'. There was a question as to what Crale's wife thought about it – and the significant reply that she must be used to that sort of thing by now, to which someone demurred by saying they'd heard that she was jealous as hell and led Crale such an impossible life that any man would be justified in having a fling from time to time.

I mention all this because I think it is important that the state of affairs before I got down there should be fully realized.

I was interested to see the girl – she was remarkably good-looking and very attractive – and I was, I must admit, maliciously amused to note that Caroline was cutting up very rough indeed.

Amyas Crale himself was less light-hearted than usual. Though to anyone who did not know him well his manner would have appeared much as usual, I, who knew him so intimately, noted at once various signs of strain, uncertain temper, fits of moody abstraction, general irritability of manner.

Although he was always inclined to be moody when painting, the picture he was at work upon did not account entirely for the strain he showed. He was pleased to see me and said as soon as we were alone: 'Thank goodness you've turned up, Phil. Living in a house with four women is enough to send any man off his chump. Between them all they'll send me into a lunatic asylum.'

It was certainly an uncomfortable atmosphere. Caroline, as I said, was obviously cutting up rough about the whole thing. In a polite, well-bred way, she was ruder to Elsa than one would believe possible – without a single actually offensive word. Elsa herself was openly and flagrantly rude to Caroline. She was top dog and she knew it – and no scruples of good breeding restrained her from overt bad manners. The result was that Crale spent most of his time scrapping with the girl Angela when he wasn't painting. They were usually on affectionate terms, though they teased and fought a good deal. But on this occasion there was an edge in everything Amyas said or did, and the two of them really lost their tempers with each other. The fourth member of the party was the governess. 'A sour-faced hag,' Amyas called her. 'She hates me like poison. Sits there with her lips set together, disapproving of me without stopping.'

It was then that he said: 'God damn all women! If a man is to have any peace he must steer clear of women!'

'You oughtn't to have married,' I said. 'You're the sort of man who ought to have kept clear of domestic ties.'

He replied that it was too late to talk about that now. He added that no doubt Caroline would be only too glad to get rid of him. That was the first indication I had that something unusual was in the wind.

I said: 'What's all this? Is this business with the lovely Elsa serious then?' He said with a sort of groan: 'She *is* lovely, isn't she? Sometimes I wish I'd never seen her.'

I said: 'Look here, old boy, you must take a hold on yourself. You don't want to get tied up with any more women.' He looked at me and laughed. He said: 'It's all very well for you to talk. I can't let women alone – simply can't do it – and, if I could, they wouldn't let me alone!' Then he shrugged those great shoulders of his, grinned at me and said: 'Oh, well, it will all pan out in the end, I expect. And you must admit the picture is good.'

He was referring to the portrait he was doing of Elsa and, although I had very little technical knowledge of painting, even I could see that it was going to be a work of especial power.

Whilst he was painting, Amyas was a different man. Although he would growl, groan, frown, swear extravagantly, and sometimes hurl his brushes away, he was really intensely happy.

It was only when he came back to the house for meals that the hostile atmosphere between the women got him down. That hostility came to a head on Sept. 17th. We had had an embarrassing lunch. Elsa had been particularly – really, I think *insolent* is the only word for it! She had ignored Caroline pointedly, persistently addressing the conversation to Amyas as though he and she were alone in the room. Caroline had talked lightly and gaily to the rest of us, cleverly contriving so that several perfectly innocent-sounding remarks should have a sting. She hadn't got Elsa Greer's scornful honesty – with Caroline everything was oblique, suggested rather than said.

Things came to a head after lunch in the drawing-room just as they were finishing coffee. I had commented on a carved head in highly polished beechwood – a very curious thing – and Caroline said: 'That is the work of a young Norwegian sculptor. Amyas and I admire his work very much. We hope to go and see him next summer.' That calm assumption of possession was too much for

Elsa. She was never one to let a challenge pass. She waited a minute or two and then she spoke in her clear, rather over-emphasized voice. She said: 'This would be a lovely room if it was properly fixed. It's got far too much furniture in it. When I'm living here I shall take all the rubbish out and just leave one or two pieces. And I shall have copper-coloured curtains, I think – so that the setting sun will just catch them through that big western window.' She turned to me and said: 'Don't you think that would be rather lovely?'

I didn't have time to answer. Caroline spoke, and her voice was soft and silky and what I can only describe as dangerous. She said: 'Are you thinking of buying this place, Elsa?'

Elsa said: 'It won't be necessary for me to buy it.'

Caroline said: 'What do you mean?' And there was no softness in her voice. It was hard and metallic.

Elsa laughed. She said: 'Must we pretend? Come now, Caroline, you know very well what I mean!'

Caroline said: 'I've no idea.'

Elsa said to that: 'Don't be such an ostrich. It's no good pretending you don't see and know all about it. Amyas and I care for each other. This isn't your home. It's his. And after we're married I shall live here with him!'

Caroline said: 'I think you're crazy.'

Elsa said: 'Oh, no, I'm not, my dear, and you know it. It would be much simpler if we were honest with each other. Amyas and I love each other – you've seen that clearly enough. There's only one decent thing for you to do. You've got to give him his freedom.'

Caroline said: 'I don't believe a word of what you are saying.'

But her voice was unconvincing. Elsa had got under her guard all right.

And at that minute Amyas Crale came into the room and Elsa said with a laugh: 'If you don't believe me, ask him.'

And Caroline said: 'I will.'

She didn't pause at all. She said: 'Amyas, Elsa says you want to marry her. Is this true?'

Poor Amyas. I felt sorry for him. It makes a man feel a fool to have a scene of that kind forced upon him. He went crimson and started blustering. He turned to Elsa and asked her why the devil she couldn't have held her tongue.

Caroline said: 'Then it *is* true?'

He didn't say anything, just stood there passing his finger round inside the neck of his shirt. He used to do that as a kid when he got into a jam of any kind. He said – and he tried to make the words sound dignified and authoritative – and of course couldn't manage it, poor devil: 'I don't want to discuss it.'

Caroline said: 'But we're going to discuss it!'

Elsa chipped in and said: 'I think it's only fair to Caroline that she should be told.'

Caroline said, very quietly: 'Is it true, Amyas?'

He looked a bit ashamed of himself. Men do when women pin them down in a corner.

She said: 'Answer me, please. I've got to know.'

He flung up his head then – rather the way a bull does in the bull-ring. He snapped out: 'It's true enough – but I don't want to discuss it now.'

And he turned and strode out of the room. I went after him. I didn't want to be left with the women. I caught up with him on the terrace. He was swearing. I never knew a man swear more heartily. Then he raved: 'Why couldn't she hold her tongue? Why the devil couldn't she hold her tongue? Now the fat's in the fire. And I've got to finish that picture – do you hear, Phil? It's the best thing I've ever done. The best thing I've ever done in my *life*. And a couple of damn fool women want to muck it up between them!'

Then he calmed down a little and said women had no sense of proportion.

I couldn't help smiling a little. I said: 'Well, dash it all, old boy, you have brought this on yourself.'

'Don't I know it?' he said, and groaned. Then he added: 'But you must admit, Phil, that a man couldn't be blamed for losing his head about her. Even Caroline ought to understand that.'

I asked him what would happen if Caroline got her back up and refused to give him a divorce.

But by now he had gone off into a fit of abstraction. I repeated the remark and he said absently: 'Caroline would never be vindictive. You don't understand, old boy.'

'There's the child,' I pointed out.

He took me by the arm.

'Phil, old boy, you mean well – but don't go on croaking like a raven. I can manage my affairs. Everything will turn out all right. You'll see if it doesn't.'

That was Amyas all over – an absolutely unjustified optimist. He said now, cheerfully: 'To hell with the whole pack of them!'

I don't know whether we would have said anything more, but a few minutes later Caroline swept out on the terrace. She'd got a hat on, a queer, flopping, dark-brown hat, rather attractive.

She said in an absolutely ordinary, every-day voice: 'Take off that paint-stained coat, Amyas. We're going over to Meredith's to tea – don't you remember?'

He stared, stammered a bit as he said: 'Oh, I'd forgotten. Yes, of c-course we are.'

She said: 'Then go and try and make yourself look less like a rag-and-bone man.'

Although her voice was quite natural, she didn't look at him. She moved over towards a bed of dahlias and began picking some of the overgrown flowers.

Amyas turned round slowly and went into the house.

Caroline talked to me. She talked a good deal. About the chances of the weather lasting. And whether there might be mackerel about and, if so, Amyas and Angela and I might like to go fishing. She was really amazing. I've got to hand it to her.

But I think, myself, that that showed the sort of woman she was. She had enormous strength of will and complete command over herself. I don't know whether she'd made up her mind to kill him then – but I shouldn't be surprised. And she was capable of making her plans carefully and unemotionally, and with an absolutely clear and ruthless mind.

Caroline Crale was a very dangerous woman. I ought to have realized then that she wasn't prepared to take this thing lying down. But like a fool I thought that she had made up her mind to accept the inevitable – or else possibly she thought that if she carried on exactly as usual Amyas might change his mind.

Presently the others came out. Elsa looking defiant – but at the same time triumphant. Caroline took no notice of her. Angela really saved the situation. She came out arguing with Miss Williams that she wasn't going to change her skirt for anyone. It was quite all right – good enough for darling old Meredith anyway – *he* never noticed anything.

We got off at last. Caroline walked with Angela. And I walked with Amyas. And Elsa walked by herself – smiling.

I didn't admire her myself – too violent a type – but I have to admit that she looked incredibly beautiful that afternoon. Women do when they've got what they want.

I can't remember the events of that afternoon clearly at all. It's all blurred. I remember old Merry coming out to meet us. I think we walked round the garden first. I remember having a long discussion with Angela about the training of terriers for ratting. She ate an incredible lot of apples, and tried to persuade me to do so, too.

When we got back to the house, tea was going on under the big cedar tree. Merry, I remember, was looking very upset. I suppose either Caroline or Amyas had told him something. He was looking doubtfully at Caroline, and then he stared at Elsa. The old boy looked thoroughly worried. Of course, Caroline liked to have Meredith on a string more or less, the devoted, platonic friend who would never, never go too far. She was that kind of woman.

After tea Meredith had a hurried word with me. He said: 'Look here, Phil, Amyas *can't* do this thing!'

I said: 'Make no mistake, he's going to do it.'

'He can't leave his wife and child and go off with this girl. He's years older than she is. She can't be more than eighteen.'

I said to him that Miss Greer was a fully sophisticated twenty.

He said: 'Anyway, that's under age. She can't know what she's doing.'

Poor old Meredith. Always the chivalrous *pukka sahib*. I said: 'Don't worry, old boy. *She* knows what she's doing, *and* she likes it!'

That's all we had the chance of saying. I thought to myself that probably Merry felt disturbed at the thought of Caroline being a deserted wife. Once the divorce was through she might expect her faithful Dobbin to marry her. I had an idea that hopeless devotion was really far more in his line. I must confess that that side of it amused me.

Curiously enough, I remember very little about our visit to Meredith's stink room. He enjoyed showing people his hobby. Personally I always found it very boring. I suppose I was in there with the rest of them when he gave a dissertation on the efficacy of coniine, but I don't remember it. And I didn't see Caroline pinch the stuff. As I've said, she was a very adroit woman. I do remember Meredith reading aloud the passage from Plato describing Socrates's death. Very boring I thought it. Classics always did bore me.

There's nothing much more I can remember about that day. Amyas and Angela had a first-class row, I know, and the rest of us rather welcomed it. It avoided other difficulties. Angela rushed off to bed with a final vituperative outburst. She said (*a*) she'd pay him out, (*b*) she wished he were dead, (*c*) she hoped he'd die of leprosy, it would serve him right, (*d*) she wished a sausage would stick up his nose, like in the fairy story, and never come off. When she'd gone we all laughed, we couldn't help it, it was such a funny mixture.

Caroline went up to bed immediately afterwards. Miss Williams disappeared after her pupil. Amyas and Elsa went off together into the garden. It was clear that I wasn't wanted. I went for a stroll by myself. It was a lovely night.

I came down late the following morning. There was no one in the dining-room. Funny the things you do remember. I remember the taste of the kidneys and bacon I ate quite well. They were very good kidneys. Devilled.

Afterwards I wandered out looking for everybody. I went outside, didn't see anybody, smoked a cigarette, encountered Miss Williams running about looking for Angela, who had played truant as usual when she ought to have been mending a torn frock. I went back into the hall and realized that Amyas and Caroline were having a set-to in the library. They were talking very loud. I heard her say: 'You and your women! I'd like to kill you. Some day I will kill you.' Amyas said: 'Don't be a fool, Caroline.' And she said: 'I mean it, Amyas.'

Well, I didn't want to overhear any more. I went out again. I wandered along the terrace the other way and came across Elsa.

She was sitting on one of the long seats. The seat was directly under the library window, and the window was open. I should imagine that there wasn't much she had missed of what was going on inside. When she saw me she got up as cool as cucumber and came towards me. She was smiling. She took my arm and said: 'Isn't it a lovely morning?'

It was a lovely morning for her all right! Rather a cruel girl. No, I think merely honest and lacking in imagination. What she wanted herself was the only thing that she could see.

We'd been standing on the terrace talking for about five minutes, when I heard the library door bang and Amyas Crale came out. He was very red in the face.

He caught hold of Elsa unceremoniously by the shoulder.

He said: 'Come on, time for you to sit. I want to get on with that picture.'

She said: 'All right. I'll just go up and get a pullover. There's a chilly wind.'

She went into the house.

I wondered if Amyas would say anything to me, but he didn't say much. Just: 'These women!'

I said: 'Cheer up, old boy.'

Then we neither of us said anything till Elsa came out of the house again.

They went off together down to the battery garden. I went into the house. Caroline was standing in the hall. I don't think she even noticed me. It was a way of hers at times. She'd seem to go right away – to get inside herself, as it were. She just murmured something. Not to me – to herself. I just caught the words: 'It's too cruel . . .'

That's what she said. Then she walked past me and upstairs, still without seeming to see me – just like a person intent on some inner vision. I think myself (I've no authority for saying this, you understand) that she went up to get the stuff, and that it was then she decided to do what she did do.

And just at that moment the telephone rang. In some houses one would wait for the servants to answer it, but I was so often at Alderbury that I acted more or less as one of the family. I picked up the receiver.

It was my brother Meredith's voice that answered. He was very upset. He explained that he had been into his laboratory and that the coniine bottle was half-empty.

I don't need to go again over all the things I know now I ought to have done. The thing was so startling and I was foolish enough to be taken aback. Meredith was dithering a good bit at the other end. I heard someone on the stairs, and I just told him sharply to come over at once.

I myself went down to meet him. In case you don't know the lay of the land, the shortest way from one estate to the other was by rowing across a small creek. I went down the path to where the boats were kept by a small jetty. To do so I passed under the wall of the battery garden. I could hear Elsa and Amyas talking together as he painted. They sounded very cheerful and careful. Amyas said it was an amazingly hot day (so it was, very hot for September), and Elsa said that sitting where she was, poised on the battlements, there was a cold wind blowing in from the sea. And then she said: 'I'm horribly stiff from posing. Can't I have a rest, darling?' And I heard Amyas cry out: 'Not on you life. Stick it. You're a tough girl. And this is going good, I tell you.' I heard Elsa say, 'Brute,' and laugh, as I went out of earshot.

Meredith was just rowing himself across from the other side. I waited for him. He tied up the boat and came up the steps. He was looking very white and worried. He said to me: 'Your head's better than mine, Philip. What ought I to do? The stuff's dangerous.'

I said: 'Are you absolutely sure about this?' Meredith, you see, was always rather a vague kind of chap. Perhaps that's why I didn't take it as seriously as I ought to have done. And he said he was quite sure. The bottle had been full yesterday afternoon.

I said: 'And you've absolutely *no* idea who pinched it?'

He said none whatever and asked me what *I* thought. Could it have been one of the servants? I said I supposed it might have been, but it seemed unlikely to me. He always kept the door locked, didn't he? Always, he said, and then began a rigmarole about having found the window a few inches open at the bottom. Someone might have got in that way.

'A chance burglar?' I asked sceptically. 'It seems to me, Meredith, that there are some very nasty possibilities.'

He said what did I really think? And I said, if he was sure he wasn't making a mistake, that probably Caroline had taken it to poison Elsa with – or that alternatively Elsa had taken it to get Caroline out of the way and straighten the path of true love.

Meredith twittered a bit. He said it was absurd and melo-dramatic and couldn't be true. I said: 'Well, the stuff's gone. What's *your* explanation?' He hadn't any, of course. Actually thought just as I did, but didn't want to face the fact.

He said again: 'What are we to do?'

I said, damned fool that I was: 'We must think it over carefully. Either you'd better announce your loss straight out when every-body's there, or else you'd better get Caroline alone and tax her with it. If you're convinced *she's* nothing to do with it, adopt the same tactics for Elsa.'

He said: 'A girl like that! She couldn't have taken it.'

I said I wouldn't put it past her.

We were walking up the path to the house as we talked. After that last remark of mine neither of us spoke for some few seconds. We were rounding the battery garden again and I heard Caroline's voice.

I thought perhaps a three-handed row was going on, but actu-ally it was Angela that they were discussing. Caroline was protest-ing. She said: 'It's very hard on the girl.' And Amyas made some impatient rejoinder. Then the door to the garden opened just as we came abreast of it. Amyas looked a little taken aback at seeing us. Caroline was just coming out. She said: 'Hallo, Meredith. We've been discussing the question of Angela's going to school. I'm not at all sure it's the right thing for her.' Amyas said: 'Don't fuss about the girl. She'll be all right. Good riddance.'

Just then Elsa came running down the path from the house. She had some sort of scarlet jumper in her hand. Amyas growled: 'Come along. Get back into the pose. I don't want to waste time.'

He went back to where his easel was standing. I noticed that he staggered a bit and I wondered if he had been drinking. A man might easily be excused for doing so with all the fuss and the scenes.

He grumbled.

'The beer here is red hot. Why can't we keep some ice down here?'

And Caroline Crale said: 'I'll send you down some beer just off the ice.'

Amyas grunted out: 'Thanks.'

Then Caroline shut the door of the battery garden and came up with us to the house. We sat down on the terrace and she went into the house. About five minutes later Angela came along with a couple of bottles of beer and some glasses. It was a hot day and we were glad to see it. As we were drinking it Caroline passed us. She was carrying another bottle and said she would take it down to Amyas. Meredith said he'd go, but she was quite firm that she'd go herself. I thought – fool that I was – that it was just her jealousy. She couldn't stand those two being alone down there. That was what had taken her down there once already with the weak pretext of arguing about Angela's departure.

She went off down that zigzag path – and Meredith and I watched her go. We'd still not decided anything and now Angela clamoured that I should come bathing with her. It seemed impossible to get Meredith alone. I just said to him: 'After lunch.' And he nodded.

Then I went off bathing with Angela. We had a good swim – across the creek and back – and then we lay out on the rocks sunbathing. Angela was a bit taciturn and that suited me. I made up my mind that directly after lunch I'd take Caroline aside and accuse her point-blank of having stolen the stuff. No use letting Meredith do it – he'd be too weak. No, I'd tax her with it outright. After that she'd have to give it back or, even if she didn't, she wouldn't dare use it. I was pretty sure it must be her on thinking things over. Elsa was far too sensible and hard-boiled a young woman to risk tampering with poisons. She had a hard head and would take care of her own skin. Caroline was made of more dangerous stuff – unbalanced, carried away by impulses and definitely neurotic. And still, you know, at the back of my mind was the feeling that Meredith *might* have made a mistake. Or some servant might have been poking about in there and spilt the stuff and then not dared to own up. You see, poison seems such a melodramatic thing – you can't believe in it.

Not till it happens.

It was quite late when I looked at my watch, and Angela and I fairly raced up to lunch. They were just sitting down – all but Amyas, who had remained down in the battery painting. Quite a normal thing for him to do – and privately I thought him very wise to elect to do it today. Lunch was likely to have been an awkward meal.

We had coffee on the terrace. I wish I could remember better how Caroline looked and acted. She didn't seem excited in any way. Quiet and rather sad is my impression. What a devil that woman was!

For it is a devilish thing to do, to poison a man in cold blood. If there had been a revolver about and she caught it up and shot him – well, that might have been understandable. But this cold, deliberate, vindictive poisoning . . . And so calm and collected.

She got up and said she'd take his coffee to him, in the most natural way possible. And yet she knew – she must have known – that by now she'd find him dead. Miss Williams went with her. I don't remember if that was at Caroline's suggestion or not. I rather think it was.

The two women went off together. Meredith strolled away shortly afterwards. I was just making an excuse to go after him, when he came running up the path again. His face was grey. He gasped out: 'We must get a doctor – quick – Amyas—'

I sprang up.

'Is he ill – dying?'

Meredith said: 'I'm afraid he's dead . . .'

We'd forgotten Elsa for the minute. But she let out a sudden cry. It was like the wail of a banshee.

She cried: 'Dead? Dead?' And then she ran. I didn't know anyone could move like that – like a dear – like a stricken thing. And like an avenging Fury, too.

Meredith panted out: 'Go after her. I'll telephone. Go after her. You don't know what she'll do.'

I did go after her – and it's as well I did. She might quite easily have killed Caroline. I've never seen such grief and such frenzied hate. All the veneer of refinement and education was stripped off. You could see that her father and her father's mother and father had been mill hands. Deprived of her lover, she was just elemental woman. She'd have clawed Caroline's face, torn her hair, hurled her over the parapet if she could. She thought for some reason or other that Caroline had knifed him. She'd got it all wrong – naturally.

I held her off, and then Miss Williams took charge. She was good, I must say. She got Elsa to control herself in under a minute

– told her she'd got to be quiet and that we couldn't have this noise and violence going on. She was a tartar, that woman. But she did the trick. Elsa was quiet – just stood there gasping and trembling.

As for Caroline, so far as I am concerned, the mask was right off. She stood there perfectly quiet – you might have said dazed. But she wasn't dazed. It was her eyes gave her away. They were watchful – fully aware and quietly watchful. She'd begun, I suppose, to be afraid . . .

I went up to her and spoke to her. I said it quite low. I don't think any of the two women overheard.

I said: 'You damned murderess, you've killed my best friend.'

She shrank back. She said: 'No – oh, no – he – he did it himself . . .'

I looked her full in the eyes. I said: 'You can tell that story to the police.'

She did – and they didn't believe her.

End of Philip Blake's Statement

— 2 —

NARRATIVE OF MEREDITH BLAKE

DEAR M. Poirot.

As I promised you, I have set down in writing an account of all I can remember relating to the tragic events that happened sixteen years ago. First of all I would like to say that I have thought over carefully all you said to me at our recent meeting. And on reflection I am more convinced than I was before that it is in the highest degree unlikely that Caroline Crale poisoned her husband. It always seemed incongruous, but the absence of any other explanation and her own attitude led me to follow, sheep-like, the opinion of other people and to say with them – that, if she didn't do it, what explanation could there be?

Since seeing you I have reflected very carefully on the alternative solution presented at the time and brought forward by the defence at the trial. That is, that Amyas Crale took his own life. Although from what I knew of him that solution seemed quite fantastic at the time, I now see fit to modify my opinion. To begin with, and highly significant, is the fact that Caroline believed it. If we are now to take it that that charming and gentle lady was unjustly convicted, then her own frequently reiterated belief must carry great weight. She knew Amyas better than anyone else. If *she* thought suicide possible, then suicide *must* have been possible in spite of the scepticism of his friends.

I will advance the theory, therefore, that there was in Amyas Crale some core of conscience, some undercurrent of remorse and even despair at the excesses to which his temperament led him, of which only his wife was aware. This, I think, is a not impossible supposition. He may have shown that side of himself only to her. Though it is inconsistent with anything I ever heard him say, yet it is nevertheless a truth that in most men there is some unsuspected and inconsistent streak which often comes as a surprise to people who have known them intimately. A respected and austere man is discovered to have had a coarser side to his life hidden. A vulgar money-maker has, perhaps, a secret appreciation of some delicate work of art. Hard and ruthless people have been convicted of unsuspected hidden kindnesses. Generous and jovial men have been shown to have a mean and cruel side to them.

So it may be that in Amyas Crale there ran a strain of morbid self-accusation, and that the more he blustered out his egoism and his right to do as he pleased, the more strongly that secret conscience of his worked. It is improbable, on the face of it, but I now believe that it must have been so. And I repeat again, Caroline herself held steadfastly to that view. That, I repeat, is significant!

And now to examine *facts* – or, rather, my memories of facts – in the light of that new belief.

I think that I might with relevance include here a conversation I held with Caroline some weeks before the actual tragedy. It was during Elsa Greer's first visit to Alderbury.

Caroline, as I have told you, was aware of my deep affection and friendship for her. I was, therefore, the person in whom she could easily confide. She had not been looking very happy. Nevertheless, I was surprised when she suddenly asked me one day whether I thought Amyas really cared very much for this girl he had brought down.

I said: 'He's interested in painting her. You know what Amyas is.'

She shook her head and said: 'No, he's in love with her.'

'Well – perhaps a little.'

'A great deal, I think.'

I said: 'She is unusually attractive, I admit. And we both know

604

that Amyas is susceptible. But you must know by now, my dear, that Amyas really only cares for one person – and that is you. He has these infatuations – but they don't last. You are the one person to him and, though he behaves badly, it does not really affect his feeling for you.'

Caroline said: 'That is what I always used to think.'

'Believe me, Caro,' I said. 'It is so.'

She said: 'But this time, Merry, I'm afraid. That girl is so – so terribly sincere. She's so young – and so intense. I've a feeling that this time – it's serious.'

I said: 'But the very fact that she is so young and, as you say, so sincere, will protect her. On the whole, women are fair game to Amyas, but in the case of a girl like this it will be different.'

She said: 'Yes, that's what I'm afraid of – it will be different.'

And she went on: 'I'm thirty-four, you know, Merry. And we've been married ten years. In looks I can't hold a candle to this Elsa child, and I know it.'

I said: 'But you know, Caroline, you *know* – that Amyas is really devoted to you.'

She said to that: 'Does one ever know with men?' And then she laughed a little ruefully and said: 'I'm a very primitive woman, Merry. I'd like to take a hatchet to that girl.'

I told her that the child probably didn't understand in the least what she was doing. She had a great admiration and hero-worship for Amyas, and she probably didn't realize at all that Amyas was falling in love with her.

Caroline just said to me: 'Dear Merry!' and began to talk about the garden. I hoped that she was not going to worry any more about the matter.

Shortly afterwards, Elsa went back to London. Amyas was away, too, for several weeks. I had really forgotten all about the business. And then I heard that Elsa was back again at Alderbury in order that Amyas might finish the picture.

I was a little disturbed by the news. But Caroline, when I saw her, was not in a communicative mood. She seemed quite her usual self – not worried or upset in any way. I imagined that everything was all right.

That's why it was such a shock to me to learn how far the thing had gone.

I have told you of my conversations with Crale and with Elsa. I had no opportunity of talking to Caroline. We were only able to exchange those few words about which I have already told you.

I can see her face now, the wide dark eyes and the restrained emotion. I can still hear her voice as she said: *'Everything's finished . . .'*

I can't describe to you the infinite desolation she conveyed in those words. They were a literal statement of truth. With Amyas's defection, everything was finished for her. That, I am convinced, was why she took the coniine. It was a way out. A way suggested to her by my stupid dissertation on the drug. And the passage I read from the Phædo gives a gracious picture of death.

Here is my present belief. She took the coniine, resolved to end her own life when Amyas left her. He may have seen her take it – or he may have discovered that she had it later.

That discovery acted upon him with terrific force. He was horrified at what his actions had led her to contemplate. But, notwithstanding his horror and remorse, he still felt himself incapable of giving up Elsa. I can understand that. Anyone who had fallen in love with her would find it almost impossible to tear himself away.

He could not envisage life without Elsa. He realized that Caroline could not live without *him*. He decided there was only one way out – to use the coniine himself.

And the manner in which he did it might be characteristic of the man, I think. His painting was the dearest thing in life to him. He chose to die literally with his brush in his hand. And the last thing his eyes would see was the face of the girl he loved so desperately. He might have thought, too, that his death would be the best thing for her . . .

I admit that this theory leaves certain curious facts unexplained. Why, for instance, were only Caroline's fingerprints found on the empty coniine-bottle. I suggest that after Amyas had handled it all prints got smudged or rubbed off by the soft piles of stuffs that were lying over the bottle and that, after his death, Caroline handled it to see if anyone had touched it. Surely that is possible and plausible. As to the evidence about the fingerprints on the beer-bottle, the witnesses for the defence were of opinion that a man's hand *might* be distorted after taking poison and so could manage to grasp a beer-bottle in a wholly unnatural way.

One other thing remains to be explained. Caroline's own attitude throughout the trial. But I think I have now seen the cause for that. It was *she who actually took the poison from my laboratory.* It was *her* determination to do away with herself that impelled her husband to take his own life instead. Surely it is not unreasonable to suppose that in a morbid excess of responsibility she considered herself responsible for his death – that she persuaded herself that she *was* guilty of murder – though not the kind of murder of which she was being accused.

I think all that could be so. And if that is the case, then surely it will be easy for you to persuade little Carla of the fact? And she can marry her young man and rest contented that the only thing of which her mother was guilty was an impulse (no more) to take her own life.

All this, alas, is not what you asked me for – which was an account of the happenings as I remember them. Let me now repair that omission. I have already told you fully what happened on the day preceding Amyas's death. We now come to the day itself.

I had slept very badly – worried by the disastrous turn of events for my friends. After a long wakeful period whilst I vainly tried to think of something helpful I could do to avert the catasrophe, I fell into a heavy sleep about six a.m. The bringing of my early tea did not awaken me, and I finally work up heavy-headed and un-refreshed about half-past nine. It was shortly after that that I thought I heard movements in the room below me, which was the room I used as a laboratory.

I may say here that actually the sounds were probably caused by a cat getting in. I found the window-sash raised a little way as it had carelessly been left from the day before. It was just wide enough to admit the passage of a cat. I merely mention the sounds to explain how I came to enter the laboratory.

I went in there as soon as I had dressed, and looking along the shelves I noticed that the bottle containing the preparation of coniine was slightly out of line with the rest. Having had my eye drawn to it in this way, I was startled to see that a considerable quantity of it had gone. The bottle had been nearly full the day before – now it was nearly empty.

I shut and locked the window and went out, locking the door behind me. I was considerably upset and also bewildered. When startled, my mental processes are, I am afraid, somewhat slow.

I was first disturbed, then apprehensive, and finally definitely alarmed. I questioned the household, and they all denied having entered the laboratory at all. I thought things over a little while longer, and then decided to ring up my brother and get his advice.

Philip was quicker than I was. He saw the seriousness of my discovery, and urged me to come over at once and consult with him.

I went out, encountering Miss Williams, who had come across

from the side to look for a truant pupil. I assured her that I had not seen Angela and that she had not been to the house.

I think that Miss Williams noticed there was something amiss. She looked at me rather curiously. I had no intention, however, of telling her what had happened. I suggested she should try the kitchen garden – Angela had a favourite apple tree there – and I myself hurried down to the shore and rowed myself across to the Alderbury side.

My brother was already there waiting for me.

We walked up to the house together by the way you and I went the other day. Having seen the topography you can understand that in passing underneath the wall of the battery garden we were bound to overhear anything being said inside it.

Beyond the fact that Caroline and Amyas were engaged in a disagreement of some kind, I did not pay much attention to what was said.

Certainly I overheard no threat of any kind uttered by Caroline. The subject of discussion was Angela, and I presume Caroline was pleading for a respite from the fiat of school. Amyas, however, was adamant, shouting out irritably that it was all settled, he'd see to her packing.

The door of the battery opened just as we drew abreast of it, and Caroline came out. She looked disturbed but not unduly so. She smiled rather absently at me, and said they had been discussing Angela. Elsa came down the path at that minute and, as Amyas clearly wanted to get on with the sitting without interruption from us, we went on up the path.

Philip blamed himself severely afterwards for the fact that he did not take immediate action. But I myself cannot see it the same way. We had no earthly right to assume that such a thing as murder was being contemplated. (Moreover, I now believe that it was *not* contemplated.) It was clear that we should have to adopt *some* course of action, but I still maintain that we were right to talk the matter over carefully first. It was necessary to find the right thing to do – and once or twice I found myself wondering if I had not after all made a mistake. Had the bottle really been full the day before as I thought? I am not one of those people (like my brother Philip) who can be cock-sure of everything. One's memory does play tricks on one. How often, for instance, one is convinced one has put an article in a certain place, later to find that you have put it somewhere quite different. The more I tried to recall the state of the bottle of the preceding afternoon, the more uncertain and doubtful I became. This was very annoying to Philip, who began completely to lose patience with me.

We were not able to continue our discussion at the time, and tacitly agreed to postpone it until after lunch. (I may say that I was always free to drop in for lunch at Alderbury if I chose.)

Later, Angela and Caroline brought us beer. I asked Angela what she had been up to playing truant, and told her Miss Williams was on the warpath, and she said she had been bathing – and added that she didn't see why she should have to mend her horrible old skirt when she was going to have all new things to go to school with.

Since there seemed no chance of further talk with Philip alone, and since I was really anxious to think things out by myself, I wandered off down the path towards the battery. Just above the battery, as I showed you, there is a clearing in the trees where there used to be an old bench. I sat there smoking and thinking, and watching Elsa as she sat posing for Amyas.

I shall always think of her as she was that day. Rigid in the pose, with her yellow shirt and dark-blue trousers and a red pullover slung round her shoulders for warmth.

Her face was so alight with life and health and radiance. And that gay voice of hers reciting plans for the future.

This sounds as though I was eavesdropping, but that is not so. I was perfectly visible to Elsa. Both she and Amyas knew I was there. She waved her hand at me and called up that Amyas was a perfect bear that morning – he wouldn't let her rest. She was stiff and aching all over.

Amyas growled out that she wasn't as stiff as he was. He was stiff all over – muscular rheumatism. Elsa said mockingly: 'Poor old man!' And he said she'd be taking on a creaking invalid.

It shocked me, you know, their lighthearted acquiescence in their future together whilst they were causing so much suffering. And yet I couldn't hold it against her. She was so young, so confident, so very much in love. And she didn't really know what she was doing. She didn't understand suffering. She just assumed with the naïve confidence of a child that Caroline would be 'all right', that 'she'd soon get over it'. She saw nothing, you see, but herself and Amyas – happy together. She'd already told me my point of view was old-fashioned. She had no doubts, no qualms – no pity, either. But can one expect pity from radiant youth? It is an older, wiser emotion.

They didn't talk very much, of course. No painter wants to be chattering when he is working. Perhaps every ten minutes or so Elsa would make an observation and Amyas would grunt a reply. Once she said: 'I think you're right about Spain. That's the first place we'll go to. And you must take me to see a bull-fight. It must be wonderful. Only I'd like the bull to kill the man – not the other way about. I understand how Roman women felt when they saw a man die. Men aren't much, but animals are splendid.'

I suppose she was rather like an animal herself – young and primitive and with nothing yet of man's sad experience and doubtful wisdom. I don't believe Elsa had begun to *think* – she only *felt*. But she was very much alive – more alive than any person I have ever known . . .

That was the last time I saw her radiant and assured – on top of the world. 'Fey' is the word for it, isn't it?

The bell sounded for lunch, and I got up and went down the path and in at the battery door, and Elsa joined me. It was dazzling bright there coming in out of the shady trees. I could hardly see. Amyas was sprawled back on the seat, his arms flung out. He was staring at the picture. I'd so often seen him like that. How was I to know that already the poison was working, stiffening him as he sat?

He so hated and resented illness. He would never own to it. I dare say he thought he had got a touch of the sun – the symptoms are much the same – but he'd be the last person to complain about it.

Elsa said: 'He won't come up to lunch.'

Privately I thought he was wise. I said: 'So long, then.'

He moved his eyes from the picture until they rested on me. There was a queer – how shall I describe it? – it looked like malevolence. A kind of malevolent glare.

Naturally I didn't understand it then – if his picture wasn't going as he liked, he often looked quite murderous. I thought *that* was what it was. He made a sort of grunting sound.

Neither Elsa nor I saw anything unusual in him – just artistic temperament.

So we left him there and she and I went up to the house laughing and talking. If she'd known, poor child, that she'd never see him alive again . . . Oh, well, thank God she didn't. She was able to be happy a little longer.

Caroline was quite normal at lunch – a little preoccupied; nothing more. And doesn't that show that she had nothing to do with it? She *couldn't* have been such an actress.

She and the governess went down afterwards and found him. I met Miss Williams as she came up. She told me to telephone a doctor and went back to Caroline.

That poor child – Elsa, I mean! She had that frantic unrestrained grief that a child has. They can't believe that life can do these things to them. Caroline was quite calm. Yes, she was quite calm. She was able, of course, to control herself better than Elsa. She didn't seem remorseful – then. Just said he must have done it himself. And we couldn't believe that. Elsa burst out and accused her to her face.

Of course she may have realized, already, that she herself would be suspected. Yes, that probably explains her manner.

Philip was quite convinced that she *had* done it.

The governess was a great help and standby. She made Elsa lie down and gave her a sedative, and she kept Angela out of the way when the police came. Yes, she was a tower of strength, that woman.

The whole thing became a nightmare. The police searching the house and asking questions, and then the reporters, swarming about the place like flies, and clicking cameras and wanting interviews with members of the family.

A nightmare, the whole thing . . .

It's a nightmare, after all these years. Please God, once you've convinced little Carla what really happened, we can forget it all and never remember it again.

Amyas *must* have committed suicide – however unlikely it seems.

End of Meredith Blake's Narrative

— 3 —

NARRATIVE OF LADY DITTISHAM

I HAVE set down here the full story of my meeting with Amyas Crale, up to the time of his tragic death.

I saw him first at a studio party. He was standing, I remember, by a window, and I saw him as I came in at the door. I asked who he was. Someone said: 'That's Crale, the painter.' I said at once that I'd like to meet him.

We talked on that occasion for perhaps ten minutes. When anyone makes the impression on you that Amyas Crale made on me, it's hopeless to attempt to describe them. If I say that when I saw Amyas Crale everybody else seemed to grow very small and fade away, that expresses it as well as anything can.

Immediately after that meeting I went to look at as many of his pictures as I could. He had a show on in Bond Street at the moment, and there was one of his pictures in Manchester and one in Leeds and two in public galleries in London. I went to see them all. Then I met him again. I said: 'I've been to see all your pictures. I think they're wonderful.'

He just looked amused. He said: 'Who said you were any judge of painting? I don't believe you know anything about it.'

I said: 'Perhaps not. But they are marvellous, all the same.'

He grinned at me and said: 'Don't be a gushing little fool.'

I said: 'I'm not. I want you to paint me.'

Crale said: 'If you've any sense at all, you'll realize that I don't paint portraits of pretty women.'

I said: 'It needn't be a portrait and I'm not a pretty woman.'

He looked at me as though he'd begun to see me. He said: 'No, perhaps you're not.'

I said: 'Will you paint me, then?'

He studied me for some time with his head on one side. Then he said: 'You're a strange child, aren't you?'

I said: 'I'm quite rich, you know. I can afford to pay well for it.'

He said: 'Why are you so anxious for me to paint you?'

I said: 'Because I want it!'

He said: 'Is that a reason?'

And I said: 'Yes. I always get what I want.'

He said then: 'Oh, my poor child, how young you are!'

I said: 'Will you paint me?'

He took me by the shoulders and turned me towards the light and looked me over. Then he stood away from me a little. I stood quite still, waiting.

He said: 'I've sometimes wanted to paint a flight of impossibly coloured Australian macaws alighting on St Paul's Cathedral. If I painted you against a nice traditional bit of outdoor landscape, I believe I'd get exactly the same result.'

I said: 'Then you will paint me?'

He said: 'You're one of the loveliest, crudest, most flamboyant bits of exotic colouring I've ever seen. I'll paint you!'

I said: 'Then that's settled.'

He went on: 'But I'll warn you, Elsa Greer. If I do paint you, I shall probably make love to you.'

I said: 'I hope you will . . .'

I said it quite steadily and quietly. I heard him catch his breath, and I saw the look that came into his eyes.

You see, it was as sudden as all that.

A day or two later we met again. He told me that he wanted me to come down to Devonshire – he'd got the very place there that he wanted for a background. He said: 'I'm married, you know. And I'm very fond of my wife.'

I said if he was fond of her she must be very nice.

He said she was extremely nice. 'In fact,' he said, 'she's quite adorable – and I adore her. So put that in your pipe, young Elsa, and smoke it.'

I told him that I quite understood.

He began the picture a week later. Caroline Crale welcomed me very pleasantly. She didn't like me much – but, after all, why should she? Amyas was very circumspect. He never said a word to me that his wife couldn't have overheard, and I was quite polite and formal to him. Underneath, though, we both knew.

After ten days he told me I was to go back to London.

I said: 'The picture isn't finished.'

He said: 'It's barely begun. The truth is, I can't paint you, Elsa.'

I said: 'Why?'

He said: 'You know well enough why, Elsa. And that's why you've got to clear out. I can't think about the painting – I can't think about anything but you.'

We were in the battery garden. It was a hot sunny day. There were birds and humming bees. It ought to have been very happy and peaceful. But it didn't feel like that. It felt – somehow – tragic. As though – as though what was going to happen was already mirrored there.

I knew it would be no good my going back to London, but I said: 'Very well, I'll go if you say so.'

Amyas said: 'Good girl.'

So I went. I didn't write to him.

He held out for ten days and then he came. He was so thin and haggard and miserable that it shocked me.

He said: 'I warned you, Elsa. Don't say I didn't warn you.'

I said: 'I've been waiting for you. I knew you'd come.'

He gave a sort of groan and said: 'There are things that are too strong for any man. I can't eat or sleep or rest for wanting you.'

I said I knew that and that it was the same with me, and had been from the first moment I'd seen him. It was Fate and it was no use struggling against it.

He said: 'You haven't struggled much, have you, Elsa?' And I said I hadn't struggled at all.

He said he wished I wasn't so young, and I said that didn't matter. I suppose I might say that for the next few weeks we were very happy. But 'happiness' isn't quite the word. It was something deeper and more frightening than that.

We were made for each other and we'd found each other – and we both knew we'd got to be together always.

But something else happened, too. The unfinished picture began to haunt Amyas. He said to me: 'Damned funny, I couldn't paint you before – you yourself got in the way of it. But I *want* to paint you, Elsa. I want to paint you so that that picture will be the finest thing I've ever done. I'm itching and aching now to get at my brushes to see you sitting there on that hoary old chestnut of a battlement wall with the conventional blue sea and the decorous English trees – and you – you – sitting there like a discordant shriek of triumph.'

He said: 'And I've got to paint you that way! And I can't be fussed and bothered while I'm doing it. When the picture's finished I'll tell Caroline the truth and we'll get the whole messy business cleared up.'

I said: 'Will Caroline make a fuss about divorcing you?'

He said he didn't think so. But you never knew with women.

I said I was sorry if she was going to be upset, but after all, I said, these things did happen.

He said: 'Very nice and reasonable, Elsa. But Caroline isn't reasonable, never has been reasonable, and certainly isn't going to feel reasonable. She loves me, you know.'

I said I understood that; but, if she loved him, she'd put his happiness first and, at any rate, she wouldn't want to keep him if he wanted to be free.

He said: 'Life can't really be solved by admirable maxims out of modern literature. Nature's red in tooth and claw, remember.'

I said: 'Surely we are all civilized people nowadays?' and Amyas laughed. He said: 'Civilized people my foot! Caroline would probably like to take a hatchet to you. She might do it, too. Don't you realize, Elsa, that she's going to suffer – *suffer*? Don't you know what suffering means?'

I said: 'Then don't tell her.'

He said: 'No. The break's got to come. You've got to belong to me properly, Elsa. Before all the world. Openly mine.'

I said: 'Suppose she won't divorce you?'

He said: 'I'm not afraid of that.'

I said: 'What are you afraid of, then?'

And he said slowly: 'I don't know . . .'

You see, he knew Caroline. I didn't.

If I'd had any idea . . .

We went down again to Alderbury. Things were difficult this time. Caroline had got suspicious. I didn't like it – I didn't like it – I didn't like it a bit. I've always hated deceit and concealment. I thought we ought to tell her. Amyas wouldn't hear of it.

The funny part of it was that he didn't really care at all. In spite of being fond of Caroline and not wanting to hurt her, he just didn't care about the honesty or dishonesty of it all. He was painting with a kind of frenzy, and nothing else mattered. I hadn't seen him in one of his working spells before. I realized now what a really great genius he was. It was natural for him to be so carried away that all the ordinary decencies didn't matter. But it was different for me. I was in a horrible position. Caroline resented me – and quite rightly. The only thing to put the position quite straight was to be honest and tell her the truth.

But all Amyas would say was that he wasn't going to be bothered with scenes and fusses until he'd finished the picture. I said there probably wouldn't be a scene. Caroline would have too much dignity and pride for that.

I said: 'I want to be honest about it all. We've *got* to be honest!'

Amyas said: 'To hell with honesty. I'm painting a picture, damn it.'

I did see his point of view, but he wouldn't see mine.

And in the end I broke down. Caroline had been talking of some plan she and Amyas were going to carry out next autumn. She talked about it quite confidently. And I suddenly felt it was too abominable, what we were doing – letting her go on like this – and perhaps, too, I was angry, because she was really being unpleasant to me in a clever sort of way that one couldn't take hold of.

And so I came out with the truth. In a way, I still think I was right. Though, of course, I wouldn't have done it if I'd had the faintest idea what was to come of it.

The clash came right away. Amyas was furious with me, but he had to admit that what I had said was true.

I didn't understand Caroline at all. We all went over to Meredith Blake's to tea, and Caroline played up marvellously – talking and laughing. Like a fool, I thought she was taking it well. It was awkward my not being able to leave the house, but Amyas would have gone up in smoke if I had. I thought perhaps Caroline would go. It would have made it much easier for us if she had.

I didn't see her take the coniine. I want to be honest so I think that it's just possible that she may have taken it as she said she did, with the idea of suicide in her mind.

But I don't *really* think so. I think she was one of those intensely jealous and possessive women who won't let go of anything that they think belongs to them. Amyas was her property. I think she was quite prepared to kill him rather than to let him go – completely and finally – to another woman. I think she made up her mind, right away, to kill him. And I think that Meredith's happening to discuss coniine so freely just gave her the means to do what she'd already made up her mind to do. She was a very bitter and revengeful woman – vindictive. Amyas knew all along that she was dangerous. I didn't.

The next morning she had a final showdown with Amyas. I heard most of it from outside on the terrace. He was splendid – very patient and calm. He implored her to be reasonable. He said he was very fond of her and the child and always would be. He'd do everything he could to assure their future. Then he hardened up and said: 'But understand this. I'm damned well going to marry Elsa – and nothing shall stop me. You and I always agreed to leave each other free. These things happen.'

Caroline said to him: 'Do as you please. I've warned you.'

Her voice was very quiet, but there was a queer note in it.

Amyas said: 'What do you mean, Caroline?'

She said: 'You're mine and *I don't mean to let you go*. Sooner than let you go to that girl *I'll kill you* . . .'

Just at that minute, Philip Blake came along the terrace. I got up and went to meet him. I didn't want him to overhear.

Presently Amyas came out and said it was time to get on with the picture. We went down together to the battery. He didn't say much. Just said that Caroline was cutting up rough – but for God's sake not to talk about it. He wanted to concentrate on what he was doing. Another day, he said, would about finish the picture.

He said: 'And it'll be the best thing I've ever done, Elsa, even if it is paid for in blood and tears.'

A little later I went up to the house to get a pullover. There was a chilly wind blowing. When I came back again Caroline was there. I suppose she had come down to make one last appeal. Philip and Merdith Blake were there, too.

It was then that Amyas said he was thirsty and wanted a drink. He said there was beer but it wasn't iced.

Caroline said she'd send him down some iced beer. She said it quite naturally in an almost friendly tone. She was an actress, that woman. She must have known then what she meant to do.

She brought it down about ten minutes later. Amyas was painting. She poured it out and set the glass down beside him. Neither of us were watching her. Amyas was intent on what he was doing and I had to keep the pose.

Amyas drank it down the way he always drank beer, just pouring it down his throat in one draught. Then he made a face and said it tasted foul – but at any rate it was cold.

And even then, when he said that, no suspicion entered my head; I just laughed and said: 'Liver.'

When she'd seen him drink it Caroline went away.

It must have been about forty minutes later that Amyas complained of stiffness and pains. He said he thought he must have got a touch of muscular rheumatism. Amyas was always tolerant of any ailment and he didn't like being fussed over. After saying that he turned it off with a light: 'Old age, I suppose. You've taken on a creaking old man, Elsa.' I played up to him. But I noticed that his legs moved stiffly and queerly and that he grimaced once or twice. I never dreamt that it wasn't rheumatism. Presently he drew the bench along and sat sprawled on that, occasionally stretching up to put a touch of paint here and there on the canvas. He used to do that sometimes when he was painting. Just sit staring at me and then the canvas. Sometimes he'd do it for half an hour at a time. So I didn't think it specially queer.

We heard the bell go for lunch, and he said he wasn't coming up. He'd stay where he was and he didn't want anything. That wasn't unusual, either, and it would be easier for him than facing Caroline at the table.

He was talking in rather a queer way – grunting out his words. But he sometimes did that when he was dissatisfied with the progress of the picture.

Meredith Blake came in to fetch me. He spoke to Amyas, but Amyas only grunted at him.

We went up to the house together and left him there. We left him there – to die alone. I'd never seen much illness – I didn't know much about it – I thought Amyas was just in a painter's mood. If I'd known – if I'd realized – perhaps a doctor could have saved him . . . Oh, God, why didn't I—? It's no good thinking of that now. I was a blind fool. A blind, stupid fool.

There isn't much more to tell.

Caroline and the governess went down there after lunch. Meredith followed them. Presently he came running up. He told us Amyas was dead.

Then I knew! Knew, I mean, that it was Caroline. I still didn't think of poison. I thought she'd gone down that minute and either shot him or stabbed him.

I wanted to get at her – to kill her . . .

How *could* she do it? How *could* she? He was so alive, so full of life and vigour. To put all that out – to make him limp and cold. Just so that I shouldn't have him.

Horrible woman . . .

Horrible, scornful, cruel, vindictive woman . . .

I hate her. I still hate her.

They didn't even hang her.

They ought to have hanged her . . .

Even hanging was too good for her . . .

I hate her . . . I hate her . . . I hate her . . .

End of Lady Dittisham's Narrative

— 4 —

NARRATIVE OF CECILIA WILLIAMS

DEAR M. Poirot,

I am sending you an account of those events in September 19– actually witnessed by myself.

I have been absolutely frank and have kept nothing back. You may show it to Carla Crale. It may pain her, but I have always been a believer in truth. Palliatives are harmful. One must have the courage to face reality. Without that courage, life is meaningless. The people who do us more harm are the people who shield us from reality.

Believe me, yours sincerely,

Cecilia Williams

My name is Cecilia Williams. I was engaged by Mrs Crale as governess to her half-sister Angela Warren in 19–. I was then 48.

I took up my duties at Alderbury, a very beautiful estate in south Devon which had belonged to Mr Crale's family for many generations. I knew that Mr Crale was a well-known painter, but I did not meet him until I took up residence at Alderbury.

The household consisted of Mr and Mrs Crale, Angela Warren (then a girl of thirteen), and three servants, all of whom had been with the family many years.

I found my pupil an interesting and promising character. She had very marked abilities and it was a pleasure to teach her. She was somewhat wild and undisciplined, but these faults arose mainly through high spirits, and I have always preferred my girls to show spirit. An excess of vitality can be trained and guided into paths of real usefulness and achievement.

On the whole, I found Angela amenable to discipline. She had been somewhat spoiled – mainly by Mrs Crale, who was far too indulgent where she was concerned. Mr Crale's influence was, I considered, unwise. He indulged her absurdly one day, and was unnecessarily peremptory on another occasion. He was very much a man of moods – possibly owing to what is styled 'the artistic temperament'.

I have never seen, myself, why the possession of artistic ability should be supposed to excuse a man from a decent exercise of self-control. I did not myself admire Mr Crale's paintings. The drawing seemed to me faulty and the colouring exaggerated, but naturally I was not called upon to express any opinion on these matters.

I soon formed a deep attachment to Mrs Crale. I admired her character and her fortitude in the difficulties of her life. Mr Crale was not a faithful husband, and I think that that fact was the source of much pain to her. A stronger-minded woman would have left him, but Mrs Crale never seemed to contemplate such a course. She endured his infidelities and forgave him for them – but I may say that she did not take them meekly. She remonstrated – and with spirit!

It was said at the trial that they led a cat-and-dog life. I would not go as far as that – Mrs Crale had too much dignity for that term to apply, but they *did* have quarrels. And I consider that that was only natural under the circumstances.

I had been with Mrs Crale just over two years when Miss Elsa Greer appeared upon the scene. She arrived down at Alderbury in the summer of 19–. Mrs Crale had not met her previously. She was Mr Crale's friend, and she was said to be there for the purpose of having her portrait painted.

It was apparent at once that Mr Crale was infatuated with this girl and that the girl herself was doing nothing to discourage him. She behaved, in my opinion, quite outrageously, being abominably rude to Mrs Crale, and openly flirting with Mr Crale.

Naturally Mrs Crale said nothing to me, but I could see that she was disturbed and unhappy, and I did everything in my power to distract her mind and lighten her burden. Miss Greer sat every day to Mr Crale, but I noticed that the picture was not getting on very fast. They had, no doubt, other things to talk about!

My pupil, I am thankful to say, noticed very little of what was going on. Angela was in some ways young for her age. Though her intellect was well developed, she was not at all what I may term precocious. She seemed to have no wish to read undesirable books, and showed no signs of morbid curiosity such as girls often do at her age.

She, therefore, saw nothing undesirable in the friendship between Mr Crale and Miss Greer. Nevertheless, she disliked Miss Greer and thought her stupid. Here she was quite right. Miss Greer had had, I presume, a proper education, but she never opened a book and was quite unfamiliar with current literary allusions. Moreover, she could not sustain a discussion on any intellectual subject.

She was entirely taken up with her personal appearance, her clothes, and men.

Angela, I think, did not even realize that her sister was unhappy. She was not at that time a very perceptive person. She spent a lot of time in hoydenish pastimes, such as tree climbing and wild feats of bicycling. She was also a passionate reader and showed excellent taste in what she liked and disliked.

Mrs Crale was always careful to conceal any signs of unhappiness from Angela, and exerted herself to appear bright and cheerful when the girl was about.

Miss Greer went back to London – at which, I can tell you, we were all very pleased! The servants disliked her as much as I did. She was the kind of person who gives a lot of unnecessary trouble and forgets to say thank you.

Mr Crale went away shortly afterwards, and of course I knew that he had gone after the girl. I was very sorry for Mrs Crale. She felt these things very keenly. I felt extremely bitter towards Mr Crale. When a man has a charming, gracious, intelligent wife, he's no business to treat her badly.

However, she and I both hoped the affair would soon be over. Not that we mentioned the subject to each other – we did not – but she knew quite well how I felt about it.

Unfortunately, after some weeks, the pair of them reappeared. It seemed the sittings were to be resumed.

Mr Crale was now painting with absolute frenzy. He seemed less preoccupied with the girl than with the picture of her. Nevertheless, I realized that this was not the usual kind of thing we had gone through before. This girl had got her claws into him and she meant business. He was just like wax in her hands.

The thing came to a head on the day before he died – that is, on Sept. 17. Miss Greer's manner had been unbearably insolent the last few days. She was feeling sure of herself and she wanted to assert her importance. Mrs Crale behaved like a true gentlewoman. She was icily polite, but she showed the other clearly what she thought of her.

On this day, Sept. 17, as we were sitting in the drawing-room after lunch, Miss Greer came out with an amazing remark as to how she was going to redecorate the room when she was living at Alderbury.

Naturally, Mrs Crale couldn't let that pass. She challenged her, and Miss Greer had the impudence to say, before us all, that she was going to marry Mr Crale. She actually talked about marrying a married man – and she said it to his wife!

I was very, very angry with Mr Crale. How dared he let this girl insult his wife in her own drawing-room? If he wanted to run away with the girl, he should have gone off with her, not brought her into his wife's house and backed her up in her insolence.

In spite of what she must have felt, Mrs Crale did not lose her dignity. Her husband came in just then, and she immediately demanded confirmation from him.

He was, not unnaturally, annoyed with Miss Greer for her unconsidered forcing of the situation. Apart from anything else, it made *him* appear at a disadvantage, and men do not like appearing at a disadvantage. It upsets their vanity.

He stood there, a great giant of a man, looking as sheepish and foolish as a naughty schoolboy. It was his wife who carried off the honours of the situation. He had to mutter foolishly that it was true, but that he hadn't meant her to learn it like this.

I have never seen anything like the look of scorn she gave him. She went out of the room with her head held high. She was a beautiful woman – much more beautiful than that flamboyant girl – and she walked like an empress.

I hoped, with all my heart, that Amyas Crale would be punished for the cruelty he had displayed and for the indignity he had put upon a long-suffering and noble woman.

For the first time, I tried to say something of what I felt to Mrs Crale, but she stopped me.

She said: 'We must try and behave as usual. It's the best way. We're all going over to Meredith Blake's to tea.'

I said to her then: 'I think you are wonderful, Mrs Crale.'

She said: 'You don't know . . .'

Then, as she was going out of the room, she came back and kissed me. She said: 'You're such a comfort to me.'

She went to her room then and I think she cried. I saw her when they all started off. She was wearing a big-brimmed hat that shaded her face – a hat she seldom wore.

Mr Crale was uneasy, but was trying to brazen things out. Mr Philip Blake was trying to behave as usual. That Miss Greer was looking like a cat who has got at the cream-jug. All self-satisfaction and purrs!

They all started off. They got back about six. I did not see Mrs Crale again alone that evening. She was very quiet and composed at dinner, and she went to bed early. I don't think that anyone but I knew how she was suffering.

The evening was taken up with a kind of running quarrel between Mr Crale and Angela. They brought up the old school question again. He was irritable and on edge, and she was unusually trying. The whole matter was settled and her outfit had been bought, and there was no sense in starting up an argument again, but she suddenly chose to make a grievance of it. I have no doubt she sensed the tension in the air and that it reacted on her as much as on everybody else. I am afraid I was too preoccupied with my own thoughts to try and check her as I should have done. It all ended with her flinging a paperweight at Mr Crale and dashing out of the room.

I went after her and told her sharply that I was ashamed of her behaving like a baby, but she was still very uncontrolled, and I thought it best to leave her alone.

I hesitated as to whether to go to Mrs Crale's room, but I decided in the end that it would, perhaps, annoy her. I wish since that I had overcome my diffidence and insisted on her talking to me. If she had done so, it might possibly have made a difference. She had no one, you see, in whom she could confide. Although I admire self-control, I must regretfully admit that sometimes it can be carried too far. A natural outlet to the feelings is better.

I met Mr Crale as I went along to my room. He said goodnight, but I did not answer.

The next morning was, I remember, a beautiful day. One felt

when waking that surely with such peace all around even a man must come to his senses.

I went into Angela's room before going down to breakfast, but she was already up and out. I picked up a torn skirt which she had left lying on the floor and took it down with me for her to mend after breakfast.

She had, however, obtained bread and marmalade from the kitchen and gone out. After I had had my own breakfast I went in search of her. I mention this to explain why I was not more with Mrs Crale on that morning as perhaps I should have been. At the time, however, I felt it was my duty to look for Angela. She was very naughty and obstinate about mending her clothes, and I had no intention of allowing her to defy me in the matter.

Her bathing-dress was missing and I accordingly went down to the beach. There was no sign of her in the water or on the rocks, so I conceived it possible that she had gone over to Mr Meredith Blake's. She and he were great friends. I accordingly rowed myself across and resumed my search. I did not find her and eventually returned. Mrs Crale, Mr Blake, and Mr Philip Blake were on the terrace.

It was very hot that morning if one was out of the wind, and the house and terrace were sheltered. Mrs Crale suggested they might like some iced beer.

There was a little conservatory which had been built on to the house in Victorian days. Mrs Crale disliked it, and it was not used for plants, but it had been made into a kind of bar, with various bottles of gin, vermouth, lemonade, ginger-beer, etc., on the shelves, and a small refrigerator which was filled with ice every morning and in which some beer and ginger-beer was always kept.

Mrs Crale went there to get the beer and I went with her. Angela was at the refrigerator and was just taking out a bottle of beer.

Mrs Crale went in ahead of me. She said: 'I want a bottle of beer to take down to Amyas.'

It is so difficult now to know whether I ought to have suspected anything. Her voice, I feel almost convinced, was perfectly normal. But I must admit that at that moment I was intent, not on her, but on Angela. Angela was by the refrigerator and I was glad to see that she looked red and rather guilty.

I was rather sharp with her, and to my surprise she was quite meek. I asked her where she had been, and she said she had been bathing. I said: 'I didn't see you on the beach.' And she laughed.

Then I asked her where her jersey was, and she said she must have left it down on the beach.

I mention these details to explain why I let Mrs Crale take the beer down to the battery garden.

The rest of the morning is quite blank in my mind. Angela fetched her needle-book and mended her skirt without any more fuss. I rather think that I mended some of the household linen. Mr Crale did not come up for lunch. I was glad that he had at least *that* much decency.

After lunch, Mrs Crale said she was going down to the battery. I wanted to retrieve Angela's jersey from the beach. We started down together. She went into the battery – I was going on when her cry called me back. As I told you when you came to see me, she asked me to go up and telephone. On the way up I met Mr Meredith Blake and then went back to Mrs Crale.

That was my story as I told it at the inquest and later at the trial.

What I am about to write down I have never told to any living soul. I was not asked any question to which I returned an untrue answer. Nevertheless, I *was* guilty of withholding certain facts – I do not repent of that. I would do it again. I am fully aware that in revealing this I may be laying myself open to censure, but I do not think that after this lapse of time anyone will take the matter very seriously – especially since Caroline Crale was convicted without my evidence.

This, then, is what happened.

I met Mr Meredith Blake as I said, and I ran down the path again as quickly as I could. I was wearing sandshoes and I have always been light on my feet. I came to the open battery door, and this is what I saw.

Mrs Crale was busily polishing the beer-bottle on the table with her handkerchief. Having done so, she took her dead husband's hand and pressed the fingers of it on the beer-bottle. All the time she was listening and on the alert. It was the fear I saw on her face that told me the truth.

I knew then, beyond any possible doubt, that Caroline Crale had poisoned her husband. And I, for one, do not blame her. He drove her to a point beyond human endurance, and he brought his fate upon himself.

I never mentioned the incident to Mrs Crale and she never knew that I had seen it.

Caroline Crale's daughter must not bolster up her life with a lie.

However much it may pain her to know the truth, truth is the only thing that matters.

Tell her, from me, that her mother is not to be judged. She was driven beyond what a loving woman can endure. It is for her daughter to understand and forgive.

End of Cecilia Williams's Narrative

— 5 —

NARRATIVE OF ANGELA WARREN

DEAR M. Poirot,

I am keeping my promise to you and have written down all I can remember of that terrible time sixteen years ago. But it was not until I started that I realized how very little I *did* remember. Until the thing actually happened, you see, there is nothing to fix anything by.

I've just a vague memory of summer days, and isolated incidents, but I couldn't say for certain what summer they happened, even! Amyas's death was just a thunderclap coming out of the blue. I'd had no warning of it, and I seem to have missed everything that led up to it.

I've been trying to think whether that was to be expected or not. Are most girls of fifteen as blind and deaf and obtuse as I seem to have been? Perhaps they are. I was quick, I think, to gauge people's moods, but I never bothered my head about what *caused* those moods.

Besides, just at that time, I'd suddenly begun to discover the intoxication of words. Things that I read, scraps of poetry – of Shakespeare – would echo in my head. I remember now walking along the kitchen-garden path repeating to myself in a kind of ecstatic delirium 'under the glassy green translucent wave' . . . It was just so lovely I had to say it over and over again.

And mixed up with these new discoveries and excitements there were all the things I'd liked doing ever since I could remember. Swimming and climbing trees and eating fruit and playing tricks on the stable boy and feeding the horses.

Caroline and Amyas I took for granted. They were the central figures in my world, but I never *thought* about them or about their affairs or what they thought and felt.

I didn't notice Elsa Greer's coming particularly. I thought she was stupid and I didn't even think she was good-looking. I accepted her as someone rich but tiresome, whom Amyas was painting.

Actually, the very first intimation I had of the whole thing was what I overheard from the terrace where I had escaped after lunch one day – Elsa said she was going to marry Amyas! It struck me as just ridiculous. I remember tackling Amyas about it. In the garden at Handcross it was. I said to him: 'Why does Elsa say she's going to marry you? She couldn't. People can't have two wives – it's bigamy and they go to prison.'

Amyas got very angry and said: 'How the devil did you hear that?'

I said I'd heard it through the library window.

He was angrier than ever then, and said it was high time I went to school and got out of the habit of eavesdropping.

I still remember the resentment I felt when he said that. Because it was so *unfair*. Absolutely and utterly unfair.

I stammered out angrily that I hadn't been listening – and anyhow, I said, why did Elsa say a silly thing like that?

Amyas said it was just a joke.

That ought to have satisfied me. It did – almost. But not quite.

I said to Elsa when we were on the way back: 'I asked Amyas what you meant when you said you were going to marry him, and he said it was just a joke.'

I felt that ought to snub her. But she only smiled.

I didn't like that smile of hers. I went up to Caroline's room. It was when she was dressing for dinner. I asked her then outright if it were possible for Amyas to marry Elsa.

I remember Caroline's answer as though I heard it now. She must have spoken with great emphasis.

'Amyas will only marry Elsa after I am dead,' she said.

That reassured me completely. Death seemed ages away from all of us. Nevertheless, I was still very sore with Amyas about what he had said in the afternoon, and I went for him violently all through dinner, and I remember we had a real flaming row, and I rushed out of the room and went up to bed and howled myself to sleep.

I don't remember much about the afternoon at Meredith Blake's, although I *do* remember his reading aloud the passage from the Phædo describing Socrates's death. I had never heard it before. I thought it was the loveliest, most beautiful thing I had ever heard. I remember that – but I don't remember when it was. As far as I can recall now, it might have been any time that summer.

I don't remember anything that happened the next morning, either, though I have thought and thought. I've a vague feeling that I must have bathed, and I think I remember being made to mend something.

But it's all very vague and dim till the time when Meredith came panting up the path from the terrace, and his face was all grey and queer. I remember a coffee-cup falling off the table and being broken – Elsa did that. And I remember her running – suddenly running for all she was worth down the path – and the awful look there was on her face.

I kept saying to myself: 'Amyas is dead.' But it just didn't seem real.

I remember Dr Faussett coming and his grave face. Miss Williams was busy looking after Caroline. I wandered about rather forlornly, getting in people's way. I had a nasty sick feeling. They wouldn't let me go down and see Amyas. But by and by the police came and wrote down things in notebooks, and presently they brought his body up on a stretcher covered with a cloth.

Miss Williams took me into Caroline's room later. Caroline was on the sofa. She looked very white and ill.

She kissed me and said she wanted me to go away as soon as I could, and it was all horrible, but I wasn't to worry or think about it any more than I could help. I was to join Carla at Lady Tressillian's because this house was to be kept as empty as possible.

I clung to Caroline and said I didn't want to go away. I wanted to stay with her. She said she knew I did, but it was better for me to go away and would take a lot of worry off her mind. And Miss Williams chipped in and said: 'The best way you can help your sister, Angela, is to do what she wants you to do without making a fuss about it.'

So I said I would do whatever Caroline wished. And Caroline said: 'That's my darling Angela.' And she hugged me and said there was nothing to worry about, and to talk about it and think about it all as little as possible.

I had to go down and talk to a police superintendent. He was very kind, asked me when I had last seen Amyas and a lot of other questions which seemed to me quite pointless at the time, but which, of course, I see the point of now. He satisfied himself that there was nothing that I could tell him which he hadn't already heard from the others. So he told Miss Williams that he saw no objection to my going over to Ferriby Grange to Lady Tressillian's.

I went there, and Lady Tressillian was very kind to me. But of course I soon had to know the truth. They arrested Caroline almost at once. I was so horified and dumb founded that I became quite ill.

I heard afterwards that Caroline was terribly worried about me. It was at her insistence that I was sent out of England before the trial came on. But that I have told you already.

As you see, what I have put down is pitiably meagre. Since talking to you I have gone over the little I remember painstakingly, racking my memory for details of this or that person's expression or reaction. I can remember nothing consistent with guilt. Elsa's frenzy, Meredith's grey worried face, Philip's grief and fury – they all seem natural enough. I suppose, though, someone *could* have been playing a part.

I only know this: *Caroline did not do it.*

I am quite certain on this point, and always shall be, but I have no evidence to offer except my own intimate knowledge of her character.

End of Angela Warren's Narrative

PART III

— I —

CONCLUSIONS

CARLA LEMARCHANT looked up. Her eyes were full of fatigue and pain. She pushed back the hair from her forehead in a tired gesture.

She said: 'It's so bewildering all this.' She touched the pile of manuscripts. 'Because the angle's different every time! Everybody sees my mother differently. But the facts are the same. Everyone agrees on the facts.'

'It has discouraged you, reading them?'

'Yes. Hasn't it discouraged you?'

'No, I have found those documents very valuable – very informative.'

Poirot spoke slowly and reflectively.

Carla said: 'I wish I'd never read them!'

Poirot looked across at her.

'Ah – so it makes you feel that way?'

Carla said bitterly: 'They all think she did it – all of them except Aunt Angela, and what she thinks doesn't count. She hasn't got any reason for it. She's just one of those loyal people who'll stick to a thing through thick and thin. She just goes on saying: "Caroline couldn't have done it." '

'It strikes you like that?'

'How else should it strike me? I've realized, you know, that if my mother didn't do it, then one of these five people must have done it. I've even had theories as to why.'

'Ah! That is interesting. Tell me.'

'Oh, they were only theories. Philip Blake, for instance. He's a stockbroker, he was my father's best friend – probably my father trusted him. And artists are usually careless about money matters. Perhaps Philip Blake was in a jam and used my father's money. He may have got my father to sign something. Then the whole thing may have been on the point of coming out – and only

my father's death could have saved him. That's one of the things I
thought of.'

'Not badly imagined at all. What else?'

'Well, there's Elsa. Philip Blake says here she had her head
screwed on too well to meddle with poison, but I don't think that's
true at all. Supposing my mother had gone to her and told her that
she wouldn't divorce my father – that nothing would induce her to
divorce him. You may say what you like, but I think Elsa had a
bourgeois mind – she wanted to be respectably married. I think that
then Elsa would have been perfectly capable of pinching the stuff
– she had just as good a chance that afternoon – and might have
tried to get my mother out of the way by poisoning her. I think
that would be quite *like* Elsa. And then, possibly, by some awful
accident, Amyas got the stuff instead of Caroline.'

'Again it is not badly imagined. What else?'

Carla said slowly: 'Well, I thought – perhaps – *Meredith*!'

'Ah – Meredith Blake?'

'Yes. You see, he sounds to me just the sort of person who would
do a murder. I mean, he was the slow dithering one the others
laughed at, and underneath, perhaps, he resented that. Then my
father married the girl he wanted to marry. And my father was
successful and rich. And he did make all those poisons! Perhaps he
really made them because he liked the idea of being able to kill
someone one day. He had to call attention to the stuff being taken,
so as to divert suspicion from himself. But he himself was far the
most likely person to have taken it. He might, even, have liked
getting Caroline hanged – because she turned him down long ago.
I think, you know, it's rather fishy what he says in his account of it
all – how people do things that aren't characteristic of them.
Supposing he meant *himself* when he wrote that?'

Hercule Poirot said: 'You are at least right in this – not to take
what has been written down as necessarily a true narrative. What
has been written may have been written deliberately to mislead.'

'Oh, I know. I've kept that in mind.'

'Any other ideas?'

Carla said slowly: 'I wondered – before I'd read this – about
Miss Williams. She lost her job, you see, when Angela went to
school. And, if Amyas had died suddenly, Angela probably
wouldn't have gone after all. I mean, if it passed off as a natural
death – which it easily might have done, I suppose, if Meredith
hadn't missed the coniine. I read up coniine, and it hasn't got any
distinctive post-mortem appearances. It might have been thought
to be sunstroke. I know that just losing a job doesn't sound a very

adequate motive for murder. But murders have been committed again and again for what seem ridiculously inadequate motives. Tiny sums of money sometimes. And a middle-aged, perhaps rather incompetent, governess might have got the wind up and just seen no future ahead of her.

'As I say, that's what I thought before I read this. But Miss Williams doesn't sound like that at all. She doesn't sound in the least incompetent—'

'Not at all. She is still a very efficient and intelligent woman.'

'I know. One can see that. And she sounds absolutely trust-worthy, too. That's what has upset me really. Oh, *you* know – *you* understand. You don't mind, of course. All along you've made it clear it was the truth you wanted. I suppose now we've *got* the truth! Miss Williams is quite right. One must accept the truth. It's no good basing your life on a lie because it's what you want to believe. All right, then – I can take it! My mother wasn't innocent! She wrote me that letter because she was weak and unhappy and wanted to spare me. I don't judge her. Perhaps I should feel like that, too. I don't know what prison does to you. And I don't blame her, either – if she felt so desperately about my father, I suppose she couldn't help herself. But I don't blame my father altogether, either. I understand – just a little – how *he* felt. So alive – and so full of wanting everything . . . He couldn't help it – he was made that way. And he was a great painter. I think that excuses a lot.'

She turned her flushed face to Hercule Poirot with her chin raised defiantly.

Hercule Poirot said: 'So – you are satisfied?'

'Satisfied?' said Carla Lemarchant. Her voice broke on the word.

Poirot leant forward and patted her paternally on the shoulder.

'Listen,' he said. 'You give up the fight at the moment when it is most worth fighting. At the moment when I, Hercule Poirot, have a very good idea of what really happened.'

Carla stared at him. She said: 'Miss Williams loved my mother. She saw her – with her own eyes – faking that suicide evidence. If you believe what she says—'

Hercule Poirot got up. He said: 'Mademoiselle, because Cecilia Williams says she saw your mother faking Amyas Crale's finger-prints on the beer-bottle – on the beer-*bottle*, mind – that is the only thing I need to tell me definitely, once for all, that your mother did not kill your father.'

He nodded his head several times and went out of the room, leaving Carla staring after him.

POIROT ASKS FIVE QUESTIONS

'WELL, M. Poirot?'

Philip Blake's tone was impatient.

Poirot said: 'I have to thank you for your admirable and lucid account of the Crale tragedy.'

Philip Blake looked rather self-conscious.

'Very kind of you,' he murmured. 'Really surprising how much I remembered when I got down to it.'

Poirot said: 'It was an admirably clear narrative, but there were certain omissions, were there not?'

'Omissions?' Philip Blake frowned.

Hercule Poirot said: 'Your narrative, shall we say, was not entirely frank.' His tone hardened. 'I have been informed, Mr Blake, that on at least one night during the summer Mrs Crale was seen coming out of your room at a somewhat compromising hour.'

There was a silence broken only by Philip Blake's heavy breathing. He said at last: 'Who told you that?'

Hercule Poirot shook his head.

'It is no matter who told me. That I *know*, that is the point.'

Again there was a silence; then Philip Blake made up his mind. He said: 'By accident, it seems, you have stumbled upon a purely private matter. I admit that it does not square with what I have written down. Nevertheless, it squares better than you might think. I am forced now to tell you the truth.

'I *did* entertain a feeling of animosity towards Caroline Crale. At the same time, I was always strongly attracted by her. Perhaps the latter fact induced the former. I resented the power she had over me and tried to stifle the attraction she had for me by constantly dwelling on her worst points. I never *liked* her, if you understand. But it would have been easy at any moment for me to make love to her. I had been in love with her as a boy and she had taken no notice of me. I did not find that easy to forgive.

'My opportunity came when Amyas lost his head so completely over the Greer girl. Quite without meaning to I found myself telling Caroline I loved her. She said quite calmly: "Yes, I have always known that." The insolence of the woman!

'Of course I knew that she didn't love me, but I saw that she was disturbed and disillusioned by Amyas's present infatuation.

That is a mood when a woman can very easily be won. She agreed to come to me that night. And she came.'

Blake paused. He found now a difficulty in getting the words out.

'She came to my room. And then, with my arms round her, she told me quite coolly that it was no good! After all, she said, she was a one-man woman. She was Amyas Crale's, for better or worse. She agreed that she had treated me very badly, but said she couldn't help it. She asked me to forgive her.

'And she left me. *She left me!* Do you wonder, M. Poirot, that my hatred of her was heightened a hundredfold? Do you wonder that I have never forgiven her? For the insult she did to me – as well as for the fact that she killed the friend I loved better than anyone in the world!'

Trembling violently, Philip Blake exclaimed: '*I don't want to speak of it*, do you hear? You've got your answer. Now go! And never mention the matter to me again!'

II

'I want to know, Mr Blake, the order in which your guests left the laboratory that day.'

Meredith Blake protested.

'But, my dear M. Poirot. After sixteen years! How can I possibly remember? I've told you that Caroline came out last.'

'You are *sure* of that?'

'Yes – at least – I think so . . .'

'Let us go there now. We must be *quite* sure, you see.'

Still protesting, Meredith Blake led the way. He unlocked the door and swung back the shutters. Poirot spoke to him authoritatively.

'Now, then, my friend. You have showed your visitors your interesting preparations of herbs. Shut your eyes now and think—'

Meredith Blake did so obediently. Poirot drew a handkerchief from his pocket and gently passed it to and fro. Blake murmured, his nostrils twitching slightly: 'Yes, yes – extraordinary how things come back to one. Caroline, I remember, had on a pale coffee-coloured dress. Phil was looking bored . . . He always thought my hobby was quite idiotic.'

Poirot said: 'Reflect now, you are about to leave the room. You are going to read the passage from the death of Socrates. Who leaves the room first – do you?'

'Elsa and I – yes. She passed through the door first. I was close behind her. We were talking. I stood there waiting for the others to come so that I could lock the door again. Philip – yes, Philip come out next. And Angela – she was asking him what "bulls" and "bears" were. They went on through the hall. Amyas followed them. I stood there waiting still – for Caroline, of course.'

'So you are quite sure Caroline stayed behind. Did you see what she was doing?'

Blake shook his head.

'No, I had my back to the room, you see. I was talking to Elsa – boring her, I expect – telling her how certain plants must be gathered at the full of the moon according to old superstition. And then Caroline came out – hurrying a little – and I locked the door.'

He stopped and looked at Poirot, who was replacing a handkerchief in his pocket. Meredith Blake sniffed disgustedly and thought: 'Why, the fellow actually uses *scent*!' Aloud he said: 'I am quite sure of it. That was the order. Elsa, myself, Philip, Angela and Caroline. Does that help you at all?'

Poirot said: 'It all fits in. Listen. I want to arrange a meeting here. It will not, I think, be difficult . . .'

III

'Well?'

Elsa Dittisham said it almost eagerly – like a child.

'I want to ask you a question, Madame.'

'Yes?'

Poirot said: 'After it was all over – the trial, I mean – did Meredith Blake ask you to marry him?'

Elsa stared. She looked contemptuous – almost bored.

'Yes – he did. Why?'

'Were you surprised?'

'Was I? I don't remember.'

'What did you say?'

Elsa laughed. She said: 'What do you think I said? After Amyas – *Meredith*? It would have been ridiculous! It was stupid of him. He always was rather stupid.'

She smiled suddenly.

'He wanted, you know, to protect me – to "look after me" –

634

that's how he put it! He thought like everybody else that the Assizes had been a terrible ordeal for me. And the reporters! And the booing crowds! And all the mud that was slung at me.'

She brooded a minute. Then she said: 'Poor old Meredith! Such an ass!' And laughed again.

IV

Once again Hercule Poirot encountered the shrewd penetrating glance of Miss Williams, and once again felt the years falling away and himself a meek and apprehensive little boy.

There was, he explained, a question he wished to ask.

Miss Williams intimated her willingness to hear what the question was.

Poirot said slowly, picking his words carefully: 'Angela Warren was injured as a very young child. In my notes I find two references to that fact. In one of them it is stated that Mrs Crale threw a paperweight at the child. In the other that she attacked the baby with a crowbar. Which of those versions is the right one?'

Miss Williams replied briskly: 'I never heard anything about a crowbar. The paperweight is the correct story.'

'Who was your own informant?'

'Angela herself. She volunteered the information quite early.'

'What did she say exactly?'

'She touched her cheek and said: "Caroline did this when I was a baby. She threw a paperweight at me. Never refer to it, will you, because it upsets her dreadfully." '

'Did Mrs Crale herself ever mention the matter to you?'

'Only obliquely. She assumed that I knew the story. I remember her saying once: "I know you think I spoil Angela but, you see, I always feel there is nothing I can do to make up to her for what I did." And on another occasion she said: "To know you have permanently injured another human being is the heaviest burden anyone could have to bear." '

'Thank you, Miss Williams. That is all I wanted to know.'

Cecilia Williams said sharply: 'I don't understand you, M. Poirot. You showed Carla my account of the tragedy?'

Poirot nodded.

'And yet you are still—' She stopped.

Poirot said: 'Reflect a minute. If you were to pass a fishmonger's and saw twelve fish laid out on his slab, you would think they were all real fish, would you not? But one of them might be stuffed fish.'

Miss Williams replied with spirit: 'Most unlikely and anyway—'

'Ah, unlikely, yes, but not impossible – because a friend of mine once took down a stuffed fish (it was his trade, you comprehend) to compare it with the real thing! And if you saw a bowl of zinnias in a drawing-room in December you would say that they were false – but they might be real ones flown home from Baghdad.'

'What is the meaning of all this nonsense?' demanded Miss Williams.

'It is to show you that it is the eyes of the mind with which one really sees . . .'

V

Poirot slowed up a little as he approached the big block of flats overlooking Regent's Park.

Really, when he came to think of it, he did not want to ask Angela Warren any questions at all. The only question he did want to ask her could wait . . .

No, it was really only his insatiable passion for symmetry that was bringing him here. Five people – there should be five questions! It was neater so. It rounded off the thing better.

Ah, well – he would think of something.

Angela Warren greeted him with something closely approaching eagerness. She said: 'Have you found out anything? Have you got anywhere?'

Slowly Poirot nodded his head in his best china mandarin manner. He said: 'At last I make progress.'

'Philip Blake?' It was half-way between statement and question.

'Mademoiselle, I do not wish to say anything at present. The moment has not yet come. What I will ask of you is to be so good as to come down to Handcross Manor. The others have consented.'

She said with a slight frown: 'What do you propose to do? Reconstruct something that happened sixteen years ago?'

'See it, perhaps, from a clearer angle. You will come?'

Angela Warren said slowly: 'Oh, yes, I'll come. It will be interesting to see all those people again. I shall see *them* now, perhaps, from a clearer angle (as you put it) than I did then.'

'And you will bring with you the letter that you showed me?'
Angela Warren frowned.

'That letter is my own. I showed it to you for a good and sufficient reason, but I have no intention of allowing it to be read by strange and unsympathetic persons.'

'But you will allow yourself to be guided by me in this matter?'

'I will do nothing of the kind. I will bring the letter with me, but I shall use my own judgment, which I venture to think is quite as good as yours.'

Poirot spread out his hands in a gesture of resignation. He got up to go. He said: 'You permit that I ask one little question?'

'What is it?'

'At the time of the tragedy, you had lately read, had you not, Somerset Maugham's *The Moon and Sixpence*?'

Angela stared at him. Then she said: 'I believe – why, yes, that is quite true.' She looked at him with frank curiosity. 'How did you know?'

'I want to show you, Mademoiselle, that even in a small unimportant matter I am something of a magician. There are things I know without having to be told.'

— 3 —

RECONSTRUCTION

THE afternoon sun shone into the laboratory at Handcross Manor. Some easy chairs and a settee had been brought into the room, but they served more to emphasize its forlorn aspect than to furnish it.

Slightly embarrassed, pulling at his moustache, Meredith Blake talked to Carla in a desultory way. He broke off at once to say: 'My dear, you are very like your mother – and yet unlike her, too.'

Carla asked: 'How am I like her and how unlike?'

'You have her colouring and her way of moving, but you are – how shall I put it? – more *positive* than she ever was.'

Philip Blake, a scowl creasing his forehead, looked out of the window and drummed impatiently on the pane. He said: 'What's the sense of all this? A perfectly fine Saturday afternoon—'

Hercule Poirot hastened to pour oil on troubled waters.

'Ah, I apologize – it is, I know, unpardonable to disarrange the golf. *Mais voyons*, Mr Blake, this is the daughter of your best friend. You will stretch a point for her, will you not?'

The butler announced: 'Miss Warren.'

Meredith went to welcome her. He said: 'It's good of you to spare the time, Angela. You're busy, I know.'

He led her over to the window.

Carla said: 'Hallo, Aunt Angela. I read your article in *The Times* this morning. It's nice to have a distinguished relative.' She indicated the tall, square-jawed young man with the steady grey eyes. 'This is John Rattery. He and I – hope – to be married.'

Angela Warren said: 'Oh! – I didn't know . . .'

Meredith went to greet the next arrival.

'Well, Miss Williams, it's a good many years since we met.'

Thin, frail and indomitable, the elderly governess advanced up the room. Her eyes rested thoughtfully on Poirot for a minute, then they went to the tall, square-shouldered figure in the well-cut tweeds.

Angela Warren came forward to meet her and said with a smile: 'I feel like a schoolgirl again.'

'I'm very proud of you, my dear,' said Miss Williams. 'You've done me credit. This is Carla, I suppose? She won't remember me. She was too young . . .'

Philip Blake said fretfully: 'What *is* all this? Nobody told me—'

Hercule Poirot said: 'I call it – me – an excursion into the past. Shall we not all sit down? Then we shall be ready when the last guest arrives. And when she is here we can proceed to our business – to lay the ghosts.'

Philip Blake exclaimed: 'What tomfoolery is this? You're not going to hold a *séance*, are you?'

'No, no. We are only going to discuss some events that happened long ago – to discuss them and, perhaps, to see more clearly the course of them. As to the ghosts, they will not materialize, but who is to say they are not here, in this room, although we cannot see them? Who is to say that Amyas and Caroline Crale are not here – listening?'

Philip Blake said: 'Absurd nonsense—' and broke off as the door opened again and the butler announced Lady Dittisham.

Elsa Dittisham came in with that faint, bored insolence that was a characteristic of her. She gave Meredith a slight smile, stared coldly at Angela and Philip, and went over to a chair by the window a little apart from the others. She loosened the rich pale furs round her neck and let them fall back. She looked for a minute or two about the room, then at Carla, and the girl stared back, thoughtfully appraising the woman who had wrought the havoc in her parents' lives. There was no animosity in her young earnest face, only curiosity.

Elsa said: 'I am sorry if I am late, M. Poirot.'

'It was very good of you to come, Madame.'

Cecilia Williams snorted ever so slightly. Elsa met the animosity in her eyes with a complete lack of interest. She said: 'I wouldn't have known *you*, Angela. How long is it? Sixteen years?'

Hercule Poirot seized his opportunity.

'Yes, it is sixteen years since the events of which we are to speak, but let me first tell you why we are here.'

And in a few simple words he outlined Carla's appeal to him and his acceptance of the task.

He went on quickly, ignoring the gathering storm visible on Philip's face, and the shocked distaste on Meredith's.

'I accepted that commission – I set to work to find out – the truth.'

Carla Lemarchant, in the big grandfather chair, heard Poirot's words dimly, from a distance.

With her hand shielding her eyes she studied five faces, surreptitiously. Could she see any of these people committing murder? The exotic Elsa, the red-faced Philip, dear, nice, kind Mr Meredith Blake, that grim tartar of a governess, the cool, competent Angela Warren?

Could she – if she tried hard – visualise one of them killing someone? Yes, perhaps – but it wouldn't be the right kind of murder. She could picture Philip Blake, in an outburst of fury, strangling some woman – yes, she *could* picture that . . . And she could picture Meredith Blake, threatening a burglar with a revolver – and letting it off by accident . . .

And she could picture Angela Warren, also firing a revolver, but not by accident. With no personal feeling in the matter – the safety of the expedition depended on it! And Elsa, in some fantastic castle, saying from her couch of Oriental silks: 'Throw the wretch over the battlements!' All wild fancies – and not even in the wildest flight of fancy could she imagine little Miss Williams killing anybody at all! Another fantastic picture: 'Did you ever kill anybody, Miss Williams?' 'Go on with your arithmetic, Carla, and don't ask silly questions. To kill anybody is very wicked.'

Carla thought: 'I must be ill – I must stop this. Listen, you fool, listen to that little man who says he knows.'

Hercule Poirot was talking.

'That was my task – to put myself in reverse gear, as it were, and go back through the years and discover what really happened.'

Philip Blake said: 'We all know what happened. To pretend anything else is a swindle – that's what it is, a bare-faced swindle. You're getting money out of this girl on false pretences.'

Poirot did not allow himself to be angered. He said: 'You say, *we all know what happened.* You speak without reflection. The accepted version of certain facts is not necessarily the true one. On the face of it, for instance, you, Mr Blake, disliked Caroline Crale. That is the accepted version of your attitude. But anyone with the least flair for psychology can perceive at once that the exact opposite was the truth. You were always violently attracted towards Caroline Crale. You resented the fact, and tried to conquer it by steadfastly telling yourself her defects and reiterating your dislike. In the same way, Mr Meredith Blake had a tradition of devotion to Caroline Crale lasting over many years. In this story of the tragedy he represents himself as resenting Amyas Crale's conduct on *her* account, but you have only to read carefully between the lines and you will see that the devotion of a lifetime had worn itself thin and that it was the young, beautiful Elsa Greer that was occupying *his* mind and thoughts.'

There was a splutter from Meredith, and Lady Dittisham smiled.

Poirot went on.

'I mention these matters only as illustrations, though they have their bearing on what happened. Very well, then, I start on my backward journey – to learn everything I can about the tragedy. I will tell you how I set about it. I talked to the counsel who defended Caroline Crale, to the junior counsel for the Crown, to the old solicitor who had known the Crale family intimately, to the lawyer's clerk who had been in court during the trial, to the police officer in charge of the case – and I came finally to the five eye-witnesses who had been upon the scene. And from all of these I put together a picture – a composite picture of a woman. And I learned these facts:

'*That at no time did Caroline Crale protest her innocence* (except in that one letter written to her daughter).

'That Caroline Crale showed no fear in the dock, that she showed, in fact, hardly any interest, that she adopted throughout a thoroughly defeatist attitude. That in prison she was quiet and serene. That in a letter she wrote to her sister immediately after the verdict, she expressed herself as acquiescent in the fate that

640

had overtaken her. And in the opinion of everyone I talked to (with one notable exception) *Caroline Crale was guilty.*'

Philip Blake nodded his head. 'Of course she was!'

Hercule Poirot said: 'But it was not my part to accept the verdict of *others*. I had to examine the evidence for *myself*. To examine the facts and to satisfy myself that the psychology of the case accorded itself with them. To do this I went over the police files carefully, and I also succeeded in getting five people who were on the spot to write me out their own accounts of the tragedy. These accounts were very valuable for they contained certain matter which the police files could not give me – that is to say: (*a*) certain conversations and incidents which, from the police point of view, were not relevant; (*b*) the opinions of the people themselves as to what Caroline Crale was thinking and feeling (not admissible legally as evidence); (*c*) certain facts which had been deliberately withheld from the police.

'I was in a position now to judge the case for *myself*. There seems no doubt whatever that Caroline Crale had ample motive for the crime. She loved her husband, he had publicly admitted that he was about to leave her for another woman, and by her own admission she was a jealous woman.

'To come from motives to means, an empty scent-bottle that contained coniine was found in the bureau drawer. There were no fingerprints upon it but hers. When asked about it by the police, she admitted taking it from this room we are in now. The coniine-bottle here also had her fingerprints upon it. I questioned Mr Meredith Blake as to the order in which the five people left this room on that day – for it seemed to me hardly conceivable that *any-one* should be able to help themselves to the poison whilst five people were in the room. The people left the room in this order – Elsa Greer, Meredith Blake, Angela Warren and Philip Blake, Amyas Crale, and lastly Caroline Crale. Moreover, Mr Meredith Blake had his back to the room whilst he was waiting for Mrs Crale to come out, so that it was impossible for him to see what she was doing. She had, that is to say, the opportunity. I am therefore satisfied that she did take the coniine. There is indirect confirmation of it. Mr Meredith Blake said to me the other day: "I can remember standing here and smelling the jasmine through the open window." But the month was September, and the jasmine creeper outside that window would have finished flowering. It is the ordinary jasmine which blooms in June and July. But the scent-bottle found in her room and which contained the dregs of coniine had originally contained jasmine scent. I take it as certain, then, that Mrs Crale decided to steal the coniine, and surreptitiously emptied out the scent from a bottle she had in her bag.

'I tested that a second time the other day when I asked Mr Blake to shut his eyes and try to remember the order of leaving the room. A whiff of jasmine scent stimulated his memory immediately. We are all more influenced by smell than we know.

'So we come to the morning of the fatal day. So far the facts are not in dispute. Miss Greer's sudden revealing of the fact that she and Mr Crale contemplate marriage, Amyas Crale's confirmation of that, and Caroline Crale's deep distress. None of these things depended on the evidence of one witness only.

'On the following morning there is a scene between husband and wife in the library. The first thing that is overheard is Caroline saying, "You and your women!" in a bitter voice, and finally going on to say, "Some day I'll kill you." Philip Blake overheard this from the hall. And Miss Greer overheard it from the terrace outside.

'She then heard Mr Crale ask his wife to be reasonable. And she heard Mrs Crale say: "Sooner than let you go to that girl – I'll kill you." Soon after this Amyas Crale comes out and brusquely tells Elsa Greer to come down and pose for him. She gets a pullover and accompanies him.

'There is nothing so far that seems psychologically incorrect. Everyone has behaved as they might be expected to behave. But we come now to something that *is* incongruous.

'Meredith Blake discovers his loss, telephones his brother; they meet down at the landing-stage and they come up past the battery garden, where Caroline Crale is having a discussion with her husband on the subject of Angela's going to school. Now that does strike me as very odd. Husband and wife have a terrific scene, ending in a distinct threat on Caroline's part, and yet, twenty minutes or so later, she goes down and starts a trivial domestic argument.'

Poirot turned to Meredith Blake.

'You speak in your narrative of certain words you overheard Crale say. These were: "It's all settled – I'll see to her packing." That is right?'

Meredith Blake said: 'It was something like that – yes.'

Poirot turned to Philip Blake.

'Is your recollection the same?'

The latter frowned.

'I didn't remember it till you said so – but I do remember now. Something *was* said about packing!'

'Said by Mr Crale – not Mrs Crale?'

'Amyas said it. All I heard Caroline say was something about it being very hard on the girl. Anyway, what does all this matter? We all know Angela was off to school in a day or two.'

Poirot said: 'You do not see the force of my objection. Why should *Amyas Crale* pack for the girl? It is absurd, that! There was Mrs Crale, there was Miss Williams, there was a housemaid. It is a woman's job to pack – not a man's.'

Philip Blake said impatiently: 'What does it matter? It's nothing to do with the crime.'

'You think not? For me, it was the first point that struck me as suggestive. And it is immediately followed by another. Mrs Crale, a desperate woman, broken-hearted, who has threatened her husband a short while before and who is certainly contemplating either suicide or murder, now offers in the most amicable manner to bring her husband down some iced beer.'

Meredith Blake said slowly: 'That isn't odd if she was contemplating murder. Then, surely, it is just what she *would* do. Dissimulate!'

'You think so? She has decided to poison her husband, she has already got the poison. Her husband keeps a supply of beer down in the battery garden. Surely, if she has any intelligence at all, she will put the poison in one of *those* bottles at a moment when there is no one about.'

Meredith Blake objected.

'She couldn't have done that. Somebody else might have drunk it.'

'Yes, Elsa Greer. Do you tell me that, having made up her mind to murder her husband, Caroline Crale would have scuples against killing the girl, too?

'But let us not argue the point. Let us confine ourselves to facts. Caroline Crale says she will send her husband down some iced beer. She goes up to the house, fetches a bottle from the conservatory where it was kept and takes it down to him. She pours it out and gives it to him. Amyas Crale drinks it off and says: "Everything tastes foul today."

'Mrs Crale goes up again to the house. She has lunch and appears much as usual. It has been said of her that she looks a little worried and preoccupied. That does not help us – for there is no criterion of behaviour for a murderer. There are calm murderers and excited murderers.

'After lunch she goes down again to the battery. She discovers her husband head and does – shall we say? – the obviously

643

expected things. She registers emotion and she sends the governess to telephone for a doctor. We now come to a fact which has previously not been known.' He looked at Miss Williams. 'You do not object?'

Miss Williams was rather pale. She said: 'I did not pledge you to secrecy.'

Quietly, but with telling effect, Poirot recounted what the governess had seen.

Elsa Dittisham moved her position. She stared at the drab little woman in the big chair. She said incredibly: 'You actually saw her do *that*?'

Philip Blake sprang up.

'But that settles it!' he shouted. 'That settles it once and for all.'

Hercule Poirot looked at him mildly. He said: 'Not necessarily.'

Angela Warren said sharply: 'I don't believe it.' There was a quick hostile glint in the glance she shot at the little governess.

Meredith Blake was pulling at his moustache, his face dismayed. Alone, Miss Williams remained undisturbed. She sat very upright and there was a spot of colour in each cheek.

She said: 'That is what I saw.'

Poirot said slowly: 'There is, of course, only your word for it . . .'

'There is only my word for it.' The indomitable grey eyes met his. 'I am not accustomed, M. Poirit, to having my word doubted.'

Hercule Poirot bowed his head. He said: 'I do not doubt your word, Miss Williams. What you saw took place exactly as you say it did – and because of what you saw I realized that Caroline Crale was not guilty – could not possibly be guilty.'

For the first time, that tall, anxious-faced young man, John Rattery, spoke. He said: 'I'd be interested to know *why* you say that, M. Poirot.'

Poirot turned to him.

'Certainly. I will tell you. What did Miss Williams see – she saw Caroline Crale very carefully and anxiously wiping off fingerprints and subsequently imposing her dead husband's fingerprints on the beer-bottle. On the beer-*bottle*, mark. But the coniine was in the glass – not in the bottle. The police found no traces of coniine in the bottle. There had never been any coniine in the bottle. *And Caroline Crale didn't know that.*

'She, who is supposed to have poisoned her husband, didn't know *how* he had been poisoned. She thought the poison was in the bottle.'

Meredith objected: 'But why——?'

Poirot interrupted him in a flash.

'Yes – *why*? Why did Caroline Crale try so desperately to establish the theory of suicide? The answer is – must be – quite simple. Because she knew who *had* poisoned him and she was willing to do anything – endure anything – rather than let that person be suspected.

'There is not far to go now. Who could that person be? Would she have shielded Philip Blake? Or Meredith? Or Elsa Greer? Or Cecilia Williams? No, there is only one person whom she would be willing to protect at all costs.'

He paused: 'Miss Warren, if you have brought your sister's last letter with you, I should like to read it aloud.'

Angela Warren said: 'No.'

'But, Miss Warren—'

Angela got up. Her voice rang out, cold as steel.

'I realize very well what you are suggesting. You are saying, are you not, that I killed Amyas Crale and that my sister knew it. I deny that allegation utterly.'

Poirot said: 'The letter . . .'

'That letter was meant for my eyes alone.'

Poirot looked to where the two youngest people in the room stood together.

Carla Lemarchant said: 'Please, Aunt Angela, won't you do as M. Poirot asks?'

Angela Warren said bitterly: 'Really, Carla, have you no sense of decency? She was your mother – you—'

Carla's voice rang out clear and fierce.

'Yes, she was my mother. That's why I've a right to ask you. I'm speaking for *her*. I *want* that letter read.'

Slowly, Angela took out the letter from her bag and handed it to Poirot. She said bitterly: 'I wish I had never shown it to you.'

Turning away from them she stood looking out of the window.

As Hercule Poirot read aloud Caroline Crale's last letter, the shadows were deepening in the corners of the room. Carla had a sudden feeling of someone in the room, gathering shape, listening, breathing, waiting. She thought: '*She's* here – my mother's here. Caroline – Caroline Crale is *here* in this room!'

Hercule Poirot's voice ceased. He said: 'You will all agree, I think, that that is a very remarkable letter. A beautiful letter, too, but certainly remarkable. For there is one striking omission in it – it contains no protestation of innocence.'

Angela Warren said without turning her head: 'That was unnecessary.'

'Yes, Miss Warren, it was unnecessary. Caroline Crale had no need to tell her sister that she was innocent – because she thought her sister knew that fact already – knew it for the best of all reasons. All Caroline Crale was concerned about was to comfort and reassure and to avert the possibility of a confession from Angela. She reiterates again and again – *It's all right, darling, it's all all right.*'

Angela Warren said: 'Can't you understand? She wanted me to be happy, that's all.'

'Yes, she wanted you to be happy, that is abundantly clear. It is her one preoccupation. She has a child, but it is not that child of whom she is thinking – that is to come later. No, it is her sister who occupies her mind to the exclusion of everything else. Her sister must be reassured, must be encouraged to live her life, to be happy and successful. And, so that the burden of acceptance may not be too great, Caroline includes that one very significant phrase: "*One must pay one's debts.*"

'That one phrase explains everything. It refers explicitly to the burden that Caroline has carried for so many years ever since, in a fit of uncontrolled adolescent rage, she hurled a paperweight at her baby sister and injured that sister for life. Now, at last, she has the opportunity to pay the debt she owes. And, if it is any consolation, I will say to you all that I earnestly believe that in the payment of that debt Caroline Crale did achieve a peace and serenity greater than any she had ever known. Because of her belief that she was paying that debt, the ordeal of trial and condemnation could not touch her. It is a strange thing to say of a condemned murderess – but she had everything to make her happy. Yes, more than you imagine, as I will show you presently.

'See how, by this explanation, everything falls into its place where Caroline's own reactions are concerned. Look at the series of events from her point of view. To begin with, on the preceding evening, an event occurs which reminds her forcibly of her own undisciplined girlhood. Angela throws a *paperweight* at Amyas Crale. That, remember, is what she herself did many years ago. Angela shouts out that she wishes Amyas was dead. Then, on the next morning, Caroline comes into the little conservatory and finds Angela tampering with the beer. Remember Miss Williams's words: "Angela was there. She looked guilty . . ." Guilty of playing truant was what Miss Williams meant but, to Caroline, Angela's guilty face, as she was caught unawares, would have a different meaning. Remember that on at least one occasion before Angela had put things in Amyas's drink. It was an idea which might readily occur to her.

'Caroline takes the bottle *that Angela gives her* and goes down with it to the battery. And there she pours it out and gives it to Amyas, and he makes a face as he tosses it off and utters those significant words: "Everything tastes foul today."

'Caroline has no suspicions then – but after lunch she goes down to the battery and finds her husband dead – and she has no doubt at all but that he has been poisoned. *She* had not done it. Who, then, has? And the whole thing comes over with a rush – Angela's threats, Angela's face stooping over the beer and caught unawares – guilty – guilty – guilty. Why has the child done it? As a revenge on Amyas, perhaps not meaning to kill, just to make him ill or sick? Or has she done it for her, Caroline's sake? Has she realized and resented Amyas's desertion of her sister. Caroline remembers – oh, so well – her own undisciplined violent emotions at Angela's age. And only one thought springs to her mind. How can she protect Angela? Angela handled that bottle – Angela's fingerprints will be on it. She quickly wipes it and polishes it. If only everybody can be got to believe it is suicide. If Amyas's fingerprints are the only ones found. She tries to fit his dead fingers round the bottle – working desperately – listening for someone to come . . .

'Once take that assumption as true, and everything from then on fits in. Her anxiety about Angela all along, her insistence on getting her away, keeping her out of touch with what was going on. Her fear of Angela's being questioned unduly by the police. Finally, her overwhelming anxiety to get Angela out of England before the trial comes on. Because she is always terrified that Angela might break down and confess.'

— 4 —

TRUTH

SLOWLY, Angela Warren swung round. Her eyes, hard and contemptuous, ranged over the faces turned towards her.

She said: 'You're blind fools – all of you. Don't you know that, if I had done it, I *would* have confessed! I'd never have let Caroline suffer for what I'd done. Never!'

Poirot said: 'But you did tamper with the beer.'

'I? Tamper with the beer?'

Poirot turned to Meredith Blake.

'Listen, Monsieur. In your account here of what happened, you describe having heard sounds in this room, which is below your bedroom, on the morning of the crime.'

Blake nodded.

'But it was only a cat.'

'How do you know it was a cat?'

'I – I can't remember. But it was a cat. I am quite sure it was a cat. The window was open just wide enough for a cat to get through.'

'But it was not fixed in that position. The sash moves freely. It could have been pushed up and a human being could have got in and out.'

'Yes, but I know it was a cat.'

'You did not *see* a cat?'

Blake said perplexedly and slowly: 'No, I did not see it—' He paused, frowning. 'And yet I know.'

'I will tell you *why* you know presently. In the meantime I put this point to you. Someone could have come up to the house that morning, have got into your laboratory, taken something from the shelf and gone again without your seeing them. Now if that someone had come over from Alderbury it could not have been Philip Blake, nor Elsa Greer, nor Amyas Crale nor Caroline Crale. We know quite well what all those four were doing. That leaves Angela Warren and Miss Williams. Miss Williams was over here – you actually met her as you went out. She told you then that she was looking for Angela. Angela had gone bathing early, but Miss Williams did not see her in the water, nor anywhere on the rocks. She could swim across to this side easily – in fact she did so later in the morning when she was bathing with Philip Blake. I suggest that she swam across here, came up to the house, got in through the window, and took something from the shelf.'

Angela Warren said: 'I did nothing of the kind – not – at least—'

'Ah!' Poirot gave a yelp of triumph. '*You have remembered*. You told me, did you not, that to play a malicious joke on Amyas Crale you pinched some of what you called "the cat stuff" – that is how you put it—'

Meredith Blake said sharply: 'Valerian! Of course.'

'Exactly. *That* is what made you sure in your mind that it was a cat who had been in the room. Your nose is very sensitive. You smelled the faint, unpleasant odour of valerian without knowing, perhaps, that you did so – but it suggested to your subconscious mind "Cat". Cats love valerian and will go anywhere for it. Valerian is particularly nasty to taste, and it was your account of it the day before which made mischievous Miss Angela plan to put some in her brother-in-law's beer, which she knew he always tossed down his throat in a draught.'

Angela Warren said wonderingly: 'Was it really that day? I remember taking it perfectly. Yes, and I remember getting out the beer and Caroline coming in and nearly catching me! Of course I remember . . . But I've never connected it with that particular day.'

'Of course not – because there was no connection *in your mind*. The two events were entirely dissimilar to you. One was on a par with other mischievous pranks – the other was a bombshell of tragedy arriving without warning and succeeding in banishing all lesser incidents from your mind. But me, I noticed when you spoke of it that you said: "I pinched, etc., etc., *to put it* in Amyas's drink." You did not say you had actually *done* so.'

'No, because I never did. Caroline came in just when I was unscrewing the bottle. Oh!' It was a cry. 'And Caroline thought – she thought it was *me*—!'

She stopped. She looked round. She said quietly in her usual cool tones: 'I suppose you all think so, too.'

She paused and then said: '*I didn't kill Amyas*. Not as the result of a malicious joke nor in any other way. If I had, I would never have kept silence.'

Miss Williams said sharply: 'Of course you wouldn't, my dear.' She looked at Hercule Poirot. 'Nobody but a *fool* would think so.'

Hercule Poirot said mildly: 'I am not a fool and I do not think so. *I know quite well who killed Amyas Crale.*'

He paused.

'There is always a danger of accepting facts as proved which are really nothing of the kind. Let us take the situation at Alderbury. A very old situation. Two women and one man. We have taken it for granted that Amyas Crale proposed to leave his wife for the other woman. But I suggest to you now *that he never intended to do anything of the kind.*

'He had had infatuations for women before. They obsessed him while they lasted, but they were soon over. The women he had fallen in love with were usually women of a certain experience – they did not expect too much of him. But this time the woman did. She was not, you see, a woman at all. She was a girl and, in

Caroline Crale's words, she was terribly sincere . . . She may have been hard-boiled and sophisticated in speech, but in love she was frighteningly single-minded. *Because* she herself had a deep and over-mastering passion for Amyas Crale she assumed that he had the same for her. She assumed without any question that their passion was for life. She assumed without asking him that he was going to leave his wife.

'But why, you will say, did Amyas Crale not undeceive her? And my answer is – the picture. He wanted to finish his picture.

'To some people that sounds incredible – but not to anybody who knows about artists. And we have already accepted that explanation in principle. That conversation between Crale and Meredith Blake is more intelligible now. Crale is embarrassed – pats Blake on the back, assures him optimistically the whole thing is going to pan out all right. To Amyas Crale, you see, everything is simple. He is painting a picture, slightly encumbered by what he describes as a couple of jealous, neurotic women – but neither of them is going to be allowed to interfere with what to him is the most important thing in life.

'If he were to tell Elsa the truth, it would be all up with the picture. Perhaps in the first flush of his feelings for her he did talk about leaving Caroline. Men do say these things when they are in love. Perhaps he merely lets it be assumed. He doesn't care what Elsa assumes. Let her think what she likes. Anything to keep her quiet for another day or two.

'Then – he will tell her the truth – that things between them are over. He has never been a man to be troubled with scruples.

'He did, I think, make an effort not to get embroiled with Elsa to begin with. He warned her what kind of a man he was – but she would not take warning. She rushed on her Fate. And to a man like Crale women were fair game. If you had asked him, he would have said easily that Elsa was young – she'd soon get over it. That was the way Amyas Crale's mind worked.

'His wife was actually the only person he cared about at all. He wasn't worrying much about her. She'd only got to put up with things for a few days longer. He was furious with Elsa for blurting out things to Caroline, but he still optimistically thought it would be "all right". Caroline would forgive him as she had done so often before, and Elsa – Elsa would just have to "lump it". So simple are the problems of life to a man like Amyas Crale.

'But I think that that last evening he became really worried. About Caroline, not about Elsa. Perhaps he went to her room and she refused to speak to him. At any rate, after a restless night, he took her aside after breakfast and blurted out the truth. He had been infatuated with Elsa, but it was all over. Once he'd finished the picture he'd never see her again.

'And it was in answer to that that Caroline Crale cried out indignantly: "You and your women!" That phrase, you see, put Elsa in a class with others – those others who had gone their way. And she added indignantly: "Some day I'll kill you."

'She was angry, revolted by his callousness and by his cruelty to the girl. When Philip Blake saw her in the hall and heard her murmur to herself, "It's too cruel!" it was of Elsa she was thinking.

'As for Crale, he came out of the library, found Elsa with Philip Blake, and brusquely ordered her down to go on with the sitting. What he did not know was that Elsa Greer had been sitting just outside the library window and had overheard everything. And the account she gave later of that conversation was not the true one. There is only her word for it, remember.

'Imagine the shock it must have been to her to hear the truth, brutally spoken!

'On the previous afternoon Meredith Blake has told us that whilst he was waiting for Caroline to leave this room he was standing in the doorway with his back to the room. He was talking to Elsa Greer. That means that she would have been *facing* him and that *she* could see exactly what Caroline was doing over his shoulder – and that she *was the only person who could do so*.

'She saw Caroline take that poison. She said nothing, but she remembered it as she sat outside the library window.

'When Amyas Crale came out she made the excuse of wanting a pullover, and went up to Caroline Crale's room to look for the poison. Women know where other women are likely to hide things. She found it and, being careful not to obliterate any fingerprints or to leave her own, she drew off the fluid into a fountain-pen filler.

'Then she came down again and went off with Crale to the battery garden. And presently, no doubt, she poured him out some beer and he tossed it down in the usual way.

'Meanwhile, Caroline Crale was seriously disturbed. When she saw Elsa come up to the house (this time really to fetch a pullover), Caroline slipped quickly down to the battery garden and tackled her husband. What he is doing is shameful! She won't stand for it! It's unbelievably cruel and hard on the girl! Amyas, irritable at being interrupted, says it's all settled – when the picture is done he'll send the girl packing! *"It's all settled – I'll send her packing, I tell you."*

'And then they hear the footsteps of the two Blakes, and

Caroline comes out and, slightly embarrassed, murmurs something about Angela and school and having a lot to do, and by a natural association of ideas the two men judge the conversation they have overheard refers to *Angela*, and "I'll send her packing" becomes "I'll see to her packing".

'And Elsa, pullover in hand, comes down the path, cool and smiling, and takes up the pose once more.

'She has counted, no doubt, upon Caroline's being suspected and the coniine bottle being found in her room. But Caroline now plays into her hands completely. She brings down some iced beer and pours it out for her husband.

'Amyas tosses it off, making a face, and says: "Everything tastes foul today."

'Do you not see how significant that remark is? *Everything* tastes foul? Then there has been something else *before* that beer that has tasted unpleasant and the taste of which is *still in his mouth*. And one other point. Philip Blake speaks of Crale's staggering a little and wonders "if he has been drinking". But that slight stagger was the *first sign of the coniine working*, and that means *that it had already been administered to him some time before Caroline brought him the iced bottle of beer.*

'And so Elsa Greer sat on the grey wall and posed and, since she must keep him from suspecting until it was too late, she talked to Amyas Crale brightly and naturally. Presently she saw Meredith on the bench above and waved her hand to him and acted her part even more thoroughly for his behalf.

'And Amyas Crale, a man who detested illness and refused to give in to it, painted doggedly on till his limbs failed and his speech thickened, and he sprawled there on that bench, helpless, but with his mind still clear.

'The bell sounded from the house and Meredith left the bench to come down to the battery. I think that in that brief moment Elsa left her place and ran across to the table and dropped the last few drops of the poison into the beer-glass that held that last innocent drink. (She got rid of the dropper on the path up to the house – crushing it to powder.) Then she met Meredith in the doorway.

'There was a glare there coming in out of the shadows. Meredith did not see very clearly – only his friends sprawled in familiar position and saw his eyes turn from the picture in what he described as a malevolent glare.

'How much did Amyas know or guess? How much his conscious mind knew we cannot tell, but his hand and his eye were faithful.'

Hercule Poirot gestured towards the picture on the wall.

'I should have known when I first saw that picture. For it is a very remarkable picture. It is the picture of a murderess painted by her victim – it is the picture of a girl watching her lover die . . .'

— 5 —

AFTERMATH

IN THE silence that followed – a horrified, appalled silence – the sunset slowly flickered away, the last gleam left the window where it had rested on the dark head and pale furs of the woman sitting there.

Elsa Dittisham moved and spoke. She said: 'Take them away, Meredith. Leave me with M. Poirot.'

She sat there motionless until the door shut behind them. Then she said: 'You are very clever, aren't you?'

Poirot did not answer.

She said: 'What do you expect me to do? Confess?'

He shook his head.

Elsa said: 'Because I shall do nothing of the kind! And I shall admit nothing. But what we say here, together, does not matter. Because it is only a question of your word against mine.'

'Exactly.'

'I want to know what you are going to do.'

Hercule Poirot said: 'I shall do everything I can to induce the authorities to grant a posthumous free pardon to Caroline Crale.'

Elsa laughed. She said: 'How absurd! To be given a free pardon for something you didn't do.' Then she said: 'What about me?'

'I shall lay my conclusion before the necessary people. If they decide there is the possibility of making out a case against you, then they may act. I will tell you in my opinion there is not sufficient evidence – there are only inferences, not fact. Moreover, they will not be anxious to proceed against anyone in your position unless there is ample justification for such a course.'

Elsa said: 'I shouldn't care. If I were standing in the dock, fighting for my life – there might be something in that – something alive – exciting. I might – enjoy it.'

'Your husband would not.'

She stared at him.

653

'Do you think I care in the least what my husband would feel?'

'No, I do not. I do not think you have ever in your life cared about what any other person would feel. If you had, you might be happier.'

She said sharply: 'Why are you sorry for me?'

'Because, my child, you have so much to learn.'

'What have I got to learn?'

'All the grown-up emotions – pity, sympathy, understanding. The only things you know – have ever known – are love and hate.'

Elsa said: 'I saw Caroline take the coniine. I thought she meant to kill herself. That would have simplified things. And then, the next morning, I found out. He told her that he didn't care a button about me – he *had* cared, but it was all over. Once he'd finished the picture he'd send me packing. She'd nothing to worry about, he said.

'And she – was sorry for me . . . Do you understand what that did to me? I found the stuff and I gave it to him and I sat there watching him die. I've never felt so alive, so exultant, so full of power. I watched him die . . .'

She flung out her hands.

'I didn't understand that I was killing *myself* – not him. Afterwards I saw her caught in a trap – and that was no good, either. I couldn't hurt her – she didn't care – she escaped from it all – half the time she wasn't there. She and Amyas both escaped – they went somewhere where I couldn't get at them. But they didn't die. *I* died.'

Elsa Dittisham got up. She went across to the door. She said again: '*I died* . . .'

In the hall she passed two young people whose life together was just beginning.

The chauffeur held open the door of the car. Lady Dittisham got in and the chauffeur wrapped the fur rug round her knees.